Catherine Cookson was born in Tyne Dock, the illegitimate daughter of a poverty-stricken woman, Kate, whom she believed to be her older sister. She began work in service but eventually moved south to Hastings, where she met and married Tom Cookson, a local grammar-school master. Although she was originally acclaimed as a regional writer – her novel *The Round Tower* won the Winifred Holtby Award for the best regional novel of 1968 – her readership quickly spread throughout the world, and her many bestselling novels established her as one of the most popular of contemporary women novelists. After receiving an OBE in 1985, Catherine Cookson was created a Dame of the British Empire in 1993. She was appointed an Honorary Fellow of St Hilda's College, Oxford, in 1997. For many years she lived near Newcastle upon Tyne. She died shortly before her ninety-second birthday, in June 1998, having completed 104 works, nine of which are being published posthumously.

CATHERINE COOKSON

THE
Silent Lady

BANTAM PRESS

LONDON · NEW YORK · TORONTO · SYDNEY · AUCKLAND

TRANSWORLD PUBLISHERS
61–63 Uxbridge Road, London W5 5SA
a division of The Random House Group Ltd

RANDOM HOUSE AUSTRALIA (PTY) LTD
20 Alfred Street, Milsons Point, Sydney
New South Wales 2061, Australia

RANDOM HOUSE NEW ZEALAND
18 Poland Road, Glenfield, Auckland 10, New Zealand

RANDOM HOUSE SOUTH AFRICA (PTY) LTD
Endulini, 5a Jubilee Road, Parktown 2193, South Africa

Published 2001 by Bantam Press
a division of Transworld Publishers

A catalogue record for this book is available
from the British Library.

ISBNs 0593 044665 (cased)
0593 04665X (tpb)

Typeset in 12/14½pt Sabon by
Phoenix Typesetting, Ilkley, West Yorkshire

Printed in Great Britain
by Mackays of Chatham plc, Chatham, Kent

7 9 10 8 6

Dedication

This story was not meant to be written. I thought I had done my last one with *The Branded Man*. However, I had forgotten the machine I had set in motion fifty years ago.

This last year has proved more than trying. My blood trouble seems to have gone wild: not only have I had my nose packed frequently, but there have been more sojourns in hospital for operations to deal with the bleedings in my stomach. I will not add to these with all the other bodily afflictions . . . I was finished.

Apparently, the machine did not hear me, for one day it presented me with a very good idea for a story. It was then I said to it, 'How on earth shall I be able to get down a story now? First, I cannot see either to read or to write; only with guidance can I write my signature. Secondly, what time have I got? Doctors are forever coming and going; Tom is forever attending to my bodily needs, which do not stop at the end of the day; there is the post to be answered by my dictation, and the constant discussions on the phone about business and television; moreover, there is my editing of film scripts through dictation to Tom, who reads them aloud to me; also the editing through the same source of scripts ready for the printer; and so it is no wonder that exhaustion takes me into bouts of ME.'

A part of my mind told me that I had to face up to what 'they' were all saying: I was old and no longer fit to carry on at this rate. And so the writing of another story was definitely off.

But, try as I might, the old machine would not listen to me. 'It's a good idea,' it kept saying; 'different from the way you have tackled anything else. All right, but you are not going to be able to put it down; but thinking it through might help to take your mind off your miseries.'

I must have said to it, 'Well, what is it going to be all about?' and the answer came, 'Well, first, I think a good title for it will be *The Silent Lady*.'

'What? *The Silent Lady*?'

'Yes; and in her you have the whole story, right from beginning to end, the Silent Lady.'

Only once before has this happened to me. The result – *The Fifteen Streets*. This was after the publication of my first book, *Kate Hannigan*. The follow-up did not suit my publishers, who wished to cut it, particularly those parts dealing with religion. I wouldn't have it: I asked for it back.

So there I was on this freezing cold morning, just after the war (coal rationed to a ton a year) in a freezing cold house, and I was dead cold inside, for my mind was a void – I hadn't an idea in it.

I was in a breakdown; I was fighting against religion – I had definitely discarded God – but there I sat, huddled in a vast cold room. I've never known, even now, what made me resort to my dramatic gesture: I threw back my head and looked up to the ceiling and cried, 'If there's anybody there, give me a story!'

It might be unbelievable, but within an hour I had the complete story of *The Fifteen Streets*, right from the first line to the last, and I sat down and started on it straight away; and I did not alter one word or incident in that book over the weeks it took me to get it down in longhand.

The whole plan came over as it had first been presented to me: every character and incident in that story now has been filmed and staged all over the country, even in small village halls.

Well, the same thing was happening again. My mind gave me every character, every incident from the beginning to the end, and I found it to be a kind of salve: instead of my mind rambling on, always negative thinking – I had little to look forward to – it would pick up where I had left off in this story and continue as if I had never stopped.

This went on for some months, and one day I said to Tom, when he was trying to break the sameness of my life with reading to me, 'I have a good story in my mind, but it will always remain there.'

'Why?' he said. 'Couldn't you put it down on to tape?'

Even to myself, my voice was cold as I said, 'Don't be silly. There are times when I can hardly hear my own voice. And I am no longer able to yammer into that machine.' And truthfully, I wasn't.

But the damned rusty old wheel said, 'Here I am, grinding away listening to your complaining, your criticising, and your self-pity; and I am warning you, your self-pity will take over and bottle those all up; and one day you'll have just too much of it, when you'll find you're not able to think coherently. And then, what little time you have left will be wasted. And where has all the big noise gone – the one that keeps preaching "Never say die!" or "I *can* and I *will*"?'

Tom says he has stopped being amazed at anything I say or do, because one day, only a short time after having my nose packed, I muttered, 'Put my table so that I can handle my microphone,' and without comment or protest, he did so. And there it began.

I knew the story was going to be different: as a character was born I seemed to emerge from the womb of it and live its life. As in *The Fifteen Streets*, I knew every piece of dialogue that had to go down and every incident; and when I came to Bella Morgan, I was in her body more than I was in my own. Although, because of the comings and goings of doctors and bed attention and the like, I could put it down only in bits

7

and pieces, with my voice often inaudible, it became something I looked forward to; in fact, I just seemed to live for the time I could return to this 'family' and to the Silent Lady herself.

Then one day, after what seemed a long, long time since I had joined them all, it was finished, and I said to Tom, 'When did I start this?' And he said, 'Exactly a month ago today.'

'Never!'

'Yes,' he assured me, 'a month ago today! And now you are utterly exhausted in all ways, aren't you?'

I lay thinking: Yes, I was. I was utterly exhausted. But how could I have got all that down in just a month? And how could I say to him now, 'There are two places where I have repeated myself, and three others that I know I must cut because the descriptions are too long'?

He looked at me in utter amazement: 'You can remember it all like that?' he asked.

'Yes; every word,' I said.

It went to the typist. Some weeks later I got it back – 876 pages of it.

I do not believe in the dogma of any religious denomination but, as I have said before, I believe there is a spirit coming from some power or source that runs through all of us. In some strange way that I do not question, I have been able to tap into that source. This is what has enabled me always to say 'I *can* and I *will*'; and it is working still and helping me through this traumatic time of illness; and sometimes so strongly that one could say I have been given the power to create little miracles for myself; and for it, I am thankful.

So this story I dedicate to all those faithful readers who have become my faceless friends over many years, and I thank you for your loyalty to me.

I hope you will enjoy this last effort of mine, which came as an inspiration to me when I needed it most.

Catherine

PART ONE

1955

1

The woman put out her hand towards the brass plate to the side of the half-open door. She did not look at the name on the plate, which said, 'Alexander Armstrong & Son, Solicitors', but seemed to find support from it by touching its frame while she stood drawing in deep, shuddering breaths.

When she finally straightened herself and stepped through the doorway into a carpeted hall, she made her faltering way towards the desk to the left of her, behind which stood a young woman with her mouth agape.

The receptionist did not greet the visitor with a customary 'Can I help you, madam?' or 'Have you an appointment?' because, to her, it was instantly evident that this woman was a vagrant and had no business here; so she did not wait for her to speak but said, 'What d'you want? I . . . I think you've come to the wrong place.'

When the woman answered, 'Mis-ter Armstrong,' the girl was again surprised, this time by the sound of the voice, for it didn't match the woman's appearance. Although it was only a husky whisper it had, she recognised, a certain refinement about it.

But the appearance of the woman definitely outweighed

the impression her voice made, for the girl now said abruptly, 'He only sees people by appointment.'

The woman pointed to her chest, then to her eyes and, opening her mouth wide, she brought out three words, 'He see me.'

'He's – he's very busy.'

Again the head went back and the mouth opened, and the woman said, 'Mrs Baindor.'

Again the voice made an impression on the receptionist, so much so that she turned quickly and, pushing open the glass-panelled door of her office, she picked up the phone, at the same time watching the woman now turn from the counter and grope her way to a chair that was set near a small table on which stood a vase of flowers.

'Miss Fairweather?'

'Yes. What is it?'

'There's a . . . a person here.' Her voice was very low.

'What did you say? Speak up!'

'I said there's a person here. She . . . she looks like a vagrant but she says Mr Armstrong will see her.'

'A vagrant! What makes you think she looks like a vagrant?'

'Well, Miss Fairweather, you want to look at her yourself and see if my opinion is wrong.' The receptionist was daring to talk like this to Miss Fairweather, but she felt there was something very unusual about this woman.

'Did you get her name?'

'Yes, but it sounded funny, like Barndoor.'

'Barndoor?'

'That's what it sounded like.'

At the other end of the phone Miss Fairweather sat pondering. Should she go downstairs and see who this person was who looked like a vagrant, or should she mention the name to Mr Armstrong to see if he knew any such person? She decided on the latter. She tapped on the door that separated her office from that of her employer and when that gentleman raised his head from reading a large parchment set out in front of him and said, 'What is it?' she coughed before saying, 'Miss Manning says there's an odd-looking person downstairs who says she wants to see you. Apparently she doesn't seem able to get rid of her. From Miss Manning's tone the woman appeared to think that you would know her name.'

'Well, what is it? I mean her name.'

'It sounded to Miss Manning, so she says, like Barndoor.'

'*What?*'

'Well, that's what she said . . . Barndoor.'

Miss Fairweather was absolutely astounded at her employer's reaction to the mention of this name, for he jumped from his seat and shouted, yes, actually shouted aloud, 'Baindor, woman! Baindor! My God!'

She saw the parchment that he had been dealing with almost slide off the back of the desk as he thrust his chair back, then he ran across the room, almost knocking her over where she stood holding the door half open.

She had been with Mr Armstrong for fifteen years and had never seen him act like this. He was a placid, middle-aged man, strict in a way but always courteous. His excitement touched her. And now she was on the landing watching him almost leaping down the stairs.

When Alexander Armstrong reached the hall he stood for a moment gripping the stanchion post as he looked across at the woman, her body almost doubled up in the chair. He couldn't believe it: he couldn't and he wouldn't until he saw her face.

The woman did not lift her eyes to his until she saw his legs standing before her; then slowly she looked up and he gasped at the sight of her. The face might have been that of her skeleton, with the skin stretched over it, so prominent was the bone formation. Only the eye sockets tended to fall inwards

13

and from them two pale, blood-shot eyes gazed up at him.

Two words seemed to fill Alexander Armstrong's mind and body and they kept repeating themselves: My God! My God! Then, too, was added the knowledge that sitting here looking at him with those almost dead eyes was a woman for whom he had been searching – at least, for whom he and his business had been searching – for twenty-five years. No, nearly twenty-six.

The words he brought out were in a muttered stammer: 'M-M-Mrs Baindor.'

She did not answer but made a small movement with her strangely capped head.

He held his arms out to her now, saying, 'Come upstairs with me, Irene.'

When she made the attempt to rise she fell back into the chair and her body seemed to fold up again. At this he swung round to where Miss Fairweather was standing at the foot of the stairs and yelled at her, 'Call my son!' and when she answered shakily, 'He's out, Mr Armstrong; you know, on the Fullman case.'

'Then get Taggart – anybody!'

The chief clerk Taggart's office was at the other end of the building, and Miss Fairweather ran back up the stairs and along the corridor. Within two minutes Taggart was standing beside his employer, saying, 'Yes, sir?'

'Help me to get this lady to my office.'

For a moment Henry Taggart hesitated while he took in the lady's garb. She was a vagrant, if ever he had seen one in his life. But he did as he was bidden. Not only did he help the weird long-coated bundle to her feet, but, seeing that she was unable to stand and there wasn't room for three of them on the stairs, he picked up what the boss had called a lady, carried her up the stairs into the main office and laid her, as directed by Alexander, on the leather couch that was placed next to the long window overlooking the square.

Then, again almost shouting at his secretary, Alexander said, 'Make a cup of tea . . . strong, plenty of sugar.' From a cupboard he took down off a shelf a brandy flask and poured from it a measure into the silver-capped lid. This he took to the couch and, kneeling down by the woman, he put it to her lips, saying gently, 'Drink this.'

She made no effort to stop him pouring the liquid into her mouth; but when it hit her throat she coughed and choked and her whole body trembled. He turned and said to the clerk, 'Go down to the office and get the girl to phone for an ambulance.'

It must have been the sound of the word 'ambulance' that roused the woman, brought her head up and a protesting movement from her hand. At this Alexander, bending down to her, said, 'It's all right, my dear. It's all right. Not a big hospital . . . I understand. I understand.'

She lay back now and stared at him; then he turned quickly from her and, going to the phone on his table, he rang a number. When, presently, a voice answered him, saying, 'Beechwood Nursing Home,' he said curtly, 'Get me the Matron, quick!'

'Who's speaking?'

'Never mind who's speaking, get me the Matron quick!'

'But, sir . . . !'

'I'm sorry. I'm Miss Armstrong's brother.'

'Oh. Oh yes, yes,' came the reply; and then there was silence. As he stood waiting, he turned and looked at the wreckage of a life lying on his couch, and again his mind cried, 'My God!'

'What is it, Alex?' said his sister's voice.

'Listen, Glenda. I'm sending you a patient.'

'You're not asking if we've got any room.'

'You'd have to make room somewhere. This is important.'

'I cannot make rooms—'

'Listen, Glenda. Have you a room?'

15

'Yes, as it happens I have, Alex; and may I ask what is up with you?'

'You'll know soon enough. Get that room ready; there'll be an ambulance there shortly and I shall be following it.'

The voice now was soft: 'What is it, Alex? You sound troubled, very troubled.'

'You'll know why in a short time, Glenda. Only tell the staff that there must be no chit-chat about the condition of your new patient. I mean how she appears . . . is dressed. For the moment just get that room ready.' Then, his voice changing, he said, 'This is a serious business, Glenda, and I can't believe what I am seeing lying on my office couch. Bye-bye, dear.'

When he put the phone down and turned round, Miss Fairweather was standing with a cup of tea in her hand, looking as if she was afraid to touch the weird bundle lying there. He took the cup from her; then, kneeling down again, he put one hand behind the woman's head to where the cap affair she was wearing bulged out into a kind of large hairnet, which fell on to her neck. It had been half hidden by the large collar of her worn, discoloured and, in parts, threadbare coat. Lifting her head forward, he said, 'Drink this, my dear.'

Again she was staring into his face; but now she made no movement of dissent when he put the cup to her lips. After she had taken two gulps of the strong tea and it began to run from the corners of her mouth, he quickly handed the cup and saucer back to Miss Fairweather and, taking a handkerchief from his pocket, he gently dabbed the thin lips.

When he saw her make an effort to speak again, he said softly, 'It's all right, my dear. There'll be plenty of time to talk later.'

But she still continued to stare at him; and what he heard her say now brought his eyes wide, for she murmured, 'My son . . . tell my son . . . He will come.'

He knew he was shaking his head slowly. She thought her son would come to her after all these years? She could know nothing about him; yet her last words 'He will come' had been spoken in an assured tone. Poor soul.

There came a tap on the door now; and Taggart stood there, saying, 'The ambulance is here, sir.'

'Tell them to bring up a stretcher.' Alexander turned swiftly to his secretary, saying, 'Fetch that old travelling rug out of the cupboard.'

Although still amazed, Miss Fairweather was quick, and after taking the rug from her Alexander pulled it open and tucked it about the thin body of the woman, gently lifting her from one side to the other until it overlapped.

The ambulancemen picked up the wrapped body from the couch, making no comment, not even on the woman's head-gear, but asked politely, 'Where to, sir?'

'Beechwood Nursing Home.'

His description did not get any further before one of the ambulancemen said, 'Oh, yes; we know it, sir. Beechwood Nursing Home, Salton Avenue, Longmere Road.'

It was almost two hours later and brother and sister were in the Matron's private sitting room; and there Glenda Armstrong stood holding the long dark coat up before her, saying, 'Can you believe it?' And not waiting for an answer, she went on, 'I can't. I remember putting this on her. It was such a beautiful coat and very heavy. I thought that even then, for it was lined to the very cuffs with lambswool. But look now, there is not a vestige of wool left in the lining, just a mere thin skin. And the coat was such a beautiful dark green; made with such thick Melton cloth you couldn't imagine it wearing out in two lifetimes. Well, it has almost worn out in one, God help her! Where d'you think it has been?'

'I don't know. I haven't any idea, but it's been on the road somewhere. Yet, looking as she did, surely she would have been detected, especially with that hat or whatever it's supposed to be.'

17

Glenda now picked up the hat from a chair and said, 'It was very smart, French, a cross between a turban and a tam-o'-shanter with a brim round it. Look, the brim is still in place.' She touched the almost bare buckram-shaped rim with her fingertips, then lifted the pouch at the back as she said, 'She must have had it made for her to fit the bun she wore low down on her neck. Look at the dorothy bag! That's the same one she had with her when it happened.' Glenda pointed to the patched handbag lying on the seat of the chair. 'Every-thing she owned was in that bag. I remember I made her take her rings with her for she had taken them all off, even the wedding ring; and there was a necklace and a card case.'

Glenda sat down now on the edge of the large chesterfield beside her brother. 'When we heard nothing from her I always blamed myself for not sending someone with her to Eastbourne. When I put her on the train I said, "Now, let me know, won't you, how things are, and I shall come and see you in a few days or so." And that's the last I saw of her. Do you remember when you told her husband she had gone to her aunt's, and he went for you for not seeing that I had obeyed his orders and sent her to Conway House? My God! If ever there was an asylum under the name of rest-home! Yet I would have liked to have pushed her aunt into that place when I got to Eastbourne the next day and she told me that she wouldn't give her niece house room and had turned her away. She said that Irene's place was at her husband's side, and she deserved all she had got for carrying on with other men. Dear Lord in Heaven!' Glenda now hitched herself on to the cushions as she repeated, 'Dear Lord! We know now that the poor girl dared not lift her eyes to another man, never mind carry on with him.' Then she went on, 'Oh, and the vest or the shift, whatever you like to call it. It was made by old Betsy Briggs. She used to clean for Irene's father after her mother died and Irene was still at school. It was one of Betsy's expert pieces, a long, slim, clinging woollen shift. It was more like the sort of dress girls wear today. She had knitted one for Irene's mother because she was afflicted with a weak chest, and then she made one for Irene. And what d'you think? She still had it on today, or the remnants of it, for although it was clean it was held together not with wool but mending threads of different colours. And on top of it she was wearing what was left of the rose red velvet dress she wore that night at the concert. You remember it?'

'Yes. Yes, Glenda,' Alexander said wearily. 'I remember it. How did you manage to get her undressed?'

'Without much protest, until we came to the vest. Then her strength was renewed for a time, because she grabbed at it, at least at the waist part. When I reassured her she could keep it by her, but that I must take it off for the present, she allowed us to do so. And when we put it into her hands she grabbed at the middle of it and, slowly, she turned it inside out, and pointed to a small brown-paper-covered package about two inches square. It was pinned to the garment, top and bottom, with safety pins, and she attempted to undo them. After I undid them for her she held on to the package. She held it to her bare chest, then let us take the flimsy woollen garment away from her. She made no resistance when the sister and nurse washed her. The sister said after: "It was eerie, like washing a corpse." Yet her body is covered with little blue marks, faint now but which at one time must have been prominent, you know, like the marks left on a miner's forehead from the coal.'

'Has she still got the package?'

'Yes. We left it in her hand, and she seemed to go to sleep. That was until Dr Swan came in. He stood looking down at her where she lay with her hair now in grey plaits each side of her face. I had already put him in the picture because he had attended her – you remember? – all those years ago. At the time, he was a very young man and must have had hundreds of patients through his hands since, yet he remembered her. "Dear Lord!" he said.

'It was when he took hold of her wrist that once more she seemed to be given strength, for she pulled her hand away and pressed it on top of the other, which held the little parcel. And although his voice was soft and reassuring when he said, "Don't worry, my dear, I'm not going to hurt you," there was fear in her eyes and her whole body trembled. His examination was brief, and she trembled violently throughout.

'When we were outside he said, "Her chest's in a bad way, but it's malnutrition that'll see her off. She can't have eaten properly for God knows how long. I've never seen a live body like it. Where has she been all these years?"

'"I don't know," I said to him. "That's what we hope to find out. But she has difficulty in speaking. It's as if she doesn't want to speak." Anyway, he said he'd call back later and we'd have a talk.'

Musingly, Alexander said now, 'I wonder what's in that package? Perhaps it might give us a lead.'

'Well, we'll not know until we can take it from her, or she gives it to us, which I can't see her doing as long as she's conscious.'

He turned to her and said, 'You know who her son is, don't you?'

'Yes, of course I do. And he'll have to be told: it's only right he should be. But how we're going to do it, and how soon, I don't know. The latter, I think, will depend on Dr Swan's opinion, and for the present all we can do is get some food into her. But it'll have to be slowly.'

Now Alexander rose to his feet, went to the fireplace and put his hands up on the marble mantelpiece. He looked down into the fire as he muttered, 'I'm shaking. I . . . The last two hours have brought the past rushing back at me as if it had happened yesterday.' He lifted his head and, turning towards her, he said, 'D'you think I might have a drink?'

'Of course; we both need one. Brandy or whisky?'

'Whisky, please.'

Glenda went into an adjoining room, and brought back with her a tray on which stood a decanter of whisky and two glasses. She poured out a large measure for her brother, a comparatively small one for herself.

After taking two gulps from his glass, Alexander said, 'I'd better get back to the office and put James in the picture. He, of course, knows nothing about this business; he was only a small boy when it all started.'

'Yes, I understand you must tell him, but you must also emphasise at the same time that he says not a word about it to anyone. Otherwise it'll be in the papers by the end of the week.'

His voice was serious as he answered her, 'Well, Glenda, that goes too for your staff. You must tell them that this must not be talked about, because if a hint of it got round that old scandal would erupt and no matter what the great-I-am did, he would not be able to buy off justice this time, and as much as I would like him to get his deserts there is the son to think about.'

'Don't you worry. This won't be the first secret my girls have kept.' Then she added, 'Will you come back to dinner later on?'

'No. I'm sorry, Glenda, I can't, but I'll phone before I go out because it'll be too late when I get back. All right?'

'All right; but I don't expect there'll be much change in her before then.'

2

It was about an hour later when Miss Fairweather brought in a tray of tea and set it on the end of Mr Alexander's desk. She looked from him to Mr James and asked, 'Shall I pour out?'

'No, thanks; we'll see to it. And,' he added, 'don't bother waiting; we'll lock up.'

'I don't mind staying on, Mr Armstrong.'

'There is no need, Miss Fairweather. We are likely to be here some time yet.'

It was a very stiff secretary who made her exit, and James Armstrong looked at his father and smiled as he said, 'There goes a disappointed lady. Is she still after your blood?'

'Don't be silly, James; she's a very good secretary.'

'Yes, but I suspect she thinks she'd make a better wife. Anyway, what's all this about? I've only got to leave the office for a couple of hours and the excitement starts. It never happens when I'm here. Taggart tells me—'

'Doesn't matter what Taggart tells you. Now, pay attention. I've got rather a long story to tell you and I'm going to start at the beginning. You were a child of six when it happened, but since you've come into the firm you've had quite a few dealings with the Zephyr Bond, haven't you?'

'Yes. Yes, I have. It's doing very nicely now and—'

'Yes, yes, I know all about that,' his father cut him off, 'but the lady who should have been receiving the interest on that bond for the last twenty-five or twenty-six years or so has never touched a penny of it for the simple reason that I couldn't find her. There was quite a bit of money spent in trying to trace her but to no avail until this afternoon when a vagrant, and yes, she must have been one for some very long time, came into this office and asked to see me.'

'Really?' The word was just a murmur.

'Yes, really. You know all about the Edward Mortimer Baindor Estate. Well, she was the wife – is still the wife – of that beast of a man. That's what I say he is, and that's what I've thought of him all these years, and although the affairs of his estate bring us in a good part of our earnings I would have told him to take it with himself to hell many a time if I hadn't been stopped by some instinct. I cannot put a name to it, except to say I felt that one day I would live to see him made to suffer for all the cruelty he had ladled out to others, and to the woman who came to us today in particular.'

His son made no remark on this, only leant slightly forward in his chair and waited for his father to go on speaking.

'My father,' Alexander now went on, 'took me with him as a young man to Wellbrook Manor, near Weybridge. He was breaking me in to the business at the time and when he received orders to go and see his client – old Edwin, Edward's father – who was crippled with gout and couldn't get around, we would make a day of it because my father had an old friend in the village of Wellbrook called Francis Forrester. He was the schoolmaster. He had taken this poor situation to get his wife away from the city because she had chest trouble. He'd had a very good job in a London school before this. Anyway, they had one daughter called Irene. She was about ten when I first saw her, a very pretty, sweet child. By the way, her mother had been something of a singer until she got this chest trouble, and her child took after her, and it was quite something to hear them singing together. The child went to the village school where she became friends with one Timothy Baxter. He was four years older than Irene, and apparently since the Forresters had come to the village six years before he had taken the little girl under his wing. His father owned a small grocer's shop in the village and when the boy was fourteen he left school and went to work for his father. His spare time was devoted to what he called his charge, who was Irene. They grew up together like brother and sister – that was, until the First World War broke out in 1914. He was eighteen then, and was only too ready to join up, but it turned out that he was colour blind. Moreover, he had had a nasty fall from his bike when he was younger and it had left him with bouts of migraine. But apparently he wasn't greatly troubled at being unable to join the Army because what he wanted to do was act. He had a good singing voice and was a natural on the stage. He had appeared in amateur concerts after he had left school and also had joined an amateur theatrical group. I don't know how it was wangled, but he got himself into a company of actors that set out round the country to entertain the troops.

'It was about this time that Irene's mother died and her father was devastated. But he looked after Irene and continued to send her for singing lessons, as his wife had wished, although he knew that his daughter would never make an opera singer. He confided to my father that, thinking the girl wasn't making any progress under the local singing teacher, he took her into town to one who had been recommended as the best. And after she had been tested the man was quite plain and honest. He said to them both it would be a waste of money to take her any further. She would do well in light musical theatricals and amateur concert singing and such, but she simply didn't have a big enough voice for anything more ambitious.

'When she told Timothy this he pooh-poohed the man's

opinion and said she had a lovely voice and that he would do his best to get her work. Her father wasn't for this, and said so, so she remained at home, keeping house for him and doing light voluntary war work during the next few years. But it was on the day war ended in 1918 that she found him dead in bed. He was clasping a photograph of his wife and by his side was an empty box of pills and on the floor an empty whisky bottle.

'Since there was now less call for entertaining the troops, Timothy was home. But the war to end all wars had left many people destitute and this included his parents; the war had ruined their little business. When they left the village to join his mother's sister in the north, he stayed on because, in a way, he still felt responsible for Irene and he could still get acting jobs in London. How they both scraped through, I don't know, but I am fairly sure it was my father who helped them both financially over this rough patch. I only know for certain that she clung to Timothy, so my father said, not only as a father and brother but also as someone she loved. That he did not feel that way towards her hadn't, Father said, dawned on her. As far as she was concerned, she would always have him and he would always have her. That was her childish idea until a friend told Timothy he could get him a job in the chorus of a musical if he came up to town at once. Naturally he did so.

'Anyway, Timothy Baxter did not remain in the chorus for long but got himself a walking-on part. He was a natural actor and had a good voice. The next thing I remember about the whole affair at that stage was that Timothy had got her a part in the chorus of the same musical he was in, so their association continued and life must have been bliss for her. That was until he told her that the main members of the cast had the chance to take their show to America and had offered to take him with them, and of course he couldn't refuse such a chance. But as soon as possible he would send for her.

'For the first six months or so they exchanged letters, hers very long, his, I understand, getting briefer and briefer. And then his communications changed to postcards. She was twenty when he went away. She was nearly twenty-two when the communications stopped altogether, and I suppose she was wise enough to know that he must have found someone else. And also I'm sure she must have told herself, as she told me later, that he had never spoken one word of love to her.

'She herself by then was taking on different jobs during what the actors called resting periods. When she was twenty-three she had a part in an operetta that was getting good reviews. It was a kind of Cinderella story. She was a house-maid and she sang Offenbach's "Barcarolle", "Night of stars and night of love fall gently o'er the water". On the stage she suddenly stops and faces the mirror and sings to herself and imagines herself as a great star. Apart from that one solo it was a small part, because it led nowhere in the story, and I often wondered why it was pushed in. Although she sang beautifully her voice really hadn't the strength to reach the heights the song deserved, yet she was always enthusiastically applauded, until the real star of the show appeared. Anyway it was in that show that Edward Mortimer Baindor, old Edwin's son, saw her for the first time, and that's where I come in.'

'What d'you mean, Father, you come in?'

'Just what I say. Bear with me and you'll know why shortly.

'Well, now, first of all I'm going to go back some years, to the manor house at Wellbrook. This is how my father told it to me, exactly as Edwin told it to him. Edwin sent for his son. Apparently Edward had just come down from Oxford and had planned to go on an extensive holiday abroad to pursue his hobby of archaeology, but the old man had different plans for him. He wanted him at home to carry on the name. There were no other relatives left either on Edwin's or his wife's side. He told his son in plain words: "What you've got to do," he said, "is get yourself married; and there's one ready, if not waiting, for the chance. She is the best bred around here, as good as her horses, I understand, and the Spencer-Moores are at rock bottom financially. Lillian's father'll throw her into your lap because there's money here. She's three years older than you, but what's that? You look older, always have done, like myself. And if she can breed as well as she can ride, this house soon should be filled with children." '

Alexander stopped here and nodded at his son, who was laughing now, saying, 'He actually told Grandfather that?'

'Yes, word for word. Funny, but there was a kind of understanding between him and my father. It was never to be the same with Edward and me.

'But anyway, I understand there was a helluva dust-up and Master Edward only succumbed after an ultimatum had been presented to him. What the ultimatum was Father didn't tell me. I don't think he knew. I should imagine it was along the lines of his allowance would be cut down to the very minimum if he didn't do as he was told. Anyway, there was an engagement announced in *The Times* and six months later there was a very grand wedding. But what neither the father nor the son bargained for was Miss Lillian's character. In a way she became a match for both of them because she showed them that horses were her priority and nobody on this earth was going to stop her riding. But young Edward did his duty as was expected of him and straight away she became pregnant, only to lose the first baby at three and a half months. Within three years she'd lost the third.

'Edward banned horses from the stables except the two that were needed for the carriage when she became pregnant again, and he practically became her gaoler. He never left the house for months on end. My father said he had the look on him of a chained and frustrated bull. He was a big man, six foot one and broad with it. Even at that age he looked like his father, though he had a violent temper, and was prone to wild

27

bursts of anger. He had none of his father's understanding or, at times, kindness. And it would seem he was by now more determined than his father that he should have an heir.

'Whether Lillian was very unhappy I couldn't say, because she too had a temper, which showed itself in a deep irritation towards another member of the household. Her husband had engaged a nurse-companion for her, and the woman seemed never to leave her side. Her lady's maid, a girl called Jane Dunn who had been her maid before she was married, one day unintentionally pointed out to Lillian how she could escape for an hour or so. While standing at the window, she saw Edward mount the carriage that was to take him to the station to catch a train into London for the day. After the nurse-companion had been into the bedroom to check that her charge was lying down and resting, the maid saw her, too, leave the house and make for the kitchen garden, which led to the bailiff's cottage. She had long suspected that there was something going on between those two, and that day she remarked on it to her mistress. Lillian sprang up from the bed, pulled on her underclothes, a pair of riding breeches, and a short jacket and hat. She ran out of the room, down the back stairs and into the yard, where she demanded of a fear-filled groom that he should help her to saddle an old horse, one considered past his prime who had been put out to grass.

'Lillian was out for two hours, and when she returned the nurse-companion was almost in hysterics at the disappearance of her charge. Lillian laughed at her. And she laughed at her husband when he returned and found her having dinner with his father and actually making *him* laugh. He was surprised at the bright face she turned to him, asking if he had enjoyed his temporary escape. But two days later she was no longer smiling . . . Nor was he, for he had learnt of her escapade. She was only seven months gone and the birth had begun prematurely. She was in labour for two days and the

28

young doctor did everything in his power to ease her pain and fetch the child out alive. But he suspected it was dead before she made the last effort. Yet the midwife still did everything in her knowledge to bring life into the tiny body. But she was unsuccessful.

'Edward was in the room, and when he looked down on the well-formed male child he let out a sound like the wail of an animal, then turned his back on it. Going to the bed where the doctor was working to staunch the blood from the patient's womb, he looked down on his wife's pallid face and screamed at her, "You did it again, didn't you, and on purpose? You and your horses have killed my child. Well, I hope they gallop you into hell!" He gripped her by the shoulders and shook her like a dog shaking a rat. He let her fall back on the pillows only when the doctor's bloodstained hand came across his face and the midwife's arms were about him from behind.

'The room was a shambles and now, as he was pressed towards the door, he yelled at the nurse-companion whom he had left on guard, "I'll throttle you if you're not out of this house . . ."

'His words were muffled by the doctor yelling at him, "Shut up, man! Get out and calm yourself!"

'What Edward Mortimer Baindor did next was to go down to the yard and beat the groom into a state of insensibility.

'Lillian died the next day and it was after the funeral that he was presented with a summons on the charge of assault and battery on one Arthur Briggs.

'It was only Father's work with Briggs's solicitor, and the offer of a substantial sum to the man made by old Edwin in order to stop any further scandal, that saved Baindor from facing the charge in court.

'Edwin, being aware of the feeling against his son in the community, willingly agreed now to his going abroad to pursue his hobby because he knew it was partly his own doing that had brought about the unhappy marriage between Edward and his dead wife.'

James rose and went to the cupboard. He handed his father a small measure of brandy. They both sat in silence sipping their drinks for a moment until James said, 'Well, I'm waiting. Go on. There's much more to come, and worse, I'm sure.'

'Yes, you're right. Well, young Edward was about twenty-seven when this happened. He would come home for short periods, then go off again, and my father said the old man never pressed him to stay. Then it was eight years later when, on one of his short stays, his father had a seizure and died, which left Master Edward in sole charge of the extensive business his father had built up. As my father said, Edward also inherited a great deal else from the old man, and that was business acumen, for now he was in control he dived into it with enthusiasm. Nothing escaped him. From the beginning Father didn't like him, nor did I, but he was a client and an important one. And what Father soon found was that the man disliked advice. He gave plenty of it himself, but by way of orders.

'Then came the night of the show I was telling you about. I was in the stalls and, happening to look up at the boxes, I saw him there. Well, that must have been when he spotted Irene and apparently fell for her, hook, line and sinker. I don't know how he arranged to meet her, I only know that from then on his whole attitude seemed to change. Not that he was any less businesslike, but he was pleasanter. Yes, that is the word, he was pleasanter.

'Then one day I had an unexpected visit from her. She said the show was closing, and I said I was sorry to hear that, but she smiled and said that wasn't what she had come about. She wanted my advice. She knew that I was Edward's . . . Here she stopped herself, then went on, Mr Baindor's solicitor, and she recalled the happy times of my visits to her father. But did I know, she asked me, that she was . . . well, what was

30

the word she should use? Being courted. And I repeated, "Being courted? Do you mean to say that you are being courted by my client?"

'She blushed slightly and nodded and said, "Yes, that is what I mean to say."

'"Well, well." I recall sitting back in my chair and smiling at her as I spoke. "So that is the reason for the change." At which she asked, "What change?"

'I said, "Well, you have altered his character already. He's lost most of his abruptness."

'"Well, I've known him less than three months, and now what d'you think? He has asked me to marry him."

'"Really?"

'"Yes," she answered, "just as you say, really. He has been very attentive and has been taking me here and there in his free time and mine. I told him about my family because he asked about them, but I didn't mention how my father died," and to this I remember replying, "No, of course not. There's no need for him to know." Then she said, "What d'you think I should do?"

'She might have been asking this question of her father, and I hesitated for a long moment before I said, "Do you like him?"

'Her answer came quite swiftly. "Oh, yes, I like him. He's so very – well, so nice and kind."

'Then I said, "Well, you like him but may I ask if you love him?" Now it was she who hesitated before she replied, "I loved Timothy first as a brother and then as a parent, both father and mother, but he didn't love me in the way I came to love him. I haven't heard from him for nearly two years now, so what feeling I had has naturally died. But do I love Edward?" The pause was longer before she said, "I don't know, but I think I could come to love him dearly."

'"Well, go ahead, my dear," I said.

'Her smile widened then vanished as she said, "But he has

31

that great manor house and the estate, and I understand he is a very rich man."

'"In all three you are right," I said to her, "and by the sound of it you are being offered the three, and wholeheartedly, I should say, because you have already made a change in him. I have seen him happy, and for the first time in his life, I should imagine."

'"You think so?"

'"Yes. And my father would confirm this and will, though he and my mother are away at the moment."

'She now said, "Yes, I know; but I came to you purposely because, well, you're younger and . . . and I thought you would understand my feelings. You see I am only twenty-three, but he is thirty-seven."

'"All the better," I said. "He'll know how to look after you, and probably much better than a younger man would. In a way I think you are a very lucky girl."

'At this she smiled at me and said, "I would too, if I could only realise what's happening to me. It's too much of a fairy-tale to take in, really."

'"Well," I said, "you continue to make it a fairy-tale, my dear . . ."

'Six months later they were married and our whole family was invited to the wedding. She had no relatives except an aunt who lived in Eastbourne. She looked the most beautiful of brides, but in a way very childlike. She didn't look her twenty-three years. I recall they were sent off in a glorious fashion at five in the afternoon to start their honeymoon, first stop Venice. There was a ball for the staff and their friends that night at the manor and any of the guests who had a mind to stay. This was all arranged by the butler, Mr Trip, and the housekeeper, Mrs Atkins. I remember recalling that I had been to that house a number of times with my father and never seen the staff so happy.

'But that wedding was nothing to when Irene gave him a

32

son. Talk about a doting father! He really did lose years, and Irene adored the child from the moment she first held him. So said my mother, for she was allowed to visit her the day after the birth.'

At this point Alexander leant forward, picked up the glass from the table and drained the remainder of the brandy. Then his tone changed as he said, 'When was it I first noticed a change in her? In a way it showed first in her voice and attitude. On her wedding day, as I said, she was like a very young girl, but she was now a woman. Moreover, she was a mother who never wanted to leave her child's side, but apparently – I was given to understand much later – she had to, once her husband was in the house. It wasn't that he wanted desperately to be with her, although he did, oh, yes, he really did, but he also wanted to monopolise the boy. Wherever he was so must the boy be.

'After their honeymoon abroad, they had attended dinners and, to my knowledge, went to two balls. One was a charity affair. Your mother and I were also there, and we remarked how he danced with her, yet when she was dancing with anyone else he just sat watching her. I think the dancing must have ended when she informed him she was going to have the child, for he would have remembered what had happened to his first wife. But nevertheless they entertained and we were many times invited to dinner. It was on these occasions that I detected another change in her. She had become very quiet, her natural gaiety had disappeared. Although she laughed and chatted to her guests, there was no spontaneity in her as there had been before. There was no sign of any other babies coming, and although his manner was still cordial then, there were also glimpses of his domineering side. When my father wasn't available and he had to deal with me, there was in his manner the unspoken words, "Why isn't he available? Doesn't he know who I am and what I mean to this firm? See that he makes himself available next time, young man." At least, that's how I interpreted his attitude, and in the end I found I wasn't far wrong.

'He rarely left home, and, I was told, when he wasn't visiting his companies and agents abroad, he spent his time with the boy. Rarely did she come to town, and when she did he accompanied her. She seemed to have very few friends of her own to visit, only us. He would leave the boy for a few hours, and a few hours only, for they never stayed in town to go to a theatre or to dine with friends. Twice they went on holiday, and the child was taken with them.

'It was about a fortnight before the boy's fourth birthday when Edward was forced to take a trip to Germany. There was to be a big takeover concerning the Flux firm, and it was imperative that he should be there. At the time I was running a charity for children's holiday camps. It had succeeded in getting a lot of poor boys off the streets or out of the gutters. It showed them a different way of life, and your mother and I were so interested in it that we had gathered together some quite big names for a charity concert. It was she who suggested we should ask Irene to come and sing. I recall her words: "Her gaoler is away, so what's to stop her? She still keeps up her singing when she can. I know because she told me. She probably sings to the boy when his papa is absent. One thing I'm certain of," she added, "she misses the stage and the company. That girl's lonely; I know she is."

'I felt I had to say to her, "I don't suppose she would dare do it without his permission."

'"Well, we can but try," was her response.

'During the past two or three weeks I had noticed that when we happened to be together Irene used to become rather agitated. It was as if she wanted to talk to me about something, to tell me something, but seemed afraid to. But this time she seemed to jump at the chance to get out on her own. The concert was to be held on a Sunday evening in one of the big theatres, and the stars would be giving their services free. It

34

was a wonderful do – the concert, I mean. We had gone to the manor and picked Irene up, and both your mother and I were in the nursery and were never to forget when she kissed her son and hugged him close, saying, "Mummy won't be long, she's just going out to sing for her supper." And he laughed at her and cried, "Well, Cook could give you some, Mummy." She threw her arms about him and kissed him, not once but three times. She didn't know it was the last time she would ever kiss her child.'

Alexander paused again. And then he put his hand on the table and brought his fingers into a fist and thumped the table with it three or four times before he again spoke to his son, who was now staring wide-eyed at him. He went on, 'It was a costume do and your mother had got her the most elaborate-looking Edwardian gown. It had a rather low neck, and apparently when your mother and the dresser went to help her on with it they saw there was an obstacle because Irene was wearing a kind of woollen shift affair that was, as your mother said, more like a fine woollen dress because it came to her knees. The dresser said she hadn't seen one for years and certainly not such a finely knitted one. Ladies used to sleep in them at one time, she said. Anyway, without it the costume fitted Irene perfectly, and when she put on the huge straw and feathered hat she looked the part, and for the first time in many a long day she looked happy . . . And she sang the "Barcarolle" beautifully. It was as if she had never stopped singing. In fact, it seemed that her voice had improved: it had become stronger. Anyway, she brought the house down. It was arranged that the main performers of the evening and their guests were to have a supper at the Carlton. So your mother took your grandmother out to the car that was waiting, leaving me behind to accompany Irene in a cab and join them at the supper as soon as she had finished changing. I recall the hall was soon cleared.

'As I waited, a young man who looked vaguely familiar

came rushing in, wound his way between the chairs and made for a door that led to the dressing rooms. Then a few minutes later, I could not believe my eyes: Irene's husband came into the theatre. He wasn't running like the young fellow, but he was hurrying, and I recognised the look on his face. Oh, dear me, I thought.

'He did not see me. Now, what I've got to say next is third hand. My information came later from the hysterical dresser. She said, "The lady had just got her costume off and had pulled on the cosy garment when the door was flung open and a man stood there with his arms outstretched, crying 'Irene!' and she jumped round and without hesitation rushed to him. He flung his arms about her and she hers about him, and they laughed at and with each other, and she cried, 'When did you arrive?'

'"'About an hour ago,' he said. 'I've just heard that you were singing here, and I rushed from the hotel. I saw Mr Armstrong's mother getting into a car outside and she said you were in the dressing room. Oh Irene!' He held her at arm's length and said, 'Why, miss, did you not ask my permission to marry, eh?'

'"'You weren't here,' she said; 'you weren't here.' Then again she threw her arms around him, and this time they kissed. Their lips were tight and their bodies close when the door opened and, at the sight of the man looking at them, she let out a sort of high-pitched scream.

'"'The young fellow turned and said, 'Oh, hello. You must—' That's as far as he got because that man sprang on him. Like a tiger, he was, and the young fellow was so surprised that under the first blow he fell backwards and never seemed to regain himself, because that man battered him to the floor. All the while the lady was screaming; and then he snatched up one of the props. It was a china vase, and he brought it down on the young fellow. It hit him across the chest and the side of the face. The attacker then turned to her,

36

and he shook her as if she was a rat. Then his fists pounded her face as he screamed at her: 'You dirty whoring slut, you!' The cleaners were rushing into the room now, but he wouldn't let go of her. By the time they dragged him from her she was quite senseless." That's all my informant remembered, because at that point she passed out.'

Alexander took a handkerchief from his pocket and wiped the sweat from his brow; but his son said nothing, just sat staring fixedly at him. Presently, his father gave a deep sigh and closed his eyes as he said, 'I can still see them lying there: her bleeding body had fallen across the young fellow's crumpled legs. His face was obliterated by blood. Somebody was yelling, "Get the police!" Another, "Get an ambulance." Another, turning to where Baindor was leaning against the wall, yelled at him, "You murdering bugger, you! Wait till the police get here!"

'The word "police" seemed to bring Baindor to his senses, and he was about to stumble out when he came face to face with me, and his words came out on a deep growl as he said, "She's a whore!" and I, forgetting for the moment who he was, cried at him, "And you're a bloody madman!" He just stumbled past me; and I went into the room and said to two of the men who were trying to straighten the young fellow's legs, "Don't touch him! Leave him until the ambulance men come."'

Alexander had not opened his eyes and James, after sitting silent for some time, said, in a very small voice, 'What happened to them?'

'Oh,' Alexander pulled himself up in his chair, 'it's a wonder she survived. They were in a dreadful state, both of them. I recall wishing the fellow would die and that mad beast would be brought up for murder. It happened that at that time Aunt Glenda had her nursing home going; Father had set her up with it. In those days she could only take six patients and within a week we had brought Irene from the general hospital ward into Glenda's care. From the accompanying report, she learnt that Irene hadn't spoken since regaining consciousness. Nor did she utter a word for the next three weeks. It appeared that the brutal beating had not only marred her body it had also marred her mind in some way, for although she understood all that was said to her, she couldn't give a verbal answer, only make a motion with her head.'

When Alexander again paused James said, 'What happened to the young fellow?'

'Well, he was in a very bad way for some weeks. One side of his face from the front of his ear to his lower jaw had been split open, and this undoubtedly would leave a scar, but at the end of the first week he was able to speak. It appeared that the manager of the troupe he was with, which had come over for a short run in England, wanted to take the matter to court, but he would have none of it. He was thinking of Irene and did not want her name to be plastered all over the papers and Baindor's reason given as to why both she and he had been battered by the husband.'

'But didn't the police take it up?'

'No; it appeared that they went to the manor and saw him, and he said the woman in question was his wife. Had she made any complaint? And when they said no, he had asked about the other person: had he taken up the case? And again the answer was no. He said it was a family affair, quite private. It was nothing to do with them.

'I did not see him for nearly six weeks and I thought he had gone abroad; and then one day he stormed in here and demanded to see my father. At that time Father was retiring gradually and was enjoying himself, seeing to the alterations of the house he had bought next door to Glenda's in order to extend her business. The idea was to take the inner wall down and make comfortable private quarters for her and a sitting room for her nursing staff. This would still leave space for eight more bedrooms. He was like a child with a new toy. My mother had said, "Let him alone, you can manage the firm, and he's happy."

'Anyway, as I was saying, Baindor came in here like a wild bull. He stood where you're sitting now, and I sat here. I did not rise to my feet as was usual when a client entered the room, and he said to me, "Where is your father?" I, lying gently, said, "At home; he has a cold, he's in bed." I remember there was a long silence before he said, "Who gave you the authority to take my wife from the hospital and put her into your sister's nursing home?" I wonder now how I dared to answer him as I did, but what I said was, "Since you had almost beaten your wife to death and seemingly did not care any more what happened to her, I took it upon myself to move her from the hospital to quieter quarters."

'"You had no right!"

'"I had every right," I said. "It was a humanitarian act. She needed personal nursing."

'There was another long pause before he said, "I understand from the doctor that she also needs mental attention, so I am having her transferred to Conway House."

'This, James, brought me to my feet immediately and I cried, "Conway House! Attached to the convent? It's practically a lunatic asylum under the name of a nursing home."

'"It is not a lunatic asylum, it is for disturbed patients, and at the present time my wife is a disturbed woman. So will you be good enough to let me get down to the business I came to discuss with your father. As he is not available I will have to talk to you. You will have come across the Zephyr Bond?"

'I remember I couldn't speak for a moment but then I said, "Zephyr Bond? Yes, of course." The Zephyr Bond was the remnants of a company his father had bought up years ago. It never produced much interest although it remained steady but, whatever the market, it would never set the place on fire. He went on, "I wish to pass this deed wholly over to your father or to you, who unfortunately seem to be in charge now, in order that you will allot to my wife the sum of five pounds a week – no more, no less – from it. This will be paid to the matron of Conway House as long as she stays there, or to wherever they may transfer her. As a Catholic I cannot divorce her, but I wish to have no more mention of her name made to me, ever. And should she at any time in the future attempt to visit the manor there are orders – strict orders – that she is to be forcibly removed. In fact, should she resist and try in any way to get in touch with the child, I shall have the matter taken to court, and I shall be given sole custody of my son because his mother was an adulteress."

'I remember saying to him in deep anger, "You've no proof of that. She was welcoming back home after an absence of three years a man she thought of as a brother, a young man who had helped to bring her up from a child."

'The cool answer came, "So you say, but I don't believe it; and more than once she has spoken of this man with affection. In fact, I once told her, and only recently, to desist. But he is not the only man in question. There was my valet, Cox, whom I dismissed three months ago. She had him so fascinated that one day when I was out he was accompanying her on the piano as she sang."

'This,' Alexander now said, 'was news to me at the time, but I also then recalled how the poor creature had looked on various occasions when I had seen her.

'He now thrust on the table the case he had brought with him and, after opening it, he placed beside it a folded bond, and with it a long, typed letter. Pushing them both towards me, he said, "This is the old bond. It has never been of great significance, but it has revived somewhat since the war, and will bring in enough to provide for my wife's maintenance at the rate of five pounds a week. I wish you to sign the acceptance in the name of your firm, and it can be witnessed. Send for your clerk."'

Alexander was now breathing heavily as he said, 'I recall,

James, that I had the greatest desire to pick up that glass inkwell' – he pointed along the desk to where it was set in a brass tray – 'and smash the thing into his face. Nevertheless, at the same time I knew that five pounds was better than nothing. She could exist on that in those days. Moreover, he hadn't mentioned anything about what was to happen to the money should she die. Were we to accept it as ours or return it to him? But I left this. That was in the future and it made no matter just then.

'The only thing I wanted at that moment, James, was to get him out of this office in case I did something that would not only ruin me but deprive the business of its most profitable client, one with whom Father had borne for years and whose business had helped greatly towards his putting me through university, buying a new home for Mother and setting Glenda up in her nursing home. Anyway, when old Watson, the clerk, came in he showed no deference to the client, because he knew what had recently happened. Although it wasn't in the papers the news had certainly got round and, as it was no doubt also said openly, Baindor should have been exposed for what he really was. My heart went out to the old fellow for his courage because, looking down at the letter on the table, which was obviously a document, he turned to the great man and demanded, "What am I signing?"

'Baindor was taken aback; then he almost shouted, "It is no business of yours. You are paid to do what you are told to do."

'Before Watson could make any further remark on this I said to him, "It's all right. It is to do with the firm and it is in order. Just sign."

'The old fellow did as he was bidden but very slowly and reluctantly. Then, straightening his back, he gave the important client one long stare before walking out.

'I fully expected Baindor's next remark: "Dismiss him, and at once!"

41

'"He is my father's clerk, and that is his business," I retorted.

'His last words to me before leaving were, "Tell your sister that my wife will be collected tomorrow, and *that*, let me inform you, sir, is the last word I want to hear about her." He stood waiting for me to make a reply of some kind, but when he didn't receive one he went out without closing the door behind him.'

'I wouldn't talk any more for a moment. I'll pour you another drink,' said James, getting to his feet now, but his father stayed him with a gesture of his hand: 'No; no more.'

He smiled wanly. 'But I'll tell you something, even remembering this business has brought back to me the awful feeling I had, once that man walked out of the office. I felt so full of rage, real rage. I'd never experienced anything like it in my thirty-odd years before and I almost felt I was going to pass out. The only thing that brought me to was the fact that I had to see Glenda, as quickly as possible, and make some other arrangement for that poor girl.

'When I told Glenda she couldn't believe it. She said that Irene wasn't fit to be left on her own yet, she still hadn't spoken. Although her body had mended in a way, it was covered with odd marks and indentations. Her face, too, was still bruised, and her mind in some way was also affected. As Glenda said, we would have to get her away from the nursing home, but to where? If she took her to our place he would certainly come there. The only thing she knew about Irene's relatives was that she had an aunt in Eastbourne, the one who had come to the wedding. And it was on this basis that we got to work and talked to Irene. We had to explain what her husband was about to do, and when we asked her if he knew anything about her aunt in Eastbourne she made a small movement with her head, which meant no. Then Glenda asked her aunt's name. I can see Irene now, slowly pointing to a table on which were a pencil and pad, and as

42

slowly she wrote down the name of her aunt, and the address. When I said to her, "Do you think you could get there – go on the train by yourself?" she made a desperate move with her head, nodding twice.

'Glenda got her into her outdoor clothes, and took her to the station. As she told me later, she kept thinking all the time that she should go with her and see her settled. But, in my presence, she had suggested to Irene that one of the nurses should go with her to Eastbourne and Irene's head had moved desperately from side to side. Then, for the first time, she spoke. Pointing to herself, she said, "All right." It was just a murmur, but it definitely was those words. Then she spoke again to me when I took her hand and helped her into the cab. Slowly and hesitantly the words came, "Thank . . . you," and that was the last time I saw her until yesterday, when she fell into this office in what looked like a vagrant's garb, but were the identical coat and hat she was wearing when she left Glenda's all those years ago. She was wearing them at the concert on that fatal Sunday night. How she has lived in them for the last twenty-seven years I don't know. But one thing is evident, she has existed on the streets.'

James's head was shaking in disbelief and his voice was low as he said, 'What about the aunt? Didn't she go there?'

'Yes, she did, but when we didn't hear anything from her for a week Glenda and I went to the house. And there I met the woman. God! My hatred for that woman almost matched my feelings about Baindor. Irene had come to her. Oh, yes, she told us she had come, but she had soon shown her the door. Irene was drunk, she said, or on drugs or something, for she wouldn't speak but wrote some disjointed words on a paper. One was "distress", the other was "husband misunderstood". So what did she say to her, this poor distressed creature? She told her that she was a married woman and must go back to her husband. Anyway, she herself was about to leave Eastbourne and live in Yorkshire.

'You know what I said to her?'

James shook his head.

'I hope you die a slow and painful death.'

'You said that?'

'I did. At that moment it was the worst thing I could wish on her.'

James now put his elbow on the arm of his chair and rested his head on his hand. They remained silent until James said, 'And you haven't the vaguest idea where she might have been all this time?'

'None whatever. And we won't have if she doesn't speak before she dies. But one thing I've promised myself, she will see her son before that happens.'

'Oh, yes.' James was sitting up straight now. 'The son. What d'you think he'll do when he knows?'

'That's to be seen. But I'm sure he's not like his father at all. He doesn't look like him or act or speak like him.'

'And he must have a will of his own to have rejected taking on the business and going in for medicine. Where is he now?'

'I don't know – in one of the London teaching hospitals, I think. I understand he's aiming to become a plastic surgeon.'

'How old is he now?'

'Oh, let me think. He was just on four when all this happened and that's twenty-six years ago, in 1928. He's thirty, I should say, just a couple of years younger than you. I should imagine he might be a consultant by now. But I don't really know when he started; I only know he was at Oxford until he was twenty-two or so. We'll soon find out, though.'

'When do you intend to see him?'

'It all depends on how the poor woman is. As she is now I don't think she'd be able to recognise anyone. Yet there must be a deep pain inside her that has lingered all these years, because that's what she said to me, the only words she spoke, "My son," which I took to mean she wanted to see him. And then she said, "He'll come." It was as if she was sure. At the moment, I only wish I knew what is in that package she keeps a tight hold of. It might give us some clue to her whereabouts all these years. Otherwise I doubt we'll ever find out.'

But he was to find out, and in a comparatively short time, and his knowledge was to come in as strange a way as the appearance of his informant herself. The story she was to tell Alexander Armstrong about where Irene had spent twenty-six of the missing years was as strange, if not more so, than the story he had just related to his son.

PART TWO

1929–1955

1

Big Bella Morgan closed the door on No. 10 The Jingles, then walked a couple of yards to her left and inserted a key into the lock of a rusty iron gate, which led into a large yard. It would have looked larger still, had it not been for the piles of broken wooden fruit boxes and the rotten fruit scattered here and there. Down the middle of the yard was a clear pathway that led to a stone building, at the end of which was a large wash-house. Thrusting open its door she cried, to the two sleeping forms lying there on thin palliasses, 'Come on! Show a leg and get on your way.'

One of the men sat up, rubbing his knuckles into his eyes and saying, 'What time is it, Bella? It's early like.'

'Aye, it's early enough,' she replied; 'early enough for you to get to Robson's and see if you can bring some decent stuff back. I don't mind yesterday's but not the day before's lot. Give Pimple Face a kick there. He'll sleep until he dies, that one.'

Now the other man grunted, then stretched his limbs, gave a loud yawn and sat up, saying, 'God! What I'd give for a cup of char.'

'You'll have it after your first run. You know the ropes – you should by now.'

'You're a hard woman, Bella.'

'I'd be harder still if I left that bloody gate open at night, wouldn't I? Because they'd be lyin' on top of you, two double, and you know it.'

'I'll just have a swill, Bella; I've got a stinkin' head.'

This came from the big man who seemed to tower over the small fat woman, and Bella said, 'Do that, Joe, but don't make a bath of it, because you know what Robson's made of. He's as likely to hand some of the offshoots to the others who'll pay a penny a box extra. We made a deal, but I don't trust him. And, the both of you, I want this yard cleared up before you get anything to eat or a kip tonight.'

'What if, when I get to the warehouse, Baker has a job on for me? How about it then, Bella?'

'Well, it's up to you,' and she grinned, 'whether or not you eat and kip here tonight. As for you, Pimple Face, I think it's about time you gave up that whistle you play on the streets or learnt a few more tunes on it. Your takings would hardly keep a hen in corn. There are bound to be some jobs left that don't end in gaol.'

'Oh, Bella.' The smaller man shook his head. 'We've been over this, haven't we? I've been there once, I've told you, and I'm not going back again. Anyway, if I can give the cops the tip-off I'll get more than coppers.'

'Aye, you'll get more than coppers,' the woman said now, 'but as like as not you'll get a slit throat as well. The villains'll be on to you, I'm sure. Anyway, get moving.'

The two men did as she said, and pushed a long barrow through the iron gate. The woman followed them; then she turned and locked the gate again, before returning to her front door and opening it with a Yale key.

Once inside, she took off her coat and the man's cap she was wearing, and hung them on a mahogany coat-stand by the side of the door. Then she walked across the sizeable hall, which was covered with brown linoleum, past the foot of a flight of broad stairs, one side of which was open to the hall and its banister supported by a stout mahogany pillar, then through a door into a large kitchen, which was warm and surprisingly comfortably furnished. An ornamental wood-framed sofa-couch stood against one wall, and there were two easy chairs which, like the couch, were covered with faded, worn tapestry. A wooden table stood in the middle of the room. The fireplace was a large open fire with an oven at one side and a boiler at the other. To the right of this was a Delft rack on which stood an assortment of odd pieces of china. There were four wooden rail-backed chairs tucked under the table, and to the side stood a basket chair, the seat well sunken with use. At the far end of the room was a larder with a marble-topped shelf running along one side, with, next door to it, a walled-off scullery area. Opposite was a door, which the woman opened and, switching on a light, passed through. She went down a flight of stone steps into what appeared to be a huge cellar, and which, fifty or so years ago, had been the kitchen of the house and the place for the servants below stairs. Like many such apartments for the lower classes in those days, it was not only below stairs but below ground and exceedingly damp.

The little fat woman now walked past the large disused rusty stove and the various cupboards going off the wall to her right side, and through another door and into a large back-yard. This had no boxes or stinking fruit lying about, but in it was built a modern flush closet. While she sat on the wooden seat there she wondered yet again, as she so often did, what could be done with the yard and the cellar. Of course it would need money, and although old Ham had been kind in leaving her the house, he hadn't left her any money, thinking that she could make a living from the business he had started long years ago of the fruit stall outside his house. Of course he had been right. She did make a living of sorts from it, but the extras had to come from other sources. Risky odds and

51

ends, such as harbouring Mr Weir's vans in this very yard at night sometimes.

Funny that. He was the only man she knew who hadn't a nickname, and he was always referred to, by his van men or those about, as Mr Weir. He was an unknown quantity, old Ham had said. They were the words he had used, Weir was an unknown quantity, and that was many years ago, because no one had ever seen him. But whoever he was he still owned remainder warehouses and sometimes dealt in questionable goods, and used more yards than her own for storing these last. However, he paid well and she couldn't but say it was a godsend at times; even though she was always glad to come down of a morning to do her business and see the yard empty. She hadn't given his main driver a key for the back door to the cellar – there was no need to. The stuff in the vans was a varied assortment of goods, cheap and otherwise, but one thing she wouldn't allow, she had stuck out against it, and that was letting them have the cellar for storage. No! She could talk herself out of a police raid by saying that she had no knowledge of what was in the vans that spent the night in her yard, but she would never get away with the same tale about her cellar, which was a part of her house . . .

By eight o'clock she had her fruit stall in place in front of the window to the right of her front door. The window had a deep sill, and boxes of fruit were piled on it. On the two front shelves of her narrow stall she had arranged various fruits. To the side stood a sack of potatoes and two orange boxes, their divisions now filled with leeks, carrots, turnips, cabbages and bunches of radishes.

There were four other decaying houses in the short street known as The Jingles, and each was used as a business of sorts. The front room of the one next to Bella's was a cobbler's shop. Next to that was a butcher's, which, it was rumoured, sold only horse meat. The fourth had been turned into an outdoor beer shop, and the ground-floor rooms of the last house held an assortment of second-hand – or you could say fourth, fifth or sixth-hand – clothing, but in them could be found something to suit all ages from the cradle upwards. It was a Paddy's market, all right, and well patronised.

The patrons of this little side-street, as one could imagine, were the lowest in the human scale, yet the businesses in it provided their owners with just enough sustenance to live. It was also frequented by those who had no money with which to buy: they came either to beg or to steal; those deciding on the latter course were naturally good runners.

On a Friday and Saturday Big Bella's stall could be cleared by dinner-time, but on Monday, Tuesday or Wednesday half her goods would find their way at the end of the day into the side-yard, which once had housed a horse, carriage and tack room with a groom's quarters situated above. These uses had long gone and there remained now what had been the wash-house, and was still the wash-house.

Today was a Friday, and the boxes her boys had brought her from the market were naturally all seconds or, you could say, thirds, but in their way they were good and there was little she'd had to pick out, and even that could be sold for a copper later in the day. So now she sat on her stool, which today, because the air was sharp, was placed just within her partly open front door.

She was not afraid, while attending her stall, to leave her door a little way open for, should anyone try to push it further, it was so arranged that it would knock over an old ship's bell, and this was always a deterrent more telling than a police whistle.

So her day began. She would leave the stall at ten o'clock when she would go indoors to make a drink; and again at twelve midday till half past when she would make herself a meal. At these times the stall was taken over by one-arm Peg-leg, a description that spoke for itself. He was a 'remnant' left from the Boer War, who had taught himself to read and write; he could also count, so in different ways he was invaluable to the small business people of The Jingles. Moreover, he was known to be trustworthy. However, by seven o'clock that evening Bella was sitting comfortably in the old basket chair in her kitchen with a glass of porter at her side on the table. The day's takings had been gone over and found to be satisfactory. She'd had no stuff to throw into the yard, only empty boxes; and now she was giving herself a half-hour's break before she started cleaning the room, which, keeping to the pattern of years, she did every Friday night. She was looking through the pictures in an illustrated magazine. The 'boys' always brought in any picture paper they came across because they knew she liked to look at them.

She was about to take her last mouthful of porter when she heard a dull thumping on the wall to the right side of the fireplace. That meant someone wanted her attention, but why? It was only an hour ago that she had given the men their nightly bowl of soup and a shive of cheese and bread, with the warning that before they turned in they were to get that yard cleaned up as much as they could. If not, there would be no beds for them tomorrow night. With this false warning she had closed the gates on them. But now she felt something must be amiss because only once before had she heard the thumping; and that had been when Pimple Face had the jitters and Joe could do nothing with him. Joe had been concerned for his friend. The closeness of the two very different men had always puzzled her. There was Geordie Joe, all of six foot and Pimple only five foot four. She knew where Geordie Joe had come from: she herself had engaged him when she couldn't understand a word he said, for he was from the north-eastern end of the country where they spoke a different language. Where Pimple came from in London she didn't know; she didn't think he knew himself. Ham had taken him on, likely out of the gutter. At first she used to think they hadn't a penn'orth of brains between them, but she had learnt differently, for she had found they were both wily, yet also in a way wise, and they weren't greedy.

Hurriedly she picked up the keys from a little table standing by the hall-stand, and from there she took her coat, pulled it about her and went out, making sure, as always, to lock her door behind her. When she opened the rusty gates, there they both stood in the dim light waiting for her. 'What's happened?' she demanded.

It was Joe who answered her in a thick whisper: 'We've got a visitor.'

'A visitor? What're you talking about?'

Joe jerked his head towards Pimple, saying, 'He knows more about her than I do.'

'It's a woman?'

'Yes, it is.' Pimple was nodding at her, his high squeaky voice now a whisper. 'It's the one that's been knocking around the market for some time. Sleeping rough. She looks like a scarecrow. Well, you'll see for yourself. We had cleared this side,' he turned his head towards where the stables had once been, then thumbing over his shoulder, he said, 'when we heard this rustle in the far corner where the boxes are piled up.'

Joe put in, 'We thought it was rats like. We thought we had got rid of them but you never can, not proper like.'

That word 'like' was another thing that identified Joe. Whether it was anything to do with the area he came from, she didn't know, although she could place many of the lads who came begging by the way they spoke.

Joe nodded towards the smaller man, who went on, 'She's not like the ordinary dossies. It's her get-up. It's obviously been classy, but she's a bit wrong in the head. The market fellows said she was dumb. And she's not after making coppers on the game because, they tell me, she's petrified of men. But only yesterday I heard Mickey Robson talking about her. He said a funny thing happened. It was early on and she must have sneaked in in the dark and he caught her taking an apple from a box, and he gripped her hand, saying, 'What're you up to?' And when she dropped the apple he said she shivered like a jelly. He said he had heard of her afore and thought she was one of the meths lot, but apparently she wasn't. As delicate as she looked she had almost torn one of the men's eyes out when he tried to get her to the floor. They give her a wide berth down there now. He said he didn't know where she kips out, but kip out she does, because her clothes are in a mess, but they must've been stylish at one time. Funny but stylish. She wears a hat, velvet one with a peak on it like a clerk's shade.'

'What d'you mean by a clerk's shade?' Bella asked abruptly.

'Well, you know, men in newspapers and offices, they wear a greenish eye-shade against the light. Hers is only a narrow brim, yet it covers her eyes. It got round too that she's dumb, but not deaf because she seems to understand every word that's spoken. But all the time she looks terrified, Mickey Robson said. He had picked up another apple and handed it to her, and then he found she wasn't dumb because she muttered very quietly, 'Thank you', and as Robson said himself, it was no working lass's voice that spoke. And then Sullivan, who was there, said he had once seen her go into a pie and pea shop. Somebody, too, must have told the Salvation Army lasses about her and the way she was dressed, and when they came back with one of their officers and he went to take her arm, she thrust him off and ran. And now we've got her.'

'What d'you mean, "we've got her"?' said Bella harshly. 'And how, in the name of God, did she get in here? What have you two been up to? Have you been out and left that gate open?'

It was Joe who answered: 'No, Bella. No. Except for a few

minutes when I took a barrowload of muck to the tip and I left Pimple here sweeping.'

'It must've been then,' said Pimple. 'I went into the wash-house for a minute to see if the fire was all right: we had filled a pot of water, we were going to have a swill down.'

Bella was making her way through the debris to the far corner of the yard; and there she stopped and looked down into a white face from which two large eyes, expressing plain terror, stared back at her. The woman's legs were drawn up under what appeared to be a long dark coat; she looked like a bundle of rags. Bella took a deep breath, then said quietly, 'It's all right; nobody's going to hurt you.'

The two men standing to the side of her exchanged glances; and they were more surprised when their boss, as they thought of her, said, 'Come on! Stand up! Let's see you!'

When the creature made no move Bella put out her hands and, gripping the woman's shoulders, pulled her to her feet, at the same time being surprised at the lightness of her; the large coat would have suggested quite a big body underneath. When she said, 'Why don't you go in a kip somewhere?' she knew it was a stupid thing to say. If the woman had any money that's likely what she would have done. She now had to put her hand out quickly to stop the form that was standing lopsidedly before her from swaying.

Pimple cried, 'Watch it! she's gonna pass out.'

Geordie Joe's big arms prevented the woman collapsing to the ground again, and as he held her limp body he looked at Bella, saying, 'What now, eh? What now?'

'Take her to the wash-house.'

'What? You mean carry her there like . . . ?'

'Well, as far as I can see, you big stook, she's not going to fly, is she? Or trot, or run?'

'She might be lousy.'

'Well, it won't be the first time you've had them crawl over you, will it? So stop your chatter and come on.'

In the wash-house, Joe hesitated. 'Where might I put her?'

'Where d'you think? On the floor!'

So he laid the unconscious woman on the floor, and there Bella leant over her and, pushing the peak of the cap upwards, she touched the fair hair that spread from under the velvet rim. Then, her hand going to the back of the head, and feeling the large pouch there, she remarked, as if to herself, 'Must have a lot of hair to tuck in there.'

'I wonder where she's from,' said Pimple. 'I wonder what's happened to her.'

'That's what I'd like to know too, Pimple. Anyway, she'll have to stay in here tonight.'

'What? With us?'

'Yes, Joe, with you. That is, unless you'd like to sleep outside in the boxes.'

'Well, from what I hear and Pimple says, she's scared of men.'

'Then you've got to reassure her, haven't you?' Bella's voice had risen. 'Will you take it on yourself to put her back among the boxes or out into the street? Tomorrow I'll let you do it. Yes, in fact I'll tell you to do it. But for tonight I say she sleeps here.'

'There's no other mattress.'

'As I understand it, Joe,' said Bella now, 'you're sleepin' on a decent one. Well, you can let her have it for the night. Pimple there kips on two thin pallets; I'm sure he'll share one with you. That right, Pimple?'

'Aye. Aye, Bella,' the words were tentative, 'if . . . if Joe's willin'.'

'Joe has no option in the matter.' Bella's voice was loud now, and it must have disturbed the woman for she put a hand to her face; then, her eyes opening, she stared up again into the face of the short fat woman bending over her and she did not move; that was until her glance turned sideways and, through the light of the swinging oil lamp, she saw the figures of two men, one very big, the other very small. Quickly pulling her legs up under her, she shuffled her body away towards the boiler. Another foot and she would have been touching the fire door, but Bella's hand stopped her as she warned, 'Look out, if you don't want to be burned! Now, it's all right, you've got nothing to be afraid of from these two. D'you hear me? D'you know what I'm saying to you?' Bella was kneeling on the floor now by the side of the woman and her face was on a level with hers as she said, 'You passed out, and you're in no fit state to go trudging the streets tonight. You may stay in here until the morning; and I promise you these two men won't touch you. D'you hear me? Do you understand what I'm saying to you?'

There was no vocal answer, but after a long moment the head made a small downward movement, although the eyes still remained full of fear.

'What's your name?'

The woman's head drooped forward, and Bella took her meaning: she wasn't going to say. So she said to her, 'Lift yourself on to this mattress here; and don't worry, I promise you you'll be safe until the morning.'

The woman did as she was told; then Bella said, 'I'd take off me shoes if I was you.' But for answer the woman drew her feet upwards and tucked them under the long coat, at which Bella said, 'Well, have it your own way. They're your feet and as far as I can see they're wet. Are you hungry?' But as she said this Bella thought she needn't have asked, and immediately turned to the men and said, 'I don't suppose either of you has a sandwich or anything tucked away in your pocket?'

Big Joe said nothing, but Pimple said somewhat shyly, 'Well, I've got a couple of buns in me coat.' Then he added quickly, 'I bought them, I didn't nick them. I got them along at the bakery, you can ask.'

'Shut up! Anyway, hand one over.'

59

Bella offered it to the woman, who was now sitting half upright propped against the warm wall side of the boiler. She looked at the hand holding the bun and her lips moved each over the other before her hand came out and picked it from the extended palm. She did not immediately put it to her mouth; but, her head turning slowly, she looked towards the small man, and there were the two words that she had been known to utter before, only this time in a croak as she said, 'Thank you.'

The effect of this on Pimple was to make him move swiftly from one foot to the other. It was as if he was about to do a jig. Then he looked at his companion, and from Joe to his boss, and what he muttered was, 'She's a different kettle of fish.'

Bella looked at him. He had a feeling in him, had Pimple: as he said, that one sitting there *was* a different kettle of fish. For a moment she wondered how long it had been since she'd had a square meal – her arms felt fleshless. On an impulse she said, 'You come with me, Joe, and I'll give you a bowl of soup for her; and if you're civil I might find a can of cocoa for you both.' And then she added as she went out of the door, 'I must be going up the pole;' and to this Joe said on a laugh, 'Just as you say, boss, just as you say: you must be going up the pole.'

Ten minutes later Joe was being pushed back through the gates by Bella. He was carrying a small straw basket in which stood a bowl of soup with a plate over it, and on the plate was a large bacon sandwich, and to the side of this was a lidded can of steaming cocoa. And as she stood locking the gates he did not walk away, but turned to look back through the rusted iron tracery and say to her quietly, 'You're a bit of all right, you know, Bella. A bit of all right. There's never been a better.'

Bella Morgan watched the big fellow disappear into the darkness; then she walked slowly to her front door, unlocked it, and entered her house.

After locking the door, she sat down in the basket chair, and she repeated, 'You're a bit of all right, you know, Bella. A bit of all right. There's never been a better.' That was a compliment and a compliment indeed. And nobody in her life, not even Ham, after she had nursed him all those years, had said, 'You're a bit of all right, Bella. A bit of all right.' It had taken that big rough galoot of a fellow to pay her the first compliment of her life. Here she was, thirty-eight years old. She was five foot two, fat, and as plain as a pikestaff, so marriage hadn't been for her. Men ignored her. No, not all men. Her father hadn't . . . She got swiftly to her feet and shook herself: she had never cried in her life and she wasn't going to start now.

2

The following morning, Bella was eager to get into the yard to see what had transpired during the night. Her first surprise was that both her helpers were up and dressed. They met her half-way up the yard, and she said to them, 'Where is she?'

'Where you left her last night, and she's sound asleep. It must be the warmth of the boiler – she's as close to that wall as to be almost inside it,' said Joe.

'Did she eat her soup?'

'Eat her soup?' Pimple put in. 'Bella, she wolfed it; and the sandwich an' all; and I gave her a can-lid full of cocoa; and she took it from me without shrinking back.'

'She shrinks from me,' said Joe. 'It must be me size. What you goin' to do with her? Give her a job of some sort?'

'Ask yourself, man, what job have I got to give her? Anyway, it takes me all me time to keep you two goin'.'

'By the looks of her,' said Pimple, 'I don't think she'd expect much, only to be warm and have a bite. I thought . . . well,' he swung his head from side to side, 'I'm sort of sorry for her. She's not like others about . . . I mean any of them sleeping rough. And she looks so scared. I've a feeling she must've had a great shock of some kind and it's turned her head, because she can speak. Well, you know, you heard her; but she won't talk; she can hear all right, though . . . everything. I'd like to know where she comes from. One thing seems certain' – his voice was firm now, unusual for him – 'it wasn't the gutter, because in spite of the muck, I mean the state her clothes are in with mud and that, I swear she's known a different class.'

'My! She's got you, hasn't she?' said Bella, on a laugh.

She left them, to go into the wash-house. As they had said, the woman was still fast asleep and curled up against the wall, which held the warmth from the dead fire. She did not know whether or not to waken her, and she asked herself, waken her to what? To go out on the road again to scratch for food, just as, apparently, she had been doing, and sleeping rough? Yes; and by the sight of that coat, very rough indeed. But, then, what was she going to do with her? She had no work to offer her; in fact, she thought, if, as Pimple surmised, she was a real lady, she might never have dirtied her hands in her life. But if that was the case why weren't her people looking for her? She was not one who could be easily overlooked. Somebody would surely have remembered seeing her: hereabouts she must have stuck out like a sore thumb. That coat and funny hat had not been bought at any second-hand stall, of that she was certain. She had felt the cloth of the coat when she had gripped the woman's arms. It was blanket thickness, and under the collar it was still a bonny green, as was the top of the cloche or turban or whatever name you could put to the hat.

She went out, thinking, I'll leave her for a while, but she must be out of there before I set up me stall.

It was some time later when she had got the can of tea and a breakfast bite ready for her workers that the knock came on her front door again, and there stood the two men, both grinning widely as they said, 'You want to come and see what's happening.'

'What d'you mean what's happening?'

'What she's doing, the one we left asleep.'

She handed them the straw basket holding their food and drink, then accompanied them back through the gates and into the yard.

It was broad daylight now and there was the woman. She was sweeping the remnants from the boxes into a heap in the middle of a cleared piece of the yard. A number of boxes in good condition were standing neatly piled one on top of the other against the far wall, broken ones were placed on the ground at the foot of them.

Bella turned and looked at the two men, and Joe said, 'What d'you make of that now?'

'What I make of it,' she said tartly, 'is that she's startin' to clear the yard, as you should've done a long time ago.'

'Oh, Bella.'

'Never mind oh, Bella.' She walked from them now and when she approached the woman whatever she meant to say was checked by the refined but muffled voice saying, 'Thank you – work.'

To this Bella answered, but only after a moment, 'There was no need; but thank you all the same.'

Then pointing to the rest of the disordered yard, the woman again said, 'Work.'

Bella looked from one to the other of her men; then, turning to the woman again, she said, 'You mean you're asking to work for me here?'

Now the head made a downward motion, and to this Bella said, 'But . . . but I can't afford to take anybody else on.'

Now the woman's head was shaking, and she turned and pointed towards the wash-house and then to her mouth, and it was Pimple who translated her seemingly deaf and dumb language by muttering to Bella, 'I think she's trying to say she doesn't want pay, just somewhere to kip and something to eat.'

The woman's gaze was now on Pimple, and she was nodding.

'You mean you'll sleep with the men?' said Bella.

Immediately the woman stepped backwards quickly, her body seemed to shrink inside the big coat and her head drooped on to her chest; again Pimple translated, saying, 'She doesn't want to sleep along of us. That's awkward, isn't it, Bella, 'cos that's our kip?'

Bella made no comment, for she was experiencing a most strange feeling as she stared at this long-coated odd creature, and the feeling told her that whatever arrangement had to be made she couldn't let the woman go into the outside world, of which she sensed she was afraid and where she would certainly be taken down by some man and probably end up in the river.

She turned to the men: 'Get your bait, then before you go I'll give you a bite to put in the wash-house for her. You, Pimple, try and explain to her – I mean about me locking the gate. Make it plain to her she can't get out even if she wants to.'

'By the look of things I don't think she'll bother too hard to get out,' said Joe.

'You leave that to me; but when you're out look about and see if you can get your hands on a single mattress of some kind; but see it's clean, not walking.'

'Aye, Bella. Aye, I'll do that,' Joe assured her. Then they all turned and looked at the woman, who was sweeping again as if her work had not just been interrupted . . .

She was still sweeping, but more slowly, when at ten o'clock Bella went out to her and said, 'Drop that,' nodding towards the brush, 'and come into the wash-house and have this.'

The woman obeyed her. When they were inside Bella handed her the can of tea and a paper plate on which there was a thick slice of bread and dripping, and she said, 'Sit down and take it easy; if you mean to clean that yard it'll take days. And another thing, I don't know where you're going to sleep because you won't sleep in here with the men, will you?'

The woman turned her head away, and Bella, a little irritably, said to her, 'What's your name?' and when the head did not turn towards her, Bella said, 'You must have a name I can call you, for goodness' sake!' The woman muttered something, and Bella repeated, 'Rain?'

The woman now stared at her; then wetting a finger, she went to the dirty window and on it she traced out the letters RE, and Bella said, 'R . . . E? RE?' Then almost on a laugh, she said, 'Ren-e?' The woman's head was nodding now. 'Reenee! Reenee! Aye. Aye.' Bella was nodding too. 'I see now: not rain, but Reenee.' Then more nodding, and Bella said, 'Nice name, Reenee.' Then, being the practical woman she was, she asked, 'You found the privy in this yard, did you?' And to the unspoken confirmation, she said, 'Well, that's something. And that's a place now that wants cleaning out. Those two beggars should've seen to it. But don't you bother with it; I'll have a go at them. I'll be back around twelve.' And with this she turned and left Reenee, wondering, as she did so, why the woman should bother her. But bother her she did; as did wondering where she was going to let her kip that night. She certainly wouldn't let her stay in the house. Oh, no; she wasn't going to have any of that. But there was the cellar. It was as cold as charity, but there was the fireplace. Old Ham used to have that fire on when he brought in pieces of old furniture, what he called antiques, and at such times the fire would be lit while he worked at mending them. Well, that seemed the only solution; but God in heaven, why was she bothering? It was Saturday and she had a decent lot of stuff to sell, the best she'd had for some time . . .

At a quarter past twelve, after she had finished her own meal, she took a bowl of soup and a meat pie into the girl, as she now thought of her, with the name Reenee, and found her chopping up boxes into kindling. In the wash-house the boiler was already full of water and the fire on. She called her in,

66

then said, 'My word, you've been busy, haven't you? And you've cleaned this place up an' all. I've not been able to look through that window for years. Now sit yourself down and have this bite.'

Reenee's eyes were on the little fat woman now and there was no longer any fear in them.

'I've thought of where you might kip. I – I mean sleep. But it couldn't be tonight because you'd freeze. It's in the cellar. There's a fireplace down there. It used to be the kitchen of the house, you know, and it's a good burner, and once that's lit . . . well . . . well, you could sleep down there. That's if the lads can get a mattress.' And then she added thoughtfully, 'And nobody would be able to get at you 'cos the door to the outside is bolted top and bottom, and the only way you can enter it is from my kitchen. So you wouldn't have to worry. You understand?'

Reenee nodded; then, her hand going slowly out, her fingers touched the little fat woman's wrist. It was only a featherlight touch but it brought a rush of feeling into Bella's body such as she had never experienced before. She did not realise it to be compassion, she knew only that she felt sorry for the creature, sorry to the bottom of her heart. But the reason for feeling like this she couldn't fathom. She was experiencing the strangest emotions. Look at last night: that big galoot had spoken to her like he did, and now the feeling for this broken reed.

Why, she asked herself sternly now, should those words come into her head – broken reed? Then she remembered seeing them in a magazine somewhere when somebody's sad life was being described. They were a broken reed, it had said. 'Get on with your bite,' she said, as she turned abruptly and went out.

Her stall was cleared by half past three in the afternoon. There wasn't even a cabbage leaf left, and the little guttersnipe gathered up the empty boxes, together with the trestles, and took them to the iron gates. When she opened them he carried the stuff inside and, as usual, went to throw the boxes into a heap, only to be stopped by Bella yelling at him, 'Stack them up! D'you hear me? Take them over to that wall where the other ones are.' She pointed to the far end of the yard and, much surprised, the youngster made three journeys with the boxes and stacked them against the wall. Then, still obeying orders, he put the trestles and the planks into what had once been a coalhouse. But he was a bit peeved when Bella added nothing to the twopence she gave him daily for running errands and clearing up.

She did not go to see what the new acquisition to her staff was about, but went into the house and made herself a cup of tea, then sat thinking about the girl and her sleeping quarters. If she let her stay in the cellar she would have to come through this house to get to it, because in no way could Bella risk giving her a key to the back door. Let's face it, she told herself, she didn't know what the creature might be up to. The word 'creature' had kept popping into her mind when she thought of the girl, probably suggested by the weird coat and hat she wore. Of one thing she was certain, the girl wasn't quite normal: something had happened to her to knock her off balance. What it was she would like to know, and she was sure she would come to know eventually; but it would take time because she would be dealing with a still very frightened creature. One thing more, there must be somebody, some-where, looking for her: a girl like that wouldn't be without a family. Surely not. Whoever had been the cause of her distress must be known to others, and they must definitely, if they had any heart at all, want to know what had become of her. Yet she had been in the gutter, so to speak, for at least some months now. Well, she told herself, there was no use sitting here mulling over something she couldn't get to the bottom of, not as yet anyway. She'd take the girl down and see her reactions to the cellar.

When Reenee entered Bella's house for the first time she stopped abruptly within the small hall and gazed about her; and Bella, seeing this, said, 'Surprised, are you? You didn't expect to see it clean and tidy and holdin' decent pieces. Well, come and see something better still.' Pushing open the door, she said, 'This is my kitchen and sitting room. I have a parlour but I don't use it. No need to; but it would also surprise you.'

Again Reenee had stopped and looked around her. Then her eyes became fixed on the fireplace, where a large iron pan stood on the hob, something quietly bubbling within it.

'This wasn't really the kitchen,' Bella said, 'it was a sort of dining-room. The kitchen's downstairs in the cellar. Come on.'

At the top of the stone stairs, she switched on a light, then another when they reached the bottom. And this showed up the long room, bare but for a pile of broken furniture in one corner.

Bella pointed to the rusted iron range. 'That's what I was talkin' about. It's a good fire, had to be in those days for all the cookin' they did. But it eats wood, and needs coal.' The word coal immediately presented her with the idea that she could pay Reenee by giving her a bag of coal each week. Aye, that would be an idea.

She unlocked the back door and, pointing towards a door across the yard, she said, 'That's the privy, a better one than the other; but if you intend to sleep down here, don't go out to it in the middle of the night because . . . well, there might be vans in the yard. That's another thing. Don't take any notice of the commotion there might be around late evenings or in the dead of night. There's nobody trying to get in, they just . . . well, they just store their vans there until the next morning. You understand?'

Reenee indicated that she did. Then she looked up and down the large yard and the look of bewilderment on her face made Bella ask, 'What is it? I told you, nobody can get in

69

except the vans and the men on them. Look yonder: there are two stout gates and they are locked. You'll be all right here, only always keep your door bolted because somebody might get curious if they see smoke coming from the chimney. You never know; there's always a sharp one among them. Oh, for that matter' – she was talking as if to herself now – 'they're all sharp, a weird lot.' She pointed again to the lavatory. 'Do you want to go to the lav?' And when Reenee indicated that she did, Bella stepped back into the room to wait. Looking about her, she asked herself again why the hell she was doing this and going to all this trouble. Was she lonely? Did she want company? Well, if she wanted company she had picked on the wrong one, hadn't she, because the girl had hardly opened her mouth. Most of the time she talked in sign language like someone dumb.

When the girl joined her again, she walked past Bella and straight to the fireplace. There, with excitement, she pointed to the grate, then acted as if she were lighting a fire. Next, she pointed towards the ceiling and, as if somewhat exasperated, Bella said, 'Look, you can do nothing until tomorrow. That fire eats wood.'

Again Reenee pointed upwards, and Bella said, 'Aye, I know there's plenty of wood up there, but down here that wouldn't last you a week.'

Then, facing her and closing her eyes tightly, Reenee put her hand to her throat. It would seem she had to press the words upwards and into her mouth and through her lips as she said, 'Tonight.' She then put her hand on her face and bent her head, indicating sleep.

'You want to sleep here tonight?'

The indication was yes.

'But, woman, there's not a spare mattress unless Pimple gives you one of his spare pads; although they might find one when they're out and about today. And look' – she turned and swept her hand as if she were taking in the whole large

70

room – 'you'll catch your death; it would be as bad as lying in the gutter.'

The girl's head now drooped on to her chest, then moved slowly from side to side, and Bella's voice was soft as she said, 'All right. All right, lass. Come on; we'll see what we can do. They should be in about six and I'll set them to work cleaning that stove with emery paper.'

The head came up sharply and shook at the suggestion, and Reenee pointed to herself, which Bella took to mean that she would clean it. She said, 'It'll be some job. But come on. I'm freezing already down here.'

They were about to pass through the kitchen when suddenly Bella stopped and, catching hold of the girl's arm, she said, 'Look; sit yourself down on that chair and I'll make a cup of tea.'

Reenee remained perfectly still and she stared at Bella, who, looking into the pale grey eyes, saw in them an expression she could not fathom.

For a moment she thought the girl was going to cry, but the lids drooped and the eyes were closed. Then she watched her turn round slowly and sit down in the chair she had indicated.

Bella lifted the heavy pan dextrously from the hob and put it on the side plate. Then she thrust the kettle into the heart of the fire, and all the while she talked.

'If you decide to stay down there, as I said, you'll need coal. Now, you indicated earlier on when I told you I couldn't afford to pay you that you would work for your board and keep, so to speak. I can promise you a decent board but I think it's a very poor keep sleeping down there. However, it's up to you. But, as I said, that fire eats wood and won't keep on without coal. So I'll pay you with a bag of coal each week. How much you use of it each day will be up to you. Now, as regards work.' She was taking cups and saucers down from the Delft rack and placing them on a tin tray, which stood towards the end of the table and already held a teapot stand.

'When the yard is finished what d'you think you can do? One thing, I think, is already certain: you don't want to go out and about, so you'll be no good going to the market. Anyway, they'd likely chase you in that get-up thinkin' you were on the pinch again. Oh, I heard about you and takin' the apple from Mickey Robson's box. So as far as I can see there's only housework.' She was now pouring the hot water into the teapot, in which she had previously placed three large spoonfuls of tea from a wooden caddy that resided on the mantelpiece, as she added, 'You've likely never been used to housework, but on the other hand have you ever been used to clearing up a yard like that one outside? I doubt it, but you did it. It was a case of needs must where the devil drives, I suppose.

'I don't know how long you've been on the road, lass, but you must've learnt a bit about work in that time. There, I'll let it draw a bit. I can't stand weak tea. D'you take sugar? Anyway, I'll put two in. You can help yourself to more if you want it; and there's milk there an' all. Could you clean this house, d'you think? I mean sweep and dust and polish and things like that, like a housewife does. I did it meself for years until I had to take over the stall when old Ham died. I'll tell you about him some time.'

She went to the Delft rack again and took down a plate; then from a cupboard standing to the side she took two large iced buns and put them on the plate; and this she placed before the girl. She poured out a cup of tea, and put it and the milk jug next to the plate. And her surprise was evident as she saw Reenee's hand go out to the cup but not lift it, just stroke the side of it with her fingertips, then the saucer.

For the first time, too, Bella noticed that the girl's finger-nails were clean. She decided that she must have scrubbed them well under the tap in the wash-house. But why had she stroked the cup and saucer? She was an odd creature if ever there was one. And she was more surprised now to see the

72

girl turn from the table, stand up and walk towards the wall at the left side of the fireplace, and there point to an ornamental glass rolling pin hanging by a piece of string from a hook. Tapping it, she turned to the table and made the action of rolling it, and Bella cried, in a sort of childish delight because she had translated this action, 'You mean you can cook?'

The affirmation was firm.

'Well, that's good, that *is* good. All right; sit down and have your bite and then we'll take it from there. Cooking. Well I never!'

On this Bella became silent as her thoughts raced and she began to sum up the creature, as she would still think of her. Here she was, wearing a coat and bonnet-cum-hat, which was class stuff; and her shoes, too . . . well, what was left of them . . . had been of the best. Moreover, the few words she spoke weren't common like. There was no trace of the Cockney or yet of anything like Geordie Joe's twang, or Welsh, or Scots. She would've detected Scots in the voice because hadn't Ham, or Hamish as was his name, been a Scot to the marrow? Then there was a certain twang – no, not a twang, more a haughty tone like some ladies used when jabberin' away to each other, when their words sounded as if they were comin' out of the top of their heads. No, it wasn't like that. She couldn't put a name to the way this girl spoke. One thing was sure, it wasn't common. It wasn't la-di-da either, but it certainly wasn't common. Yet she could do all these common things, and now the latest, she could cook. Dear, dear. There was something very strange about her, very strange indeed. And Bella would very much like to get to the bottom of it. Aye, she would that. But who knew? Food and warmth, and that fear she seemed to have of men taken from her, that might loosen her tongue.

As she said, 'Get that tea down you, and the bun,' there was a knock on the front door. She opened it to her two helpers

73

standing there, and straight away she said to them, 'Did you get it, the tick?'

'Yes.' Pimple was nodding at her.

'Well, where is it?'

It was Joe who answered: 'We've got one, Bella; and it's a good one, a new one. But it won't be' – he was going to say 'delivered' when she said, 'Shut up! and come inside,' and practically hauled the two of them over the step, finishing, 'You want the street to know? Wipe your feet, then come into the kitchen and let me know the rest.'

She left them, and in a minute they followed her to the kitchen where they stood like two awkward youngsters near the head of the couch looking at the table, then at Reenee sitting there. She was looking at them, and there was now no fear in her eyes.

'Out with it!' said Bella sharply. 'What about this delivery? What're you talkin' about?'

'Well, I was in the warehouse. You know, helpin' to straighten up.'

'Aye,' Bella cut in now. 'What were you straightenin' up this time? Dinner services or chamber pots?'

The two men laughed. 'Nothing like that, Bella. Loads of Army boots, old style, and hundreds of tin plates and mugs. They must've been clearing out some barracks.'

'It must've been on the level an' all,' said Bella.

'Oh, aye, this job was on the level. Half his stuff's on the level, that's why he gets off with the other half, I suppose.'

'You're right there. Well, go on and tell me what happened about the mattress.'

'I put it to one of the fellows what I was on the look-out for like. A damaged one; I said it wouldn't matter. Well, it was just before I came away, and he called me aside and said there'd be a new one dropped off late when the vans came into the yard.'

'Oh, they're comin' tonight, are they?' said Bella. 'They

74

haven't been for a while. What is it this time?'

'Oh, I wouldn't even guess, Bella. And I've no idea of the time; but how they get those horses and vans in there without making much of a rattle at night I'll never know.'

'Oh, aye, the horses.' Bella now turned to Reenee. 'Don't worry if you hear the jingle of harnesses and horses' hoofs. You see, they take the horses away for the night and bring them back in the morning, about seven or so. At least most times.

'But anyway, you two, for tonight you'll have to let her have one of your pallets 'cos she's goin' to sleep in the cellar.'

'In the cellar!' This came on a high note from Joe. 'It's like death down there.'

'Yes; that's why you're goin' to the depot for a hundred-weight of coal; but you're not takin' one of the standard sacks; I'm not payin' for coal dust, I want roundies. Understand?'

'Aye, Bella.'

'And you, Pimple, bring your pallet round here; I'll give you the key to the gate. And bring in all the kindling she's chopped. The wash-house fire's already on; it's been goin' for half the day I should think. And you'll get your grub when you come back. All right? Stop eyeing the teapot, Joe.' Bella went to the cupboard in the dresser, bent down and took out two china mugs. After filling them with tea and four teaspoonfuls of sugar each she handed one to each of them. 'I'm doin' you an honour, for that's real good china with its name on the bottom.'

Joe made pretence of turning his mug over, then said, 'I'll empty it first, Bella.'

The men emptied the large mugs in almost two draughts. Then they were giving her their thanks as she ushered them to the front door where, in a low, changed tone, she said, 'I know it's Sunday in the morning and it's your free day when what you do and where you get to is no business of mine, but I'd like to know if you'll do something for me.'

They spoke and nodded together. 'Anything, Bella. Anything.'

'Well, will you go into that cellar down there and sweep the walls of the cobwebs and help to wash that floor, then see if there's anything worth mending among that lot of odd pieces and bits of furniture in the corner? Ham left them like that, and I must say I haven't bothered with them since – too busy. You'll lose nothing by it.'

'Oh, we'll do that, Bella. We will.'

And it was Pimple now who said, in a very quiet voice, 'She's no ordinary woman, is she? She's a sort of a lady.'

Bella looked at him closely for a moment before she said quietly, 'Aye, Pimple. I suppose in a way you could say that. She's a sort of a lady.'

3

Bella Morgan wasn't given to pondering. She had always been too busy looking for a way to fend for herself and go on living, or too tired to think at all. One thing had puzzled her when she had come to this part of London: she had been called Big Bella though she was only five foot two. Likely it was because of her voice: that was big and loud, and she wasn't afraid to raise it. But during the last month she had been made to ponder on how her existence had changed, been transformed, because this woman or girl or creature, as she had first thought of her, had turned into a sort of companion. But not only had her life, as it were, been changed, so had the lives of Geordie Joe and Pimple Face; not in their main occupations but in themselves. They were cleaner; she could even say they looked smarter, because they had been to Ginnie's clothes store down the road and rigged themselves out with some respectable fifth-hand gear. Moreover, they washed more often.

Washed. The word conjured up the first of the two incidents in the past month that had strengthened her interest in the girl, if that was needed. It had had to do with washing.

It happened on a Tuesday. There had been next to nothing to trade and it had rained all morning, and by two in the afternoon she had got her little helper to clear her stall and had presented him, to his delight, with two boxes of very questionable fruit, from which, nevertheless, she knew he'd make some coppers before the day was out; and she had walked down the now absolutely clean yard. She had never known it to be as clean in her time. As Pimple Face said, 'You could eat your bread off it.'

The rain had stopped and when she saw no sight of the girl as she usually would around this time, sitting on the log chopping the previous day's boxes into kindling, she knew she would be in the wash-house. As she neared it, she noticed the door was closed, which in itself was odd; the door of the wash-house was hardly ever closed except at night. Another thing that took her notice was that the window was covered up from the inside.

She made her approach quietly and looked at it. A sheet of newspaper was tucked into the frame. But it didn't actually fit it; there was a good half-inch gap at the side. She put her eye to this, and what came into her line of narrowed vision was a pile of clothing laid across the top of an orange box. There were two petticoats and a pair of fancy bloomers, which she immediately recognised as silk. Real silk. The bloomers had a lace frill, and round the band of the frill were garters, fancy garters, almost an inch deep slotted with ribbon. To the side was that coat. It was half open and she could glimpse the lining, of a light grey colour and the material like lamb's wool. A pair of stockings was hanging over the top of the box; the legs were a light grey but the feet were almost black, and she could distinctly see that one was badly holed.

There was the sound of faint splashing. Then the girl came into view: her whole body was bare and she was rubbing herself down with one of the two clean coarse towels Bella had given her only that morning for the boys. She was fascinated by the sight of her. She had a beautiful figure but it was so thin. She watched her now take up a garment she hadn't noticed. It seemed to be made of fine wool, and when she put it on it covered her like a skin and reached below her knees. It wasn't a chemise or anything in that line. She had never seen anything like it. It could have been a kind of fine woollen frock if it hadn't been so clinging. And now what did intrigue her was: when she saw her step into her bloomers she pulled out a little bag that was pinned to the inside of the hem, and she pulled it open by a silken cord at the top, and she put her fingers into it, then closed it again. It was like one of the small dorothy bags Bella had heard that ladies used to take to dances and such dos. They would hold only handkerchiefs and smelling salts and bits like that. When Reenee pulled her bloomers high the bag lay against her flat stomach and did not make a bulge. The first petticoat she put on was a waist one, the second had a bodice and straps, but she had no corsets. Funny that she had no corsets; and she was not even wearing a camisole that would hold her small breasts, but the long woollen garment was so shaped that it held them. At this point Bella had turned quietly away and made a hasty retreat from the yard.

In the kitchen she sat down in her basket chair. She did not bother to make herself a pot of tea but sat there; and now she did muse, not only muse but kept saying to herself that something should be done about that poor creature. She had come from good people, rich people, oh, yes. She knew finery when she saw it. And then there were the coat and hat. The coat might be mucky now but it had quality still.

And cap all this with her voice and what had you? Somebody who shouldn't be around here. Somebody who was off her head; well, not right off her head, but there was something wrong. She could speak, but she didn't; she seemed afraid to. She was petrified of men. Now that was an odd thing, for in the class she came from she would have met dozens and dozens of men. Had she been married? She didn't

79

wear a ring but that didn't signify. Something had happened to her, an accident of some kind that had affected part of her brain, because in other ways she was sensible and she took everything in.

Ah, but then – Bella now moved uneasily in her chair – how could she account for the lady, as presented by her voice and her clothes, working as she had been like a scavenger in that yard for weeks? And now in this very house: look how she had cleaned those rooms upstairs; and, above all, look at her cooking. Somebody somewhere had taught her to cook. She could make a roast, a stew, and she knew how to bake bread.

Oh – Bella rose to her feet – she wished she could get to the bottom of it all. Nothing had ever before intrigued her like this. What she knew she should do was to go to the authorities, not the local police station, but a big central one, and tell the top brass there all about Reenee, and say somebody must be looking for her somewhere. But what would happen then? They would send men here, and she would be off! Oh, yes, in that coat and hat and her worn-out shoes, and that would be the last she would see of her. And what then? She paused for a long while before she said, 'I'd miss her. She feels like a . . .' She couldn't put the word 'daughter' to the girl nor yet 'friend', and she wasn't much of a companion for she hardly ever opened her mouth, except to bring out the odd word, and this would be accompanied by sign language. But there was something about the girl, the woman, that touched Bella in some way. She felt she wanted to put her arms around her and comfort her. Aye, she did . . . as she would a child or someone in trouble. And, oh, aye, that girl was in trouble, or at least had been, in bad trouble . . .

The second event that had aroused Bella's interest even further happened on the day the old cobbler next door died. It was about the third week of Reenee sleeping in the cellar kitchen.

The cellar had taken on a new face, thanks to the work both Geordie Joe and Pimple Face put in every Sunday: they had not only swept the walls but painted them. They had acquired, from where Bella did not ask, three large tins of paint. One was an off white and the other two a deep blue.

By erecting the trestles and planks used for the fruit stall they had painted the grubby ceiling white. This part of the business had taken them over two weekends for first they had to clear the ceiling of its layers of smoke and dust gathered over the years. Their efforts in this particular line were rather messy: they endeavoured to clean it with wet mops. However, during the second weekend they painted it. If the result was a somewhat streaky white there was no one to grumble. Following this they painted the walls blue, which was quite successful because after two coats, as Bella herself said, you couldn't recognise the place. Moreover, they scrubbed the floor, during which time Miss Reenee, as they now called her, endeavoured, as she had been doing for some time, to finish cleaning the range of rust. Also its companion fender, which had turned out to be made of brass.

What was more, among the rubbish that had been thrown into the corner of the room the men had found a seatless basket chair, and nailed some boards across it to form a seat. To this Bella had added a large pillow to soften it, but which could also be used when the girl was sleeping on the comfortable mattress that had been left, as promised, in the yard, together with a good blanket still in its shop wrappings – both, as Joe informed her the next day, gifts from Mr Weir; and he had also added that he was told the message had come from the boss personally. Undoubtedly he thought they were for Bella's use alone.

Another concession had been made to the visitor. She was eating her evening meal with Bella. Not that she ate much, and what she did she seemed to nibble at slowly as if she had to make it last. Likely, Bella thought, she had taken up this

81

habit when she had first been thrust on to the road.

She looked at her now. She was sitting to the side of the fireplace staring into the fire, and she wondered what she was thinking about, if her muddled mind allowed her to think. She looked different, and of course she would without that coat and hat on her. Oh, what a job that had been to get them off her; she had seemed determined to go around doing the housework in them. Even to doing the cooking. She had allowed an apron to be put round her waist, but she had kept the coat on, until Bella had said, 'Now, look here, we've got to come to some new arrangement if you're going to stay with me. That coat and headgear's got to come off, at least while you're workin'.' She recalled the pained look the girl had given her as if she were depriving her of something she valued. She had suddenly taken her by the hand and almost run her up the stairs and through one of the four doors on the landing; and once inside the room she had flung her arm out, saying, 'Now look at it! There's nothing frightening up here, is there? There's a wardrobe and a dressing-table and a wash-stand with a little chest of drawers, together with a single bed. I can tell you, I thought I had reached heaven when I first slept in this room, and I can also tell you there's not many furnished like it in this row of houses. Now, you can come up here and you can take your hat and coat off in the morning and hang them in that wardrobe. Nobody's going to go near them. But if I were you, when you're so busy cleaning up all my belongings, I think you should take a brush to that coat and also sponge it down and iron it out. What've you got underneath? Let me see. Come on! Come on, now!' She had unclasped the hands that were holding the buttons of the coat; she was determined to have her way in this instance, so she unbuttoned the coat, opened its flaps and exclaimed, 'Well, now, a red velvet frock. What is there to be ashamed of in showing that? Certainly, being velvet, it's all creased and marked – velvet gets like that when it's roughly treated, which it's bound to be with you sleeping in it.'

The girl had turned from her and, pulling the coat close around her again, she sat on the edge of the bed, while Bella continued with her tirade: 'And that frock won't last for ever. Look, I know; I know it's no good suggestin' you goin' down to Ginnie's 'cos I know you won't; but I could, and it isn't all Paddy's market down there. She has a cupboard where she keeps lots of decent things. Two or three times she's tried to rig me out, but look at the shape of me. The clothes are either too narrow or too big for me; but she keeps me in skirts and things like that, and if I was any use with me needle I'd be able to alter things. I'm not, I know, never have been in that way, but there's no need why I can't bring a couple of frocks up to let you have a look at.'

When the head she was addressing drooped further down she said, 'All right. All right. But I'm goin' to insist on you leavin' that coat and hat up here. I can give you a kind of old cloak to put over your head when you go out of the front door to the gates. Now, I'm goin' to leave you here to think about it.'

As she reached the door she turned and said, 'You can take them downstairs at night when you go to your bed if you're so worried about them, but during the day when you're in the house I'm havin' to put me foot down.'

The girl had come down in the red dress, and Bella had gone on with her chattering as if she hadn't noticed any change in her new companion, and that was how she had come to think of the girl, as a sort of companion.

This particular night was a Friday night, and when her other two workers came into Bella's kitchen, as they often did now, on this occasion they were dressed in their Sunday best.

'Goin' somewhere?' said Bella, in surprise. At this they both looked awkward and grinned, and it was Joe who answered, 'We thought of goin' to the Tivoli. We hear there's some good turns on, and on a Friday night you can get up in the gods for threepence.'

'Can you now?' said Bella. 'And when did this idea attack you?'

The men exchanged glances; and then it was Joe who, inclining his head towards his friend, said, 'It was Pimple's. He'd like to hear the music, he said. He used to go at one time, didn't you, Pimple?'

Pimple nodded his lowered head. 'Well, well!' said Bella. 'It's better than the bars, I'll give you that.'

'Oh . . . I don't know if you know, Bella, but old Frankie next door died this afternoon. They said it was a heart-attack.'

Bella straightened up from where she had been going to put the kettle on the hob. 'He died this afternoon, you say? Well, well. Young Frankie will come into his own now; he's worked hard enough for the old niggard for years. Eeh, how Ham hated that man!' She laughed now. 'I wonder if they've met up wherever they've gone. Something happened between them long before I came on the scene. I only mentioned his name once in this house and never again because one night, I remember it like yesterday, he was standing where you are, Joe. I was cleaning the table there' – she thumbed towards it – 'and I said on a laugh, "Mr Francis next door offered me a job today. He said I could go and work for—" Well, that's as far as I got because . . . because he turned on me like, well, I don't know what, and he thrust out his arm and stabbed his finger towards me and growled at me, saying, "Don't speak ever again . . . about that man in my house; I can't abide . . ."'

She didn't finish, for she was looking at the two men who were staring over her shoulder towards where Reenee had been sitting in the chair, and she turned swiftly, and what she saw amazed her too: the girl was now as stiff as a ramrod. Her body was stretched out, supported by her bottom in a straight line across the front edge of the chair. From her head to her feet she was like a corpse and her arms were upraised as if she were pushing someone off her.

They all rushed towards her, the two men gripping her arms and Bella patting her face, saying, 'Come on, lass, come on.'

Then suddenly the middle of her body from her shoulders to her thighs began to heave up and down, up and down.

'She's havin' a fit,' whispered Pimple.

'Shut up!' muttered Bella.

Of a sudden they watched the whole body collapse and fold into the chair. The girl's head turned to the side and her hand came up and partly shaded the face, as if she were warding off a blow.

'It's all right. It's all right, love.' Bella's voice was reassuring. 'You're among friends; there's nothing to be afraid of. Come on; don't shrink back like that. Wake up. Come on; wake up from wherever you are.'

As if obeying an order Reenee's eyes slowly opened, and if Bella had never seen a look of terror on anyone's countenance before she saw it now. And again she was patting Reenee's face, saying, 'It's all right, lass, it's all right. You're among friends. I told you, there's nothing to be afraid of. Come on now.'

Bella straightened up and, pointing to the cupboard, she said to Joe, 'There's a bottle in there at the back. It's got some gin in it. Pour a drop out.'

As might have been expected, Reenee did not choke on the drink. She swallowed a mouthful, then lay back and closed her eyes again.

The three of them were standing apart now, and Pimple said, 'I wonder what brought that on, because just a minute before she was lookin' at you, at least at your back and the way you were pointing to Joe here and telling him about old Ham goin' for you.' Pimple nodded. 'It's funny, but it was as soon as you spoke that she suddenly stiffened out like that. It

85

was so sudden. I couldn't say anything to you.'

'Well,' said Bella tersely, 'what could I have said that would've caused that spasm? I only said, "Don't speak that man's name in this . . ." well, in fact I didn't finish, did I?'

It was Joe who repeated softly now, '"Don't speak." Perhaps that's why.'

'That's why what?' Bella demanded. 'Come on, tell me what you think that's why.'

'Well' – Joe moved from one foot to the other – 'I can't explain, really, but you sounded like somebody givin' an order, like old Ham used to do 'cos he had been in the Army once, I understand, in his young days, and what you said was, "Don't speak!" And, you see . . . well, she doesn't speak, does she? I mean it's an effort for her to say one word. D'you see what I mean?'

Yes; Bella saw what he meant, and now she groped for the back of a chair, turned it about and sat down where she could look at the almost crumpled body of this poor girl or woman or whatever she was, and she repeated softly, 'Don't speak.' Then, looking at Joe, she said, 'D'you think somebody must've told her that once?'

'Shouldn't be surprised, Bella, 'cos look at what she did with her hand, she put it up as if to save her face like.'

There was silence for a moment until Pimple said, 'Well, whatever happened she must have ended up with her head bein' bashed. That's probably what turned her brain a bit. What d'you say, Bella?'

'I don't know what to say, Pimple. That's the God's honest truth. I don't know what to say. But I'm more puzzled now than I was before about who she is and where she's come from.'

'I think she should lie down, Bella,' said Joe. 'We've got to help her downstairs; the state she's in, you'd never be able to hold her up.'

'No; you're right there, Joe.' She got up from the chair now and, bending over Reenee, she said, 'Come on, lass. We're goin' to get you down on to your bed.'

Reenee opened her eyes. The dreadful look had gone from them, but in them was such sadness that it affected all three of them, and when she tried to speak Bella checked her, saying, 'Don't try to get anything out, lass. Have a good night's rest and you'll feel better in the mornin'.'

The lads helped her to the top of the stairs, but there they knew they couldn't help her down, one on each side of her, and without any further words Joe picked her up in his arms and walked tentatively down the flight of stone steps and into the transformed cellar, where the new mattress lay to the side of the fireplace and on it a neatly folded blanket. To the other side of the fireplace there stood a half-full sack, and in front of this a lidless box in which there were some large pieces of coal. To the side of the bag was a pail covered over with a fruit box.

After Joe had laid her on the mattress, Bella grabbed the pillow from the old basket chair and put it under Reenee's head, and before she went to cover her with the blanket she pulled off the worn shoes, saying under her breath as she did so, 'I'll get these in to young Frankie tomorrow; he'll fix them within an hour. The uppers are still good, but look at the soles, they're through, and there's hardly any heels left. Anyway' – she straightened up – 'she'll be all right now. I'll see to her; thanks very much for your help. Get yourselves off to the show.'

It was Pimple Face who said, 'I'm not bothered any more, Bella, and you never know . . .' He turned and, looking at Joe, said, 'Do you . . . ? What I mean is, there might be need of somebody goin' for a doctor or something.'

'Aye; you're right,' said Joe. 'Yes, you're right, Pimple.'

The figure on the bed moved uneasily, and Bella pushed at them, saying, 'You see? She can hear all right again. She doesn't want to see any men at all, of any kind. Oh, I wish I knew the bottom of this. Anyway, get yourselves away.'

'We'll see,' said Joe. 'But before we go I'd better bank that fire up.' And so saying, he took a pair of old tongs from the hearth and put the roundie coals from the box one by one on to the smouldering fire until the grate was heaped up. Then he filled up the box from the sack before dusting his hands one against the other and repeating, 'We'll see, Bella.'

When the two men had gone up the steps, Bella, kneeling by the mattress, put her hand inside the blanket and took hold of Reenee's arm, and she stroked it gently before she asked, 'How're you feelin' now, lass?'

The woman turned from her and when, after a moment, Bella put out her hand and gently turned her face towards her, it was only to see it was running with silent tears. She murmured, 'Oh, my lass! Don't.' She felt in her pocket to see if she had a handkerchief, and not finding one she took the end of her apron and wiped Reenee's face with it; and then she said softly, 'Don't be feared of anything, me dear. Nobody's goin' to hurt you here. Those two lads that's just gone away, they'll see to that. And if you don't want to go beyond the door, except to the yard next, well, that's good enough for me. I won't press you in any way, lass. There now. Don't distress yourself.'

But Reenee was gasping in her throat and her mouth opened wide before she brought out a single word, a broken 'Sor-ry.'

'Oh, girl, you've got nothin' to be sorry for. You had a kind of . . .' She paused. What was she going to call it? Not a nightmare . . . nor was it like a fit. '. . . a bit of a turn.'

Reenee was now gripping the chubby hand, and Bella placed her other hand on top of it, patting it all the while, saying, 'I used to have turns when I was a lass. I've never told you how I got here, have I? We all have our troubles, you know, in this life. Very few of us get off without troubles, but mine started young. By God, they did!' Again she paused, while she told herself not to go on. Then she remembered a saying of old Ham's, 'If you want people to stop talkin' about their troubles, you tell them yours. That'll soon shut them up.' Well, her troubles couldn't shut this poor creature up more than she was, but nevertheless they might distract her from any painful thoughts, so she said, 'I came from Liverpool, you know. I was thirteen and I couldn't get away quick enough, 'cos I'd had a hell of a life. I didn't have to come to this part of London to know men. Oh, no. I knew them in me own home, such as it was called. She, me mother, she never saw daylight and me dad, unfortunately, he had to work before he could start drinking in the bars. There were three rooms and you couldn't swing a cat in any of them, and from when I can remember I was crushed between lads in the bed. Top or bottom, it was the same. I slept under it for God knows how long to get out of their way. They were all older than me, and they went off one after the other, until there was me left with a pair of them. I tried to go to school as often as I could. I got there enough to learn to read, when she didn't send me to the pawn shop or make me scour the place, which was like a pigsty. She was me mother, but she was a dirty bitch if ever there was one. A dirty, lazy bitch.

'"Love thy father and thy mother," so the big book says. If ever I hated two people in me life it was those two, especially him, for now the lads had gone he was gettin' at me. And she let him. I had the bed to meself now, and he came in one night paralytic and went straight for me. He was a big fellow, but I had means of protectin' meself. I'd used it on the lads, and by God, didn't I use it on him that night! It was a bodkin needle, you know, that you use for mats and helpin' to cut leather. It's curved at the end like. And I left a mark on him that would take some healin' for months, if ever it did, and I flew, just as I was, out of that house. Slept in me clothes. I had managed to grab me coat, me old coat, and that's all I had when I left Liverpool around one o'clock in the morning. It was early March and cold.'

She stopped and looked down into the pale eyes that were looking into hers and she said, 'Am I talkin' too much, lass?' and when there was a slight movement from the head she went on, 'Well, that's all right, then. But I won't go on about how I got to London. I only remember that I slept in a couple of barns and scared the feathers off a number of hens. Believe me, I couldn't look a raw egg in the face now. I got two lifts on my journey; and on each one I had to show my little carved knife and—' She laughed again. 'When one of them threatened to put me off on the road in the black dark somewhere from nowhere I told him what I would do to him before he got me there and to keep on driving.' She was giggling now, like a girl, as she said, 'And you know, Reenee, he did. He just did. Although I was small made and only thirteen I knew I looked a lot older. Well, I'd had a lot of experience to make me look like that, I can tell you, girl.

'I've lost count of the days it took me to reach the big city, and also,' she added grimly, 'of the number of men who wanted to be kind to me.' Her voice was slow and low. 'I'd been brought up among drink and squalor, and all those around me lived by their wits, so now I put mine into practice. But when I think back, I must still have looked like a lost schoolgirl, except for my face. It was old. It was old then, and it has never seemed to change.'

Her smile widened here. 'But I must tell you how I came to own this house and the fruit business, and about Hamish McIntyre. I had learnt how to live rough and exist for days at a time on rotten fruit or what I could scavenge from dustbins, those near hotels. But you had to fight your way to get at them because the ones near the big hotels, as I said, they had what the posh people called their own clientele. You had to be there pretty early in the morning to pick out anything worthwhile, and one day a cop almost nabbed me. I'd gone into a cook shop and pinched a couple of pies and I almost ran into him head-on as I left the shop and he gave chase. The shop had been near the fruit market and I dashed through there and passed what I now know is the Opera House and up some alleys. In and out I went until I lost him. But,' she shrugged her shoulders, 'I suppose I'd lost him in the market. I was just one of hundreds of kids on the same game. Anyway, I wasn't to know that then, and I wove in and out, in and out, then up through a narrow roadway, and I recall there were shrubs on one side of it. Anyway, I was gasping when I saw a pair of iron gates and, beyond, a yard littered with boxes and rotten fruit, and I did what you did, lass: I went in and I hid in a corner behind some boxes and I waited for that bobby comin'. I could've waited till next week, had I known it, but I was so exhausted and weak with hunger that I fell asleep. I sort of dreamt that someone came and stood over me, then went away, but when I woke up there was nobody about.

'Then I did wake and looked about me. There was squashed fruit of every kind that had been swept into piles here and there, but though I was very hungry and I'd eaten worse I couldn't touch them, 'cos I wanted to be sick; and I was. I vomited but it was mostly water. After a while I sneaked out, and when I got past the gates I saw just a few yards away a man selling fruit from a stall, and again I made a run for it. But that night, not bein' able to find anywhere to kip, I thought of that yard and that pile of boxes, and when it was dark I made my way there. The gates were shut, but they weren't locked, and I carefully lifted the latch, went through them, closed them gently behind me, and took my sleepin' quarters among the boxes.'

Again she stopped. 'You all right, dear?' she said. 'Shall I go on?' When the head made a movement, she said, 'All right, then. Well, to cut this bit of the story short, I stole what I could to eat during the daytime. I'd found it was no good offerin' your services to anybody, there were so many in the same boat as meself, but each night I went back through those gates and slept behind the boxes. That was until one morning when I tried to get out and found the gates locked. Eeh, lass, was I in a pickle! The place was walled in. There was a kind of stone buildin' at the end of it, which looked as if it was droppin' to pieces, like most of the houses round about. In panic I started to shake the gates. Then there was this man. He'd come and stood in front of the gate and said, "Well, now, what can I do for you?" His voice, I recognised, was Scots. A thick Scots. "Let me out," I said, "else I'll bloody well scream!"

'"Oh, yes? Do that," he said. "By all means. That's what I want you to do so I can bring the polisman, and he can take you where you should be, behind bars."

'"I've done nowt," I said.

'"No," he answered, "only used my premises as sleepin' quarters for the last week or so."

'Eeh! I began to tremble, lass. So he had seen me that first night, but why had he left me alone till now? When he suddenly unlocked the gate and stood before me I backed from him and got me knife out. I said, "You come near me, mister, and you'll be sorry. If I do nothin' else I'll leave a mark on you."

'"Yes, I suppose you would, miss," he said. "But let me tell you, I wouldn't touch you, my dear, with a ten-foot barge-pole if I had one in my hand this minute. But seein' that you've used my premises for sleepin' quarters I don't see why you shouldn't pay for your night's rest by some work, like sweepin' up this yard."

'Well, Reenee, I stood and gaped at him. Then, me wits returnin', I said, "What'll you give me?"

'"Give you?" he said. "It's you who owes me, miss. I've told you, you've got to pay for your sleepin' quarters."

'I glared at him. Then, as if I had any power to bargain, I said, "I'll do it if you give me a bite of food."

'"Oh! Oh, I see. You're not only askin' for a bed you're askin' for board too, is that it?"

'I nodded at him and said, "Aye."

'Now in that thick voice of his, he said, "I'll give you a meal," he said, "about ten o'clock, after I've seen what work you do. You see that buildin' down there?" He pointed down the long yard. "Well, there's a hut next to it, and it's got tools in it. You'll find something that you can use to clear up. And don't attempt to do a bunk, because if you do you won't find any sleepin' quarters here tonight. The gate will be locked. Understood?"

'I didn't answer him, but I turned away and went down the yard to find the hut with the tools in.'

And now Reenee smiled as Bella went on, 'My cleanin' up wasn't like anything you did, me dear. But he gave me a meal, and it was a good one. Of course, he bein' Scottish, it was a bowl of porridge, and with it a slice of bread and pig's fat. Also a can of black tea – neither milk nor sugar in it, but I can tell you, it was like wine to me. And that state of affairs went on for almost a week, because after I'd done my stint and eaten the food I went out and about my scroungin'. But I always returned hungry and longed for the mornin' and that porridge. Then one day he said to me, "Where're you from?"

'"Liverpool," I said.

'"How old are you?"

'I recall lookin' from one side to the other before I said, "Sixteen."

'"You're not." His words came back like a shot. "You can't be more than fourteen. Why are you here? Haven't you got any people? Are you from a home of some sort?"

'"Aye, mister." I *was* from a home of some sort. Yes, you could say that all right. And I didn't know I was cryin', actually cryin' – me!

'He bawled, "Oh, for God's sake! Don't come that. I've

93

never been softened by tears before, and I'm not likely to be now."

'You know what I said to him in reply? "Who's askin' you to be bloody well softened. I don't want any of your sympathy or kind words, if you have any in you, that is. I'm me own boss and always will be. So there. Nobody's goin' to tell me what to do; if I don't want to do it, I don't do it. Get that, mister!"

'And you know what he did, Reenee? He put his head back and he laughed. He was a man, I found out later, who wasn't given to laughter. He had to have something really to laugh about. That morning I heard him laugh until he nearly choked. And then he said, "D'you want a job?"

'"What?" said I.

'"You heard. You heard, big woman. I said, d'you want a job?"

'"Depends."

'"On what?"

'"On what you're gonna pay me." I saw him swallow deeply before he said, "A shillin' a week, and your food and board. You see that buildin' down there next to where you got the brushes? Well, it's a wash-house. The first thing you do is clean it up. There's a good boiler in there. You fill it with water from the pump just beyond it. Then you chop up some of these boxes and put the fire on. You'll have to chop enough to keep it goin' because it eats wood. Then you can kip there. But first this yard's got to be cleaned as it should be, not played at like you've been doing these last few days. That wash-house is to be clean in order that you can do my washing in there, and this includes the bedding. Have you ever done any washing before?" When I didn't answer, he said, "Well, you'll learn. And if it's all to my satisfaction you'll get a shilling a week and your grub."

'Well, lass, in the next six months I learnt what work was. Aye, I did it for six months, and then one day he said to me,

"Don't you think it's about time you went along to Ginnie's and got a change of rags? If you come out lookin' decent I'll take you on as me housekeeper. Can you cook?"

'"No."

'"Well, that doesn't matter very much," he said; "except you'll have to learn how to make porridge. I generally eat out anyway. But what about it?"

'"What wage?" I said.

'At this he laughed again: "Half a dollar."

'"Your housekeeper?" I repeated, lookin' up into his big hairy face.

'"Yes," he said, "my housekeeper, and" – he thumped me in the chest – "you won't need to bring out your knife. Be quite sure on that point, Bella. What did you say your second name was?"

'"Morgan."

'"Well, Miss Bella Morgan, you will be safe with me. Even when you grow up I can't see you lookin' much different from what you do now; so you have no need to worry on that score."

'I recall now, lass, how hurt I felt. I knew I was small, with a thick-set body, and me face was plain. But, anyway, that's how it started: I became his housekeeper. I must have been just turned fourteen at the time and I worked for him sixteen years – the last three he spent a lot of time ill in bed – and I knew as much about him at the end of his life as I did when I first saw him. I can only put it like this: he was a man of many parts. His routine never changed in all those years until he took to his bed.

'He didn't always attend the stall; he had a man who would come in and take over. At such times he'd be up in his bedroom. He had a little desk there and he was always writing down notes or figures. I got that much from the torn-up scraps that were in the wastepaper basket. But I also know that he didn't deal in much second fruit, it was nearly all good stuff. I understand it hadn't always been like that: he had started very much on seconds, and that's why he hated old Frankie next door. One day they had an awful row and Frankie said, "You're nowt but a bruised-fruit vendor." Anyway, as I was to find out, he had a number of different suits in his wardrobe and they were all good ones.

'He had a pattern like a timetable. The stall was cleared at five. He never did it himself, not while I was there anyway. By six o'clock he'd be washed and dressed for out. Some nights he'd be back about nine. Others he would say to me, "Don't wait up. I won't want anything." I don't think he had ever said please or thank you in his life, and he always made me feel I was of no importance, just someone to clean the house, do his washing and get his breakfast. There were nights I knew he didn't get back till twelve o'clock, and I used to wonder what he got up to. But in all those years I never saw him the worse for drink, though of course I didn't see him when he came in that late.

'At the end he had a doctor to him, who told me he had a sort of wasting disease. I've learnt since it must've been what they call leukaemia. Something to do with the blood. Another thing that was odd, he wouldn't let me wash him except to put a flannel round his face on bad days.

'Shortly after he had taken to his bed—' She stopped here and said, 'You interested, lass?' and when Reenee made her usual nod of confirmation, she went on, 'Well, that's all right. As I said, he hadn't been long in his bed when he called up the man who saw to the stall and told him to carry on; but first, he gave him a letter to take to the warehouse for a Mr Weir. That very night he said to me, "I want you to get to your room and stay there. I'm going to have a visitor. He will be able to let himself in, he's got a key." I just stared at him and then he croaked at me, "D'you hear what I say? I'm sayin' to you, make yourself scarce. Keep to your room until my visitor goes. Your lugs will be wide open and you'll hear him leave. You understand me, now?"

'I never said a word but I went out. It was over an hour later when I heard someone coming up the stairs; it was over two hours later when the footsteps went down the stairs. Through the window I could see no sign of a cab or anything. The next day he sent for his solicitor, who brought two clerks with him. Well, as they were up there a long time I went and tapped on the door, opened it and was about to ask if they would like a cup of tea when there was a bawl came from the bed, "Get out!"

'At a glance I could see that the bed was covered with bits of paper and things like parchment rolled up, and the solicitor man was sitting on a chair to the side of the bed with the clerks standing beside him.

'I closed that door none too quietly. Sometimes I considered him a pig of a man, and that was one of the times. I forgot he had been kind in givin' me house room; yet he had never broken his neck over paying promptly for my services. Anyway, it was the very next afternoon when I went into his room that he handed me a closed envelope, and on it was simply the name "Mr Weir", and he said, "Get that to the warehouse as soon as possible."

'I went downstairs and I was about to pick up my coat and put it round me, when the bell rang and there, outside, stood the doctor. He was a nice, civil man, middle-aged and kindly, and I led him upstairs, opened the door and stood aside for him to pass. Then we both let out an exclamation. There was nobody in the bed, and to my knowledge Mr McIntyre hadn't been able to move out of it for weeks. But there he was, all crumpled on the mat at the foot of the bed and in his hand, of all things, was an open clasp knife. It was one of those, you know, like Scouts have that hold a screwdriver and a file as well as a knife. Well, on this occasion only the blade was showin', and it was still in his hand, and when the doctor turned him over he said, "Dear God, he's had a stroke! What on earth brought him from the bed?"

'I helped to carry his twisted body back to the bed, and it was no lightweight, and the doctor said, "This'll finish him surely." Then he said, "Now give me a hand. I have to get him on to his side to examine him."

'The examination proved that Mr McIntyre had certainly had a stroke all down his left side, and his face was twisted and he was unable to speak.

'"You can't manage him on your own any more," the doctor said. "He'll have to have a nurse. I'll see about it first thing in the morning. He'll take no harm lying as he does now. Don't agitate him in any way by trying to get him to talk. Will you be all right by yourself tonight? Perhaps you know someone who will stay with you?"

'"No, I won't need any help," I said; "I'll be all right, Doctor. I've seen to him so far."

'"Yes, indeed you have," he said, "and it's been too much for anyone, let alone someone of your size."

'I tell you, Reenee, it was the most uneasy and frightening night I've spent in me life, and even before I left Liverpool, and after. I can tell you I had some frightening nights. On that road I was scared to death many times but nothing like the night I watched him die, because that's what he was doing and I didn't know. He kept opening one eye and staring at me as if willing me to do something, and I recalled the past two or three days when he had been struggling for breath. Time and again he would point through the iron bars at the foot of the bed, and twice he distinctly said the word "lino"; once I thought he said, "Lift the lino." So after he fell asleep I quietly pulled up the mat that lay across the foot of the bed. There was no break in the lino there. Then I looked around the edge of it where it was all tucked neatly underneath the skirtin' boards, which were agape with shrinkage for nearly half an inch. There was no break at all in the lino. Definitely, though, he had been trying to get at the lino with that knife, but why?

Then I thought of the way he had been lyin': he might have pointed to the window. Something under the window-sill? Well, I examined that; and there was a kind of gap between the bricks and the bottom of the wooden sill, and I put my fingers into this, but there was nothing there. Anyway, I must've dozed and when I woke up I had no need to ask any more questions: his head had fallen to the side and I knew he was dead. I wasn't sorry, no, I wasn't; although I still felt I owed him something for giving me the job. Four days later he was buried, and during that time I'd been sweating, wondering what was going to happen now. I had a few shillings saved up, but most likely I'd be on the streets again, because I couldn't imagine he would have left me anything in his will.

'He was a mean man, and those, Reenee, are the very words the solicitor said to me the day of the funeral. He said, "Your master, Miss Morgan, was a mean man, I'm very sorry to say."

'"Oh, I know that," I said.

'"Well, come and sit down, my dear," he said, and I can remember the kindly man leading me to the kitchen table, and we both sat down. "He hasn't left you entirely bereft," he said. "I don't know whether you'll be pleased or not, but he has left you this house."

'I gasped and said, "He's what? He's left me the house?"

'"Yes, he's left you the house, but not a penny with which to support it. He feels that there's the vegetable and fruit business outside and you should be able to make enough to keep the house going. I even dared to suggest to him that he could leave you a little something, but he bit my head off, saying you wouldn't know what to do with money."

'I think the kind man was withholding something, for I'm sure Mr McIntyre would have added, because she's a numskull. You see, I couldn't talk to him. I couldn't tell him what I thought or even anything I'd read in the papers. He didn't stop near me long enough for anything like that. Then the solicitor surprised me. He said, "You might not believe it but he has died a very rich man."

'"A rich man?" I repeated.

'"Yes," he said; "a very rich man. Your employer, I'm afraid, led two different lives."

'I remember' – she laughed here – 'saying naïvely, "Well, what did he do in the other one?" and the solicitor man, he laughed too and said, "I don't suppose you know anything about what is called the Stock Exchange? Well, he worked on that, but not alone. He had a friend, a rather superior friend, and they must have worked together looking to the future, for when businesses were failing and dropping to pieces they bought shares in them and in many cases profited greatly by it. Some are still hanging fire, but will one day surely rise. But it's a pity for him he won't be here to see the result of his labours in that direction. And I must tell you too, my dear, he made no real profit out of the fruit business; he paid the man who looked after it quite a decent wage. I feel the fruit business was a cover-up for his other life, because he detested this house and also this district. I think he moved in a different circle once he was away from it. Twice I saw him with a particular man. I was very surprised, but I didn't show myself. It was his business, but he was my client, and I charged him quite high fees for my services, for I don't like mean individuals, and I found him out to be mean in more ways than one. It is more than mean of a man, I think it is cruel, to watch a business die before his eyes, knowing that with just a very small effort he could save it. No, I am not going to be a hypocrite and say I am sorry to see Mr McIntyre leave this world. I don't know about you, Miss Morgan. I think, in fact I am sure, you have more than enough to feel aggrieved about."

'You know what I said, Reenee? I even made him laugh when I said, "Me? I hope he's in heaven at this minute, Mr Travis, because he's left me this house. It mightn't mean much to you, but it's been home to me. You see, Mr Travis, I've had a bad four days thinking I'd be thrown out on the road again, because that's where he picked me up from, you know. He found me sleepin' among the filthy fruit boxes in the yard. So, yes, I do hope he's in heaven."

'The solicitor patted me on the shoulder, "You are a very kind little woman, Miss Morgan," he said; "I'm sure you'll make a success of the fruit business, because you'll look after it yourself and not have to pay anyone else. If at any time I can be of use to you, you've just to call on me and I can promise you," he wagged his finger at me, "I won't treat you as a client and put you on my charge book."

'Oh, he was a nice man, Reenee, and still is, for since then he's called in once or twice to see how I'm gettin' on. But to get back to the night Ham died. I'd been about to take that note to Mr Weir. He seemed to be the boss of the warehouse. Well, with all the fuss I never got the letter to him and I must confess I opened it. All it said was: "Come tonight." So one day when he called I asked Mr Travis, "Have you met Mr Weir?"

'"No, I've not, Miss Morgan."

'"You don't know the man who owns the big wholesale warehouses?" I asked him.

'"Yes, I know the man who owns the big warehouses, but it isn't Mr Weir," Mr Travis said.

'"Oh, I thought it was. Anything I've wanted for the house or anything like that has come through Mr Weir. Mr McIntyre used to say, "Just tell Mr Weir what you want and you'll get it if it's for the house."

'"It was Mr Weir who was the visitor who came to see him?" asked Mr Travis.

'"I don't know, sir," I said. "I only know that I wasn't allowed to see him. Mr McIntyre made me stay in my room."

'"He did? While a gentleman was here?"

'"Yes. Oh, yes. The gentleman seemed to have his own key,

and I didn't come out of the room until I heard him leave."

'"Well, well. You learn something every day, Miss Morgan," he said. "Remember that."'

Bella now looked down on the white face turned towards her on the pillow, and she realised that her listener had fallen asleep. Eeh, she said to herself, I've talked her to sleep. She had heard of people being talked to death but never talked to sleep.

Gently now she lifted the blanket and placed it over Reenee's shoulders. Then she pulled her own cramped body upwards. She went to the fire and pushed the little brass tidy close to the bars to make sure that if anything fell out it wouldn't roll on to the hearth. The fire had burnt down somewhat and there was no fear of any of the coal pieces toppling forward. Well, she told herself, she'd leave it like that for a time; then later she'd bring Reenee a night drink, although she wouldn't disturb her if she was still asleep.

After she made her quiet way back up the stone stairs to the kitchen, she was surprised to see Joe and Pimple sitting there.

'Why haven't you gone?' she demanded.

'Oh, well—' They rose together to their feet, and it was Pimple who said, 'There's always another night, Bella; we thought the state she was in and you here on your own . . . well, it was better if we hung around.'

'What d'you think happened to her?' asked Joe. 'It wasn't an ordinary fit, like, was it?'

'No, it wasn't an ordinary fit,' agreed Bella; 'but I don't know what happened to cause it, unless, as you said, it was me repeatin' Hamish's words when he went at me that night: "Don't speak," he almost ordered me. Well, that's what I think it must have been. Those words hit her then as they must have done before when somebody yelled at her, "Don't speak!" Dear God.' She shook her head. 'But to knock her out of her wits like that, it must have been something terrible that happened. Anyway' – her voice changed – 'I tell you what. If you're not goin' to spend your money on the idle life you can go and spend a bit of mine. What about goin' to the bakery for pies and peas and a roll, and bringin' them back here, and we'll have them round the fire? What about it?'

Like children who had been given a treat, their faces lit up, and straight away Pimple said, 'Oh, yes, Bella, we'd like that fine. I'll get the basins, will I?'

'Do that; and here's the money,' she said, picking up a tin box from the mantelpiece. She took two shillings out of it, saying, 'That should cover a good supper,' as she smacked it on the table.

'By aye!' said Joe, as he picked it up, then added, 'What if I scarper with it?'

'You try it, and I'll put the polis on you, that's all.'

The two men went out laughing, and Bella flopped into the easy chair by the fire and laid her head back. Then folding her hands in her lap and speaking to someone she knew not, she said, 'Thank you. I've got a lot to be thankful for this night.'

4

It was towards the end of October. Autumn was here: there had been the first heavy frost in the night and now the day was bright and crisp.

Over the past months the routine of the house had continued to run along with little change, but on that day three small incidents were to occur that would change the routine and the occupants' way of living. The first happened around dinner-time.

Reenee was cleaning the small window at the end of the hall through which the street could be seen. She was looking at four men, a street band, who were standing in the gutter. They had been playing a Strauss waltz, one man strumming a banjo, one beating a small drum, another blowing a flute, and the fourth playing the fiddle. The sound coming from the last suggested that the strings were slack. But they had stopped playing now, and one of them, the man with the drum, was talking to Joe, and they were smiling at each other. Bella had come in from the kitchen to tell Reenee to come and have her dinner break, and she had gone to her side and had looked out: 'Poor souls,' she said. 'God help them! They're walkin' on their uppers. That one's got paper stickin' out of his shoe. What's Joe on about? He seems to know the fellow.' And she went out, saying, 'I'll soon find out.'

Outside, Joe turned to her from the man. 'He's from my part of the country, Bella. Just up the coast, Whitley Bay way.' Then, addressing the four-man band, he said, 'This is my boss, Miss Morgan.'

The men all nodded, saying, 'Pleased to meet you.' Bella said nothing, she just stared at their starved faces. She had seen so many, more and more every day up this street. But this lot seemed to be welded together in their poverty.

Joe said to her, 'Would . . . would you mind, Bella, if I took them down to our place?' He pointed to the gate. 'We've still got the soup you gave us and some pies an' that and—'

'Stop your jabberin'. What use is your drop of soup and a couple of pies going to be to four of them? Take them down there, then send Pimple back and I'll see to him.'

'Ta, Bella. Ta.' And as he turned to the other man Joe said, 'Would you like to come down and see where we hang out?'

'Me and me mates?'

Their faces alight, they followed Joe through the iron gates and down to the wash-house, which was no longer just a wash-house: an iron flap had been welded on to the front of the fire, and on it a tin kettle was bubbling away. And near the wall a bench had been constructed. On it stood a little oil stove, a frying pan, and above that a rack holding two tin plates, two mugs and some cutlery. The beds had been rolled up to form seats, a mat was on the floor and a curtain at the window, a real curtain that could be pulled across at night. Reenee had made it for them.

Back in the house, Bella went hurriedly to the kitchen and said to Reenee, 'God help them. That's the worst lot of semi-starvation I've seen. And one of them comes from Joe's part, that's at the other end of the country, what Joe calls the North-East. There must be many worse than these men. There'll be trouble in the towns, you'll see; things are desperate. But what am I talkin' about? Get a tray out,

Reenee, and some basins and cut up a new loaf.'

Like a well-trained servant, Reenee did as she was bidden, and eagerly. After cutting the slices of bread she pointed to a dish of margarine on the table and looked at Bella, who nodded, and she spread the bread, then stuck the slices together until there were four large sandwiches. Then she took from her own plate two shortbread biscuits and placed them on top of the bread, and Bella, seeing what she had done, said, 'Well, two won't go very far among four;' so she picked the two off her own plate and put these with the bread. 'Bring me that bowl and I'll fill it with soup. Can you manage this tray?' she said, turning to where Pimple had come in, and he answered her, 'Oh, yes, Bella. I'll manage any tray with food on it.'

'They're a poor lot, aren't they?' Bella said.

'I'd say they are, Bella. There's dozens, even hundreds, like them on the road. But this lot, apparently, have clung together all the way from the North. Between them they haven't a sound boot to their feet or a spare shirt to their back. They've been travelling round since eight o'clock this morning and haven't taken a penny.'

'Here.' Bella went to the tin box again and, taking out a shilling, she said to Pimple, 'Give them that. It won't help much but likely it'll go towards gettin' them a kip tonight.'

After Bella had let Pimple out of the door with the laden tray, she returned to the kitchen. Reenee was shaking her head, and as if she had spoken, Bella said, 'Yes, it is a terrible state to be in. It's not right, it's the government; but what can you do with the government? I don't know, and people with more brains than me don't know either. Here! Let's make some fresh tea; that teapot is cold enough for layin' out.'

It was as they sat drinking their tea that there was a knock on the front door again, and Bella said, 'That's Joe's knock.' As she rose to go to the door she was thinking it a pity the lass couldn't push herself to open it; but when she faced Joe she said, 'What is it now? You should be back at work.'

'Aye, I know, Bella, but listen: they'll not get anywhere to kip tonight for what they've got today. They're determined to keep together through thick and thin, and they've already been through God knows what. Well, I've got two sheets of tarpaulin. They were thrown away from the warehouse, and you know there's a leak in the wash-house roof, and I thought there might come the time when I'd have to cover the roof over. So if they've got nowhere else to go would you let them lie inside the gates? Well, I mean against the wall of the wash-house. It would be warmish there. They could lie on one piece and cover themselves over with the other.'

Bella hesitated, then said, 'Well, as long as they don't make a rule of it, all right.'

'And, Bella?'

'Aye, what is it now?'

'You know you've rigged us both out with Mr Ham's things wherever they would fit us, shirts, pants and things like that. Coats an' all. I know the one you got me is a size too big, but I always wear an old sweater under it, to push it out like. One of those fellows is about my size – at least, he's big-boned, which is about all that's left of him. D'you think—'

'Yes, I think,' barked Bella; 'and I'll see what I can do. If they're not here in the morning you can tell them to call back. But don't you make a habit of this, d'you hear? You could pick up hundreds you lived next door to at your end of the country if you had a mind.'

'Aye, I could, Bella. I could at that.' He was grinning at her. 'But thanks all the same. I'll tell them. And they're grateful.'

She closed the door upon him and quickly went back to the kitchen. There she said to Reenee, 'I've got to get back to the stall, but you go upstairs now, into my room, and the big chest in the corner. You'll see it's still got piles of his vests and pants and shirts and things in it. Spread them out on the bed.

107

Then see what coats and trousers are left. Put them over the end of the bed so I can get at them. The small chest of drawers is mine, and what I've got to hang up I put in the single wardrobe next door. That's where I used to keep me clothes before I went into the big room.' She laughed now as she repeated, 'The big room. His room. Eeh, I had a job to make meself get into that bed! I didn't for two or three weeks, you know, not after he went. Then I scrubbed the whole place down and turned the tick over. But one day I promised myself I'd have a carpet in that room, not that old lino. Now I have to go out and face the blast. It's chilly out there. I'm certainly not lookin' forward to the winter.

'Oh, don't look like that, lass. I wasn't meanin' that you should help or come out. Please don't take things to yourself. I understand your feelings. Don't worry, lass. Don't worry.' And when Reenee's hand came out and her fingers touched Bella's sleeve it was a way of saying, 'Thank you for under-standing,' and Bella always took it as such, and she said, 'Of course. Of course I understand. Now let's get on with it.'

And they got on with it, and were waiting for the two lads to come in and take their meal down to their abode.

When the special knock came on the door and Bella said, 'That's Joe,' she was more than surprised, amazed, when Reenee sprang up and, almost at a run, went to the door, opened it and let the two men in.

In the hall they turned and looked at her and their surprise showed. It was Joe who expressed it by saying, 'You opened the door for us. That was good of you, Reenee. Ta . . . ta . . . thank you.'

'Yes,' put in Pimple; 'thank you very much, Reenee.'

'Will you come and get this and stop your jabberin' out there?' Bella's voice came to them, and the two men went into the kitchen smiling. Neither of them remarked on what had just occurred, but Joe said, 'I've got news for you, Bella.'

'Aye, news? What kind of news?'

'Well, you won't have any more horses' hoofs in your yard at night, that's one thing I know.'

'You do? Where did you hear that?'

'Oh, that and a lot more. There's been some fun, I can tell you, fun in the whole warehouse this afternoon. Talk about skittering! You know me and the likes of me are never allowed near the horse-driven vans when they're being loaded, but this morning I knew they had been loaded because the horses had been put into trim. Then this afternoon Mr Dixon, the real head of this end of the show, well, he comes out quick and orders the pieces in the vans to be taken out and put here and there among bits of furniture in one of the removal vans, the big long ones you know. And then two other fellows came and led the horses out of the yard to God knows where. Then the furniture van, with all household oddments as if somebody was just moving house, was driven out of the yard. Now what d'you make of that, Bella?'

'Well, I don't know,' said Bella; 'you seem to know much more about it than I do. One thing I'm glad of, though, they won't be coming here again.'

'Nor any of their removal vans,' put in Pimple, ''cos they could never get round that corner and into the gate. The horses were manoeuvrable.'

'Oh.' Bella laughed and, turning to Reenee, she said, 'We'll be able to go to the lav now any time we like.' And when Reenee hung her head, Bella said, 'Oh, lass, see the funny side of it.' On a sober note now, she went on, 'They've still got a key to that gate.'

'Oh, I can soon fix that,' said Joe. 'I didn't work with joiners and carpenters for nothing. I can twist a lock until it wishes it was dead.'

They were all laughing now; even the corners of Reenee's lips were moving upwards. Although her lips remained tight it showed that she was indeed enjoying this joke.

'What about your own orphans of the storm?' Bella said to

Joe. 'Have you given them a time limit to come back?'

'Aye, I have, Bella. I said if they weren't there at nine o'clock the gate would be locked.'

'Good. Anyway, if they come, I'll give them a bite before they leave in the morning, and you can tell them we've got some odds and ends of clothing that might be of use. You two have had your share and even in your case, Joe, they only fitted where they touched. But poor Pimple there . . .'

She nodded at Pimple, but he, smiling at her, said, 'Oh, I'm very glad with what I got, those lovely warm pants and vests and a decent shirt. But it's better to wear me own togs on top of them, because if people saw me decently dressed I'd get less than I'm gettin' now, and that's not sayin' much.'

'Not a good day?'

Pimple shook his head sadly, saying, 'People don't appreciate opera. I've stood outside that Opera House for hours and picked up every note, and when I play it comes out as clear as a bell although I say it meself. But do folks take any notice? No. It has to be "Tipperary" or "All Alone on the Telephone" or some drivel like that, and if they're in a picture queue they'll hum along with you. But will they put their hands in their pockets? No. Just here and there, when it'll be a penny, sometimes even a halfpenny. I feel like spittin' in their eye for the halfpenny; yet once inside they'll likely take tickets for the circle. Such is life.'

'Aye,' said Bella, 'such is life, Pimple. Could be worse.'

'Oh, aye. I'm not really grumbling, Bella.'

'Why d'you do it, then?' asked Bella. 'I mean go around playing.'

'Oh, you know why, I pick up things.'

'Oh, you've tried that game before, but what did it fetch you? Nothing. As I've said before, you could end in the gutter with your throat slit one of these nights if any of them villains you've shopped found out.'

'Aye, you're right,' said Pimple, 'you're right. But I don't know what else I can do.'

They all turned now and looked towards the young woman, who was writing or drawing on a piece of paper. Bella went and stood near her, and the other two followed. Reenee did not lift her head, but went on drawing. Eventually what she had drawn amounted to two lines down the middle of the paper with, on each side, shorter lines running to the edge, ten short lines on one side and only seven on the other. At the end of these she had made two squares. In one she was now laboriously writing the name Joe; then in the other Pimple.

'Well, what does all that mean?' said Bella tersely.

Down the middle of the paper she now wrote the word beds.

'Beds!' Bella looked from one man to the other and she repeated, 'Beds! What d'you think she means?'

It was as if Reenee answered for herself: getting to her feet, she pointed towards the steps leading downstairs, then cupped one side of her face in her hand and closed her eyes.

'I know. I know,' said Pimple quickly. 'You're making downstairs into a kip house, aren't you?'

Irene nodded, the while making a sound they took as yes.

'Oh, lass,' said Bella, impatiently now, 'and where d'you think you'd sleep?'

It was as if Reenee was trying to smile now as she thumbed towards the ceiling, and Bella came at her, saying, 'So, you would go up there, would you? I've asked you twice if you'd take my old room but, no, you preferred to be downstairs by yourself.' Then, looking towards the men, Bella said, 'What an idea! How does she think we're goin' to get to the lav walkin' through a line of mattresses every night?' However, she turned to the girl again and acknowledged, 'It was a good idea, my dear. Aye, it was. And if it could've been worked I would have had a new business set-up, and you know where the fruit could go to, and as far beyond. But no, lass; there's no way that that can happen because the main thing for us is the lavatory. There's nobody gonna get me to go out me front door and through that back gate and down to that dirty old hole next to your abode.' As she spoke she turned to the lads and shook her head as though emphasising her decision.

'You could have a lav put up here.'

'Where, man? Where, I ask you? In this kitchen?'

Joe looked about him, then shrugged his shoulders. 'Something could be done.'

'Look!' cried Bella. 'Ten to twenty men sleeping downstairs and that one lav across the way? What's goin' to happen d'you think in that yard? Oh, no, thanks; I'd rather have the old horses back. We could shovel up their mess.'

'Aye; you're right,' said Joe. 'You're always right. But it was a good idea;' and he turned to acknowledge Reenee.

She hung her head as if in disappointment, but brought it up sharply again when Bella almost shouted, 'And where's the money comin' from for mattresses, lavatories, new lavs up here? And that will only be the beginning. God, let's talk sense! I'm sorry, lass. I'll admit it was a marvellous idea, but what money I make now just manages to get us through, and that's with a squeeze at times, I can tell you. Go on, now, you two, take your meal and get out of it. And if those fellows turn up tonight, have you enough tea down there to give them a drink?'

'Oh, aye,' said Pimple. 'We don't have it strong, and there's quite a bit from the last quarter you gave us.'

'Well, then, go on, get yourselves away.'

'Good night, Bella.'

'Good night, Bella.'

'Good night, lads.'

'Good night, Reenee.' The two men spoke as one, and her lips opened as if she was about to speak; but no words came, yet the look on her face was telling them good night . . .

The next morning the four players stood in the hallway and looked in amazement at the pile of underwear, socks and boots that Bella had spread out on the bottom of the stairs, and at the coats and trousers that were hanging over the stair-rail.

'The vests and pants and socks,' she said, 'you can make fit you somehow, but I'm afraid the trousers and coats are way beyond your size, except for you,' and she pointed to the biggest of the men and she said, 'What's your name?'

'Andy Anderson.'

'What was your trade?'

'I was a bricklayer, ma'am.'

'Well, here! Try this coat on.'

The coat was a size too big, but it did not deter the man. He turned the cuffs up, then pulled one side of the coat over the other, saying, 'Oh, I could fix this, ma'am. Willie there is good with his needle. He'd make new buttonholes for me, wouldn't you, Willie?'

Willie did not answer, and Bella said to him, 'What's your name, son?'

'Willie Young, ma'am.'

'And what was your trade?'

'I was a baker.'

'I'm surprised you're out of work,' she said.

'Oh, ma'am, you shouldn't be surprised at anything that happens when you're among starvin' men and bairns. They broke into the shop one night and cleared the lot. It was a Sunday and the bakin' had been done for the Monday mornin'. There was nothin' left and the boss had had enough. That was the third time it happened, so there were five of us without work.'

'Dear, dear.' Bella picked up another coat, and handed it to the third man. 'That's miles too big for you, but put it on and see.'

They all laughed gently when they saw the shorter figure

lost in the depths of the big jacket, but the man said, 'I'll take it, ma'am, if you wouldn't mind. I can put a belt round the middle and Willie could see to the cuffs for me.'

Bella laughed. 'Willie's goin' to have his work cut out. Now what d'they call you?'

'Tony Brown, ma'am,' and before she could ask the next question he added, 'I was a plumber.'

Turning to the last man, she said, 'That only leaves you.'

'I was a ship's carpenter, ma'am. Me name's John Carter.'

'And these trousers' – Bella had taken them from the rail – 'they're very good stuff and they won't fit any of you, I'm sure, but you could pawn them. You might get a bob or so on them because they're tailored an' all.'

'We can't thank you enough, ma'am,' said Andy Anderson; 'and for lettin' us stay the night.'

'Oh, I couldn't see you had a very comfortable time of it lyin' on tarpaulin, and over you, too.'

'Oh, it's amazin', ma'am, how warm it was near that wall, and after the lads had given us a mug of tea. You've got a pair of good lads there, ma'am.'

'Yes. Yes, I suppose so.'

'They think the world of you,' said Willie Young.

'Oh, aye?' said Bella. 'Well, that's on good days. What they say about me on bad 'uns can't be repeated.'

They all laughed as they gathered up the clothes from the stairs, and it was John Carter, the carpenter, who said, 'Can we go back, ma'am, down to the boys' place and fit ourselves out?'

'Yes; yes, of course.'

'We wish we could do something for you, miss . . . ma'am,' said Tony Brown now. 'It isn't often one meets with such kindness.'

'Well, you haven't got me to thank, really, but that big thick-headed Geordie Joe who recognised a neighbour's voice. But go on now, and better luck today.'

They trooped out, still voicing their thanks; Bella returned to the kitchen, and said to Reenee, now standing at the farthest end of it, 'I doubt from the looks of two of them they'll see the winter through. It's scandalous, scandalous.' She shook her head, then said, 'Well, we can't do any more. That's the end of it, so let's get on with the day's work.'

But apparently it wasn't the end of it, only the beginning, for when Joe and Pimple came for their morning meal Joe said, very quietly, 'Don't go for me, Bella, I'm only doing things for the best; but those lads were tellin' me last night of some of the kips they'd had to sleep in, and they were disgraceful, while the decent ones charged a shilling a night for a bowl of soup, a can of tea the next morning and a wash. I told them about Reenee's idea for the kip made out of the cellar kitchen, and how it sounded impossible. Well, Bella, Andy the brickie said nothing's impossible when altering a house, and he knows that 'cos he's helped with many, and he wondered if you'd let him . . . well, look around and see what might be done here and work out how much it would cost like. What about it, Bella?'

'Oh, my God!' said Bella. 'What next?' She looked across at Reenee. There was an expectant look on the girl's face, so she said, 'Oh, all right. There can be no harm in that. Tell him to come in before they go.'

About half an hour later Bella nearly laughed outright at the assembly of different men standing at her front door. They must have put the new gear on top of the old, for even their trousers looked well padded now and two of the men, who were wearing the coats, appeared to be twice their size, at least in breadth. It was the bricklayer who spoke to her. 'Ma'am, if you wouldn't mind, would you let us have a look round? We might be able to work something out, and that might help you with your plan the lads were telling us about last night.'

'My plan?' Bella cried. 'I have no plan. It was a pipe dream of somebody's.' She didn't name Reenee.

115

'Well, ma'am, we feel we want to do something for you, and it will be no harm leaving you with a few suggestions if ever the idea should come to anything.'

Bella was stopped from answering by seeing Reenee scampering up the stairs.

'Have we frightened her, ma'am?' said one of the men.

'No, you see, she's lost her memory, or most of it, and whatever's happened to her . . . Well, men had something to do with it, and between you and me she can't bear the sight of them. But about your suggestion. You seem set on repaying me, so if it's going to please you, do as you say and have a look round. But I'm warning you, that's as far as it'll go. I haven't any money and I have enough to worry about in keeping my little business going.'

'Now, you two, listen to me,' said Bella. 'As I've told you, I haven't the money to see this thing through. And I can understand those fellows' enthusiasm: they're in such a state they'd go to any length to have a settled place to kip and a regular bite in their bellies. It's all very fine, talk and planning, but it's happening too swiftly for my liking. No, I'm not for it. Up till now I've lived quietly without all this fuss and bother; for what is it going to come to in the end? As far as I can see, nothing. They'll be back where they started, and our lives will go on as before.'

Suddenly she turned on Reenee, almost yelling now, 'And don't you look like that, lass! It's me that has to pay the piper, as the saying goes. So let's hear no more about it. I'll tell them in the morning. They've gone mad with their measuring and planning.'

But she didn't tell them in the morning for she had something more serious to think about. Reenee had gone. My God, she would go mad!

This was the outcome of last night. Why had she allowed the men to go up in the attic to see what was there? She had given way to her own curiosity and thought she might as well make use of them while they were here. And what had they found? Everything you'd find in a children's playroom: broken dolls' houses and all kinds of toys, including two moth-eaten teddy bears, besides broken furniture.

Joe had discovered a beam running across the ceiling and through the wall into the cobbler's place, indicating that at one time perhaps the two houses had been one.

But what had caused the upset with Reenee was the larger moth-eaten teddy bear. After the four men had gone, having taken all the oddments of furniture down into the yard, Reenee had come down from her bedroom, and when she sat by the fireplace Bella had picked up the moth-eaten bear she had kept back and taken it to her, saying, 'What d'you think about this, what's left of the poor thing?' as she dropped it on to Reenee's lap, only to exclaim, 'Oh dear!' as Reenee, suddenly grabbing the bear, began to rock herself back and forth, moaning what seemed to Bella and the two men the same word over and over again. Bella was gripping Joe's arm as she said, 'God in heaven! She's had a bairn at some time.'

Neither Joe nor Pimple made any comment, they just stared at the wailing figure, for now Reenee's voice had risen as she rocked the bear.

'She'll make herself ill going on like that,' said Bella. 'We should try to get it from her.'

'I wouldn't,' put in Pimple. 'Just leave her.' And they stood watching the swaying figure hugging to her the remnants of the teddy bear until, slowly, she seemed exhausted and lay back in the chair, but still with the bear clutched to her breast, its head tucked under her chin.

Bella had approached her quietly, saying, 'There you are, lass. There you are.' She looked down into the streaming face and the tears came into her own eyes. She'd never had a child of her own, never wanted one, having been brought up among too many, so she had never known the love of a child, or for one, but she was experiencing it now. This girl was acting out of passion, of feeling. It was as if she had found her child again, long lost.

It was a good ten minutes later that the tension in Reenee's body seemed to seep away and she lay limply in the chair.

Quite suddenly, Pimple turned and walked to the far end of the kitchen, opened the door and went out, and Joe, about to follow him, said something that amazed Bella. He looked at her and murmured, 'Things happen in life that are too hard to bear. They are much worse than being hungry and frozen at nights,' and at this he, too, turned and left her.

It was at the twelve o'clock break that Bella left the stall to Peg-leg and went indoors, but Reenee wasn't in the kitchen.

Bella went to the top of the stone stairs, but told herself not to be silly, she wouldn't be down there: those fellows were probably still about. She turned round and went to the foot of the hall stairs and called, 'Reenee!'

When there was no reply she called again. Then she went quickly up the stairs and unceremoniously into the second bedroom. She pulled open the wardrobe door, then emitted the words, 'Oh, my God!' because neither the discoloured coat nor the weird cap were hanging there. But the bear was lying at the bottom of the wardrobe. What was there too was the dress Bella had got from Ginnie's a few weeks ago and had persuaded Reenee to wear round the house. The velvet dress was gone as well.

'Oh, my God!' She sat on the edge of the bed. Where would she have gone to in her state of mind? It had been bad enough until last night, but the hugging of that moth-eaten old bear must have brought back something in her past in a way that had driven her out to find it. She must send somebody looking for her. But Joe wasn't here, at least not for another half-hour, and you could never depend upon Pimple. But she must get Joe. Yes, she must get Joe.

She was running down the stairs quicker than she had done for a long time, through the kitchen and into the backyard where two of the men were standing talking; and she cried at them, 'You know the warehouse where Joe works?'

'Aye, ma'am. Aye.'

'Well, go and fetch him. Tell him that she's gone, the lass . . . the woman . . . she's gone.'

'You mean your . . . that . . . your girl?'

'Never mind who I mean, he'll know who I mean. Get yourself away!'

Within fifteen minutes Joe was standing in front of her, saying, 'You don't mean it?'

'I do. I do. Her coat, hat and the red velvet dress. All she ever owned. In fact, just what she came in here with she's gone out with, and I don't know where to send you lookin'.'

'Somebody must've spotted her. She'll stand out, always did.'

As Joe was hurrying from her she shouted to him, 'Where d'you think Pimple will be playin'?'

'God knows, Bella; he gets around. But I'll away.'

It was half an hour before Joe returned. He stood before her silently and shook his head.

Bella plumped down on to a kitchen chair, laid her head on her folded arms on the table, and began to cry. When she felt his hand patting her shoulder she straightened herself, wiped her face quickly with the end of her apron and said, 'I – I can't tell you, Joe, how I've come to like that lass. I know half her mind's been lost in the past but I'd an idea it would come through one of these days. But till then I wanted to look after her. And it's selfish in a way because she has brought light into my life that wasn't here before I saw her lyin' that day among the boxes and the rotten fruit.'

119

5

During the time Bella was baring her soul to Joe, Irene was standing in a pawn shop facing an old man who wore a skull cap, and he was looking at something she had taken out of a bag inside her coat pocket. It was a ring and he looked at it for a long time before he put his hand under the counter and brought out an eye-glass. It was some minutes later when he said to her in a thick tone, 'You want to pawn this article?'

When she nodded he paused a moment or two before speaking again, then said, 'Have you any idea of its worth?' His words were slow as if he were talking to a child, and again she inclined her head towards him.

He now picked up the ring and once more put the glass to his eye. Then, after a moment, he called, 'Joseph!' and was answered by a younger edition of himself coming from a back room and taking a position by his side. When his father held out the ring silently to him the younger man looked at it for quite some moments before, taking the eye-glass from his father, he too peered through it. Then he muttered one word: 'My!'

The elderly man was speaking once more to Irene and he said, 'You will, I am sure, be asking a large loan for this article, but first I must ask you, does it really belong to you?'

The word came out quick, utterly clear and loud: 'Yes!'

Its tone was so different from the appearance of this person that the men's eyes met again for a moment, and they were still more astonished when their customer's small fist thumped her chest, exclaiming loudly, 'Mine! Mine!'

'All right, madam. We believe you, but as I was about to say, we don't often take into pawn articles of this value. Ours is a very poor district, as you can see, and really we must tell you our loans don't go much beyond ten shillings, if that. So you will understand my questioning about this most wonderful ring. Nevertheless I am used to stones, madam. Good stones.'

Again there was an exchange of glances; and then the old man gave his full attention to Irene, saying, 'What did you think about asking, I mean as a loan?'

They both waited and the same sum was in both their minds. She would ask at least for fifty pounds but they would beat her down, naturally, as it was their business to do so. But this ring here was worth a great deal of money, if he knew anything about stones. Oh, yes. Rubies and diamonds.

She surprised them both by saying, 'Thirty pounds.'

It was the son who repeated, 'Thirty pounds.' Then he looked at his father and repeated, 'Thirty pounds.'

He turned quickly to a shelf before him on which were small pockets of articles with tickets hanging from them and he pushed one here and there before he muttered, 'Don't haggle. Don't haggle, Father.'

The older man seemed to consider a moment, and then he said, 'Thirty pounds. Well, I don't see why you can't have thirty pounds. Do you mean to leave it lying for some months or a year?'

She stared back at the men who were now facing her, and they saw that she was making a great effort to speak again because her mouth opened and closed convulsively. She put a hand to her throat and such was her agitation that the elder

121

man said, 'Don't worry yourself, my dear lady.' Yes, he had called her a lady, for he was sure, under that dreadful garb, that that's what she was, a lady, but in distress of some kind because her words came out only as syllables.

Quietly and slowly, he said, 'You mean that it may be more than a year before you come back? But I must tell you, madam, that if you do not return in a year and pay back your loan then by law we are allowed to keep what you pawned and sell it. You understand?'

They both saw that she didn't, and it was the younger man who said, 'You can insure it. I mean, you can pay so much to insure it if you don't mean to return in a year. You could cover it for a year, two years, three years or more, and it will always be here when you come back. That's if you can afford to insure it. You could perhaps use some of the thirty pounds in insurance?'

She shook her head vigorously. Then she seemed to think for a moment and, putting her hand quickly inside her coat, she fumbled about a bit before placing before them another ring.

'A wedding ring?' asked the elderly man.

She nodded.

The younger man took the ring and, turning it round in his fingers, he said to his father, 'Do you see those?'

'I would be blind, my son, if I didn't. Diamonds are diamonds, even if they're only pinhead size,' and his fingers now traced the band of small diamonds running round the centre of the circle.

'You would like to pawn this also?'

Irene's head bobbed again, and then with a great effort she brought out the word in stilted form, 'In-sur-ance.'

'Oh, yes. Yes.'

Then she added another word to it, 'Part.' This word was clear.

Both men considered; and then the younger one said, 'You

want to know how much you can borrow on this ring, and you want to leave part of it by way of insurance on both the dress ring and this one?'

Irene looked at him for a long moment, and then, taking a deep breath, she brought out again the single word, 'Yes.'

'Well, madam' – the older man was speaking again – 'you know that this hasn't the value of the first ring? It is very nice, oh, very nice indeed, and of value, and it is wise that you are using it by way of insurance.' Then he turned to his son. 'For how many years would five pounds cover the insurance on the article?'

Once again the young man turned his back on his father and addressed himself to arranging the things in the small cubby-holes, and he whispered, 'Offer ten.'

'But . . . but, son . . .'

'Offer ten, Father, please.'

The older man's whispered words were audible to Irene: 'Have you gone soft in the head already? Does she hold a charm?'

'No, Father,' the younger man did not turn to his parent, 'let us say compassion of some sort. I don't know why, but compassion.'

'Dear, dear. I think, my son, you will soon have to be looking out for another post,' and the two men laughed together. Then they were both looking at Irene, whose face was now showing some anxiety, and the father said, 'Oh, quite a small amount would cover the insurance for a number of years, so if we offer you ten pounds you would be able to add most of that to your thirty. Would that be suitable?'

They both watched the look of relief on the face across the counter. Then it was as if she were making another great effort to speak. Seeing a scrap of pencil, she picked it up, together with the newspaper that was lying there and she wrote, very slowly, 'How many years will five pounds cover insurance?'

'Oh,' the older man looked at his son, then said, 'Well,

that'll have to be worked out. What d'you think, Joseph?'

Joseph had taken a pen from his pocket and was writing hastily, and when he finished he said, 'Eighteen years.'

She seemed quite satisfied with their answer. Then the elderly man said, 'Will you be coming back before then?'

Maybe. Her lips framed the word but no sound came, but he seemed to pick up her dumb language and he translated it to, 'Perhaps?' and she nodded.

It was the young man who spoke next. 'Do you live around this way?'

Her answer, he had surmised, would be a definite no; but her head drooped a little, then gave an affirmative nod. She lived around here then. Whereabouts? Why hadn't he seen her? But, then, he rarely went out during working hours; when he did it would be to visit other similar business houses that included family ties, cousins and half-cousins.

His father was now writing out four tickets, and he himself placed the two rings in a small box that he had taken from under the counter and wrote something on the lid. Then, looking at her, he said, 'Your name, please?'

She hesitated for a long moment before, on the margin of the sheet of newspaper, she wrote 'Forrester'. He said, 'Christian name?'

She wrote the letter C, and he repeated, 'C. Forrester,' as he wrote it on the box lid. Then he opened a ledger that was beside him and wrote in this too. Meanwhile his father had finished writing on the tickets, in a small neat hand, the descriptions of the pledges; and he handed two of the tickets to her saying, 'Keep them safe because, you know, they are your only proof that you have lodged your precious jewellery with us. You understand? If you were to lose them, someone else might try to claim them.'

It was the son now who put in quickly, 'We shall also give you a receipt for the insurance of five pounds on the articles.' He turned and looked at his father, who said, 'Yes, of course.'

Within a few minutes she was handed another small piece of paper with 'Isaac Gomparts, Pawnbroker and Dealer' stamped on it, and above this a few words saying that she had insured the said articles for five pounds which would cover the period of eighteen years.

Irene picked up the two tickets and folded them in the piece of paper, which just covered them; then she stood waiting as she watched the younger man count out thirty-five pound notes, which he handed to her, saying, 'Count.' But she shook her head, and he said, 'I shall put them in an envelope for you, yes?'

She nodded, and after he had handed them back to her in the envelope, she put the tickets in with the money, then placed the envelope in a pocket of her coat. Then the three of them stood looking at each other, until the younger man said, 'I hope the transaction will help you.' She looked straight at him and bowed her head once to him. Then, looking at the older man, she brought out, again seemingly painfully, the words, 'Thank you.'

'Never has a customer been more welcome, madam. Good day to you.'

Inclining her head, she nodded from one to the other and went out. Then the older man, turning to his son, said, 'Well, well! And what came over you, may I ask, Joseph Gomparts?'

'I don't know,' said his son. 'I can only say we've been dealing with a beautiful maimed woman with the face of a lost angel.'

At this he turned and walked away, leaving his father patting the counter and shaking his head as he muttered to himself, 'Dear God, it is as you say, don't look for the reasons of life in your own kin. They are of you and you can't fathom it.'

Bella was sitting looking up at Joe. She was making no attempt now to dry the tears that were still running down her face, and her voice was cracked as she said, 'It was that damned teddy bear; it did something to her. And yet, when she came down this morning, I was amazed at the sight of her. She looked so . . . well, so much more alive, much more conscious of everything. That's the only way I can put it. At one time I thought she looked excited, and I thought, Good, perhaps the bear has straightened out part of her mind in some way, and on the quiet, when she was down here, I looked in her room to see if it was on her bed – she'd likely been sleeping with it – but no, it wasn't, and when I was lookin' in the wardrobe to see if her coat was still there, I saw it pushed right into the corner. Now if it was the incident of the bear that brought her to herself, she wouldn't have pushed it into a corner, would she? She would have left it somewhere where she could still see it. Nevertheless, it must have done something to make her clear out.' She had hardly finished the last words when the door that led down from the kitchen to the stone stairs burst open and Pimple, almost breathless, hurried in and held on to the table as he said, 'She's on her way! She's on her way! She'll be here any minute.'

'How d'you know about it?' Joe demanded. 'We've been lookin' all over for her.'

'Yeah, you might have, but I didn't know anything about her walkin' out until there I was at the end of Brampton Street. It's a long street, and I saw the figure at the other end. Now, she's unmistakable in that get-up. At first I thought I was seeing things; and then she disappeared – into where d'you think? A pawn shop.'

'What?'

'That's what I said, Bella, into a pawn shop. Now, look. I'm not goin' to stop because she'll be in in a minute.'

'Oh!' Bella got to her feet. 'Wait till I see her.'

'Bella! Bella!' Pimple now spoke in a tone of command and with a voice that could have come from someone twice his size, so deep and firm was it. 'You'll do nothing of the sort.

If you'll take advice, for once in your life, you'll do nothing of the sort. You'll open your arms to her because, if she went into that pawn shop, it was to pawn something, wasn't it? And who would she pawn for? Not for herself, I'm sure, but for you or whatever you're doing. At least, that's how I see her. Anyway,' he grabbed Joe's arm, 'let's get out of this. I came the back way, running like a hare, 'cos I knew she would be making for home and I didn't want her to see me. So she'll come in the front way. Now, I've told you, Bella.'

Bella gazed at him in amazement, and she watched him almost pull Joe towards the staircase door. As it banged closed the front door opened, and Bella stood trembling, holding tightly with one hand to the edge of the table to steady herself.

Then, there she was, the girl, the woman, the strange one, as she had first seen her in that long, stained coat and weird hat. Only her face looked different today. She came slowly forward and when she stood before her Bella found she was quite unable to speak. She only knew she loved this poor creature and then, just as Pimple had said, she put her arms out, and Reenee went into them. Her own arms went round Bella's stubby body, and they held each other close; and like this they stood for a full minute before Bella, pressing her slightly away, looked up into her face and said, 'Oh, lass! You . . . you did frighten me! I thought you'd gone for good, or at least gone somewhere.' And now she made herself ask, 'Where . . . where have you been?'

Reenee's eyes were bright and her throat swelled as she endeavoured to get out the words, 'Pawn shop.'

'Pawn shop!' exclaimed Bella. And although she knew this was where Pimple told her she had been, it was with genuine surprise that she repeated, 'Pawn shop!'

Reenee now indicated that Bella should sit down, and she herself sat as well. Then, unbuttoning her coat and putting her hand inside it, she brought out a brown envelope, out of which she slowly pulled a thick wad of pound notes. She did not lift out the tickets but pressed them into a corner of the envelope, which she then doubled and returned to her pocket. Then, looking at Bella, who was staring wide-eyed at the money, she began to count it out silently on to the table. When she reached thirty she stopped; and the last notes in her hand she counted separately; then putting them to one side, she pointed to them and then to herself as she again made an effort to speak. The word she muttered now was 'Mine.'

Bella simply gazed at her. She couldn't believe her eyes. There were thirty pounds on the table; and when Reenee pushed them towards her, she exclaimed, 'Oh, lass! How on earth did you get . . . ? But why? Why had you to . . . ? I mean—' She stopped talking and gazed down on the money and said, 'Thirty pounds. Thirty pounds,' and added the word, 'How?'

Reenee pointed quickly to her left hand and the second and third fingers, then indicated what Bella clearly understood as rings.

'You've pawned your rings? You had rings? Your wedding ring?'

She watched the look on Reenee's face change: the brightness went off it, but nevertheless she acknowledged Bella's concern with a movement of her head, before she pointed again to her third finger and made two circles over the top of it.

For a moment Bella was puzzled, and then she said, 'Engagement ring.'

Again Reenee's head nodded downwards.

Bella's voice was hushed as she said, 'Must have been a very, very good ring to bring all that money. But why? Why, lass?'

On Bella's last words Reenee tried to speak. When she wasn't successful she pulled the newspaper towards her, and going to the mantelpiece where Bella kept a pencil she took it down and wrote along the border of the newsprint, 'Men's plan. Need something. Poor.'

Bella looked at her and there were tears in her eyes again as she said, 'Oh, love. Fancy you thinking of them and you frightened to death of them. There's nothing to be afraid of, they wouldn't hurt a hair . . . All right,' she held up a hand as she saw Reenee almost shrink back from her, 'I didn't mean that you should talk to them or recognise them, but I still maintain they're good blokes and they would never hurt you in any way. Oh' – she laughed to herself – 'if they as much as said a wrong word to you our two would murder them, Joe and Pimple, you know.'

The words did not bring a smile to Reenee's face but she pointed to the five pounds that were to the side, and she said again, 'Mine.'

'Of course, lass. Of course you've got to keep something for yourself.' The head was shaking but in denial, and Bella said, 'It isn't for yourself, but you want to keep it? Is that it?'

The nod told Bella that she had said the right thing; and again looking at the money, she muttered, 'I'll have to put it some place safe. And, lass,' she suddenly lifted her head, 'I . . . I'll tell the lads what you've done, and for them and the others, but I won't tell them how much there's here. Oh, no, because that will put more ideas into their heads of how it could be used. Shall we say ten pounds and bring out the other bit by bit for what is needed? How d'you feel about that?'

The two nods from Reenee brought from Bella, 'Good lass. Good, we're both of the same mind. But where am I goin' to put the remainder?'

Reenee was now standing with her head slightly to one side as if thinking; then that semblance of a smile came to her face and she made a gesture that Bella should gather up the notes. She herself picked up the five pounds from the table and pushed them into her inner coat pocket. Then, taking Bella's arm, she led her down the room and through a door into the little-used parlour.

After the brightness of the kitchen this room appeared as if they had already reached late evening; Reenee led Bella to the far blank wall against which stood a roll-top desk. She pointed to the key in the lock, turned it, pushed open the lid, then pulled out one of the lower drawers that were fitted along the back of the piece and, putting her hand inside, she picked up a smaller key, pushed in the drawer and locked it. She turned and gave the key to Bella who, now smiling widely, said, 'Eeh, lass, you must have investigated all this. But that's the very place. Yes, yes, you're right.' She counted off ten of the notes and put them into her apron pocket, unlocked the drawer and laid the other twenty carefully in it, locked it, then turned . . . and handed the key to Reenee. At this Reenee shook her head vigorously and waved Bella's hand to one side. Then she pulled down the lid, locked it and handed the second key to Bella. Then once more she found herself clasped in the arms of the little woman, who was whispering, 'Oh, Reenee, if ever there was a light came into me life it's been you. But God knows, my dear, how you have suffered along the way to get here. I only wish I knew.' She put her hand up and touched Reenee's face. 'Oh, I wish you would speak and try to tell me all that you remember. That's if you remember anything.

'Oh, dear me! What have I said? I'm sorry, lass. I'm sorry. Don't look like that. You have nothing to fear, ever. Whoever did what they did to you I hope they rot in hell. But come on, lass, come on, else we'll both be blubbing again. Wait till I tell the lads. And . . . and what say I give the fellows five shillings at the end, will that please you?'

The light slowly returned to Reenee's face and she made one small movement with her head, then they both left the room hand in hand together, the slight, grotesquely dressed girl and the little homely woman.

6

It was three weeks later and the changes that had already taken place both in the house and downstairs in the cellar were unbelievable. There was now going off the kitchen a bathroom, formerly the big larder and the long broom and oddments store. That the colour of the bath, the basin and the lavatory yelled their bold red at you as soon as you opened the door was of no account. The walls had been painted what John called a dove grey. Next to the wash-basin was a two feet by eighteen inches long window covered with a floral-patterned curtain. Looking through this window across the yard you knew something was happening to the wash-house, but that was as yet unfinished.

Downstairs, in what had been Reenee's sleeping quarters, a great transformation had taken place. At the far end were two doors leading into separate rooms, each holding a single iron bed on top of which was a good mattress and a quilted bed-cover. Besides this there was a chest of drawers and a curtained-off corner that acted as a wardrobe, and a repaired chair rescued from the attic. Neither Joe nor Pimple could believe that these rooms had been furnished for them alone. Such was the effect on Pimple that he had dared to put his arms around Reenee and kiss her cheek. This had been done, it must be admitted, at a rush and had taken her off her guard. But as he had stood back from her, he said, 'I had to do that, Reenee, because the miracle could never have happened without you.' He did not add 'pawning your rings'.

Along two sides of the long room were roughly constructed low wooden platforms waiting for mattresses.

Then there was the outside, the new latrines and the wash-place that held two basins, each with its roller towel. The material of the towels was rough but that did not lessen the men's appreciation of them.

That the four men had worked wonders was said over and over again by Bella. But now there was a snag, and they were having a meeting about this down in what was to become the bunk-house or, to give it its common name, Big Bella's Pad. It was Joe who had thought up the title.

They were now sitting on forms at each side of the long central table. This had been constructed from two cement-covered planks found amongst a heap of builders' rubbish. They had picked up the trestles for it and the forms while scrounging in the dump yard, the same place in which they had found the red bathroom suite. The condition of the latter had amazed them: as John had said, probably somebody had been unable any longer to stand the colour. Nor could they believe their luck when the old grubber asked only four pounds five shillings for the lot.

Bella sat at the end of the table. To one side of her were Joe and Pimple, and next to Pimple sat Willie. On the other side were Andy, Tony and John. It was Willie who now put in plaintively, 'I wouldn't be in the way, ma'am.'

'I know that, laddie, I know that. We all know that. But she's a sick woman in her head, at least half of it, and I don't know how it's gonna be overcome. Perhaps, as she got used to Joe here and Pimple, she might get used to the rest of you, if you stay that long.'

'Oh, if the plan works out, ma'am,' came from Tony, 'you've got me for life.'

'And me,' said John.

But what Andy said was, 'I wish I could say the same, but I have a wife and two bairns back there, and if things get turned round I'll have to go back. In fact, to be truthful I'd want to go back. As I've said, I miss me bairns and they're growin' up without me. But I can't see it happenin' for a year or so, not from readin' the papers.

'About the lass, though, ma'am, what are we gonna do? We can't keep out of the way all the time, can we? Now that things are about to get working? Willie there is a very good cook – I know that just from the experience of the last few weeks – but he tells me he's best at makin' bread and pastry, so if you would let him make bread,' he was nodding at Willie now, 'each man could have a shive with their broth at night and, in the morning, a slice with their mug of tea. If they wanted to buy a pie, a meat one that is, it would cost them twopence, or they might want just a bun for a penny. But he said quite a lot of money can be made out of that kind of thing, and if it got round there was a wash-up place as well as a place around a big fireguard where they could dry their boots or hang their clothes if they were wet, you would have your beds filled every night, I can tell you.'

'But would they, if they're on their uppers, be able to pay a shillin' a night?' put in Bella.

'Aye, that's a point, because there's many a night we hadn't a shilling among us, let alone one each. Yet there were other nights when we had, and what we got for a shilling . . . well, I've told you all about it. But here, what are you offering? They can have a wash straight away; they can come in and they can get warm sitting on the forms around a fire; then they can have a bowl of soup and a shive, and the soup isn't just soup, it'll be broth with plenty of vegetables in. Joe there said

133

he could get all the vegetables he could carry from the market every morning, like he does the fruit, and all that's needed to go with them is a couple of penn'orth of bones, preferably with meat on them,' he laughed now, 'and half a pound of hough meat.'

'What's hough meat?' said Bella, looking from one to the other.

Joe said, 'Oh, it's the rough end of the cow. But one of the main things I would say, Andy, besides having a good few taties in it, is the barley. Add half a pound of barley to that and that kale pot will have more nourishment in it than any restaurant in London town. What d'you say, Willie, 'cos you'll be the one that's doin' it?'

'Oh, aye. Aye. But . . . but remember, I won't be the only one that's doing it. The missis here, she'll be running things and she'll see what is used, and know how much she can spend and what she can make in order to carry on 'cos, as she's said, there'll be no fruit stall outside once it gets going.'

'The way I see it,' put in Tony, 'the ones we'll get here are mostly those fellows with part-time jobs, and for a shillin' a night they'll be only too damn glad of the chance to come.'

'Well,' said Bella, quickly now, 'this all brings us back to the point, what about the lass? How are we goin' to get her to accept that you're goin' to be in that kitchen all day, Willie?'

'If I talk to her . . .' said Willie.

'No. No, that wouldn't be any good.' This came from John. 'I have an idea. I don't know what you'll think about this, ma'am, but I've only been in your front room, or parlour as you call it, once. To me, it was a dark, dingy place, and I'm quick at taking in things. There was a great big sideboard that could be halved in size by the middle part being taken out. They're as old as the hills, those things. One day they'll be worth money, but they're not now. And there's two big leather chairs in there, besides a roll-top desk. The window . . . well, it hardly lets any light in at all.'

'You're not touchin' the roll-top desk, John. That stays as it is, no matter what else you change.'

'Oh, aye, and it's a very good piece of furniture; but that window could be made twice its size. The sideboard could be made half its size and look better for it. Then fresh wallpaper and a bit of paint and that room could be a very comfortable place. And I saw there was quite a good grate in the fireplace, which had a tiled surround. It could be made cosy like, and I'm sorry to say it's anything but cosy to me now. Well, there you are, ma'am. What d'you think? What I'm getting at, really,' John finished, 'is that it will be some place for her to . . . well, she seems to want to hide, and it will be comfortable and nice, in fact, for you both, because there's no place in the house I can see that provides the two of you with any privacy, not even the kitchen.'

Bella looked at him, and she smiled and said, 'You must have taught yourself a lot, lad, decoratin' those boats. You've got an eye for things, haven't you?'

'Aye, ma'am, I pride meself on having an eye for how things should be in a room. It hasn't brought me very far, as you can see, but I'm never happy unless I'm fixing something or altering something to look better.'

'Well, I can say this to you, laddie, you have my go-ahead about that room. Anything you do in it, I say carry on. Only leave the roll-top desk where it is.'

'You mean that, ma'am, after . . . after we finish extending the wash-house?'

'Yes, I mean it. And was it your idea to extend the wash-house?'

John hung his head for a moment, then quickly raised it as he said, 'Aye, it was; and it'll be fine when it's finished. We'll have two double bunks, and some bare necessities. We'll make it a comfortable pad for as long as you need us. Isn't that so?' He looked round the table.

'Yes. And we've been very grateful for it,' said Andy.

135

'You'll never know, ma'am, how grateful. And to think you're paying us what you can, an' all.'

'Five shillings a week isn't much, lad.'

'It's a bank roll when you haven't got owt,' said Tony. 'By, it is! But as you said last night, we know you can't go on doing that until you see how this business is going to work. So if you stop after this week we'll understand, won't we?'

John said, 'It'll be enough payment to be working on your parlour, ma'am.'

'You're good lads. They are, aren't they?'

She had turned to Joe and Pimple, and Joe said, 'Never better. But you see, Bella, they're from my part of the country, they couldn't be otherwise, could they now?'

She reached out her hand to slap his face, but he leant back from her and they all laughed.

Joe said now, 'I must tell them at the warehouse about the mattresses tomorrow, Bella, because I know they're goin' to move the lot. Supposedly for the retail business, but that lot of mattresses they've brought in was for no ordinary order. There must be a hundred of them if there's two, and they want rid of them as quick as possible. He was asking five shillings each, and I got him to phone through to the other warehouse and tell them that they were for you, and the word came back 'half price'; but that'll cost thirty bob, Bella, and there's the blankets. They're full size, there's no singles, and he wanted four bob each, but you could have them for two. That will be another twenty-four bob.'

Bella shut her eyes and put her head back for a moment, as if considering, and then she said, 'Dear Lord, I don't know where the money's comin' from. Anyway, you'd better get them, 'cos there won't be another chance like it. We can always take in sewing – there's an old Singer machine in the boxroom upstairs and nobody to use it. We'll manage. All right, then.'

But Willie stopped her rising by saying, 'I can't start in that kitchen, ma'am, knowing that I'm puttin' that lass out or hurtin' her in some way.'

'You won't have to,' said John quickly. 'You lot can carry on with finishing off the wash-house. I'll set to work in the parlour. The only thing is,' he turned to Andy, 'I'll want you for the window, but that won't be for, say, a day or so. All right?'

He had addressed this last remark to Bella and she said, 'All right, if you can do it in a couple of days; we'll manage till then.'

She rose slowly and heavily from her chair, saying, 'Good night, lads.'

'Good night, ma'am. Good night. And thanks again. And that's from all of us.'

She nodded at Andy; then, looking at Joe, she said, 'You and Pimple come upstairs for a minute or two, will you? I want a word with you.'

The kitchen was empty and Bella stood looking at the two men as she said, 'It isn't only the cookin' business that's worryin' me. It's that damn coat. She's taken to wearin' it every minute of the day. It's all since the lads have come into the yard and, of course, up in the house, and when I cornered her yesterday morning in the bedroom and said, "Look, lass, you're not naked underneath, so why do you . . . ?" That's as far as I got. It was the word "naked". Her eyes seemed to pop out and then she stiffened on the bed and, believe me, lads, she went into one of those up and downers, you know her stomach risin' and fallin', as if it were bein' pumped up and down. And as she was coming round she looked at me as if she didn't recognise me, but when she really came to she said, "Sorry," like she does, you know; and then she said, "Coat," and she hugged herself as if she was huggin' the coat to her. And I said, "All right, then you must wear it; but there's one thing I can't understand, lass . . . You don't wear it in front of Joe and Pimple." Then I saw a look come on her face as if

137

she was trying to question something, you know when you're trying to think something out and the corners of your eyes crinkle up. She even bit on her lip as if she was tryin' to fathom why she didn't wear the coat in front of you two.'

'Oh, I shouldn't worry,' said Joe, 'not so much about the coat. The lads wouldn't mind her wearin' the coat, but it's the business of her acceptin' Willie in the kitchen here. And, you know, you've got to have him because, as he says, the bit of money you'll make after you settle up everything will come from the extras on pies and things that he turns out. He says there's money in the bakery lark, but for that he needs an oven and a kitchen.'

'There might be money in it,' said Bella, 'and he's right, but what else can I do about it? There's no way of persuading her. And although John's going to alter the parlour, she can't stay in there all her days.'

'Listen,' said Pimple, 'leave it, will you? I have an idea that might bring her round. But . . .'

'Well, let's have it, then.'

'I can't, it'll just have to be worked out when the opportunity arises. Leave it for now. You might be downstairs and she'll be washing up or something, but just leave it. It might work and it might not. I only know this: half her brain's gone into the past, into a fearful past, I should say, but what's left is quite clear and she understands much more than any of you imagine. Now, just leave it.'

'Well, if you say so, mister,' said Bella, mockingly now, 'we'll do as you ask. Won't we, Joe?'

Joe did not grin, he just said, 'Well, he does get things right at times, you know, Bella.'

'Go on with you. Get along! I've got enough to think about without any more new ideas.'

After they left the room Bella turned and went into her new bathroom. She switched on the electric light, then stood looking around. Eeh! She'd never thought to have a bathroom like this. And, oh, how she would love to get into that bath. Yet, somehow, she was a bit frightened. But fancy having your own bath and being able to lie in it. She had been amazed when Tony tapped into the boiler at the side of the fireplace so they could have hot water in the bath and the basin. Of course it would mean more coal and more stoking up, all that, but she put out a hand and stroked her red acquisition and she said to herself, I'll get in one night when Reenee's in the kitchen, to be on guard, and then I'll do the same for her.

Thinking back to what she had seen through the window of the wash-house, she said to herself, She'll love a real bath; oh, I bet she will. But if only we could make her see that with Willie in the kitchen everything would run smoothly. Well, as smoothly as it can, because this is a big concern I'm taking on and, really, God only knows how it's gonna turn out.

Pimple had made sure that Bella was downstairs with the men sorting out the mattresses and the blankets, and he had taken Joe aside saying, 'Come on upstairs with me for a minute. No, not that way, she'll see us as we go in. Come on round through the gate.'

They came in quietly through the front door, and when they entered the kitchen Pimple knew that Reenee was down at the scullery end of it, washing up. He said quite clearly to Joe, 'There's nobody here. Reenee must be upstairs. So what d'you think we should do about it, Joe?'

Joe didn't for the life of him know what the little fellow was alluding to, but he said, 'I don't know, Pimple. Bella's put all she has into it, you know; she must've spent every penny; and now she's faced with buyin' new glass for that sittin'-room window because they can't get that second-hand. They couldn't get a frame small enough, and they've had to get one made. She's not goin' to like that when she hears about it. And, you know, her fruit and veg stall will stop once the pad opens downstairs. And what she'll make out of the pad

139

business will just get her by and nothin' more; and she certainly won't be able to pay the fellows the bit she's givin' them now.'

'She won't be skinty with the broth either, that's for sure,' said Pimple, 'and although we'll get the vegetables cheap, and as much as she'll be able to take, there's the washing of them and chopping up. And then there's the shoppin' to do, which'll take her out. She's said she's got to try to make a deal with the grocer 'cos she'll want quite a lot of barley and sugar and tea; and, too, there's the butcher along there. He's not much cop, I hear, but who's to question as long as there's a bit of meat floating about in the broth. She just can't do all that herself. Willie must be allowed up here. He's used to a bakery and ordering and how they do things. It would take a load off her mind – and, as he said, there would be a further profit in the pies and oddments he would make. She'll need that if she's goin' to give them a shive of bread with the soup.'

'Well,' said Joe, 'we've been all over this you know, and she won't disturb the lass. Anyway . . .'

There was a pause now before Pimple said, 'Such a pity, 'cos he's such a quiet, nice lad and, oh, what he'd give to get back to his own job again. I can't understand it. He wouldn't hurt a hair of her head. Look how she puts up with us, she's all right with us.'

'Yes,' said Joe, 'but it took time. Don't forget, it took time. And then there's her coat, and Bella can't get her to go about without that coat. She's tried all ways. Tried to fathom it out. It's as if she feels safe behind it.'

'I don't know about that,' said Pimple. 'She never looks safe. At times there's a look of terror in her eyes. Different words bring it out; I've noticed that, and you have yourself. Anyway, I suppose we'll get through, but not as well as we might. Isn't it funny when she was the one who thought up the idea? Remember the night she drew the lines on the paper? And the beds goin' down, and the lads turnin' up as a group like that? Who would've thought there'd be a bricky and a plumber and a carpenter and a cook? What a pity there weren't another two, such as a bank manager and a solicitor; we might have got somewhere!'

'Aye,' said Joe, on a laugh, 'if they'd had a bobby with them then we all know where we would've got. Oh, let's get down.'

'Look, I'm not goin' down the stairs just yet, I'm going to have a look at the wash-house and see how they've got on. They're geniuses, that lot, you know.'

The room was empty again except for Irene standing tight-pressed against the wall of the scullery. Her mind was in a whirl. In the kitchen all day, he wouldn't hurt a fly. He wouldn't hurt a fly. And Bella wanted him there. So much to do. All those vegetables to wash and clean. Shopping. Washing up. Piles, piles of washing up. Tin plates, tin bowls. Spoons. The words were whirling round in her mind. But my coat. I'd have to wear my coat. Oh, yes, I'd have to wear my coat. If I didn't it would come back again. All that. Oh, no! And she pressed her hand to her brow then took a long, slow, deep breath and said firmly, 'I must wear my coat.'

No one could have been more surprised than Bella, not even the men, the next morning when Reenee appeared downstairs in her coat, but over it was one of Bella's voluminous aprons, or pinnies, as she called them; and although the broad waist gave some covering to the coat, the length of it only touched her knees. And if it hadn't been that Bella knew laughter was the last thing she must give way to, she would have laughed her head off. But apparently Reenee was in a serious mood, for she had come straight to Bella and, pointing to the oven, said with some difficulty, 'Cook.'

'You want to cook, lass?'

Reenee shook her head; then to Bella's further amazement she beckoned her to come downstairs with her; and so, lead-ing the way, she entered the room that was stacked with bedding, towels and piles of tin cutlery, besides other odds and ends.

Seated at the table were the four men, and they all rose to their feet when the young lady, as they referred to Reenee, approached them with the missis following. And, stranger still, they watched her go to Willie. She did not look directly at him, her head was bowed, but she spoke, and what she said was, 'Cook,' and she thumbed towards the ceiling. And when Willie stammered, 'Aye, miss. Aye, miss, I'd love to cook. And . . . and I won't disturb you, I promise.'

She turned swiftly from him now; and after glancing from one to the other of the three men she directed her gaze on John. Then she extended her hands to a measurement of about two feet.

Quick off the mark, John said, 'You want a board, miss, about two feet, eh? What kind of a board?' He closed his fist and started to rub on the top of the board. 'Polished?'

She shook her head vigorously; then, with her hand she made a chopping movement across the end of the table; and he exclaimed, 'For chopping?'

She now turned her lowered gaze towards Willie again, and he said quietly, 'Like a board for chopping vegetables on, ready for the broth and meat and things like that?'

She gave a quick nod, and Bella said, 'Well I never!' and with the four men she watched the girl go up the stone stairs.

It was Willie who asked quietly, 'What's brought her round, Bella? Oh! I'm sorry . . . ma'am.'

'That's fine with me, Willie; that's me name. Now don't ask me about the miss, I don't know. And yet I think it's got something to do with Pimple, because he said to me yesterday, "Just leave it. Just leave it." He talked as if he had something up his sleeve. And yet, although when I've been with him and Joe talking about the goings-on here, I've not heard him open his mouth about you or the cooking or anything else. But I'll find out. Oh, I am relieved, and you are too, Willie, aren't you?'

'Relief isn't the word for it, Bella. I'm dying to get my hands into some dough.' He turned to look across at John and said, 'Can you knock her up a big chopping board?'

'I've got the very thing. There's the section of wood out of the sideboard in the parlour, Bella. You'll not want to make use of that, will you? If she uses the unpolished side of that, it'll do fine. The decoration of the parlour can wait another day now that the lass hasn't got to hide herself while I do the sideboard. Dear, dear, poor lass. And, you know, she's got a bonny face, hasn't she?'

'It isn't bonny, John,' said Willie, 'it's beautiful.'

'Well, just as you say; but I can add I think it's a Goddamn shame she's like she is 'cos somebody's to blame. It's a wonder she hasn't been searched for.'

'Oh, hush now,' Bella put in. 'She likely has, but who would think of looking in this neck of the woods? And, anyway, there would have been plenty of time to find her before she reached this part, I bet. But I say to you all, every one of you, don't probe and don't talk about her outside . . . I mean in a pub, anywhere like that. She's happy here, she feels safe. Aye, that's the thing, she feels safe, because whatever's happened to her she's afraid of the world outside, and them in it. And now let's get to work and no more chit-chat.' On this, she turned abruptly and went upstairs.

7

It was three weeks later and, as Joe said, the business was indeed going like a house on fire. They'd had to turn some customers away. The gates were opened at seven in the evening and closed on the last sleeper at half past nine in the morning. Each of the four men had his allotted task. Joe and Pimple continued to bring the vegetables from the market first thing in the morning and sometimes a box of fruit, but Joe kept on his part-time work at the warehouse for, as he said, there were pickings there from time to time that might be of help to Bella and the business.

With Pimple it was slightly different: the offerings he received from his tin-whistle playing in the local streets were meagre, but they were supplemented occasionally through his keen sense of spotting trouble here and there. His perspicacity in this line had earned him five pounds from the local police station in the last two weeks. He had heard muffled voices coming up through a pavement grid outside an empty building. What was more interesting to him was that the building was next to a bank. The street was practically deserted, so he stood for a moment, his ears strained; but he could not make out anything that was being said. And so he made it his business to take his whistle to a street not far away, from where he had been moved on more than once by its regular police-man, and sure enough, this happened again. He gave the constable some backchat and in the backchat was a message. This incident had happened a week or so ago.

When he had told Bella she had said, 'Oh, lad, that's no game to play, it's dangerous. I've told you before, they'll get you one of these days, and then God help you. You've done one stretch and you didn't like that, did you?'

'No, Bella,' he said. 'As I've told you, that's why I went over to the police's side; but as the rumour has it on the street, I'm the fellow who can't stand cops. It's a great help.' He had grinned at her, and Joe, who was there at the time, had said, 'I'll give you this, Pimple, you've got more guts than me.'

The other four men, the band, as Joe called them, saw to the admission of the men and the distribution of the food. They had formed a rota of duties that seemed to work well. There was no admission to drunks or wineys, those who stank of meths. Both Joe and Pimple helped the men out on such occasions because they knew more about the street types round the market than any of the four men.

It got that a queue would begin to form down the lane to the yard gates an hour before opening time, and on very wet or cold nights Bella would allow them to be let in earlier, even to have them put an extra mattress or two down the middle of the room rather than turn the shivering creatures away. There were written notices inside the doors in the lavatory, the urinal and the washplace to the effect that anyone known to have messed up these places unnecessarily would not be admitted again. Also, there was no fear of wet beds because the plastic covers had been left on the mattresses.

Naturally the unfortunate men slept in their clothes, but were they to take off their boots and their top coat they rolled them up and laid them alongside them in the bed, experience at this level of life having proved that they couldn't trust any of their fellow men. But if a man's coat was sodden wet

145

he would ask if it could be laid over the large iron fire-guard in the kitchen, and whoever was on duty saw to it that it was still there when its owner woke up.

The ample slice of new bread cut from a fresh loaf and supplied with a bowl of broth at night and the mug of tea in the morning, was so appreciated that, as John said, it was pitiful to see their pleasure, but nevertheless dreadful to see a man foretelling what he expected the rest of the day to be like when he broke the morning slice in two and deposited half in his pocket.

Big Bella's Pad soon made a name for itself, and when Bella was visited unexpectedly one day by an inspector all he said, with a grin as he left, was, 'Why don't you put sunshades up in the yard, Bella, and make it into a holiday home?'

Bella had never been happier. There was her lass . . . her lass sitting at that kitchen table day after day chopping away at vegetables; then later, after scouring her hands, she might fill the pie tins with their rounds of pastry ready for the meat. This delighted Willie, and time and again he would whistle as they worked together . . . together but at a distance. She never stood close to him.

One day as he whistled he glanced at her face. It looked bright. She had stopped what she was doing and seemed to be looking into space, which she was, into a space where there was music and something else . . . For a moment she seemed to experience the most wonderful feeling, and then it was gone when Willie spoke, saying, 'Do you know that? It's a piece from *La Traviata*?'

As she turned to him, the sound of the music was still in her head; she was looking straight at him and her eyes were bright as she nodded twice. But when he said, 'Do you like operas?' a puzzled look came over her expression and she shook her head.

'You likely would if you heard them. I'll tell you what,

146

some night before we open we'll get together, the four of us – no, the five of us because Pimple can make his tin whistle speak. Anyway, we'll play you some tunes. What about that, eh?'

She looked down, but the corners of her mouth were moving slightly upwards and he could see that she was pleased. A few minutes later, when Bella returned from her shopping and her ordering for the day and came into the kitchen, saying, 'It's freezing out there. You know when you're well off in here,' Willie turned a bright face to her, saying, 'Miss here recognised a piece I was whistling. It was from *La Traviata*, the opera, you know.'

'Aye?' said Bella cautiously, then added, 'Well, what about it?'

'Well, I've just said to her, one night before we open we'll get together the band and Pimple and we'll give her some tunes.' Here he paused, then looked at the straight face of the little woman and said, 'Of course, if that's all right with you, Bella.'

'Oh, it's all right with me, yes, definitely. There's nothing I like better than a bit of music.'

'Oh, we can play well together when we're given the chance. I know John's fiddle sounds a bit ropey but, as he said the other night, he'll soon be able to buy himself some new strings. The ones he has on are past tightening.'

There was a glint of laughter in Bella's eyes now but her lips looked prim as she said, 'I don't suppose you'd take on the job of playing our visitors to sleep?'

'Oh, now that's not a bad idea, missis. We could add another twopence to the bill.'

At this Bella said firmly, 'If I hear of a new idea in any shape or form coming from you lot, there'll be some sackin' to do. That I promise you.' Her attention was quickly drawn to Reenee who was bending over her table as she scraped a carrot on the grater. Bella could have sworn that she had

147

heard a gurgle from her, so she said, 'Would you like to hear that band play their pieces, lass?'

Reenee looked up, and Bella saw the tentative smile showing around her mouth, and when her head made one small movement of agreement Bella said, 'Oh, well, then, that's that.' Turning to Willie she said, 'We'll be havin' our tea around five. Tell the men to come in and do their stuff. But inform them they're not goin' to make a practice of it. If they want to practise they can do it in the wash-house.'

Willie laughed now, saying, 'They do, Bella, on the quiet, stuffin' a mattress in the bottom of the door to dull the sound. But I tell you something, you wouldn't believe the good stuff that comes out of Tony's flute and Pimple's whistle. You wouldn't believe the tunes Pimple knows; and the two together, just them two, by, it sounds good!'

That very evening Bella had to admit to herself that, aye, it did sound good. She had brought the two armchairs to the end of the table where she and Reenee could sit comfortably and listen. The door to the stone flight was pushed well back and Joe was standing there. He could see where the men had assembled near the bottom of the stairs and when they started to play Bella's head went to the side. It wasn't like the stuff they rendered in the street, this was different. It was nice. She turned and smiled at Reenee, and Reenee nodded back at her. They played first a number of the well-known tunes of the time; one or two they had used on the road, such as 'All Alone on the Telephone', but now it was with a difference. It was all softer, clearer. Bella tried to find the word 'harmonious', but couldn't. She only knew that it was all very nice indeed and that she was enjoying it.

They had been playing for about fifteen minutes when they stopped, and then there came the combined sound of the flute and the tin whistle, and when the silvery notes of 'The Barcarolle' floated up the staircase Bella thought, Eeh, my! Fancy the two of them being able to play like that together.

Reenee had been sitting back in her chair, but now she brought herself upright and there came into her head the most odd feeling. She was floating. And as she floated to the music she heard a voice singing. She knew she was thinking like this because the voice . . . oh, she knew the voice and she knew the words it was singing: 'Night of stars and night of love falls gently o'er the waters.' Her body stretched upwards, her mind was clear. There was no obstruction there, nothing, no fear, nothing but a great emptiness and in it the voice singing:

> 'Falls gently o'er the waters.
> Heaven around, below, above,
> No more will reach the shore.'

And then it was rising. The voice was soaring: 'Night of stars and night of love,' on and on . . . and then she was standing up: her arms outstretched, her eyes wide, she was trying to walk past Bella, when Bella, pulling herself out of the chair, said, 'What is it, lass? What's the matter? Sit down.' And looking towards Joe, she said, 'It's the music, tell them to stop.'

Immediately on Bella's command Reenee's arm shot out towards Joe, and she flapped her hand at him, which meant he hadn't to tell them to stop, so he turned his puzzled gaze back to Bella, and she said, 'All right, let them go on. But sit down, lass, sit down.'

She found she had to force Reenee's stiff body back into the chair, and it wasn't until the music stopped that the stiffness went and her whole body became limp. Now Bella did say, and firmly, to Joe, 'Tell them that's enough.'

Again Bella was surprised to see Reenee's hand go out to stop Joe. Then she was sitting up and, turning towards the mantelpiece and pointing. Bella said, 'Pencil?' but without waiting for an answer she went past Joe and took the pencil and loose-leafed pad and, handing them to Reenee, she

149

watched her slowly tear out a page and just as slowly, even laboriously, write the word 'beautiful' on it. With an effort she handed it to Joe who, looking at it, said, 'You want me to give it to the lads?'

Again there was the slight inclination of the head and he, after turning and looking at Bella and showing her the piece of paper, went down the stone steps, to be greeted with, 'Did they enjoy it?' from Tony and Pimple.

'Yes, she said to say it was beautiful; but something happened to her when you played that last piece. I swear to God she was singing. Her mouth was opening and shutting and her tongue was moving, you know, as you do when you sing. Not so much when you talk but when you sing. And I'm sure,' he looked at Pimple, 'I'm sure, Pimple, she was back wherever she came from for those few minutes and there was music there. I tell you, lads, it made me feel awful to see her.'

'What's she like now?'

'Oh, I think she's back to what she was before. Whatever it was, it was like a flash in the pan, but she must have recognised where she had once been. It was eerie. She was going to come downstairs.'

'Come down?' said Willie.

'Yes; she had her arms outstretched as if she were walking to someone and singing. It's shaken Bella. Anyway, I know nowt about music, but I can say you all played lovely. Thanks, lads.'

It was two days before Christmas Eve. The kitchen was warm, as usual, and today it had a special aroma. This was from a large basin of mixed sweet mincemeat, all ready to fill pies, for which Willie's slab of pastry had already been turned and rolled and turned and rolled.

Dressed for outdoors in a brown felt hat and a grey coat, and with a large woollen muffler round her neck, the ends of which were tucked under the lapels of her coat, Bella came in, and after taking a basket from the bottom of the cupboard she turned and looked towards the vegetable board, saying, 'Where's the miss, Willie?'

'Haven't seen her this morning, Bella.'

'You haven't seen her? When I went upstairs to get changed she was just finishing washing our breakfast things. Then she usually goes upstairs and tidies her room before coming down and starting on the veg. Well, you know she does.'

'She didn't this morning, Bella.'

Bella stared at Willie for a minute. Then dropping the basket on to a chair, she hurried out and up the stairs. She did not tap on Reenee's door but went in.

The room was empty; but she noticed the wardrobe door was half open, and when she looked inside she exclaimed, 'Oh, my God! No! No!' Her coat had gone; but she still nearly always wore that downstairs, except sometimes she would take it off in the evening when she was sitting sewing something; but the hat, that weird hat had gone, too. 'Not again, Reenee,' she said aloud; 'not again. Oh, lass, don't, please! Not at this time of the year.'

She almost ran back down the stairs and called to Willie, 'She's gone!'

Willie stopped his cutting, his hands flat on the board. 'What d'you mean she's gone? You mean the miss has gone?'

'Who the hell am I talkin' about, Willie? Yes! She's gone.'

'Well,' he swallowed deeply, 'she went off before, but she came back, didn't she?'

'Yes, she might have; but I'm gonna tell you something; she's never been the same since she heard Tony and Pimple playin' that piece. It did something to her. It must have penetrated to something from her past. At times she'd sit, her eyes crinkled at the corners as if she was thinking, thinking hard. I tell you, she's never been the same since.'

'We meant it for the best. I'm sorry.'

'Oh, lad, of course you did, and it was lovely, really lovely.

151

And she loved it and all. Look what she wrote on that piece of paper . . . "beautiful". But it took her back somewhere, I know that. Twice she's come down without her coat on and then, as if remembering, she's gone back for it.'

Bella sat down on a chair. 'I'll go mad if anything happens to her, lad. I really will.'

'Oh, nothing'll happen to her. You know, we've talked about it when we're down there together, the lads and I, and she's got a very sensible side. We all agreed on that, and she takes everything in. It's only part of her that's got funny and, as Pimple said, that part of her is dominated by fear. Look how she won't move out among people. She's never been out of the doors, he says, for months on end. And I think we all agree, she'll never come fully to herself until she faces up to that fear.'

'And that's what she can't do,' said Bella, 'else she wouldn't be here if she could face up to it, would she? And I can tell you, and I shouldn't say this, but I dread the day she does face up to it, 'cos then I'll lose her. She wouldn't stay in this life two minutes if she was all right, now, would she?'

After a moment of consideration Willie said, 'No, you're right, missis. The likes of us, the lads an' that, well, we're different. Most of us have had to rough it all our lives, but she must have been brought up different. She's known a different way of living.'

'Oh, be quiet, lad. What am I goin' to do?'

'I would just sit still or, better still, go out and do your orderin' and your shoppin'.'

'I can't do that, I just can't. If only . . . if only Pimple or Joe were here, they'd know what to do.'

'No, they wouldn't, missis; no more than you. It's my opinion that she's gone out. She knew where she was heading for and why she was goin'. There's part of her mind that is as sane as your own. Perhaps it's only a small part, but it's there. Anyway, she's likely gone shopping.'

'Shopping! What would she go shopping for?'

'Aye, I agree. But then she wouldn't have any money, would she? Joe says she won't take money.'

'Oh, she's got money. She's got a bit of money of her own.'

'She has?'

'Yes, she has.'

'Well, then, she's likely gone shopping.'

'Look at the weather! It's sleeting, and it'll freeze her out there.'

'Well, she has that big coat on, missis, and it looks like a blanket because it's fleecy lined.' Then, more to himself, he muttered, 'It's a wonder that she hasn't been spotted before now in that rig-out.'

At that very moment Irene was being spotted in the rig-out by someone who had seen her before. She had entered the pawn shop, and there stood the younger of the two pawnbrokers. He was attending a customer, saying 'Half a dollar, I'm sorry; no more, just half a dollar,' and the customer said, 'Well, better than nothing.'

Irene stood aside and watched the man behind the counter write out a ticket, then hand over half a crown to the waiting woman, who had a woollen scarf round her head and who was definitely wearing two coats of different colours, for the upper one dropped just as far as her knees.

Mr Joseph Gomparts's smile was wide as he greeted Irene. 'How pleased I am to see you, madam. Have you come to retrieve your jewellery?'

She shook her head, and at this he said, 'No?' and again she shook her head. Then she pointed towards the shop window, and he said, 'Something in there?' She nodded; then, putting her hands together, she imitated the handling of a flute or whistle and he said, 'Oh, a musical instrument?' Again she inclined her head.

'Oh, yes,' his head was bobbing now, 'I remember there

153

was a flute there. Yes, there was and . . .' He thought a moment, then looked along the shelves and across the shop to where there were more shelves, and he said, quite suddenly, 'He never came back for it. Can you wait? My father's in bed with a cold but he'll know whether or not he has sold that.'

It seemed no time before he was back again, almost hopping to his place behind the counter and saying, 'It wasn't sold. It's in the store-cupboard with the rest. We get a lot of musical instruments, you know. I must look it up in the book. Just a moment.' He turned to where a thick-backed ledger lay towards the end of the counter, and thumbing through it, with his finger tracing each entry, stopped suddenly and said, 'Ah, eighteen months ago, seven and sixpence. Just a moment.' Again he was gone from her; and it was slightly longer before he reappeared. In his hand was a flute. He handed it to her.

It looked as if it were made from ivory. After stroking it she looked at the tag hanging from it which said, ten shillings; and again her eyes met his, and he, putting his head on one side, laughed and said, 'It is our little bit of profit, but in this case, madam,' his voice dropped, 'we will say seven and six. Will that suit you?'

His last words were almost whispered, but she nodded. Then, opening her mouth and making an effort, she said, 'Thank you.'

'You are very welcome, madam. Very welcome. Any time . . . any time. I will wrap it up for you. Is it going to be a present for someone?'

She nodded.

'Well,' he said, 'seeing as it's Christmas, I have a piece of Christmas paper here which,' he added, with a grin, 'we don't usually go in for. I will make it into a little parcel.'

This he did, and sealed it with a bit of wax before handing it to her, saying, 'I am sure the recipient will be delighted with it.'

She paused; then slowly lifting her hand, she extended it to him and he, as slowly taking it, pressed it gently. No word was spoken but they looked at each other; then she turned and left the shop, and as he looked after her he experienced a feeling that was new to him, but he had no words in his fertile mind to express it.

The sleet had turned to snow. It was falling in large flakes and clung to vehicles and passers-by, leaving them white-coated. Only the roads looked dark and muddy.

She had been walking for fifteen minutes before she came to the first real shopping centre. She knew she had been this way before and, instinctively, she also knew what she was looking for. Eventually she stopped outside a window, which showed winter woollies of all kinds, from pom-pom hats to large fringed scarves, woollen jumpers and even a complete knitted suit on a model. She did not linger to examine the different pieces displayed but went straight into the shop. However, once inside, she stood for a moment while her snow-covered head and shoulders dripped moisture down her coat. Then, blinking rapidly in the bright light, she approached a curved counter, at one end of which was a long rack with a notice which read, 'Half price. Making way for new stock'.

Very few customers were in the shop, and none at this counter; and the girl behind it stood looking at the figure before her. She did not see the woman's long coat and hat as odd, because they were both bespattered with snow that was still to melt, but she greeted her with a smile and said, 'Yes, madam, can I help you?'

When the customer indicated by putting her hand around her neck that she wanted a scarf, the assistant thought, Poor soul, she's deaf, but immediately she turned to a rack and brought down two scarves.

Irene could see that they were long and made of thick wool, and that they were priced at fifteen shillings each. Her mind was endeavouring to work fast: she must have four scarves; and then she must have enough money left for Bella's present, and something for Joe. She shook her head and indicated by measuring the scarf that half the length would do.

The snow from the woman's headgear had melted fast, as had that from her shoulders, and the assistant could see now that the coat she was wearing, although it appeared bulky and might be warm, also looked rather dirty.

Irene's eyes had strayed to a rack on which she saw a number of scarves hanging and the assistant, noticing this, said, 'Yes, madam. They have been reduced by more than half but some have fringes only on one end.' Then she added with a smile, 'Manufacturers' mistakes, you know.'

Irene nodded and, going to the rack, she lifted down one scarf which was about two and a half feet long and six to nine inches wide and, yes, it had fringing on one end only. There was a tag on this particular scarf, which she looked at. Noticing this, the assistant came round the counter and said, 'It is less than half price, being, as I said, a kind of mistake. They are very good value at five shillings.'

Irene laid the scarf on the counter next to the expensive one. It was only two-thirds as long and not so wide, but it was of the same quality and she nodded quickly and pointed to it, then to the other three that were on the rack.

'You'll take them all, madam, the other three too?' the assistant said. 'They're really a bargain. I'll wrap them for you.'

Irene's hand was touching what looked like a silk blouse and the girl said, 'Oh, miss, that wouldn't fit you. It's a pity, because it's a lovely material, but it comes out time and again at sale time. You see, it was made up in the sewing room here, but the customer never turned up again. There are people like that, you know, madam,' and straight away the thought flashed into her mind that she was treating this person as she

156

would a lady. Yet there was something about her; she didn't know what. Anyway, if she could make another sale, that was all to the good, because it had been a very dull morning – people weren't out shopping on a morning like this. She unhooked the blouse from the rack and laid it on the counter. It was an odd shape for a blouse, and this she pointed out, remarking that the person who had ordered it in the first place must have been very broad and with a very short waist. But then she lifted it up and ran her fingers through one of the sleeves, saying, 'It's real silk, it's beautiful, isn't it?'

Irene stared down at the odd-shaped multi-coloured blouse, and already she could see Bella in it. Something told her it would need altering here and there, but it was indeed a beautiful material. She looked at the tag. It was marked ten shillings and sixpence and as she stared at it the assistant said, 'Believe it or not, madam, it was priced at seven pounds before it was put on the rack, and it has been reduced three or four times since. It's a gift to anybody who's good with their needle.'

At this Irene nodded affirmatively, then pressed it towards the scarves before turning again to the rack. There, fingering a woollen garment, she looked at the assistant for guidance. The girl said, 'That is really a waistcoat, madam. As you see, it's sleeveless and it's large; but it isn't wool, it's what you would call a composition. It would be very nice for a gentle-man. You see it has two short leather belts on each side, which would clip in the middle.' She demonstrated how this could be done. 'These were very fashionable with men at one time, though generally in suede or leather.' And now she smiled as she said, 'It isn't everyone who can afford suede or leather, but this would make a nice Christmas present for a . . .' she hesitated '. . . for a gentleman. That is, if he had a large frame. Do you know someone it might fit?'

At this Irene nodded vigorously: she was thinking of Joe.

The assistant said, 'Well, now, let's reckon this all up . . . One pound eighteen shillings,' she said finally. 'Is that what you make it, madam?'

Irene did not nod but, putting her hand inside her coat, she withdrew from the pocket two pound notes.

As the assistant was pushing the change and receipt across the counter towards Irene, she bent forward and exclaimed, 'You haven't a bag with you, madam? Oh, well, I can supply you with one, and I'll do so with pleasure.' She was somewhat surprised when the customer put out her hand and touched her gently on the sleeve, then pointed to some fancy wrappings on the counter, at the same time emitting one word, 'Please.'

The word had a slightly husky sound, but the assistant, after staring at this strange lady, who had an unusual, beautiful yet colourless face, said, 'You would like them wrapped?'

At this Irene bent her head and her lips gave a slight quirk of a smile, which brought an answering smile from the girl, as she said, 'It'll be a pleasure, madam.' And so she rolled up each in a fancy Christmas bag and closed it with a Father Christmas adhesive sticker. Then, from under the counter, she drew a pretty figured paper bag large enough to take all Irene's purchases, and when at last the girl handed them to her, Irene was still smiling.

When the customer's hand came out and her fingers touched her sleeve, the girl was surprised, but more so when Irene, seeming to gasp for breath, said, 'Thank – you.'

'It's been my pleasure, madam. And a happy Christmas to you.'

At this Irene's head bobbed two or three times before she turned and walked from the shop. The girl, looking at her back and seeing the long, stained coat, was wondering who on earth her customer was or had been. Yes, those were the words, had been, for although the woman could hardly get out her words, the tone of them wasn't common. And the face . . . she had never seen a face like it, and she had, over the years in the shop, looked at hundreds. But that one, that face had the most lost look she could ever imagine. What a strange incident! They won't believe it at home when I try to tell them, she said to herself.

Pimple gasped when, through the falling snow, he saw a figure he knew immediately to be Reenee's. She was more than ten minutes' walk from home. No, he wasn't seeing things, he hadn't made a mistake in identifying her; how could he with that coat? He hurried towards her, and was soon by her side, matching his steps to hers. 'You been out shopping?' he asked.

She turned her head quickly, and on a sharp gasp her lips formed his name, but they made no sound.

'You do pick your days, don't you, to take a stroll? Oh, look out!' he said, as he took her arm and, quite roughly, pushed her further on to the pavement when a lorry, its wheels in the gutter, splashed the muddied snow into the air. 'Look,' he said now, 'let me carry that bag.'

But she shook her head vigorously and held the bag quite tightly in front of her.

'All right, all right,' he laughed, 'I'm not goin' to pinch it, miss,' which, he noticed, caused her lips to move upwards into a smile, but he couldn't see her eyes for her body was leaning forward against the falling snow.

Presently, he said merrily, 'There's a saying, you know, Reenee, does your mother know you're out? I bet Bella doesn't know you're out, does she?'

Irene did not turn to look at him, but she shook her head.

'Well, look out for squalls, for there'll be hell to pay. She'll go mad, you know, wondering where you might be. She's very fond of you, but I suppose you know that. I've never known anybody so fond as she is of you. Look,' he took hold of her

159

arm, 'let's take a short-cut else we'll be covered with mud before we get in.'

He led her up some side-streets, and then there they were in The Jingles. There was Ginnie's and the outdoor beer shop and the butcher's and the cobbler's, and then, as Pimple put it, they were at their own front door.

He rapped smartly on it, and when it was opened by Willie, he said, 'You take your time, don't you? Footmen are supposed to be already behind the door waiting for a knock. I'll talk to you later, sir.'

'You idiot,' said Willie, under his breath; 'she's nearly up the pole. Oh, miss,' and he went to help her off with her coat. She pushed him away, yet her lips were curved upwards.

In the kitchen Bella stood quite dumbfounded, so much so she couldn't speak. Not even when Irene lifted up the pretty coloured bag and brought out the word, 'Shopp-ing,' did she utter a word; but she sat down slowly on a chair and, leaning her elbow on a table, she laid her face on the palm of her hand. She did not look at the pretty bag or at Reenee, but she turned and gazed at the two men now standing looking at her, and she said, 'It'll happen one of these days. It will. I'll have heart failure and you'll find me on the floor. Nobody seems to care what happens to me, what they do or what they don't do.'

'Oh, Bella,' said Willie now. 'And all our dear friend here has done,' he put his hand out towards Reenee, 'has been to go out shopping. Bet your life that bag's full of goodies.' And now he turned to Reenee and said, 'I hope you bought something for me.'

She actually smiled at him before turning away, walking out of the kitchen and up the stairs.

Bella asked them both, 'What d'you make of her? What can you make of her?'

And it was Pimple who answered, 'Only that she's full of love. She wants to give and there's a barrier stopping her in some way. But she overcomes it enough to go out on a morning like this to buy us Christmas boxes of some kind. That must be what was in the bag. It was just by chance I spotted her: she was walking along as if she was used to bein' out every day in Brandley Street.'

'That's away down near Holborn.'

'Yes; and that's where she's been, I imagine. And I bet you a shilling we won't know till Christmas Day what's in that bag. If I could dare to give you a little more of my wisdom, Bella, I would say to you, act as if nothing had happened. Don't go for her in any way, please.'

Bella looked at the face peering at her. Except for the cheek-bones and the sockets round the eyes it had the scars of smallpox on it. But behind that marred face she now knew lay a keen brain, a wise brain, and below, the kindest heart of any man she had ever known, and she wasn't forgetting Joe as she said it to herself . . .

Christmas Eve came. The snow was lying. All but four of their patrons had told her that they had been given a ticket to this or that place for dinner, tea and entertainment on Christmas Day: some in church halls, others were going to a room taken by a number of thoughtful people to provide both the work-less and the down-and-outs with at least two hot meals that day and the next.

When Bella learnt of the plight of the four, she told Joe to tell them that they were welcome to stay for their Christmas dinner downstairs. The four men from the wash-house had already been invited upstairs to have dinner in the parlour. The kitchen table had been carried in there and would seat eight, although four might have to sit on a bench. Moreover, the parlour had been decorated with pieces of holly, and paper chains stretching along the mantelshelf.

Pimple did not go out at all on Christmas Eve but helped Willie with the cooking and the preparations for the following day: besides a large Christmas pudding there was a still larger Christmas cake, to be decorated with pink icing and holly leaves.

It was while Bella was out doing the last remnants of her shopping that Reenee went upstairs; then returned and, placing a pound note on the baking table, she looked from Pimple to Willie, then back to Pimple again and, putting up three fingers, slowly mouthed the word 'wine'.

'Wine?' said Willie. 'You want to buy some wine?'

She nodded, but kept her gaze still on Pimple, and extending two fingers, she pointed to the parlour. Then, with only her index finger held up, she pointed towards the stairs and the room below.

It was Pimple who, after a moment, said, 'You want three bottles of wine, two for upstairs, us, and one for those fellas who are staying for their Christmas dinner?'

She nodded two or three times, and the corners of her mouth moved upwards. He smiled widely back at her and said, 'Have you anything in mind, madam, as to what kind of wine you would like?'

She shook her head, then looked at Willie, and he said slowly, 'A dry one for . . .' he pointed towards the stairs '. . . and us, one bottle of red wine, and for the ladies one bottle of Muscat.'

'How d'you know about wines, Willie?' said Pimple.

'Because, sonny boy,' said Willie playfully, 'at one time I was a waiter too, and in a good-style restaurant. It didn't last long, just a year, but nevertheless I learnt a lot. But you won't get any of the wines along the street at the outdoor beer shop.'

'No, I know that,' said Pimple; 'but not five minutes away is a very good wine shop. I sniff it every time I pass it.'

They now looked at Reenee who was tapping the pound note as she tried to get out the word 'enough?' and they both said together, 'Oh, aye, enough. Plenty . . . plenty. And it's very kind of you,' said Willie; 'very kind of you indeed, miss.'

162

Pimple said nothing, but he took up the pound note, folded it and put it inside his breast pocket; then, looking at Reenee, he said softly, 'I'll see that everything goes just as you plan it. Like you planned downstairs.'

He now turned to Willie. 'You know that, don't you? It was she who planned all that outfit that you and the other three are running now. Yes, it was she who planned it on a piece of paper.'

Reenee had turned from them to go to the vegetable board. Here, she sat down and started to work at her daily chores. But there was a light on her face that neither of the men had seen there before.

Christmas Day: they had all been up since very early, and breakfast was over. Now, while Tony and Andy were seeing to the clearing up of the big room and the toilets, helped now by the four men that were staying on, Willie was at his baking table being helped by Pimple, and on one corner of it Reenee, still wearing the big coat, the sleeves turned well back, was at her board; but today she was not chopping the vegetables, she was just preparing them for boiling and braising to accompany the turkey that Bella had brought in yesterday with her shopping.

It was around lunch-time that she told the band, as she called the four men, and Pimple and Joe to get themselves cleaned up and that she would see them in the parlour in half an hour's time.

At this order, Reenee rose from her board and went upstairs. Then Bella herself went into the parlour, telling herself she was as clean and tidy as ever she would be, and there she sat looking quietly at the fire. She had never in her life known a Christmas like this, never. She was happy in a way she had never imagined possible. It was, she said smilingly to herself, like being in love for the first time. She had never been in love, never, not with a man. Yet she was

163

now surrounded by men who all seemed to give off, and to her, a certain amount of love. You could call it respect, but then, above them all she had the gift of what she thought of now as a daughter, because that was what Reenee had become to her, a beloved daughter. She couldn't imagine life without her, and she didn't mind in the least if the girl never put her nose outside the door again in her lifetime because she felt that, one day, if she was seen out and about, someone would come and take her away. Someone was bound to recognise her: once seen that face could not be forgotten.

The men came in one by one: first Joe and Pimple; then Andy and Tony and John and Willie. Just as they were seated the door opened and there appeared before them a lady, because not one of those men doubted but that they were looking at a lady, a real lady. Reenee was wearing her red velvet dress. To the waist it was unmarked, and not one of those men looked further to where the bottom of the skirt was badly stained. But what they noticed most was her beautiful hair. It was no longer screwed into a tight bun lying on her neck, but was laid in two loose coils on the back of her head up to the crown.

She seemed unaffected by the silence and their staring until Willie, springing forward, placed a seat for her and she sat down. That seemed to loosen their tongues and they said, one after the other, 'Happy Christmas, miss. Happy Christmas.'

She nodded to each of them; and then she looked at Bella, who now said, 'I suppose I'd better start the ball rolling. Now, I haven't bought any of you handkerchiefs or socks or such-like, but there you are: there's five shillings each for you. You may do what you like with it except get drunk, because if you do you won't be admitted into this pad.'

At this there was general laughter, while each man, as he took the two half-crowns from her hand, offered her his thanks most sincerely.

Then it was Andy who said, 'Now it's our turn. Our

presents might be very small, ma'am, but they come with our combined feelings for you,' and he handed her two boxes.

When she opened the first one she saw underneath the top glazed cover a tablet of soap, a bottle of scent, a jar of face cream, and a tin of talcum, and next to it, of all things, a little bottle of red nail varnish. At the sight of this she let out a laugh and said, 'Well, thank you, boys, very, very much and for not forgettin' me nails.'

There was general laughter now, and it was Tony who said, 'We couldn't find one without nail varnish, Bella, but there's always a first time for everything.'

'You've said it, lad; but it'll be on me toe nails I'll use it.'

Then she opened the second box and out of it she picked up a soft woollen shoulder shawl which, they could see, pleased her greatly; but what she said was, 'Why had you to go and spend your money on a thing like this for me? You need every penny I give you.'

'Simply,' put in John now, 'we wouldn't have any money to buy anything, my dear Bella, if it wasn't for you and your kindness.'

'Nonsense! But, oh, lads, thank you very much indeed.' And she looked now from Joe to Pimple and said, 'I suppose you were in on this, an' all?'

'Oh, yes,' said Pimple; 'they made us do it. We didn't want to, but they made us do it.' There was more laughter now.

Then Willie handed two boxes to Reenee, and she put her hand on her breast as if to say, 'For me?' She put the bag she was carrying on to the floor and opened the first box. It was very similar to the one Bella had received, and she smiled at them, then tapped the nail varnish while her lips moved upwards and her mouth opened wide as she brought out one word that sent them all into peals of laughter, for the word was 'vegetables'.

And Willie said, 'Yes, I'll demand that you paint your nails before you do any more vegetables, miss.'

165

Now she opened the second box. In it was a bottle of perfume and half a dozen white lawn handkerchiefs, arranged uniformly round the scent, to show the initial R. She stared down at the box, and her head drooped further. Then she gulped and brought out the words 'Thank you', before bending down quickly to the floor and picking up the bag that she had brought in with her. Now she handed the first parcel to Bella, the second small parcel to Pimple, and the third parcel to Joe. Then, one after the other, she gave each of the other four men similar size parcels. Nobody had attempted to open his own, and she looked at them, then spread out her hands.

It was Tony who said, 'Go on, Bella. You open yours first.'

Bella took out a garment and held it up, and immediately saw the odd shape of it. It was meant, she supposed, to be a blouse, and it was made of silk; it was so wide that she could see her own quite firm and large-breasted body being lost in it. She looked towards Reenee who now, with another great effort, uttered the words, 'Me. Alter.'

'Oh, yes; yes,' said Bella, 'that'll be the easiest thing in the world. But it's beautiful. Lovely material. What on earth made you buy that? It must have cost the earth, woman.'

Reenee shook her head.

'Well, thank you, love. It was so thoughtful of you. I can't get over it, I've never had a silk blouse in my life.' She turned to Joe and said, 'Well, come on, let's see what more money she spent on you.'

Joe undid the Christmas wrapping and held up what looked like a woollen waistcoat, and he exclaimed in true astonishment, 'My, lass! Where on earth did you get this? It's fine.' And immediately he pulled off his coat and put the garment on; and although he had to pull in his stomach quite a bit to link the two leather straps together he managed it, then said, 'It's lovely. And it's warm, and it reaches to the bottom of my back, which is where I want it. Oh, miss, thank

166

you. Thank you.' Now they all looked at Pimple. Pimple's present looked thin and long compared with Bella's and Joe's, and after he had unwrapped it he slowly placed it across the palm of his hand and stared at it. They all stared at it; and it was Tony who gasped as he said, 'Good Lord! It's a flute. And what a flute! Oh, look at it!'

Pimple looked at it; then he threw the Christmas paper to one side and brought the instrument to his lips. But that's all he did with it: he did not blow on it, but he stroked it. Then it was Tony speaking again: 'That's real ivory, man,' he said. 'Do you know that's real ivory? God in heaven! Where,' he turned now to Reenee, 'did you get that, miss? You . . . you could never have bought it. That must have cost a packet, and I know what flutes cost. I've never seen a better one than that.'

'Don't be so mouthy.' It was Bella speaking to Tony now. 'She wouldn't go out and steal it.'

'Oh, Bella, I wasn't meaning anything like that, but that kind of flute is rare. It's ivory!'

Reenee looked at Bella; then she moved the index finger and thumb of her right hand around two fingers of her left as if turning a ring, and Bella said, 'Oh. Oh yes, I understand lass. Gomparts.' Reenee nodded, and Bella, turning to Tony, said, 'The pawn shop. She got it in the pawn shop where she pawned her rings.'

Pimple hadn't spoken, but now he almost darted across the room, and startled Reenee as he dropped on his knees before her. Taking her hand, he kissed the back of it, saying, 'I'll keep it till the day I die, Reenee.'

And now she surprised them all: she actually lifted her other hand and stroked his disfigured face, saying with a gasp as she did so, 'Your name?'

'My name?' His voice was a whisper now. 'You want to know my name, Reenee?'

She inclined her head deeply towards him. He glanced

around the company, then looking back at her, he said, 'Carl.'

At this she repeated, 'Carl', and again, 'Carl.' Then, pointing to his face, she said, quite plainly, 'No more. Never. No more.'

'You mean you will never call me by my face now, but by my name?' And at this she nodded again.

He uttered no word, but his head fell on to his chest and he remained still for quite a while. No one spoke until Andy, taking in the situation, said loudly, 'If somebody would like to know what I've got I'll open my parcel now.'

At this there was a murmur of forced laughter round the room, and when he unwrapped his parcel he exclaimed, 'A muffler! A real woollen muffler. Oh, thank you, miss. Thank you.'

Then one after the other, Tony, John and Willie opened theirs and all exclaimed in the same way, 'Mufflers! Oh, you couldn't've got us anything better, miss.'

As this was going on Carl got to his feet, and he was now standing near the window as if intent on looking out, and nobody passed any remark on it.

Then Bella said, 'Well, now, would anyone like to know what I've bought her? John, hand me that box off the side-board, will you? There, lass; and that's with my love.'

Slowly unwrapping the paper, Reenee lifted the lid and stared down for a full minute at the soft blue wool garment before picking it up and holding it before her. She held it at face level, but the bottom of it folded on to her knees, and she saw she was holding what appeared to be a coat. 'It's a house-coat. It can be worn at any time of the day, and although it's very pretty it'll be warm. Come, stand up and let me put it on you.'

At this, Reenee's body stiffened just a little, and when Bella's voice came to her, saying softly, 'It's all right, lass, you need only wear it when you want to, just when you want to, but I'd like to see if it fits you.'

It was John who took the box away from Reenee's lap, and it was Willie who put out his hand and helped her to her feet. Then she stood, and Bella stood behind her, saying, 'Just slip your arms into it.'

Slowly Reenee obeyed her, and there she was standing in this very pretty housecoat. It had a row of self-covered buttons down the front, and it hung down to just below her hips, and at each side there were pockets.

Bella now put out her hands and turned down the collar, saying as she did so, 'They called it azure, the colour. I would have said it was a soft blue but, no, that's what they said, it was azure. Now look at that, boys!'

Bella turned to the men now, and they all exclaimed, each in his own particular way and not out of politeness. 'It's lovely, miss. It suits you down to the ground; well, I mean, half-way.'

'You would think it had been made for you.'

On and on the compliments went until Carl, who had turned from the window some minutes earlier, said quietly, 'Nothing could make you more beautiful than you already are, but it suits you and I hope, for all of us, we'll see you in it often.'

Reenee looked across the room at Carl and she smiled at him – actually smiled, for the length of her lips had moved up much further than ever before.

Now Bella broke the tension again with her practical common sense. 'The next item on the programme, ladies and gentlemen, is eating, and we ladies will sit here and be waited upon, so you can all get busy and scramble around.'

They all trooped out to the kitchen, laughing, to bring in the food, and there was only Bella and Reenee in the room. Reenee had sat down in the chair again, still in the housecoat, and Bella drew up a wooden chair towards her. Taking Reenee's hand, she said, 'You like it?'

There was a crackle in Reenee's throat as she turned now

169

to Bella and whispered her name, 'Bell-a. Oh, Bell-a.' And as she leant forward and placed her head on the older woman's shoulder Bella put an arm about her and hugged her, knowing with this gesture that her day of happiness was complete. To herself, she said, Don't let anybody dare tell me that this girl has lost her mind.

8

It had been a long, hard winter, but this was a morning in March and the sun was shining and spring was in the air and the postman had left one letter. It was addressed to Mr Andrew Anderson. He was the only one who ever received a letter, and as Bella was about to take it downstairs she fingered it and looked at Reenee. 'This will be from his wife. He's been waiting for it for days, if not a couple of weeks or more. Yet I know he's quite regular in sending her every penny he can spare. And it's funny she didn't take the chance to bring the bairns and come up to see him. I told him I'd pay for their fares; and, as you said, lass, you'd put a mattress in the boxroom and they could have your room.'

Bella often referred to Reenee's kindnesses as 'she said', or 'you said', because they spoke for themselves.

As she opened the front door she remarked, as if to herself, 'I wonder what she has to say to him this time?'

She wasn't to know the answer until later that evening.

It was when Joe and Carl came upstairs to bid her the usual goodnight that Joe said, 'Andy got a letter this morning. Well, you know that, you brought it down the yard. By! There was nearly sparks flyin' when he told us about it; I've

171

never seen him turn on anybody like he did on Tony.'

'Turn on Tony? What for?'

'Well, you see . . .' He looked at Carl, and Carl said, 'It was the contents of the letter, Bella. He must have said in one of his that he was going to make a trip home somehow and see how they were, and the answer told him that he needn't bother, that she was goin' back to Wales to live with her parents. All her people are in Cardiff, you see. Anyway, from what I gather she told him that her little job in the North-East had been cut down to three hours and that, anyway, she couldn't go on; she had no life there.

'Apparently, her sister in Cardiff has a second-hand clothes shop. She's single and she's run it for years, and now she wants some help. As Andy said, if anybody's goin' to get a job it should be somebody in the family, and she's offered it to his wife; so she's gone there and taken the bairns with her.

'When John pointed out that things were as bad in Wales as any other place in the country, Andy said nothing. But when Tony put in quietly, "I bet it's because she has a man on the side," my, you should've seen the way Andy jumped up and turned on him! I thought he was goin' to hit him, and he yelled, "She's not like that! She's not like yours!" I can tell you, Bella, the tension rose. And when Andy got up and walked out, Joe there went after him.'

'Aye,' put in Joe now, 'he was as mad as a hatter. He was grippin' the gates as if he could break them. Anyway, he says he's goin' through to Wales to see just what the set-up is. In any case, he hasn't seen his bairns for nearly four years. But he'll be back, he said. The fare will be over a pound; we're clubbing up to see to that, but he'll have to have a penny in his pocket. That's why we've come up to see you, Bella.'

'You needn't worry about that,' said Bella quickly. 'I'll see he's got enough for the journey, and a bit over.'

An incident was to arise out of Andy's decision to visit Wales. Its effect wouldn't be shown for the next three years, and then it would change Bella's little business and all those connected with it.

The coat that had belonged to Hamish McIntyre and which Bella had given to Andy had always been too big for him, but that hadn't mattered because he wore it only when he wanted to look tidy, perhaps on a Sunday when they walked into the City or the West End. But now he was facing a journey, and he said to Willie, the only man of the little group handy with his needle, 'If I were to open the side seam of the coat, Willie, and cut a piece off the front of the jacket, would it hang just the same or would it affect the shoulders?'

Willie had said, 'I don't see why it should affect the shoulder. Yes, open the seam and I'll pin it up and see how much you could take in.'

In the afternoon of that day, Andy started on the task of unpicking the side seam of the coat. To get a better grip on the material he thrust his thumb and finger into the small breast pocket as a means of pulling the material taut while he picked out the machine stitches.

It was as his finger slipped into the fob pocket, as these pockets were often called in which gentlemen could keep a small watch, that he felt a crinkle under his fingers as if from a piece of paper beneath the lining. On closer investigation, he saw that the lining of the small pocket had at one time been cut and neatly stitched over.

Intrigued to know why the piece of paper or whatever it was had been inserted in the lining, he cut away about two inches of it. Inside was a piece of stiff paper; he also discovered that the lining of the pocket was quite separate from the lining of the coat. In fact he could feel that this was a pocket inside a pocket. But now he had the piece of stiff paper on the table in front of him, and he saw immediately that it had been folded up tightly. Slowly he straightened out the folds and, to his amazement, he saw he was looking simply at the flap of an envelope. There was nothing on it; that was, until he turned it over and was confronted by line after line of small writing, starting at the top of the flap and following in shorter and shorter lines until it reached the gummed tip.

It was a dull day and the light in the wash-house was dim, and he realised that he couldn't read what was written here unless he had a light. He went to a cupboard at the end of the room and took out a small torch.

Slowly, word by word, he picked out the following:

My Dearest Fellow, As I'm breaking the rule, and this is the only love letter you are likely to receive, take care of it. I'm in the train from Harwich. I only had a moment's notice. There's a meeting at four. Be at the flat at seven o'clock tomorrow night. I can't wait to see you, my love – five weeks is too long, too long. Lots of pretty bits of glass. Couldn't get word to you sooner. Came without a case or anything – high command – I can't wait for tomorrow night, my love. Nelson will get this to you at your business. Business? Ha! ha! Bring quite a bit of loose cash. Couldn't go to bank, not supposed to be here. Switzerland the day after tomorrow. Can't wait to see you. Too long away. Must be a better cover than fruit. Until then, beloved. Yours

Andrew had reached the end of the writing but could hardly make out the signature which was written across the gummed section. But holding it to the side he could discern the name 'Jason'.

Then he sat looking ahead through the window into the yard. That coat had belonged to Bella's boss – a big hairy Scot, she said he was – and all the time he was a . . . His mind stopped for a second on the word, and then he said it aloud, 'Poofter.' Good God!

There was someone crossing the yard now. It was John. He jumped up and knocked on the window first, then opened the door and beckoned him.

'What is it?' said John.

'Just this. Come in. Close the door for a minute. You'll have to take the torch, but just read that, will you?'

'Well, what is it? Where did you get it?'

'Just read it, and then I'll tell you where I got it.'

Slowly John began to read, but before he was half-way through he lifted his head and stared at Andy, then made a sound in his throat before going on.

After he had read it all he sat looking at Andy and said, 'He's one of those. Where did you get it?'

Andy showed him where he had found the hidden letter; then he said, 'Can't believe it, can you? Remember what Bella said her boss had been like, a big hairy Scot, and she did say she never liked him because he didn't give her a civil word in his life.'

'No, no; of course he wouldn't. He had no room for skirts, had he? My God!'

'What d'you think I should do?'

'I would show it to Bella, and just let her see what kind of a fellow he was.'

'You think so?'

'I do.'

They went together and asked if they could have a word with her, and Bella, thinking it was about Andy's journey, said, 'I told Joe to tell you everything would be all right. If you want to come back, your place is there, and the lads would be very pleased to see you again, I know that, so . . .'

'It isn't that, Bella,' said John quietly. 'Andy was undoing the seam of the coat you had given him – you remember it was too big for him? It was all right goin' about the place, as he said, but he was goin' to travel and he wanted it a bit smaller across his chest, so Willie told him how it might be done.'

And now he turned to Andy and let him finish the tale. Having done so he handed her the envelope flap and said,

175

'Will you be able to read that? The writing's small, but I've brought the torch with me.'

Like John, Bella had only read a short way when she stopped and looked from one to the other, and before going on she said, 'You got this out of his coat?'

'Yes, yes; I can show you the place.'

After she finished reading she sat back in the chair and what she said now was, 'The dirty, rotten swine of a man! He was one of those!'

'Aye,' said John now; 'he was not only one of those but one of the worst kind. There are some just ordinary fellows in the same boat, I know. I've worked with them, and, really, left to themselves they wouldn't hurt a fly. In fact, they were terrified half the time because it would be gaol for them if they were found out, you know.'

Bella shook her head and said slowly, 'To think I worked for him for sixteen years! He used me as a cover-up an' all. He must have, mustn't he?'

The two men nodded.

'I should think so, Bella, yes. And the fruit business, as it says there. But you can't do anything about it, can you?' said John. 'And this other chap was askin' for loose cash, as if he had a pile stacked somewhere.'

'Well, I wish I knew where it was,' said Bella. 'If I could get an inkling of where he stacked his stuff I'd give him away, dead as he is, and whoever this other one is, this Jason. But I tell you what I shall do. I've told you I never liked him; I also had the feeling that his solicitor never did either. Twice, these last few years, Mr Travis has called in to see how my business is goin' because, he said, the man was a mean man not to leave me a penny to run the house on, but to say I had to keep that little business goin' in order to have a shelter over me. He . . . he left a lot of money, you know. Well, I know what I'm goin' to do, I'm goin' to show this to Mr Travis because I'm sure he'll be interested to read it. He's a solicitor and a good man. He was concerned for my welfare at the time. I'm not sure of his address, but when Carl comes in I'll get him to find out.'

Bella now tried to explain to Reenee, who had been sitting listening to what was being said, that her late boss was a bad man, and in more ways than one, and that Andy had found proof of this from the piece of a letter that had been sewn inside the lining of the coat she had given him, and which had belonged to her employer.

Reenee did not seem to understand fully what it was all about, nor did she seem interested, only in the fact that Andy was going home to see his children and that he would be coming back . . .

The following day she took eight half-crowns from the large children's money box that Bella had placed on her window-sill and into which she put two half-crowns every week, because Reenee herself had refused to handle the money, shaking her head that she did not want it. But on such an occasion as this she seemed pleased to resort to the box, and she gave the money to Willie, indicating that she wanted him to give it to Andy.

Bella had made no remark on Reenee's gesture, but Willie, in his kindly way, had thanked her for Andy, saying, 'You're one in a million, miss. We all say that.'

Before Andy returned, four days later, Mr Travis came to the house. Carl had found out where the solicitor's office lay and had taken a letter there from Bella.

Mr Travis was now sitting in Bella's parlour, on which he had remarked the moment he entered: 'What a different room this is from that dark hole you were left with.'

And she had answered, 'Yes, it is, Mr Travis, but that's thanks to the lads.'

Mr Travis knew all about the lads. He also knew about someone he had heard called the Silent Lady, someone, he imagined, who had agoraphobia and whom Bella had taken into her kindly care. And now he went on, 'You said in your note, Miss Morgan, that you have something to show me that might be of interest.'

She went to the roll-top desk and from a drawer took the flap of the envelope, but before handing it to him she explained how one of her men had come across it.

Mr Travis looked at the small writing on the flap; then he felt in his inner pocket and took out an eye-glass and, using it with his right eye, he scanned the lines. He did not lift his head until he came to the signature and, like the others, he had to turn the piece of paper on end before he could make out the name written across the gummed area. Then looking at Bella, he said, 'Well, well, well!'

'That's what I said when I first read it, but I may add, Mr Travis, I said much more than that, I swore about him. He was clearly a bad man in some other ways, from what that writing suggests, not just that he was . . . well, one of those, you know, but that reference to the pieces of glass.'

'Oh, yes,' he nodded at her, 'the reference to the pieces of glass. You know, Miss Morgan, you have done me a great service this day.' Then again picking up the flap from the table, he looked at the signature and said, 'Jason. This, Miss Morgan, this nasty piece of paper, has given me a lead that a number of people will find very helpful.'

'May I ask what you mean, Mr Travis?'

'Your late employer and his fruit business acted as a screen for part of a very big smuggling concern. You know, he was under suspicion long before he died, yet nothing could actually be tacked on him, because we did not know his associates. Only twice . . . twice did I see him with his so-called friend, and once in a restaurant. That was when I realised who Jason was, and that our Mr McIntyre was moving in very elevated social circles.

'I wondered then why a man who ran a fruit stall could be

in such high company. It wasn't a restaurant in London but well outside, and it was quite by chance that I went in. Fortunately I saw them before your employer saw me, and I made my escape, so to speak. But that night I had found out something that was of great interest to those in authority.'

'The police?' asked Bella.

'Well, not exactly the ordinary police. There are all kinds of police, you know, especially among the Customs. They are called undercover men. You know, you cannot accuse people of any crime unless you have proof, and proof is very difficult to get. But a Christian name can be of great help; and the pieces of glass mentioned in this so-called love letter, Miss Morgan, were diamonds, and this was only one kind of glass that was being dealt with.' He shook his head slowly now. 'No wonder his dear friend warned him that this was the only letter of this kind he would ever be likely to get. Your employer imagined that he had a very safe place for it; and he must have valued it to hang on to it as he did.'

'Mr Travis,' Bella said quickly now, 'what about the loose cash, a lot of it? He had no loose cash in this house, and these last two days I've searched the place from top to bottom again, wonderin' if I would come across something, you know what I mean, like you read in stories. The only place he would have left any money is in that' – she pointed to the roll-top desk – 'and it hasn't any secret drawers; I've had them all out. All the rooms, too, were linoed up to the skirtin' boards, except this one which is a cord carpet. But that was stripped out when the lads painted the room: they hosed it down in the yard and dried it and, look, it's as good as new. But there can be no loose boards underneath it, else, by gum, they would've found them! And then there was the attic. They cleared everything out of that and made use of much of it in the wash-house.'

'Yes; yes, indeed. I've seen round and they've done a splendid job. They were so fortunate to find you. Yet again, you were fortunate that they had that combination of different trades.'

She laughed and said, 'My, yes. I couldn't have picked better, could I? But to get back to this loose cash. Where could he store loose cash? Have you any idea, Mr Travis?'

'When loose cash was referred to, Miss Morgan, I think it would perhaps mean that it was in a bank, somewhere he could easily get his hands on it during the time he had before their meeting because, by the sound of it, the term loose cash might have covered several hundreds of pounds. His cover-up was the stock market. My accountant used to deal with that for him; but after the night I saw him in the restaurant I surmised he must have different channels.' He now patted the paper again. 'Oh, and the name Jason . . . Well! That's the biggest mistake he made in sending that note to his friend.'

Bella looked at him enquiringly now and said, 'What will happen – I mean to the friend or the others he was associated with?'

'I wish I were able to tell you, Miss Morgan, but I can only say that this piece of paper has tied "Jason" in with an organisation that nobody suspected he had any dealings with. And another thing, your former employer might have kept decent clothes to change into in this house, but he had another source of income for his wardrobe. I'm sure of that now. I promise you, Miss Morgan, if anything dramatic should come out of this you will be the first to know; although I might have to ask you to keep it to yourself, which I know you will. And I would add, although I've said it before, that if at any time there's a way in which I could assist you, that is I or my company, we should be only too glad. How are you managing . . . for money, I mean, and to pay your staff?'

'Oh, that's all right, Mr Travis. I get by well and can put a little aside, not a lot but something. It means I can give these poor fellows work, as well as a dry bed to the needy, and more and more of them seem to be pouring into the city.'

'Yes, indeed, Miss Morgan, there are, the country's in a dreadful state – the world's in a dreadful state at this moment, and it seems to my mind at times that any move that is made only leads us further into disaster. But, anyway, we can't do much about it, you or I, can we? Yet we are both doing our bit in an unseen way.' He leant toward her, and his words were hardly above a whisper as he said, 'If we were to prevent hundreds of thousands, even millions being creamed off from this country to find their way to Switzerland, the place your employer's friend mentions in this epistle, we'll have done a great deal.'

Bella could only nod, saying, 'Yes; yes,' although she did not understand exactly what he meant.

They parted affably, Mr Travis emphasising again that she had only to call on him for help, and she promising faithfully that if ever the time came she would do so. As yet she wasn't to know that the time wasn't so very far away.

The following morning she was a bit late in getting up, and when she entered the kitchen and saw Willie and Reenee busily working she apologised, saying, 'Eeh, my! I overslept. I think I've got a bit of a cold on me. You've had your breakfasts?'

'Yes, Bella, we've had our breakfasts, and all is running well, as usual, except . . .' Willie stopped what he was doing at the table and repeated '. . . except for Andy. He came back last night, Bella.'

'He did?'

'Aye, but he's in a bit of a state. He sat there with his head down and his hands hanging between his knees. Carl had just made a pot of tea, and he handed Andy a mug, which he took but didn't say anything. Yet he drank it straight down. Then John said, "Well, lad. Come on, tell us how you got on. It's better when it's out." At that Andy straightened up in his chair, and he looked from one to the other of us before he spoke. He said he had caught them on the hop. He hadn't told

181

his wife he was comin' and he walked into a full kitchen. Of all things, they were havin' a party, a birthday party. The widower next door had a six-year-old boy, and there the two of them were, all merry and bright. So were her mum and dad, her sister – the married one – and two of her bairns, and the single one and Andy's wife and her bairns. He must have appeared like a bomb dropping on to the middle of the table. Anyway, if they were surprised by the sight of him, he said, he was surprised at the sight of that table: he had never seen such a well-laid table for years. No one would think there was a slump or anybody out of work in Wales, at least in Cardiff. It was laden with ham and tongue and tarts and cakes of all kinds.

'It was she who spoke first, he said. She jumped up from her chair and almost yelled at him, "Why didn't you tell us you were comin'?" And nobody asked him to sit down until her father stood up and told him to take a seat. Apparently Andy told them to finish their party and that he would come back later. And he went along to a pub and got himself a pint and a sandwich, and there, he said, he sat for nearly two hours. When he went back, the kitchen was clear except for her and the two bairns. They seemed to be waitin' for him, he said, for she turned straight away to the bairns and said, "This is your da."

'He must have made to go towards one of them because he told us the younger, Betty, backed away and said, "You're not me da. I don't like you." And with this, she had run from the room.'

Willie now looked from Bella to Reenee, and said, 'What could you say to that? We just sat there like dummies. And then his wife must have said the only place he could sleep was on the couch in the front room as there was nowhere else, and she must have left him. He said to the older girl, "Don't you remember me?" and she answered that she remembered him taking them up the river on a Sunday afternoon in a sculler.

His head must have drooped once more when she turned on him and in a voice, which must have been just like her mother's, she said, "I'm not goin' back there. I don't like it. I like it here and I want to stay."' Here Willie paused, then said slowly, 'He asked Carl if there was any more tea in the pot and we all jumped up at once to pour it out. It was a dreadful experience, Bella, awful.

'And in the morning his wife said she had lived like a widow for the last four years and fended for herself for most of the time; now she was home and intended to stay there.

'He must have said something to her like, "You won't stay a widow long, by the look of things," for she said that perhaps he was right, and her sister had pointed out earlier that long before she had met him, the fellow next door and she had been courting, and it was a pity she had ever left Wales.

'He said he doesn't remember anything more, only that he went into the front room and took his attaché case from under the couch, and then that he was at the station. And . . . and you know what he said then, Bella? I nearly burst out cryin' meself. He said he didn't feel like a man any more. He said all the rough times he'd had with us chaps long before we came here and met you, Bella, the cold, the hunger, the misery, standin' and beatin' that little drum out in the rain hour after hour, nothing like that had ever made him feel as small as he did on that station.'

When Willie did not continue, Bella asked quietly, 'How is he this morning?'

'Very down in the mouth. We told him to stay indoors and just clean up the wash-house.'

'I'll go round,' said Bella, 'and have a word with him.'

'Well, if I were you I'd wrap up well. You shouldn't go out today at all, that cold's heavy on you.'

'Thanks, Father, I'll do that.'

After she had left the kitchen, Willie turned his attention to

Reenee. She was sitting with her hands idle on her lap while there was still a pile of vegetables before her. He knew she was thinking about what she had just heard, and he said, 'I'm glad I'm not married; it must be awful to have kids and then they turn against you. Of course, you've got to see their side of it: they haven't seen him for some years. That wasn't his fault either; Bella's invited them down here more than once. It looks to me as if Tony was right about the wife.'

Willie now watched Reenee's mouth open, and then she brought out the single word 'Lost.'

'Yes, Reenee. As he himself said, he felt he was no longer a man. And as you say, he feels lost. It must be an awful feeling.'

There was a silence, then he sighed and said, 'Well, we'd better get on. Broth doesn't make itself, does it, Reenee?' She began to chop the vegetables. Yet it wasn't ten minutes before she suddenly laid down her knife and walked away from the table, bringing from him the reprimand, 'Where're you going?' and the immediate apology, 'Oh I'm sorry. It isn't my business.' Yet two minutes later, he thought it was, when she came back into the kitchen, the sleeves of that great coat pulled down and on her head that weird article which was supposed to be a hat. At the sight of her standing just inside the door he almost rushed at her, saying, 'Oh, please! Please, Reenee! Don't leave the house. Bella gets so upset when you leave.' She put up a hand and held it in front of his mouth, but she didn't touch it; she waved her hand in denial, then pointed, first to the door, then to the left as though towards the gates. With her head going back and her mouth opening, she said, 'Wash.' And again, 'Wash.'

He translated quickly, 'Wash-house? You're goin' to the wash-house?'

She nodded, and the corners of her lips moved upwards, and he suggested, 'To . . . to see Andy?' Again she nodded, brightly now, and he added, 'Nice. Nice,' and immediately went before her to open the front door, from where he watched her go along to the gates and through them.

The sight of the weirdly dressed figure coming towards her caused Bella almost to drop the wash-basket she was carrying out of the wash-house, and she muttered under her breath, 'Oh, my God, what now? She's not goin' out again, surely.'

Andy was standing behind her and he murmured, 'That's the miss.'

'Who else?' murmured Bella. Then on Reenee's approach she said, 'And where d'you think you're off to on this soft summer's morning that would cut your throat?'

For answer Reenee pushed past her and went into what Bella would always call the wash-house, causing Andy to step back and Bella to re-enter and close the door after her.

Reenee held out her hand to Andy, and when he took it she spoke two words, almost plainly now, 'Home . . . friends.'

Bella smiled widely and with not a little pride translated, 'She means, Andy, that you're home and among friends.'

'I know. I know,' Andy said softly. He put his other hand on the one he was holding, and there was a break in his voice when he said, 'Thank you, miss. I'll never forget what you have just said: I am home and among friends and the one I hold most dear is your very kind self.' He knew he should have said the one he held dear next to Bella was herself but, glancing at Bella, he felt that she understood because she was nodding at him and her eyes were bright.

Slowly now Reenee pulled her hand away from Andy's and, looking round what was now quite a large room, she made a sound in her throat that could not be translated, for she was trying to say, 'So big and comfortable.'

She walked over to the addition the men had built on, which was larger than the wash-house itself. Against the far wall were stacked three wooden bunks; alongside the right-hand wall was a wooden platform with a mattress on top, forming another bed; and in the intervening space were two renovated easy chairs and a table about three foot square.

185

Now taking on the role of guide, Bella said, 'They play cards in here at night and gamble for monkey-nuts; they'll have the police on them.' Then she pointed to what had been the far wall of the actual wash-house and where there now stood a large cupboard. She opened it, to disclose shelves on which were pieces of crockery. The plates might be cracked and the cups and mugs be without handles, but nevertheless they were china; and on the bottom shelf was a box with an assortment of rough cutlery in it. The companion door of the cupboard contained an array of tins and covered dishes, and did duty as a food cupboard. The boiler top was no longer to be seen, for this was covered with what Bella recognised to be part of the spare leaf to the kitchen table. The boiler fire had an enlarged grate, on the hob of which stood a bubbling kettle, and, most surprising of all, along the left side of what had been the original wash-house was a chintz-covered sofa. That the chintz had seen better days made no difference; it looked clean and comfortable, and Bella, turning to Andy, whose whole being seemed to have lightened during the last few minutes, said, 'I've meant to ask you: how did get you that in?'

'Oh, we put it in before we finished building the end' – he thumbed over his shoulder – 'and we were lucky that it never reached a tip. We saw it being taken from a house and being given to the dustmen, and we asked them if we could have it and, never letting anything go for nothing, one of them said, "It could cost you a bob," so we gave him a bob willingly.'

'Eeh!' Bella went over and examined the couch. 'It's got a carved frame. Really, it's beautifully done.' And she turned to Reenee and said, 'Haven't they made a fine place of it? And what was it, just an old wash-house? You lads are a clever lot.' She was addressing Andy again, and he answered her, without a smile now, 'Not me, Bella. I can only handle bricks; I haven't got an eye for finer things, just bricks.'

'Well, where would they've been without you and your bricks?' said Bella briskly. 'They could never have built this place without you. Anyway, come on now, you're not gonna sit mooning here all day. Take us back in, and tonight we'll crack a bottle. Yes, we will,' she emphasised, waving her hand; 'we'll crack a bottle to welcome you home.'

And this they did, and Andy, who yesterday had felt he was nothing, knew that among friends like these he couldn't help but grow into a man again.

9

Bella's cold was a bad one, and she passed it on to Reenee.

Unfortunately, Reenee's cold attacked her chest, and one morning when she didn't appear at breakfast Bella went up to her room and found her in a fever, hardly able to get her breath.

'Oh, my dear,' she said, 'you've got it right and proper, haven't you? I'm sorry, lass; I'm sorry I gave it to you, but mine was never like this. Nevertheless, I know what'll cure it, a lemon in some boiling water with a drop of whisky in it.'

Reenee was past making comment of any kind: all she could do was hold her chest tight, trying to press down the pain and the tightness of it and to prevent herself from having another bout of coughing.

'Just lie quiet now; I'll be back in a minute.'

But three doses of hot lemon with dashes of whisky did nothing to alleviate Reenee's condition. As the day wore on she became worse. This frightened Bella, and when she saw Carl in the yard, talking to one of the boys, she called down to him.

When he hurried into the kitchen she said, 'Look, you know the doctors round here. I know there's only two, but who's the better?'

'Why, Bella?'

'The lass, Reenee, she's bad, real bad. I think she's in a kind of fever.'

'Oh, there's Dr Brown and Dr Harle. Dr Harle's the assistant. He's a young man, but they say he's good. Well, I know he is: I saw him pull a fellow's shoulder back into place without him havin' to go to hospital.'

'Well, go and get him. Ask him to come as soon as he can.'

It was almost two hours later when the doctor arrived, and straight away Bella liked the look of him. He wasn't all that young, perhaps in his late thirties, and he was only of medium height, but broad, and his voice was nice, as she put it to herself, kindly like. She noticed that he seemed a little surprised at the inside of the house. Being at this end of the market area, he had likely expected it to be a muck-heap, and as they made their way upstairs, he said, 'Have you lived here long, Miss Morgan?'

'Touchin' on thirty years.'

'Really! And you've never had the doctor in?'

'No; not often, Doctor, we haven't. As I recall, you're the first since Mr McIntyre died.'

On entering the bedroom, he stopped for a moment just inside the door and looked at the waxen-faced figure on the bed. Reenee's chest was heaving; the sweat was running from her brow. Her eyes were wide open, and as she turned them towards him she pulled the rest of the bedclothes right up under her chin with a convulsive movement, making a guttural sound in her throat.

Immediately Bella went to her. 'Now it's all right, love. It's all right. This is the doctor. He's a nice man and he's come to make you better.'

The head on the pillow turned from side to side, and the doctor, having put down his bag and taken off his overcoat, gently eased Bella to the side and, bending over Reenee, said, 'It's all right, my dear, it's all right. I'm only going to take your temperature and look at your chest.'

189

A sound came again from her throat, and now her two hands were flat on his shoulders and she was pushing him away. Bella, taking the doctor's arm, whispered to him, 'She's afraid of men.'

'What?' His face was puzzled.

'Just what I said, Doctor, she must've had a shock in her time, a great fright. She's afraid of men, most of them anyway. She's got to get very used to them before she'll let them come near her.'

He looked at her closely before turning back to the bed and saying to Reenee, 'My dear, I am not going to hurt you. I am a doctor and I just want to help ease that cough of yours.' He now forcibly took one of her wrists in his hand, and when he had felt her racing pulse he laid it down and said, 'I must explain to you. You're in a high state of fever and you must be examined before I can help you.' Again the hand came out to push him, and to his amazement he saw the large eyes in the pale face close tightly and the bedclothes heave up and down, not from her chest but from her stomach.

Pulling the heavy eiderdown to the foot of the bed, Bella said, 'Oh, she's gonna have one of her turns, Doctor. Her stomach always goes like that beforehand, up and down, up and down, as if it was bein' pushed up and then down.'

'Has she epileptic fits?'

'No, I've seen people in them, Doctor. What she has isn't a fit, not ordinarily, but it's something. She's . . . she's afraid of something, and she genuinely yells out in one of these turns. You see, she can hardly speak, it takes her some time to get a word out; but in the turns . . . well, she does, I mean speak, and clearly at times, but just a single word or two.'

He turned from the bed. 'She's in a very low state. She can't go on like this, I must examine her.'

'She won't let you, Doctor. She rarely takes her clothes off, I mean even in front of me. She's got a kind of what they would call phobia: she wears a big dark coat all the time, mostly in the house, as if she's hiding behind it or something. But she's a lovely girl and she's not really mental – I mean, I think she's lost just part of her memory. Something happened to her, something awful, but otherwise part of her brain's all right because she knows everything that's goin' on, and . . . and is kindly.'

He said quietly, 'I can't struggle with her and make her undress, so I shall have to give her a little jab. It will put her out for perhaps half an hour, but in that time we'll be able to see what has to be done. Otherwise, I am telling you, Miss Morgan, she could die.'

'Oh, God, Doctor! I couldn't have that . . . I love her. I love her like a daughter.'

'How long has she been with you?'

Bella had to think. 'Oh, since late 'twenty-nine,' she said. 'Two years or more. She's happy here, I know she is. She never goes out, not unless she must, and then it's only to help somebody.'

He stared at her for a moment then went to his bag, took out a phial and a needle, then gripped Reenee's arm, and jabbed the needle into it. She was now yelling, 'No! No! I won't! I won't! Please!' She turned her face into the pillow and, lifting up her arm, she covered her eyes, muttering as she did so. 'I won't, not like that. No! no, I won't.'

Slowly the arm fell from her face, her body sank and went limp in the bed. He said, 'Does she always struggle like this?'

'Oh, yes; yes.'

'Well, let's get her things off.'

'Oh, Doctor.'

'Woman!' His voice was sharp. 'I've got to examine her chest.'

'Yes, Doctor.'

Bella now pulled down the sheet and the blanket to expose Irene's body covered in the woolly shift she remembered seeing through the wash-house window. It was clinging to her

191

skin showing her slight form, and it looked grey and dirty, but Bella knew it wasn't. This was the garment, together with her underclothes, that she washed in the basin last thing at night when they were all in bed, and which she dried before the fire and over the fireguard. It used to be that she crept downstairs in the dark at night; that was until they got the bathroom. Now, sometimes three times a week, she would bathe herself last thing at night when they were all in bed, and likely she would wash her clothes in the bath and dry them over the kitchen fire as she had before. Poor girl.

Bella couldn't tell the doctor all this, and when he said, 'Does she always wear this thing?' she could only nod at him. 'Well, help me to get it off her shoulders; it goes right up to her neck.'

When they handled the woollen garment they found it was wringing wet. He said, 'That's got to come off; she's got to have something dry on. Come along; pull it right down.'

'It's her I'm thinking about; but I suppose it's all right, she doesn't know. Thank God she doesn't know.'

'Get a couple of towels, warm ones. She must be rubbed down.'

After Bella had hurried from the room, he examined the heaving chest and found what he already suspected. It was pneumonia. If she survived this she would be lucky. He now touched her breast where a blue mark ran for about half an inch under the nipple, and he peered at it for a moment. The breast was running with sweat, and he looked about him to see if there was a towel at hand. There wasn't, so he took a handkerchief from the side pocket of his coat and wiped it dry. Again he looked at the mark.

The other breast, he saw, showed two blue marks, but further down, and his eyes narrowed. Then he looked at the girl's stomach. It was quite flat, and he passed over it until he came to her groin. There, using his handkerchief, he again wiped away the sweat, and he could see now what looked like a dark stain on the skin. It was like the imprint left after skin had been flailed with a whip or rope. He had seen sailors' backs criss-crossed with this sort of scar from old floggings, but no, surely this couldn't have been caused by a whip or a rope?

Gently he heaved her over on to her side. There were no marks on her back but there, on her buttock, the one visible to him, were blue stains, like those on her breast. They were very like the stains left from pieces of coal that punctured miners' brows, but he knew that these marks were not from a whip or a rope, they were from teeth. He lifted the other buttock carefully, and yes, there they were again, more of them. He stood up. This woman had been abused, and savagely too.

The door opened and Bella brought in a couple of warm towels, and together they gently dried Reenee's body.

When he came to her feet he lifted up one foot and examined her ankle, and there again was scarring. Why on earth hadn't somebody found this out before? Yet who would have recognised the marks and the stained skin unless they had knowledge of how they had come about? They might have termed the bluish marks love bites, but there were love bites and love bites. These marks were in another category. Poor woman.

'Have you a dry nightgown?'

'Aye, I have a couple, but they're calico and stiff; she's not used to . . .'

'No matter what she's used to, she has to be changed into dry clothes at regular intervals during the next forty-eight hours or so.'

Again Bella darted from the room, and when she returned it was to see that the doctor had covered the sweating form with the sheet and blanket.

It was about fifteen minutes later when he sat at the little table near the window writing out a prescription. When he handed it to Bella he said, 'Get that made up as quickly as possible and give her a spoonful every three hours. The directions will be on the bottle. Also, there is a salve to rub into her chest. The main thing, though, is to keep her warm and dry. To my mind, Miss Morgan, she should really be in hospital.'

'Oh, no! No, she would hate that, she couldn't bear that, Doctor.'

He stared at her. 'What do you know about her?'

'Very little,' she admitted dolefully, 'only that she's a lady and I'm sure has been very well bred.'

He put in quietly, 'Very badly treated by someone.'

'Yes, Doctor?' It was a question.

'Oh, yes. Her body is marked where it shouldn't be. I'll tell you this much, Miss Morgan, and it might sound very crude, but if she had been a prostitute I could have understood it, but not if, as you say, she is a lady. But my examination has indicated that she has been very badly treated by someone she must have known well. Do you think she was married?'

'Oh, yes, she was married.'

'How do you know that?'

'Well,' Bella pointed to two ring fingers on the left hand, 'she went to the pawn shop once. It must have cost her something to do that: she pawned a wedding ring and an engagement ring. They must have been of some value because she got thirty-five pounds on them.'

He raised his eyebrows as he said, 'Thirty-five pounds! Yes, they must have been of value. But why did she do that?'

'She . . . Well, to tell you the truth, Doctor, it was she who suggested in her deaf and dumb way that the poor people who travel the streets or sleep rough should have a bed, and it was she who suggested starting up my business. She wrote it out on a piece of paper, a kind of design, and we had four men here, members of a little street band, and they were of all trades, building trades, I mean. So, you see, although there are times when she could be taken as being mental, she's not. She worked out that these men could do this job if there was enough money for materials. But I hadn't the money that it would cost. I said this, naturally, in front of her, and to the men, and one day she slipped away. I thought I'd lost her for ever, and I nearly went mad because . . . well, I've got very fond of her, and that's what she did.'

He stared at her before he said, 'Why on earth would she still have two valuable rings on her if she was in the condition you said you found her? Why didn't she sell these before and get a lodging or food to eat?'

'That's what I've asked myself dozens of times, Doctor, but I think they must have meant something to her.'

He turned now and looked at the bed and the face lying there, and he said quietly, 'How strange. And she's been a very beautiful woman. She still is in a way. Well, Miss Morgan, I must go now. Take that to the chemist' – he pointed to the prescription on the table – 'as soon as possible, and I shall call back this evening. If she's awake I won't attempt to examine her further. At the moment, sleep is what she requires; and, as you say, she's afraid of men. And well she may be,' he said, as he took up his bag and made for the door. 'Yes; well she may be.'

For the next week Bella had her work cut out; and she didn't know how she would have managed if it hadn't been for Carl, who gave up his daily street travelling and acted as help and housemaid, running between the kitchen and the bedroom.

On the third day after the doctor had seen her, Reenee had certainly passed through a crisis, when both Bella and Carl had thought she was dying. But the next morning the fever subsided. Now, after a week, she lay limp in the bed and seemingly lifeless, and she did not protest at Bella's ministrations. Nor had she made any comment on the stiff calico nightdress that covered her. Surprisingly, too, she did not object to Carl's

195

help, for example when he put his hand behind her head and lifted it up in order that she should drink . . .

It was three weeks before she was able to get out of bed and sit by the small fire that Carl had kept going day and night. She was wearing the housecoat Bella had given her, but her lower body was shrouded in a large blanket.

She did not make any reference to the whereabouts of her underclothes: two silk undergarments, a cotton petticoat, the woollen shift and her long stockings had all been washed and ironed. Then there was her velvet dress hanging over the back of the chair. If she noticed, she did not remark, even to herself, that an attempt had been made to clean the marks and mud-stains off the bottom of the skirt by washing it, which had improved it little.

For some days now she had been aware that she was feeling different. More quiet inside; her mind wasn't groping so much. It seemed as if it were resting, like her body.

There was one thing that, in a small way, did disturb her. It was when she felt the approach of the strange man, the doctor. She had never raised her eyes to his face; she only knew that his chin was clean-shaven and that he always wore a soft white collar, not a stiff one, and that his voice was kind. Yet some part of her mind would remind her that this man had seen her body.

Today he stood in front of her and said, 'It's bitterly cold outside. This little fire gives off a good heat, doesn't it? But you will soon be able to get downstairs into the sitting room, where you'll feel more comfortable.'

As she listened to him, she thought she was very comfortable where she was and she would like to stay here always, just sitting, never moving, never being forced to take notice of anything or anyone, and never, never being forced to speak.

When he took her hand to feel her pulse she made no resistance. He remarked, 'That's good.' Then, as if he were talking to an ordinary patient, he added, 'But you must take care, you know, of that chest. Always see that you wrap up well when you go out.'

Outwardly she remained unresponsive. He had said 'when you go out'. She was never going out. She would never leave this house again, this security and Bella. Oh, Bella, Bella. And Carl . . . yes, Carl.

She did not tell herself that Carl was a man. No, he was just Carl . . . like Andy and the rest of the men she now thought of as family.

She knew there was a change in her, but she couldn't question it or tell herself why she should think of those four men as being part of Bella's family. But they were, and she could look at them without fear.

Something in her mind moved swiftly: the word 'fear' had stirred something. She recalled that she hadn't thought of that word for a long time – at least, it seemed a long time, although she could vaguely recall when the doctor had struggled with her.

The word 'struggled' now became prominent in her mind, and she shook herself. The quick movement of her body caused the doctor to say, 'You're not feeling cold, are you?'

She shook her head, and Bella indicated to the doctor that he should come with her out of the room. And this he did, but not before saying, 'Well, my dear, I'm glad to see you so much better. I won't pop in again for a week, and then just to make sure you are perfectly fit again. Goodbye.'

She went to raise her head, then stopped; her mouth opened and she made a sound in her throat, but it did not form any word.

Out on the landing, Bella said, 'She often gives that shudder, and I think it is when she is recalling something, or her mind is troubling her in some way, but it didn't seem as if she was troubled today. And she hasn't been, not for days; well, I would say, since she got over the bad bout.'

'Yes, I'm sure your diagnosis is quite right, Miss Morgan.'

197

'If you will come into the parlour, Doctor, I will settle your bill, and gladly.'

'Oh, there's no hurry for that.'

She said, on a laugh, 'Well, if you don't take it now you might never get it. I might go out and spend it.'

'Well, I wouldn't mind if you did, Miss Morgan, because you really have had a very strenuous three weeks. And, may I say, I don't know what you would have done without your butler.'

As they went down the stairs she said, 'I'll tell Carl your new name for him, he'd like that.'

Then her voice sobered. 'He's a good fellow is Carl, Doctor. God, or the devil, put a curse on him, but get behind that face and you'll find he's got a mind and that it works. He thinks a lot and is wise. I suppose it's because of his reading – he reads anything and everything he can get his hands on.'

'Well, I'm sure all you say about him is true, but what *I* say is that in his misfortune he has found a very good mistress in yourself, Miss Morgan.'

10

As the months wore on and another winter approached, the routine in the little business seemed to carry on much the same day after day. But outside in the streets in the daytime men begged for work or bread; at night on park benches, in shop doorways, under bridges there seemed to be more and more humanity lying huddled in disarray, for unemployment and starvation were driving men into London where, night after night, shivering creatures had to be turned away from the gates that led into the yard. This would be after they had taken in perhaps an extra half-dozen and let them sleep on the warm bare boards up the centre of the room, and perhaps another four in the men's wash-house next to the urinal. As this place was cold the men were provided with thin pallets and a blanket; but there was always a bowl of soup before they lay down and a breakfast of tea and new bread in the morning.

Things were coming to such a pitch in this way that the four men of the original band were now in Bella's kitchen, together with Joe and Carl. Reenee had gone to her room. What John was suggesting was that if Bella could afford to get the wood they would knock up a kind of shelter at the far end of the backyard. It would be a rough affair, but nevertheless it could be made to take eight mattresses. Joe had said there was to be a clearing out of the warehouse and there were still some mattresses there, which might be going cheap. He had already told her that there was something astir in the warehouse. The far sheds were being cleared of everything, but not the retail part: 'The legal and above board part,' Carl put in, thereby somewhat relieving the gravity of the looming situation.

'As I told you, Bella,' Joe said, 'they're scared about something. The mattresses, mats and things like that have all been brought over to our side for what they call a big sale. They're packed up to the roof there.'

Bella said, 'Whatever sale there is, Joe, mattresses will still cost money. As for the wood, well, I'll have to know how much it's goin' to cost because I can only do so much. You know that.' Recognition of the fact echoed through the group.

'Leave it until tomorrow,' she said. 'I'll think it over because I'm as concerned as you are about those fellows standing outside the gates at night. Talk about the Bible and the beggar at the gates. Dear, dear! Well, as I said, lads, I'll see you in the morning.'

The four men made their departure, only Joe and Carl staying behind, as they always did, to have a last word with Bella. And apparently Joe had something special he wanted to say.

'Sit down a minute, Bella. I want to tell you something, or ask you something. You've always said you hate the lino in your bedroom and that you'd like a nice carpet.'

'Yes, yes, I have. I've said many other things too that I'll never get, and often.'

'Well,' said Joe, 'there's one going. Dixon took me on the side and said, "There's a carpet left over there, lad," and he pointed to one of the stores. "It's a lovely thing – they say it's Chinese – but they daren't take it out to sell it because it's of such quality they would get nabbed for it. And then there's the size," he said. And then it came: "D'you think your missis would be interested in it?" and I said, "Well, I'll ask her; but how much?" And . . . well . . .'

'Go on,' said Bella; 'go on, spill it.'

'Ten pounds.'

'Ten pounds!'

'Aye, that's what he said. Well, what he said was it was worth hundreds. If it was sold in one of the big shops it would bring hundreds; but I know they want to get rid of it. Why they didn't take it to the other place I don't know, but I think they're cleaning that up too. There's certainly a scare on of some kind, aye. Well, Bella, the rumour is that your Mr Weir, you know the one who always lets you have things half price, he's in trouble, and I think he's on the run. He's not showin' his face anyway, we'll say that much. They're cleanin' up the place before there's an inspection by the police. You know, ours – I mean where I work – isn't the only warehouse he's got, he has two or three in the city, I understand, or he had.'

Bella was staring at Joe now, and she said again, 'Ten pounds! You couldn't beat him down?'

Joe drooped his head and said, 'I already did, Bella. He was askin' fifteen, and I said I knew you couldn't go to that, so he said he would take ten for it, ready money, if it was moved out the morrer night.'

'What if the police were to come here and find it?'

'Well, you would say you bought it second-hand from the store, and you didn't know what kind of carpet it was. It could be from Timbuktu or John O'Groats or anywhere else. But Dixon seems to know his stuff, and he said it's a spanker and that he would've had it himself, only it's too big for his front room. They're not askin' around about it, because some of his fellows might get a drink and open their mouths too wide.'

Bella looked at Carl, and he nodded at her and said, 'I think it's about time in your life, Bella, you gave yourself a treat. You've always said you hated the lino in that room. So go on. We'll all pig in and help.'

'You'll do nothin' of the sort. If I'm goin' to have a carpet for my room I'll buy it.'

Bella turned to Joe and said, 'All right, get it. I'll give you the money in the morning. But where will we put it until I get the room ready?'

'We can leave it down by the hall in your sitting room; in fact it'll go behind the couch and the roll-top desk. It would fit in lovely there, I'm sure. Anyway, wait till you see it.'

As Bella said goodnight to the two men she did not realise that the buying of that carpet was going to alter not only her life but all their lives, in much the same way as Reenee's plan had created the room downstairs.

The carpet arrived the next night, and as it was half unrolled in the parlour Bella gazed at it in awe. It was, in a way, plain-ish, a sort of silver-grey with flowers woven at each corner; but the strange thing about it was the pile. It seemed to be almost two inches thick, so thick that you could not insert your finger in it and touch the canvas.

Reenee was present when Joe and Carl stretched out the carpet, and she looked from them to Bella, then down at the carpet. Kneeling, she felt it; then again looking up, she gazed into Bella's face and nodded before her mouth opened and the word that came out sounded like something that ended in 'ease'. And it was Carl who said, 'Chinese, Reenee?' and she turned quickly to him and nodded.

Bella looked at the two men and said, 'She knows . . . She knows quality.' This to her was another proof that her dear girl came from a good home.

The carpet was rolled up quickly and placed behind the couch and the roll-top desk, and was quite unobtrusive there. When Joe said, 'We'll pull up the lino tomorrow night,' Bella interrupted him, saying, 'No; you leave that alone. Me and Reenee here will see to that.' What she didn't add was, 'I don't want two men messing around in my room when they might see more than is good for them. Her wooden box was under the bed, and she had no key to it, and what surplus money she had every week went into it. The main money for paying out the men and bills she kept in the roll-top desk.

The following day she and Reenee started to take up the lino.

They found it to be in four pieces. The three larger pieces came up easily. The last piece, to the side of the window, was, like the others, tucked under the skirting board, but no matter how they pulled at it they could not release it.

'I'll have to get a knife,' said Bella, 'and cut it right along there. Stay where you are; I'll be back up shortly and bring some tea with me. I'm as dry as a fish, and I'm sure you are too.'

Reenee was kneeling opposite the end of the window-sill, and, feeling rather tired with pulling and pushing at the sheets of lino, she rested her hand on the sill. In front of her hung an old brocade curtain that must have been put up years ago, and as she felt it she pulled it to one side, exposing the paint-work. She thought, Paint; yes, paint before carpet is laid. She rubbed her fingers up the stanchion of the window and as she did so some of the paint practically flaked away under her touch. As she brought her fingers down to the sill again she saw what looked like a round rusty patch. She had seen patches like this before, where a brass fitting had been screwed in to hold the swathes that held back the curtains during the day. She had a flash in her mind of a curtain hanging somewhere . . . somewhere. She groped in her mind but could not remember where she had seen a curtain pulled back to the brass holder and, as if in affection, she put her thumb on the patch. To her amazement she felt it move. She looked behind her to see if Bella was coming. But there was no sight nor sound of her, so she pressed her thumb again on the dark patch and when it moved downwards and she heard a rustling sound, she looked to her left . . . and saw the lino slip from underneath the skirting board. Wide-eyed and open-mouthed, she gazed on it. Then she was on her knees pulling it further from the wall and gazing down into a narrow trough in which lay neatly piled bundles and bundles of what looked like bank notes. Letting her eyes travel to the far end near the wall, she could see a number of small chamois-leather bags.

She slumped back on her knees for a moment, then sprang up and was rushing towards the door when it opened and Bella entered carrying a tray on which were two cups of tea and a plate holding two buns and a knife. She was amazed when it was seized from her hands and thrust on the bed. 'What is it, girl?' she cried. 'What's the matter with you?'

Grabbing her arm, Reenee pulled her towards the window and on to her knees, and now she was kneeling looking at a trough, all of three feet long, under the window and her mind kept repeating, Oh, my God! That's money down there, a lot of money. She picked up a bundle of the notes but dropped it as if it had burnt her.

She turned and stared at Reenee, whose face was aglow as she thrust out her arm and grabbed one of the chamois-leather bags. Pulling open the top, she dipped her hand in and brought out a number of gold sovereigns; then let them drip back into the bag.

'In the name of God!' Bella's words were awe-filled, 'Sovereigns! Gold sovereigns. What are we to do? What are we to do with all this?' She stared at Reenee and, in a trembling voice, she said, 'I must get Mr Travis. He'll know.'

Now Reenee stabbed her finger into Bella's chest and quite clearly she brought out the words, 'Yours!'

'Eeh, lass. I'd get into trouble for hoarding all that. In any case, I wouldn't know what to do with it. God knows what it'll amount to when it's counted up.'

Again Reenee spoke, but haltingly now as she said, 'Trav-is. Trav-is.'

'Yes; yes, you're right. We must see Mr Travis. He'll know.

But hide it. Look, put the lino back the way you got it. D'you know how?'

For answer Reenee pushed the lino underneath the skirting board, and there it was as it had been before; the curtain was hanging down covering the rusty patch, which seemed to have returned automatically to sill level. And Bella stood up and held Reenee's face in both her hands as she said, 'Nobody else must know about this, you understand? Until after Mr Travis has seen it. I'll get Carl to go and fetch him. I can trust Carl, but I won't tell him about this' – she pointed down to the floor – 'I'll just say I want to see Mr Travis on business.'

Carl was about to go out when Bella said, 'Would you run a message for me, Carl?'

'Anything for you, Bella. You know that, don't you?'

'Go to Mr Travis's office and ask if you can have a word privately with him. Put on your decent coat. Tell him that Miss Morgan would like to see him.'

'I'll do that, Bella. I'll go and put me good togs on. Is it about the property next door?'

She screwed up her eyes as she exclaimed, 'What? You mean the cobbler's shop?'

'What else?'

She slapped his cheek playfully, saying, 'You mind your own business. Go on with you.'

After he had departed, grinning, she remained standing at the foot of the stairs: she was not looking up them, but along the passage to where the wall divided this house from the next. The cobbler's shop had been empty these past two or three months. Frankie had found that, these days, not so many people could afford to have their shoes mended, never mind buy second-hand ones, so he had put the shop on the market. Apparently there had been no buyers; well, who in their right mind would buy a place like that? But Carl had said, 'Is it about the cobbler's shop?' Oh, my God! What was she thinking? There was enough money in that cubby-hole or whatever it was to buy six cobblers' shops, she thought, then hastily reminded herself that it wasn't hers. Anyway, the idea was a good cover-up for her wanting to see Mr Travis.

She went upstairs to her room. Reenee was still on the floor, her fingers moving along the skirting board, and in this position she turned to Bella, her eyes bright, and she muttered something.

'What are you saying?' Bella said.

Reenee's fingers moved backward and forward; then again her mouth opened and, gulping in her throat, she brought out, 'Spring.'

'Oh, a spring.'

Reenee was nodding vigorously now, and she indicated the whole length of the trough and Bella said, 'Well, well,' then bitterly she repeated, 'A spring. He must have made that, the bugger; all that money there, all that time. That's what he was trying to get at just before he died. I hope where he's burning in hell now this minute he knows we've found it. Aye, *we* have. No matter who gets it *we*'ve found it. All his hidden cash that was mentioned on the back of the envelope flap,' and she repeated, 'Loose cash, indeed!'

Carl was back within half an hour. His face was bright as he said, 'Mr Travis is a very nice gentleman. He greeted me very civilly. He said he would call upon you in the next hour and would be only too pleased to do so. Wasn't that nice of him?'

'Aye, it was. Now, don't mention to Joe or anybody else that I sent for Mr Travis, you understand?'

His face became solemn for a moment, and he said, 'Yes, Bella, I understand. And don't worry, you know me.'

Mr Travis was as good as his word, and Bella took him straight into the sitting room. Closing the door after them, she asked him to sit down, which he did, but only after she was seated. 'What can I do for you, Miss Morgan? Have you some news for me?'

'Well, in a way, I suppose you could say I have.' And she told him what they had discovered, and as she did so she watched his face lengthen and his eyebrows move upwards.

'A great deal of money?' he asked.

'I would say so, sir, a great deal. But I haven't counted it.'

He stood up. 'I am intrigued, Miss Morgan. Will you take me, please, to where you found this hoard.'

A few minutes later he was kneeling on the floor of Bella's bedroom, with Bella by his side, and Reenee standing at the far end of the room near the head of the bed. After taking up one pile of five-pound notes and straightening them out, he flipped through it quickly before turning to Bella and saying, 'You're a rich woman now, Miss Morgan. Do you know that?'

'It's not mine, sir.'

'Miss Morgan, I want to say to you' – his voice had changed – 'don't be silly. This is your house, isn't it? It was left to you, and all in it.'

'But that,' she pointed down to it, 'isn't honest money.'

Here Mr Travis laughed and he said, 'It's as honest as you'll find today, Miss Morgan. Now listen to me. The only people who might lay any claim to this would be the tax man or the Customs, and they have already, through your help – oh, yes, through your help and that piece of an envelope – been able to save this country many hundreds of thousands of pounds. Oh, much more. That one signature, Jason, did so much towards clearing up what had been troubling both the Customs and the tax people for a long, long time. There are not many people in this town with the name of Jason and who deal in pieces of glass. This Jason had been suspect for a long time but he was such a figure that no one dared put a finger on him without proof. I may tell you he was only one of a number who had to make a hasty retreat from this country, so hasty that the documents that they left condemned them. That gentleman has never yet been found, but 'nevertheless the powers that be remain hopeful.'

Bella looked at him in awe now, as she said, 'You found all this out by yourself?'

At this, he put his head back and laughed, 'No, Miss Morgan. But I will tell you this much. My grandfather was in the diplomatic service and an ambassador for years. I have two brothers. They are both now in the civil service. You know, there are many kinds of detectives in the civil service; my brothers are two of them. They are very ordinary-looking men, soft-voiced, but one is connected with Customs and the other with . . . oh, things along the same lines and gentlemen who, like your late master's friend, spend much time in Holland and Switzerland. We often get together, and my firm is very interested in all they have to say. Over the years we have occasionally been of help in different ways to them, through clients such as yourself, Miss Morgan, who bring into the open scoundrels such as your Mr Hamish McIntyre who, through you, led us to his friend Jason. Our firm owes you a great deal, Miss Morgan, as do my brothers. I have told them a lot about you and your business. And now we come to this.'

He pointed to the row of notes and bags on the floor, and when he saw Bella shudder he said, 'My dear Miss Morgan, you should be overjoyed.'

'I'm far from that, Mr Travis, I'm scared. I've never seen so much money in my life, and I can't believe what you say, that it belongs to me or that I can claim it, 'cos I won't know what to do with it.'

'Don't worry about that, Miss Morgan, we will deal with all that business, and to your satisfaction. The first thing we must do now is to find some place of safety for this money, at least for the moment. Have you a large holdall?'

'There is that up there.' Bella was now pointing to the top of the wardrobe. 'He used that at times.'

Mr Travis looked up at the bag. 'The very thing,' he said.

'Wait a minute, Mr Travis,' Bella put her hand on his arm.

'How am I goin' to explain to anyone, I mean the lads and
. . . well, people I want to buy from, where on earth I've got
. . . How much would you say there was?'

Mr Travis replied, 'I'm not sure, but at a rough guess over
four thousand pounds. The sovereigns, being gold, will be of
more value now than when they were purchased because the
price of gold fluctuates.'

'Oh, dear God!'

'Come . . . come, sit down there, Miss Morgan,' and he
pushed her gently on to the side of the bed. Then, looking
straight at the figure standing stiffly against the wall, he said
to Reenee, 'Don't you think, my dear, that your friend here
is absolutely entitled to consider this money her own?'

To Bella's surprise, for she had swung round and looked at
her, Reenee opened her mouth and said a definite, 'Yes.'

'There you are, Miss Morgan, there is confirmation, and
firmly said, and from the one you say who actually found it.
Now listen to me. We must think up something plausible to
explain your change of fortune, but this will come later. At
the present moment, we must put this money in a safe place
until tomorrow morning, by which time I shall have talked
the matter over with my partner. Tomorrow, Miss Morgan,
I would ask you to get into your best bib and tucker and I
shall take you to see him and my father. Now, let us get this
money packed away.'

The following morning, Mr Travis arrived carrying a large
briefcase. Bella herself had opened the door to him, and he
said to her quietly, 'I thought it best, Miss Morgan, to come
and help you transfer our luggage out of the house as un-
obtrusively as possible, because you can't carry it in that big
bag. I have brought my briefcase, and between that and your
shopping bag and handbag I'm sure we can get your goods
from the house without any comment. What d'you say to
that?'

'Yes. I was wonderin' meself how we were goin' to get it out, and I'll be glad to see the last of it.'

He laughed gently, then said, 'Well, come along and let us get on with the business.'

Half an hour later Mr Travis ushered his client into his well-appointed offices, which took up two floors of a very ordinary-looking building in a side-street off a main market piazza. He led her across the foyer, past an interested receptionist at a desk, into a lift and on to the second floor. There he was met by a tall man, who immediately relieved him of his heavy briefcase and helped him off with his coat. 'They're waiting for you in the board room, sir.'

Mr Travis had to place a firm hand between Bella's shoulders to press her forward across the carpeted hall, to a heavy oak door and into a room that smelt of leather and cigar smoke and something else to which she could not put a name.

The room seemed full of men, yet there were only four, including Mr Travis, who now took her handbag and shopping bag and laid them on the leather couch next to his briefcase, then directed her towards an armchair into which she sank. Her body seemed smaller than ever.

'This is my father, Miss Morgan.' Mr Travis directed her gaze to an old man, whose presence filled the room.

The voice that came from the chair was more like that of somebody in his hale fifties, for it boomed at her: 'I am very pleased to make your acquaintance, Miss Morgan. Excuse me not rising. I may add that this is not the first time I have heard of you, for in the past you have been of some assistance to my family.'

What could she say to this? Nothing. She did not even smile because, as she said to herself, she was all at sea, in that lovely room, with paintings on the walls of men dressed like mayors.

'And this,' said Mr Travis, directing his hand towards the tall man sitting to Bella's left, 'is my partner and, unfortunately, my cousin,' which caused a ripple of laughter to sound round the table.

The man, standing up and bending over Bella, took her hand, saying, 'That remark is reciprocated a thousandfold, Miss Morgan. However, I must say I am more than pleased to make your acquaintance. I, too, have heard about you and the good work you do for others less fortunate.'

All Bella could find to say was, 'Thank you.'

'And this very important person, who controls us all,' said Mr Travis now, 'is our accountant, Mr McLean.'

A small man rose from the far side of the table and came to her chair and, holding out his hand, said, 'It's an honour to meet you, Miss Morgan.' Then bending further towards her, he said, on a broad smile and in a loud whisper, 'Fortunately I am not related to the family.'

'We can thank God for that!' came the voice from the big leather chair. Again there was laughter, and Bella thought, They're just like an ordinary family.

Mr Travis now lifted his briefcase on to the table and, stooping, he picked up Bella's handbag. 'Has it only the necessary requirements in it, Miss Morgan?'

'Yes; I emptied it of all its bits and pieces.' She smiled, and he smiled back at her. Then, taking his seat close to hers, he said, 'Mr McLean will count out your little gold mine for the benefit of my father. He cannot believe that all this money was stored secretly in your house and probably would have lain there until the house was demolished if it hadn't been that you were going to give yourself a present of a carpet for the floor.'

The accountant and the other partner now began to check the money, their fingers flying over the notes so quickly that she couldn't imagine they were counting it all. When they came to the bags, the sovereigns were poured on to the table, which elicited an exclamation from the armchair: 'Well, well, well! I haven't seen so many together for years.'

At last the money was arrayed on the table piled in rows, and the accountant said, 'As the market stands now, the sovereigns would bring the amount to well over four thousand pounds; but these will rise in price, and I should imagine, once things begin to turn in the country, and they must shortly, then they could soon be worth half their value again, so it would be wise to keep them in a deposit box for the present.'

Mr Travis now took hold of Bella's hand and said, 'Please, Miss Morgan, don't look so aghast. We have had many clients in our time, but not one that shivered with the knowledge he had a little more money than he expected.'

At this her wits seemed to return and she repeated, 'A little more? That lot's too much for anybody.'

'This is what we propose to do, Miss Morgan, with your permission. We shall bank for you two thousand in safe bonds. This investment will have what you might call a proviso, meaning that should you decide to take the money out within five years you will forfeit their accumulated interest. Do you understand me?'

Bella paused for a long moment before she said, 'Just so that it's safe for five years.'

'Yes, that's a way of putting it. It's safe for five years and will eventually give you good interest. The next thousand, my accountant thinks we should use to, as he calls it, play the market when favourable. This means buying and selling shares, you understand?'

She didn't, so she just looked at him and he said, 'Well, it doesn't matter. It will mean he will try to double your money for you. Sometimes, unfortunately, he might lose some of it. How about that?'

She smiled and said, 'Well, I think,' she paused, 'we will be able to afford it.'

The laughter now was quite loud. 'Now, about the last thousand. I think this should be banked and used for your current purposes. For example, you might wish to improve your house or business.'

This she did understand, and nodded, saying, 'Yes, I was going to ask your advice on that, Mr Travis.'

'Yes?'

'Well, you see, the house next door, really it was joined on to mine, they used to be all one, and when it was divided, next door became a shoe shop. Then it went downhill and turned into an ordinary cobbler's; and now it's up for sale. I know it isn't everybody's choice, but if I could buy it I could extend my business – we have to turn a lot away most nights.'

'I think that would be a very good idea, Miss Morgan. Would you like us to see about it?'

'I would, Mr Travis.'

'Does the shoemaker still own it?'

'Yes.'

'Do you know where he lives?'

'I'm sorry, I don't.'

'Oh, well, don't worry about that, we'll find out. That'll be quite easy. Now about banking it for you,' and he turned to his father, saying, 'James has a small branch in that area, hasn't he? He could be told she has been left the money by a friend.'

'Yes, yes,' said the old man.

'Well, then, I think, Mr McLean, if you will put, say, three-quarters of this into the vault and the rest into Miss Morgan's handbag, we'll be ready to do some signing of documents and such before we go to the bank. But first, I think, we all deserve a drink, and not just coffee or tea. Would that suit you, Miss Morgan?'

She smiled. 'I never object to a gin,' she said.

Of a sudden Bella found herself relaxed and not sitting upright in the middle of her chair but leaning back. She had never experienced anything like this in her life and she knew she never would again. Well, she would be able to tell Reenee all about it, but would the lass be able to take it in? And how could she expect her to when she herself could hardly take it in?

The old man was speaking to her now, and she had to quell her thoughts to give him her full attention. He was saying, 'You have given us a very interesting morning, Miss Morgan. I know quite a bit about secret drawers and hidden hoards. You see, before he died, one of my sons was captain of a ship – and the stories he told of what sailors got up to below decks in order to smuggle in gold!

'Henry, my son, actually showed me some of the places in his ship which had been carved out, and so skilfully that at times they fooled the Customs. But Arthur there tells me that this trough under the lino was a work of art. The lino, I gather, was just a shield to cover a three-inch wide trough, fully lined with kid. He said that whoever contrived it must have been an expert in this particular field. The lengths to which some people will go to acquire riches!'

'Ah!' exclaimed Mr Travis. 'Here's Tom with our life-savers.' After handing one to Bella he then passed glasses round to the others. And when he raised his own the other men followed suit, and with him said, 'Cheers, Miss Morgan.' Then he added, 'And to a successful business life ahead of you.'

Looking at the half-filled glass of gin, Bella said, 'Thank you, Mr Travis. Thank you all,' and she nodded to each in turn; 'but I know I shall not be able to start on a business career for some time if I now drink all this.'

Oh, they were nice people. But no; she wouldn't drink it all, because she didn't want to go home under the influence, as it were. She had a lot to tell them, and plans to make, plans that would affect them all, and for the better. She would see to that.

11

Two nights later Bella got her little band together in the kitchen and told them of her plans. She was buying the house next door and opening it up into hers, but before anything could be done with it it must be thoroughly cleared out. Her solicitor had suggested that she should get an architect to design the best way of altering the cellar floor and the yard. That would take in more people than she really intended, but she had told Mr Travis that they themselves were so full of ideas that she would put it to them first, to see what they thought could be done.

With the exception of Carl, they had all gaped at her. 'Have you come into a fortune, Bella?'

'No,' she replied politely, 'but I have found an oil well,' which caused them all to laugh, but self-consciously. Then she told them a tale of having been left, quite unexpectedly, a few hundred pounds by someone she had helped years ago and had never thought to hear from again. It showed you there were good people in the world. But this was the point: she hadn't money to throw away but she had enough to alter that house next door into something like this one; anyway, it would enable her to provide for more men off the street.

'I was advised to have a look at that place along the river that is run by the council,' she told them. 'The mattresses there are on raised platforms. They also have a row of single rooms which are taken by the week by men who are in some kind of work but haven't a house or flat to go to.'

'Aye,' put in John now. 'We tried to get in there one night, but it was full. The beds might be on platforms, but there's no big fire in the room, nor do they get soup and breakfast, and they still charge a shilling a head. But you can have a wash and a shower for that too.'

'And are those rooms really let as private rooms and just for men?'

'I wouldn't know anything about that,' said John.

At this they were all quite startled when Reenee made a sound in her throat and, pointing to herself, nodded.

'You know about them, Reenee,' said Carl now, 'about the rooms?'

Again she nodded.

'You stayed there?'

Her head drooped and she raised one finger. 'For one night?'

Again her head gave a slight movement.

'What were they like? I mean, how big? How many of them?'

'Give her a chance,' said Joe. Then, 'Do you want a pencil and paper, Reenee?'

She looked up at him and nodded. He went to the mantelpiece and took from it Bella's shopping list and a pencil, and when he laid them before her she turned the pad longways, then drew a long line, which she then made into ten divisions, causing Willie to ask softly, 'Those are rooms?'

She did not look at him but her head moved again, and now it was John who asked, 'How big are they, miss?'

She looked at him and thought, then pointed from the fireplace to the middle of the table; and it was Carl who got up

216

and measured the distance, saying, 'About ten feet long?' She nodded. Then he asked, 'How wide?'

She had to think again, then pointed to the fireplace and the front of the table; and again he measured and said, 'About eight feet?'

It was John who now put in, 'Ten by eight . . . really, not bad.'

'What was in the room?' asked Bella. And at this Reenee turned over a page of the notebook and quickly drew what looked like a bed; then to the side of it a drawing of what could only be a small chest of drawers, and between that and the end of the wall, she drew a line perpendicular to the wall, with a hook on the further side; and John immediately said, 'A place for hanging up your clothes in the corner between the walls?'

Reenee nodded brightly at him. Lastly, she pointed to the wall to the side of the chest of drawers and drew a rectangle. Joe exclaimed, 'A mirror! We haven't got one in our room, have we? That's something that will have to be seen to,' which caused Tony to bark at him, 'Don't be so bloody dim, man. Everybody doesn't want to look at their face.'

Quietly, Carl put in, 'It's all right. I see my face every day in the shop windows. Don't worry, Joe.'

'I didn't mean nowt,' stammered Joe.

'I know you didn't, you great big fathead, so shut up,' said Carl, who then turned to Reenee, saying, 'What about if women came in like you? Were you in a different section?'

She now put up three fingers, which said to them that there had been three rooms for women.

'But what about if they weren't filled?' asked Willie now.

There was a quirk to Reenee's lips as she looked back at Willie, and she put her finger across her top lip, which indicated a moustache.

And he laughed and said, 'They were given to the men?'

She nodded. Then, as practical as ever, Andy said, 'Where

did they wash, miss? Not in the men's place?'

She shook her head, then wrote along the edge of the paper, 'Small room off;' and Andy said, 'There was a washbowl in the small place?'

She smiled from one to the other as she demonstrated washing her face; and now, turning over the paper, she drew a small circle with a sort of chain through it, and next to it she wrote soap.

'They chained up the soap?' Carl said in surprise.

She nodded vigorously; then swiftly her hand moved down the table and, picking up the knife and a small piece of bread, she proceeded to cut pieces off each corner until there was hardly anything left in the middle.

The room was filled with laughter, and there was a sound in her throat that might also have been laughter.

'Good for them,' said John. 'They cut pieces off it?' She nodded to him, but as she did so Bella thought, I don't think she was laughing the night she was there, poor soul. She put out a hand and placed it over Reenee's.

They looked at each other, and it was as if Reenee was reading Bella's mind because the smile went from her face and there was a silence in the room. Then, as if to break the tension, Carl said, 'How long did they leave the lights on? Right through the place, I mean.'

At this she lifted up one finger and he said, 'One hour? After closing?'

She nodded.

'They weren't givin' much away,' said Tony.

Bella broke in, saying in a firm voice, 'Well, lass, once again you've given us a pattern to work on. What d'you say, boys?'

The chorus was general and loud, 'Oh, yes, yes. We could get ten rooms across the bottom of that yard; but of course they would mean extra latrine and washin'-up places.'

'But how're we goin' to provide the soap?' Joe put in.

'They won't need to steal,' said Bella; 'there'll be ha'penny pieces of soap, and it won't be blue-mottled any more. That in future will only be used for the floors, which goes for indoors too.' She was nodding towards Willie now. 'But let's get down to facts. If the place is goin' to provide for twice as many people as we already cater for, then the six of you can't work it all alone. I've been thinking about it, and you, Joe, can give up most of your job now. And I'll put you on the same rate as the others. We mightn't be able to get much more on the cheap, but you never know, so you can still remain good friends with the warehouse people. Also, it'll be your job to see to the vegetables for both places. Get them from the market as you usually do, then it's up to you to clean them and chop them, because Reenee, here, has had enough of that, I think,' to which Reenee shook her head, but Bella went on, 'I know what's best, lass, and I feel that you would very much like to help Willie with pastry and bread-making and things. Now, wouldn't you?'

Reenee was looking at Willie now, and he at her, and he said, 'I'd love to have you help me, Reenee.' And at this she lowered her head a little and nodded twice.

Bella said, 'Well, that part's settled. Now there's you, Carl. I know you like your walk-about, and you could still do it for a couple of hours a day, but the rest I'd like you to give up for me. Although you can't cook like Willie, you can make broth, which could be done in the new kitchen. Besides which you could help with the cleanin' up of the rooms and the outbuildings. But now, you other three, Andy, Tony and John. You can't see to everything and I can tell you there'll be much more work to be done than you imagine, so I'm going to employ two young fellows who wouldn't mind doin' the dirty work of the wash-houses and keepin' the yards clean. You other three'll have your work cut out with practically rebuildin' that place next door. From the little I've seen of it, it's goin' to take time and hard labour. I'll start you all off on a pound a week, and we'll wait and see how business goes. The better it goes the more your wage will go up; and when you're thinkin' of a pound a week, it might seem very small compared with what you used to make in the shipyards and places like that, but don't forget you've got board and lodgings.' And she laid stress on these last words. 'Your quarters might've been just a wash-house, but now it's as good as any house.'

'You're right there,' said Andy, a sentiment the others echoed.

'As for the two other residents,' Bella now looked from Joe to Carl, 'I really think they should pay rent for their accommodation, rooms to themselves with every convenience. Tut-tut. I'm too soft-hearted, that's me.'

They were all laughing now, and it was Joe who paid another of his rough and rare compliments, saying, 'You said that in fun, Bella, but it's right in earnest.'

12

And so on these lines began Bella's new business, which was to prosper and keep them all happy in the years that followed. That period lasted until a name became known to every individual in the western world and beyond – Adolf Hitler. War was declared on 3 September 1939, and London became a scene of activity: trains, buses, all kinds of vehicles were filled with children and families to get them away from the danger zone, because it was feared that London would be the main target for air raids. But it was not until almost a year later that London was first bombed.

When that happened, Bella found she could hardly cope with the nightly inrush of families, trying to find shelter from the heavy bombing. They would make their way down to the two large basement sleeping rooms that were considered safest because they were below ground level. Many of the families hadn't parted with their children at the beginning, while others had children who had returned, having found that they didn't like either the country or the people with whom they had been boarded. Often one of Bella's mattresses, all of which lay now on high wooden frames, would have to hold three children, with their mother lying on the floor beside them. Many openly welcomed this rescue place rather than go down into the underground stations or government-built shelters.

Bella had little fear of losing any of her men in the call-up because even the youngest among them was well over thirty-five years old. But they all signed up for civilian service in the Fire Brigade or as fire-watchers and, with the work they did for Bella, they were kept busy for never less than twelve hours a day. As for food, at first there had been no worries, because vegetables were still plentiful. By 1940, however, rationing had come in. Each person was allotted a booklet that entitled him or her to have a small amount each week of meat, tea, sugar, butter, bread, bacon, eggs and sweets, maybe small amounts but nevertheless fair to all. Vegetables became scarcer and dearer. If a night visitor to Bella's wanted fat on his bread, he had to provide it. Nevertheless, even if the broth was a little thinner and was seasoned by bones alone, it was always more than welcome to every occupant of a mattress. The tea in the morning was a different thing. Boiling water was plentiful, but there was no longer free tea and sugar.

A change had come over Reenee during this time. Although she still could not bear to be near strange men, she spent hours helping mothers with fractious children; and Bella noticed that, just as she had once hugged the old bear to her, now she hugged a child, while making a humming sound in her throat. So much had she changed in this way that Bella wouldn't have been surprised if, of a sudden, she had got her memory back, though she herself dreaded the idea of it.

Also to Bella's amazement, she seemed to enjoy the singing, especially when the four original band members got together and rattled out not only tunes from the old days, but also modern ones, especially funny ones like 'Kiss Me Goodnight Sergeant Major, Tuck Me in My Little Wooden Bed'. If Reenee could have laughed, Bella knew she would, and then wondered if she was able to laugh inside.

It took only one small incident to change all this. Reenee was near the door one night, where she had been seeing to a woman and her children who were sitting on a mattress. The small band was going out and Willie said, 'Did you enjoy it?' and Reenee was nodding to him and smiling, when one of the husbands who had come in from the outside pulled her round and grabbed at her coat, saying, 'Why the hell must you always wear that dirty black nightgown? It spoils the look of the place!'

That he was half drunk was no excuse, but before he knew where he was Andy's big fist had caught him under the chin and levelled him. Then the others dragged him from the room and to the gate and threw him outside.

By this time, away from the hubbub, Bella was assisting Reenee up the main staircase into her room, saying, 'There now . . . there, lass. He was drunk. He meant no harm, not really, he was drunk. Don't tremble so, lass. You're all right.'

In the bedroom, Reenee threw herself on the bed and, putting her hands behind her head, gripped the iron rails of the bedhead while her body stiffened and her middle began its old form of jerking up and down.

'Oh, my God!' wailed Bella. 'You've not had one of these for years! If I had him here I'd kill him meself, and not only him, but also the one who first caused you to go on like this.' And now she put a hand under Reenee's back and the other one on her stomach and tried to still the movement. But, just as she had found before, this only seemed to accentuate the motion, until Reenee suddenly let go of the railings and her body crumpled into a heap inside the old coat.

'It's all right, my love. It's all right.' Bella was holding her and stroking her face, which was wet with tears.

That's new, Bella thought. She had never seen Reenee cry like this: her eyes had always become wet, but now the tears were raining down her cheeks. Bella muttered, 'Oh, that swine! There's always somebody to spoil things. Don't worry, love. Don't worry. You'll not see him again, I can assure you of that.'

But no matter how she tried on this night she couldn't get Reenee to take off the coat; so she took off her shoes, covered her over with a blanket and said, 'I'm off downstairs, love, to make a hot drink. Now, you'll be all right.'

Bella wasn't surprised to see the six men down there in the kitchen waiting for her; and it was Carl who said, 'Has she had one of her turns?'

'Aye,' said Bella; 'the first in God knows how long. I had thought she was finished with them.'

'A bad one?'

'Yes, very bad. She's cried as I've never seen her cry before. But go on now, the lot of you, and thank you for coming up. But don't worry, I'll get her round again. I only know this, if it wasn't for the few married couples that come in together, I would see that the men kept to the room in the basement of the other house and the women to the one in this house.'

'It could be done,' said John. 'Most of the fellows are either in the Army or the Air Force or at sea. Others are on night shift and sleep in the houses during the day. We could give it a try.'

'Oh, well, I don't want to disturb them,' said Bella. 'They've got a lot to put up with, especially those with kids. Leave it; she'll likely have come round by the morning . . .'

Reenee didn't come round in the morning, or the next day, or the next: she got up and sat huddled in her coat near the window of her bedroom. It was on the third day that she went down into the kitchen, where Willie greeted her as if nothing had happened, saying as she took her place at the table, 'I don't know what we'll do, Reenee, if they ration flour. I'd hate to have to cut out the bread, wouldn't you?'

She looked at him and he looked back at her. There was an expression in her eyes that he hadn't seen there for a long, long time. He couldn't put a name to it, only that she looked lost.

224

No amount of talking, all the kind messages sent up with Bella from down below by the regular patrons that they hoped her cold would soon be better because they missed her, left any impression on her. She just looked at Bella, then went on with what she was doing. The patrons of what was called Bella's Pad all looked upon the poor lass as being a bit simple, not quite right in the head, but kindly nevertheless; and a number of the mothers did miss her, especially her attention to the youngest members of their families.

The air raids on London were renewed after the Luftwaffe had finished off, as they thought, the fighter airfields on the edge of the city. The four members of the band were now all fire-watchers, helping the air-raid wardens. Andy and Tony were generally on together, as were John and Willie in their turn. Each pair had their own area. It was left to Joe and Carl to see to the patrons of Bella's houses on nights when they were free of their own duties. This meant keeping watch on the gates until they were closed at eight o'clock; then, with the help of some of the regulars, distributing the bowls of soup and newly baked bread, on which each person would gladly put his own margarine or jam. Afterwards one or the other would go outside to be on fire-watch for the area.

Generally, the first siren would indicate a coming raid sufficiently early for people to take cover. But this night there was no time after the wail of the siren ended and the thunder of bombs shook the house, penetrating to the pads. Bella had been sitting in the kitchen with Reenee, who could not be persuaded to go down the stairs into the basement again.

That the bombing was quite close was evident, and Bella put her arms around Reenee and held her. She was amazed that Reenee's body was not shaking with fear as hers was. In fact, it was Reenee who put her hand on Bella's head and stroked her hair back from her brow, making sounds of sympathy in her throat.

When daylight came to London the next morning it showed the first horrors of many more to come: houses still burning, whole streets laid flat like fallen packs of cards.

The men were disturbed that Bella now had to sit out the raids with Reenee upstairs when there was more protection in the two basement rooms underground. It wasn't until Willie got the idea of getting an Anderson shelter and putting it near the gate of the yard that Bella's trouble was eased, because without any demur Reenee would go out of the front door, along the street, through the gate and into the shelter, which had been made as comfortable as such places could be.

They had arranged two separate bunks and a little calor-gas stove on which they could boil a kettle for a cup of tea. Also there were tins holding buns and biscuits, though they never seemed to eat them. There wasn't much singing done downstairs either, these days, not since Dunkirk when the remains of the British Expeditionary Force were taken off the shores of France on 3 June 1940. One young woman's husband had died of his wounds on the rescue boat coming over to England, and another's husband had been rescued from the Dunkirk beach only to be drowned when the small boat in which he was being taken to a Navy frigate was bombed.

Every now and again Mr Travis would visit Bella, but these days he was a sad man, for his two nephews, both in the Navy, had died when their ships had been torpedoed in the Atlantic while shepherding convoys of merchant ships from America.

Bella could offer little comfort; she could only take his hand and pat it. And now he said, 'I shouldn't be talking to you like this, my dear, you who've had such a rough time of your own, so much to put up with . . .'

'Oh, Mr Travis, I feel I've had nothing but luck in my life since I was fourteen. Although I hated working for Mr McIntyre, it was by luck that I came to do it, and I was very lucky then to meet you. And I look back and think what my life would have been without my dear Reenee; and there again you come into it, for not another man in your business would have guided me so honestly through that side. Had it not been for you, I know now that I couldn't have let myself claim that money. I would have been afraid. But your advice and that of your family has made me comfortable for the rest of my days, and through that I have been able to make many others comfortable too. And you know, Mr Travis, I'm going to say this, I look upon you as a friend.'

'Oh,' he said, 'then I am honoured, Miss Morgan, that you should think so of me. But what we have done for you is nothing to what you have for others and particularly for one of my brothers, and, incidentally, for the country at large.' And when, later, they shook hands at the front door, it was as close friends they parted, he promising to look in again soon, and she telling him how welcome he would be.

The war went on and so did the bombing. Many patrons of Bella's Pad had lost their homes; some had also lost relatives. But nothing so serious touched Bella and her little family till one night in 1943. The sirens had gone, the shelters were full, the bombs were dropping, the fires were blazing, and the raid seemed never-ending. At last the All Clear sounded, and some settled down to sleep while others got up to go and see if their homes were still standing.

Down in the Anderson shelter Bella was sitting on the edge of her lower bunk. She had a strange worried feeling on her. All the lads were out: Andy, Tony, John and Willie were all fire-watching; Joe was now with an ambulance team, and Carl was doing his turn in the communications office of the Fire Brigade.

Bella waited until the autumn dawn broke before she left the shelter and made her way along to the wash-house. There were no lights on in there, so she went back to the shelter and said to Reenee that she was going indoors. Reenee, too, got up. She had been sleeping in her coat, so she pulled a scarf round her head and went out and upstairs with Bella.

Bella had thought she might find either Joe or Carl indoors but there was no one.

At seven o'clock, when not one of her lads had returned, she said to Reenee, who was making tea, 'I've an awful feeling on me that something's happened. They always come straggling back, but so far there's not one of them in.'

It was as she sat drinking the tea that Joe and Carl came slowly up the stairs and into the kitchen. They were both covered with dust and looked utterly weary.

Immediately Bella was on her feet. 'Had a bad night?'

Neither man spoke, and she demanded, 'What is it? What's happened?'

'There's bad news, Bella,' Carl muttered.

'Bad news! Who?'

It was Joe now who said briefly, 'Andy.'

'Oh, no! Not Andy!'

Neither of them spoke; and Bella, her face blanched, turned to look at Reenee who had dropped into a chair and laid her head on her folded arms on the table. Bella wanted to go to her and say, Don't have another turn, for God's sake, not now, but she couldn't speak. After a moment she turned again to Carl: 'Is he dead?'

'Yes. From what Tony tells me, the house next door had had a direct hit, and this one was on fire. There was a woman screaming, and he went in. He must have got to her because after the house collapsed they were found together. Joe was helping with the injured' – he thumbed towards Joe – 'but nothing could be done. Tony was there. His hands were burnt. John and Willie had been directed there, and arrived as they were taking the bodies to' – he gulped and choked before he went on – 'the mortuary. Tony went to the dressing-station, he wouldn't go to hospital. The three of them are now back in the house,' he tilted his head towards the wash-house, 'but I'd leave them, Bella, for a bit; they . . . they're so cut up. You see, they weren't just like Joe and me here, odd bods, they were more like a family, like brothers. They'd been through a lot together.'

It was a strange feeling for Bella. She felt she couldn't cry, yet she wanted to do something like scream or throw something, break something. In this moment she realised that as Reenee was like a daughter to her, those six fellows were like the sons she had never had, and that the one who had laid bricks, built walls and, although not the cleverest of the four, seemed to lead the band, would not return home again.

Andrew Anderson was buried four days later. The only mourners were his adoptive family, with the exception of Reenee who had not offered to attend and to whom no one had suggested it.

The amazing thing to all of them was that not one of his relatives had come from Wales. They had fully expected his wife to put in an appearance, but no. Carl had written to tell her that Andy had died, but did not receive a reply, although he had written on the back of it, 'If undelivered return to sender'.

After the ceremony, when they returned to the house, they found that Reenee had set out the tea table in the sitting room. She had brought out the new china tea service Bella had bought for herself before the war, and the table was set with bread and butter, corned-beef sandwiches, and a plate of Willie's buns, made with liquid paraffin, which Willie had discovered was a good substitute for fat.

'Oh, that's nice of you, lass,' Bella said, and the men nodded their approval. What conversation there was among the six of them at the table touched only on their inability to understand how a wife and two daughters could ignore the fact that their husband and father had died saving someone from a burning house.

'Now she can get married,' Tony said bitterly. 'She'll be living with the fellow anyway.'

'He never said anything about her from the day he came back that time, did he?' Willie put in quietly. 'And I don't think he ever wrote to her again.'

'That's no excuse,' said John; 'those lasses could have sent a note, if not his wife.'

Bella put in quietly, 'He's goin' to be missed in more ways than one. D'you want to take on somebody else?'

The chorus came, 'No, Bella, we'll manage.'

'Anyway,' said John, 'we couldn't stand another fellow in his place. We'll manage, at least for a time. Don't worry, Bella; we'll rearrange things.'

'How nice it was of that Mr Travis to send that holly wreath,' Carl said, to which Bella replied, 'He's a good man, is Mr Travis, and a gentleman.'

To everyone's surprise, and Bella's most of all, Reenee went downstairs that night, for the first time in months, to help the mothers with their children. Life went on and so did the war.

The men were often asked by the 'patrons' to play again, but since Andy's death they hadn't done so.

London was bombed continually; there was hardly a district that didn't show skeleton houses or streets of rubble. Coventry had been laid flat, and many other cities, among them Liverpool and Plymouth, had been terribly damaged; more ships were sunk; food became scarcer; it looked as if the war would never end. Yet there were towns that never experienced a raid; others where a single plane had attacked, such as the one at Hereford that dropped a bomb near the munitions factory there. The spirit that prevailed over the whole nation, led by their great wartime Prime Minister Winston Churchill, was amazing.

When American troops arrived in England, Bella said many girls and women, who should have known better, seemed to go mad; and all done under the guise of making the men feel at home . . .

Then one day, 6 June 1944, an invasion fleet ferried armies of many nations across the Channel, and over the following months defeated the Germans in territories they had occupied: France, Holland, Belgium and Scandinavia. At last the Allies were winning, but at a terrible price.

It wasn't until 8 May 1945 that the slaughter in Europe came to an end. They called the day it was celebrated VE Day. The British, the Russians, the Americans and the French had won, and there began the huge task of reconstruction. In the meantime there were still the Japanese to defeat. One day a pilot dropped a bomb and devastated a Japanese city and everyone in it in one terrible flash. Now the war really was over, though the age of the atomic bomb had arrived.

13

On the day the war ended in Europe almost everyone in England danced in the streets – they'd all gone through so much together. Now it was over, though there were many who mourned that they no longer had anyone with whom to dance.

Bella's two rooms and the yard saw their share of gaiety and dancing: the boys even got their band together again and played jigs and waltzes and all the songs that were asked for . . .

But joy is an emotion that cannot be held. Normality flowed back: there were houses to rebuild and repair; there were jobs to find. Not every man returning from service life found that his old job was open to him: new hands had been taken on; women had taken men's places in many factories and were doing the work for less pay.

Bella expected that soon her beds would no longer be needed, and she talked this over with the boys. 'Wait and see,' they said. 'There are the single rooms, they are always booked up. Young fellows starting in jobs again are finding staying in those rooms is cheaper than going into digs or living with relatives. As for the beds, there'll always be tramps on the road,' to which Bella had whipped back, 'I don't want tramps, not real tramps. You lot weren't tramps: down-and-outs, yes, but there's a difference. The others do it from choice.'

'Don't worry, Bella,' they said; 'just leave it for a time. As long as you can keep us on, we're satisfied.'

'Oh, lads, I can keep you on. I can promise you that. If it comes to a push we could turn all of next door into single rooms.'

'You're right there, Bella.'

For about six months or so after the war the beds were indeed fully occupied, mostly by single men who could not find any cheaper or better place in which to kip than Bella's, so for a while they were kept busy. When things did begin to slacken off, the men cleared out the large room next door and redecorated it; then set about not only redecorating the latrines and wash-basins but tiling them. By 1947 the business was showing a big drop in those who needed a single night's kip; so it was decided, starting next door, to convert all of the downstairs into double rooms. And in each of these was to be the luxury of a wash-basin.

People had believed that rationing would end, at least by a year after the war had finished, but no, it went on, as did the black market.

And life went on in Bella's Pad according to the same pattern until 1950. Bella was now sixty years old, and feeling her age. Her boys, as she still called them, were in their fifties. Perhaps Joe and Carl were a little younger, and Reenee, she imagined, was about fifty. Bella had never been able to find out her real age when she first came to her. She guessed Reenee had been twenty-nine or thirty. Strangely, her face hadn't seemed to alter, perhaps because of its fine bone formation; but the skin was tighter and paler. But what did worry Bella at times about her dear girl, as she still thought of her, was the habit she now had of sitting for hours staring ahead. Sometimes she would blink rapidly and press her lips tightly together, as one does when trying to remember or recall something. And another thing, too, was worrying: she was eating less. Her body, Bella thought, really looked like a skeleton underneath those clothes. In the winter she'd had to call in Dr Harle again because Reenee's chest was so bad, but although Reenee tolerated him she still did not look at him unless she was forced to.

Dr Harle had not said anything to Bella about his patient seeing a doctor who could deal with her mind, but she knew that Mr Travis must have had a talk with him. It was odd, she thought, that the only man with whom her girl seemed completely relaxed was Carl. At times, she would give her hand to him, or pat his sleeve gently. These were times, Bella noticed, after she herself had scolded Carl when he had been out for longer than the two-hour walk-about, as he called it. Once she had said to him, 'One of these days you'll get done over by the villains. You'll push your nose in so far that they'll see you or guess at it.' And it was at times like this that Reenee seemed to show concern for the small man with the disfigured face . . .

World events, even events in London, did not seem to penetrate the quiet routine and placidity of the life that went on at numbers 10 and 12 The Jingles. That was until 1955, when something took place that altered their lives for good.

It was a simple incident and it happened to Carl. He no longer played his flute in the street, but he continued to keep his eyes open, and once or twice had earned a few pounds from the police. But on that day he wasn't looking around for the smallest detail that might have a bearing on something bigger, because a severe wind was blowing and he had his head bent and his cap pulled down over his brow.

He was walking along a residential street in which there were a few shops, a large public house and a hotel. A number of vehicles lined up along the kerb were delivering goods to different establishments, and he was both surprised and shocked when he found himself tripping face forward over a hatchway, and then, still face forward, sliding down into a cellar, there to hit his head against a barrel, which knocked him into blackness. He came round to a voice saying, 'What the hell's going on here?' and another voice that seemed to come from above, shouting, 'The silly bugger fell over the hatch. Is he out?'

'Aye, I'd say he's out. You don't hit your head on a barrel and say "hello".'

Another voice from somewhere said, 'Give him a drink of beer.' And the answer to this was, 'Don't be a bloody fool, I can't tap a hogshead down here. Go an' get a mug of water – that'll bring him round.'

He was round; he was lying with one side of his face flat on the stone floor, but his legs still seemed to be in the air. Someone took him by the shoulders and pulled him forward, and then, slowly, he opened his eyes and looked along what seemed to be a stone passage lined with barrels and, at the end of it, two men working. One of them yelled, 'What's all the commotion about?'

The answer came, 'This idiot's slipped down the chute. He's out for the count.'

Carl gave no sign that he wasn't out for the count; he had come round, but his eyes were fixed on the two men beyond the barrels, from one of which they were pulling things. He could see only half the barrel and the back of one man, and the things he was pulling from the barrel had wooden handles. But the light from a window caught the gleam from what must have been a metal tube attached to the handle. First one handle, then another came out before a voice above his head bawled, 'Get that bloody lot back! He'll be round in a minute.'

The barrel was pulled out of view and the other man disappeared with it. He now gave a gasp as some cold water drenched his face and head and a voice said, 'That's done it. He's round all right. Sit him up.'

235

They sat him up, but he kept his eyes closed. 'You all right, chum?'

He didn't answer, only put his hand to his head as if it were aching, and it was. The man said, 'What d'you mean by taking a slide down the barrel roll, eh?'

Still with one hand on his head, Carl said, 'I think I've hurt me ankle.'

'Well, let's get you to your feet and see.'

When Carl limped towards the bottom of the chute the man said, 'Can't see much wrong with it. Can't be sprained, else you wouldn't be able to put it down. Well, now you're goin' out the way you come in. Lie on that board and stretch your arms upwards. Bill!' he yelled. 'Give him a hand out.'

Carl did as he was ordered. He lay face down on the slippery board, stretched his hands upwards and found them gripped; then his feet were pushed, and the next minute he was hauled into the street, with one of the men holding him, a man with red hair, saying, 'D'you walk about with your eyes closed?' And then, looking at him closely, he said, 'I know you. You're Pimple Face, the whistle player. Haven't seen you about for ages.'

Carl took a deep breath before he said, 'Lost me wind.'

A bellow came from the cellar: 'Get on with it up there. What d'you think we're waitin' for?'

The man who had been speaking to him gave Carl a slight push and said, 'Well, get on your way and keep your eyes open in future.'

Carl got on his way. He had hurt his ankle but he hurried on until he reached the house where he told Bella of how he had tumbled down into a beer cellar because he hadn't looked where he was going. He made no mention of what he had seen in that cellar. But the next day, although he was still limping, he went out against Bella's protests for his usual walk-about. This time he took a different direction. It was towards a police station; but he didn't go in, he went straight past it, and stood on the kerb about twenty yards away. Presently, a police car drew up outside the station and the policeman who got out happened to glance first one way, then the other down the street before he went in. A few minutes later, as Carl was walking slowly back and about to pass the station door, it opened and out came the policeman as if he had timed Carl's arrival. Carl, looking up at him, said, 'Nice day.'

'It all depends what you're doing,' the policeman answered.

Carl smiled, he even laughed, but as he did so he said, under his breath, 'Number six Boar's Head, very important.' Then he added, 'Aye, it all depends what you're doing. At present I'm limping because I've got a bad ankle.'

'Get along with you!' said the policeman, then got into the car, and Carl got along.

But that evening, after saying he felt like a pint, he went out again and along to the Boar's Head. He sat on a bench near the wall some distance from the counter and sipped at his beer. The bar was full and the men were standing about in groups. He had almost reached the bottom of his mug when a man plumped down beside him. He was holding a pint mug in his hand, and after taking a drink from it he said, 'That's better. What a day! All sixes and sevens. There are days like that, you know, when nothing seems to go right.'

'Yeah, I agree with you.' Carl had to raise his voice above the din of the room as he added, 'I've had one like that meself.' Then he muttered, 'Fell down into a cellar yesterday, wasn't lookin' where I was goin', knocked meself out for a minute or so, and then I saw something interesting.' His voice dropped to a whisper. 'I'd hit a barrel with me head and they thought I was knocked out and went to get water to bring me round.'

His partner interrupted, saying loudly, 'D'you want another?'

'No. No, thanks. I can't see you getting to the counter for the next fifteen minutes or so and I must be off.'

Then he went on, under his breath, 'The Phoenix cellar, unloadin' guns from a barrel, what looked like a beer barrel the same as the rest. The delivery lorry was from the QX Breweries.'

The man sitting next to him took a long drink from his mug, then said, 'Did they spot you?'

'No, I was supposed to be out. They brought me round by throwing water over me. Then they pushed me up and out the way I had dropped in.'

'You're sure of this?' The voice was very low and Carl answered, 'Beer hasn't wooden handles and steel pipes on the end.'

'Sure you won't have another pint?' said the man.

'No thanks; I've got to get back. I hurt me ankle yesterday and it's still givin' me gyp. Be seein' you sometime.'

'Yeah.'

Carl pushed his way through the crowd; then made his way back to The Jingles, knowing as he did so that this time he had unearthed something very worthwhile.

It was about three weeks later when there were reports in most of the papers that the police had caught a gang of arms smugglers, and that a naval patrol boat had stopped a cargo vessel. When it had been searched, the holds had contained what were supposed to be barrels of beer but were full of guns. Twelve men had been arrested. These included the manager of a private brewery and the owner of a hotel and public bar. The police were still looking for four men wanted for questioning in this affair.

Well, well. Carl had preened inwardly; he had really done something at last! What he had seen was gun-running all right.

He said nothing to anyone, but waited anxiously for the trial. They had caught three of the other suspects, who were now being held in custody, but the fourth was still to be found. Previously, two other suspects had had to be released for lack of evidence to hold them.

So important was the case that the result of the trials, three months later, again filled the front pages of the newspapers. Two of the ring-leaders were each given ten years. Of the others, sentences ranged from six to five years.

That night Carl sat on the form at the end of the bar and sipped at his pint. He wasn't a regular at this bar, but he was recognised as dropping in now and again, and the barman would have a word with him.

As usual, it was full, and after a while a man looking for a seat came and sat on the end of the form. He gave a long sigh, and said. 'Another day over; all sixes and sevens.'

To this Carl remarked lightly, 'But there's always a silver lining.'

His companion laughed and said under his breath, 'It could be gold in this case.'

It was a promise, and it warmed Carl and confirmed that he had at last done something big.

After draining his mug, the man said quietly, 'Bob's tea stall Monday, round eleven.'

Then he rose slowly and said. 'Be seeing you.'

Carl went on sipping at his mug of beer, which was only half full. It wasn't so much the money he was pleased about, although he wouldn't turn his nose up at it, it was the appreciation he had heard in the man's voice.

This was Friday night. He'd have the weekend to get over, and it would be a good weekend, a happy weekend. He'd take in a few bottles for the lads then play cards with them.

He left the bar and walked along the street. There were two blocks before he'd have to turn into The Jingles, and these he could walk blindly, even on a black night like this.

He had reached the turning when a car drew up slowly at the pavement, and its lights brought his head up. A man had got out and was now standing in front of him. He couldn't make him out, but he said, 'What is it? What d'you want?'

'Oh, we just want a chat, Mr Spotty Face. You don't remember me, do you?'

The man now pulled him to where the light was shining from inside the car, and Carl, who felt his guts turn into a knot, was looking up into the face of the red-haired man who had pulled him out of the cellar and had recognised him as once playing the whistle on the streets. 'Remember me now?'

Carl could not answer, and the man said, 'Well, it doesn't matter, chum, does it? Because you won't remember very much after this.' Carl found himself heaved up bodily and thrust into the back of the car, which immediately moved off swiftly. Another man was already seated in the car, and he said, 'Hello, chum. Did you enjoy your chat with the disguised copper? We hope you did, because it'll be the last enjoyment you'll ever know,' and immediately Carl felt a blow first to one side of his head, then to the other, and hazily heard a voice saying from somewhere in the distance, which might have been the front seat, 'Leave him be until we get him there.'

And that's all Carl ever remembered.

Bella was angry. She looked at the clock again, then said to Joe, 'It's eleven o'clock. He's never been out as late as this before. Where d'you think he's got to?'

'If I knew, Bella, I'd tell you; and I've told you afore that all he said to me was that he was goin' along for a pint. He'd be only half an hour or so, he said, and I didn't say to him, like I've wanted to many a time when he's been goin' along for that pint, that if he wanted a pint so badly we would get a few bottles in. But, Bella, you know . . . well, you know yourself, he's still doin' that other business.'

'Yes; and that's what I'm frightened of. He'll do it once too often and it'll get him . . . Oh, dear God! Where is he?' She turned to Reenee, who was sitting by the table. There was an

anxious look on her face and she pointed, first at Joe, then to
her eye, and he said, 'I'm pickin' up her meanin', Bella. But
where would we start to look, Reenee?'

'Anywhere,' Bella said irritably now. She did not add, 'He's
likely lying in some back lane,' but she went on, 'Go and wake
the lads and tell them what's happened. Then go to the bar
and ask what time Carl left.'

'Aye, I could do that . . .'

Two hours later the men were in the kitchen. Nobody they
had spoken to had seen Carl. The barman said he did not
know at what time he had left, because the bar had been full
and he hadn't noticed him going.

'Should we phone the police?' said Tony.

'I wouldn't,' said John. 'If anything's happened they'll find
out soon enough; they generally do. In the meantime he might
come staggering in.'

They didn't go to bed until three o'clock and Carl hadn't
come staggering in; and when they all met in the kitchen again
the following morning, Bella said, 'They've got him. God
knows where he is, likely in the river. One thing I feel sure,
we'll never hear from him again. Poor lad. What he's had to
put up with. That face alone has been a drawback to him.
He'd got a mind and could've used it in some business. But
lookin' like that, who would take him on? And he knew it.'

'If he doesn't show up before dinner-time,' Joe said, 'I'm
going to the polis station.'

Joe had no need to go to the police station for at about
eleven o'clock that morning there was a knock on the front
door. When Bella opened it and saw two uniformed police-
men standing there, she put her hands over her eyes and
muttered, 'I knew it. I knew it. Something's happened to him.'

'May we come in, Miss Morgan?' said one.

'Aye. Aye, come in and tell me the worst. Is he dead?'

They didn't answer, but she led them away from the
kitchen, where she knew Reenee would be standing pressed

241

against the wall in the scullery, and into the parlour, and there one of them said, 'I should sit down if I were you, Miss Morgan.'

She sat down, and they sat opposite, and she said, 'Well, go on, for God's sake, and tell me.'

'We've found him, in fact he was dropped outside Wall Street police station at six o'clock this morning, what was left of him, yet he is still alive.'

'Oh, my God! My God! Where is he now?'

'He's in hospital, Miss Morgan,' said the other man. 'They're doing everything possible to keep him alive. The last news we heard was that he was out of the theatre.'

'Was – was he badly battered?'

The first man said, 'I'm afraid so, Miss Morgan. They didn't mean him to survive. He must have a very strong constitution under his frail exterior.'

'May I go and see him?'

'Yes; yes, of course. But he won't be conscious for some hours.'

Her body suddenly stiffening, she said, 'This is because he was workin' for you lot, isn't it? Now, isn't it?'

They both looked away and then one of the men said, 'Yes, I suppose so.'

'You don't suppose so at all, you know so.'

Again the man said, 'Yes, Miss Morgan, you're right. He . . . well, he was a great deal of help, more than that, in bringing those gun-runners to justice. Some of those still around were bound to take their revenge, for we cannot hope we have caught everyone concerned, but we're all very sorry that the little fellow has had to pay for it.'

'Aye,' said Bella, brokenly now, 'and he won't get any medals for it, will he?'

Neither man spoke for a moment. Then one said, 'No. I'm sorry, there's very few medals given out in this business; but I can tell you one thing, he's appreciated up top because, you know, he's one of the few straightforward . . .' he paused '. . . helpers to the force. A lot of them are on both sides: they give so much away and, under that, they can carry on with their own line. Oh, we know all that. But we've always known that the Pimple—' He stopped. 'I'm sorry, but he's been known by that name.'

'His name is Carl.'

'Carl,' repeated the policeman. 'Well, well. Anyway, I can tell you that all of us working on these very dangerous cases have appreciated his help. It's been small at times but always straight, and we were always able to go on that. And now here's one who hopes he . . . well, he lives to know that we appreciate him.'

The other officer spoke now and said, 'If I were you, Miss Morgan, I wouldn't go to the hospital until tomorrow. You see, as I said, he won't be round for hours and then . . . well, I'm afraid he won't be able to speak to you much, if at all.'

'That's if he's still here,' Bella persisted bitterly.

'Well,' said one of them quietly, 'we can only hope, and we're all hoping. Believe that.'

After an awkward silence the two men rose, and she too, and as she let them out she said, 'You didn't tell me which hospital he's at.'

'He's in the Royal, in a side ward. One of our men is sitting with him all the time so that if he does recover he might give us a lead about who attacked him. Whoever they were, I'm sure they never expected him to survive.'

When she closed the door on them she had almost to grope her way to the bottom of the stairs, and there, dropping down on to the last step, she bent forward, picked up her apron, buried her face in it and began to cry as she hadn't done before, even after Andy's death.

She had known Carl before Andy and the others had come on the scene. He had been pitiable in many ways: he had had his looks to contend with, and she was convinced he had been sleeping rough for a long time. She knew that he was sharp-witted; later, she recognised he was wise in many ways and also that he had a brain, that he was intelligent. When she felt the arm go round her she turned and put her head on Reenee's shoulder; and Reenee held her and rocked her gently, and her face, too, was wet. Presently, she pushed Bella away gently; then she brought out the word, 'Dead?'

Bella's throat was so tight she couldn't speak, but she stood up and tugged Reenee to her feet. Then she said haltingly, 'Not . . . yet,' and repeated, 'not . . . yet.'

Reenee now put her joined hands against her breast as if she were praying, and the guttural sound that came from her throat repeated the words, 'Not yet.'

Bella was in her best coat and hat. Joe had on a good suit; he'd even had his hair cut, and his brown shoes were well polished. The police had arranged that they would be met outside the Royal Hospital's main entrance at eleven o'clock this morning and they were now waiting for the taxi to take them there. Willie was in the hall, Reenee was there, too, but standing further back near the kitchen door, and Bella, turning towards her, said in quite a loud voice, as if she were some far distance away, 'Don't worry, love, we won't be long; and if he's awake we'll tell him you're thinking about him.'

'Here's the taxi,' said Willie, as he opened the door. Then, looking at Bella, he said, quietly, 'She'll be all right.' Then even lower, he added, 'Don't expect miracles; he likely won't know you.'

For a moment she stared at him as if in disbelief, then went out into the street, with Joe following her, and they got into the taxi. The driver had not bothered to leave his seat and open the door for them, an action that seemed significant – fares from this end of town wouldn't expect courtesy.

However, his manner changed, just the slightest, when he drew his cab to a stop and was turning to ask for his fare before they let themselves out. To his surprise, a policeman hurried along the pavement towards the taxi, opened the door and gave his hand to the woman. Then, looking at the taxi driver who had now opened his door and was about to get out, the policeman asked, 'What is it?' The man, inspecting the meter, gave him the price, and at this the policeman turned to Joe, saying, 'It's all right, I'll see to it.' Bringing some silver out of his pocket, he picked from it the exact amount and said to the driver, 'You were a bit late in opening the door, weren't you?'

The man glared at him, reached back and banged the door shut, then drove off.

Bella had recognised the policeman as one of the two men who had called at the house yesterday to give her the dreadful news, and she said, 'Thank you. Thank you, Officer.'

Placing a hand gently on her elbow, and with Joe walking at her other side, he guided them to the main door of the hospital.

Although she had lived in London all these years she had never seen the Royal London Hospital and she was awed by its size, but more so by the bustle that was going on all around her as they were led through corridors and past wards until the policeman brought them to a halt. He stopped a nurse, and said, 'We have permission to visit Mr Carl Poze. He is, I understand, in a side ward.'

The nurse looked from him to the little woman and the tall man and she said, 'Oh, yes. Wait a moment, I'll get Sister.'

The sister came and the policeman addressed her, 'Good morning, Sister;' then, motioning to Bella and Joe, he explained, 'These are relatives of Mr Carl Poze and have permission, I understand, to visit him.'

The sister looked at the two visitors before she said, 'Yes; just come this way.'

She led them into a short corridor, but paused before opening the door and, looking at Bella, she said, 'Please don't

245

be distressed by the condition in which you'll find . . . your son?' she enquired.

'Yes, you could say so,' said Bella softly.

'I must ask you, if possible, not to disturb him in any way by . . . well, your reactions. Also I think that ten minutes will be sufficient.' She now opened the door to allow them to pass into the room.

A man was seated at the far side of a bed. Bella had taken only three steps towards it when she found she couldn't move further. Joe's arm came about her, and with the sister's help, he placed her in a chair.

She sat staring at the thing in the bed. At first, all her blurred gaze could make of it was that it was attached to wires and tubes, all joined to the head and face and neck. The little of the face she could see was just a slit that might have been the mouth, and if there was a body it was lying under a cage, with the exception of the arms. Yet here again there was no flesh visible, because right down to the wrists they were bandaged, and from there the hands lay in what looked like bags.

There was a whirling in her mind. The sister had said only ten minutes: that was a long, long time ago; something was happening to her . . .

For the first time in her life, Bella had fainted.

She knew she was dragging herself up out of some terrible blackness. She had never felt like this in her life before. What was the matter with her? Where was she?

She opened her eyes and gasped for breath, and a voice said, 'That's it. Take deep breaths. That's it, deep breaths. You'll feel all right in a moment. I'm sure you'd like a cup of tea.' It was a nice voice, soothing. She felt relaxed. She didn't know why she was here. What had happened to her? Then slowly, slowly, there came into her mind the picture of the thing she had seen lying in the bed, and she wanted to cry out against it. But the soothing voice was going on: 'Ah, here comes a cup of tea. Now will you sit up? That's it. Open your eyes. There, that's better, isn't it? I'll put this cushion behind your head. Now sip this tea; you'll feel better. That's it, open your eyes.'

She opened her eyes and looked up into a bright round face, a young face, and what she said to it was, 'Joe?' and Joe's voice came to her from the foot of the couch or whatever she was lying on, and he said, 'It's all right, Bella. It's all right. I could've passed out meself. I could that.'

She looked up again at the bright face. She had to put her head well back, for the nurse was standing, and she said, 'Is . . . is he gone?'

'No, no. Don't worry. The doctor's just finishing on the ward; he's going to come in and have a word with you. Now, just finish this tea,' she said, placing the cup on a small table to Bella's side.

'Thank you.'

'Rest there now; I'll be back in a moment.'

'Joe.'

Joe went to her and knelt down by her side. He took her hand, and said, 'They say he's holding his own. Try not to worry.'

'But, Joe . . . did you see him? There . . . there must be nothing left of him.'

Joe did not answer for almost a minute. Then he said, 'He's tough inside, is Carl, and he's got pluck. I always knew he had much more pluck than me. Me, I was all brawn and mouth, but Carl, well, he had brains – and pluck.'

For a moment she forgot the picture in her mind as she patted his hand and said, 'You've always been a good man, Joe, always. You were like two brothers together, and he was very fond of you. Very. He – he once told me that you were the best mate anybody could have.'

'He did, Bella?'

'Yes. Yes, he did, Joe, and that's the truth.'

When the door opened, Joe pulled himself to his feet and

looked to where a young man in a white coat, accompanied by the sister, was coming towards them.

'This is Dr—' Bella did not catch the name, it sounded foreign, but the sister went on, 'He is seeing to your son, Mrs Morgan.' She now pulled a chair forward and the young man sat down on it. Leaning towards Bella, he said, 'How are you feeling now?'

'I – I couldn't really tell you, Doctor. It was the shock.'

'Of course. Of course.'

'Will . . . will he live, Doctor?'

The young man did not answer for a moment; and then he said, 'If we can possibly make him, he will live. If he gets over the next three or four days then we'll be able to say he's going to be all right.'

'He must've been in a dreadful state.'

Again there was a pause before the young man said, 'He was, Mrs Morgan, in a dreadful state. Whoever did this to him didn't intend him to live. Even if for nothing else, I would hope that he does survive to give us some idea of the culprit or culprits whose intention was to murder him. Perhaps you noticed that there was a policeman sitting by his bedside. They, too, are hoping, even willing him to live so that justice can be done. Anyway,' he patted Bella's hand, 'rest assured everything that possibly can be done medically will be done.'

As he went to rise from the chair Bella caught at his hand and said, 'How – how long will it be before . . . well, before he will know anybody?'

'That's hard for me to tell you at the moment, Mrs Morgan, but give us a week and then I'm sure we shall know much more. And may I suggest, for your own good as well as the patient's, that you don't come to see him for, say, another three or four days? Will you agree to that?'

She stared up at him. 'Yes,' she said flatly.

As if to lighten her anxiety, he said, 'But you can phone every day and Sister will tell you how he is. All right?'

She nodded and he said, 'Goodbye, then, Mrs Morgan.' He inclined his head towards Joe, then went out with the sister.

Bella sat up on the side of the sofa and realised she was in a rest room. 'Let's go home, Joe,' she said.

Quickly, he replied, 'Stay there a minute while I go and see if the polis is still there, 'cos we'll never find our way out of this place on our own.'

The policeman was still there, and he got them home; and now, her hand in Reenee's, Bella was sitting facing her four boys and listening while Joe related to them what they had found in the ward and how Bella couldn't stand it and had passed out; and he gave them word for word what the doctor had said about Carl, finishing with, 'There's nothing for us now but waitin'.'

At this point Willie put in, 'Aye, and prayin'. I've never prayed in me life that I can remember, not even from a bairn, but I'll do it now.'

John added his voice. 'I won't do any prayin'; I can only hope that the police catch those buggers before one of us get wind of who did it, because what they've done to him would be nothin' to what we'd do to them. I can promise you that,' then turned and went down the stone steps to the room below.

Without further words, the other two followed him, and Bella was left with Joe and Reenee. She whimpered, 'It was awful. Awful, the sight of him. He wasn't there; it was a mummy of some kind, all wired up.'

'Don't distress her, Bella. Don't distress her.'

'I'm not! I'm just tellin' her. The only good thing about it, he's under a very good doctor. He's a nice fellow, young, and he said I can phone every day, but . . . but we haven't got to go yet.'

Bella phoned every day for a fortnight. The first week the sister's replies were mostly the same, kindly but firm: there was little change; she would be advised not to visit for a while. At the end of the week a different voice came on the phone and a nurse said, 'Oh, I think he's turned the corner. Anyway, they're taking him down again to theatre this afternoon, so he must have.'

Bella had repeated, 'Theatre! Another operation?'

'Oh, yes. But they wouldn't be giving it to him if he wasn't fit to have it, you see, so it's good news in a way. Don't worry.' She rang off.

Such were the answers, too, during the following days. The sister must have been absent, for different nurses answered Bella's calls and they all said yes, definitely he was holding his own; and they had great hopes for him, and perhaps, yes, they would tell her tomorrow when she could come and see him again.

Carl came to himself gradually. He knew he had no body, but he could move a few fingers on his right hand; but then they stiffened. All he had left was a head, and it ached. Sometimes it ached so badly that they would stick another needle into him. He welcomed the jabs, because they took him away from everything and into a warm blackness where there was nothing. But one morning he woke up to see a face looking at him. It wasn't a nurse's face, this face he didn't know, but he knew the voice and what it was saying, because it was saying, 'You're feeling better this morning, not all sixes and sevens.'

Sixes and sevens. He was sitting once again on the bar bench and a man was saying, 'Oh, it's been a day. All sixes and sevens.' And whenever the man said that Carl would give him a message. What kind of a message? The man's voice came to him again, saying, 'You won't remember me, because I don't look as I did when we talked in the bar.'

He could see only out of one eye, for the other was bandaged, and he fixed it on the face. This was a thin face,

250

sharp. The chin was pointed. He always noticed people's features. He could see that the man was smiling at him, and the voice said, 'If I told you I had thick tidy brown hair, a moustache and plump jaws, and I talked with a Cockney accent, saying, "It's been a day, all sixes and sevens", would you recognise me? A wig and some gum shields and an imitation 'tache can change a man.'

The man in the bar, the police bloke.

His voice was soft. 'I'm sorry about what happened to you. Sorry to the heart, chum. You did a good job but, my God, you've had to pay for it! And I'm still looking for them; but, believe me, I'm grateful for what you did. That's a poor way of saying thank you, but if, in the future, there's ever anything I can do, you've just got to say, "What a day it's been! All sixes and sevens,"' and he laughed, still softly, then said, 'We were wonderin' if you could remember anything that happened before the attack.'

Carl thought . . . Before the attack. Before they murdered him. He knew they had been going to murder him. Oh, yes; yes. It was the ginger-haired fellow, the one who had pulled him out of the brewery. He didn't know the other two with him, but his face he'd never forget. It was the last thing he remembered. Carl's eye turned towards the man and he muttered, 'Ginger-haired.'

'He was ginger-haired?'

'Yes.'

'Sure?'

'Yes . . . and . . .'

'Yes? Can you remember anything more about him?'

Could he remember anything more about him? The teeth? Oh, yes, the teeth, because that day he himself had had the toothache, which was why he was walking with his head down and his hand across his mouth. And that's also why he saw the tooth like a tusk. When the man said he had remembered him playing the whistle, he had grinned, and there, at

251

the side, yes . . . yes, he had seen what he had thought looked like a little tusk. It must have been two teeth growing together. Two growing out of the one place. He remembered thinking it was a good job the point went straight down else it would have ripped his lip. Yes. 'The tooth.'

'The tooth? Something about his teeth?'

'Yes. This side.' He was trying to lift his hand up to his face, but found it too difficult. Then he said, 'Right side . . . No, left side. Two teeth, one—' He paused for breath and the man said, 'Take your time, don't hurry. Just try to remember,' and his voice sounded excited.

'Well . . . two from, like, one root. One half over the top of other, like – like a fang.'

'Oh, Carl. You're a marvel! You really are a marvel. I must tell you, straight away, I've got them. I know where he is, and where I get him I'll get his mates. I've got him. Red hair and a crooked tooth. God!' He put his hand on the bandaged arm and said, 'You're a wonderful fellow, so observant. You should've never been in the position you are. I must go now, but you'll see me again, and many others of my lot, I promise you. And I promise you this also, if I can do anything about it, he'll get life.'

The detective hurried from the room and almost bumped into the doctor, who said, 'My, you're in a hurry! What is it?'

'You wouldn't believe, Doctor! He's just given me a piece of most vital information. He's actually given me the features of the man who intended to murder him, and I know exactly who this fellow is. We've grilled him for four days, but he got out of it – supposed to be in the house with a cold or something, never near the brewery. And he was backed up by his mates.'

'And you know where he is?'

'Oh, yes! We can put a finger straight on him.' He leant towards the doctor. 'He thinks he's safe, lying low, he's assisting in a brothel.'

The doctor laughed gently now and said, 'How exciting for him.'

'Yeah. And there's more excitement to come. I'll keep you in touch, Doctor. Well, anyway, it'll make headlines shortly, if I've got anything to do with it.' He jerked his head back towards the door. 'That poor fellow in there. He should've been in the police force, in the special end. He's got an eye for small details, and it's small details that can move mountains. Well, be seein' you, Doctor.'

'Be seeing you,' and smiling now, the doctor went into the room, saying to the nurse, 'There goes a happy man.'

He turned to the figure on the bed.

'Good morning, Mr Poze. Oh, you're looking a bit brighter. How are you feeling?'

'I still don't know, Doctor.'

'Of course not. But you are improving, and as you know, you're for another ride down the long corridor this afternoon. We're going to see to that nose of yours; you won't recognise yourself when they're finished with it. And also, as I said yesterday, we'll be dealing with some of those marks on your face. It could've been done years ago if you'd only come to the hospital.'

'Too old, Doctor.'

'Nonsense! How old are you?' He turned to the nurse. 'How old is he, Nurse?'

Before the nurse could say anything, Carl said, 'Kickin' sixty.'

'Oh, what's sixty? By the way, what is your Christian name, Mr Poze?'

'Carl, sir.'

'Oh, that's a nice name. Well, our acquaintance has been very close of late so I don't see why you shouldn't be Carl.' The doctor straightened up. 'Is there anything you need, Carl, I mean anything you fancy? You've got to eat, y'know.'

Carl attempted to shake his head. Then his eye turned

towards the table, banked with flowers, near the wall at the foot of the bed and he said, 'Who sent those?'

'Oh, well, I've seen your mother bring some in.' He knew now that Mrs Morgan was really Miss Morgan and that this poor fellow here was not her son. Yet presumably she had cared for him for years and thought of him as her son. But his name was Poze, foreign in a way. He turned to the nurse, saying, 'Who else were the flowers from?'

The nurse went to the table and said, 'Someone called Reenee, and this other one, the last visitor brought yesterday, and there are just two initials on them. Well, they're not initials, they're numbers, a six and a seven.'

The doctor said, 'Do you know what those numbers stand for, Carl?'

And Carl said simply, 'Yes, I know who they're from. It's very kind of him.'

The nurse said, 'There's another bunch with a card on. "From the lads. Come home soon."'

Carl closed his one eye. Come home soon, they said. Would he ever be able to walk? As it was, he still felt that he hadn't any body left on him; he was numb from the neck downwards. Perhaps he was paralysed. He didn't know and was afraid to ask.

The voice above him was saying quietly, 'That's it, rest. I'll see you this afternoon. Don't worry, you're going to be fine.'

The young doctor left the room and walked briskly along the corridor; but at the end he was stopped by the little woman, Miss Morgan . . . She was looking quite happy at the moment, so different from when he had first made her acquaintance. She must indeed love that fellow very much, son or no son. It was a strange world. 'Good morning, Miss Morgan,' he said. 'On your way once again? You'll find him much better this morning.'

'Oh, thank you, Doctor. Thank you.' Her hand went out now and caught at his wrist. Looking up into his face, she said, 'I'll never forget you as long as I live and what you've done for him, and what you're doing for his poor face.'

'Oh, the credit is not due to me, Miss Morgan, I can assure you. Professor Baker is the plastic surgeon, I just assist him.' He leant towards her now, saying, 'I've not yet reached the eminence of being a consultant. I have nearly two more years to go as a registrar.'

Quite slowly she brought out his name, but in two syllables, 'Bain-dor. It's a difficult name to remember and, I must tell you, I've made a mess of it a number of times.'

He was laughing now. 'You're not the only one, Miss Morgan, and it's clever of you to pronounce it so accurately, because it is sometimes Baindoing, or I have even known it to be Barndoor.' She laughed and Joe did too. 'But, then, what's in a name? Nothing, really.'

'There's something in yours, Doctor. As I said, I'll never forget it, or what you have done for my lad.'

'Well, go along now and see your lad. You will find him much brighter. He's even asked about the flowers on the table.'

'He has?' Bella was surprised.

'Yes.'

'Eeh! Well, that shows he can think.'

'Oh, yes, of course he can think. Whatever those brutes did to him they didn't manage to knock his brains out. He has still got those.'

'Thank God for that, and you.'

He waved at her and walked quickly away, and she, turning to Joe, moved on along the corridor, saying to him, 'Isn't he a lovely man?'

'None better,' Joe said; 'and I understand from one of the porters he's from the top drawer. His father's a millionaire and they live in a mansion.'

'No!'

'Aye; one of them told me yesterday when I spoke about

255

him. He said he was well liked, not like some out of the top drawer, who think they're God Almighty because they have the tag of doctor on them and hold their noses in the air. Not him. It was rumoured, the porter said, he had to fight his father to take up this career. But he still lives in the mansion.'

'Well I never!' said Bella. 'And he talks so ordinary. Well, I mean not ordinary but kindly.'

'Aye; well, he's a gentleman.'

14

It was the same evening, and John, Tony and Willie had come upstairs to find out the latest news from the hospital. Bella regaled them with the incidents of her visit. First, of Carl's apparent improvement and of how plain now were the few words he could utter; and of how interested he was in the flowers. And, lastly, of their meeting with the doctor in the corridor. She laughed as she said, 'He was . . . he was so nice, so lovely, and I think he was pleased that I got his name right. It's a very funny name and everybody seems to get it wrong. He said some people called him Barndoor. Did you ever hear anything like it?'

'What is his real name?' put in John.

'Well, it sounds foreign, but it is pronounced Bain-dor. I suppose when you say it quickly it could sound like Barndoor,' and as she repeated the name she turned to include Reenee in the laughter, only for her face to change quickly as she got to her feet, saying, 'No, no, lass! No!' because Reenee's body had stiffened. It wasn't jerking, as it usually did, it was just stiff. She seemed to have no middle; her head rested against the back of the chair and her heels were stuck in the rug on the floor, and from her heels to her head she was stiff.

257

With Willie now to one side of her and Bella to the other, they endeavoured to break the rigidity by forcing her to sit up again; but she remained as she was. Then slowly her right hand moved up to her head and her mouth opened to emit a guttural sound; then she brought out a word. They couldn't understand what it was, but John immediately suggested, 'She's been struck again by something that was said. Perhaps it was the name of the doctor or something.'

'How could it be?' snapped Bella. 'It was only his name.'

'Well, that could've done it,' said Tony.

'Done what?' demanded Bella.

'Stirred her memory. It's things like that that do.'

'Oh, my God!'

'She's comin' round,' said Willie. 'Lift her back in the chair.'

They eased her back; but she didn't open her eyes, she just sat there, her body limp now but her hand still to her head.

'I'll have to get her upstairs to bed,' said Bella; 'that's where she should've been long before now 'cos she coughed her heart out all last night. I'll have to get the doctor to see to that chest of hers again. And, what's more, she's not eating. Oh, there's always something! I thought things were goin' too smoothly. Help me to the bottom of the stairs with her, Willie. I'll manage after that.'

Reenee did not need much helping upstairs. She walked, each step slow and deliberate, and in the bedroom she went straight to the bed and lay down on top of the eiderdown. Bella said, 'Aren't you goin' to take your things off, lass?' And when there was no reply, she said soothingly, 'All right, then. All right. I'll just take your shoes off and cover you up, then perhaps you'll get to sleep and feel better in the mornin'.'

She lit a night-light, then turned off the electric table lamp and went quietly downstairs.

The men were still there, and it was John who said, 'That doctor's name is an odd one. I've never heard a name like that before, and nobody's ever spoken such a name in this house, have they?'

He was looking at Bella, who flopped down into a chair as she said, 'But he's a doctor, and he must be thirty if a day. And she's been with me . . . well, how long? It must be all of twenty-six years. I don't know how long she was roaming before that.'

It was Willie who asked now, 'And she had no sign of identification on her clothes, Bella? Not on her underwear or anything?'

'No. It's worn to ribbons now with her wearin' it, like that coat, but it was of very high quality at one time. All her underwear was silk. She used to have a little bag; it was pinned to her knickers.'

She thought of that little bag. She had seen inside it the time the doctor had come and given her that dose that had knocked her out, and all there was in it was a cheap-looking necklace affair, like a chain dog collar, and on the end of it there hung three red balls. It was like something you would buy in the market. There was a flat case, too. She didn't know whether it was brass or gold, and no matter how she had tried to open it she couldn't. She had gone round the sides of it and pressed it as if it might have a spring. She had even inserted one of her nails between the two pieces of metal, but could make no impression. She stopped at using a knife because perhaps it wouldn't close again, and then the lass would be upset and know that she had been messing about with her things. So she had put them back in the bag.

'It's a long time since she had a turn, isn't it, Bella?' said Willie.

'Oh, yes; and ages ago since she walked out.'

That had been another scary time, Bella thought. It was the day after she had said to her, 'D'you know how long we've been together, lass? Nearly seventeen years.' The next morning she was gone, dark coat, funny hat and all. Bella had

259

nearly gone round the bend again, and once more it had been Carl who had warned her that Reenee was on her way back; and she hadn't been gone an hour. She had asked him if he knew whether she had been to the pawn shop. He had said he didn't know; he had just seen her turning the corner on her way back up the street. And yet, that was an odd thing, she recalled now. She'd had to call the doctor in to her because her chest had gone very bad again, and she had looked in the bag, and that cheap-looking chain had gone; as also had the case that she had been unable to open. But in its place there was a piece of brown paper folded neatly; and when she opened it there were four pawn tickets and a faded piece of cardboard. She remembered she couldn't quite make out the figure on the cardboard. She thought it might have been that of a little boy; then again, no. It was as if it had been torn off a postcard with a picture on it, but the years had dimmed the colours and it had seemingly been wet, so it had a smudgy look. But that was all that was in the bag, and it had been wrapped in this square of brown paper. She had wondered about it for a long time. She must have gone to the pawn shop again and pawned those things. They must've been of some value else they wouldn't have taken them. But she didn't come back with any money this time. Nothing at all. So why had she pawned them? Bella remembered Reenee had taken off her hat and changed her shoes, then rolled up her coat sleeves and gone downstairs to the kitchen and got on with her work as if nothing had happened. She had been a puzzle, that girl. She had been the light of Bella's life, but at the same time she had been a worry, and now here she was going off her head again because of the mention of a name, Baindor. Why should a name like that affect her? Oh, dear me, she'd have to keep a close watch on Reenee else she'd go off on her wanderings again. In her mind she must be looking for somebody.

She wished Joe was back. He had gone out to get himself a pair of shoes.

In her mind Irene was looking for somebody connected with that name of Baindor. Baindor. Was it her own name? Yes; yes, it must be her name. It *was* her name. She was Mrs Baindor. And there was a child. Oh, yes; there was a child.

She turned over in bed, grabbed a pillow, hugged it to her and rocked herself as she said, a child, a child, a birthday . . . Richard.

The name filled the room, it filled the world. Richard. Richard. The echo was like bells ringing. Dozens and dozens of church bells. They became a din. She dropped the pillow and put her hands to her head, covering her ears. Richard, he was a child. He was four. Yes. She knew he was four. Where was he?

There came a great rush of feeling in her, and she could hear a voice saying, 'It's all right, dear. It's all right. We are going away, far, far away, on a boat. No one must know.' He would kill her. He would kill her. Who? Who would kill her? She was staring into the blackness . . . the blackness of her mind where a face was forming, a large face, a terrible face; and then it was staring down into hers, and she was crying out against it. Then her body stiffened and she could hear herself shouting, 'No! No! No more! Not that! I won't! I won't!' Her body was paining all over; and she became stiff. That was until the great hands were on her stomach and were on her back, pushing her up and down, up and down, the voice crying at her, screaming at her just one word: 'Respond! Respond!' Then her body was lifted and thrown about, and she screamed again, 'Not that! Please!'

There were arms about her and a different voice was saying, 'There, lass. There, lass. You're dreaming. Come on. It's a nightmare.'

She fell against the body, then she clung to it, and her shaking was making the body shake; but she gripped it tight because she knew it would save her.

261

'There now. Just look at the sight of the bed. And that chest of yours. You'll have to see the doctor again. Come on! Let me take your coat off.'

'No, no!' The words came hoarsely from Irene's throat. She must never take her coat off. He must never get at her body. No man must get at her body, ever, ever, ever. Timothy.

Timothy. Who was Timothy? She opened her eyes, then murmured, 'Oh, Bella!'

'Yes, love; it's me. You're quite safe. Now, be a good lass and let me take your coat off; just your coat, that's all; and I'll get you a hot drink, and give you one of your tablets to ease that chest . . . That's a good girl. I'll hang it up.'

Bella took the worn threadbare coat to the wardrobe and hung it up, shaking her head as she did so. All this because she had used the name of that doctor. It had done something. It had hit Reenee's mind – her other mind – and she had recalled something. Oh, she hoped it would stop there.

She settled Reenee down and covered her up, saying, 'Lie quiet now; I'll be back in a minute.'

Reenee lay quiet, and her mind was repeating, Bella. Bella. She loved Bella. But there was a name that had come back. Timothy. Who was Timothy? Slowly the sound of the name seemed to soften her. For an instant, she felt warm inside; the name was acting like a balm on her troubled thinking.

It would come back, she told herself. Oh, yes, it would come back, because he wasn't in the nightmare. No, that man, that dreadful, dreadful man; she didn't want *him* to come back, not into her mind. Oh, she didn't want to see that man again. He was cruel, dreadful. Oh, she hated him. Why? Who was he, the one who brought the blow on to her head and knocked her into darkness, into another world, into another life? And her child had gone. Yes, her child had gone. But now he was back. Bella. Bella had brought him back. Baindor. Baindor. That was her name. That was her child's name. But he was not a child, not any more. Bella said he was a doctor.

How long ago was it since she had held him and rocked him, the child? Weeks, months, years, aeons of time. Words were coming into her head that hadn't been there before.

'Is your head still aching, dear? Take your hands down. Now drink this cocoa and take this pill. It'll ease your chest, and you'll have to see the doctor again. Now lie down and go to sleep; everything will be different in the morning. Don't worry; your coat's in the wardrobe.'

She lay quietly. The door had closed; the night-light was glowing softly in the room and her coat was in the wardrobe. Her shield was in the wardrobe. She couldn't live without her coat; they would get at her if she wasn't covered up. Men with hands that clawed at you. His hands had clawed at her all over. Oh, what his hands had done. Whose hands? The hands of the face. The hands of that awful face. She was tired. Bella said it would be all right in the morning. She would think a lot better in the morning. She knew she would.

She woke at dawn. It was as if she had spent the hours of sleep in a life that must have been hers at one time. She got up and went to the wash-stand and, pouring some ice cold water into a basin, she washed her face and hands. She got into her velvet dress, then put on her coat and what was left of her hat, pushing the bundle of her greying hair into the net at the back of her head. Amazingly, the net was about the only part of the hat still intact. Then she took the money-box from the mantelpiece and, turning it upside down, she twisted the lever at the bottom until there was a gap, and a shower of half-crowns fell into her lap. These she dropped into the inside pocket of her coat, then replaced the box on the little mantel-piece.

She went down the stairs as softly as a cat and let herself out of the front door, but once the cold morning air hit her she began to cough, and so, her hand tightly over her mouth, she hurried away down the street into the lightening day . . .

263

How long it took her to reach the hospital she didn't know, she had twice lost her way; once she actually stopped and, opening her mouth, she forced herself to speak to a woman, saying, 'Royal Lon-don hos-pital.' And the woman, obviously puzzled by the weird-looking creature, pointed, saying, 'Along the main road there. Then two streets . . . no, three. Somebody will show you the way after that, but keep to the main road here.'

Irene nodded her thanks, then walked on.

However, when she reached the hospital she was neither amazed nor distressed by the bustle of people around her – she seemed to have been here before – but a number of times she was pushed aside or jumped at the sound of an ambulance or a car horn, before a porter who was helping someone into a car banged the door closed and, in standing back, nearly fell over her.

He was about to say, 'I'm sorry, miss,' when he stopped and surveyed her. She was coughing desperately and he said now, kindly, 'You want the Outpatients?'

She did not answer him, but he said, 'Well, come along this way.'

He led her to a door and into a kind of hallway, and at the reception desk he said, 'She's wandering about; I think she's looking for Outpatients. She's got a bark on her like a dog.'

Exhausted, Irene leant on her forearms on the desk and brought out the word, 'Doc-tor Bain-dor.'

At the desk two girls were attending to phones that seemed never to stop ringing, and the receptionist said to her, 'Dr Baindor?' Then she said, 'You want Outpatients.'

At this Irene shook her head and repeated, 'Bain-dor.'

The girl stared at the weirdly dressed individual: she was definitely a vagrant of some sort, but she wanted Dr Baindor.

She pressed a button at the side of her desk, and to the woman who came to the counter she said, 'This one wants Dr Baindor; she doesn't want Outpatients.'

The newcomer leant forward on the desk and surveyed the dirty-coated, weird-hatted individual. She looked at the deathly white face, and then Irene again put her head back and brought out the word, 'Baindor.'

'Get ward six,' the woman said; 'and find if he's on duty.'

Irene stood waiting. She heard the receptionist speaking on the phone and she heard part of what she said; one of the words was 'weird' another was 'insists'. Then the woman was nodding into the phone; and after she had put it down she came to the desk and said, 'Dr Baindor has gone off duty for the weekend; he won't be back until Monday.'

Irene looked at her for a long time, then slowly she turned, tottered out of the hall and made for the entrance. Outside, she was confused. There were so many cars, so many ambulances, so many people. She walked down a side-road, but before she reached the end of it she knew that she was going to fall. She looked about her: by the kerb was a large wooden box, as if someone had just delivered it or put it there to be picked up. She dropped on to it and sat with her head bowed and her hands in her lap. What was she to do? She couldn't wait here until Monday and she couldn't walk back to Bella's; she didn't know the way. But she had money, she could get a taxi.

At the sound of laughter, her head lifted. Three men had turned the corner into this side-road and were coming towards her; and at the sight of them her whole body seemed to leap into the air: the man in the middle, yes, the man in the middle, that was Richard! He looked like her father; he had her father's features and his mouth. This she had always said and been so proud that it was so.

She wasn't aware of jumping up and of approaching the men, or that they had stopped and one was saying, 'What now? Look at this!'

What she did, and to all their surprise, was grip the wrist of the man in the middle, who, now more surprised than

265

the rest, said, 'What is it? You want Outpatients?'

She stared into his face. It was Richard. He was just like her father.

A man to the side of her said under his breath, 'She's a nut. She's begging.'

She turned towards the man, and such was the look she gave him that he stepped back; and now opening her mouth wide, she brought out, 'Rich.'

'What did I tell you?' said the man. 'She's begging. She says you're rich; she's heard about you.'

'Shut up!' said the man in the middle.

But the man on the other side had put his hand in his pocket and was handing her a shilling. She looked at it, then slapped the back of his hand so hard that the coin went spurting into the air, bounced on the ground and rolled into the gutter.

The man in the middle said, 'She's . . . she's not after money. She's in trouble of some sort. Sit down,' he said, and, his wrist still held tight, he led her back to the box. As she started to cough again he said, 'Oh, my goodness! You must get to Outpatients. They'll see to you there.'

She shook her head, and the talkative man now put in, 'It's you she's after. You do this to the women.'

'Shut up, Alex! For God's sake, shut up!'

This was Richard; he looked like her father. Her father was never handsome like him but the features were the same.

The young man now loosened her fingers from his wrist, saying, 'I've got to go. I've got a car waiting, but my friend here' – he now pointed to the other man – 'my friend here will take you to Outpatients.'

He backed away from her; then, turning to the man called Alex, he said, 'See to her, will you, Alex? That chest is bad, very bad.'

Alex. Help. Alex helped. He helped her father. Alexander? Yes, Alexander. For the moment she saw the dreadful face hovering over her; then in its place came another, a nice face.

Alexander. Armstrong. Her head went back and she said the word aloud, 'Armstrong.'

The kindly man said, 'You want to see Mr Armstrong?'

She shook her head. Then in a flash it came to her, Alexander Armstrong. He was a solicitor. He came to the house, the great house. Alexander Armstrong the solicitor. Beverley Square. She had been to Beverley Square. The young man bent over now and said, 'Come along, my dear. Come along; you can't sit here all day. And that box will soon have to be moved.'

She looked up at him and said one word, 'Taxi.'

'Taxi?'

She nodded, then put her hand inside her coat and brought out some silver and showed it on the palm of her hand.

'Oh, I see what you mean, my dear, you can pay for a taxi. Do you know where you want to go?'

She put her head back, then tried to bring out Beverley but couldn't. Suddenly he said, 'Could you write it?'

She nodded, and he brought from his inner pocket a small book with a pencil. It was an address book, and turning to a plain page, he said, 'There. Write it there.' And so, in large letters that almost covered the small sheet, she wrote 'Beverley Square. Armstrong, Solicitor.'

After reading it he did not say anything for a moment; then he repeated to her, 'You want to go to Beverley Square and a solicitor there called Armstrong?' She bowed her head deeply, and he said, 'Come along. I'll get you a taxi.'

When he stopped a taxi, he opened the back door, then said to the cabby, 'This lady wants to be dropped at Beverley Square near the office of a solicitor called Armstrong. Will you do that?'

The cabby looked from him back to his passenger, and he muttered, 'That's what I'm here for, sir.'

'She has enough money to pay you, so don't worry.'

About ten minutes later the taxi entered the square and

cruised slowly, until it stopped opposite a flight of steps at the top of which was a large brass plate with, imprinted on it, Alexander Armstrong and Son, Solicitors.

He got out and opened the door for her, and again from her pocket she brought a palm full of half-crowns. Being a moderate man, he took only what was his due, one half-crown, and when she nodded to him, he said, 'Thank you, ma'am,' and watched her stagger up the steps and into the remainder of her life.

PART THREE

1955

1

⚜

She lay, as it were, between two worlds. One in which soft voices spoke to her as they dripped food into her mouth and washed her body. That was a nice feeling. Why had she ever been afraid of her body? But had she been afraid of it? Oh, yes; she had in that other world that kept coming and going. She was still afraid of her body, and of hands going over it. Nails digging into her. Leather straps striking her. But these hands were as soft as the words that were spoken. The voices talked above her head as if she couldn't comprehend. She could, though; she had always been able to comprehend, hadn't she, even in the other world? She mustn't try to bring back that world because in this present one were Mr Armstrong and Glenda. Oh, yes, Glenda. Glenda had put her on the train, but she hadn't told her about the other world. And her son. Her son was coming. Glenda had promised her that. And he was grown-up. He was more than four. She closed her eyes tightly. Of course he is, she said to herself, in a very strange voice that seemed to come from the past. Don't be silly. He is a doctor. You've held his hand. But Alex has promised to bring him back and we will have dinner together.

Will Mrs Atkins be there to serve it? Mr and Mrs Atkins knew a lot of what was going on, and she was so kind, she wasn't like an ordinary housekeeper. And Trip knew too. Oh, he knew what was going on. He hadn't been a butler to father and son for nothing. He and Mrs Atkins talked. They talked about her, but kindly. They knew what she was going through, especially Trip. He was the only one who slept in the main house, and he must have heard her at night.

There it was again, the face! Oh, no! She didn't want to see it. She was in this soft, soft bed. They were washing her body, or they had washed her body. Yes, they had and she was resting. But why? Why had he to come again? He was haunting her. She heard her voice yelling, yelling, 'Don't! Don't! You filthy swine! I am not an animal. I hate you! I hate you!' Then the lifting up and the throwing of her body here and there. And now she was in that last night when she knew it was the end. She had planned to escape and she was going to escape or she would die under his hands. And he was shaking her as she yelled at him, 'You are worse than any animal. You are a filthy pervert!' Yes, she had yelled at him; and that was when he shook her until her brains seemed to rattle in her head. She could feel them, and his voice must have vibrated through the house when he said, 'Don't you ever dare speak again.' Then there was more shaking, and, his voice deeper, louder, more terrible, now screaming, 'Don't you ever dare open your mouth again!'

She couldn't remember how those words finished, only that they put a stamp on her mind. She must never speak again. Never, never, never. He had screamed that at her, and he had beaten her body back and forward on to the bed, his great hands lifting her shoulders, then throwing her back; and then he had done what he usually did, and she could fight no more.

But there was one hope. The escape was planned. Mr Cox, dear Mr Cox, whom that devil had sacked just because he played the piano for her. Cox had taken the money, more than a thousand pounds. She had saved this over the years, not spending her lavish allowance, and now he had booked a passage on a liner and she and Richard were going to America where Timothy was. Timothy was her very dear childhood friend. He was married, oh, yes, but that wouldn't matter. He would hide her somewhere, because her husband would have her followed. But it was all arranged. She only wished she could tell dear Alex. But Trip knew, at least she thought Trip knew. But Freda McArthur could be trusted because she, too, knew what went on at night and how she suffered, because she had helped to bathe her on many a morning, when the tears had run down her face. And she would have helped her anyway, because Freda was in love with Mr Cox and, she knew, she was going to leave soon and they were to be married. It was all planned. They were just waiting for his next trip abroad, and it had come. She had been so full of joy that she wanted to please Alex and sing at his concert. And how she had enjoyed that. Oh, it was in defiance, because he would never let her sing; never mind stand on a platform. The beast, the horrible filthy beast of a man. And then she hadn't time to think about the plan of going to America to see Timothy, because there he was and she was in his arms, and then the world broke up: there was nothing but screams and blows and terror and the voice yelling again, 'Don't you dare speak!' She had tried to explain the surprise visit but the voice had bawled her down. Then a great weight had come on her head and she had fallen into another world; and there she had remained until now.

And the old world was on her again and she screamed out, 'I hate you! I loathe you! You dirty, dirty . . .'

She knew her voice had trailed away.

The prick in her arm brought her back into the softness of the bed, and there were voices all around her, some saying, 'Dreadful. Poor creature.' Who were they talking about? It didn't matter, she was going to sleep.

2

'I can't do this on my own, Father. I just can't. You'll have to talk to him.'

Alexander sighed and lay back in his chair. Then he said, 'Shall we have him here?'

'No,' James said. 'I don't think this is the place to break such a story. I think it should be at Glenda's, where he'll be able to see her clothes and the rags and tatters she must have worn under that dreadful coat. Dear Lord! Well, you'd better get on the phone and invite him to hear the change that's going to take place in his life. Where d'you think he'll be?'

'Back in the hospital,' said Alexander. 'But it's Monday and they'll all be on different times. I'm certainly not going to ring his home; for if he shouldn't be in I'd be put through to his father, and the thought of that man makes my gall rise.'

He picked up the phone but didn't, as would have been usual, ask his secretary to get him the number, but dialled the hospital himself.

He was told he would be put through to Dr Baindor's ward, where a curt voice said, 'Yes, Dr Baindor is on duty, but he's busy.' Alexander almost shouted, 'Well, please will you tell him wherever he is that Mr Alexander Armstrong wishes to speak to him on a very important matter, and now!'

There was silence, and when he glanced across the table at his son, he saw that he had covered his ear with one hand. James said softly, 'They're probably too frightened to bother the great man if he's on a ward round.'

Alexander turned quickly to the phone, saying, 'Hello there! Is that you, Richard?'

'Yes. Yes, it's me. And what a way to send a message. You are a bully of a man, you know. What is it now?'

'Richard, when will you be off duty?'

'In half an hour's time.'

'Well, I would ask you, in fact I would tell you, that you must come straight to the nursing home where James and I will be waiting for you. There is a patient here you must see.'

'A patient in the nursing home? But, Alex, what have I to do—'

'Be quiet! Just listen to what I say. This is most important.'

'Something to do with me?'

'Everything to do with you.'

'Concerning my father?'

It was almost a yell into the phone, 'Yes, concerning your father! Now don't ask any more; and, please, don't phone home and tell them where you're going. We'll expect you . . . well, within the next hour. Now get here, Richard, as quickly as you can.'

There was silence at the other end of the line for a moment; then came the words, 'As you say, Alex. As you say.'

They were in Glenda's sitting room, Alexander in an easy chair and James at the end of the couch. Glenda was standing by the sofa table, and her fingers were beating on it as if keeping time to something. She was saying, 'I hope she comes back a little to herself before he arrives, because she's had an awful turn. I wouldn't like him to hear her repeat what she was saying. His father must have been quite inhuman. At one point she must have imagined she was in bed with him. Dear

275

God! It was awful. You know what she said?' Glenda now looked from her brother to her nephew. Then, her head drooping, she said, '"I am not an animal! I won't be treated like an animal!" And then her body heaved in that strange way again, up and down, up and down, and then she was begging him, actually begging him, not to do something. Then quite suddenly she croaked – in her mind she must have been screaming, you know, like in a dream – but she croaked, "I hate you. You're worse than any animal. You're a filthy pervert!" Then her body began to lift from the bed as if she were being pushed back and forward. We had to try to hold her down in case she injured herself. I don't know where she got the strength, because she's so frail. And then she was gasping, "Don't dare speak! But I will! I will!" And then it was as if her body seemed to be lifted in the air and thrown on to her face, because she heaved herself round in Sister's arms and fell on her face. I had to give her an injection. It'll be a wonder if she survives this one. This is the first time I've seen her in this state.

'Before that, she imagined she was back in the house talking to Mrs Atkins and Trip, and she mentioned Mr Cox, the valet, and was on about something like an escape he had planned for her. Do you remember Cox, the valet?' She looked at her brother.

'Oh, yes. Yes.'

'And she mentioned her lady's maid and the nurse. She was talking to the nurse as if she were standing beside the boy's bed. It was pitiable. Her chest has eased a little but she can't last much longer. This has taken away the very little energy she's got left.'

Her fingers were again beating on the table and she said, 'What I'd like to know is how Richard's been kept in ignorance all these years, I mean of what actually took place.'

'Simply because, my dear, his father is a clever man. If you remember, he took him straight away to Italy, and they stayed there for more than two years. The boy was seven or so when he brought him back and put him in that Catholic boarding-school. It was only he who visited him, and immediately the holidays came he was whisked off abroad or away somewhere. He was about twenty when the war ended; but before that he had made up his mind as to what he wanted to be, once he got out of the Army, and he stood his ground against his father for the first time. He was going to be a doctor and, of all things, he chose plastic surgery. This caused such a row that things have never been the same between them since.'

Alexander now pulled himself to his feet and stood with one hand gripping the mantelshelf as he looked across to his son. 'Whether you are with me or not in this, James, our firm is no longer going to see to the Wellbrook Estate. I know what it'll do to the firm's income, but as it is, we both know we're doing quite well now and can live comfortably without his business.'

James's reply was quiet: 'I'm with you there.'

'There's the bell,' Glenda put in. 'That'll be him. I'm away. You can call me later, if you like, but I can't be in on this. I just couldn't sit through it; and anyway there was my share, and I'm not proud of it. I'll never forgive myself for letting her go alone on that train to Eastbourne.'

When Richard Baindor entered the room his handsome face looked strained and his voice held an anxious note as he said, 'Well, here I am, at your command, Alex. And I'm still wondering what it's all about.'

'Sit down.' Alexander pointed to an armchair; then he resumed his seat, as did James. There followed a long, awkward silence as they surveyed each other; then, haltingly, Alexander said, 'What do you know about your mother, Richard?'

'About my mother? Only that I was about four years old when she left me and . . . well, she went away. My father told me later that she had died and that he didn't want to hear me

277

speak of her again. It seemed to annoy him. Even as a child, I had noticed it when I asked him something like "When is Mama coming back?" And this happened a number of times while we were in Italy; and because at that time I was a little afraid of him, even more than a little, I kept my thoughts about my mother to myself. Then one day, some years later, without any lead-up, he said, "Your mother is dead, Richard, and I don't want you to mention her name to me ever again." I don't know how old I would have been then, ten or eleven. It was during a school holiday, and I remember, when back at school and hearing other fellows talking about their mothers, feeling a bit lost somehow, as if I had missed out on something.'

'You had indeed missed out on something, Richard. You had indeed.' Alexander was nodding at him. 'Now, I'm going to start at the beginning, and it'll be the second time I've had to go through it, and this is a painful process. I told James here the story and he found it almost unbelievable, as no doubt you will yourself.'

Richard said quietly now, 'You're going to tell me about my mother?'

'Yes, I'm going to tell you about your mother, and also about your father. And I warn you that you will be disturbed. But you must know the truth before it is too late.'

And so Alexander began. For a full half-hour he talked, and for a full half-hour Richard Baindor sat staring at him, not uttering a word or asking a question, not even when Alexander finished, 'Nearly twenty-seven years have gone by. We don't know what has happened to her in all that time, only that she must have worn the same clothes practically every day, I think, and that, for a time, she must have been sleeping rough. Very rough.'

Again there was a painful silence. Then both Alexander and James watched the young man fall back in his chair and cover his face with his hands. They made no move, but waited until the spasm had eased. Then they watched him pull a handkerchief from his pocket and wipe his face. He did not say he was sorry or make any apology for his tears, he just sat staring at them. It was some minutes before he spoke: 'It's . . . unbelievable,' he said.

'Yes,' said James, 'it does seem unbelievable, but when you see her, Richard, you will believe all right.'

'He turned her mind?'

'Yes,' said Alexander. 'He definitely turned her mind. It is slipping back now, into Wellbrook Manor when you were a boy of four. I recall the night she last held you: she put her arms around you and hugged you while she promised you you were both going on an adventure. I didn't know anything about it then. She had told me nothing, but her manner had been rather odd – odd for her, that is, because usually she was not placid exactly, but just quiet. That evening she seemed excited, even highly excited, especially when she went on the stage, and she had never sung better. In her heart she must have known it would be her last appearance there because she was going to escape. It was only some time after the terrible scene in the dressing room that Cox called on me and gave me what money was left over from the purchase of two second-class tickets to America. At that time, your father was away, but she was determined, even if he hadn't been, that she would still make a run for it, and take you with her. Trip has told me that he was in on this.'

'Trip? Old Trip?'

'Yes, old Trip.'

'Why has he never said anything to me?'

'Because, I should imagine, he knew what it would do to you: you thought she was dead and it was better to leave it like that. He didn't know what had happened to your mother and, what is more, he was middle-aged even then, and the manor had been his home since he was a boy working in the yard. He had no other home, but he knew that if he dared to say anything to you he would be out on his neck; and so would Mrs Atkins.'

'And . . .' Richard hesitated '. . . have you thought she was dead all these years?'

'Not really. No. For years we had detectives looking here and there, but we decided, at least I did in my own mind, that when one reported that a strange lady had been sighted on the London docks, she must have gone abroad after all. But no; she must have just been wandering there, knowing with half her mind that that was the place of escape.'

Richard rose to his feet and began to pace the room almost from the window to the door. Neither Alexander nor James did anything to stop him or uttered a word until he looked at them and said, 'I can't take it in. You say she looked like a vagrant and probably had been exactly that for years, judging from the condition of her clothes?'

It was Alexander who answered, saying, 'Yes, Richard, and we shall show you the clothes so that you will see what I mean by a vagrant.'

Now Alexander rang a bell, and when a maid arrived he said, 'Would you please ask Matron if she will step in here a moment?'

Glenda came in. She looked at Richard, who was now standing by the far window, gripping the framework.

At her entry he turned slowly.

She did not speak to him and it was a moment or so before he murmured, 'Oh, Glenda. Glenda.'

'I know, Richard. I know just a little of how you must feel, because I, too, am staggered.'

It was here that James broke in, 'Do you think you could get the coat and hat and other garments?'

She paused, then said, 'Yes, I can do that,' and went off.

It was more than five minutes later before she returned, and during that time not half a dozen words had been exchanged between the three men.

Glenda drew away the white sheet covering the garments that were laid across her arm. She put them on the couch and, turning to James, she said, 'Hold that up, will you?'

He took the dirty-looking, worn coat and held it so that Richard could see it. Then, when Glenda took the weird contraption of a hat and placed it on the neck of the coat there came a loud exclamation from Richard. 'I've seen her! I've met her! Oh, dear God! Yes.' He put his hand to his head and turned to face them again. 'She was sitting on a box on the drive of the hospital. She—' He couldn't go on: his eyes were tightly closed and his lower lip was caught between his teeth, before he recovered sufficiently to say, 'She gripped my wrist. She must have recognised me somehow. Why she was there, I don't know; but the chaps – there were two with me – they thought she was begging. And' – he closed his eyes again – 'one of them offered her a shilling, and she knocked his hand flying and the shilling went into the gutter. She still had hold of my wrist and was trying to say something.' He looked at Alex now and asked, 'Is . . . is she partly dumb?'

'In a way, yes, Richard, or, at least, she's fearful of speaking.'

'She kept opening her mouth and putting her head back, and one of my friends suggested that what she said was "Rich", and went on to explain: "She thinks you're rich, she's begging." And I remember now how that dreadful pale face changed. I – I had to ease her fingers from my wrist and I kept telling her she must get to Outpatients. She – she needed atten-tion for her chest. Intermittently she was absolutely croaking, and I recall I backed away from her saying I had a car waiting. And, you know, I almost went at a run. And she had come in those clothes when she first saw you?'

'Oh, yes. Just like that. She must have worn them for years.'

Richard now took the coat from James's hands and, holding it in front of him, he stared at it before pulling it to his chest and saying, 'Poor woman! I'll – I'll kill him! I know

281

now that I've always had two overriding emotions with regard to my father. Fear and dislike. But not any more. It isn't just dislike. I'll kill him!'

He laid the coat gently over the arm of the couch and said to them, 'But where has she been all this time? She couldn't have been going round in such a state. She would have been picked up by the Salvation Army or some organisation like that.'

'We don't know where she's been, Richard,' said Alexander, 'and I doubt if we'll ever find out, because she still has great difficulty in speaking, though I think part of it is her weakened state. She's in a bad way.'

Glenda was now holding up the tattered remains of two other garments. She hadn't brought the drawers with her; that would've been too embarrassing; but she had brought what was left of the woollen shift, and he took it in his hands, and saw that it had been stitched here and there, with stitches over stitches. The woollen garment was still long but very fragile and worn.

Glenda said to him: 'It's as I told Alex, she has terrible memories, and she thinks she's back in the manor, and what she reveals happened at night in it becomes more horrifying. But how, I ask myself now, did she ever expect to escape from that man? I'm sure he would have hunted her to the ends of the earth and taken you back, Richard. Then God knows what he would have done to her, because he must have certainly intended to kill both her and Timothy on that night of the concert. When I saw her body I couldn't believe it. I know she has a delicate skin, it still shows in her face, but I don't think she bruises easily. But her body is almost covered with marks left by deep cuts and tears of some kind. Even after all these years they are still evident, faint but evident, like stains on the skin. They're especially noticeable around the ankles. I'm telling you this, Richard, to give you some indication of the reason for her mental condition. The last battering must have turned her mind and impeded her speech. But why she has worn these clothes all these years, I don't know. At some time she might have had a change in circumstances, but we'll probably never know. She has clung to these clothes as if . . . well, I have my own theories, but we won't know until we find out where she's been.'

Richard sat down, his elbows on his knees, and rested his face between his hands. No one spoke until he lifted his head and, looking at Glenda, asked, 'May I see her?'

Glenda hesitated before saying, 'Well, she's asleep now; she became so agitated that I had to give her a jab. It might be an hour or so before she's round. But of course you may see her; and,' she smiled now, 'it will be wonderful, I'm sure, when she wakes to see your face.'

'She must have recognised you that day, as you say, when she gripped your hand,' Alexander said.

'But how? If I was four when she last left me.'

After a moment's thought Alexander said, 'Probably because you bear a strong resemblance to her father. Yes,' he nodded, 'the more I look at you the more I see Francis, your grandfather. And you have her mouth. But there's no sign of your . . . begetter in you, and none as yet shows in your nature, and I've known you since you were a baby.'

'Well, I suppose I can thank God for that,' said Richard bitterly. 'But when I think how my poor mother was allowed to suffer so much all those years . . .' In quite a different tone he appealed to Alexander, 'What am I going to do?'

'You'll have to see him and tell him.'

'*Tell him?* If I were to see him at this moment I'd strangle him. I'll have to think, because this puts an end not only to my way of life but also to his.' He stood up again and once more began to pace. Then he stopped and, looking at them, he said, 'I'll never live in that house again. I'll set foot in it once and that will be to tell him what I know of him and think of him. I've felt guilty all my life about my feelings regarding him because everything he did seemed to be for my welfare. Until I decided for myself what I was going to be he was for pushing me on into business so that in time I could take over his empire. And it is an empire he's got, as you know only too well.'

He turned to Alexander now. 'And what has he made most of his money out of? Property. A lot of it in the slums, dropping to pieces. That has always upset me; but I was so afraid of him for years that I daren't say anything to him. Twice only I have witnessed how he reacts when he is thwarted in any way. On each occasion he became violent. Once only, though, did he attempt to lift his hand against me, when he kept his doubled fist in mid-air before dropping back to his seat. It looked as if he was going to have a seizure. I recall now, it was in my teens on the day I dared to say to him, "I would like to know more about my mother, Father." That day I was once more forbidden ever to mention her name again: she had been a wicked woman, he said, she had left me without a thought. On and on he went, before finishing in a dreadful, terrifying voice, "Don't ever speak her name to me again as long as we live."

'From that day I began to question, but daren't voice my thoughts. It was Trip who, one day, took me aside and said, "Your mother was not a bad lady. Just remember that." I could never get him to go on and tell me more, although I begged him, and he said . . .' Richard paused. 'He said, "I've lived in this house all my life, as has Mrs Atkins. We both came when we were very young; we look upon it as home. We want to finish our days here in peace, Master Richard. Do you understand me?" I didn't, but I said yes. It would be easy to condemn his attitude, but when I think that only a few days ago I pushed her off me, I want to bury my head in shame.'

'Don't be silly!' Alexander said sharply. 'You weren't to know.'

'Come along, Richard,' said Glenda, 'but she won't be round yet.'

A few minutes later he was entering his mother's bedroom. He walked slowly to the bedside and looked down on the emaciated face with the two long grey plaits lying, one each side of it. He was so pale himself that the sister pushed a chair towards him.

As he sat there, staring into the face of his mother, there was no way to describe the emotions that flooded him. He could say the main one was love, but there was sorrow, anxiety, remorse and, through it all, a strong vein of anger. For a moment he felt it would overpower all his other emotions, because it was linked with hate, and deep within him he knew that, if nothing else, he had inherited those two emotions from the man who had begotten him, and he knew he would use them to the full.

How he would do this, he did not yet know. He knew only that he wanted to lift the figure from the bed and hold her in his arms and tell her he remembered her. Oh, yes, he remembered her. He could even now recall the last time she had held him in her arms. She had looked so lovely, and she had worn that coat and that hat, which had made her extraordinarily beautiful then. He could even recall his nurse of that time . . . Flora. Flora Carr. But where had his mother been all these years? Why hadn't she come back and sought him out?

Well, she had, hadn't she? She had sat on the box on the hospital drive and held his wrist. In some way her mind had cleared and she remembered the past. But who or what had brought her into the present?

Someone was speaking to him. He turned to see a nurse at his side who said softly, 'Matron says will you stay to dinner?'

He couldn't give her an answer, his mind was in a whirl. He muttered, 'I don't know. I'll see.'

He recalled that he had promised to meet Jackie later on for dinner; he wasn't due back in the hospital until nine tomorrow morning. But he wasn't going back to the hospital and he'd have to tell them. But Jackie? He'd have to get word to her as well. Just now, though, the only thing that mattered was that he meant to stay with his poor mother for as long as she needed him.

During the next hour he drank two cups of coffee, sitting where he was, holding the long-fingered, blue-veined hand. It was the hand of an old woman, yet the face did not show many wrinkles. The skin was too tightly drawn for that. He was staring down into it as the lips moved and the eyelids lifted; and then she was looking at him. Now her mouth opened and she brought out one word in a husky whisper, 'Richard.'

As his arms went about her, hers went around his neck and he murmured, 'Oh, Mother, Mother.'

The sister and a nurse were standing at the foot of the bed. Both turned away and busied themselves at a table by the door. It was too much to witness.

'My love, I should have known you the other day.'

The arms tightened about his neck.

How long they clung together he didn't know; only when she released her hold on him did he let her slip back on to the pillows and, stroking her damp hair from her forehead, said, 'I'll never leave you again. Never.'

'Richard.' The name was clear although throaty.

'Yes, talk to me. Tell me where you've been all this time. Just a little bit at a time.'

She put up her hand and stroked his cheek, and now she said another name, 'Bella.'

'Bella? Who is Bella?'

He watched her eyes close and her lips move up into what could have been a smile, and the next word she used was, 'Good.'

Again he repeated, 'Good?' Then said, 'Bella was good?'

She made a small motion with her hand.

Glenda was by his side now and she said softly, 'Don't tire her, Richard. It's wonderful. She spoke clearly; I could hear it. A little at a time. Let her rest.'

He leant forward now and placed his lips on his mother's forehead, and again her arms were up and around his neck.

'Richard.'

'Yes, dear Mother? I'll be here, all the time. I'll not leave you unless you're asleep. Try now . . . try now to rest.'

Slowly her arms slid from his neck and on to the counterpane, and again the smile was taking up the corners of her mouth.

Passing the sister, he went to the window and stood looking out. He knew what was about to happen to him: he was going to cry again, and he mustn't. His heart was so full of love for her that it had become an unbearable pain. He knew what it was to love. He loved Jackie; but it had never caused this pain. Pain that was built on sorrow and regret for the years that had gone and would never return. Years during which he had missed the love of a beautiful girl, a beautiful woman, who was now lying behind him, a mere skeleton of herself. But at least now she was here although it could never fill the great gap that had built up in him since he was a boy . . . It had closed a little when he met Jackie, who had filled his heart with warmth.

Glenda was by his side once more, and she said softly, 'She's asleep. Now, come and have something to eat.'

'I'm going to stay tonight.'

'Yes; I'll have a chair-bed made up for you alongside her. But you can't go on if you don't have rest and food; you know that. Come on now.'

She took his arm and, after one more glance towards the sleeping figure in the bed, she led him from the room.

She was saying, 'Alex is still here; I'll bring a drink into the sitting room before we eat. Go on in.'

'Presently, Glenda. I must get in touch with Jackie; I

promised to meet her. I must also get through to the hospital. But tell me, how long do you think she's got?'

'Oh, I couldn't say, my dear. Dr Swan says that if we can get a little nourishment into her and if her chest eases, she could hang on for a few weeks.'

'A few weeks! Really? Oh, well, then, I shall ask for leave.'

'What are you going to tell Jackie?'

'You mean about this business? Nothing at the moment. I'll ... I couldn't talk about it to anybody else, not just yet. I'll try to explain to her. Will you excuse me? And may I use the phone in your office?'

'Certainly. Go along.' She pushed him down the short corridor, and at the corner, she said, 'It's the end door.'

He went into the small, neatly arranged office, sat down on a typist's revolving chair at the end of a desk and pulled the phone towards him. His first call was to the hospital and his head of department. He knew that David Baker would still be at work and he asked to be put through to him. When the voice came on the phone, he said, 'David ... it's Richard.'

'Yes, Richard? You want to have a word with me? Anything wrong?'

'I can't put you in the picture yet. Something very important has happened, and I want to ask if you think I could take my leave as from now for the next month or six weeks.'

'For four to six weeks?'

'Yes. I know I'm asking a lot, but I was due for a month anyway.'

'It's all right. Tell me honestly, are you in trouble?'

'No, I'm not in trouble, not that kind of trouble, but someone I love, should have loved for years, I have found and she is dying ... and ... and I want to be with her.'

There was silence at the other end of the line; then David's voice was saying, 'Someone you have found? You intrigue me.'

'I'm sorry, David. I would like to give you the whole story

now, but I shall later on, I promise you. I must ask, though, if it would be putting you out too much.'

'No, no. I'll fix something up. Your main work was on the little fellow, but he's getting on amazingly and a few weeks more in bed won't do him any harm. Anyway, he's got to learn to walk. But may I keep in touch?'

'Yes, of course.'

'Where are you now? At home?'

'No.' Richard's voice was harsh. 'No, David, I'm not at home; and I'll never be at home again. I can tell you that much.'

'Oh, my goodness. Anyway, where'll I find you?'

'At Beechwood Nursing Home.'

'Oh, yes, I know it. And I can get you there?'

'Most of the time.'

'Well, go ahead. I'll phone you again in a day or two.'

'Yes. Thanks, David, thanks very much indeed. Goodbye.'

For a moment longer he sat thinking, then rang a number and a stiff voice said, 'Beaumont Lodge.'

'This is Richard Baindor. Is Miss Jackie at home?'

The voice at the other end changed: 'No, sir. She left for her office not half an hour ago. Would you like to speak to his lordship?'

'No, thank you. I'll contact her. Thank you. Goodbye.'

In answer to his next call the voice that answered was abrupt, but said, 'Yes?'

'Is Miss Franks in her office?'

'Yes. Who's speaking?'

'Richard Baindor.'

A moment later and Jackie was on the line. 'Hello, Richard. What's up? We haven't to meet for another hour, have we? I've been home to get all togged up, but there are some papers I need for tomorrow's journey and I thought I'd pick them up before I went on to your little grey home in the west and . . .'

'Jackie, stop it and listen to me. I can't see you tonight.'

There was a pause, and then she said, 'I knew it. One of those blasted nurses has got you at last! I said they would.'

'Jackie, please! Stop kidding. Listen to me. Something serious has happened. I can't tell you what it is on the phone and I can't see you tonight.'

'What d'you mean, something serious has happened? To your father?'

He barked, 'No, not my father.'

'All right! All right, don't shout!'

'I can't explain now, but just believe me, I'm desperately sorry about tonight but—'

'Where are you? Where are you speaking from?'

'Glenda's nursing home.'

'Who in there can be keeping you, then?'

'Someone very important; but I've told you I can't talk about it over the phone, and I'm in no state to see you tonight. What's more, whatever you do, don't phone the house.'

'Well, you'll see me tomorrow, will you? Look' – her voice was soft now – 'if you're in trouble of some kind . . .'

'No, I'm not in trouble, Jackie, of any kind. I'm only in – Oh, I can't explain! But look, do me a favour, go off on your assignment to Wales tomorrow. It's a very good one. You know it is; you've been looking forward to it.'

'To hell with Wales and assignments! I'm not going to leave you—'

'Jackie. Something good and something awful has happened to me . . . well, not to me, but has come into my life. It's something you'll have to share, but it's something I'm so upset about at the moment I wouldn't be able to talk to you coherently. Now, do as I ask, you'll be there only for a day. He's a big catch. Get his story, then come back; and as soon as you're home ring me up. Then we'll make arrangements to meet and I'll tell you all about it. It's a long story and it's going to change our lives.'

'Our lives? You mean we're . . . ?'

290

'Oh, no. No, I don't mean we'll have to part or anything like that. I could never part from you, Jackie, you know that. Believe me, I'm going to need your help and your advice. So will you do as I ask?'

There was a pause before she said, 'Yes. And I'll say it again, I love you very, very much whatever happens.'

'And I love you, Jackie, more than words will ever express. Goodbye, darling, for the present.'

'Bye-bye, my love.'

Richard put down the receiver, took a long, deep breath, then again rested his elbows on the table and put his head on his hands.

3

Bella was at her wits' end. She'd had them out searching all day and nobody seemed to have seen the odd figure in that awful dirty coat and weird headgear. They must have made Reenee stand out, yet no one seemed to have noticed her. Bella was tired. They were all tired. She couldn't go to the hospital today to see Carl; she had sent Joe to tell him that she had a filthy cold and was lying up for a day or so, because she knew that once he heard that Reenee had gone again he'd be upset because he was unable to do anything about it . . .

The following morning she asked them all again to go out looking and asking if anyone had caught sight of her, and they all returned with the same message. John refrained from mentioning again that he had been to the river police to ask if they had come across a body in the water.

They were about to break up that evening when Willie remarked, 'She's never gone off like this for years, has she, Bella? Then you mentioned the doctor's name and she went into one of her turns.'

They all looked from one to the other, and Tony said, 'None of us knows her real name. I wonder, do you think that might be her name? You never know.'

'No,' said Bella quickly; 'it was the name of the doctor.'

'Well, the doctor, that special doctor, works in the hospital an' he's been lookin' after Carl, hasn't he?'

'Yes.' She nodded.

'Well, d'you think she might have gone to the hospital to try to see Carl?' asked Tony.

'If she had,' put in Joe, 'I'd have been the first one to know. But it wasn't Carl's name that upset her, it was the doctor's. And I think our next step, Bella, is to go to the hospital tomorrow morning and find out if she's been there.'

The following morning Bella and Joe took a taxi to the hospital. They did not go straight to Carl's ward but to the reception area and enquired if a woman had been asking to speak to Dr Baindor.

One of the girls behind the desk looked at her and said, 'Lots of people come here enquiring for this doctor and that.'

'Yes, I know what you mean,' said Bella, 'but this woman would look different. She would look very odd to you with a weird hat and an old dirty coat.'

'Was she ill?'

'Yes; she had a very bad chest.'

'Well, she would likely go to Outpatients. Look, go outside and you'll see the directions to Outpatients.'

'Thank you.'

In the outpatients' department Bella put the same question to a girl standing behind the counter, but the girl took no heed of her because she was busy dictating something to a doctor who was at the end of the counter writing on a pad; and when again Bella put the question, the girl said, 'What? An odd woman? This is a place for odd people.' She laughed and turned to another receptionist, further along the counter, who was using a phone.

'But this person would stand out,' persisted Bella stiffly. 'She was wearing a long, dirty-looking coat and a weird head-piece.'

293

'Well, I'm sure I haven't seen anyone like that.'

The girl who had been using the phone put it down and said, 'Oh, yes. I was on the main desk the day she came. She was asking for a doctor, a special doctor. She wouldn't go until we made enquiries about where he was. When she was told he had gone on leave she went away.'

Bella turned and looked at Joe, who said, 'Thank you,' but then added, 'Do you know whether or not she left the hospital?'

The woman thought for a moment, then said, 'I suppose she did. She went,' and she pointed to a window, 'down the drive there.'

Outside, Bella said, 'I can't go and see Carl, I'm too upset. But she must be about somewhere.'

They were walking down a side drive when they heard running footsteps behind them. They turned and saw a young man in a white coat. He called, 'Pardon me, but . . . but I think I have seen the woman you are looking for. She was dressed very oddly, had a weird contraption on her head.'

'Yes, yes,' Bella was nodding at him, 'that's her.'

'Well, you see, she was enquiring for Dr Baindor.'

'Yes, I'm sure she would be, a doctor of that name, yes. You see, I know that doctor, he's looking after one of my boys.'

'Oh,' the young man said, and Bella went on, 'Do you know where she went?'

'Yes, I do, as it happens. I was with Dr Baindor at the time. She seemed to recognise him and hung on to him. But he had a car waiting and he asked me to see to her. She should have been in hospital, she had an awful chest.'

'Oh, my!' Bella said. 'And you don't know where she went?'

'Yes, I do, because she had difficulty in speaking, as if she were partly dumb.'

'That's her,' said Joe now.

'Do you know where she's gone?' asked Bella quickly.

'Yes, because she asked me to get her a taxi. She wrote the address in my diary here . . .' He put a hand into his breast pocket and brought out a little book. He opened it, and said, 'There,' pointed to a page and read, ' "Beverley Square. Armstrong, Solicitor." I got her a taxi and I told the driver where to take her. That's the last I saw of her.'

'Oh, thank you, young man!' Bella grabbed his hand and shook it up and down. 'You have been a help! Thank you. And you helped *her* too.'

'I hope you find her,' he said; 'I'm sure you will.'

Fifteen minutes later they were walking up the steps and into the hall of the solicitor's office.

The receptionist asked Bella, 'Have you an appointment?'

'No, I haven't, but I must see him,' said Bella curtly.

The girl looked at the pair, the tubby little old woman and the big, gangling middle-aged man, and she said, 'He never sees anyone unless they have an appointment.' She didn't like the look of either of these two. Common. 'What is your name?'

'Miss Bella Morgan.'

Once more the young girl picked up the phone and contacted Miss Fairweather. 'There are two people down here,' she said softly, 'who want to see Mr Armstrong. The woman's called Miss Bella Morgan.'

'Have they an appointment?'

'No.'

'Well, what are they like?'

The receptionist's voice was very low now as she answered, 'Common.'

'Miss Manning, please don't judge people by their dress. Remember the other day?'

Yes, Miss Manning remembered the other day all right, and that weird woman, and all the fuss and the ambulance and everything, as if she were somebody important; and apparently, from the little she had heard, she was. Then why was she looking like a vagrant? Nobody could explain that to her. She again spoke into the phone: 'Well, what am I going to do?'

'Get them to wait.'

Miss Fairweather now tapped on her boss's door and straightway went in, saying, 'There are two people in the foyer, Mr Armstrong, and their appearance doesn't seem to impress Miss Manning. She described them as common.'

'Did she now? And those two common people want to see me? What is their name?'

'If I remember rightly, it is Miss or Mrs Bella Morgan.'

'Bella?' He repeated the name again, before saying, 'Send them up straight away.'

Bella and her companion were shown into Alexander's office. He was standing ready to greet them and immediately he offered Bella a chair. Then, after looking from one to the other, he sat down and asked quietly, 'How can I help you?'

'A woman came to see you the other day,' said Bella. 'She was very oddly dressed in a long dark coat and a weird hat or whatever. Am I right?'

'Yes, Miss Morgan; you are right; she did come to see me and—'

'And you know where she is now?'

'Yes, I do indeed. She's well tucked up in bed in my sister's nursing home, and I must tell you, my firm and I have been looking for her for the past twenty-seven years.'

Bella took a deep gulp of air and said, 'Twenty-seven years? And that's nearly as long as I've had her.'

'No!'

'Yes. Yes, sir, it is. She's like . . . well, she's more than a daughter to me, more than a companion. She brought something into my life that I'd never had, and I've looked after her. She wasn't right in the head then, and I'm afraid it hasn't improved much, but I've looked after her to the best of my ability. The only thing I couldn't get her to do was change her clothes, I mean that coat and the hat. But she has never been out of my house for . . . well, nigh on ten years until two days ago, and only two times before that.'

Alexander was gazing at her in amazement and his voice was just a whisper as he said, 'She wore the coat all the time?'

'Most of the time, yes. It was a sort of protection somehow. You see, she was afraid of men. I've got five lads – well, I call them mine – and I've looked after them for years. One got killed in the war, but Joe here, and Carl, they were lads when I took them on years ago because I had a fruit stall attached to the house. It took her some time to get used to them, but she had only to see another man or anybody come to the door and she flew out of the way. It was as if she was expecting somebody to come and do for her, or something like that.

'Oh, it's a long story, sir. Joe here, and Carl – he's in hospital under Dr Baindor – they found her lying in a dirty old yard of mine that was filled with broken fruit boxes and quite a bit of rotten fruit. She was sleeping among the boxes. I don't know how long she had been on the road or sleeping rough, I never could get that out of her, but it must have been for some months because she was in a dreadful state. But, anyway, I've had her, sir, for all these years. And I thought I'd lost her for good.'

She stopped for want of breath, and Alexander said, 'Miss Morgan, at this moment I don't know anybody I'm more pleased to see than you and your friend there' – he nodded towards Joe – 'because you've filled in the great gap of her life. And, do you know, twice she has said the name Bella.'

'Has she?' Bella's face was a-beam now.

'Yes, it was as if she missed you.'

'Would . . . will I be able to see her?'

'Of course. You'll be very welcome. I'm sure you've got a long tale to tell us, and I've got, I can assure you, Miss Morgan, a longer and more terrible tale to tell you.'

Her face drained of colour. She looked at him and said, 'Aye, I bet you have, sir. I knew something terrible must have happened in her early life because she used to go into spasms at the mention of a name or a word that seemed to recall some terrible past. Her body would go into contortions as if she was fighting somebody.'

'And indeed she was, Miss Morgan. But you'll know all about it later. Now, I'm not going to ask you if you would like a cup of tea here, I'm going to take you to my sister's nursing home where you'll be made more than welcome, I can assure you. And there you will see your—'

'I call her my lass.'

'Well, you'll see your lass.'

He rang a bell, and when Miss Fairweather entered he said, 'I am going with these good friends to my sister's, Miss Fairweather. And when Mr James comes back, tell him to come straight along, will you, please?'

'Yes, Mr Armstrong.'

He took his hat and coat from a hallstand near the door, and led them out, down the stairs and into the hall. There he paused. 'Will you just wait one tick, I forgot to tell my secretary something.'

At this he went back up the stairs and surprised Miss Fairweather by going to her desk and saying in a low voice, 'I've left quite a number of letters I've already drafted on the desk. Some others I haven't got down to yet, but they're not very important and you'll know how to deal with them. Will you see to them for me?'

'Of course, Mr Armstrong. Don't you worry, just leave them to me.'

'Thank you, Miss Fairweather.' He patted her arm then left her with a strange look on her face. He would have been surprised if he had seen her eyes turn to her arm where he had laid his hand, for it was the first time he had made such a gesture to her in all the long years she had worked for him.

Bella could not believe all this was happening to her and Joe. Wait till she told the others! The car was a large one, though she did not appreciate the luxury of it for she was so taken up with the fact that in a short while she would see her lass. The words kept repeating themselves in her mind: she would see her lass . . .

The lady who was introduced to her as the solicitor's sister was kindness itself. She took them both into a fine sitting room, where she informed them that before they did any visiting they must have a cup of tea and a little talk with her and her brother.

The little talk filled Glenda and Alexander with astonishment. For twenty-six years this little woman had looked after Irene. They could hardly believe it, nor that the poor dear thing had lived in a house for years and years without going out of its doors. But was it any more astounding than the life the patient was revealing to them all bit by bit, demonstrating the time she had suffered under that brute, that filthy brute of a man, who was now a multi-millionaire and sitting comfortably in his mansion?

When Glenda opened the bedroom door, Richard rose to his feet from the side of the bed and stared at the little woman and the tall fellow by her side, and exclaimed softly, 'Bella?'

She stared at him: this was Carl's doctor, Dr Baindor, whose name had knocked her lass into one of her turns. Baindor. This, then, was the boy, the son. She thrust out a hand towards him and he grasped it; then he put his finger to his lips and pointed to the chair. She sat down, still looking at him, before she turned slowly to the bed and looked at the face that was lying there. That dear, dear face, but how different: the long plaits hanging down each side of her shoulders, the pretty nightdress, the long sleeves ending in frills at the wrists. Gently, she lifted up the thin hand from the counterpane and held it almost reverently against her breast.

Slowly the eyes opened and to her utmost delight there was recognition in them, and her name came out quite clearly, though slightly huskily. 'Bella. Oh, Bella.'

The arms lifted and were about her neck, and she was enfolding her lass, crying as she did so, 'Oh, my lass! Oh, my love! To see you here lookin' so lovely! I've been so terribly worried. I thought I'd lost you.'

'Bella. Bella.'

'Yes, I'm your Bella. I'll always be your Bella.'

Then the face below hers turned and looked at the man standing to the side of the bed, and Irene said, 'My son.'

'Yes, lass, your son.' Bella was looking up into Richard's face and she said, 'I can't believe it, but I always knew she had a child somewhere;' and turning back to Irene, she said, 'Remember the teddy bear?'

'Teddy bear.' Those words were clear too.

'You hugged it and rocked it, and I knew then you had a child.'

Bending down to his mother, Richard said softly, 'Bella and I have met before. I look after one of her boys. You know . . . Carl.'

'Carl. Oh, dear Carl.' The name, too, was clear.

'Bella came to visit him.'

'Carl here?'

'Not here, Mother, in the hospital.'

Irene looked at Bella and, lifting one hand, she stroked her cheek, saying as she did so, 'Kind. Kind.'

'And who wouldn't be kind to you, lass? Who wouldn't? The lads'll be overjoyed. Joe's here.' Bella looked over her shoulder. 'Joe! Come and say hello.'

Irene now looked up into the big rough face, and the smile came to her lips again and she said, 'Joe.'

'Yes,' put in Bella, 'Joe and Carl. They were pals. Always pals.'

'Lovely to see you, Reenee . . . 'tis,' said Joe. 'By! We've missed you.' Then, bending closer to her, he said, 'Worn my shoes down lookin' for you.'

The lips went higher up into a smile. Then Glenda's

300

quiet voice broke in on them: 'I would let her rest now.'

After they had left the room, Richard sat by the bed, and Irene, looking at him, said, 'Bella . . . so kind, so kind,' and he answered softly, 'Yes, I'm sure she is, my dear; and she loves you.'

Irene's eyelids drooped and there was a smile on her lips as once again she drifted into sleep.

It had been agreed between Alexander, James and Glenda that before he approached his father Richard should talk to Jackie and give her the full picture, because although the result of the interview might not alter his choice of profession, it would certainly affect his way of living. The old swine would definitely cut him off without a penny.

They imagined they all knew exactly how Jackie would react, but it was better, they thought, that it should be put to her, so here he was at the station, greeting her from the train.

After their warm embrace Richard said, 'May we go to your flat?'

'Yes, of course; but what about yours?'

'I . . . I don't want to go back there.'

When she glanced sideways at him, he said, 'It will all be made plain to you shortly.'

'Well, I hope so; you've had me worried for the last forty-eight hours.'

'How did you get on?'

'Well, I suppose you could say the interview was successful but to sit for two solid hours in the company of a man who has the intelligence of a rabbit and an ego the size of an elephant, there you have my answer. I suppose he was born with a photographic mind and at school he could read through a book and remember every page of it, so was dubbed one of the clever clogs, and he has built on that. He could tell me every law that has been passed since 1066, oh, and long before that, and that has got him where he is today. But ask him to solve any of the problems that are being created by his lot, and he'll give you an answer by reference to page so-and-so in a book by so-and-so. There were times when I had to tell myself to sit still, to stay put, that this was a job: I wasn't there to dissect his character, only to know how he felt about his new title.'

Her tirade stopped as he brought the car to a halt outside her flat, but as soon as she was indoors and they were settled in a comfortable but small and rather cluttered sitting room, she went on, 'I was saying about how that had got him where he is today. Now, Richard, give my father his due, and I know, as do a few other people, that in a way he bought his title. You don't shovel heaps of money into your party without expecting something in return. He has always aimed at being somebody, after having pulled himself up by his boot-laces, and not having had much of a so-called education. Yet he's got more intelligence in his head than many of his so-called friends in the House of Lords, especially that big lump of egotism I've been dealing with all day. Well, now, that's the answer to your question at the station; and now it is your turn to tell me whatever is making your face the colour it is. Before that, however, d'you want a drink? Something hard? Or tea or coffee?'

'Coffee, please. It'll keep hot longer.' He gave her a wry smile.

'Oh, that means it's going to be a long session.'

'Yes, it means just that.'

It was an hour and a half later. They were both still sitting on the couch and they were silent. He had told her everything, right from the beginning, as Alexander had told him, up to the present day when his mother had given him four pawn tickets and a faded picture of himself when he was a boy. As yet he didn't know what the pawn tickets represented; but he or Alexander would find out. And lastly he had told her what he meant to say to his father, and that he knew he would be disinherited.

Slowly she put out a hand, caught his and held it against her cheek. She said softly, 'The usual thing to say would be that I can't believe it, but I can, every word of it; and I'll tell you now, darling, I might not have said so but I have always disliked your father. As for my old man, he can't stand him either, for he knows only too well your engagement to me would never have been countenanced if it hadn't been for his title.'

'I'll not have any income other than what I earn, you understand that?' Richard said.

'Of course I understand. But very shortly you'll be a consultant, and I haven't seen your present superior or any of the others like him living from hand to mouth. And then there's me. I have my job, which I might tell you I'm going to change.'

He took her other hand. 'What d'you mean you're going to change?'

'I'm . . . Oh, I'm going to stay in the same business, but I'm not going to go on tour any more. That one assignment abroad finished me. I realised then that I wasn't made to witness children dying of hunger or people fleeing for their lives, and one tribe slaughtering another. I thought I was until I got there; but no. It takes years to find out what you do best, and I've just found out what I can do best' – and now her voice changed – 'and one of the things is staying near to you, because I love you, Richard.'

He was now holding her tight, and they were lying on the couch and his eyes filled as he said, 'I'm ashamed of myself. I'm doing this so often.'

'You can't find a better way of release. Go on, darling, let go. As long as you want to cry on my breast I'll be happy all my life.'

After a moment he muttered, 'It's . . . it's her . . . Mother. I . . . I can't get her out of my mind. The sight of her and what she must have gone through at his hands. To have turned her mind, because it is still not right. She slips back and forward between the past and the present, and nearly always a terrible past. It's pitiable to see her fighting and struggling when she's remembering him again. I don't know how I'm going to face him, Jackie, I really don't. I know I must; but how am I going to keep my hands off him?'

'You will. After what you've told me you'll be able to cut him to shreds with your tongue. The final fact that you're walking out on him for ever will finish him.'

They lay quiet for a moment before she asked softly, 'Will you take me to see your mother?'

'Yes, darling. I'll take you to meet her, and you will be able to see for yourself the devastation that one human being can wreak on another.'

It was nine o'clock the next morning when Richard rang the number of what was called the house phone. This was placed in Mrs Atkins's office so that she could deal with the ordering and the household necessities quite apart from what was called the main phone.

When she picked it up and heard Richard's voice saying, 'Is that you, Mrs Atkins?' she exclaimed, 'Oh, Mr Richard, the master has been so worried—' only to be cut off by his voice saying sharply, 'Listen, Mrs Atkins. I need your help and Trip's. Now, listen carefully: get Trip to the phone, but don't let the master know I'm calling. You understand?'

'Yes, Mr Richard. I'll get him.'

When Trip came to the phone, he said, 'Oh, sir, I'm glad to hear you. We wondered what had happened to you.'

'Listen, Trip, there isn't much time. Has he got anyone looking after him now?'

'Not at the moment, sir. You know he's had nurses, but the last one left a week ago. He's been seeing to himself since.'

'Well, now, I want you to do something for me; and should

304

it go wrong and he finds out that you have helped me, let me assure you and Mrs Atkins that you will not lose by it. What is more, there is a position awaiting you both at Beaumont Lodge, Miss Jackie's home, you know. Now, listen, I want you to get my cases, or better, tell Mrs Atkins to take a maid up with her and fill the cases with as much of my clothing as they can get in. Don't bother with any folding or messing about; just throw everything in from my drawers and cupboards. Then I want you to have them carried down the back stairs where my car will be waiting near the old barns. Who can you trust? Benson?'

'Oh, yes, sir. Benson, of course.'

'And old Tollett?'

'Both of them. They would do anything for you . . . like myself.'

'Thank you, Trip. Thank you. As I say, don't worry. Whatever happens, you'll all be taken care of. That's a promise. I shall be there within the next hour. That should give Mrs Atkins time to get those cases downstairs, shouldn't it?'

'Oh, yes, sir. You are leaving, then, sir?'

'Definitely, Trip. To put you in the picture, I shall tell you one thing: I have found my mother. Yes . . . yes, I heard you gasp. I gasped too. She was turned into a vagrant on the roads. It's a long, long story, but if you stand in the hall this morning, you and Mrs Atkins, you will hear all about it. But do this for me first and as quickly as possible. You will, won't you?'

'Oh, yes, sir, we'll see to it. Don't worry.'

Richard put down the receiver, and stood breathing deeply. Then he looked at Glenda, who was standing nearby, and said, 'Glenda, I'm full of fear, like a soldier who has been sent into battle and ordered to kill somebody.'

'Oh, Richard, don't talk like that; and you're not full of fear, at least of him, are you?'

'Oh, no! Not of him. Never again of him, ever. But I've a fear of myself and what I might do.'

305

'Well, you know what Jackie said to you: slay him with words, that will be enough. And another thing, you're not sleeping on that chair-bed any more. There is a room vacant, it's just two doors away, and you're going to take that as yours for the present.'

He put out his hands to her and drew her gently to him and said, 'You're a lovely person, Glenda Armstrong, a lovely person. And, like your brother, you are the best friend a man could ever have, and I'll never stop being grateful to you.'

'Get yourself away! We don't want any more tears, do we? That'd be the end of me if my staff see me with a wet face; they'll know they have made a mistake and that I'm human after all.'

She pushed him away from her on a laugh, and he too, entering her mood, laughed and said, 'Poor staff; I understand how they feel.'

The road along which he drove was so familiar. He knew every hedgerow, every copse, every field. He felt he even knew the cows in the fields; the same ones seemed to have been there for years. And then there was the river gleaming in the distance. How many times had he fished in there? But never again. When he came to the gates of the manor he drove past them and for some distance until he came to two more iron gates. These were plain ones and were open; he drove through them and along an avenue of beech trees. They ended at a high wall, beyond which were the kitchen gardens. He drew the car to a stop, picked up a case from the passenger seat, then got out and walked round the side of the house on to the terrace.

Within a few seconds he was standing at the front door. He had no need to ring, it was open, and Trip stood there as if he had been waiting for him.

'Where is he?' asked Richard quietly.

'In the drawing room, sir. He's been using it a lot of late.'

'Are my things in order?'

'Just as you arranged, sir; and your sports gear, too.'

'Thank you very much, Trip. We'll be talking later. Don't worry,' and he put out his hand and patted the old man's shoulder as he emphasised, 'And tell Mrs Atkins the same.'

It seemed a long distance before his steps had covered the hall and he was at the drawing-room door. He did not knock but went straight in and closed the door behind him. Then he stood looking at the man who had brought himself forward in the big armchair, muttering, 'Richard.' His name, though, wasn't spoken in welcome but in a growl of disapproval. As the great bony figure pulled itself up from the chair, the voice went on, 'And where do you think you have been, sir, on your month's leave? Answer me.'

'I'll answer you, sir,' Richard replied, in a similar tone. 'I've been seeing my mother. I've been by her bedside for days now.'

He watched the face before him change colour as if it had been lit by a red-hot fire beneath the skin. The voice that came now was not from the throat but as if from some distant high place: 'You're mad! What is this? A game? Your mother died years ago.'

'My mother did not die years ago. Under your treatment my mother lost most of her mind and became a vagrant. And for more than twenty-six years she would have remained as a vagrant had it not been for the kindness of a poor woman who took her in and has looked after her all these years. And such was the condition of my mother's mind that she never left the little house where that woman lived but four times in all those years. And during all that time she wore the same clothes she had worn the night you attempted to murder her and her friend.'

'Her lover! He was her lover. I saw them.'

'You saw them meeting after years of separation. He had come to the theatre on a surprise visit, just as you had. But

307

long before then you had not only bruised her body, but tortured it! And also tortured her mind, and to such an extent that she became afraid of men. Her only shield against them was the coat and hat she had bought herself, and which you didn't approve of. Remember? It was too striking; it brought men's attention to her more than usual. You couldn't stand it. But she defied you and wore it. Here it is, sir!' and, bending down, he opened the case and brought out the dirty coat and the hat, and swung them before his father's eyes, saying, 'Look at it! It's in a terrible state; but how else would you expect it to look after all this time? You will recognise the shape, at least that of the hat, the French hat you forbade her to wear. But she defied you, as she did in many other ways.'

'That could have been anyone's coat and hat. Somebody found it. The woman is an impostor.'

'Such an impostor sir, that she still has nightmares, which have been witnessed by two doctors, who have sometimes to hold her down because she continues to fight you off. You! With your filthy, rotten, perverted hands. That is just what you are, a filthy pervert. All your life you have been one.'

'How dare you?' It was a scream that filled the room and echoed from the walls.

'I dare! And I'll go on: it is known that you as good as murdered your first wife. I have talked with her maid, who saw you ignore the dead son she had just pressed from her dying body, then take the poor woman by the shoulders and shake her, almost throttle her, until you were dragged from her. But she, too, had defied you, hadn't she? She died within hours, and what did you do? You left the country. People talk and you couldn't bear it. You should have been locked up then.

'But my mother's case was worse; oh, much worse. You must have instilled in her the fear that burnt into her brain: you commanded her not to talk. "Do not speak!" You ordered her. And those words, after all these years, she still repeats. And added to them is a description of the things you did to her body. You are *vile*!'

'Shut up!' It was another scream. 'It's you who are mad! How dare you say such things? You know nothing about it; you were only a child.'

'But she wasn't, was she, Father? She wasn't a child. You married her when she was twenty-three. Following that she had five years of torture with you, at least after the first year, when you started to show your true self. Your toothmarks are still on her body, faint maybe, but still evident to two doctors.'

'I will not have this! I shall go and see her and prove she is—'

Now it was Richard's turn to raise his voice, 'You move one step towards her, you make one enquiry as to her whereabouts and I'm telling you, believe me, I shall see that the whole story is in every paper in this country, as well as in France and Germany and Italy where so many of your assets lie, and where you are known as a great businessman. I shall tell the world exactly what you are: a filthy pervert who used a young woman so vilely, and the mother of your child at that, that you turned her brain. Now I promise you: make one move out of this house and I shall do as I've said. I shall see your story reaches America – there first. So, I'm warning you, for the rest of your life you will live in this same cage in which you have tortured two women.'

'Do you know what you are doing? I'll – I'll disinherit you.'

The laugh that came from Richard was scornful and he cried, 'Disinherit me! Do that by all means – you'll be doing me a service, for I am no longer under your control, your ownership. That's what you think, don't you? That you own me, as you owned your poor wife. Well, you made a mistake with me because – let me tell you now: yes, you are my father, and I've feared you, but I have never, never liked you. Now, sit and think about that. I no longer fear you, nor do I even pity you; and this is going to be your gaol, this house, which, if you are wise, you won't leave, because once I know you have I'll do as I promised and carry out my threat, and there won't be a country in which you'll be able to hide your head under your money-bags any more.'

He gazed around the room now as if looking for something, and then his eyes fell on the Ming vase standing on a tall carved-wood Indian pedestal. This vase, he knew, was one of his father's greatest treasures, because he had won it from other collectors who had gathered in London many years ago at an auction to bid for it. It had cost a fortune then, and today it would be priceless. So much did his father value the vase that he would not allow even Trip to dust it. Only he himself handled it.

With a dive, Richard grabbed the precious object, and lifted his arms high, before bringing it down on the marble-tiled hearth.

It was with a cry of rage that his father now sprang at him, but Richard's arms were up and his fists ready.

Of a sudden the great man, who was now almost towering over Richard, stopped. His face had lost its fiery colour and had drained to a sickly grey, and when slowly his arms dropped to his sides, Richard turned from him, grabbed Irene's coat and hat, thrust them into the case, then made for the door.

In the hall, huddled together, were three maids, Trip and Mrs Atkins.

Edward Baindor tottered backwards and fell into a chair. There, gasping for breath, he brought out a sound that was recognisable only to Trip. But it was only with measured tread that he entered the drawing room. When he saw the condition of his master he hurried forward, saying, 'I'll ring for the doctor, sir.'

At this the great head was shaking and the word that came

out was 'Solicitor.'

Trip gazed in amazement at the pieces of china splayed all over the hearth rug and the hearth, and he thought, Oh, my God! *That* vase. It will kill him. But he turned and hurried to the phone and rang Alexander's office. 'Let me speak to Mr Armstrong straight away, please,' he said.

When Alexander came on the line he said, 'This is Trip, Mr Armstrong. The master wants you. I will take the telephone to him.'

When he handed the phone to the gasping man, Edward Mortimer Baindor said, 'Get here! Now!'

'I'm sorry, Mr Baindor, but I can't, not just now.'

'Now, I said, Armstrong,' and then there were only gasps to be heard before the voice came again, 'Listen! I want you *now*.'

'I have to be at a meeting in fifteen minutes' time. It's very important. I am sorry, I can't be with you today at all. Perhaps tomorrow.'

'Don't dare!' There was another silence before the voice came again: 'Leave meeting, everything. Get here now!'

The phone at the other end was put down, and only then did Edward Baindor turn his head towards Trip and gasp, 'Doctor!'

It was two o'clock in the afternoon and Miss Fairweather was sitting at the end of Alexander's desk taking down in shorthand a letter he was dictating when the door swung open and a very presentable young woman bounced in, saying, 'Sweetheart, I just had to—' At the sight of Miss Fairweather rising quickly to her feet she said, 'I'm very sorry, my dear. You're busy.'

'I'm always busy, but not too busy to see you. Come and sit down, you . . .'

What the end of his sentence would have been Miss Fairweather did not wait to hear. She gathered up her

311

notebook and swiftly left the room, closing the door noisily behind her.

'I've annoyed her – you were busy?'

'No, no. But what on earth are you doing here?'

'I've come to look for my intended.'

'Well, I too would like to know where he is.'

Jackie's tone changed now as she said, 'I'm getting a bit worried. I knew he had gone to see the old man and that he had made arrangements with Trip to have all his things brought down to his car. Well, I've been to his flat and can't get in. And then I went along to Glenda's and she, like you, hasn't seen hide or hair of him since he left the house just after nine this morning. And you know, as she says, he has hardly left his mother's side for . . . well, not for this long anyway. Glenda was a bit worried that she hadn't heard from him. She phoned Trip and he said Richard had left the house by car with his luggage as arranged just after eleven this morning.'

After a moment, Alexander said, 'He phoned me . . . the old man. It must have been just after Richard left, and he told me he wanted me there immediately. Well, I knew what that meant, the changing of the will, and he meant it all right. In fact, Trip phoned not fifteen minutes later to say that I had to bring documents and my clerk. I had already told him that I had a meeting and that I wasn't coming today, but you know him: he speaks and you obey or else. Well, this time it's or else: I told him I wasn't able to get there until tomorrow.'

Jackie sat back in her chair, closed her eyes and said, 'One tries to put a cheerful face on things but, oh, I really am worried about Richard; he was in such a rage inside. I've been saying to him, do your blows with your words, they'll be more effective, but I'm afraid that something may have happened and they came to blows and . . . well . . .'

'You needn't worry about that,' put in Alexander, 'because as I said, Trip told me he had left the house.'

Jackie said slowly, 'I saw her yesterday.'

312

Alexander had no need to ask whom she had seen but said, 'Yes, and what did you think?'

'I . . . I seemed to stop thinking. It was a shock to see the face so emaciated. Twenty-six years of living in the dark, you could say, being afraid to speak. Probably the fear kept her from recalling the past, which Glenda tells me she's doing frequently now and also talking a little more clearly, linking her words together as she hadn't done earlier. But, oh dear, dear! What a tragedy; what a wasted life! I wanted to cry just looking at her.'

'Did she speak to you?'

'Yes, she did; and it was odd how Richard transmitted her meaning, because when she put out her hand towards me and said, "Nice," I didn't know how to answer, but Richard, looking at her, said, "Yes, isn't she? She's very nice," to which she again nodded and repeated his words, "Very nice." When Richard said softly, "She's going to be your daughter-in-law and you're going to be at our wedding," she turned to him and her face was very sad when she said, "Soon." He looked at me then, and said, "Yes, soon." It was too much; I just had to get out of that room. I knew I was going to cry, as he had.'

Alexander's voice was low and soft as he leant across the table, saying, 'You're a very nice person, Jackie, and Richard is a lucky man to have found you.'

'I'm lucky, too, Alex. My work takes me among a lot of men, especially in offices, and some of them are . . . well, pigs; they are the kind that look down on women as an inferior species and, being so, won't object to a little mauling.'

'No-o.'

'Oh, yes. You in your small world don't know what goes on in the big one. I learnt how to give an upper-cut by the time I was twenty.'

'You didn't!'

'Oh, yes, I did. But, going back to your remark, I know, Alex, I'm a lucky girl in finding Richard.'

At this there was a buzz from the button at the end of his table and a voice said stiffly, 'Miss Armstrong on the phone for you, Mr Armstrong.'

He picked up the phone and said, 'Hello there.'

'He's back.'

'Oh, good! Where on earth has he been?'

There came a short laugh; then, 'Two places. To a lock-smith to have the lock changed on his flat, because he wouldn't put it past the old fellow to send somebody down to clear it, for he, too, has a key and, of course, it's his property. The other is' – here she began to laugh as she continued – 'he went and had a drink. It must have been more than one. Oh, he's not drunk, although he's not far from it; he would need something after that ordeal, I should think. I wish you had been here. He went in to his mother and, Alex, I'm sure she nearly laughed.'

'Why was that?'

'Because after apologising to her for being away so long, he said, "Mother, I'm drunk. I'm drunk because I've achieved something today that I've wanted to do for years."

'I'm sure she didn't know what he was talking about, really, but she made a sound like laughter in her throat and put her hands up to his face and held it, before drawing him gently into her arms. It was good to see, Alex. I'll tell you all about it later.'

After he put the phone down Alexander looked at Jackie and said, 'Did you get the gist of all that?'

'He's had a lock changed or something and he's drunk.'

'Yes; and that's about the whole of it,' said Alexander, laughing.

'Poor Richard. He must have gone through it. I'll go now, because I'm dying to see what he looks like tight.'

As he led her towards the door, she said softly, 'I love him so, Alex.'

He had opened the door and now, when she lifted her head

up towards him and kissed him, she added, 'And I love you too.'

'Go on!' he said, pushing her, and she went past Miss Fairweather's desk, meaning to give the woman a smile, but Miss Fairweather had her back towards her and was doing something at the filing cabinet.

For the next half-hour or so Alexander got on with the special business of the next day, when he must go to see that damned man. As the will stood, there were no other beneficiaries; everything was simply left to his son, Richard Mortimer Baindor. Alexander rang for Miss Fairweather to come and take the dictation on the rest of his letters.

After about three minutes, when there had been no reply to his signal that he was waiting for her, he rang again; and when, once more, there was no reply he got up and looked into the next room and towards her desk. She wasn't there. At the end of the corridor there was a rest room where the staff had their breaks, but he didn't like to go in. However, he had no sooner seated himself at his desk again than his door opened and James came in.

James did not sit down but addressed his father straight away: 'What have you done or said to Miss Fairweather?'

'Me! What have I said to whom?'

James's voice rose, 'To your secretary.'

'What did I say to her? I only dictated the letters. What are you getting at?'

'She's going to give her notice in. That news to you?'

'She's what?'

'You heard what I said, she's going to give her notice in. She says she's had enough, over fifteen years of it.'

'Had enough of what?'

'Enough of you, Father.'

James pulled a chair close up to the desk and sat down. 'You are sometimes very blind and stupid about other people's needs behind that keen law-filled mind of yours.'

315

'Would you mind telling me what you are talking about?'

'I'm talking about your secretary and your conduct towards her.'

'My conduct? It has been impeccable.'

'Yes, damn you, and I mean that . . . too impeccable. You've never unbent with her all these years: Miss Fairweather this and Miss Fairweather that. Miss Fairweather will see to this and Miss Fairweather will see to that. Yes, and Miss Fairweather, let me tell you, will be a very great loss to the firm. Go down into the storeroom and look at the files. She can lay her hands on anything, right back practically to the day she came. She was twenty-five years old then, and a highly trained secretary, and since that time she has looked after our interests in a way nobody else would or could. Do you know that?'

Alexander sat back in his chair. Then he said, 'What in the name of God are you getting at?'

'I'm getting at you, Father.' James's voice sounded weary. 'Even when Mother was alive that girl had a crush on you.'

'*What?*'

'Well, call it what you like. As I said, it started before Mother died, and that's ten years ago.'

'But what have I done today to make her change her mind?'

'Only that you are, she understands, about to marry a girl who is young enough to be your granddaughter.'

'I'm *what*? I've never said anything to her about marrying again or—'

'No; but you've had a young lady in here today, haven't you?'

'Yes, I have, and that young lady was Richard's fiancée. She came looking for Richard, just as we've all been doing.'

It was James's turn now to sit back and he spluttered as he said, 'Oh, that's it, is it? How did you part with her?'

'Part with whom?'

'With Jackie, of course.'

Alexander sat thoughtfully for a moment, then he suddenly began to chuckle and he said, 'Oh, my God! Just before I opened the door she'd told me how much she loved Richard and we'd had a long talk about this and that and then . . . well, as I opened the door for her, she leant up and kissed me and said she loved me too.'

'Well, that must have done it. Miss Fairweather's been in the rest room crying her eyes out. But she means it about leaving. Even when she knows that it was Richard's girl, it won't make any difference. I think, as she said, she's had enough.'

'And what d'you expect me to do?'

'Melt.'

'*Melt?*'

'Yes. You treat her like a machine. She is Miss Fairweather. She is the one who can lay her hands on anything you want at any moment. Because of her you can walk out of this office at any hour of the day and the work will get done. She is just Miss Fairweather.'

Alexander sat back in his chair, an expression of wry dismay on his face. Then he voiced his thoughts: 'Look at me,' he said, 'I'm almost sixty. She's a woman in her prime – she's only forty.'

'She's older than Jackie.'

'Oh, Lord!' Slowly Alexander shook his head. 'If there wasn't enough trouble here and there as it is. Now this. How on earth am I going to face her?'

'That's up to you, but she'll give you her notice in the morning, I know that, if not today. Apart from Jackie, and I'll explain that to her, I don't think it'll make the slightest difference. She knows and I know and you know that any firm in this city will just jump at her once they know she's free. And I'll tell you something else you didn't know. Rankin

317

– yes, Rankin, your kindly associate at the Bar – offered her a job about three years ago and at much more than she's getting here.'

'Rankin did that? The swine!'

'No; he's a businessman. He'd lost his secretary and he'd heard about her. None of your papers ever went astray nor was a word misspelt, nor the grammar anything but perfect. Oh, no, he knew what he was after. He put it to her quietly one day. "If ever you want a change, Miss Fairweather, just come and see me," he said. I was there; well, I was within earshot when he said it; and I remember when I passed him I said, half in fun and wholly in earnest, "Do you want your throat cut?" He burst out laughing, and he said, "All's fair in love and war."'

'Well I never!'

'Yes; that's something else for you to think about. So, if I were you, I wouldn't ring for Miss Fairweather tonight. I would put your things on and get yourself away home, or along to Glenda's.'

'What I want to say to you now,' said Alexander tartly, 'is, go to hell!'

'Yes, I know you do; but I'm going along now to tell your secretary, who is going to be your secretary no longer, that she made a mistake. Not that it'll do any good. I'll be seeing you, Father.'

James went out, laughing now, and Alexander put his head in his hands and said, 'Oh, my God! What have I done?'

Glenda was laughing heartily as she said, 'And what advice do you expect to receive from me, dear brother?'

'Oh, Glenda! Don't take it as a joke. I'm in a fix here . . . Miss Fairweather and me!' His voice had sunk to a scornful note.

'It's as James said, you're a blind idiot.'

'Oh, he's been on the phone already and told you?'

'Yes; and you deserve all you're getting. It's as he said, even when Miss Fairweather knew who the girl was, she was still adamant that she was going to leave. And, you know, I don't blame her. When I've been in your office I've noticed your manner towards her. You *do* treat her like a machine.'

'I do nothing of the sort. I've been a very good boss to her.'

'Moneywise, oh, yes, perhaps, but there are other bosses who'll be glad to give her the same, or more, to get some-body who's so efficient. James may have laughed about it, but I can tell you he's right.'

'But what can I do about it, Glenda? Look at me. I'm nearly sixty. I've never thought of anybody since Mary went, and she's . . . well, she's not forty yet, I don't think.'

'She's forty and she's a very good-looking woman. I've seen her out of her office gear and she's attractive.'

'Then why the devil hasn't she been married before now?'

'Because, you idiot, she fell for you and, what was more, years ago she was tied to her home and her mother. Her mother was riddled with arthritis, and she stayed at home after office hours and saw to her. Did you know she was brilliant at school and heading for university when her father died? He wasn't as well insured as he should have been, leaving barely enough to keep them both, so she had to change her thinking. She went to a managerial college for a year and sailed through. Then she became a secretary and she landed with you when she was twenty-five.'

'How do you know all this?'

'Because we've chatted. The first time was when I met her in the restaurant round the corner from Beverley Square and she recognised me from my visits to you at the office. That was when James was just starting and I came and set up his office for him, if you remember, for he had as much idea then of order as he has now. He's very like you.'

'Look here,' put in Alexander now, 'you're going too far. You'd think we were a pair of idiots.'

'Well, that's what you are when it comes to running an office. You're all right on the law and on the courtroom floor, and with the clients, because it's already been set up for you.'

'Good God!' Alexander got up from his seat, went to the sideboard and poured himself out a whisky from the decanter standing there, threw it back and said, 'How strange it is that our firm has managed to get where it is.' Then, as if asking a question of the air, he continued, 'How on earth did we manage until fifteen years ago?'

'All right, but you were very much smaller then, and even so you were often in a muddle; changing secretaries and other office staff as often as your coat. You look back.'

He sat down again and his voice now had an almost pathetic note about it when he asked, 'How am I going to get through the next month with her?'

And the answer that came was, 'That's up to you, Alex. Have you ever thought of looking at her? Have you ever asked yourself if you like her?'

'Oh, I like her. Yes, I like her. I admire her. But honest to God! I've never thought past that.'

'Well, once again,' said Glenda, 'have you ever *looked* at her?'

He thought. Yes, he had looked at her. She had an oval face with a very small nose. It was a snub nose. He couldn't remember what her mouth looked like. Her eyes . . . he couldn't remember the colour of her eyes either.

Glenda's voice came at him now, saying, 'Try looking at her during the next few days.'

As he was answering, the phone rang. 'Yes? This is . . .' She got no further for a voice said, 'Is Mr Richard Baindor with you?'

'Who's speaking?'

'Dr Bell.'

'Yes, Richard is here.'

'Well, will you tell him his father is dying and that I think he should be here.'

'I will do no such thing.'

'What did you say?'

'I said, I will do no such thing. He saw his father this morning.'

'Yes; and the heart-attack and stroke have followed that meeting.'

'Dear, dear!' she said; then, 'My brother, Mr Baindor's solicitor, is here. Would you like a word with him?'

She handed the receiver to Alexander. 'Yes, this is Armstrong here.'

'Hello there! We know each other.'

'Yes; yes, we do, and I understand from the little I have heard that your patient is dying.'

'Yes, he is.'

'Do you like him? Have you ever liked him?'

'That is a very odd question to ask of me.'

'But I am asking it of you. Do you like him?'

'No, I don't. Never have.'

'Good. Well, I can say the same.'

'Nevertheless, no matter how we like or dislike anyone, it isn't good for a man in his state to die alone.'

'He deserves nothing else. You say he's dying; well, so is his wife.'

'What d'you mean? His wife died years ago.'

'His wife didn't die years ago. It might be news to you, Doctor, that she's lying here, but she is also dying, and her son is with her. When your patient tried to murder her he didn't finish off her body but he almost finished off her mind. She lost her memory and for a time was a vagrant on the roads and would have been still but for a kindly woman who looked after her for these twenty-six years or so. That'll be news

321

to you, and I would ask if you will keep it to yourself until I see you, which will be after you have rung to tell me that your patient has died.'

The voice that came over the phone was very low now as Dr Bell said, 'Will you tell his son?'

'No; not until you phone me finally.'

'Very well. Goodbye.'

Alexander turned to Glenda and said, 'So he's going. Thank God I didn't answer his demand this morning, for Richard would now be without a penny.'

'That wouldn't have troubled him.'

'It mightn't have, but it's his due and he can now use his father's ill-gotten gains to put things to rights. I'll see to that.'

It was three o'clock in the morning and the voice on the phone was Trip's. The night nurse took the call and Trip said, 'Could I speak to Miss Armstrong, please?'

'She's asleep. But I could give her your message as soon as she wakes. Is it important?'

'No. Not all that important. Just say Mr Baindor died at half past two this morning . . .'

By nine o'clock Richard had telephoned both Alexander and James and asked them the same question, should he tell her? And the answer was similar from both. It was up to him. If he thought it would ease her mind, yes. But what did Glenda think? Glenda thought she should be told and added that she had had a quiet night and seemed rested this morning.

Now, as he sat in Glenda's office, Richard said to her, 'I don't know how I'm going to put it to Mother because, although I have no regrets whatever, I know our meeting yesterday morning caused the attack.'

'He would have had it in any case, and shortly. I spoke to Dr Bell first thing and he told me that of late he'd had minor heart-attacks and that he wouldn't have been surprised if he had dropped dead straight away. But he rallied, then had the stroke.

'Knowing him, he'd make himself rally until Alex appeared and he'd had time to change his will. But all I can say is, thank God for the stroke. So don't let his going worry you in any way.'

'It's not. It's not; believe me, Glenda. And you know something? It wasn't what I said that upset him most, I'm sure it was the breaking of that vase. I only wish there had been more of the wretched things I could have smashed.'

There was a tap on the door now and a voice said, 'May I come in?'

When it opened Jackie entered, and Richard, getting to his feet, said, 'You're early. I thought you'd be at work.'

'I've taken the day off . . . no, the week off.' And then she added, 'How d'you feel?'

'All right. All right in one way but worried in another. We've just been discussing if it would be wise to tell Mother of his going.'

Taking a seat near Glenda, Jackie looked at her and said, 'What d'you think?'

'I think he should tell her.'

'So do I.'

'Will you come in with me?' Richard asked her.

Jackie paused, then looked at Glenda and said, 'Yes, if it's all right with you, Glenda.'

'Of course. But I would suggest that you get it over as quickly as possible.'

Irene was lying with her eyes closed, but she wasn't asleep; she was thinking, thinking it had been a strange night because of the dream she had had, and she could remember it. That was very odd because she often dreamed but when she woke she could never recall details. Her mind was mostly in a jumble, and she made it worse when she tried to think.

She had seen herself as a young woman walking through

323

some kind of hall; she went upstairs and into a room where a man was lying on a bed; and she walked up to the side of the bed and looked at him. She saw that he looked frightened; then she realised why – he was wearing handcuffs, and they were clamped to each side of the bed. Yet, strangely, his plight did not move her to pity for him, or sympathy. His brow was running with sweat, but she made no effort to wipe it.

She had no feeling whatever for the figure on the bed; so she turned away from him, and was now in a garden, a beautiful garden, and there was pulsing through her such a feeling of relief that she wanted to skip and dance. But she shouldn't, you only did that when you were a child. But there she was, she was jumping over narrow streams; she was running through woods; and then, of a sudden, she stopped and found herself back in the bedroom. But there was no one in the bed, the man had gone. She turned about and ran down the stairs and out into the garden again. She looked up at the sky and began to sing – she could hear herself singing – and then a voice spoke to her, saying, 'Would you like a drink, dear?' She had looked at the kind nurse and shaken her head slightly. Then she had gone to sleep again, and went once more into the garden. But now she was walking slowly and her body had a strange feeling. There was a lightness about it as if it were about to fly away from her. It was as if she had been released from somewhere. She sat on a seat. Everything about her was peaceful.

Then she was on her feet again, walking once more into a kind of light. Beautiful light. Rosy light. She was watching the dawn breaking, feeling so happy to be in the light, for the night had been so long, so very long. She was still walking in the light when a nurse's voice said, 'There you are, dear. Let me put a pillow behind your head. That's it. Now drink this. That's right. You've had a good night. The night nurse told me you only woke up once, and that was early on. Do you feel better?'

For a moment she did not answer, because she was asking herself if she did feel better. She felt something, she felt different, she didn't know how, or why she should feel different, but she did; and she enjoyed the tea. Her answer was plain and clear, 'Yes.' And then after a moment she added, 'Thank . . . you. Thank . . . you.'

'Oh, that's splendid! Your throat's a lot better. Now rest easy; we won't disturb you for a while, you look so comfortable there.'

It was odd, but she did feel comfortable. Her body did not seem to trouble her any more. She made a great effort to swallow some porridge when breakfast came, which brought murmurs of approval from the nurse; and further murmurs when she ate three teaspoonfuls of the beaten-up softly boiled egg mixed with thin pieces of bread and butter.

When later she was washed and her hair combed and she was lying waiting for the time when her son would come back into the room she slid into a light doze, to waken and see not only Richard but that nice girl he was going to marry looking down at her. It was the girl who said, 'Good morning.'

And she answered her with a smile and said, 'Good . . . morning.'

'Oh,' said Richard, 'you sound much better this morning. That proves your chest is easier.'

He turned from the bed, pulled a chair forward and motioned Jackie on to it so that she could be closer to his mother's head; and he took his mother's frail hand and, bending over her, said in a low voice, 'You do sound stronger this morning, Mother; do you feel better?'

She looked at him, then nodded. He turned now and looked helplessly at Jackie. Jackie knew he was afraid to start, so taking hold of Irene's other hand, she stroked it for a moment before saying, 'Richard's got something to tell you, my dear, and he's afraid it might worry you.'

Irene was staring at her son and to his amazement she

325

said, quite clearly, 'I know . . . He's gone . . . dead.'

They stared at each other for a long time; then slowly she withdrew her hand from his and stroked his face, and there was even a smile on hers as she said, 'Free.'

He turned from the bed and walked blindly towards the window. All the tears of his childhood that he'd had to clamp down on for fear of his father seemed to have formed a well inside him that was now overflowing, and he seemed unable to stop it.

He heard Jackie saying to his mother, 'You're wonderful . . . wonderful.'

And she was wonderful; but, he realised suddenly, she would soon be leaving him.

4

The funeral of Edward Mortimer Baindor took place four days later. It did not make headlines in any paper, but in one of the leading journals it was stated in so many words that it was a great surprise that the financier had been cremated with less attention than would have been given to most men of his position. It was a private occasion and was attended only by his solicitors, Alexander and James Armstrong, and representatives from his businesses in America, Germany, France, Italy and Holland. It was regrettable that his only son had been unable to attend the service; he was indisposed. A near neighbour, Lord Blakey, father of Miss Jacqueline Franks who was engaged to Mr Richard Baindor, was also present.

Mr Richard Mortimer Baindor would inherit what amounted to a financial empire.

After the funeral, Alexander, James and Richard had been tied up for hours each day talking to the managements of the overseas companies of the firm. They had come to the conclusion that a chief executive should be appointed to oversee all the separate businesses and report back on whether some of the companies should be dissolved or sold off.

When at last the three men had the office to themselves, Richard burst out, 'I can't handle this, Alex. You can see they all expected me to take his place and run them all more or less as he did.'

'As I've told you and we've told them, a new chief executive will take his place,' said Alexander.

'Well, it'll be a very tough man who could deal with that lot. What I suggest you do, Alex, is sell as many of the companies as you can.'

'I'll do nothing of the sort. As for a candidate, I know the very man.'

'You do?'

'Yes.'

'Well, why haven't you mentioned him before?'

'Because I couldn't. I haven't spoken to him yet. But I know he's a man who will be delighted to analyse these various companies and get the general feel of the best way forward.'

'And who is he?'

'George Peacock. He's the senior partner of a firm of accountants across the square. He's only in his late forties. Like me, he was pushed into a family firm to follow his father's footsteps. What is more, he's had wider experience than I ever had; he's a very good accountant with receivership experience and investment banking contacts. Now he would just jump at the chance to immerse himself in the reorganisation and scaling down of the Baindor empire. Anyway, we can talk to him, but I know before I start what his answer will be. And he can quite easily leave what he's doing to his younger brother, who, like his father, has a feeling for the more general side of accountancy.'

'Whatever happens,' said Richard, 'I'm going on with my career. I've only another two years or so and I'll be fully fledged, and I love the work.'

'Well,' put in James now, 'I see no reason why you

shouldn't go on and leave it to Father and me to fleece you, because we will, you know.'

'Yes; yes, I know that.' Richard smiled now and looked from one to the other; then, turning to Alexander again, he said, 'When can we see this fellow?'

'I'm going over to see him today.'

'The sooner the better. Now I must get back to Mother. I've hardly seen anything of her these last few days.'

'Get along there then,' said Alexander. 'James and I will join you tonight. By the way, one of us must go and see that pawnbroker. I meant to do so before the funeral, but one thing and another held us up.'

'Why not forget about the things there? She'll never need them again.'

'She didn't carry those tickets about with her for years for nothing. Glenda said that she mentioned the tickets yesterday, at least she said, "Gomparts," and then followed this with "Tickets, pawn tickets." So she knows that those things are still in pawn, and I'm sure she would like them. So I'll go tomorrow.'

'All right.'

'Lastly,' put in James, 'you really can't carry out your intention about the manor, Richard.'

'I can, James.' Richard's voice rose as he opened the door. 'The minute she's gone I'm going to burn the whole damned place down.'

In the silence after his departure neither of the other men spoke. Then, looking at his father, James said, 'He means it.'

'He can't do it.'

'Who's going to stop him? It's his place; he can do what he likes with it.'

'It would be a sin, and what good would it do?'

'Apparently it'll do him some good. What's more, doing it is a kind of last tribute to her.'

329

'By the way,' Alexander said, 'she's failing. I would say he won't have very long to wait.'

James sighed as he rose, but at the door he paused and, looking back at his father, he smiled and said by way of a little light relief, 'May I ask how things are going with . . .' his voice dropped '. . . Miss Fairweather?'

'Oh, now, don't start on that again.'

'I won't; but how *are* things?'

'I can do nothing. She told me that she's going at the end of the month and I told her how sorry I was, and asked if I had upset her in any way, and so on, and so on.'

'And what did it come to?'

'Nothing, except I told her that I would miss her a lot.'

'Did you say just that, or did you add, "in all sorts of ways"?'

'Get yourself out before I start swearing. Go on!'

'In today's paper it says that your star's in the ascendant.' Then James made a hasty escape before his father could make any comment.

It was on the Saturday evening, and through the misty autumn twilight Alexander and Richard hurried in to Beechwood.

They were taking off their overcoats when Glenda appeared from her private quarters, saying, 'You're back, then. How did it go? Did you get them?'

'Yes; Alex did,' said Richard, smiling at her. 'Come along and see how she takes them.'

'No, no; I can't. Anyway, Bella is with her. The boys dropped her off. She has bought them an old banger, which they have done up. Really, it's a marvellous little car. Talk about four kids with a Christmas box. Anyway, they're going to pick her up later. And I have visitors, too.'

'Anyone we know?' asked Alexander.

'Of course. Anyway, go and get this business over. She's had a quiet day, but take it easy with her, not too much

330

emotion, mind.' She had spoken the last words to Richard. He did not answer, but both men turned and walked towards the stairs.

As soon as they opened the door Bella rose from the bed-side, saying, 'Oh, I'm about to be on me way. I've stayed too long as it is; I always do. But she's lovely today, aren't you, love?' She bent over Irene and kissed her, and Irene put up her hand and stroked the grey-white hair.

'You stay where you are,' said Alexander, 'because you know more about this little business than we did a couple of hours ago.'

Richard was bending over his mother now and asking, 'All right?'

'Fine. Fine, dear.' She smiled up at him, and the hand was once more raised, but touching his cheek now. Alexander had pulled up two chairs to the bedside, one on each side of Bella, and it was Richard who said, 'Do you know where Alex has been?'

Irene gave a slight movement of her head, then contradicted this by saying slowly, 'Yes . . . and . . . no.'

Richard now put his hand into the inner pocket of his coat and brought out the small brown envelope. After opening the flap he took one of her hands and tipped the contents on to it; and she was looking down on her wedding ring, her engagement ring, the beautiful necklace that Bella had taken for a fairground trinket, and the little card case. She stared at them for a long moment before lifting her eyes and looking from Richard to Alex and saying, 'Mr Gom-parts?'

'Yes.' Alexander was nodding at her. 'I saw the two Mr Gomparts, two gentlemen indeed. You know, they have kept these for you all these years because, as the son said, he fully expected you to come back one day for them. The necklace had insured the other pieces for two lifetimes. They had kept them in their private safe all these years.'

Richard, now touching the articles she was holding in her

331

palm, said, 'Alex says the younger one spoke so wonderfully of you. You know what he said? He has never been able to get you out of his mind, and he's always thought of you as . . .' He paused here and his voice dropped. There was a crack in it as he said, 'The Lost Angel.'

Irene's eyes closed. The lids were pressed tight and when a tear fell from beneath her lashes Alexander said quickly, 'Now, now; we were warned. Glenda told us she would throw us out if we upset you.'

Irene opened her eyes, and said, 'Dear . . . Mr Gomparts . . . so good.'

Then, looking down at the jewellery in her hand, she lifted up the wedding ring, handed it to Richard and said, 'Hated that.' There was a long pause while they waited, because they knew she had something more to say. When she spoke again her words were blurred but audible: 'I . . . kept it . . . because it had . . . giv-en me you.'

'Oh, Mother.'

Alexander's voice said, 'Steady. Steady. She has more to say.'

Richard straightened up. He watched his mother pick up the beautiful engagement ring and, lifting it towards Bella, whose head was on her chest and whose face was already wet with tears, she said, 'Bella . . . my friend . . . for . . . you.'

Bella lifted her head and looked at the ring, and, being nobody but herself, she could only exclaim, 'Oh, my God!' Then, looking from one man to the other, she said, 'Eeh, no! I couldn't. Not that. It's worth a lot of money.'

'Take it.' Richard's voice was low. 'She loves you, and it is the only way she has of showing her thanks.'

Irene had to push the ring into Bella's hand, and all Bella could do now was pull her bulky self to her feet, lean over her dear lass and kiss her, saying as she did so, 'I really want no presents. You were my present.'

332

The tap on her shoulder from Alexander brought Bella slowly back into the chair.

Now picking up the little card case, Irene offered it to Alexander, saying, 'Small . . . but . . . full of . . . grat-it-tude.'

He looked down at it in his hand. Then, doubling his fingers over it, he said, 'It will always be my most precious possession.'

Irene smiled at him, then said haltingly, 'You will . . . never . . . open it.' And he, looking back at her, said, 'I won't?' Then, opening his hand again, he pressed round the edges as Bella had once done, and tried every way to open it.

Irene put out her hand and took it from him; then she squeezed the middle of the little case twice, and it opened slowly. She smiled at him and said, 'Clever.'

Taking it from her, Alexander looked at the inside for a spring but couldn't see one; then, looking at her with a broad smile, he said, 'Yes, indeed, Irene . . . clever. Wherever the spring is it must be so minute that no one could ever find it. It's wonderful.'

Irene now gave a long sigh. She lifted up the necklace, put it back into the brown paper envelope and laid it by her side on the counterpane; then, looking at Richard, she said, 'For . . . someone else . . . Jackie.'

'Yes, Mother. I'll bring her after dinner.'

Alexander now put out his hand to a small bell-pull, and when a nurse appeared the men left the room. Bella remained, wordless now but holding Irene close . . .

A minute later the three stood outside the door; and now Alexander said to Bella, 'Don't cry. Don't cry, my dear. She's happy. Dry your face and come along. Glenda's waiting. She says she's got company.'

'Eeh, no! I couldn't meet any company, Mr Armstrong, and the lads'll be waiting.'

'The lads can wait,' Richard put in. 'Come along.' And he took her elbow and led her down the stairs to Glenda's sitting room. But once inside they all stopped as, surprised, they looked at the company. It consisted of Jackie, Miss Fairweather and James.

Jackie was no surprise to Richard, but Miss Fairweather was to Alexander. However, before he could make any comment Richard, looking at his fiancée, said, 'Where on earth have you been all day? I've been trying to contact you.'

'I've been at work.'

'I thought you'd left.'

'There're more jobs than one. I've been offered two since I left the magazine, but I've turned them both down.'

'Why?'

'Because I've got another job in view.'

'For goodness' sake!' put in Glenda now. 'Sit yourselves down and let's get this over with because, if I know anything, tempers are going to rise.'

'Why should they?'

This came from Alexander, and his sister said, 'Wait and see.' Then turning to Jackie, she said, 'Well, fire away. Get it over with.'

Jackie was sitting next to Miss Fairweather and they exchanged glances. Then Jackie said, 'I've been very busy these last two weeks.' She was now looking at Richard who had seated himself opposite her on the couch.

'But so have we all,' said Richard.

'Yes, Richard, so have we all, but your projects have been different from mine. Do you want to hear about them?' and she paused for a moment, then said, 'Why am I asking that? Because whether or not you want to hear you've got to be told. First, though, I must ask you a question, and I'll have to stand on my feet to do it.' She rose from the chair and, looking straight across at him, she said, 'Are you still determined to burn down the manor when your mother goes?'

He did not respond immediately, but rose slowly to his feet also before saying, 'You know I am. Absolutely determined.'

There was a long pause, and an uneasy feeling began to fill the room, when Jackie's next words brought a gasp from all those present. 'Well,' she said, 'Richard Mortimer Baindor, if you persist in carrying out your scheme of hate, then I shall never marry you, and I won't repeat that, but I'll just emphasise it by saying that I meant every word of it.'

He glared at her. Then harshly, he said, 'What's come over you? You've known all along what I meant to do. You've never said anything against it yet.'

'No. But I've thought all the more, and I knew from the beginning that should you do such a thing it would break us up.'

'But why? In the name of God, why?'

'Simply because you imagine it will recompense your mother for all she has gone through, but you have forgotten the nature of the man who caused it, for I know he would be glad to see it burn to the ground rather than be used for the purpose I have in mind.

'He looked down on his servants as menials. Besides being a bad and evil man, he was an out-and-out snob, a social climber, and it irked him that he had never been given a title. Well, now, if you will listen to me for a few minutes more I shall tell you what I have been doing during the last two weeks – at least Margaret and I . . .

'With the help of Miss Fairweather and her cousin, who is an architect, I have, or rather we have, planned the rebuilding of the manor and would hope to make it into something that would burn your father up still more, wherever he is, because we propose it should be turned into a convalescent home for the poor.

'And when I say the poor, I mean the poor: not anyone who can afford to pay something towards having attention after an illness or any such thing. It's the poor I have seen this last week or so under the guidance of Bella there. She has shown us parts of the city which make her little house appear like a middle-class mansion, and she has introduced me to people who have never known anything but the life lived in a slum. And they are your slums now, some of them. Oh, I know you mean to do something about it, but you won't be able to change the whole world or even London, and there will always be those people who, after being in hospital or lying at home with no one but their family to see to them, who are so poor that they can't afford a week, a fortnight, a month of attention and comfort and the feeling that they are being cared for, that they are no longer the dregs. And Bella knows a lot about the dregs, because all her boys were taken from there. What did surprise me, among all the debris I saw, was how they managed to approach life with a smile and a joke.

'Well, there you have the rough outline. For more details I must tell you that Maggie,' she nodded towards Miss Fairweather, 'and George, the architect, have worked out a plan. By the way, do you know how many rooms there are in your mansion, Richard?'

When he did not answer but still continued to glare at her, she said, 'Sixty-five! That isn't counting the kitchen and the servants' quarters. And did you know that that house was built in three parts? The kitchen quarters were the original part, built at the end of the seventeenth century. It was a little homestead. Then at the beginning of the eighteenth century along came somebody and bought all the land around it, and added on an east wing. Not satisfied with that, somebody else in the nineteenth century stuck another wing on the other side of the kitchen. From the outside you would think it had all been built at the same time, because at the end of the last century a new façade was put over the lot.'

Here she paused for breath and bowed her head for a moment; then she went on, 'The proposition is this, that two-thirds of the house could be turned into a convalescent home with rooms for twenty patients, with others for nursing staff, et cetera. The other third could be a strictly private house. The original kitchen quarters could be attached to the convalescent home and that would be a big asset. The other part, the east wing, which consists of the drawing room, dining room, billiard room and so on, besides the bedrooms upstairs, could be private quarters, a home, not a showplace. Then there are the gardens. There's the river where male patients could fish, and the gardens could remain for patients to wander and sit in. The private house would have its own garden at the back. As for the cottages outside, we'll come to them later; but these, when altered, would be homes for Bella and her boys.'

Jackie looked down at her tightly joined hands which were lying in her lap; then jerking her head upwards, she returned Richard's stare and said, 'Well, Richard?'

For answer he swung round from her and made for the door. At this she jumped up and cried after him in the loudest voice she had ever raised to him before, 'That's always the coward's retreat. Why don't you stand and face an opponent?'

He turned on her, saying, 'I am not retreating, miss. I am going next door to pour myself a very stiff whisky and to ask myself how, in the name of God, I ever got mixed up with you.'

At this both of them were startled by Glenda's voice, almost as loud as Jackie's: 'Whose house is this anyway? Jackie and I will go next door and see to drinks, not only for you but for all of us, for we certainly need them. Come along, Jackie.'

When the two women were outside the door they leant against each other and Glenda said, 'Dear Lord, girl, you did give it to him!'

'It was the only way, Glenda. I know him. He would have burnt that place down, I know he would, and everything in it.'

'And you wouldn't have married him?'

'No, because what I've seen this last fortnight has wrung my heart. You know, I didn't realise that I had been brought up with a silver spoon in my mouth. Because I pushed myself into journalism I thought I was a working girl. I found I know damn all about work. I know damn all about living. It's Bella who knows about living, and the lads; and so does Margaret, in her way. I have an idea in my head and I mean to carry it out, not just the conserving of the house, but something else. I'll tell you about it later, but let's get that drink, because here's one who needs it.'

In their absence Richard had slumped on to the couch in the sitting room. His head was down, his joined hands hanging between his knees, and there was silence in the room for a moment, until Miss Fairweather spoke.

Looking across at Richard, she said, 'Dr Baindor . . . I am perhaps speaking out of turn, but I must say that she is right. That house could be used for so much good. It could vindicate all your dear mother has had to suffer. Miss Morgan here knows what it is to live in poverty, what it is to live in the gutter, as she has said. And there are still many people in such a situation. I, as you know, work during the week, but both Miss Franks and I and my cousin have spent the last two weekends under her guidance travelling through parts of London one could not believe existed. I'd like to stick my neck out further, by saying you have a great lady in your fiancée.'

Richard now raised his head, loosened his hands, lay back in his chair and looked at Miss Fairweather.

'Thank you,' he said. 'I – I suppose you are right; in fact, I know you are. But that . . . my way . . . was the only way I could see to getting him and the house entirely out of my life.'

Alexander meanwhile was looking at his secretary and what he now said to her in a soft voice was, 'You are a very secretive creature, Miss Margaret Fairweather.'

Miss Fairweather's colour changed slightly, but she kept her eyes on Alexander's face as she said, 'One learns that, Mr Armstrong, when working in the law.'

This caused an immediate guffaw from James, who put out his hand and patted Miss Fairweather's shoulder as he said, 'Maggie, all I can say is, you're marvellous. I've always known it; I haven't been blind like some people.' He grinned now as he went on, 'What we're going to do at the end of the month, I just don't know.'

'I shouldn't worry, Mr James. I've decided to stay on for a little longer until Mr Armstrong finds a suitable substitute.'

Alexander's voice cut in, addressing his son: 'You're enjoying yourself, aren't you? Well, I would thank you to mind your own business for a time, and I mean that. You understand?'

'Oh, yes, sir, I understand.'

James was still grinning when he stood up and said, 'Here come the drinks. Thank God for wine, whisky and women.'

Immediately after dinner, which had been simple and short, Richard, speaking to Jackie for the first time since their heated encounter, said, 'Mother would like to see you. Will you come along?'

Her face straight, her voice matter-of-fact, she said, 'Yes; of course,' and together they left the others. But before they reached Irene's bedroom he pulled her to a stop and, taking her by the shoulders, he said, 'I want to shake the life out of you, even slap your face and tell you that you are an interfering busybody; and for two pins I would take you at your word and go ahead with what I meant to do. Yet at the same time I know damn well I couldn't, because I can't live without you.'

She did not say anything to this, but she put her arms around his neck and his went around her waist and, their lips and bodies held close, they stood swaying for a moment; then she said softly, 'I took a risk. I knew I might be blighting my life but I had to do it, not only for my sake but for yours, because I knew that that was the last thing your mother would want you to do, and that what she would love you to do is help the poor, the lost and the lonely, as she herself was helped for so many years.'

Again he kissed her, but softly now; then they went into the bedroom where the sister was putting the last touches to her patient's comfort for the night. Turning to them, she said quietly, 'I'll leave you for a little while, but she's very tired.'

Richard nodded to her; and then she left them. Now, bending over Irene, Richard said, 'You wanted to see Jackie.'

After making a slight movement with her head, Irene took from beneath the counterpane the paper envelope that held the necklace and handed it to Jackie, saying slowly, 'For you.'

Jackie gasped as she stared down at the beautiful gold and ruby necklace, saying, 'Oh! How . . . how beautiful. For me?'

'Wedding . . . present . . . soon . . . very soon.' And when, after a deep breath, she ended, 'A week,' Richard said, in surprise but softly, 'But, Mother, we have nothing prepared. I mean, there have been no arrangements made or anything.'

Irene turned from him and looked towards Jackie. 'Licence.'

At this Jackie nodded quickly, saying, 'By special licence?'

Again Irene nodded, but now she was smiling as she brought out, 'Good girl.'

Jackie laughed softly; and, bending towards Irene, she held up the necklace, saying, 'I'll always treasure it. Always. And I won't be happy until I can call you Mother-in-law.'

Irene closed her eyes, and when they watched her lower lip tremble Richard said, 'Now, Mother, please, don't upset yourself, or else we'll have Glenda in here knocking our heads together.'

Irene opened her eyes, swallowed deeply and said, on a slight laughing sound, 'Dread-ful . . . woman.'

There was a tap on the door and Sister entered. Her voice was low but brisk as she said, 'Time, please.'

Richard bent over his mother and kissed her gently. She

held his face in her hands for a moment but said nothing. Then Jackie was looking down into her eyes, and in a soft whisper she said, 'You are a beautiful lady, and I thank you for giving him to me.' Swiftly she kissed her, then turned, and Richard followed her.

They were on the landing now and Jackie stood with her face against the wall. Richard put his arms about her and pulled her round to him, and, with tears rolling from her eyes, she muttered, 'Don't say one word. Not one word.' Then, tugging herself from his arms, she said, 'I'm going to Glenda's bedroom to tidy up. You tell them.'

'Yes, darling. I'll tell them.' He let her go, then made for the sitting room where the rest of the small company were having coffee. When he entered the room he closed the door behind him, but did not immediately step further in. He said, 'She – she wants us to be married right away. Special licence.' Then slowly he walked towards the couch and said to Alexander, 'I know nothing about this, how to go about it.'

Alexander put up his hand and caught Richard's and pulled him gently down to his side, saying, 'Don't you worry. We'll see to everything.'

5

It was amazing to them all how Irene seemed to come alive during the next few days, after Richard and Jackie had told her what they proposed doing with the manor house. Her interest was aroused and she nodded to every plan they explained to her. And when, after one or two short sessions with her, they hadn't mentioned Bella or her boys it was she who said, 'Bella . . . What . . . about Bella?'

At this Jackie had laughed and said, 'Oh, Bella was our first thought; Bella and her boys could never be left out of this scheme. You know the six cottages at the end of the estate?'

Irene had made a small nod.

'Well,' went on Jackie, 'the first two are to be made into one, in fact gutted and rebuilt. They are to house Bella, Joe and Carl. And provision has been made for Carl's wheelchair.'

Irene had nodded in agreement. 'Nice . . . Yes; nice.'

'And the other cottages,' Jackie had gone on, 'are to be gutted in the same way, and Tony, John and Willie will have one each, which they mean to rebuild themselves, like they did the wash-house, you know.'

There was a smile on Irene's face now and she repeated, 'The wash-house;' then again, her head moving, 'The wash-house . . . warm.'

'And what is more,' Jackie went on, 'Trip and Mrs Atkins and the two old gardeners who have worked outside for years are to carry on as long as they want to. In fact, they'll all keep on the same services in our part of the house and look after us because there'll be a special staff for the convalescents. It is all being arranged. You know Miss Fairweather, Alex's secretary?' and she smiled widely at Irene now. 'She and her cousin, the architect, have done marvellous work.'

'Nice . . . woman.'

At this remark, Richard said, 'Yes, she is, Mother, a very nice woman; and between you and me' – he leant over her and smiled into her face – 'we all hope that soon she will not remain Miss Fairweather.'

'No? . . . Marry?'

Richard smiled at his mother, and she, looking up into his face, asked softly, 'Who?'

And the reply came just as softly, 'Alex.'

'No!'

'Yes . . . we hope.'

Now Jackie put in, 'If he's got any sense.'

Irene lay back in her pillows and drew in a long breath before she said, 'Exciting.'

'And that's what we're doing to you, exciting you too much, and we must go, because if that sister comes in, or a nurse, we shall be in trouble.'

Irene closed her eyes and put out her hand to them, which they both patted before going quietly out.

Eight days later they were married in the local register office, attended only by Alexander, James, Glenda, Bella and Miss Fairweather.

When they kissed they did so gently, looking into each other's eyes; then they thanked the registrar and went out. There had been no talking; they went through a hall and down a flight of stone steps to the waiting limousine, followed by Bella, James and Glenda.

Miss Fairweather was about to follow them when Alexander drew her back into the hallway. Looking straight at her, and without any lead-up whatsoever, he said, 'Maggie,' and to this she merely answered, 'Yes?'

It was a question, and the next thing he said was, 'Would you marry me?'

There was a long pause before her laughter came: it was soft, but nevertheless it was laughter; then she said, 'The answer, Alex, has been a foregone conclusion for years.'

'Oh, Maggie!' He now had hold of her arms. 'I've been a selfish damn fool, and I never guessed, because you didn't give me an inkling. But really I had never thought I could feel this way ever again for anyone. But is it too late for me to say, and for you to believe, that I love you and have gone through the devil's own torture these last few weeks?'

She was smiling broadly as she put her hand up and touched his cheek, saying, 'I have no sympathy for you whatsoever, and I hope you go on suffering, because I've done my share of it over you for a long time now.'

'Oh, Maggie.' He glanced round the hallway. There was no one in sight, so quickly he thrust his arms around her and kissed her. Then as he turned towards the door, who should be standing there but James, and at the sight of him Alexander gave a short laugh and said, 'Dear God! You would have to stick your nose in, wouldn't you?' And at this, the three, laughing together, walked down the steps and towards the second car. Before they reached the pavement Alexander, his voice a hoarse whisper, now said, 'James, please . . . please don't say a word yet. Please. It's their day.'

And his son, looking at them both, said, 'All right,' and they continued the few steps to the car, which would take them back to Glenda's for a wedding breakfast.

6

Irene's joy lasted only ten days more; yet during that time it was noted that she seemed to be more at peace and happier than she had ever been.

She died in her sleep, but right to the last she was aware that her son was holding her hand and had been holding it for a long time and that his dear face was near hers.

When she closed her eyes, it was a gentle fading away, for she did not stop breathing until four hours later.

Irene was buried next to her mother, whose grave and small headstone had been obliterated for years now with moss and overgrown weeds at the far end of the cemetery, which overlooked the river.

Of her father's grave there was no trace. He hadn't had a Christian burial because he had committed suicide; yet there must have been some part of the cemetery where he lay, although there was no record of it.

The church was crowded, and so was the cemetery, with many photographers and journalists, the latter having found it difficult to get anything out of the close-mouthed family and friends who had surrounded Irene during her last days.

It had come as a great surprise to everyone that Mrs Irene Baindor had been still alive. There was a mystery here, but not one that even the cleverest journalist was able to probe, although it was felt that there must be a great sentimental story here. The nearest they could get to it was that her son had been with her when she died . . .

A fortnight later there was another gathering of all those concerned. It was in Glenda's sitting room. They were there to discuss their futures as far as it was in their power to do so.

It had already been arranged with Alexander and George Peacock that the businesses abroad that remained would eventually be managed by the accountant. The London office would be run by Alexander and his wife Margaret, leaving his own business in the hands of James.

A new post had been created for George Green, Maggie's cousin. His position now was managing director of the company that had been set up to oversee the demolition of old slum properties and the erection of new ones. His first job, however, was to get the convalescent home into working order.

Lastly there were Richard and Jackie. It was decided that Richard would finish his training during the next two years with the next step his appointment as consultant plastic surgeon. Jackie had not yet voiced her plans, but now she did, saying, 'What am I going to do? Well, I'll tell you. I've taken up a new career.'

'A new career?' This came from a surprised Richard.

'Yes, dear husband, a new career.

'First of all, I propose to be a wife and mother, but my new career is to be that of a writer.'

'Writer? What d'you mean?' said Richard. 'As a journalist, you write now.'

'No, I don't; I merely report. But now, I propose to write a book.' She had everybody's attention, and Alexander said, 'A book? A novel?'

'No; not a novel, Alex, a biography, of a man who was once known as a great financier and of how he turned his wife's brain and for twenty-seven years put her into limbo. But most of all, the main character will be Miss Bella Morgan, who was dragged up in the slums of Liverpool, and knew what it was to sleep rough. One day, when she was nearly forty years old, she came across a strangely dressed woman lying in a filthy yard, trying to find shelter under dirty fruit boxes. She took her into her life. She not only cared for her but she loved her and protected her and lived daily with her; and her charge only set foot out of the house four times in twenty-six years. The only thing, it seemed, that Miss Bella Morgan could not do for her was to get her to discard the old, tattered dress and coat and weird hat in which she had left home: her idea was that the coat protected her from men. And such was her love for it that she asked to be buried in this outfit. Her wish was granted.

'And of how, in the end, one word, one name that Miss Bella Morgan happened to mention brought back, at least partly, some of her charge's past and revealed to her that she had a son whom she hadn't seen since she had last held him in her arms as a boy of four years old. And so she went searching for him and she found him, and the great silence that had held her almost dumb was broken. And,' she finished, 'I'm calling the book *The Silent Lady*.'

No one spoke, and Richard, who had been standing by her side, dropped on to a chair and bowed his head; then, looking up at her and taking both of her hands, he brought them to his face and kissed them. Then he said, 'You are the most wonderful woman in the world.'

She stared back at him, then to break the silence that had fallen on them all she reverted to her usual joking manner and said, 'Oh, I've just been waiting for you to recognise it.'

They all laughed until Alexander said, 'And how long do you think it is going to take you to write this epic?'

'I've worked it out. Four years. In between times I hope I will have other family business to attend to: the nursery is all ready.'

Epilogue 1959

Covering the whole of Wellbrook Manor was an air of excitement: from the nursery at the top of the house, where lay two-and-a-half-year-old Alexander Franklin Baindor and his sister, one-year-old Belinda Baindor, through the convalescent area where the patients were about to celebrate with a party; to the main room in the house which was a sixty-foot drawing room and was now crowded with people. Standing in groups there were Mr Trip and Mrs Atkins, members of Glenda's nursing staff, Alexander Armstrong and his wife Margaret, James Armstrong, and in their company was Bella's kind friend and solicitor, Mr Travis, together with George Green, the architect. Lord Blakey was there, and next to him Timothy Baxter, who had flown in from America, a man now in his sixties but as handsome as ever; close by Dr Bell was talking to Dr Harle; and near the end of the long table was Mr Joseph Gomparts, his face alight with pleasure. Bella's five lads, Joe, Carl, supporting himself on two sticks, John, Tony and Willie were there; and close behind Carl stood his friend, now a high police official, Raymond Smyth, jokingly known among the family as Mr Sixes and Sevens. A group of Richard's friends had come from the hospital, and included three doctors and two nurses; and there was Bella, resplendent in blue velvet. Finally, there were Richard and Jackie, and Richard, having received a signal from Trip that the cars were on the drive, announced to the company that they must now all be on the move.

It took them exactly an hour to reach the centre of the City and their mystery destination, which had been a closely guarded secret. It was the Merchant Tailors' Hall where a reception was to be held to mark the publication of Jackie's book.

It began at half past seven with drinks and introductions to Jackie's publisher, his associates and literary friends, and Jackie's journalist friends and acquaintances she had made in the magazine and newspaper world.

The mingling with drinks went on from seven thirty to eight fifteen when dinner was announced; it was a sumptuous meal accompanied by the soft music of a string quintet that played in the background.

This was followed by the speeches, which took no more than half an hour. The last to speak was Lord Blakey, who talked of the qualities of his daughter, her husband, and of Miss Bella Morgan and proposed a toast to their health. Such were the brevity and wit of his words that they brought a hail of laughter from the assembled company and gave a final touch to a magnificent evening.

Now cameramen and television journalists were mingling among the tables. But many of them had naturally gathered in front of the top table. Cameras were clicking, lights were flashing, and, amid the hubbub of voices, one was raised above the rest. With a camera pointed at Jackie, the man cried, 'Lift it up!'

He was pointing to the book on the table, but had the good sense to add, 'Please, Mrs Baindor, lift it up!'

At this request Jackie took the book from the table, looked at it for a second, then suddenly thrust it at Bella, who was standing by her side.

Shaking her head, Bella cried, 'Oh, no! No!'

With a broad smile and a quick lifting of a hand Richard told her to do what the photographer was asking.

Bella stared down for a moment at the cover: There was her lass, draped in the long dirty coat; but the beauty of her face shone out from the dark background and drew the eye upwards to the cloth crown, all that was left of the weird hat. In the seconds that she stared at it her heart cried, 'Oh, my lass, my lass. This, as your son says, will vindicate your life.'

And on this thought her arms swung up and outwards as if she were about to launch the book into the air.

Such had been Bella's gesture that the following morning one newspaper showed the exact picture, and the editor, being in poetic mood, added, 'It was as if the little woman was opening a cage and letting free an imprisoned bird.'

Aug, $16, Mon-Fri, 8:30pm and $12 Sun, 8:30pm. The *Elizabeth II*, a representation of the ship which brought the first English settlers to North America, is moored 4 miles S on Rte 400, Manteo St across from the waterfront. $8, $5 w/ student ID, tours every 30 mins, 9am-7pm, 473-1144.

Nags Head Woods Preserve, 441-2525, 15 miles N of Manteo, is a nature preserve with two walking trails, open Mon-Sat 10am-3pm. Nearby in Kitty Hawk, the **Wright Bros Memorial and Museum** on Rte 158, 441-7430, pays homage to the great inventors. Open 9am-6pm daily. $4 p/car, $2 pp. What better way to celebrate a visit to the place where man first took flight than with an airplane tour from **Kitty Hawk Aerotours**, 441-4460, 30 min coastal tours. $29 pp for parties of one or two, $23 pp for more than three. Icarus fans may want to try the nearby hang-gliding operations: call **Kitty Hawk Kites**, 441-4124. $75 for a 3 hr lesson including training film, ground school and 5 flights.

Waterworks organises **dolphin tours**; $22 for 1 hr, 441-8875.

Lighthouses, at Cape Hatteras, Ocracoke, Corolla and Bodie. Visitors are not permitted to climb up the Bodie tower but are free to wander the grounds. The **Chicamacomico Life Saving Station**, on Hatteras Island near Rodanthe, records how private rescue companies of the 19th century operated.

Cape Fear Museum, 814 Market St btwn 8th & 9th St, Wilmington, (910) 341-4350. Dive into the background and history of the Lower Cape and learn how North Carolina earned its nickname, 'the Tarheel State.' Mon-Sat 9am-5pm, Sun 2pm-5pm. $4, $3 w/student ID.

INFORMATION

Outer Banks Chamber of Commerce, Ocean Bay Blvd, Kill Devil Hills, off milepost 8^1/$_2$, 441-8144. Mon-Fri 8:30am-5pm.

Aycock Brown Welcome Center off Rte 12 and 158 in Kitty Hawk, 261-4644, open 8:30am-6:30pm daily.

Cape Hatteras Ntl Seashore Information Centers; Bodie Island, 441-5711; Hatteras Island, 995-4474; Ocracoke Island, 928-4531. All open daily 9am-6pm.

Cape Fear Coast Visitors Bureau, 24 N Third St, (800) 222-4757, open Mon-Fri 8:30am-5pm, Sat 9am-4pm, Sun 1pm-4pm.

TRAVEL

Car Ferry btwn Cedar Island and Ocracoke Island, daily, 2 hrs, $10 car (book several days ahead on summer w/ends), $1 pp. Call (800) 345-1665 in Ocracoke, (800) 865-0343 in Cedar Island or (800) BY FERRY. Free ferries across Hatteras Inlet btwn Hatteras and Ocracoke daily, 5am-11pm, 40 mins. Taxis to and from Wilmington airport cost around $15 o/w. Call 762-3322.

TOBACCO ROAD
North Carolina's backbone consists of a 150-mile-long arc of cities stretching between **Raleigh** and **Winston-Salem**. I-40 and I-85 pass through the rolling Piedmont hills, home of major tobacco-growing farms and factories. The state capital is in Raleigh and the **Raleigh/Durham Triangle** area, home to three major universities, has the nation's highest number of PhDs per head of population.

ACCOMMODATION

In Durham: Carolina-Duke Motor Inn, 2517 Guess Rd, off I-85, exit in Durham, 286-0771/(800) 483-1158. S-$50, D-$53, XP-$3. Pool, AC, TV.

Budget Inn, 2101 Holloway St, Hwy 98, 682-5100. S-$35, D-$43, $3 key deposit. Pool, TV, laundry.

In Raleigh: Regency Inn, 300 N Dawson, 828-9081. S-$42, D-$48.

YMCA, 1601 Hillsborough St, 832-6601. $18.50 w/shared bath. Men only. Pool.

YWCA, 1012 Oberlin Rd, 828-3205. Women only. $22, $60 week. Rsvs essential,

required to fill out application form in person.

In Winston-Salem: Days Inn North, 5218 Germanton Rd, (336) 744-5755. S-$47, D-$52, XP-$5.

Motel 6, 3810 Patterson Ave, (336) 661-1588. I-40 exit to US 52 N, exit Patterson Ave. Newly renovated. $46, XP-$3.

FOOD

In Durham: 9th Street Bakery, 776 9th Street, 286-0303. Cheap pastries and bakery items, sandwiches from $3. Live folk music at w/ends. Mon-Fri 7am-5pm, Sat 9am-midnight.

Satisfaction, 905 W. Main St, 682-7397. Big Duke hangout. Pizzas, sandwiches, burgers. Lunch, dinner, Mon-Sat 11am-1am.

In Raleigh: Applebee's Neighborhood Grill & Bar, 4004 Capitol Blvd, 878-4595. American fare (burgers, chicken, steaks) $6.50-$10. Open daily 11am-11pm, w/ends til midnight.

OF INTEREST

Durham: Duke Homestead State Historic Site, 477-5498, ancestral home of the Duke family, with early tobacco factories and historic outbuildings. **Duke University** is a gothic wonderland built with tobacco money. It's also the site of **Duke Chapel**, which boasts a 210 ft tower with 50-bell carillon and over 1 million stained glass pieces fitted in 77 windows. **Duke Museum of Art,** 684-5135, features Medieval sculpture, American and European paintings, sculpture, drawing and prints, Greek and Roman antiques. **Sarah P Duke Gardens**, 684-3698, contains 55 acres of landscaped and woodland gardens with 5 mile trail among waterfalls, ponds, pavilions and lawns. General tours of most attractions from visitor centre, 2138 Campus Dr, 684-3214, Mon-Sat. Call ahead as schedules change frequently.

Chapel Hill is a college town 15 miles SW of Durham on US 15501. Home of the **University of North Carolina**, the first public university in America. Visit the **Morehead Planetarium** on Franklin St, near campus, 962-1236. Star Theatre shows cost $4, $3 w/student ID. **Franklin St** is also the place to find cheap food and student bars and clubs. For those who have had enough of sight-seeing, **Cane Creek Reservoir**, 8201 Stanford Rd, 942-5790, offers boating, fishing, canoeing, swimming, picnic and sunbathing areas.

Raleigh: Mordecai Plantation House Historic Park, 1 Mimosa St, 834-4844. Birthplace of Andrew Johnson, features antebellum plantation house and other historic buildings. Mon, Wed-Sat 10am-3pm, Sun 1pm-3pm. $4, $2 w/student ID.

North Carolina Museum of Art, 2110 Blue Ridge Rd, 839-6262. European paintings from 1300, American 19th century paintings, Egyptian, Greek and Roman art. Tue-Thur , Sat 9am-5pm, Fri 'til 9pm, Sun 11am-6pm. Free.

North Carolina State Capitol, 1 E. Edenton St, 733-4994. Greek revival style, built btwn 1833 and 1840. 'One of the best preserved examples of a Civic Building in this style of architecture.' Mon-Fri 8am-5pm, Sat 9am, Sun 1pm. Across the street is the **North Carolina Museum of History,** 715-0200. Explore the state's history through hands-on exhibits and 'innovative' programs. 'Check out the Sports Hall of Fame and Folklife galleries.' Changing exhibits provide detailed glimpses of the past. Tue-Sat 9am-5pm, Sun noon-5pm. Free.

Winston-Salem: Reynolda House Museum and Gardens, Reynolda Rd, (336) 725-5325, houses 18th-20th century American paintings, sculpture, and prints associated with the founder of R J Reynolds Tobacco, including Church's *The Andes of Ecuador*. Tues-Sat 9.30am-4.30pm, Sun 1.30pm-4.30pm, $6, $3 w/student ID.

Historic Bethabara, 2147 Bethabara Rd, 924-8191. Reconstruction of 18th century Moravian Village, with 130 acre park, archaeological sites and other historic buildings. Settlers first came to this area in 1766. **Old Salem**, 600 S Main St, 721-7300. Costumed interpreters re-create Moravian life. Daily demonstrations, bakery,

restaurant and shops. Both are open Mon-Sat 9.30am-4.30pm, Sun 1.30pm-4.30pm. The newer art is at the **Southeastern Center for Contemporary Art**, 750 Marguerite Dr, 725-1904. Tue-Sat 10am-5pm, Sun 2pm-5pm; $3, $2 w/student ID.

Greensboro, on I-40 btwn Winston-Salem and Raleigh, was the birthplace of the 1960s national student sit-in movement for civil rights. It's here where four local African-American students sat down in Woolworths and refused to move. The legacy of their courage is chronicled in the **Greensboro Historical Museum**, Lindsay St at Summit Ave, (336) 373 2043. Tues-Sat 10am-5pm, Sun 2pm-5pm. Free. Greensboro also boasts one of the world's largest waterparks. **Emerald Point Waterpark**, 3910 S Holden Rd, (336) 852-9721, offers giant wave pool, tube slides, drop slides, drifting river and more. All day tkts $22, or $15 after 4pm. Open Sun-Fri 10am-8pm, Sat 9am-9pm. On I-85 at Asheboro, about 30 mins S of Greensboro, is the **North Carolina Zoological Park**, (800) 488-0444. The world's largest natural habitat zoo. Open 9am-5pm, 'til 4pm in winter, $8.

INFORMATION
Chapel Hill: Chamber of Commerce, 104 S Estes Dr, 967-7075.
Durham: Convention and Visitors Bureau, 101 E Morgan St, 687-0288.
Raleigh: Capital Area Visitor Center, 301 N Blount St, 733-3456.
Winston-Salem: Chamber of Commerce, 601 W 4th St, 725-2361.
Winston-Salem Visitors Center, 601 N Cherry St, 777-3796.

INTERNET ACCESS
Raleigh:
CupAJoe, Mission Valley Shopping Center, 2109-142 Avent Ferry Rd, 828-9886, Mon-Fri 7am-midnight, Sat from 9am, Sun 9am-11pm, $1.50 for 15 min.
North Regional Library, 200 Horizon Dr, 870-4000, free.
Winston-Salem:
Forsyth County Public Library, 660 W 5th St, 727-2264, free.

TRAVEL
Durham: Greyhound, 820 W Morgan St, 687-4800/(800) 231-2222.
Durham Area Transit Authority, 683-3282. Public bus service runs daily, schedules vary, fare 75¢.
Raleigh: Amtrak, 320 W Cabarrus St, 833-7594/(800) 872-7245.
Greyhound, 314 W Jones St, 834-8275/(800) 231-2222. Chapel Hill $7, Durham $7.
Capital Area Transit, 828-7228, public bus service runs Mon-Sat, schedules vary, fare 50c. Many hotels offer free shuttles to and from Raleigh-Durham airport to downtown, so ask around. Taxis cost around $22 o/w. Call 266-3015.

ASHEVILLE AND AREA Travellers to this area find the simple, unhurried charm that is fading elsewhere in the busy 'New South'. The crafts and folklore of the Appalachian Mountains flourish in the shops and markets here, and the region's natural beauty is protected from overdevelopment. If you put your feet up anywhere in North Carolina, this is the place to do it.

ACCOMMODATION
Intown Motor Lodge, 100 Tunnel Rd, 252-1811, S-$32, D-$36, more at w/end.
Log Cabin Motor Court, 330 Weaverville Hwy, 645-6546. Cabins $32-38 for two.
Thunderbird Motel, 835 Tunnel Rd, 298-4061. From D-$37

FOOD
Boston Pizza, 501 Merriman, 252-9474. Popular student hangout; pizzas from $7. Try the 'Boston Supreme!' Mon-Sat 11am-11pm.
The Hop, 507 Merriman, 252-8362. Homemade ice cream in 50's style joint. Open daily, noon-9pm.

Three Brothers Restaurant, 183 Haywood St, 253-4971, serves everything, over 40 types of sandwiches. Open 11am-10pm Mon-Fri, Sat 4pm-10pm.

OF INTEREST

Biltmore House and Gardens, 255-1776, built by the Vanderbilt family, is an opulent exception to the area's humble charms. Peter Sellers' last film *Being There* was filmed at this 250-room European style chateau. Includes garden, conservatory, winery, and two restaurants. Take exit 50 or 50B on I-40 south of Asheville. Tkt office 9am-5pm, house open 'til 6pm, winery 'til 7pm and gardens open 'til dark. $30 all inclusive.

Chimney Rock Park, (800) 277-9611, lies 25 miles SE of Asheville near intersection of US 64 and 74. A 26 storey elevator runs inside the mountain and ascends to 1200 ft. 'Spectacular views over the Appalachian Mountains.' Also various nature trails through the nearby **Pisgah National Forest**, natural rock slides at **Sliding Rock** and a 404 ft waterfall, 877-3265.

For literary interest head to **Flat Rock**, once home to poet Carl Sandburg, and current site of the **Flat Rock Playhouse**, North Carolina's State theatre, 693-0731. Sandburg's home for 22 years, **Connemara**, 693-4178, has books and videos of the writer-poet's life. His championship goat herd lives on. Tours of the home Mon-Fri, 9am-5pm, Sat-Sun 1pm-5pm, every 30 mins, $3. The **Thomas Wolfe Memorial**, 48 Spruce St (next to the Radisson Hotel), 253-8304, honours Asheville's most famous son. Wolfe's best known novel, *Look Homeward Angel* (titled after Milton's poem of the same name), was inspired by childhood experiences; his father was the town stonecutter. Asheville is a prime spot to shop for **local crafts**. Traditions are lovingly preserved. The **Mountain and Dance and Folk Festival**, 258-6111, on the first w/end in Aug has been going more than 60 yrs. The annual **World Gee Haw Wimmy Diddle Competition** is held annually in Aug at the **Folk Arts Center**, 298-7928, and includes demonstrations of this native Appalachian toy, made from laurel wood. About 70 miles NE of Asheville is **Grandfather Mountain**, (800) 468-7325, the highest peak in the Blue Ridge Mountains and the first private preserve set apart by the United Nations as a Biosphere Reserve. Known as the most biologically diverse mountain in the east, it's also the site of the annual **Highland Games**,(828) 733-1333, a celebration of Scottish dancing, piping, and Gaelic culture held each July. Entrance to the mountain is off US 221, 2 miles north of Linville. $10. Open daily, 8am-7pm.

INFORMATION/TRAVEL

Asheville Chamber of Commerce, 151 Haywood St, 258-6101. Open Mon-Fri, 8:30am-5:30pm. 'A very helpful staff.'

Asheville Transit , 253-5691. Serves city and outskirts. Fare 75¢, 10¢ transfer.

Greyhound, 2 Tunnel Rd, 253-5353/(800) 231-2222. 2 miles E of downtown, served by Asheville Transit buses #13 & #14.

INTERNET ACCESS

East Asheville Library, 902 Tunnel Rd, 298-1889, free.

GREAT SMOKY MOUNTAINS NATIONAL PARK The name 'Great Smokies' is derived from the smoke-like haze that envelopes these forest-covered mountains. The Cherokee Indians, the area's original inhabitants, called it the 'Land of a Thousand Smokes'. Part of the Appalachian Mountains near the southern end of the Blue Ridge Parkway, the popular park has been preserved as a wilderness that includes some of the highest peaks in the eastern US and 68 miles of the Appalachian Trail. *www.nps.gov/grsm/*

The **Great Smoky Mountain Railway** runs 4.5 hr trips through Nantahala Gorge and Fontana Lake, from $22. 'Waste of time. What mountains? Telephone cables obscured view of scrap yards.' 7 hour raft and rail trips, from $55 (includes picnic lunch and guided raft ride). All departures from Bryson City. Call (800) 872-4681 for rsvs.

The area near **Cataloochee** affords an excellent impression of the obstacles facing the earliest pioneers on their push into the west. Cabins, cleared acreage and other pioneer remnants dot this section of the park. Perhaps the most fascinating visit is to the **Cherokee Reservation**, (800) 438-1601. There's a recreated Indian village, and a production of *Unto These Hills*, an Indian drama about their land and the meaning it holds for them, a museum, and casinos—a controversial but commonplace feature of the modern Indian reservation.

The North Carolina entrance to the park is on US 441 at Cherokee with the visitor centre located at **Oconaluftee**, not far from the Indian reservation. Cherokee also offers numerous motels and campgrounds. Try **Oconaluftee Motel**, US 19 South, (828) 488-3712, D-$50.

SOUTH CAROLINA *Palmetto State*

In its semi-tropical coastal climate and historical background, the Palmetto State, first to secede from the Union, marks the beginning of the Deep South. South Carolina also typifies the New South. Since the Second World War, booming factories, based on the Greenville area, have replaced sleepy cotton fields and cotton itself has been replaced by tobacco as the major cash crop. Textile manufacturing and chemicals are the state's major industries, but industry has not developed at the expense of the state's traditional charm and lovely countryside.

South Carolina has, however, something of a split personality. Charleston beckons the visitor with its graceful streets and refined architecture. Myrtle Beach entices with all the subtlety of a tourist-howitzer. South Carolina has her slower country charms, but other than Charleston, few compare favourably with her neighbours. The beaches are less cluttered in North Carolina and the mountains are grander in Tennessee. *www.yahoo.com/regional/U_S__States/South Carolina.*
The area code for Columbia is 803, for Charleston and Myrtle Beach it's 843..

CHARLESTON The curtain rose here on the Civil War to the cheers of society ladies and the blasts of harbour canon. Charleston's exuberance found a less violent expression in the 1920s when a dance dubbed the *Charleston* became a national obsession. Dance was better suited to the genteel Charleston nature that epitomises Southern graciousness. Settled by aristocracy, Charleston has always been concerned with architecture, art and the length of the family tree. More recently in 1989, this lovely old town was severely battered when hurricane Hugo roared through. Many of the historic buildings suffered severe damage, so much so that the town will never look the same again.

ACCOMMODATION
Bed, No Breakfast, 16 Halsey St, 723-4450. Guest house in Harleston Village near College of Charleston, S/D-$75, T-$80. 'Comfortable.' 'Limited space.'
Rutledge Victorian Inn, 114 Rutledge Ave, 722-7551. B&B, From S-$59. AC, TV. Favourite stop for BUNAC travellers and owners helpful in finding work in area. Rsvs essential, daily 9am-5pm.
Motel 6, 2058 Savannah Hwy, 556-5144, S-$40, D-$46.
Camping: Fains Campground, 6309 Fains Blvd, 744-1005. $19 for 2, $85/wk.

FOOD
The Gourmetisserie in the City Market is junk food centre—hamburger, pizza stands. 'Great meeting place.'
Olde Towne Restaurant, 229 King St, 723-8170. Despite its name, it turns out to be Greek, with fish and meat specialities. Lunches from $6.50. Friendly. Open Sun-Thurs 11am- 10pm, w/ends 'til 11.
Papillion's Pizza Bar, 41 Market, inside the church, 723-6510. All-you-can-eat lunch buffets daily $6, dinner buffet Mon-Wed, $7. Open Sun-Thurs 11am- 10pm, w/end 'til 12.
Pinckney Cafe, 18 Pinckney St, 577-0961. Seafood etc. from about $4.50. 'A little gem. Sit outside and try the seafood gumbo.'

OF INTEREST
A tremendous city pride exists in Charleston, and there are excellent documentaries on the city shown in the downtown area. *Forever Charleston*, a slide show on the city, is shown at the Visitor Reception and Transportation Center, 325 Meeting St, 720-5678, from 9am-5pm daily; $2.50. The **Preservation Society**, 147 King St at Queen, 722-4630, is a useful place to learn about the history of Charleston and the volunteers welcome foreign visitors. Maps, pamphlets and walking books are available. Mon-Sat 10am-5pm.
   Charleston is famous for its fine houses, squares and cobblestone streets. Start your walk along **Church Street**, the vision Heyward and Gershwin used to create **Catfish Row** in *Porgy and Bess*. The **Battery**, along the Cooper and Ashley rivers, has blocks of attractive old residences. The only **Huguenot church** in the US is at Church and Queen streets while the **Dock Street Theater** is across the street. Topping the list of restorations is the **Nathaniel Russell House**, 51 Meeting St, 724-8481, probably the best house to visit. Dating from 1808, it has a famous 'free-flying' spiral staircase and lavish furnishings. Open Mon-Sat 10am-5pm, Sun 2pm-5pm. $7. Basket-weaving traditions inherited from Africa and handed down by generations of slaves can still be seen at the **Market**, Meeting and Market Sts. Fruit, veggies, masses of junk and some beautiful handicrafts. Watch the ladies making baskets—and then buy one. 'Lively and colourful.'
Daughters of the Confederacy Museum, 34 Pitt St., 723-1541. 'Rather higgledy-piggledy, but there is some unusual Confederate memorabilia at this place.' Sat and Sun 12pm-4pm, $2.
Gibbes Museum of Art, 135 Meeting St, 722-2706. Displays early art and portraiture of South Carolina and one of the finest collections of miniatures in the world. 'Worthwhile: some quite impressive early American paintings, and some even more impressive modern woodwork.' Tues-Sat 10am-5pm; Sun 1pm-5pm. $6, $5 w/student ID.
Kahal Kadosh Beth Elohim, 723-1090, founded by Serphadic Jews in 1749, the current temple was built in Greek-Revival style in 1841 and is the oldest synagogue in continuous use in the US, also an early centre of reform Judaism. Tours Mon-Fri 10am-noon.
The Charleston Museum, 360 Meeting St, 722-2996. Started in 1773, claims to be

the oldest museum in the country. Exhibits include a full-scale replica of the Confederate submarine, *HL Hunley*; you can peer into the open side of the sub. 'Creepy.' Mon-Sat 9am-5pm, Sun 1pm-5pm, $7.

The Old Exchange and Provost Dungeon, 122 E Bay at Broad St, 727-2165. Built btwn 1767 and 1771; delegates to the first Continenetal Congress were elected here in 1774. The dungeon was used as a prison by the British during the Revolution. Open daily 9am-5pm for self guided tours, $6.

Citadel Military Academy, 953-5000, is known as the West Point of the South. Female cadets have stormed and conquered West Point but the first woman who breached the staunchly male Citadel in August 1995 dropped out after a few days of 'hell week.' The male-only tradition came to a screeching halt in 1999 when Nancy Mace became the first female graduate. Now several female cadets are enrolled in the academy, proving that they are every bit as tough as the boys! The college, at Moultrie Street on banks of Ashley River, offers tours and a free museum, open Sat noon-5pm, Sun-Fri 2pm-5pm. Don't miss the dress parade every Friday at 3.45pm when the cadets are in session.

The Confederate bombardment of Federally-garrisoned **Fort Sumter**, just across the harbour, began the Civil War. Now Fort Sumter is a national monument, 883-3123, with its history depicted through exhibits and dioramas. Open daily, 9am-5pm. Fort Sumter is accessible only by boat. There are 3 boat tours daily to the fort, $10.50 for 2hr, 15 min tour that includes 1 hr on the fort itself. Boats leave from City Marina and Patriot's Point, 722-1691 for schedules. Be careful to take a boat that actually lands on the fort!

Ft Moultrie, 883-3123, on Sullivan's Island but easily reached by car, has served as the bastion of security for Charleston harbour since the revolutionary war. Visitors center open daily, 9am-5pm. Also just outside Charleston is **Boone Hall Plantation**, 884-4371, 7 miles N near US 17. Beautiful house and gardens; the stunning Avenue of Oaks leading to the mansion inspired the one seen in *Gone With the Wind*. Mon-Sat 8.30am-6.30pm, Sun 1pm-5pm, $12.50.

Charles Towne Landing, 1500 Old Towne Rd, 852-4200, 6 miles outside Charleston, marks the site of the first permanent English speaking settlement in South Carolina. See the *Adventure*, a working reproduction of a 17th century sailing vessel. Also guided tram tours, animal forest, bike paths and walkways. Open 9am-6pm daily, $5.

Summers can be scorching, but you can cool off at **Folly Beach**, off Rte 171, with public parking and showers. 15 min from downtown. 'Excellent beach, very long, deserted and clean.'

INFORMATION
Charleston Visitor Reception and Transportation Center, 325 Meeting St, 720-5678. Open daily. Good maps available. 'Helpful.' Even the **Chamber of Commerce** is historic—it is one of the nation's oldest civic commercial organisations; 81 Mary St, 577-2510/853-8000.

Also look online at *www.gocarolinas.com*.

INTERNET ACCESS
Charleston Library, 3503 Rivers Ave, 744-2489, free.

TRAVEL
Amtrak, 4565 Gaynor Ave, 9 miles W of town on Hwy 52, 744-8263/(800) 872-7245. The *Silver Meteor* calls here from NYC. Taxi from downtown, $10-$14.

Charleston Airport is located 13 miles N of downtown. Taxis $15-$20, 767-1100. Shuttle $7 available at airport.

Greyhound, 3610 Dorchester Rd, 744-4247/(800) 231-2222.

Local Bus (SCE & G), 747-0922. Daily 5.30am-midnight. Fare 75¢.

MYRTLE BEACH AND THE GRAND STRAND   The 60 mile stretch of South Carolina's northern coast known as the Grand Strand has seen almost frightening growth in the past two decades. It's loaded with countless amusements, fast food joints, and tacky boutiques with merchants selling the inevitable Myrtle Beach T-shirts and trinkets. In summer, the 30,000 population of Myrtle Beach swells to around 350,000.

Brookgreen Gardens, on US-17S, 20 min S of Myrtle Beach, 237-4218, seems out of place here. In a serene setting, the world's largest outdoor collection of American sculpture—over 400 works of art are on show, set against 2000 species of plants. The gardens also feature a wildlife park and aviary. 'Worth spending the whole day the sculptures are amazing.' Sun-Wed 9.30am-5pm, Thur-Sat 'til 9pm, $7.50.

Further south is pretty and famous **Pawleys Island**. One of the oldest resorts on the Atlantic coast, this was originally a refuge for colonial rice planters' families who fled a malaria epidemic. Residents work hard to preserve its more elegant, less commercialised feeling. The well-known Pawleys Island Hammock is hand-woven and sold here—you can watch them being made by local craftsmen.

Georgetown, on Hwy 17 at the southern end of the Grand Strand, was the first settlement in North America. It was established in 1526 by the Spaniards and named 200 years later in honour of King George II. Concentrating on the export of rice, Georgetown became a thriving port in the 18th century; in the early 19th century, it became the biggest exporter of rice in the world. Although this trade has now gone, there are still many things worth seeing, such as the old docks along the waterfront that have been converted into **Harborwalk**, a promenade of restaurants and shops. Venture to Broadway at the Beach, 29th Ave N, and check out the **Ripley's Aquarium,** 916-0888. Awarded the 1999 Governor's Cup for being the best tourist destination in South Carolina, the Aquarium gives you the unique opportunity to walk through underwater tunnels while sharks and piranhas swim over your head. Open 9am-9pm daily, $13.95.

ACCOMMODATION/FOOD/ENTERTAINMENT

For the **Myrtle Beach Reservation Referral Service**, call 626-7477.

Although hotels are everywhere, they are generally expensive in season. There are a few bargains, though. **Rainbow Cove Motel**, 405 Flagg St, 448-3857, has been recommended.

Sand Dollar, 401 6th Ave N, 448-5364. Rooms w/baths, AC, TV. BUNACers welcome—special rate, D-$70-85 weekly pp for four. Pool.

Fortunately Myrtle Beach claims 12,000 **campsites** and calls itself the 'Camping Capital of the World.' Try **Myrtle Beach State Park** on Rte 17 South, 238-2224, site $22-24, tents $18-20. Rsvs 2 weeks in advance. The Myrtle Beach Chamber of Commerce, 1200 N Oak St, 626-7444, has a complete guide to the area's campsites.

Peaches Corner, 900 Ocean Blvd, 448-7424.'Best burgers on the beach—try a famous 'Peaches Burger.' Open daily 11am- 2am.

The Filling Station, 1604 N. Kings Hwy, 626-9435. All-you-can-eat buffet for $5 lunch, $7 dinner. Salad, soup, sandwiches, pizza, desserts and more.

2001, 920 Lake Arrowhead Rd, 449-9434. Three clubs in one building. Choose from dance, country and 'shag'! Daily 8pm-2am, cover $8-$10, but check local papers and hotels for coupons.

INFORMATION/TRAVEL
Myrtle Beach Chamber of Commerce, 1200 N Oak St, 626-7444. Pick up copies of *Beachcomber* and *Kicks* for local events and entertainment listings. Open Mon-Fri 8:30am-5pm, Sat-Sun 8am-12pm. 'Also has useful accommodations directories.'
Greyhound, 511 7th Ave N, 448-2471/(800) 231-2222.
Coastal Rapid Public Transport Authority (CRPTA), 248-7277, bus service around Myrtle Beach area. Fare $1-$1.50, transfers 10c.

INTERNET ACCESS
Myrtle Beach Public Library, 4405 Socastee Blvd, 293-1733, free.

COLUMBIA   In the middle of South Carolina at the junction of three inter-states sits Columbia, the state's largest city and capital since 1786. Although growing rapidly, the city is mild by Charleston or Myrtle Beach standards. Lake Murray, with 520 miles of scenic lakefront, is less than 20 miles away. Columbia's biggest claim to fame is the success of a local band, Hootie and the Blowfish.

ACCOMMODATION/FOOD
Along the interstates are the best places to find cheap and clean rooms.
Baymont Inn, 911 Bush River off I-26, 798-3222. D-$50.
Masters Economy, 613 Knox Abbott Drive, 796-4300. S-$32, D-$40. Near the university campus.
Off-Campus Housing Office, Room 235, the Russell House, Green St, 777-6680, can direct visitors to people in the university community with rooms to rent. Open 8am-5pm. Check their Web site for information: *www.sasc.edu/ocss/homepage.htm.* For food and entertainment, head to **Five Points**—a business district at Blossom, Devine and Harden Sts—frequented by students.
Columbia State Farmer's Market, Bluff Road across from the USC stadium, 737-4664. Fresh produce daily. Mon-Sat 6am-9pm.
Groucho's, 611 Harden St, 799-5708, Columbia's renowned New York-style Jewish deli. Cheap filling sandwiches for around $6. Open daily 11am-4pm.
Yesterday's Restaurant and Tavern, 2030 Devine St, 799-0196, is an institution. Open daily for lunch and dinner, lunch from $4-7, dinner from $5-14. Open Sun-Thurs 11:30am-midnight, Fri-Sat 'til 1am. 'Friendly manager!'

OF INTEREST
Many of the city's attractions are located in or around the **University of South Carolina**. A mall-like area lined with stately buildings built in the early 19th century and called the **Horseshoe** marks the campus centre. On the Horseshoe facing Sumter St is the **McKissick Museum**, 777-7251. Large collection of Twentieth Century Fox film reels and science exhibits. Open Mon-Fri 9am-4pm, Sat-Sun 1pm-5pm.
Columbia Museum of Art, within walking distance from the McKissick at Main and Hampton Sts, 799-2810, houses Renaissance and baroque art as well as oriental and neoclassical Greek art galleries. Open Tue-Sat 10am-5pm, Wed 'til 9pm, Sun 1pm-5pm. $4, $2 w/student ID. Adjoining **Gibbes Planetarium**, takes you on a journey 'Into The Future,' find out what it would be like to live on a space-station, or wander around on Mars. W/end shows only 2pm and 4pm, 'Carolina Skies' at 3pm, what you'll see in the sky at night from the Carolinas. 50c.
South Carolina State Museum, 301 Gervais St, 898-4921, housed in a renovated textile mill, focuses on art, history, natural history, and science and technology. Mon-Sat 10am-5pm, Sun 1pm-5pm, $5, $3 w/student ID, free on the first Sunday of every month.
State Capitol, at Main and Gervais Sts, 734-2430. Built in 1855, the six bronze stars

on the outer western wall mark cannon hits scored by the Union during the Civil War. Tours hourly, 9:30-3:30 Mon-Fri, 10:30-2:30 Sat. Open 9am-5pm Mon-Fri, from 10am Sat.

INFORMATION/TRAVEL
Greater Columbia Convention and Visitors Bureau, 1012 Gervais St, on corner of Assembly, 254-0479. Mon-Fri, 9am-5pm, Sat 10am-4pm.
Amtrak, 850 Pulaski St, 252-8246/(800) 872-7245.
Greyhound, 2015 Gervais St, 799-4091/(800) 231-2222.

INTERNET ACCESS
Columbia Public Library, 931 Woodrow St, 799-5873, free.

TENNESSEE   *The Volunteer State*

Tennessee is music country. Memphis has been fertile ground for blues musicians and rock and rollers alike. Nashville brought country music down from the hills to mainstream America. The difference in music reflects deeper social differences within the state. The east is 'Hill Country'—backwoods and fiercely independent. The west is flat in texture and southern in demeanor, drawing life from the Mississippi River. The two cultures clashed violently during the Civil War, and several of the war's most costly battles were decided on Tennessee soil.

Tennessee's transition from its backwoods past into the 21st century has not been easy. After a famous trial in 1925, a Tennessee teacher named John Scopes was fined for teaching the theory of evolution. The eastern half of the state is less isolated today thanks to the Tennessee Valley Authority (TVA) built by the Franklin Roosevelt Administration. TVA was a massive effort to both tame a river and to civilise an entire region. People still argue over the proper role of government power in projects such as TVA. The state celebrated its 200th birthday in 1996. *www.yahoo.com/regional/U_S__States/Tennessee/.*
The area code for Nashville is 615. For the east it's 931 and 423. For Memphis and the west dial 901.

NASHVILLE   The Hollywood of the South, Nashville sparkles with the rhinestone successes and excesses of her country music stars. Bulging with moral character, Nashville is a centre of education and has more churches per capita than anywhere else in the country.

ACCOMMODATION
Most cheap motels are several miles outside town. 'Difficult to find cheap accommodation unless you have a car.'
Days Inn, 1400 Brick Church Pk, 228-5977/(800) 325-2525. D-$45 for four. TV, pool, bfast.
Knights Inn, I-65 and W Trinity Lane, exit 87B, 226-4500. 3 miles N of Nashville. S-$35, D-$42, XP-$5. AC, TV, pool.
Motel 6, 311 W Trinity Ln, 227-9696. Junction of I-24 east and I-65 north. AC. S-$38, D-$44.
Travelodge, 1274 Murphreesboro Rd, 366-9000. Downtown. S- $42.50, D-$48.50.
Camping: Many campgrounds are clustered around Opryland. Try **Nashville Travel Park**, 889-4225, site $20 for 2, XP-$4, $36.50 with full hook-up, or **Two Rivers**

Campground, 883-8559. Take Briley Parkway north to McGavock Pike and take exit 12B onto Music Valley Drive. Sites $27.50 for 2 with full hook-up, XP-$3.

FOOD

Bluebird Cafe, 4104 Hillsboro Pike, 383-1461. Mon-Sat 5.30pm-midnight, Sun 6pm-midnight. Live music and entertainment nightly, cover varies. Sandwiches, french bread pizzas.

Elliston Place Soda Shop, 2111 Elliston Pl, 327-1090. Mon-Sat 6am-7:30pm. Home-cooked food.

OF INTEREST

The District. Broadway, 2nd Ave, Printer's Alley and Riverfront Park, make up the historic heart of Nashville. Renovated turn-of-the-century buildings house shops, restaurants, art galleries bars and nightclubs.

Country Hall of Fame and Historic RCA Studio B, 4 Music Square East, 256-1639. Number one on any tourist list. Where Elvis Presley cut 100 records from 1963-71. See the King's solid gold cadillac, alongside exhibits, rare artifacts and personal treasures of other legendary performers. Tours 9am- 5pm daily, $10.75. 'Watch out for bogus Hall of Fame on next street.' 'Not worth it.'

Music Row, btwn 16th and 19th Aves S. The recording studios for Columbia, RCA and many others are here. For a taste of historic Nashville you can tour the 'mother church of country music,' the restored **Ryman Auditorium**, 116 Fifth Ave N, 254-1445/889-3060 for show info and tkt rsvs. The 100-yr old venue now offers daytime tours and live-performances every evening. Tours 8.30am-4pm, $6. The **Music City Queen**, 889-6611, docked at Riverfront Park offers daily sightseeing and Sun brunch cruises. Also host to blues and jazz events on Sat evenings, $12-$28, call for schedules. The recently opened 20,000-seat **Nashville Arena**, btwn 5th and 6th Aves, 770-2000, is home to the **Nashville Kats** football team and host to a variety of concerts and special events. Call for details.

Nashvillians are hot on reproductions. Their pride and joy is the **Parthenon Pavilion**, the world's only full-sized copy of the original and located in Centennial Park along West End Ave, 862-8431, Tue-Sat 9am-4.30pm, Sun 12.30pm-4.30pm, $2.50.

Fort Nashborough, 1st Ave N btwn Broadway and Church Sts, is a replica of the original fort from which the city first grew. For some real history, leave town on I-40 (Old Hickory Blvd exit) and head 12 miles E to **The Hermitage**, 4580 Rachel's Lane, 889-2941, the home of Andrew Jackson, a backwoods orphan who became US president (1829-1837). He is buried on the grounds. Open 9am-5pm daily, $9.50. **Belle Meade Mansion**, 5025 Harding Pike, 356-0501. Was the largest plantation and thoroughbred nursery in Tennessee. Mon-Sat 9am-5pm, Sun 1pm-5pm, $8.

ENTERTAINMENT

Topping the entertainment list is the show that made Nashville, **The Grand Ole Opry**, 889-6611. Radio WSU, and later television, broadcast this country music show out to a receptive nation. Tkts are tough to get during **Fan Fair**, the annual jamboree of country music held in June. The rest of the year you stand a decent chance. $18-20 admission to the 2 shows each Friday and Saturday nights with cheaper matinees in summer. You can ask to be on the waiting list. 'If you have up to number 15, you stand a chance.' 'Nothing quite like it.' Opryland veterans will note the absence of the theme park, closed in 1998. Look for its replacement, **Opry Mills**, a mega-shopping and entertainment complex, slated to open in April 2000. Walk through the garish **Opryland Hotel** where tropical vegetation, southern architecture, a Liberace impersonator and a waterfall all co-exist under one enormous roof. The **Opryland River Taxi**, 2812 Opryland Dr, offers a shuttle service btwn the Opryland complex and Riverfront park via Cumberland River, taking in Opryland and downtown attractions, $12 r/t. For info an all Opry attractions call 889-6611.

Printer's Alley is Nashville's standard club strip. **Tootsie's Orchid Cafe**, 422 Broadway, 726-0463. Top Country/Western bar, springboard for future Opry stars. Merle Haggard and other country greats may drop in to see how things are going. Nightly 'til 3am, no cover. Also try the **Station Inn**, 402 12th Ave S, 255-3307. Closed Mon. The area near Vanderbilt Campus has more student-oriented entertainment.

INFORMATION
Convention and Visitors Division, Chamber of Commerce, 161 4th Ave N, 259-4755. Mon-Fri 8am-5pm.
Visitor Information Centre at the Nashville Arena, corner of 5th and Broadway, 259-4747. Mon-Fri 8.30am-8pm.
For tourist info online, go to *http://nashville.citysearch.com*.

INTERNET ACCESS
Bean Central, 2817 W End Ave, 321-8530, open Mon-Sat 7am-11pm, Sun 9am-5pm, $2/30 min.
Davidson County Library, 1409 12th Ave S, 862-5861, free.

TRAVEL
Greyhound, 200 8th Ave and Demonbreun St, 2 blocks S of Broadway, 255-3556/(800) 231-2222. 'Use caution in this neighbourhood.'
Metropolitain Transit Authority (MATA), 862-5950. Runs Mon-Fri 5am-midnight, minimal service w/ends. Murfreesboro Rd/Airport Bus, #18M. Fare $1.40

EASTERN TENNESSEE AND THE GREAT SMOKIES The **Great Smoky Mountains National Park** is one of the most heavily visited parks in the United States. Named by the Cherokee Indians for the haze which shrouds the mountain peaks, the 800 miles of trails offer an immense variety of wildlife and landscapes. You will have to travel through **Gatlinburg** to reach the park entrance. 'Commercialism at its worst,' Gatlinburg specializes in wax museums, Elvis memorabilia, UFOs and Jesus knickknacks, all for sale to the gullible tourist. The only things worth doing, perhaps, are to ride the ski lift or to climb the space needle from where you get a good look at the mountains. *Area code is 931.*

N of Gatlinburg on US Hwy 441 is **Pigeon Forge**, home of **Dollywood**, 1020 Dollywood Lane, (800) 365-5996, the only Tennessee attraction to rival Graceland. The theme park is devoted to the life and career of Tennessee's own Queen of Country, Dolly Parton, and includes music shows, restaurants, rides and 'jukebox junction', devoted to the 50s—all with an 'old-time' atmosphere. 'You won't be disappointed!' Daily 9am-9pm, $30. For accommodation look towards **Smoky Mtn Motor Lodge**, 3661 Parkway, (423)453-9732. From D-$60.

The park has 3 visitors centres, the main one being Sugarlands, 2 miles S of Gatlinburg, on Newfound Gap Rd, where you can get maps, and info on the park's unique history and wildlife. (423)436-1200 is the park info line which links all 3 centres, the others being at **Cades Cove** and **Oconaluftee.** You must get a permit at the center in order to stay overnight at any of the 100 back-country campsites which dot the park. For 3 of the 10 developed campgrounds at **Smokemont, Elkmont** and **Cades Cove**, you have to make rsvs, call (800) 365-2267 enter code GREA, or go on-line to *http://reservations.nps.gov*, sites $15. The other campgrounds are first-come, first-served,

$6-$11. If you decide to stay over in the park, you will need to bring in your own food; there are no restaurants.

Getting around the park requires a car. The best way to see the mountain peaks is to drive along **Foothills Parkway** towards Walland, or along I-40 skirting the park's northeast flank. Only one road, Hwy 441, actually crosses the park, but it sometimes seems more like a superhighway than a drive through the country. Along the way there are numerous turn-outs and trail-heads. A ranger can direct you to quiet walkways (trailheads with only one or two parking spaces) that offer more challenging and private trails, or you can stick to the more touristed, but impressive main turn-outs at the well-known vista points. **Cades Cove** in the western part of the park offers some of the best wildlife and a collection of historic buildings. Come early if you want to see the animals. Rangers offer guided tours in the evenings from most campgrounds in summer. *www.nps.gov/grsm.*

CHATTANOOGA   In the southeastern corner of the state, this was the site of an important Civil War battle. Union troops were pinned down under siege for two months before reinforcements allowed them to break free from the mountains and down into the plains of Georgia. 'A lovely city. One of the nicest places I visited in the USA.' *Area code is 423.*

OF INTEREST
For both the view and the history, take the incline railway up **Lookout Mountain**, site of the famous Battle Above the Clouds. The mountain was an important signalling point for troops in the field. The gradient is 77.9% at its maximum; $8 r/t. There is a **Visitors Center**, 821-7786, at the top which has displays on signalling in the Civil War. Also a 13' x 30' painting, *The Battle Above the Clouds.* 'Cheaper to pay for bus right to top and back, $1.50. Bus leaves from near Greyhound.' 'While at the top, follow road to park and see the cannons and memorials, and imagine the battle. The view is still better from up here.' Just over the border with Georgia, on Hwy 27 is **Chickamauga** and **Chattanooga National Military Park**, (706) 866-9241. The Union forces were driven from here into Chattanooga after a fierce battle in which 48,000 men were wounded or killed. The **Battles for Chattanooga Museum**, (423) 821-2812, has an excellent slide and map show of the battle. Open daily 9am-6pm, last show 5.30pm, $5. If you are heading to Chattanooga from Nashville, you may want to stop at the **Jack Daniel's Distillery**, Hwy 55 in Lynchburg, (931)759-4221. Free tours daily 8am-4pm but don't expect free samples, the distillery of the potent whiskey is in a dry county. 'Best tour in America; the smell of whiskey is all around!'

MEMPHIS   Chuck Berry, WC Handy, Carl Perkins, Jerry Lee Lewis, Elvis Presley and so many others have called Memphis home. Cradled in a bend of the Mississippi River, this city gave birth (via such legends as James Cotton, Howlin' Wolf and Junior Wells) to the urban blues and to rock 'n' roll. U2, Depeche Mode and Paul Simon all have a keen fascination with the place.

After a long spell of urban decay, Memphis has reconstructed its down-town waterfront. Beale Street, famous for its blues clubs, is once again worth visiting. And Mud Island, in the Mississippi River, has several river-related attractions reachable by monorail. The river connects Memphis with the Deep South, giving the city the most southern feeling of Tennessee's large

GREAT AMERICAN BREAKFASTS

Breakfasts, and their Sunday cousin, 'brunch,' have a special place in American culture. Don't give in to the bagel-and-cream-cheese temptation without first ordering a heaping tower of warm, syrupy pancakes. For the great all-American breakfast, try: **Colony Inn,** in the main village, **Amana, IA**, (319) 622-6270, offers a plentiful spread of all the traditionals. A spicier wake-up call awaits at **Cisco's Bakery,** 1511 E Sixth St, **Austin, TX**, (512) 478-2420. Its Tex-Mex-breax include huevos rancheros powerful enough to open even the most stubborn lids. **Em Lee's** best offerings are the huge blueberry waffles, Dolores and 5th, **Carmel, CA**, (408) 625-6780. **Lou Mitchell's,** Jackson St & Jefferson, **Chicago, IL**, (312) 939-3111, serves up unforgettable Greek toast. Also in **Chicago** the **West Egg Cafe**, 280-8366, does wonderful things with eggs, from breakfast burritos to the 'veggie benedict' special. Near Chicago in **Willmette, IL, Walker Brothers Original Pancake House,** 153 Greenbay Rd, (847) 251-6000, is noteworthy for pancakes of all kinds, with apple at the top of the list. **The Bunnery**, Cathe St in **Jackson, WY**, (307) 733-5474, boasts wonderful buttermilk coffee cake and much more. At **Original Pantry,** 877 S Figueroa St, **Los Angeles,** (213) 972-9279 (24 hrs), try hot cakes or French toast. **Sara Beth's, New York City**, (212) 496-6280, makes its own preserves, homebaked muffins, sticky buns and offers a wide range of other breakfast foods. It has 3 locations on Amsterdam Ave north of 80th St, on Madison and 92nd and in the Whitney Museum. In **San Francisco, Doidges**, on Union St, serves unique concoctions: peach and walnut chutney omelettes, and a breakfast casserole with meat, cheese, potato, tomato, sour cream and a poached egg. Open 'til 2pm Mon-Fri and 3pm w/ends, (415) 921-2149. For excellent coffee, try **Cafe Trieste,** 1465 25th St in **SF**, where Kerouac probably began his day, (415) 550-0668. In **San Diego**, sample the homemade granola and delectable pumpkin waffles at **Cafe 222**, Island Ave, (619) 236-9902. **Avignone Frères**, 1775 Columbia Ave (off 18th St), **Washington, DC**, (202) 462-2050, serves continental, English and country breakfasts; great omelettes and good homemade muesli.

cities. There are excellent views of the Mississippi as she broadly sweeps away to the southwest just below the city.

Despite attempts to spruce up the city, vast sections remain depressed, reminding the visitor that this is a town where dreams have died. The number one attraction in Memphis is Graceland, where rock 'n' roll king Elvis Presley is buried. And in April, 1968, Martin Luther King, Jr was assassinated at the Lorraine Motel. *Area code is 901.*

ACCOMMODATION
Admiral Benbow Inn, 1220 Union Ave, 725-0630. S/D-$36, $5 key deposit. TV, AC, pool. Take bus 13 down Union. 'In a rough area; not for someone travelling alone.'
B&B in Memphis, 327-6129. Helen Denton provides a listing of hosts who offer B&B services and makes rsvs. D-$95-$125. Advance rsvs of 2 weeks.
Super 8 Motel, 6015 Macon Cove Rd, 373-4888. Exit 12C off I-40, 10 miles to airport. D-$55. Eating places nearby, about 12 miles to Graceland.
Motel 6, 1321 Sycamore View Rd, 382-8572. I-40 east exit on Sycamore View Rd South, 25 miles from train station. Newly renovated. S-$45, D-$52.
Memphis YMCA, 3548 Walker Ave, near Memphis State University, 323-4505. $79

weekly, $253 p/mth, $30 key deposit. Men only.
Camping: Graceland KOA, 3691 Elvis Presley Blvd, 396-7125. Pitch your tent right next door to the King's house. Sites $20, $29.95 w/hook-up.
T.O Fuller State Park, near Chucalissa Indian Village, 543-7581. $13 for two, XP-50c. 24 hrs. 'Very good.'

FOOD
Memphis is famous for pork BBQ, with over 100 BBQ restaurants.
Corky's, 5259 Poplar Ave, 685-9744, 30 mins from downtown. Renowned both nationally and locally, sit-in or drive-thru. BBQ platters with sides $6-$9. Open Sun-Thur 10:45am-10pm, Fri-Sat til 10:30.
The North End, 356 N Main St, 526-0319. Southern-style cooking; good, cheap vegetarian dishes. Open 11am-2am daily. Live music Wed-Sun.
The Map Room, 2 S Main, 579-9924. Open 24 hrs. "We spent 7 hours here drinking coffee and playing cards and chess whilst waiting for our train.'

OF INTEREST
The best sights in Memphis are her many musical shrines, the most holy of which is Elvis Presley's home, **Graceland**, 3734 Elvis Presley Blvd, 10 miles S of town, 332-3322. Open daily 8am-6pm. The 'Platinum Tour', takes in the 23-room, 14-acre mansion, the *Lisa Marie*, a 96-seat airplane/penthouse in the sky, Elvis' tour bus, a stunning car museum, plus the Meditation Garden where Elvis and family are buried. $19.50, $17.50 w/student ID. The 'Mansion Tour,' includes a 20 min video presentation and tour of the house only, $10, $9 w/student ID, but you will not want to miss the costumes, gold-wrapped grand piano, and 'jungle' playroom. Walking through the amazing 80 ft long 'Hall of Gold' lined with the King's gold records is almost breathtaking. Only by walking down this hallway can you begin to comprehend the enormity of Elvis's success. Catch the #13 bus to Graceland from just outside Greyhound, $1.10. 'last bus on Sats leaves at 5pm.' 'Free shuttle from Beale St.' 'I toured house hurriedly with 15 middle aged fans brought to tears in midst of disgusting bad taste. Plastic souvenirs are everywhere.' 'Worth it for the experience and insight into a great American icon.' *www.elvis-presley.com*.
Gray Line Elvis Tours, 384-3474. Comprehensive bus tour of Graceland and Elvis 'sites.' Pick up from most downtown hotels.
Audubon Gardens; and the 18 old buildings which make up **Victorian Village**, 680 Adams Ave, 526-1469, pleasant to stroll through and highly recommended, $5, $2 w/student ID. Mon-Sat 10am-3.30pm, Sun 1pm-3.30pm.
Chucalissa Indian Village, Indian Village Drive, T.O Fuller State Park, 785-3160. Reconstructed 1000-year-old Indian village. Choctaw Indians live on the site and demonstrate Indian crafts. Tue-Sat 9am-4.30pm, Sun 1pm-4pm, $5.
Dixon Gallery and Garden, 4339 Park Ave, 761-5250. Good collection of French and American Impressionist paintings. Tue-Sat 10am-5pm, Sun 1pm-5pm, $5, $3 w/ student ID.
Memphis Music & Blues Museum and **Hall of Fame**, 97 S 2nd St, 525-4007. 'Rare blues recordings, posters, guitars, video exhibits, photos and general memorabilia.' 'Not worth the money.' Sun-Thur 10am-6pm, Fri and Sat 10am-9pm, $7.50. The **Memphis Pink Palace and Planetarium**, 3050 Central Ave, 320-6320, is one of the largest museums in the Southeast, and specializes in science and history. Originally housed in the adjoining pink marble mansion. Mon-Wed 9am-5pm, Thur 'til 9pm (free 5pm-9pm), Fri and Sat 'til 10pm,Sun 12pm-5pm. $6 museum, IMAX theatre shows, $6 (call for show times), $3.50 planetarium. Combo tkts available.
Mud Island, 576-7230, situated offshore from main downtown area and accessible by a monorail. 52-acre park and entertainment complex devoted to life on the Mississippi River. Park entrance is $4, includes all attractions except **River Museum**, $8. Tour a towboat, see a film about disasters on the river, and the Mark

Twain talking mannequin that tells you about the river's history. The 5 block long **Mississippi River** scale model, complete with flowing water, follows the river's path to the Gulf of Mexico. Open 10am-8pm. Mud Island is also home of the *Memphis Belle*, the first B-17 bomber to successfully complete 25 missions in WW II, and subject of a Hollywood movie and Tennessee's largest swimming pool. Concerts in the summer, call Ticketmaster, 525-3000 (10am-5pm) for details. Big names who have played in the past include Don Henley, Chicago, and Sheryl Crow.

National Civil Rights Center, 450 Mulberry St, 521-9699. Houses exhibits and films on the individuals who led the civil rights movement and has two constantly changing galleries. Adjoining the centre is the **Lorraine Motel**, site of the 1968 assassination of Martin Luther King, Jr. Mon, Wed-Sat 9am-6pm, Thur 'til 8pm, Sun 1pm-3pm, $6, $5 w/ student ID.

The 32-storey, 6-acre **Pyramid**, which opened in autumn 1991, houses the **American Music Hall of Fame**, the **Memphis Music Experience**, **College Football Hall of Fame** and an arena seating 20,000. Tours Mon-Sat 9am-5pm, Sun noon-5pm on the hr.

Sun Studio, 706 Union Ave, 521-0664, launched the career of many legends including Elvis Presley, B.B King, Muddy Waters, Roy Orbison and Johnny Cash. Tours daily 10.30am-5.30pm hourly, $8.50.

ENTERTAINMENT

Beale St, 4 blocks of nightclubs, galleries and restaurants. The place where WC Handy blew the notes to make him 'Father of the Blues'. His house is now a museum, 352 Beale St. Live music nightly and outdoor entertainment year-round. Call the Merchants Association at 529-0999 for festival schedule or check the Friday section of the *Commercial Appeal*. Try **Rum Boogie Cafe**, 182 Beale St, 528-0150, 11am-2am, $5 cover. During the day, **Abe Schwab**'s, 163 Beale St, 523-9782, an eclectic and amusing drugstore, sells just about anything. 'Lively and bustling rapping, blues and loud records combine to create a unique atmosphere.' Listen to **WDIA**, 1070am, the famous black radio station where B.B. King used to spin records and an important station for the early growth of the blues, and R&B scene. Try to plan your trip for **Elvis Week** in August, 'in the week he died, there are Elvises everywhere!'

INFORMATION

Visitor Information Center, 340 Beale St, 543-5333. Mon-Sat 9am-6pm.

TRAVEL

Greyhound, 203 Union Ave, 523-1184/(800) 231-2222. Use caution in this area at night.

Amtrak, 545 S Main St, 526-0052/(800) 872-7245. 'Surrounding area very dangerous, even during the day, watch out!'

Memphis Transit Authority (MATA), Union Ave & Main St, 274-6282.

Buses to **Memphis International Airport** depart from 3rd and Beale, Mon-Fri 6.45am-6.15pm. Take the Showboat bus and transfer to #32 at the fairground, erratic service, fare $1.10. **Hotel Express** (HTS), 922-8238, is an airport shuttle and will pick you up from any downtown hotel, 8.30am-11pm, $8. For a taxi call 577-7777, $20-$23 o/w.

2. CANADA

BACKGROUND

BEFORE YOU GO

Citizens and legal, permanent residents of the United States do not need passports to enter Canada as visitors although they may be asked for identification (proof of citizenship or Alien Registration card) or proof of funds at the border. All other visitors entering Canada must have valid passports. Since Immigration officials have enormous discretionary powers, it is wise to be well dressed, clean cut, and the possessor of a return ticket if possible. The following persons do not need a visa if entering only as visitors:

1. British citizens and British overseas citizens who are readmissible to the United Kingdom.
2. Citizens of Andorra, Antigua and Barbuda, Australia, Austria, Bahamas, Barbados, Belgium, Belize, Botswana, Brunei, Costa Rica, Cyprus, Denmark, Dominica, Finland, France, Germany, Greece, Grenada, Hungary, Iceland, Ireland, Israel (National Passport holders only), Italy, Japan, Kiribati, Liechtenstein, Luxembourg, Malaysia, Malta, Mexico, Monaco, Namibia, Nauru, The Netherlands, New Zealand, Norway, Papua New Guinea, Portugal, Republic of Korea, San Marino, Saudi Arabia, Singapore, Solomon Islands, Spain, St. Kitts and Nevis, St. Lucia, St. Vincent, Swaziland, Sweden, Switzerland, Tuvalu, United States, Vanuatu, Western Samoa, and Zimbabwe.
3. Citizens of the British dependent territories who derive their citizenship through birth, descent, registration or naturalisation in one of the British dependent territories of Anguilla, Bermuda, British Virgin Islands, Cayman Islands, Falkland Islands, Gibraltar, Hong Kong, Montserrat, Pitcairn, St. Helena, or the Turks and Caicos Islands.

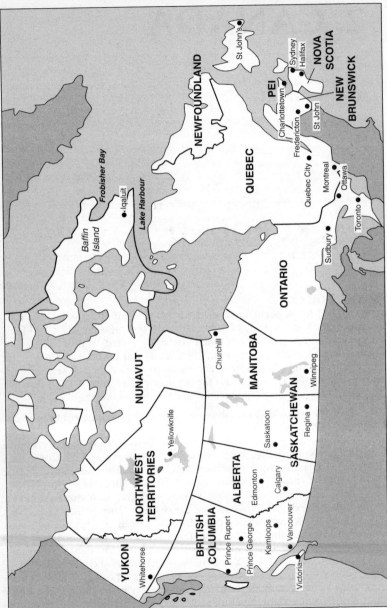

Nationals of all other countries should check their visa requirements with their nearest Canadian consular office. If there is no official Canadian representative in the country, visas are issued by the British embassy or consulate. Those requiring visas must apply before leaving home.

To **work in Canada**, a work visa must be obtained from the Canadian immigration authorities before departure. To qualify you must produce written evidence of a job offer. If you are a student, contact the **BUNAC** London office (020) 7251-3472) for information about the *Work Canada* programme which gives eligible students (tertiary level or gap year) temporary work authorisation. Similar opportunities are open to students of a few other countries. Check with your nearest consulate. If you plan to **study in Canada** you will need a special student visa, obtainable from any Canadian consulate. You must produce a letter of acceptance from the Canadian college before the visa can be issued.

Visitors who plan to re-enter the United States after visiting Canada must be sure to keep their US visa documentation and passport to regain entry into the US. (*See Background USA chapter for information on the Visa Waiver programme.*)

Customs permit anyone over 18 to import, duty free, up to 50 cigars, 200 cigarettes and 400g of manufactured tobacco.

Along with personal possessions, any number of individually wrapped and addressed gifts up to the value of $60 each may be brought into the country. Each visitor who meets the minimum age requirements of the province or territory of entry may, in addition, bring in 1.1 litres of liquor or wine or 24 x 33ml bottles / cans of beer or ale, duty and tax-free.

Further details on immigration, health or customs requirements may be obtained from the nearest High Commission, embassy or consulate. Or see the Canada Tourism Website at *www.canadatourism.com/en/ctc/travel_canada/index.html*

GETTING THERE

From Europe. Advanced booking charter (ABC) flights are available from London and other British and European cities to various Canadian cities including Halifax, Ottawa, Toronto, Montréal, Winnipeg, Calgary and Vancouver. Also available are several different types of package deal. Canadian Airlines and Air Canada offer packages including anything from bus passes, hotels, coach tours, rail passes, to car and camper wagon rental. The only way to discover the best fare and route for yourself is to get all available information from your travel agent when you are ready to book and check with airlines directly for current promotions or seat sales.

Air Canada and Canadian Airlines offer 14-day advance purchase tickets. Currently the 14-day advance purchase fare from London to Toronto is about £470 plus tax during the summer. Expect to pay about £530 plus tax to Vancouver or Calgary.

If you are not able to take advantage of the various advance booking fares, then it may make sense to fly into the USA and continue your journey from there. Using **VUSA fares** and booking before leaving for North America, you could fly on from New York for about US$175, and US$422 to Vancouver. Again, do your research before paying out your money, and bear in mind that travel from the USA, by bus, rail or air, into Canada is very easy

and can be very inexpensive (see below). Travellers to Canada via the USA will of course need to obtain a US visa before leaving their home country.
From the USA. You have the choice of bus, train, plane or car, or of course you can simply walk across on foot. It is impossible, within the confines of this Guide, to give all the possible permutations of modes, fares and routes from points within the USA to points within Canada, but, as a rough guide to fares from New York to the major eastern Canadian cities, the current fares to Toronto are: by train, about US$65-$100 o/w, US$130-$195 r/t depending on when you travel; by bus, about US$83 o/w, $168 r/t. Airline prices vary from as little as US$120 to US$209 r/t, depending on dates of travel, even if you only need a one way ticket, buy a round trip, they are always much cheaper. Don't overlook the aforementioned VUSA fares.

Should you cross the border by car it's a good idea to have a yellow 'Non-resident, Interprovincial Motor Vehicle Liability Insurance Card' (phew!) which provides evidence of financial responsibility by a valid automobile liability insurance policy. This card is available in the US through an insurance agent. Such evidence is required at all times by all provinces and territories. In addition Québec's insurance act bars lawsuits for bodily injury resulting from an auto accident, so you may need some additional coverage should you be planning to drive in Québec. If you're driving a borrowed car it's wise to carry a letter from the owner giving you permission to use the car.

CLIMATE AND WHAT TO PACK

Canada's principal cities are situated between the 43rd and 49th parallels, consequently summer months in the cities, and in the southernmost part of the country in general, are usually warm and sunny. August is the warmest month when temperatures are in the 80s. Ontario and the Prairie Provinces are the warmest places and although it can be humid it is never as bad as the humidity which accompanies high temperatures in the US.

Be warned, however, that nights, even in high summer, can be cool and it's advisable to bring lightweight sweaters or jackets. Naturally as you go north, temperatures drop accordingly. Yellowknife in the North West Territories has an *average* August temperature of 45°F (7°C) for instance, and nights in the mountains can be pretty cold. Snow can be expected in some places as early as September, and in winter Canada is very cold and snowy everywhere.

When you've decided which areas of Canada you'll be visiting, note the local climate and pack clothes accordingly. Plan for a variety of occasions, make a list, and then cut it by half! Take easy-to-care-for garments. Permanent press, non-iron things are best. Laundromats are cheap and readily available wherever you go. Remember too that you'll probably want to buy things while you're in North America. Canadians, as well as Americans, excel at producing casual, sporty clothes, T-shirts, etc. The farther north you plan to go and the more time you intend to spend out of doors, the more weatherproof the clothing will need to be. And don't forget the insect repellent.

It's important too to consider the best way of carrying your clothes. Lugging a heavy suitcase is not fun. A lightweight bag or a backpack is possibly best. A good idea is to take a smaller flight-type bag in which to keep a change of clothes and all your most valuable possessions like passport, travellers cheques and air tickets as well, but always hand carry the bag containing your passport and money. For extra safety many travellers like to carry passport documents and travellers cheques in a special neck/waist pouch or wallet. When travelling by bus, be sure to keep your baggage within your sights. Make sure it's properly labelled and on the same bus as yourself at every stop!

TIME ZONES
Canada spans six time zones:
1. Newfoundland Standard Time: Newfoundland, and Labrador (GMT – 3$^1/_2$ hrs).
2. Atlantic Standard Time: The Maritimes, far eastern parts of Québec and Nunavut (GMT – 4 hrs).
3. Eastern Standard Time: Most of Québec, and all of Ontario east of 90 degrees longitude (GMT – 5hrs).
4. Central Standard Time: Ontario west of 90, Manitoba, Saskatchewan except NW corner of the province, most of Nunavut (GMT – 6hrs).
5. Mountain Standard Time: NW Saskatchewan, Alberta, Northwest Territories, northeastern British Columbia (GMT – 7 hrs).
6. Pacific Standard Time: Most of British Columbia and the Yukon (GMT – 8 hrs).

From the last Sunday in April through the last Sunday in October, Daylight Saving Time is observed everywhere except in Saskatchewan, where Standard Time operates in most of the province.

THE CANADIAN PEOPLE
Although Canada, like its neighbour to the south, is a comparatively young country, Canadians now feel that they have finally emerged as a major world power in their own right, and gone are the days when Canada can only function in the shadow of Great Britain or the United States.

It is just 133 years since the confederation of 1867. At that time Canada petered out into trackless forest to the north of Lake Superior, and no regular communication existed to the isolated settlements of the Red River in the west. The provinces of Ontario, Québec, Nova Scotia and Prince Edward Island made up the confederation. The other six provinces and two territories only gradually joined. Of the last provinces, Saskatchewan and Alberta were formed in 1905 and Newfoundland entered the federation in 1949, all amazingly recent. For this reason, although undoubtedly proud of their country, Canadians are fiercely defendant of their home provinces, and may well declare themselves an Albertan (or Québecois, whatever ...) first, and Canadian second. The Inuit tribes of the north (don't call them Eskimos) recently celebrated a victory; Nunavut, meaning 'Our Land' in Inuit, was created in April 1999 from the eastern portion of the Northwest Territories. Isolated and arctic, settlements are few and far between and communications limited, but the element of self-rule allowed to the Inuit is a milestone for the First Americans of the whole continent.

The population of Canada is roughly 30 million, a relatively small population spread over a gigantic land mass. Practically everyone lives along the southern strip of Canada, which borders on the United States. Most of Canada is still wilderness. The majority of the Canadian people are descendants of white European types, either Gallic or Celtic. There are also Native Peoples (Indians and Eskimos) and, increasingly as Canada continues to open its doors to the rest of the world, late 20th century Canadian society is rich in cultural and racial diversity, Chinese, Eastern European immigrants, Tamils, Sikhs and other people from all corners of the world.

Canada is rich in natural resources and rich with money in the bank. There are five banks in Canada, and the influence of the big five is very strong, reaching far beyond banking. All its natural wealth did not, however, prevent Canada from joining the ranks of nations suffering from economic recession in the early '90s. Such was the economic state of the nation, that it brought an end to the long rule of the Conservative Party when overwhelmingly, Canadians voted to transfer the economic future of Canada to the care of the Liberal Party.

Continuing to maintain its centre-stage prominence is the perennial problem of Canadian politics, Québec. The main pre-election aim of the Bloc Québecois, formerly led by Lucien Bouchard, was to prepare Canada for Québec's independence. The values and traditions of the individual provinces are strong and Canadian politics is renowned for its bitter interprovincial and provincial-versus-federal rivalries. Ontario, the most wealthy province and the principal seat of the government, is often at the centre of the controversy, and one of the most bitter power struggles has been between Ontario and Québec.

There are more than 8 million French speaking Canadians; the majority live in Québec. You will notice the phrase 'je me souviens' on the license plates in Québec. This phrase (I remember) refers to the defeat of Montcalm on the Plains of Abraham by General Wolfe. This event signalled the end of a French power base in the New World. The French have felt besieged and encroached upon by the English world ever since, hence their sometimes desperate measures to protect their heritage and remain a 'distinct society' within Canada. Constitutional proposals designed to keep Québec within the federation and everyone else happy as well, have not yet gained approval; the referendum on sovereignty narrowly failed in 1995. Though many bitter feelings still stem from the conflict, there is no doubt that this unsubtle blend of French and British influence adds an extra quelque chose to the Canadian cultural picture.

The Canadians have somehow acquired something of a reputation for being puritanical, conformist, humourless and dull! Certainly there's a need there for more than a touch of Gallic charm and chic, but this image is largely the face of officialdom and bureaucracy. You will find the Canadian people charming, hospitable and anxious to share their land with you. They will also be most anxious to uphold Canada's uniqueness and to show that Canada is not the same as America—despite the apparent social similarities. Never call a Canadian 'American'!

Try and see something of the *real* Canada. Don't expect to find the stereotypical Mountie on every street corner; Native Indians don't live in teepees, and it doesn't start snowing on September 1st! Visit an Indian reservation, learn about Inuit arts and crafts, and meet with Canadians as they celebrate at the numerous fairs, rodeos and festivals across the country. (Provincial tourist authorities can supply dates and locations of the various events.) 'Man-made 21st century Canada will impress you, but it is the Canadian way of life and the natural beauty of the land that will really dazzle you.'

HEALTH

Canada does operate a subsidised health service, though on a provincial rather than federal basis. Most provinces will cover most of the hospital and medical services of their inhabitants, although three months' residency is required in Québec and British Columbia. The short-term visitor to Canada, therefore, must be adequately insured *before* arrival.

MONEY

Canadian currency is dollars and cents and comes in the same units as US currency, i.e. penny, nickel, quarter and dollar and $2 coins. The dollar coin has a great name, the 'loonie'; a loon (bird!) is featured on one side. The two-dollar coin is subsequently occasionally referred to as a 'twonie'. At present one Canadian dollar is worth about US $0.67, and you will find your dollars go a lot further here than in the US; this has not always been the case, for a long time Canadians would cross the border to make large purchases! To avoid exchange rate problems, it is a good idea to change all your money into Canadian currency or travellers cheques. (At the time of writing; £1 equals approximately CAN$2.31.)

Unless otherwise stated, all prices in this section are in Canadian dollars.

Travellers cheques are probably the safest form of currency and are accepted at most hotels, restaurants and shops. As well as American Express, Thomas Cook and Visa cheques, you can also purchase cheques issued by Canadian banks before you go. Those with student bank accounts often are able to order travellers cheques commission-free from their own bank, but it is still worth checking a few places as a better exchange rate may still mean more dollars for your pound, even paying 1-2 percent commission. They may be used in the same way as cash at major stores or businesses in Canada. **Credit and debit cards**. Barclaycard, Visa and MasterCard and are all widely accepted, and you can draw cash from these cards at banks and through ATM's (cashpoints) for a fee. You will be charged commission for every transaction you make. Switch and Delta debit cards can be used in the same way, provided, of course, you have cash in your account back home. Commission is also charged, but it differs from that for a credit card.

Bank hours are generally 10 am-4 pm, Monday to Friday, and often with a later opening on Friday. If you are planning an extensive trip to Canada and the USA, you might consider opening a bank account that offers a cash card which works on both a Canadian and US bank system. All you need to open an account in Canada is cash. It is a simple matter of filling out one form. Since opening an account with a Canadian bank means corresponding with them through the mail, you will want to look into it well in advance of your trip. The Royal Bank of Canada offers a 'client card' that is valid in Canada and at all 'Plus' system machines in the US. ATM's (Automated Teller Machines) are common in big cities and at most banks, and normally accept cards with a Visa / MasterCard sign – check with your bank for availability and charges, and make sure you know your PIN! ATM's are also (fatally!) often located in big stores and bars!

Sales Tax and Rebates. Provincial Sales Tax (PST) applies on the purchase of goods and services. This varies from province to province. In Ontario for instance the rate is eight percent, although there are exceptions such as on shoes under $30, books, groceries, and restaurant meals costing less than $4. On the other hand if your meal costs more than $4, then the tax is ten percent. Alberta, Yukon, Nunavut and the NW Territories do not have any PST. Canada also has a country-wide **Goods and Services Tax (GST)** of seven percent. Overseas visitors may be able to claim a rebate of this **GST** paid on some items such as short-term accommodation and on consumer goods; it cannot be reclaimed for travel, car hire or meals. To complicate matters further, in Newfoundland, Nova Scotia and New Brunswick, the GST and PST have been combined into the **Harmonised Sales Tax (HST)** of 15 percent. The HST and GST can all be reclaimed, and in Quebec and Manitoba, so can the PST. Keep your receipts! Each receipt must normally be for a minimum of $50 before taxes, and expenses must total at least $200. Details from: Visitors Rebate Program, Revenue Canada, Summerside Tax Centre, Summerside, PEI,C1N 6C6, (800) 668-4748, *www.rc.ga.ca*. Outside Canada phone (902) 432-5608. Application forms are also available in duty free shops and airports. In Ontario, there is a refund of the Retail Sales Tax, i.e. the PST levied on retails sales only, paid on goods permanently removed from Ontario within 30 days, and totalling $50 or more. More information from; Retail Sales Tax Branch, Refund Unit, 4th Floor, 1600 Champlain Ave., Whitby, Ontario, L1N 9B2, (800) 263-7965, or (905) 432-3332. **Tipping**, as in the USA, is expected in eating places, by taxi drivers, bellhops, baggage handlers and the like. Fifteen percent is standard.

COMMUNICATIONS

Mail. Postage stamps can be purchased at any post office or from vending machines (at par) in hotels, drug stores, stations, bus terminals and some news-stands. At present it costs 55¢ to send a letter to a US address and 95¢ to Europe and other overseas destinations. Within Canada the rate is 46¢. Canada Post is *very* slow. Post offices are not generally open at weekends. The postcode is a must if sending mail to Canada. If you do not know where you will be staying, have your mail sent care of 'General Delivery' ('Post Restante' in Quebec). You then have 15 days to collect.

Telephone. Local calls from coin telephones usually cost 25¢. As in the USA (see earlier section, the two systems are very similar) local calls from private phones are usually free. You can direct dial to most places in Canada, the United States and Europe. Dial 0 for the operator. Check local directories for the cheapest times to place a long distance call – usually between 11pm and 8am. Telephone cards are available in Canada, buying you $10 or $20 worth of time. 'Information' (Directory Enquiries in Britain) is the area code you want, followed by 555-1212. **NB:** Toll-free numbers (those that begin with 800, 887, 888, can only be dialled from within North America.

Internet Access. Email and the internet are now essential communication tools in all but the most remote areas of Canada. Access is cheaper than back in the UK (especially with free local phone calls) and subsequently more widely available. Main public libraries provide free public internet access (you may have to sign in and wait for a specified time spot) and there are many cyber cafes – phone ahead first though as they pop up and disappear rapidly. Internet kiosks also offer access, especially common in hostels.

ELECTRICITY
110v, 60 cycles AC, except in remote areas where cycles vary.

SHOPPING
Stores are generally open until 5.30 or 6 pm with late opening on Thursday or Friday, although stores in the cities may well stay open later more frequently. Usually, only shops located in tourist areas will be open on Sundays. Canada is big on shopping malls (the inventor of which was a Canadian). In the large cities there are huge underground shopping malls so that you don't need to go outside at all in the harsh Canadian winter, but can move underground from mall to mall, or mall to subway or train station.

Good buys in Canada include handicrafts and Eskimo products such as carvings, moccasins, etc. Casual, outdoors or winter wear is recommended too.

THE METRIC SYSTEM
Canada is metric. Milk, wine and gasoline are sold by the litre; groceries in grams and kilograms; clothing sizes come in centimetres, fabric lengths in metres; and, most important, driving speeds are in kilometres p/hour. See the conversion tables in the Appendix.

DRINKING
Liquor regulations come under provincial law, and although it's generally easy to buy a drink by the glass in a lounge, tavern or beer parlour, it can be pretty tricky tracking down one of the special liquor outlets which can be few and far between. Beer, wine and spirits can only be bought from a liquor store which will keep usual store hours and be closed on Sundays. The exception is Quebec, where alcohol is available in supermarkets. Restrictions on alcohol consumption in Nunavut are determined separately by each community. The drinking age is 19, except in Québec, Manitoba and Alberta, where it is 18. Carry ID just in case.

DRUGS
Narcotics laws in Canada are federal, rather than provincial, and it is illegal to possess or sell such drugs as cannabis, cocaine and heroin. Penalties (up to $1,000 or 6 months in jail for a first offence) are the same for offences involving marijuana as for heroin, etc.

CIGARETTES
Cost is currently about $4 for a packet of 25. Foreign brands are widely

available. Smoking is discouraged in public places, with penalties and level of enforcement depending on the province.

PUBLIC HOLIDAYS

New Year's Day	1st January
Good Friday/Easter Monday	Variable
Victoria Day	3rd Monday in May
Canada Day	1st July
Civic Holiday	4th Aug in all provinces except Québec, Yukon and Northwest Territories
Labour Day	1st Monday in September
Thanksgiving Day	2nd Monday in October
Remembrance Day	11th November
Christmas Day	25th December
Boxing Day	26th December

INFORMATION

In **Britain** contact Canada House, 62-65 Trafalgar Square, London WC2N 5DT. The **Visit Canada Centre** is open Mon-Fri 9am-5.30pm, Information line 0891-715000. They will also send out a free Visitors Pack. The High Commission's web address is *www.dfait-maeci.gc.ca/london/menu.htm* and has an excellent section on transportation within Canada. In *Canada* tourist information centres abound and are indicated on highway maps. Especially recommended is the information published by the provincial tourist offices. If you plan to spend any length of time in one province it is well worth writing to them and asking for their free maps, guides and accommodation information.

On the Internet: *citynet/countries/canada or canada.gc.ca*.

Provincial Tourist Offices

Alberta: Explore Alberta, Box 2500, Edmonton, Alberta T5J 2Z1, (800) 661-8888 or (780) 427-4321. *www.explorealberta.com*

British Columbia: SuperNatural British Columbia, 1166 Alberny, Suite #600, Vancouver, BC, V6E 2Z3, (250) 387-1642. BC Tourism, Parliament Buildings, Victoria, BC, V8V 1X4, (800) 663-6000, or (604) 685-0032. *travel.bc.ca*

Manitoba: Travel Manitoba, 7th Floor, 155 Carlton St, Winnipeg, Manitoba, R3C 3H8, (800) 665-0040 or (204) 945-3777. *www.travelmanitoba.com*

New Brunswick: Tourism New Brunswick, PO Box 6000, Fredericton, New Brunswick, E3B 5HI, (800) 561-0123 or (506) 453-0123. *www.gov.nb.ca/tourism*

Newfoundland & Labrador: Department of Tourism, Culture and Recreation, PO Box 8730, St John's, Newfoundland, A1B 4K2, (800) 563-6353 or (709) 729-2830. *public.gov.nf.ca/tourism*

North West Territories: Northwest Territories Tourism, PO Box 610, Yellowknife, NWT, X1A 2N5, (800) 661-0788 or (867) 873-7200. *www.nwt-travel.nt.ca*

Nova Scotia: Nova Scotia Tourism, PO Box 456, Halifax, NS, B3J 2M7, (800) 565-0000 or (902) 425-5781. *explore.gov.ns.ca*

Nunavut: Nunavut Tourism, PO Box 1450, Iqaluit, Nunavut, X0A 0H0, (800) 491-7910 or (867) 979-6551. *www.nunatour.nt.ca*

Ontario: Ontario Travel, Queens Park, Toronto, Ontario, M7A 2R9, (800) 668-2746 or (416) 314-0944. *www.ontario-travel.com*
Prince Edward Island: PEI Travel Information, PO Box 940, Charlottetown, PEI, C1A 7M5, (800) 463-4734 or (902) 368-4444 *.www.peiplay.com*
Québec: Tourisme Québec, PO Box 979, Montréal, Quebec, H3C 2W3, (800) 363-7777 or (514) 873-2015. *www.tourisme.gouv.qc.ca*
Saskatchewan: Tourism Saskatchewan, Suite 500, 1900 Albert St, Regina, Saskatchewan, S4P 4L9, (800) 667-7191 / 1-877-2ESCAPE or (306) 787-2300, *www.sasktourism.com*
Yukon: Yukon Tourism, PO Box 2703, Whitehorse, Yukon, Y1A 2C6, (867) 667-5340. *www.touryukon.com*

THE GREAT OUTDOORS

Hardly surprising with all those wide open spaces, that Canadians are very outdoors minded. Greenery is never far away and the best of it has been preserved in national parks. There are many national parks in Canada ranging in size from eight to 44,000 square kilometres, and in type from the immense mountains and forests of the west to the steep cliffs and beaches of the Atlantic coastline. In addition there are many fine provincial parks and more than 600 national historic parks and sites.

Entrance to the national parks costs $3-$5 for a one-day pass, more for season passes. All but the most primitive offer camping facilities, hiking trails, and facilities for swimming, fishing, boating and other such diversions. Most of the national parks are dealt with in this Guide. For more detailed information we suggest you write to the individual park or to: Parks Canada, 25 Eddy St, Hull, Quebec, K1A 0M5. Call (888) 773-888, for a copy of the free booklet *National Parks of Canada*, or visit their web site *parkscanada.pch.gc.ca*

A list of major parks follows:

Banff, Alberta.
Cape Breton Highlands, Nova Scotia.
Elk Island, Alberta.
Forillon, Québec.
Fundy, New Brunswick.
Georgian Bay Islands, Ontario.
Glacier, British Columbia.
Gros Morne, Newfoundland.
Jasper, Alberta.
Kejimkujik, Nova Scotia
Kootenay, British Columbia.
Kluane, Yukon.
La Mauricie, Quebec
Mount Revelstoke, British Columbia.

Nahanni, Northwest Territories
Pacific Rim, British Columbia.
Point Pelee, Ontario.
Prince Albert, Saskatchewan.
Prince Edward, Prince Edward Island.
Pukaskwa, Ontario
Riding Mountain, Manitoba.
St Lawrence Islands, Ontario.
Terra Nova, Newfoundland.
Waterton Lakes, Alberta.
Wood Buffalo, Alberta / North West Territories
Yoho, British Columbia.

MEDIA AND ENTERTAINMENT

Canada until recently was viewed as a cultural wasteland. Even now, for preference, Canadians watch US or British television programmes and read US or European magazines. Traditionally, talented Canadians moved from Canada to the USA in order to succeed. However, this has begun to change.

CANADIAN WINTER SPORTS

Canada is a winter wonderland of sports. The country's vast, untamed wilderness offers over 300 ski areas and some of the world's best snowboarding, downhill and cross-country skiing. Canadians are also mad on ice hockey.

EAST—Canada's eastern resorts are a paradise for both downhill and cross country enthusiasts and tend to be a good deal cheaper than those in the west.

Marble Mt, Corner Brook, Newfoundland, (709) 637-7600. Offers the best spring skiing east of the Rockies. Lots of trails and plenty of powder. Day pass $28, $22 for students.

Ontario and Québec are where the real action is; **Blue Mt**, Collingwood, Ontario, (705) 445-0231. This is the biggest and highest ski area in S Ontario. Great diversity of runs with new ones being cleared regularly. 'Check out Planet Collingwood, the hottest nightspot in town.' Day pass $38, $34 for students.

Loch Lomond, Thunder Bay, Ontario, (807) 475-7787. One of the best hills in Thunder Bay with a good cross section of different skill level terrain. Day pass $27, $22 w/student ID, higher at weekends.

Mt St Louis Moonstone, Coldwater, Ontario, (705) 835-2112. Downhill and cross-country trails, good spot for beginners. 'The hills are always groomed to perfection and lift lines are never too busy.' Day pass $31, $21 w/student ID..

Horseshoe Resort, Barrie, Ontario, (705) 835-2790. This is the busiest resort in the Barrie area, quieter times are during the week and at night. Good skiing for all levels. 'Helpful staff and well maintained runs.' Day pass $33, $28 w/student ID. 4 hour passes also available.

Mt St Anne, Beaupre, Québec, (418) 827-4561. Great downhill, cross-country and 24hr skiing and plenty of variety. 'A hidden treasure'. Day pass $45, $38 for students.

Stoneham, Québec, (418) 848-2411. A medium sized resort with trails for every level. 'Great variety of terrain and great nightlife around the resort'. Day pass $39, $29 w/student ID.

Mt Tremblant, Québec, (819) 681-2000. Tremblant is the ultimate definition for tons of snow, countless number of trails and variety of terrain. 'Peaceful, scenic cross-country trails'. Good employment opportunities. Day pass $52, $39 w/student ID.

WEST—The Rockies are the place to ski in the west.

Lake Louise, Alberta, (403) 522-3555. Plenty of snow and plenty of challenge, huge diversity of terrain, beautiful scenery and well groomed runs. Good employment opportunities in surrounding hotels and restaurants. 'An absolute treat for skiiers and snowboarders, their bowls are the best!' Day pass $49.75, $39 w/student ID.

Sunshine Village, Banff, Alberta, (403) 762-6500. Good powder and wide range of trails, excellent for beginners. Good employment opportunities. Day pass $46, $38 w/student ID.

Fortress Mt, Calgary, Alberta, (403) 264-5825. Heaven for snowboarders, lots of natural halfpipes, powder, trees and no one to bug you. 'Love it.' Day pass $30, $25 w/student ID.

Big White, Kelowna, BC, (250) 765-3101. Perfect for intermediates, one of the best mountains for powder with wide groomed runs. Recently expanded with lots of new facilities and fast lifts. Day pass $47, $40 for students.

Whistler/Blackcomb, Whistler, BC. Has been recognised as N America's best, most hard-core ski/snowboard resort. The most challenging peaks and the highest vertical rise in the north. Massive diversity of trails and outstanding facilities. 'Go to heaven and ski like hell.' 'Expensive but worth every penny.' Day pass $61, $51 w/student ID.
Silver Star Mt, Vernon, BC, (250) 542-0224. Home of the Canadian National Cross Country Team, with over 90 km of groomed trails. Challenging downhill runs for all levels and, of course, outstanding cross-country conditions. Day pass $46, $39 for students.
Red Mt, Rossland, BC, (250) 362-7384. One of Canada's oldest resorts, still challenging to both skiers and snowboarders. Good powder, tree skiing, quiet lifts. 'Radical expert terrain but most of it is unmarked'. Day pass $40, $33 w/student ID. For info on all mentioned resorts and more, www.goski.com/canada.htm or, www.Skinetcanada.com/.

ICE HOCKEY Hockey is by far Canada's most popular spectator sport and one of the country's most widely played recreational sports. The **National Hockey League** (NHL), is a professional league comprising of 27 North American teams including 7 Canadian based teams. Although many teams are located in the US, the majority of NHL players are Canadian. The **Calgary Flames, Edmonton Oilers, Montreal Canadiens, Ottawa Senators, Toronto Maple Leafs**, and the **Vancouver Canuks**, slug it out among the top teams for the **Stanley Cup**, a trophy symbolic of hockey supremacy in N America. Hockey season runs from Oct-Jun. www.nhl.com/.

Ringette A relatively new sport that has attracted a large following in Canada is Ringette. More than 50,000 ringette competitors play on approximately 2500 teams. Played mostly by women, ringette is similar to hockey, but a rubber ring replaces the puck.

SKATING Canada also excels at figure skating. A vast network of clubs across throughout the country has produced a long line of medalists including Barbara Ann Scott and Kurt Browning in the Olympics, and more recently, Elvis Stojka in the World's. As a spectator sport figure skating has steadily increased in popularity over the past several years. Although not as widely practised, speed skating has produced Canada's greatest Winter Olympian, Gaetan Boucher; he took home not one but two Gold medals in 1984.
For more general sports info, *http://.gc.ca/*.

This is partly because the government has legislated a minimum level of Canadian content in radio and television and implemented a strict 'hire Canadian' policy throughout the arts and entertainment business. Canadian culture is also flourishing more as a reflection of new-found Canadian pride. Visitors will be impressed with the high standards in ballet, theatre and classical music. Folk music and the visual arts thrive, and Canada boasts a number of exceptional museums and restorations well worth visiting for a glimpse of Canada past. There is also a huge annual festival scene in Canada. From major cities to small towns, from Shakespeare to jazz, you'll find a celebration of some kind wherever you go.

SPORT AND RECREATION

Canada has hosted almost every major sports competition: the summer and winter Olympics, Commonwealth Games, Pan-American Games and World University Games, including the 1999 Pan-American Games held in Winnipeg. Canadians love to camp, hike, fish, ski and generally enjoy the outdoors. Winter sports (naturally) are very popular from ice-skating to snowmobiling. Ice hockey is the biggie for watching. There is a Canadian version of American football, and baseball is also very popular; the Toronto Blue Jays won the world series in baseball in 1992 and 1993. Surprisingly perhaps, the national game is lacrosse. (See *Winter Sports* box for more information.)

ON THE ROAD

ACCOMMODATION

For general hints on finding the right accommodation for you, please read the 'Accommodation' section for the USA. The basic rules are the same.

All the provincial tourist boards publish comprehensive accommodation lists. These are obtainable from Canadian government tourist offices or directly from provincial tourist boards and have details of all approved hotels, motels and tourist homes in each town. These are excellent guides and are highly recommended.

Hotels and Motels: Always plenty to choose from around sizeable towns or cities, but if you're travelling don't leave finding accommodation until too late in the day. In less populated areas distances between motels can be very great indeed. The major difference between the hotel/motel picture here and in the US is that the budget chains like Super 8 and Motel 6 have not yet made it to Canada in force. It shouldn't be a problem to find independent, reasonably priced motels on highways between the major cities. Many highway motels will often have restaurants attached. The local tourist bureau will usually have a list of local hotels and motels. However, for the budget traveller, it is likely that a tourist home will nearly always be a less expensive alternative.

Tourist Homes: A bit like bed and breakfast places in Britain and Europe, only without the breakfast. In other words a room in a private home. Usually you share a bathroom and your room will be basic but perfectly adequate. Such establishments are scattered very liberally all over Canada with prices starting around $25-$30. Certainly if hostels are not for you, and your budget doesn't quite stretch to a motel, then these are the places to look for. Again, the local tourist bureau will be able to provide you with a list of possibilities.

Bed and Breakfasts: There is now also the firmly established bed and breakfast circuit. Singles from about $35, doubles $55-$80 and up – some can be very luxurious. Several guides to bed and breakfast establishments (town and country locations) are published in Canada and can be picked up in bookshops everywhere. Otherwise, the local tourist office will provide listings. Bed and Breakfast is often your best bet for a cheap room in remoter areas where hotel/motel accommodation is expensive.

Hostels: Hostelling International Canada has over 80 member hostels across the country with at least one hostel in each major city. The National Parks in Alberta are well covered. You can save money with an International Youth Hostel Card from your own country since non-members usually pay about $2-$5 more. There is no limit to a stay. For detailed information and lists of hostels write to: HI-Canada, 205 Catherine St, Suite 400, Ottawa, Ontario, K2P IC3, (617) 237-7884, *www.hostellingintl.ca* or else enquire via the association in your own country. Annual membership is $24 plus tax, or you can collect six 'welcome stickers at $4 each time you stay – this will also give you annual membership. It's currently cheaper to join the AYH in the UK. For information on independent hostels contact Backpackers Hostel Canada, RR 13, Site 10-1, Thunder Bay, Ontario, P7B 5E4. email: *candu@microage-tb.com* Website: *www.backpackers.ca*

YM/YWCAs: Y's have weight lifting machines, pools and aerobics classes for those in need of an exercise fix, but standards vary, and in some cities the Y is predominantly a doss-house for the local homeless. Cheaper and often better, are tourist homes. For further information, contact the Y's Way, 224 E 47th St, New York, NY 10017 or phone (212) 308-2899 for information. For a complete list and information on Canadian Y's: YMCA National Council, 42 Charles St East, 6th Floor, Toronto, Ontario M4Y 1T4, (416) 967-9622. *www.ywca.ca*

University Accommodation: There is much campus housing available during the summer. Look particularly for student owned co-operatives in cities such as Toronto which provide a cheapish service, often with cooking facilities. University housing services and fraternities will often be able to help you also. In general, college housing starts at about $20 single but can be as high as $35 single. Staying on campus usually gives access to all the usual facilities including cafeterias, lounges, etc., and often a pool and gymnasium/athletic fields. The drawback about campus accommodation is that it is usually not available after mid-late August, when Canadian students begin returning to college.

Camping: Canadians are very fond of camping and during the summer, sites in popular places will always be very full. Usually, however, campgrounds are not as spacious as those in the USA and less trouble is taken with the positioning of individual sites. Prices are about the same, $8-$25 per site. There are many provincial park campgrounds, as well as sites in the national parks and the many privately operated grounds usually to be found close to the highways. Campgrounds are marked on official highway maps.

The Rand McNally *Campground and Trailer Park Guide* covers Canada as well as the USA. Also, the Canadian Government Office of Tourism publishes guides on camping across Canada: Canadian Tourism Commission, 8th Floor West, 235 Queen St, Ottawa, Ontario, K1A 0H6, (613) 946-1000. The much recommended KOA now have about 50 campgrounds in Canada. Details from: KOA Inc, PO Box 31734, Billings, Montana 59107-1734, (406) 248-7444. They will send a directory of campsites; send a $3 fee for postage, or pick one up at a site for free. Both the provincial tourist guides and local tourist bureaux are other sources of information on where to find a campground. The government-run parks tend to have the more scenic tent sites. Most camp sites are open summer months only, July to September.

For real outdoor camping in Canada you need a tent with a flyscreen. Black flies and mosquitoes are a serious problem in June and July and the further north you go the worse the little darlings are. It gets cold at night too as early as August, so be prepared for colder temperatures and wetter weather than in the US. Other hazards of camping in Canada include bears and 'beaver fever', a rare intestinal parasite (*giardia lamblia*).

FOOD

How much you spend per day on food will obviously depend upon your taste and your budget, but you can think in terms of roughly $2-$5 on breakfast, from $4 on lunch, and anything from $6 upwards on dinner. It is customary in Canada to eat the main meal of the day in the evening from about 5 pm onwards. In small, out-of-the-way towns, any restaurants there are may close as early as 7 pm or 8 pm. Yes, McDonalds does operate in Canada, as do several other US fast food chains.

Canadian food is perhaps slightly more Europeanised than American and in the larger cities you will find a great variety of ethnic restaurants, any thing from Chinese through Swedish and French. In Québec, of course, French-style cooking predominates and in the Atlantic provinces sea food and salmon are the specialities. Remember to try Oka Cheese in Québec and wild, ripe berries everywhere in the summer.

TRAVEL

To be read in conjunction with the USA Background travel section.

Bus: Bus travel is usually the cheapest way of getting around, fares generally being less than half the airfare. Every region in Canada has different bus companies, Gray Coach, Acadian Lines, Greyhound and Voyageur are the largest.

The Greyhound (USA) Ameripasses are only valid in Canada on specific routes, e.g. Buffalo or Detroit to Toronto. There are however two unlimited travel Greyhound Canada passes, the **Canada Pass** for travel west of Ottawa/Toronto and the **Canada Pass Plus** which covers the whole of Canada. Rates for the Canada Pass are: for a 7 day pass, £99; 15 days costs £149; 30 days is £176 and 60 days costs £233. On the Canada Pass Plus, a 15 day pass is £161; 30 days is £206 and 60 days is £266. If bought before departure to Canada, travel can be on non-consecutive days, i.e. 7 days travel within 10 days, 15 out of 20 days, 30 out of 40 days and 60 within 80 days. If bought in Canada, the pass is only valid for the number of consecutive days. Unofficially, it may be possible to upgrade passes once in Canada; 'I upgraded my one month pass to two months by paying only $100 + tax. This enabled me to travel further east to the Maritimes. I confirmed that the upgraded pass would get me to the east coast at the Calgary head office.' The Canada Pass Plus Pass can only be bought before departure for Canada. All passes are non-refundable once any portion of the pass has been used. As with the USA, Greyhound have combined with Hostelling International to produce the **Go Canada** and **Go Canada Plus Passes** combining coupons for bus travel and hostel accommodation. You have to purchase the pass before leaving for Canada and must be a member of Hostelling International. For example, a 15-day bus pass combined with 7 hostel nights is £235. Passes can be bought from travel agents, Greyhound, or BUNAC in London.

Always check for the cheapest 'point-to-point' fare or excursion fare when making just one or two journeys without a bus pass. Toronto to the west coast, for instance, could cost about $212 one way.

One difference between the US and Canadian Greyhound operations worth noting is in baggage handling. Unlike the USA, the Canadian bus companies will never check baggage through to a destination without its owner. Bags cannot be sent on ahead, for instance, if you are simply seeking a way to dump them for a day or so while you see the sights. Lockers are usually available at bus stations, and don't forget to collect your bags from the pavement once they have been off-loaded by the driver.

The Canadian Adventure operates hop-on/hop-off bus routes in the east (Canabus Tours) and west (The Moose Run) with a connecting service between the two. They go off the beaten track and allow you to meet other 'like-minded' travellers. Contact Canabus at (877) CANABUS / (416) 977-9533 *www.canabus.com* or Moose Run at (888) 388-4881 / (604) 944-3091 *www.mooserun.com*.

Further Still Canadian Adventures offers east and west coast organised adventure tours, and a 3 day Toronto / Niagara package for $99. Contact (877) 371-8744 / (905) 371-8744 or *www.furtherstill.com*. ISIC card holders receive a 10 percent discount.

In Ontario and Quebec the **Rout-Pass** offers access to the routes of 35 inter-city bus companies between April and November. It offers coupons for travel within a 7, 14 or 18 day period, and can be purchased from intercity bus terminals in Toronto, Ottawa, Montreal, Quebec City and other major terminals, seven days in advance. The 14 day pass is $257. Call Montreal Bus station on (514) 842-2281.

Car: The Canadian is as attached to his car as is his American cousin. In general roads are better, speed limits are higher and there are fewer toll roads than south of the border. Canadian speed limits have gone metric and are posted everywhere in kilometres p/hr. Thus, 100 km p/hr is the most common freeway limit, 80 km p/hr is typical on two-lane rural highways, and 50 km p/hr operates most frequently in towns. Canadians, of course, drive on the right! Note that the wearing of **seat belts** by *all* persons in a vehicle is compulsory.

Car rental will cost from about $30-$45 p/day, $200 p/wk, with free mileage up to a point and a cost p/km of about 5¢-20¢ thereafter; the big companies often offer unlimited mileage. You may pay a surcharge for renting from the airport location; check with different branches of the same company. Most now have websites where you can get info and make online bookings – again these rates sometimes differ from those you pay booking in person. It's a lottery! As always, shop around for the best available rates. Finally bear in mind there will be another surcharge for more than one driver, and a hefty one if you are under 25; some companies will still refuse to rent to you at all. To hire an RV camper is a lot more expensive, but of course you wouldn't be paying as much for accommodation. RV campgrounds still charge $20-30 per night for hook-up. You would be joining a fleet of North American drivers – families and seniors especially.

Third party **insurance** is compulsory in all Canadian provinces and territories and can be expensive; it's not unusual for it to double the total amount you pay. British, other European and US drivers licences are officially recognised by the Canadian authorities. Membership of the AA, RAC, other European motoring organisations, or the AAA in the US, entitles the member to all the services of the **Canadian AA** and its member clubs free of charge. This includes travel info, itineraries, maps and tour books as well as emergency road services, weather reports and accommodation reservations. (NB: The US AAA also publishes excellent tour guides for Canada.)

Gas is sold by the litre and costs up to 50¢-60¢ a litre. Gas stations can be few and far between in remoter areas and it is wise to check your gauge in the late afternoon before the pumps shut off for the night.

One **hazard** to be aware of when driving in Canada is the unmarked, and even the marked, railroad crossing. Many people are killed every year on railroad crossings. Trains come and go so infrequently in remote areas that it's simply never possible to know when one will arrive. Be particularly alert at night.

Air: The two major airlines, Air Canada (*www.aircanada.ca*) and Canadian Airlines (*www.cdnair.ca*), offer different discount fares. There are 14-day and 21-day advance fares, touchdown fares, and late night fares to name a few. Air Canada offers **VUSA fares**, which give discounts of 25-30% on fares, however, you must book in advance before leaving for Canada. **Canada 3000** (*www.canada3000.com*) have been recommended for offering discounted flights within North America. This is a no-frills operator where a charge is made for on-board drinks and headphones, but if the price is bargain-basement... .

Canadian Airlines offer a 3-8 coupon airpass for $495-$820 off-peak / $555-$930 peak (July-August). The pass must be in conjunction with a flight into Canada with Canadian. Higher prices apply if you fly to Canada on another airline.

West Jet are a low-fare airline operating to currently eleven destinations in west and central Canada, as far east as Thunder Bay in Ontario. They have low fares all the time, and great specials, e.g. $44 from Calgary to Edmonton o/w. Call (888) WESTJET / (403) 250-5839, or visit their website at *www.westjet.com*

Students (with an ISIC card) may be able to get student discounts on flights through Travel CUTS, The Canadian Universities Travel Service Ltd, 187 College St, Toronto, (416) 979-2406, or at any of their other offices throughout Canada.

Rail: One of the conditions for the entry of British Columbia into the Confederation was the building of the Canadian Pacific Railway, and with the completion of the track in 1885, Canada as a transcontinental nation finally became a reality. Later came Canadian Northern and the Grand Trunk Pacific, nationalised into Canadian National in 1923 after both companies had gone bankrupt.

Until 1978, Canada possessed two rail systems, the privately operated but viable Canadian Pacific, and the state-owned, often floundering, Canadian National. With the formation of VIA Rail Canada in 1978, the routes and fare structures of both became totally integrated. To cross Canada by train was quite an adventure, one of the world's great railway journeys. Unfortunately, the Canadian government has now scrapped the famous transcontinental track through the Rockies via Banff as part of a mammoth, more than 50 per cent, cut in rail services nationwide. However, the more northern route via Jasper still operates but only three times a week. The one way fare coast-to-coast, is about $500, and the journey takes three days.

The service cuts mean that many small, more remote communities can no longer be reached by train.

In the East, VIA Rail runs high speed *Rapido* trains along the so-called Ontario-Québec corridor connecting Montréal with Windsor, Ontario. The Toronto to Montréal trip takes less than 5 hours and costs around $70-$90. System-wide various discount fares are available. These vary according to the time of year, day of the week, length of stay, age of traveller, etc, so always enquire about the 'cheapest possible fare' when planning a trip. If you have a student ID card, be sure to show it; discounts are often up to 40 percent.

Then there is the **CANRAIL Pass**. This gives unlimited travel on VIA trains and is good value for someone planning to do a lot of travelling. At press time, VIA offer a pass valid for 12 days within a 30-day period. During peak travel times (1st June-15th October), for the entire system a student (under 25/ISIC) pass costs $545 and an adult pass is $616. Extra days (up to 3 out of a 15 day period), are $45 (student), and $50 (adult). Low season rates are: student, $355; adult, $390. Extra days are also cheaper. NB: Seats reserved for Canarail may be limited so it is recommended you obtain tickets as early as possible. There is also a pass valid for 15 days' use within a 30-day period; $445 student/$489 adult, low season; $683 student/$772 adult, high season. In all cases tax must be added.

In addition there is a combined VIA/Amtrak **North American Rail Pass**. This pass covers travel on both rail systems for 30 days. The peak student fare is CAN $858/adult – $965; low season rates: student $608/adult $675.

The trains are comfortable, civilised, have good eating facilities and are easy to sleep on. A much recommended way to travel. Long Haul Leisurerail, PO Box 5, 12, Coningsby Road, Peterborough PE3 8XP, (0870) 7500222, are the main agents in the UK. Or call VIA up on the Internet: *www.viarail.ca*.

Hitching: Thumbing is illegal on the major transcontinental routes, but it is common to see people hitching along access ramps. Check the 'local rules' before setting out. In some cities there are specific regulations regarding hitching, but in general the cognoscenti say that hitchers are not often hassled and that Canada is one of the best places to get good lifts, largely because rides tend to be long ones—even if you do have to wait a long time on occasions.

The Trans Canada Highway can be rough going during the summer months so look for alternative routes, for example the Laurentian Autoroute out of Montréal, and the Yellowhead Highway out of Winnipeg. Wawa, north of Sault Ste Marie, Ontario, is another notorious spot where it is possible to be stranded for days. The national parks can also be tricky in summer when 'there are too many tourists going nowhere'.

Hiking and Biking: Trail walking is one of Canada's best offers. There is so much wilderness space that it really would be a crying shame to spend any length of time in the country without experiencing something of The Great Outdoors. Some of the best, of course, is in the national parks. A good guide to hiking trails in the national parks is *The Canadian Rockies Trail Guide: A Hiker's Manual to the National Parks*, by Bart Robinson and Brian Patton. Information is also available from the individual parks. For information on the best routes for cyclists, contact the Canadian Cycling Association at 333 River Road, Vanier, Ontario K1L 8H9, (613) 748-5629.

Urban Travel: Town and city bus or subway fares are generally charged at a standard rate. Exact fares are often required and are around 90¢-$1.50, and upwards. Transfers, allowing passengers to change routes or bus to subway routes, are generally available in cities, usually free.

Taxis usually are pretty expensive unless shared by two or three people. In rural areas (much of Canada outside the major population centres) there is little in the way of public transport and, failing ownership of a car, taxis may be the only way. Check under individual towns and cities for more detailed information on local travel.

FURTHER READING

History

The very readable books of Pierre Barton including: *The National Dream, Klondike, The Promised Land* and *Arctic Grail*

General

Aurora Montrealis, Monique Proulx
My Discovery of the West, Sunshine Sketches of a Small Town, by Stephen Leacock
O Canada, Edmund Wilson
The Oxford Companion to Canadian History and Literature, ed. A. J. M. Smith

Fiction

Affairs of the Art, Lisa Bissonnette
The Ice Master, John Houston
The Man from the Creeks, Robert Kroetsch
Maria Chapdelaine, Louis Hémon
The novels of Margaret Atwood, Margaret Laurence, Carol White and Robertson Davies

Travel

For extended stays in Canada we recommend purchase of one of several available in-depth guides to Canada, e.g. *Lonely Planet.*

Want to know more? Check out these sites. *http/citynet/countries/canada* or *http://canada.gc.ca/.*

MARITIME PROVINCES AND NEWFOUNDLAND

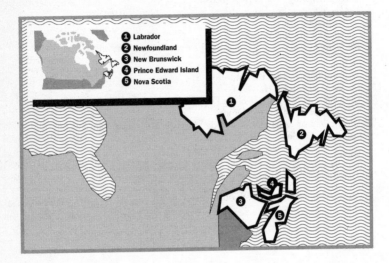

1. Labrador
2. Newfoundland
3. New Brunswick
4. Prince Edward Island
5. Nova Scotia

These Atlantic-lapped provinces were the early stop-off points for eager explorers from Europe and subsequently became one of the main battlegrounds for their colonial ambitions. The chief combatants were Britain and France and as a result, strong English, French, and Scottish threads run through Maritime culture and history. Indeed, the first recorded visitor from Europe to North America was Prince Henry St Clair, who arrived here from Scotland in 1398, almost a century before Columbus set foot on the continent. The 600th Anniversary of his voyage was celebrated throughout the Maritime Provinces during the summer of 1998.

The story of the Maritimes is the story of a people who have fished and travelled and died at sea. The Grand Banks, the huge, shallow Continental Shelf ranging from Massachusetts to Newfoundland, is the most fertile fishing ground in the world. The economy of the Maritimes is based on forestry, tourism, and the Grand Banks, with more fishery-related PhDs per capita than almost anywhere in the world.

The region is beautiful in the summer, full of lake and sea swimming, excellent seafood, forest hikes and breathtaking scenery. Winters are long and hard with much snow, ice and general wintry chills to contend with! Spring comes late and Autumn, as elsewhere in north eastern North American, is colourful and spectacular. Summer or autumn are recommended as the best times to visit the Maritimes.

NEW BRUNSWICK

New Brunswick is bounded mostly by water, with over 1300 miles of coastline—a constant reminder of the importance of the sea in this Maritime province. To the west, it is bordered by Maine, QuÈbec and part of the Appalachian mountain range. Inland, there is rugged wilderness accounting for the popularity of huntin', fishin', campin' and hikin'.

The Vikings are said to have come here some thousand years ago, but when French explorer Jacques Cartier arrived in 1535, the area was occupied by Micmac and Maliseet Indians. Later, the province became a battleground for French Acadian and British Loyalist forces. In 1713, by the Treaty of Utrecht, New Brunswick was ceded to the British along with the rest of Acadia (PEI and Nova Scotia). Many of the French fled south to the United States and settled in Louisiana. There, 'Acadian' was corrupted into 'Cajun', a word still used to describe the French in Louisiana. As a result of this early French influence, New Brunswick today remains 35 per cent Acadian, most in the north and the east of the province.

While in New Brunswick, be sure to sample the great variety of shellfish available, as well as the province's speciality—fiddleheads. Also, try a pint of the local Moosehead beer—although it is now available nationally, the sea air of New Brunswick itself is essential for a successful taste test. The coastline also has a number of whale-watching opportunities especially in the summer and early autumn.

The telephone area code is 506.

FREDERICTON The City of Elms is the capital city of the province and its commercial and sporting centre. Clean and green, this is 'a good Canadian town' which got started in 1783, when a group of Loyalists from the victorious colonies to the south made their home here, naming the town after the second son of George III. They chose for their new town a spot where there had previously (until the Seven Years War) been a thriving Acadian settlement. During hostilities the settlement was reduced by the British and the inhabitants expelled.

Fredericton's great benefactor was local boy and press baron, Lord Beaverbrook. His legacies include an art gallery, a theatre, and the university library. The latter is named Bonar Law-Bennett Library, after two other famous sons of New Brunswick, one of whom became Prime Minister of Great Britain, and the other Prime Minister of Canada.

The town is situated inland on the broad St John River, the 'Rhine of America', once an Indian highway and a major commercial route to the sea. The whole area is one of scenic river valleys and lakes.

ACCOMMODATION
Elms Tourist Home, 269 Saunders St, 454-3410. S-$45, D-$55, XP-$10.
Fredericton International Hostel, 621 Churchill Row, 450-4417, $16-20, open May-September, 2 blocks from bus station; luggage storage, laundry facilities, free parking; single, double and family rooms.

University of New Brunswick, Residents Admin. Bldg, Bailey Dr, (a red brick building with four clocks) 453-4891. S-$29, $18 w/student ID, D-$21pp, $15pp w/student ID, $80 weekly, students only. 24 hrs. Close to downtown. 'Friendly and helpful.'—university accommodation only available until mid-August.

Camping: Provincial Park, 12 miles W on Hwy 2, 363-4747. Sites $17 for four, $19.50 w/hook up, kitchen shelters, showers.

FOOD

Boyce Farmers' Market, George St, 451-1815. Sat only 6am-1pm. Have breakfast or an early lunch in the market hall, then check out the fresh produce and local arts and crafts.

Crispin's, King's Place Mall, King St, 459-1165. Deli, bakery with cafe. Great for cheap lunches, soups, salads, sandwiches, nothing over $4. Mon-Fri 6.30am-5.30pm, Thu & Fri 'til 9pm, Sat 9am-5pm.

Lunar Rogue, 695 King St, 450-2065. Good pub food and some interesting variations, $5-$10. Huge order of Rogues Nachos, $4.25. Live bands. Daily 9am-midnight.

Molly's Coffee Shop, 554 Queen Street, opposite Officers Square, 457-9305. Fine coffee and tasty snacks in this little cafe.

OF INTEREST

Beaverbrook Art Gallery, 703 Queen St, 458-8545. Has works of Dali, Reynolds, Gainsborough, Churchill, etc., plus good section on history of English china. A gift to the province from the press baron. Free tours daily Mon-Sat 10am. Summer Mon-Fri 9am-5pm, Sat 10am-5pm, Sun noon-5pm. Closed Mon in winter. $3, $1 w/student ID, 50¢ w/ISIC card.

Christ Church Cathedral, off Queen St at Church St, 450-8500. Worth a visit for its beautiful stained-glass windows. Free tours, res req. Summer: Mon-Fri 8am-6pm, Sat 10am-5pm, Sun 1pm-5pm, Call for winter times.

Kings Landing Historical Settlement, at Prince William, 23 miles W of Fredericton on Rte 2, exit 259, 363-4999. Re-created pioneer village showing the life of rural New Brunswick as it was in the 1800s. Features homes, school, church, theatre, and farm. Daily 10am-5pm; $10, $7.25 w/student ID.

Provincial Legislative Buildings, Queen & St John Sts, 453-2527. Includes, in Library, complete set of Audubon bird paintings and copy of 1783 printing of Domesday Book. Free tours include visit to legislative chamber. Summer: daily 8.30am-7pm, otherwise 9am-4pm.

University of New Brunswick, University Ave, 453-4666. Founded 1785, making it the third oldest university in Canada. Buildings on campus include the **Brydone Jack Observatory**, 453-4723, Canada's first astronomical observatory. Tours available in academic term, suggested donation. Call for opening times.

York-Sunbury Historical Museum, 455-6041. In **Officers Square**, this military museum depicts the history of Fredericton and New Brunswick. Summer: Mon-Sat 10am-5pm, Sun noon-5pm, otherwise Mon, Wed, Fri 10am-5pm. $2, $1 w/student ID. 'Kind of neat.'

INFORMATION/TRAVEL

Fredericton Tourist Information, 397 Queen St, City Hall, 460-2129. Summer: daily 8am-8pm, otherwise 8am-5pm. Very helpful.' Also another info booth on the Trans Canada Hwy btwn Rtes 640 & 101, same hours.

New Brunswick Tourism Information, (800) 561-0123 for general telephone information; also see *www.tourismnbcanada.com.web*

SMT Bus Terminal, 101 Regent St at King St.

TRIUS Taxis, 454-4444 To the airport, costs around $25 o/w.

MONCTON   This unofficial capital of Acadia is a major communications centre, but really has only two tourist sites of any importance: **Magnetic Hill** and the **Tidal Bore**. At Magnetic Hill, go to the bottom of the hill by car or bike, turn off the ignition, and by some freak of nature you'll find yourself drifting up the hill!

The Tidal Bore is at its highest when it sweeps up the chocolate banks of Petitcodiac River from the Bay of Fundy, reaching heights of 30 ft along the way. Bore Park is the spot to be when the waters rush in, all in 30 mins. Check the schedule published in the daily paper for the times when the tide is at its highest. Magnetic Hill is located at the corner of Mountain Road (126) and the Trans Canada. Bore Park is at the east end of Main St. An annual **Arts & Crafts Fair**—the biggest in the Maritimes—is held at Victoria Park in mid-August.

There is a nice beach with the warmest waters north of Virginia at **Shediac** on the Northumberland Straight. This is also the place to catch the annual lobster festival held in July. It's a short bus ride from Moncton and there is plenty of camping space nearby.

ACCOMMODATION
Ask at the Tourist Bureau, or call Tourism New Brunswick on 856-3590/(800) 561-0123, daily 8.30am-4.30pm, for a list of local B&Bs, prices from D-$40.
Sunset Hotel, 162 Queen St, 382-1163. From $45, XP-$5.
Univesite de Moncton, 858-4008. Lafebra & La France residence halls have accommodation during summer only. $44 student, $63 non-student, lower weekly rates. Go to cnrs of Crowley Farm Rd & Morton St for best entrance.
Camping: **Camper's City**, 384-7867. Sites $19, $25 w/hook up.
Magnetic Hill Campground, 384-0191. Sites $19, $20 w/hook up. Both close to Magnetic Hill, and open May 1-Oct 31.

INFORMATION/TRAVEL
Tourist Bureau, 655 Main St, 853-3590. Daily 8.30am-6pm. *www.moncton.org*
Codiac Transit, 857-2008. Public transport system serving Moncton, Riverview and Dieppe.
Bus Depot, 961 Main St. See under Saint John for other buses.
Train station, behind Eaton Centre, Main St. Services to Halifax, Montreal.

CARAQUET   Situated on scenic Baie des Chaleurs in the north of the province, Caraquet is the oldest French settlement in the area and just west of town is a monument to the first Acadian settlers who came here following their expulsion by Britain. On St Pierre Blvd there is an interesting museum of Acadian history, the **Acadian Museum**, 726-2682, Mon-Sat 10am-8pm, Sun 1pm-6pm, $2, $1 w/student ID. Off Hwy 11 to the west of town is the **Acadian Historical Village**, 726-2600, daily $10, $7 w/student ID. Daily 10am-6pm. The buildings here are all authentic, they were brought here and restored. There are also crafts and demonstrations showing the Acadian lifestyle. Also has a **Wax Museum**, 727-6424, $6, $5 w/ student ID. Self-guided audio tour, 9am-6pm.

CAMPBELLTON   This pretty waterfront has the claim to fame of hosting the world's largest salmon and an 8.5m sculpture dominates the aptly-named Salmon Plaza. A Salmon Festival takes place each July. Salmon aside, the town is an interesting base from which to explore. Mount Carleton, the highest point in the Appalachians, and Sugarloaf Mountain, which has a chairlift for the less active. You can also stay in Canada's only **Lighthouse Youth Hostel**, 1 Ritchie St, 759-7044, $12, June to mid-August only.

KOUCHIBOUGUAC NATIONAL PARK   Pronounced 'Koo-she-boo-gwack', this park hosts some wonderful beaches as well as coastal forests and boglands. The main attraction is Kelly's beach, with warm swimming water, also nature trails etc. Inland, the park is also home to vicious insects -wear repellent. The Park has a number of campgrounds—reservations taken on (800)213-7275 or call the Park directly 876-4205. There is a $3.50 entrance charge per person. Further south, the award-winning **Irving Eco-Centre La Dune de Boutoche** offers long, curving boardwalks over sand dunes and fragile marshes that are home to rare birds and plants. Open daily 10am-8pm, free of charge.

SAINT JOHN   Known as the Loyalist City, and proudly boasting a royal charter. Saint John was founded by refugees—those intrepid American settlers who chose to remain loyal to Britain after the American Revolution. The landing place of the Loyalists is marked by a monument at the foot of King Street, the shortest, steepest main street in Canada. Before the Seven Years War, however, Saint John was occupied by the French. The first recorded European discovery was in 1604 when Samuel de Champlain entered the harbour on St John's Day—hence the name of the town and the river on which it stands.

Largely as a result of its strategic ice-free position on the Bay of Fundy, Saint John has become New Brunswick's largest city and its commercial and industrial centre. Shipbuilding and fishing are the most important industries and Saint John Dry Dock, at 1150 ft long, is one of the largest in the world. The waterfront is a pleasant place to visit and the bustling downtown streets are dotted with shops, cafes and historic properties. Good times to visit are during the Festival-by-the-Sea in August and Loyalist Days, the third week in July. (Incidentally, Saint John is never abbreviated, thereby making it easier to distinguish from St John's, Newfoundland.)

ACCOMMODATION
Earle of Leinster B&B, 96 Leinster St, 652- 3275. D-from $60. Historic house, walking distance of all attractions, breakfast included.
Fundy Ayre Motel, 1711 Manawagonish Rd, 672-1125. S-$75, D-$84, XP-$8 all with private bath. Close to downtown and Nova Scotia ferry.
YM-YWCA, 1925 Hazen Ave, 634-7720. S-$30, $20 single room, plus $10 deposit. Equipment storage area, parking. Friendly and helpful.' Full use of YMCA facilities; pool, fitness centre, on-site cafe.
Camping: Rockwood Park, off Rte 1, in the heart of the city, 652-4050. Sites $14, $18 w/hook-up. Two swimming lakes, offers horseriding in the park.

FOOD
Grannan's, 1 Market Square, 634-1555, is the place if you're a lover of raw oysters (half dozen $8.95), other seafood from $6. Mon-Sat 11.30 am-midnight, Sun 'til 10pm.
Market Square, renovated building with 19th century exterior and trendy, modern interior; on the waterfront. Lots of places to eat and shop.

Old City Market, 47 Charlotte St, 658-2820. Fresh produce, crafts, antiques. Great for browsing and buying, a must. Closed Sundays and holidays.
Reggie's Restaurant, 26 Germain St, 657-6270. Imports smoked meat from Ben's, the famous MontrÈal deli. Inexpensive, filling meals $3-$7. Mon-Fri 6 m-8pm, w/ends 6 am-6 pm.

OF INTEREST

There are four self-guided **walking tours** around Saint John: Prince William's Walk, the Loyalist Trail, a Victorian Stroll and the Douglas Avenue Amble. Each takes around an hour and a half, and shows you the highlights of the historic streets of Saint John. Among these are **Loyalist House**, 120 Union St, a Georgian house built in 1816; the **Old Loyalist Burial Ground** opposite King Square; the spiral staircase in the **Old Courthouse**, King Sq; **Barbour's General Store**, fully stocked as in the year 1867, with a barbershop. Pick up a map at Tourist Information, 1 Market Sq. **Guided walking tour**, departs Barbour's Store, Market Slip at the waterfront, daily in summer at 10 am & 2 pm, $3.
Carleton Martello Tower, Charlotte St Extension, 636-4011. Fortification erected during and surviving the War of 1812. Spectacular view of the city. Summer: daily 9am-5pm, $2.50, $1.50 w/student ID.
Fort Howe Blockhouse, Magazine St. Replica of blockhouse built during 1777 in Halifax, then disassembled and re-built to protect Saint John Harbour. Good panoramic view of the city. Daily 10am-dusk, free.
New Brunswick Museum, Market Sq, 635-5381. This museum, founded in 1842, was the first in Canada. It features a variety of historic exhibits, both national and international, a natural science gallery with a full-sized whale skeleton, artwork and Canadiana. Mon-Fri 9am-9 pm, Sat 10 am-6 pm, Sun noon-5 pm. $6, $3.25 w/student ID, free Wed 6pm-9pm.
Reversing Falls Rapids. The town's biggest tourist attraction. Twice a day, at high tide, waters rushing into the gorge where the Saint John River meets the sea force the river to run backwards creating the Reversing Falls Rapids. There are two good lookouts for watching this phenomenon: the Tourist Bureau lounge and the sun deck on King St.
Rockwood Park, A beautiful park within the city limits. Fresh water lakes, sandy beaches, camping, golf, and hiking trails.

SPORT

Canoeing/Kayaking: Eastern Outdoors Inc., Brunswick Sq, 634-1530/(800) 565-2925. The place to go for rentals, guided tours, and rock climbing.
Golf: Rockwood Park Golf Course, Sandy Point Rd, 634-0090. 18 holes $26, club rental $18.
Skiing: Poley Mountain Ski Area, in Sussex 51 miles E on Hwy 1. Information 433-3230. Also, **Crabbe Mountain**, in Lower Hainsville, 94 miles N on Hwys 7 & 2. Information: 463-8311.

INFORMATION

Saint John Tourist Information, Market Sq, (888) 364-4444, 658-2855. Daily, summer 9am-8pm, otherwise 9am-6pm. In summer only: **Reversing Falls Visitor Centre**, 658-2937; **City Centre Seasonal**, on Hwy 1 west of harbour bridge, 658-2940. On the web: *www.city.saint-john.nb.ca*.

TRAVEL

Bay Ferries. There's a car ferry service from Saint John to Digby, Nova Scotia—a 2¹/₂ hr trip. Nice scenery, but rather pricey, $55 per car, $25 for walk-on passengers. Crowded in the summer. Call (888) 249-7245 for details. Saint John bus operates to Woodville St -10 minute walk to ferry terminal.
Saint John Transit, 658-4700. Local, city service.
SMT Bus Lines, 300 Union St, 648-3500. Bus to Moncton $22 o/w, 2hr 10 mins

FUNDY ISLANDS   Campobello Island: Going west on Hwy 1 from Saint John, you can catch a ferry from Back Bay that will take you, via Deer Isle and Campobello, to Lubec, Maine, call **East Coast Ferries**, 747-2159. On Campobello is the 3000-acre **Roosevelt Campobello International Park**, 752-2922. Visitors can see the 34-room 'cottage' maintained as it was when occupied by FDR from 1905 to 1921. Daily 10am-6pm, June-Oct, free. Also here is the **East Quoddy Head Lighthouse**, the last working lighthouse with the St George's Cross facing east, the cross symbolises safety and peace to those at sea.

The lighthouse stands on its own island, accessible only at low tide. In July and August, it's a great spot for whale watching from land. The **Public Library and Museum**, 3 Welshpool St, Welshpool, has some surprising artifacts retrieved from the seabed in the Bay of Fundy. Call 752-7082 for details. Free of charge, open Tue-Fri 2pm-5pm, and also Tue/Thu eves 7pm-9pm. Campobello is also linked to Maine by the Franklin D Roosevelt Memorial Bridge.

Grand Manan Island: The largest island in the Bay of Fundy is a haven for bird and whale watchers. Try **Sea Watch Tours**, 662-8552, offering boat tours to sight puffins ($44-60) or combined whale & birdwatching trips, $44, from mid June to the first week in October. Call from the mainland for weather information as cancellations due to fog are not uncommon. The island is reached from Black's Harbour on the mainland. Call **Coastal Transport Grand Manan Ferries**, 662-3724, cost $43.70 for vehicle with two people or $8.75 foot passenger. There are various guesthouses on the island, or **camping** at Seal Cove; **The Anchorage**, 662-7035, $21.50, $24 w/hook-up. Also has a bird sanctuary and hiking trails.

FUNDY NATIONAL PARK   Centrally located, the park is just over an hour from Moncton and within two hours of Fredericton and Saint John. It is only a few hours from the Maine/New Brunswick border and within a day's drive from Montréal or Boston. Fundy National Park has a spectacular setting, a vast area of rugged shore and inland forests, with unique ecosystems and rare birds; the Bay of Fundy has the world's highest tides (16 metres). This allows visitors the rare experience of strolling along the ocean floor at low tide. At **Hopewell Cape** on Rte 114, the Fundy tides have gouged four-storey sculptures out of the cliffs, $4 entrance.

The sculptures look like giant flower pots when the tide is low, and you can explore them from the ocean floor. At high tide the flower pots disappear, leaving behind little tree-topped islands. The area offers a variety of impressive maritime scenery from fog-shrouded shores to sun-dappled forests, from steep coastal cliffs to tide-washed beaches, and from bubbling streams to crashing waterfalls.

For info call the Park on 887-6000. $3.50 p/p entry fee. Just eastwards along the coast, you reach **Cape Enrage**, which houses a lighthouse, abandoned in 1988 and lovingly restored by a local school teacher and his students. The old lightkeepers cottage has been transformed into a pleasant cafe, and you can try a number of adventurous activities, including kayaking and abseiling.

ACCOMMODATION
Fundy National Park Hostel, 887-2216. Small, rustic-style cabins located right in the park. $10, $13 non-members. Kitchen, showers. Jun-Sept. 'Relaxed atmosphere.' Shuttle service upon request will pick up/drop-off in Sussex. Heated pool and organised activities. *www.fundyhostel.com*
Camping; 5 campsites within the park, res rec during summer, call the Park for res, $12, $17 w/ hook-up.

ST ANDREWS Just a short hop from Maine and the US border, St-Andrews-by-the-Sea, to give it its full title, was designated a National Historic Site in 1998, and is a pretty resort town containing many original Loyalist houses. Many were floated across the bay from Maine after the American Revolution, now safe on dry land in King Street and Water Street. Whale watching is available, May-September from several companies along the seafront and pier, approx. $30-$60 p/p. **Kingsbrae Gardens,** 529-3335, 222 Frederick St, has many flowers, plants and shrubs, $6, $4 students w/ID, open 9am-dusk. **Walking Tours** meet at 10am and 2pm, by Heritage Discovery Tours, 529-4011, $10.50 for 2 hrs. The **Huntsman Aquarium Museum**, Brandy Cove Rd, 529-1202, is not another *Seaworld*—and this is reflected in the prices—but they do have a touch pool where you can pick up starfish and the like, $3.15, 10am-4pm.

ACCOMMODATION
Salty Towers, 340 Water Street, 529-4585, bed & breakfast inn with sumptuous furnishings, $52, $62 with en-suite. **Camping: Passamaquoddy Park Campground**, 529-3439, 1km east of the town centre along Water St, great sea views, $17, $21 w/hook-up.

INFORMATION / TRAVEL
Chamber of Commerce Welcome Center 529-3555, and the **Day Adventure Center**, are located at 46 Reed Ave, next to the arena.
SMT Bus, 648-3500, from Saint John drops passengers at Water St.

NOVA SCOTIA

Known as the Land of 10,000 Welcomes and the Festival Province, Canada's 'Ocean Playground' is famous for its attractive fishing villages, rocky, granite shores, and historic spots like Louisbourg and Grand Pré. The early Scottish immigration to Nova Scotia is manifested in such events as the annual Highland Games in Antigonish and St Ann's Gaelic College. It is said that there is more Gaelic spoken in Nova Scotia than in Scotland.

Although the French were the first to attempt colonisation of the area, it was James I who first gave Nova Scotia (New Scotland) its own flag and coat-of-arms when he granted the province to Sir William Alexander. The French preferred the name Acadia, after explorer Verrazano's word for Peaceful Land, however, and so the French thereafter became known as Acadians. By the Treaty of Utrecht in 1713, the province was finally ceded to the British for good. Cape Breton Island followed later, after the siege of Louisbourg in 1758.

Many Americans also emigrated to Nova Scotia in the late eighteenth and early nineteenth centuries, among them the Chesapeake Blacks and a group of 25,000 Loyalists—possibly the largest single emigration of cultured families in British history, since their numbers included over half of the living graduates of Harvard. They settled mostly around Sherbourne.

Driving is the best way of discovering Nova Scotia. There are eight specially designated tourist routes throughout the province which cover most of the points of interest. Among these, the Cabot Trail on Cape Breton Island is particularly recommended. Autumn is the most beautiful season; in summer, the ocean breeze always has a cooling effect. Although most people visit Halifax and the South Shore, Cape Breton Island is also worth a visit and has much to offer the nature-loving traveller.

The telephone area code is 902.

HALIFAX Provincial capital and the largest city and economic hub of the Maritimes, the making of Halifax has been its ice-free harbour, so that not only does it deal with thousands of commercial vessels a year but it is also Canada's chief naval base. Settled in 1749 by Govenor Edward Cornwallis, Halifax became Canada's first permanent British town, built as a response to the French fort at Louisbourg.

Although a thriving metropolis with the usual tall concrete buildings and expressways, the town does retain a certain charm with many constant reminders of its colourful past. The historic downtown areas of Halifax, and its twin **Dartmouth** across the bay, are perfect for discovering by bicycle or on foot (don't go alone after dark). Check with the Tourist Office for information on walking tours and the many festivals that go on in and around the town. **Citadel National Historic Site** a hilltop fort in the middle of town is a good place to start exploring and to get your bearings.

Connected to Halifax by two bridges and two ferries ($1.55), Dartmouth is known as the 'city of lakes' since there are some 22 lakes within the city boundaries. 'Walk across Macdonald Bridge, free, for a very good view of both cities,' or take the #1 bus. The town is also home to the well-respected Bedford Institute of Oceanography, which collects data on tides, currents and ice formations. A comprehensive visitors guide with all the basics can be found at *www.halifaxinfo.com*

ACCOMMODATION
Dalhousie University residences, 6385 South Street, 494-8840. S-$36, $24 w/student ID, D-$54, $42w/student ID. Apartments also available. Pool and art gallery. May-Aug only.

Fenwick Place (off-campus residence), 5599 Fenwick St, 494-2075. Apartment-style accommodation, two bedrooms $51, three bedrooms $72, $19 pp for students willing to share. All apartments have kitchens and bathrooms. May-mid-Aug, rsvs recommended. Open 24 hrs.

Halifax Heritage House Hostel, 1253 Barrington St, 422-3863. YH-$15, non-members $18. Kitchen, laundry, no curfew. 'Very friendly.' Parking.

Inglis Lodge, 5538 Inglis St, 423-7950. Rooms from S-$25, D-$55, $75-$120 per week. Shared bathroom, kitchen and TV room.

Mount Saint Vincent University, 166 Bedford Hwy, 457-6286. About 15 mins from downtown. S-$35, $29 w/student ID, D-$49, $43 w/student ID. Gym and beautiful

arboretum. May-Aug only. Cheaper for weekly stays. Res req.
Camping: **Laurie Park**, 12 miles N of Halifax on Old Hwy 2, in Grand Lake, 861-1623. Sites $10 for four. 'Very basic.' June-Sept.

FOOD

Athens Restaurant, 6303 Quinpoll Rd, 422-1595. Greek and Canadian food, $6-$11. Daily 9 am-midnight. Good for breakfast.'
Midtown Tavern, Prince & Grafton Sts, 422-5213. Cheap pub-style food, nothing over $7. Mon-Sat 11am-11pm.
Satisfaction Feast, 1581 Grafton St, 422-3540. Good vegetarian food, lunch from $7, dinner from $10. People come from miles around for the homemade wholewheat bread and desserts ($3.50). Daily 9 am-10 pm, however, not an extensive breakfast menu.
Thirsty Duck, 5472 Spring Garden Rd, 422-1548. Irish and English beer; good music. Daily 11am-1am. Pub menu, very reasonable prices, $4.50-$7.

OF INTEREST

Art Gallery of Nova Scotia, 1741 Hollis St, 424-7542. Regional, national and international art. Tue-Sat 10am-6pm, Thu til 9pm, Sun noon-5pm. $5, $2 w/student ID. Free on Tues.
The *Bluenose II* sails from Historic Properties for a 2 hr cruise around the Harbour. This is the schooner stamped on the back of the Canadian dime. Many other harbour cruises are also available.
Citadel National Historic Site, 426-5080. This star-shaped fortress surrounded by a moat (now a dry ditch) was built in 1828-56, and is Canada's most visited historic site. There is a magnificent view of the harbour and the noon gun is fired daily. Free tours. 'Staff in uniform, friendly and well-informed.' There is an **Army Museum** recalling the military history of the fort. Grounds open year-round, Citadel mid-June-mid-Sept, daily 9am-6pm, $6.
Churches: **St George's Round Church**, Brunswick & Cornwallis Sts, 421-1705. An example of the very rare round church, built around 1800. In the summer, **Music Royale**, period music in historic settings, is presented. Tours available. **St Mary's Basilica**, on Spring Garden Rd, has the highest granite spire in the world. Daily tours in summer, 8.30am-4.30pm. **St Paul's Church**, Barrington & Duke Sts, 429-2240. Oldest Anglican church in Canada. Built in 1750, this is the oldest building in Halifax. **Old Dutch Church**, Brunswick & Garrish Sts, built in 1756, was the first Lutheran church in Canada.
Dalhousie University, Coburg Rd. An attractive campus with the usual facilities and guided tours. **The Art Gallery**, 6101 University Ave, 494-2403, is worth a look. Year round Tue-Sun 11am-4pm, suggested donation.
Halifax Public Gardens, on Spring Garden Rd & South Park St. 17 acres and 400 different varieties of plants and flora. Fountains and floating flower beds. Daily 8 am-dusk.
Maritime Museum of the Atlantic, Lower Water St, 424-7490. Exhibits on the 1917 Halifax explosion (which killed 2000 people and flattened 300 acres of Halifax) and relics from the *Titanic*. Docked behind the museum is *CSS Acadia*, one of the earliest ships to chart the Arctic Ocean floor. Don't miss the stunning view of the harbour. June-Oct, Mon-Sat 9.30am-5.30pm, Tue 'til 8pm, Sun 1pm-5pm. Closed on Mon in winter. $4.50, $3.50 w/student ID.
Nova Scotia Museum of Natural History, 1747 Summer St, 424-7353, 424-6099 for 24 hr recorded info. Featuring the province's natural and human history, the spectacular quillwork of the Micmac Indians, and thousands of bees in glass enclosed hives. June-Oct Mon-Sat 9.30am-5.30pm, Wed til 8pm, Sun 1pm-5.30pm. $3.50, free 5pm-5.30pm, Weds 5.30pm-8pm. Closed Mon in winter (free Oct-May).
Point Pleasant Park is 20 min from downtown. Take South Park St, then Young Ave to the park. A good place to eat lunch. #9 bus from Barrington St.

Prince of Wales Martello Tower, located in Point Pleasant Park, the tower acted as part of the 'coastal defence network' set up by the British to protect against the French. June-Sept daily 10am-6pm. Free.

Province House, Hollis St, 424-4661. Canada's oldest and smallest parliament house. Built in 1818, called 'a gem of Georgian architecture' by Charles Dickens. 'The house has very detailed plasterwork and carving, very well kept.' Summer: Mon-Fri 9am-5pm, w/ends & hols 10am-4pm, otherwise Mon-Fri 9am-4pm. Free.

York Redoubt, Purcell's Cove Rd, 15 miles W of Halifax on Rte 253. Site of historic fortification and magnificent harbour views. Daily in summer 10am-6pm; grounds 'til 8pm. Picnicing facilities. Free.

Nearby: Peggy's Cove, **Liverpool**, **Lunenberg**, **Bridgewater** and the rest. Picturesque fishing villages but overrun by tourists.

SHOPPING/ENTERTAINMENT
Barrington Street and the Historic Properties are both good places to shop. The Scotia Square Complex has the usual shopping mall attractions.

Halifax International Busker Festival, 429-3910. Annual August festival of street performers in downtown Halifax.

The Nova Scotia International Tattoo, 451-1221, at the beginning of July, is a popular extravaganza featuring both Canadian and international performers of all kinds.

Shakespeare by the Sea, 422-0295, present the Bard's works outdoors in Point Pleasant Park, July-Sep.

INFORMATION
Check In Nova Scotia, 425-5781/(800) 565-0000; *explore.gov.ns.ca/*

Visitor Information Centre, 1595 Barrington St (cnr with Sackville St) 490-5946. Daily 8.30am-8pm.

Nova Scotia Travel Info Centre, near the airport on Hwy 102, 873-1223.

The Red Store Visitor Information Centre, Historic Properties, Water St, 424-4287. Daily 8.30am-8pm. On the waterfront.

INTERNET ACCESS
Ceilidh Connection, 1672 Barrington St, 422-9800, charges $8/hr in its cafe surroundings, otherwise try the **Spring Garden Road Library**, 5381 Spring Garden Rd, 490-5700, for free access Tue- Sat.

TRAVEL
Acadian Lines Bus station, 6040 Almon St, near the Forum, in the south end of peninsula Halifax, 454-9321. Regular stops at the airport on the way from Halifax to Cape Breton and Amherst. #7 connects with downtown.

DRL, (888) 263-1852, bus service to S. Shore and Yarmouth. Also leave from the Halifax terminal, 6040 Almon St.

Metro Transit, 490-6000. Basic fare: $1.55, transfers available. Also runs the **Ferry**, to Dartmouth. Frequent departures from the foot of George St. $1.55 o/w. Bus transfers valid on ferry.

Share-A-Cab, arrangements should be made at least 4 hrs in advance of travel time. Call 429-5555/(800) 565-8669 for rates and schedules.

VIA Rail, 1161 Hollis St, (888) 842-7245. Trains are few and far between; to Truro and Montreal.

GRAND PRÉ NATIONAL HISTORIC PARK
The restored site of an early Acadian settlement. The nearby dykeland (*grand pré* = great meadow) is where the French Acadians were deported to in 1766 after failing to take an oath of allegiance to the English king, preferring to remain neutral.

Longfellow immortalized the sad plight of the deported Acadians of Nova Scotia in his narrative poem *Evangeline* (see under *Louisiana* in *USA* section). There is a museum in the park with a section on Longfellow and a fine collection of Acadian relics, everything from farm tools to personal diaries. Also in the park is the **Church of the Covenanters**. Built in 1790 by New England planters, this do-it-yourself church was constructed from hand-sawn boards fastened together by square hand-made nails. The similarly homemade pulpit spirals halfway to the ceiling.

The gardens are nice for walking and the whole park is open daily June-Sept, 9 am-6 pm, free. To get there from Halifax take Rte 101N, the park is three miles east of Wolfville. Call 542-3631 for park info.

ANNAPOLIS ROYAL   Situated in the scenic Annapolis Valley, famous for its apples, this was the site of Canada's oldest settlement. Founded by de Monts and Champlain in 1604, and originally Port Royal, it became Annapolis Royal in honour of Queen Anne, after the final British capture in 1710. The town then served as the Nova Scotian capital until the founding of Halifax in 1749. This tiny town has a **Visitor Centre** at Hwy 1, open 8am-8pm summer, 532-5454.

The site of the French fort of 1636 is now maintained as **Fort Anne National Historic Park**, and seven miles away, on the north shore of Annapolis River, is the **Port Royal Habitation National Historic Park**. This is a reconstruction of the 1605 settlement based on the plan of a Normandy farm. Here, too, the oldest social club in America was formed. L'Ordre de Bon Temps was organised by Champlain in 1606 and visitors to the province for more than three days can still become members. The park is open daily May-October, 9 am-6 pm, free. Thirty five miles to the south is **Kejimkujik National Park**, open 24 hrs, year-round, the visitors centre is open 8.30am-9pm, 682-2771. The park entrance and information centre is at **Maitland Bridge**. Admission $3.25. The area was originally inhabited by the Micmac Indians. The park is good for canoeing, fishing, hiking, and skiing in winter. Canoes can be rented for $4 per hr, $20 per day. Ask at info centre for details. 20 km away is **Raven Haven Hostel**, South Milford, 532-7320, June-Sept, $11 a night. Located on Sandy Bottom lake; lots of outdoor activities.

YARMOUTH   The only place of any size on the western side of Nova Scotia, Yarmouth is the centre of a largely French-speaking area. During the days of sail this was an important shipbuilding centre although today local industry is somewhat more diversified.

A good time to visit is at the end of July when the Western Nova Scotia Exhibition is held here. The festival includes the usual agricultural and equestrian events plus local craft demonstrations and exhibits.

ACCOMMODATION
El Rancho Motel, Rt 1, Hwy 1, 742-2408. August rates: S-$52, D-$59, overlooking Milo Lake. Kitchen facilities.
Yarmouth Hostel, 216 Main St, 742-1612. Dorm $16, private rm $30 up.

TRAVEL
Ferries to Portland (10 hrs) and Bar Harbor, Maine (5 hrs). For info on the Portland run, call (800) 565-7900 (in Canada), (800) 341-7540 (in USA); for Bar Harbor info call (800) 565-9411 (in Canada), or (902) 742-5033 (in USA). Passenger rates range from (roughly) $20-40, vehicles $60-100 and up. All the info on routes and ferry companies into Nova Scotia can be found at *explore.ns.ca/discover/howto.htm#ferr*

SYDNEY Situated on the Atlantic side of the province, Sydney is the chief town on Cape Breton Island and a good centre for exploring the rest of the island. It is a steel and coal town, a grim, but friendly, soot-blackened old place. While here you can visit the second largest steel plant in North America.

Like the whole of Cape Breton Island, Sydney has a history of struggles against worker exploitation and bad social conditions. Since France ceded the island to Britain as part of the package deal Treaty of Utrecht in 1713, hard times and social strife have frequently been the norm.

A ferry goes to Newfoundland from North Sydney across the bay.

ACCOMMODATION
Garden Court Cabins, 2518 King's Rd, Sydney Forks, 564-6201, 14 miles W of Hwy 125 on Rte 4. Rates from S-$45 - $D-70 w/kitchen .

OF INTEREST
Highland Games, July, Antigonish or St Anne's. Kilts, pipes and drums, sword dancing, caber toss, etc.

Nearby: In the picturesque, lakeside town of Baddeck, the **Alexander Graham Bell National Historic Park**, Chebucto St, 295-2069, displays, models, papers, etc., relating to Bell's inventions. Bell had his summer home in the town. July/Aug 8.30am-7.30pm, otherwise 9am-6pm, $4.25.

Also in Baddeck, the **Centre Bras d'Or Festival of the Arts**, mid-July-Sept, includes Music Fest with many famous artists, 295-2787.

Glace Bay, 13 miles E, site of the **Miners Museum and Village**, 849-4522. Includes tour of underground mine running out and under the sea, and the village shows the life of a mining community 1850-1900. Ask about Tue evening concerts by the Men of the Deeps. June-Sept, daily 10am-6pm, Tue 'til 7pm, Sept-June, Mon-Fri 9am-4pm, $3.50, w/ mine tour, $6.50.

INFORMATION/TRAVEL
Acadian Bus Lines, 99 Terminal Rd, 859-5609, from Halifax and Baddeck.
Cape Breton Tours, 55 Colby St, 564-6200, day tours to the Cape Breton Trail, $55 p/p.
Marine Atlantic Ferries to Argentia ($55p/p, $124 car, 14 hrs) and Porte-aux-Basques ($20p/p, $62 car, 5 hrs), Newfoundland, (800) 341-7981.
Visitors Information, 20 Kelpic Dr, Sydney River, 539-9876. Daily 8am-8pm.

FORTRESS OF LOUISBOURG NATIONAL HISTORIC PARK Built by the French between 1717 and 1740, this fortress was once the largest built in North America since the time of the Incas. Louisbourg played a crucial role in the French defence of the area and was finally won by Britain in 1760, but not before it had been blasted to rubble.

A faithful re-creation of a complete colonial town within the fortifications, with majestic gates, homes and formal gardens. There is a museum, and tours by French colonial-costumed guides are available.

The Louisbourg Shuttle, 564-6200, picks up from accommodation in Sydney, 26 miles S, daily 9am & 4pm return, $25 r/t, not including park entry, res rec. The park is open June & Sept, daily 9.30am-5pm, July & August, daily 9am-7pm, $11 (Visitors Information Centre, 733-2280).

CAPE BRETON HIGHLANDS NATIONAL PARK The park lies on the northern-most tip of Cape Breton sandwiched between the Gulf of St Lawrence and the Atlantic Ocean. It covers more than 360 square miles of rugged mountain country, beaches and quiet valleys. The whole is encircled by the 184-mile-long Cabot Trail, an all-weather paved highway on its way round the park climbing four mountains and providing spectacular views of sea and mountains.

In summer, however, it gets very crowded and the narrow, steep roads are jammed with cars. There are camping facilities in the park and good sea and freshwater swimming.

This is an area originally settled by Scots and many of the locals still speak Gaelic. There are park information centres at Ingonish Beach and Cheticamp, 224-2306. Admission to the park is $3.50. At **Cheticamp**, there is Trois Pignons, 224-2612, an Acadian Museum with craft demonstrations, French-Canadian antiques and glassware, $3.50 and Coop Artisanal, a rug-making centre. Both are open daily in the summer. **Camping**, $15-21 inside the park, call park info on (800) 213-7275 / 224-2306. *parkscanada.pch.gc.ca*

IONA On the way back across the Strait of Canso, a side trip here to the Nova Scotia **Highland Village**, 725-2272, may be worthwhile. The village includes a museum and other memorabilia of the early Scottish settlers. A highland festival is held here the first Sat in August. Summer hours Mon-Sat 9am-6pm, winter Mon-Fri 9am-5pm, $5. The village is off Hwy 105, 15 miles E on Hwy 223 via Little Narrows, overlooking the Bras d'Or lakes. *www.highlandvillage.ns.ca*

PRINCE EDWARD ISLAND

Prince Edward Island—known primarily as the home of *Anne of Green Gables* and as a great producer of spuds—is Canada's smallest and thinnest province, being only 140 miles long with an average width of just twenty miles, and a population of a mere 136,500. PEI was originally named 'Abegweit' by the local Micmac Indians, meaning 'land cradled on the waves'. The French colonised the island and baptized it Isle St Jean, but when it was ultimately ceded to Britain as a separate colony, the British renamed it after Prince Edward, Duke of Kent. Now known as the 'Garden of the Gulf', PEI is a popular spot for Canadian family vacations because of its great sandy beaches and warm waters, perfect for lazy summer sunning!

Note the colour of the soil in PEI: it's red because it contains iron which rusts on exposure to the air. Limits are put on billboards here: you won't see any along the side of PEI's highways. The full effect of this constraint only hits you when you are bombarded with billboards back on the mainland. A note of caution: only camp in designated campgrounds—camping is pro-hibited everywhere else (including the beach).

In 1997, 124 years after the 1873 Terms of Union between Canada and PEI placed a constitutional obligation on the federal government to maintain 'continuous communication' between the island and the mainland, PEI has finally been linked to mainland Canada, by the 9 mile-long Confederation Bridge which spans the Northumberland Strait. An engineering marvel, it is the longest continuous marine span bridge in the world. It takes ten minutes to cross the bridge by car, and there is a one-way toll of $35.50.

Alternatively, you can reach this island paradise in the good old way by ferry from Caribou, Nova Scotia, to Wood Islands, east of the capital (75 min, $10.25, $47 car). Bay Ferries, (888)249-SAIL. Queues are long in the summer, particularly if you're taking a car. Schedules vary throughout the year but in summer the ferry runs 8 times daily. Another ferry runs between Souris, PEI, and Cap-aux-Meules, Quebec, 687-2181.

The telephone area code is 902.

CHARLOTTETOWN The first meeting of the Fathers of the Confederation took place in Charlottetown in 1864. Out of this meeting came the future Dominion of Canada (hence the nickname, 'The Cradle of Confederation'). In the Confederation Chamber, Province House, where the meeting was held, a plaque proclaims 'Providence Being Their Guide, They Builded Better Than They Knew'. The citizens of PEI were not so convinced however. They waited until 1873 before joining the Confederation. Even then, according to the then Governor General, Lord Dufferin, they came in 'under the impression that it is the Dominion that has been annexed to Prince Edward Island'.

These days things are quieter hereabouts, only livening up in summer when Canadian families descend en masse, and PEI's other tourist attraction, harness racing, gets going out at Charlottetown Driving Park. The restored waterfront section of town, Olde Charlottetown, offers the usual craft shops, eating places and boutiques. You can even tour the town in a London double-decker bus!

ACCOMMODATION
Charlottetown Youth Hostel, 153 Mt Edward Rd at Belvedere, 894-9696. Near UPEI campus. $15, $16.50 non-members. Kitchen, parking, bike rentals. 25 min walk from Charlottetown. Open June-Aug only. 3km from town centre—shuttle bus twice daily—see Travel.
Uni of PEI residences: at University and Belvedere Ave, 566-0442. In **Blanchard Hall**, apartments sleep four, w/kitchenette, lounge and private bath, $76, **Marion Hall**, S-$35, D-$45. All rooms include bfast, available July-Aug only.
Plenty of Tourist Homes with reasonably-priced accommodation—res rec during July & Aug. **Blanchard Heritage Home**, 163 Dorchester St, 894-9756, May-Oct, $18-30.

FOOD
Cedar's Eatery, 81 University Ave, 892-7377. Large servings of Canadian and Lebanese food. Average price $8, lunch specials $4, dinner specials $5.
Olde Dublin Pub, 131 Sydney St, 892-6992. Specializes in seafood, moderate prices. Live Irish entertainment nightly in the summer. Daily 11am-2am.

OF INTEREST
Abegweit Sightseeing Tours, 894-9966, operate guided tours of both the South and North Shores ($60), covering most points of interest including Fort Amherst National Historic Park and Pioneer Village. Daily from Charlottetown Hotel at Kent & Pownal Sts. 1 hr guided tours ($9) of Charlottetown depart six times daily

from Confederation Centre.

Confederation Centre of The Arts, Queen & Grafton Sts, (800) 565-0278 / 566-1267 *www.confederationcentre.com*. The focal point of the town's cultural life, it has an art gallery, museum, library and three theatres. In the main theatre, a musical version of the story of PEI's favourite orphan—**Anne of Green Gables**—is staged every summer, June-Sept. Tkts $20-$38, call for performance dates. A summer festival is held here annually. Museum / gallery open daily 9am-7pm, $4.

Province House, Queen Square at Grafton St, 566-7626. The site of Confederation, Canada's founding fathers met here in 1864 to decide the fate of the Dominion. The provincial Legislature now meets here. June-mid-Oct daily 9am-6pm, otherwise Mon-Fri 9am-5pm, self-guided tours. Free.

Pioneer Village, on Rte 11 at Mont-Carmel, in the Acadian region of PEI, approx 1¹/₂ hours from Charlottetown, 854-2227. A log reproduction of an Acadian settlement with homes, blacksmith's shop, barn, school, general store and church. June-late-Sept, daily 9am-7pm, $3.50.

INFORMATION/TRAVEL
Ed's Taxi, 892-6561. Offers pre-planned tours, $30 p/hr.
PEI Tourist Information, (800) PEI-PLAY. *www.peiplay.com*
Be warned! There is no public transport on the island.
SMT/Acadian Bus Lines, 454-9321, operate from Halifax, Nova Scotia ($54 o/w) to Charlottetown, Summerside.
Shuttle Bus, 566-3242, operates twice daily between Charlottetown and Cavendish Visitors Centres, stops at the youth Hostel, $9 o/w, $15 same day rtn.

INTERNET ACCESS
Confederation Center Public Library, Queen & Richmond Sts, 368-4642. Free public access computers.

PRINCE EDWARD ISLAND NATIONAL PARK Situated north of Charlottetown, the Park consists of 25 miles of sandy beaches backed by sandstone cliffs. Thanks to the Gulf Stream the sea is beautifully warm. **Rustico** is one of the quieter beaches. $3p/p Park entry.

Ask about good places for clamming. Assuming you pick the right spot, you can just wriggle your toes in the sand and dig up a good meal.

At **Cavendish Beach**, off Rte 6, is **Green Gables**, 672-6350. Built in the 1800s, the farmhouse inspired the setting of Lucy Maud Montgomery's famous fictional novel *Anne of Green Gables*. The house has been refurbished to portray the Victorian setting described in the novel. Daily in summer 9am-5pm, til 8pm July & Aug, $5. The beach here is very crowded during summer and probably best avoided. Camping sites and tourist homes abound on the island, call (800) PEI-PLAY.

NEWFOUNDLAND and LABRADOR

Newfoundland and Labrador are a bit off the beaten track, but it's worth taking a little time and trouble to get here. The island of **Newfoundland** is rich in historic associations (the Vikings were here as early as AD 1000), 'discovered' by Prince Henry St Clair of Scotland in 1398, and more officially by John Cabot in 1497. It was the first part of Canada to be settled by Europeans, and the first overseas possession of the British Empire, now a society neither wholly North American nor yet European. Fishing and related marine research are still the main industries, although mining is important and the oil industry has reached here too. **Labrador**, the serrated northeastern mainland of Canada, was added to Newfoundland in 1763. Until recent explorations and development of some of Labrador's natural resources (iron ore, timber), the area was virtually a virgin wilderness with the small population scattered in rugged little fishing villages and centred around the airport at Goose Bay.

Strikingly beautiful, Newfoundland and Labrador offer spectacular seascapes (and an estimated two million seabirds), long beaches, and picturesque fishing villages (some still with access only from the sea); vast forests, fjords, majestic mountains, and hundreds of lakes—Newfoundlanders call them 'ponds'—some of which are nearly 20 miles long!

Newfoundlanders' speech is unique: English interspersed with plenty of slang and colloquialisms. The curious nature of the province is also evident in the names of its towns, like Heart's Content, Come By Chance, and Blow-Me-Down. The people here are very friendly and helpful—well prepared to take a visitor under a collective wing. Newfoundland is probably the only Canadian province to celebrate Guy Fawkes Day; ask about the summer folk festivals also.

There is a daily car and passenger ferry service to Port-aux-Basques from North Sydney, Nova Scotia (800) 341-7981, *www.marine-atlantic.ca*, $20p/p plus $62 car, o/w). A ferry also operates to Argentia, only 136 km from St John, $55p/p plus $124 car o/w. Once on the island the Trans Canada Highway stretches from Port-aux-Basques to the capital, St John's, via Corner Brook and Terra Nova National Park. There is a bus service from the ferry to St John's.
The telephone area code is 709. www.gov.nf.ca/tourism/.

ST JOHN'S   A gentle though weather-beaten city, St John's overlooks a natural habour situated on the island's east coast, 547 miles from Port-aux-Basques on the southwestern tip. Icebergs often float in the emerald-ocean outside the harbour, sometimes as late as July. Nearby Cape Spear is just 1640 miles from Cape Clair, Ireland, and the city's strategic position has in the past made it the starting point for transatlantic contests and conflicts of one sort or another. The first successful transatlantic cable was landed nearby in 1866; the first transatlantic wireless signal was received by Marconi at St John's in 1901; and the first non-stop transatlantic flight took off from here in 1919.

Take a walk along Gower St to view the rows of historical old houses; downtown Water St has been the city's commercial centre for 400 years and is still the place to find interesting stores, restaurants and pubs. St John's has begun to develop more after the recent discovery of off-shore oil fields. The pastel painted houses rising from the harbour look stunning from the water; on dry land however, most of the older buildings have been destroyed either by fire in the 19th century or demolished in the 20th. *www.city.st-johns.nf.ca/*

ACCOMMODATION
Bird Island Guest House, 150 Old Topsail Rd, S-$50, D-$60. Also operates whale and birdwatching tours.
The Old Inn, 157 Le Marchant Rd, 722-1171. S-$39, D-$48. Bfast $2-$4. Close to

downtown. Rsvs required.

Prescott Inn B&B, 19 Military Rd, (888) 263-3786, central location, good breakfast incl., full of Newfoundland art; D-$45.

Youth Hostel, Hatcher House, Paton College, on the campus of Memorial University of Newfoundland, btwn Elizabeth Ave & Prince Phillip Dr, 737-7933. S- $13, D-$18 non-students, D-$20, D-$30 non-students. Check-in 8 am-2 am. Open May-Aug only.

Camping: CA Pippy Park, Alandale Rd, Nagel's Place, 737-3669; $14, $20 w/hook up. Open May -Sept.

FOOD / ENTERTAINMENT

There is a good variety of reasonably priced places to eat on Duckworth St, or try; **Chess' Snacks**, 9 Freshwater Rd, 722-4083. Take-out fish. $4-$7, daily 10am-2am, w/ends 'til 3am.

St John's has a burgeoning restaurant scene, including **Bianca's**, 171 Water St, 726-9016; very elegant, res req, closed Sun.

For traditional Newfoundland cuisine, and to suit a smaller budget, try the **Classic Cafe**, 364 Duckworth St, 579-444, open 24 hrs.

The folk music scene is also renowned and dozens of pubs and clubs showcase local talent. **The Ship Inn**, 265 Duckworth St, (on Solomon's Lane), 753-3870 is open till 3am most nights.

OF INTEREST

Anglican Cathedral, Church Hill & Gower St, 726-5677. Said to be one of the finest examples of ecclesiastical Gothic architecture in North America. Begun in 1847, and following two fires, restored in 1905. Features sculptured arches and carved furnishings. National Historic Site. Daily 10am-5pm. Tours available by arrangement. Also, **St John's Haunted Hike,** 576-2087, leaves from outside the Cathedral, 9.30pm Thu, June-Aug, $6.70.

Memorial University Botanical Gardens, 306 Mt Scio Rd, 737-8590. Developed to display plants native to the province. Beautiful meandering walking trails. May-Nov daily 10am-5pm, $2.

Newfoundland Museum, 285 Duckworth St, 729-2329. St John's is rich in history and folklore and this particular museum has the only relics in existence of the vanished Indian tribe, the Beothuks. Summer daily 9.30am-4.45pm, free.

Quidi Vidi Battery, (pronounced Kiddy Viddy), 729-2977. Just outside of St John's, the battery overlooks scenic Quidi Vidi village and is restored to its 1812 appearance. Staffed by guides in period costume. Daily 10am-5pm, $2.50.

St John's Historic Walking Tours, 3 Fitzpatrick Ave, 738-3781. Guides will introduce you to the downtown area, historic landmarks, craft stores and local entertainment. By appointment only.

Signal Hill National Historic Park (accessible from Duckworth St), 772-5367, so named because the arrival of ships was announced from here to the town below through a series of flag signals, it is also the site where Marconi received the first transatlantic wireless signal in 1901. Inside the park is **Cabot Tower**, built in 1897 to commemorate the 400th anniversary of John Cabot's discovery of Newfoundland and Queen Victoria's Diamond Jubilee. 'Million dollar view' of St. John's and the Atlantic, and an interesting visitors centre. Daily in summer 8.30am-8pm, $2.50.

Nearby: Trinity, on the Bonavista Peninsula, north of St John's. This town of 350 people has several national heritage sites and pretty streets lined with brightly coloured, saltbox-style homes. One highlight is the **Cape Bonavista Lighthouse**, 468-7444, $2.50, daily 10am-5.30pm, June-Oct. Restored to the 1870 appearance and with costumed guides. The admission also covers entrance to the **Mockbeggar Property**, Roper Street, 468-7300, June-Oct, 10am-5.30pm, another restored house.

Festivals: the annual **Royal St John's Regatta** on Quidi Vidi Lake takes place the first week of August; the province's event of the year. Call 576-8921 for details. The same week sees the **Newfoundland & Labrador Folk Festival**, 576-8508; folk music, dancing and storytelling.

INFORMATION/TRAVEL
St John's Tourist Information, located on Harbour Drive on the waterfront, 576-8514.
Metro Bus, 495 Water St, 722-9400, covers downtown St John's, $1.50 base fare, for further afield you will have to take a tour. Some recommended operators are; **Legend Tours** 753-1497, **City & Outport Adventures** 754-8687, **Discovery Tours** (800) 654-5300 / 722-4533. One day tour with lunch $90.
The **airport** is situated north of town and is reached only by taxi. Call **Bugdens Taxi's** 726-4400, $14.

TERRA NOVA NATIONAL PARK In the central region of Newfoundland, around three hours away from St John's, this area was once covered by glaciers 750 ft thick which left behind boulders, gravel, sand and grooved rock. The sea filled the valleys, leaving the hills as islands. The result is the incredibly beautiful **Bonavista Bay** a picturesque wilderness, with saltwater fjords, barrens and bogs. But it's certainly not swimming country. The cold Labrador Current bathes the shores and it's not unusual to see an iceberg.

Inland the park is thickly forested, hiking trails climb headland summits and follow the rugged coast. Moose are common sights in the park, and occasionally a fox or a bear may be spotted. Fishing, canoeing and camping are available inside the park, sites cost $12-18 w/hook-up. For Park info call 533-2801, for canoe rentals and camping rsvs, call (800) 563-6353.

Access to the park is easy since the Trans Canada Hwy passes right through it for a distance of 25 miles, admission $3.25. DRL,738-8088, also provides bus transportation from St John's. 1 bus daily to nearby Eastport Junction, approx. 3hrs, $37 o/w.

GROS MORNE NATIONAL PARK This is Newfoundland's second National Park, located on the island's west coast, 10 hours away from St John's. This park, about 65 miles wide, is the more popular of the two parks because of the rugged beauty of its mountains. The landscape here is very different from that of the eastern coast of the province—colossal collisions of tectonic plates created formations as barren as the moon: 'fantastic'. Flora and fauna are abundant, orchids thrive, over thirty wild species in all, and the park is home to giant Atlantic hares, woodland caribou and moose.

You can wade along the sandy beaches of Shallow Bay, or look for 'pillow rocks' that formed along the coast as lava cooled under water. You can travel by boat winding up through the glaciated fjords of Western Brook or Trout River Ponds, and a serious hike to the top of Gros Morne Mountain (16km, 7-8 hrs) will reward you with a spectacular view of Ten Mile Pond and the Long Range Mountains. **Rocky Harbour** is the largest settlement in the Park, and the prettiest; take a walk along the Coast to the Lobster Cove Head Lighthouse. **Western Brook Pond** is reminiscent of the Norwegian fjord. The easy 3km trail leads to the dock where you can take a boat tour, $30 p/p, June—Oct, 458-2730. The **Lookout Trail**, 5km, is recommended as having some of the best views of the Park. **Trout River Pond** is another highlight.

There are many campsites within the park; site prices range from $11-$16 per night. There is also **Woody Point Youth Hostel**, 453-7254, $15 dorm, $20 private room, open year round. For groceries head for **Rocky Harbour**. For more info, call 458-2417. Entry fee $3.25, 4-day pass $9.75.

L'ANSE AUX MEADOWS NATIONAL HISTORIC SITE   At the northern tip of Newfoundland, and believed to be the site of the Viking settlement of AD 1000. According to legend, the Vikings defended this post against Indians until perils became too great and they withdrew to Greenland. No standing ruins of their buildings have survived, but excavations have disclosed the size and location of buildings, and many everyday objects have been found, making this an UNESCO World Heritage Site. Guides on site daily. Open 9am-4pm June-Oct, till 8pm July/Aug, $5, 623-2608. From St John, L'Anse aux Meadows is a 12 hr drive via Deer Lake. Alternatively there is an airport nearby at St Anthony, where you could rent a car and drive 45 minutes to the site, or fly into Deer Lake, a 6-8 hr drive via Gross Morne National Park and other places of interest.

ST PIÈRRE AND MIQUELON ISLANDS   Off the southern coast of Newfoundland, these islands constitute the only remaining holdings of France in North America. Once called the 'Islands of 11,000 Virgins', these granite outcrops total only about 93 square miles. A French territory since 1814, the natives parlent Francais, mangent baguettes and pay for them in francs. The main attraction to these wet and windy isles is the Gallic atmosphere rather than any particular sights. Historically, the primary economy of the islands was smuggling, especially during the Prohibition era when 300,000 cases of liquor a month were being taken in from Europe and Canada. Al Capone and other gangsters were frequent visitors to the islands!

Today, the islands survive on heavy subsidies from Paris, as the other industry of cod fishing is in decline. The treacherous waters surrounding the isles are said to have contributed to more than 650 wrecks. You can reach the islands by ferry (daily 2.45 pm, $60 r/t, (800) 563-2006) from **Fortune**, NF, on Rte 210. Canadians and Americans need to show proof of citizenship (driver's licence or birth certificate) and all other nationalities must have a passport. Accommodation on the island is reasonably priced, B&B $55-$65, Auberge $73. **Tourist information**, (800) 565-5118.

LABRADOR   This desolate land to the north-east of Quebec is not the ideal travelling environment. Much of the Province was, until recently, only accessible by air or sea, and that is still true of the northern wilds. Separated from Newfoundland by the Belle Isle Straits, this part of Canada was first settled by Basque whalers, followed by Irish and west country English. The region has a dialect reminiscent of Shakespeareìs era, and a lot of other things here seem to have moved on just as slowly. It is possible to explore the southernmost region on a day trip from St Barbe in Newfoundland. The sea crossing itself is reason to make the effort, often with views of whales and icebergs. The **ferry** runs between 1 and 3 times a day, call **Puddister**

Trading Co., 726-0015 for details. Passengers $9, cars $18 o/w. This, the most accessible part of the region, probably has the most significant attractions, including the **Maritime Archaic Indian Burial Mound National Historic Site**, which marks the continent's earliest known burial site, 7,500 years old. The site is located at L'Anse-Amour, off Route 510, 458-2417. Also on Route 510, is **Red Bay National Historic Site**, detailing the towns' whaling past. 9am-6.30pm, June-Oct, $5, 920-2142.

Ferries also travel between Lewisporte and Cartwright / Happy Valley, taking 33 hrs, or from St Anthony north up the coast, taking 12 leisurely days (foot passengers only), June—Sept, weather-permitting. For more information, call **Coastal Labrador Marine**, (800) 563-6353 / 535-6872. Most of the coastal villages began as fur-trading posts or are Indian settlements—the nomadic Inuit and Naskapi have managed to retain their culture and way of life unchanged for centuries. Happy Valley/Goose Bay also has an **airport** and a **Visitor's Centre,** 365 Hamilton River Rd, 896-8787, but there is no public transport—if you fly, be prepared to rent a car at the airport.

Inland, a rail track runs from **Labrador City**, a mining town with little to recommend it, on a spectacular journey to **Schefferville**, 416 km north. The train leaves only once a week, call 944-8205, $71.55 rtn. Labrador is a wilderness area, and if you visit, be prepared for extreme conditions (Happy Valley/Goose Bay has an average January temperature of minus 16c). One way of avoiding any pitfalls is to let someone else make the arrangements. Specialist Tour companies include **BreakAway Adventures**, 896-9343, offering kayak trips, or **Torngat Mountain Tours**, 896-4292, offering longer adventures into the Torngat Mountains, amongst others.

Labrador is also a great spot for viewing the **Northern Lights,** especially in the spring and autumn.

ONTARIO AND QUÉBEC

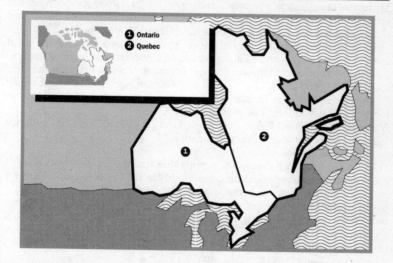

This section is devoted to those old enemies and still rivals, Ontario and Québec. Both provinces evolved out of vast wilderness areas first opened up by Indians and fur traders, only later to become the focus of a bitter rivalry as Québec was colonised by the French, and Ontario by the British and American Loyalists. In 1791 Québec became Lower Canada and Ontario became Upper Canada. In 1840 the Act of Union united the two and finally brought responsible and stable government to the area.

Cultural differences between the two provinces remain strong, but one thing which is pretty similar is the climate. Summers can be hot and humid but winters long, very cold and snowy. Both Québec and Ontario also offer progressive, modern cities as well as vast regions of wilderness great for getting far away from whatever it is you're getting away from.

ONTARIO

The 'booming heartland' of Canada is the second largest province, claims one-third of the nation's population, half the country's industrial and agricultural resources and accounts for about 40 percent of the nation's income. Since Confederation, Ontario has leapt ahead of its neighbours, becoming highly industrialised and at the same time reaping the benefits of the great forest and mineral wealth of the Canadian Shield which covers most of the northern regions.

Ontario was first colonised, not from Britain, but by Empire Loyalists from the USA. Previously there were only sporadic French settlements and trading posts in what was otherwise a vast wilderness. The ready transportation provided in the past by the Great Lakes, (all of which except Michigan lap Ontario's shores), and now the St Lawrence Seaway, has linked the province to the industrial and consumer centres of the United States, and has been a major factor behind Ontario's success story.

There is water virtually everywhere in Ontario, and in addition to the Great Lakes, Ontario has a further 250,000 small lakes, numerous rivers and streams, a northern coastline on Hudson Bay and of course Niagara Falls. On the web, try *www.ontario-canada.com* and *dir.yahoo.com/Regional/Countries/Canada/ Provinces_and_Territories/Ontario*. For a comprehensive list of cities in Ontario, try the latter net address, but at the end add */Cities*.

National Parks: Point Pelee, Pukaskwa, Georgian Bay Islands, St Lawrence Islands, Fathom Five and Bruce Peninsula.

OTTAWA Although the nation's capital has had the reputation of being a dull city, Ottawa has perked up considerably in the last few years. Dare we even say that Ottawa has become, well, almost a fun city to visit?! It has a lively student/youth emphasis and boasts a thriving cultural life, offering the visitor many excellent museums and art galleries, and top-notch theatrical performances. When the bars and restaurants start shutting down for the night, the popular solution is to cross the river into Hull, Québec, where everything is open until 3 am.

The most colourful time of year to visit is during spring when more than a million tulips bloom in the city and Ottawa celebrates its Festival of Spring. The tulip bulbs were a gift to Ottawa from the government of the Netherlands as thanks for the refuge granted to the Dutch royal family during World War II. In summer the city is crowded with visitors and there are many special festivals and activities. A lively, fun atmosphere prevails.

Even Ottawa in the winter has its charms. You can catch the Winterlude Festival in February or just enjoy the spectacle of civil servants, with their suits and briefcases, skating to work on the four and a half mile long Rideau Canal. The canal is known as the world's longest skating rink.

Samuel de Champlain was here first, in 1613, but didn't stay long and it took a further 200 years and the construction of the Rideau Canal before Ottawa was founded. Built between 1827 and 1831, the canal provided a waterway for British gunboats allowing them to evade the international section of the St Lawrence where they might be subject to American gun attacks. Queen Victoria chose Ottawa as the capital of Canada in 1857 because it was halfway between the main cities of Upper and Lower Canada—Toronto and Québec City—and therefore a neutral choice. *www.capcan.ca/* is *Canada's Capital*, an online travel guide featuring a capital tour and activity zone covering Ottawa and surrounding areas.

The telephone area code is 613.

ACCOMMODATION

B&B places are abundant, except during May and early June when student groups and conventioneers arrive for summer residence. A complete list of B&Bs can be found in the *Ottawa Visitors Guide*; information is available at the tourist office in the National Arts Centre. Also, from **Ottawa B&B**, 563-0161, from S-$50, D-$50-$80, includes cooked bfast, evening refreshments, shared bathroom, free parking.

Centre Town Guest House Ltd, 460 Somerset West, 233-0681. Clean rooms in comfortable house. Free bfast in a cosy dining room. From S-$25, D-$35. Monthly rates from $400. Rsvs recommended.

Ottawa International Hostel (HI-C), 75 Nicholas St, 235-2595. Heritage building, the former Carleton County Jail is the site of Canada's last public hanging. 'Sleep in the corridors of a former jail and take a shower in a cell.' Centrally located. Laundry, kitchen, large lounges, 'Fantastic place; unique; friendly people.' Many organised activities including biking, canoeing, tours. $17.

Regina Guest House and Hotel (HI-C), 205 Charlotte St, 241-0908. Walking distance of Parliament Hill, museums etc.; private rooms, breakfast available, kitchen, laundry, storage, parking, lounge. Open May-Aug only. Dorms $17 members, $22 non-members, private rooms D-$36/44.

University of Ottawa Residences, 100 University St, 564-5400. Easy walk from downtown. Dorm rooms and shared showers. Free linen, towels. From S-$34, D-$40, cheaper w/student ID. Bfast $2. May-Aug.

YMCA/YWCA, 180 Argyle Ave, 237-1320. Close to bus station. 'Clean and bright.' Gym, TV, pool, kitchen with microwave. Cafeteria Mon-Fri 7am-6.30pm, Sat/Sun 8am-2.30pm; bfast $4. From S-$42, D-$49. Weekly and group rates available. Payment required in advance. Res rec.

Camping: Gatineau Park, 827-2020, has 3 campgrounds: **Lac Philippe Campground; Lac Taylor Campground;** and **Lac la Peche.** All campgrounds are off Hwy 366 NW, Hull, within 45 min of Ottawa. Map available at visitors centre. Park has five beaches and boating facilities.

Also, **Camp Le Breton**, at Le Breton Flats, Booth and Fleet Sts, 943-0467. Summer $9 per night. 'Very convenient.'

FOOD

Breakfast is cholesterol-rich here and a generous helping of eggs, potatoes, meat, toast and coffee is the norm!

Byward Market, north of Rideau. Local produce, cheese, meat, fish, fruit, clothing, bits and pieces; it's been here since 1846. 'Great.' 'Not to be missed.' The area around the market is good for eating places in general. Daily 8am-6pm.

Café Bohemien, 89 Clarence, 241-8020. Innovative menu and reasonable prices usually under $10.

Father and Sons, 112 Osgoode St (at eastern edge of the U of O campus), 234-1173. Favoured by students, traditional tavern-style food and a variety of Lebanese specialities are served up. All served daily till midnight, generally Mon-Sat 7am-2am, Sun 8am-1am.

Las Palmas, 111 Parent Ave, 241-3738. Hot hot hot Mexican cuisine heaped high! Meals under $15. Mon-Thu and Sat 11.30am-10.30pm, Fri till midnight.

Wringer's Restaurant & Laundromat, 151 Second Ave, 234-9700. Kill 2 birds with one stone. Mon-Sun 9am-10pm, except Sat, till 5pm.

Yesterdays, 152 Spark St Mall, 235-1424. 'Good food at reasonable prices, $5-12.' Open daily till 11pm.

OF INTEREST

Canadian Museum of Civilisation, 100 Laurier St (at St Laurent Blvd), just across the river in **Hull**, Quebec, (819) 776-7000. This impressive museum explores the history of Canada's cultural heritage. Also an IMAX Theatre. Daily 9am-6pm, Thu till 9pm, $8, Free Sun 9am-noon.

Canadian Museum of Contemporary Photography, 1 Rideau Canal, 990-8257. Take a glimpse at modern Canadian life. Wed-Sun 11am-4pm, closed Mon/Tue. Free.

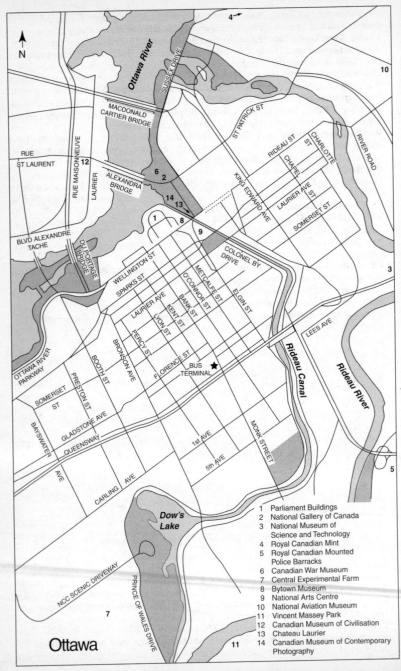

N

Ottawa River

SUSSEX DRIVE

MACDONALD CARTIER BRIDGE

RUE ST LAURENT

RUE MAISONNEUVE

LAURIER

ALEXANDRA BRIDGE

ST PATRICK ST

RIDEAU ST

CHAPEL ST

CHARLOTTE ST

RIVER ROAD

KING EDWARD AVE

LAURIER AVE ST

SOMERSET ST

BLVD ALEXANDRE TACHE

DU PORTAGE BRIDGE

COLONEL BY DRIVE

WELLINGTON ST

SPARKS ST

LAURIER AVE

O'CONNOR ST

METCALFE ST

ELGIN ST

BANK ST

KENT ST

LYON ST

PERCY ST

BRONSON AVE

BOOTH ST

PRESTON ST

FLORENCE ST

BUS TERMINAL

LEES AVE

Rideau Canal

Rideau River

Ottawa River Parkway

SOMERSET ST

BAYSWATER AVE

GLADSTONE AVE

QUEENSWAY

1st AVE

5th AVE

MONK STREET

CARLING AVE

Dow's Lake

NCC SCENIC DRIVEWAY

PRINCE OF WALES DRIVE

Ottawa

1 Parliament Buildings
2 National Gallery of Canada
3 National Museum of
 Science and Technology
4 Royal Canadian Mint
5 Royal Canadian Mounted
 Police Barracks
6 Canadian War Museum
7 Central Experimental Farm
8 Bytown Museum
9 National Arts Centre
10 National Aviation Museum
11 Vincent Massey Park
12 Canadian Museum of Civilisation
13 Chateau Laurier
14 Canadian Museum of Contemporary
 Photography

Canadian War Museum, 330 Sussex Dr, (819) 776-8600. Canada's military history from the early 1600s on. Daily 9.30am-5pm, Thu till 8pm. $4, free on Sun 9.30-noon, Canada Day (1 July) and Nov 11.

Central Experimental Farm, Maple Dr, 991-3044. Part of the **Agriculture Museum,** est. 1886 and HQ for the Canada Dept of Agriculture. Flowers, tropical greenhouse, animals. Great place for a picnic—beautiful site on the canal. Daily sunrise-sunset; greenhouse daily 9am-4pm; free. Horse-drawn wagon tours available.

Parliament Hill. The Gothic-style, green copper-roofed buildings stand atop Parliament Hill overlooking the river. Completed in 1921, the three buildings replaced those destroyed by fire in 1916. Conducted tours daily every 30 mins, 9am-8.30pm; Wknds till 5.30pm. Information (800) 465-1867 / 239-5000. Free. During the summer there are *son et lumière* displays, due to be updated for 2000 so check timings. When parliament is in session you can visit the House of Commons. The best view in the city is from the 291-foot-high **Peace Tower** in the Square. The Tower has a carillon of 53 bells and during the summer the bells ring out hour-long concerts daily at 2pm in July/Aug, or shorter recitals at noon most weekdays. In true Buckingham Palace tradition, the **Changing of the Guard**—complete with bearskins and red coats—takes place on Parliament Hill at 10am, weather permitting, from late June to late Aug. The flame located in front of the Buildings burns eternally to represent Canada's unity. There is a white **Infotent** by the visitors centre.

National Arts Centre, Confederation Sq., 996-5051 ext. 212. Completed in 1969, the complex includes theatres, concert halls, an opera house and an art gallery. Year round 9am-5pm, tours available. Box office 755-1111.

National Aviation Museum, Rockcliffe Airport, just off St Laurent Blvd, 993-2010. Offers special exhibitions in the summer, and displays over 100 aircraft. Discover the role played by aeroplanes in the development of Canada. Summer daily 9am-5pm, Thu till 9pm; Sep-May closed Mon. Free Thu 5pm-9pm. $5, $4 w/student ID.

National Gallery of Canada, 380 Sussex Dr (opposite Notre Dame Basilica), (800) 319-2787 / 990-1985. Canadian art of all periods in a modern glass building designed by Moshie Safdie. Worth visiting for insight into Canadian history. Open 10am-6pm daily, Thu till 8pm. Free except for special exhibit, around $12, $10 w/student ID (also: free with American Express card). 'Spectacular.'

National Museum of Science and Technology, 1867 St-Laurent Blvd, 991-3044. 'A must for those who like to participate.' Lets visitors explore the wonderful world of technology and transport with touchy-feely exhibits. Summer daily 9am-5pm; in winter, closed Mon. $6, $5 w/student ID.

Rideau Canal. The 124 mile waterway which runs to Kingston on Lake Ontario. The 'giant's staircase,' a series of eight locks, lifts and drops boats some 80 ft between Ottawa River and Parliament Hill. In the winter the canal is turned into the world's biggest ice skating rink and commuters skate to work. Cruises on the Canal and river are available; $12 for 1hr 15mins, from dock at the Conference Centre. Contact Paul Boat Lines, 225-6781. Or hire a bike at **Dows Lake**, 232-1001 and ride along the towpath. Near the locks is the **Bytown Museum**, 50 Canal Road, 234-4570. An interesting look at old Ottawa. May-Sep Wed-Sat 10am-4pm, Except Tue, closed, Sun 1pm-4pm; $2.50 / $1.25 w/student ID. Close by, in Major's Hill Park, is the spot from where the **Noonday Gun** is fired. Everyone in Ottawa sets their watches by it. Can be heard 14 miles away.

Royal Canadian Mint, 320 Sussex Dr. Guided tours every half hour, Summer; Mon-Wed 9am-5pm, Thu/Fri 9am-7pm, Sat/Sun 9am-4pm; Winter 9am-5pm daily; $2. Tours in groups, rsvs essential, call 993-8990 the day before or early same morning.

Parks: There is a nice park at **Somerset and Lyon** and the **Vincent Massey Park**, off Riverside Dr, has free summer concerts. If you have transport, a trip to **Gatineau**

Park, five miles beyond Hull, is worth a thought. Good swimming, cycling, hiking and fishing. 'The park gives an impression of the archetypal Canada; rugged country, timber floating down the Gatineau, etc.' **Dow's Lake Pavilion**, 101 Queen Elizabeth Driveway, rents pedal boats, canoes and bikes. Open daily 11.30am-1am. Rentals by the hour with varying prices.

ENTERTAINMENT

Read *What's on in Ottawa*. For late entertainment cross the river to Hull where the pubs are open longer. Ottawa has several English style pubs. Recommended are: **Elephant & Castle**, Rideau Centre, 234-5544 (fish 'n chips). **Marble Works**, 14 Waller St, 241-6764 (open till 10pm, except Sat—closed) and **Earl of Sussex**, 431 Sussex Dr, 562-5544 14 English beers on tap. Try **Reactor** in the Market, 241-8955, and **Hoolihans** 241-5455, on York, for dancing.

Barrymore's 323 Bank St (nr the **Royal Oak**) 233-0307, is Ottawa's big venue for popular bands.

Bon Vivante Brasserie, St Joseph, **Hull**, (613) 232-2508. French Canadian music.

Downstairs Club, 307 Rideau, 241-1155. Intimate venue, smaller live bands, jazz, locals.

At the **National Arts Centre**, 53 Elgin St, 996-5051, student standby (max 2 tkts pp) available for some performances.

If you are in town on Labour Day Sep w/end, don't miss the **International Hot Air Balloon Festival** which launches itself from the Parc de l'Abe in Gatineau and can be watched from Parliament Hill.

Festivals: Odyssey Theatre, 232-8407, hosts open-air comedy at **Strathcona Park**, end July-end Aug, $20, $17 w/student ID. Based on the Italian Commedia deli Arte—incorporating dance and drama.

Annual **Central Canada Exhibition**, 237-7222, end Aug in Lansdowne Park, includes a fair, animals, crafts, concerts, etc. 'Good fun.' During the first 3 Wknds of Feb, **Winterlude**, 239-5000 lines the Rideau Canal with ice sculptures focusing on what it is like to be an Ottawan in winter!

SHOPPING

For Indian and Eskimo stuff try **Four Corners,** 93 Sparks St, 233-2322 and **Snow Goose**, 83 Sparks St, 232-2213, open Mon-sat 9.30am-5.30pm. Also, check out **Sparks St Mall**, a 3-block traffic-free shopping section btwn Elgin and Bank. Fountains, sidewalk cafes, good shopping, etc.

Byward Market, 55 Byward Market Square, 244-4416. Shops, cafes and nightclubs.

Rideau Centre, on Rideau, 5 min walk from Arts Centre. Ottawa's primary shopping mall.

INFORMATION

Read *Usually Reliable Source* and *Penny Press* for what's happening.

Capital InfoCentre, 90 Wellington St (across from Parliament Hill), (800) 465-1867/239-5000. Open daily; 8.30am-9pm summer, 9am-5pm winter. Hi-tec, interactive tour planners and a 3D map of the City, as well as all the usual tourist info.

Hostelling International-Ontario East Regional Office, 75 Nicholas St, 235-2595. Youth hostel passes, travel info and equipment. Mon-Fri 9.30am-5.30pm, Sat till 5pm.

INTERNET ACCESS

Ottawa Public library, 120 Metcalf St (cnr with Laurier), 236-0301, Mon-Thu 10am-8pm, Fri noon-6pm, Sat 10am-5pm.

TRAVEL

One of the nicest ways of seeing Ottawa is by bike, and an extensive system of bike-ways and routes is there for this purpose. Bicycles available for hire next to Chateau Laurier Hotel and on sunny days, at Confederation Sq. For prices and info call **Rent-a-Bike**, 241-4140, $20 a day. Daily 9am-7.30pm (credit card required).

OC Public Transport, 1500 St-Laurent, 741-4390 (for all bus info). Excellent system with buses congregating on either side of Rideau Centre. $2.25 basic fare, $5 All Day Pass if bought from vendors, $6 on board the buses.

VIA Rail, 200 Tremblay Rd, (800) 561-3949. Passenger train service throughout Canada. Rail station is 2 miles from city centre. To get there catch #95 bus on Slater St or Mackenzie King Bridge, every 15 mins; $2.25.

Ottawa International Airport, 248-2000 (six miles out of town). Bus #96 takes you there along the Transitory, #97 on Sun or early am, late pm. **Kasbury Transport**, 736-9993, runs shuttles btwn the airport and various hotels. Daily every 30 mins, $9, 6 w/student ID.

Voyageur Colonial Coach, 265 Catherine St, 238-5900. Primarily services eastern Canada.

Greyhound, 237-7038, run buses bound for western Canada/southern Ontario.

MORRISBURG A small town on the St Lawrence whose main claim to fame is **Upper Canada Village**, a re-creation of a St Lawrence Valley community of the 19th century. The village is situated some 11kms east of Morrisburg on Hwy 2, in Crysler Farm Battlefield Park, (800) 437-2233. The Park serves as a memorial to Canadians who died in the War of 1812 against the United States.

The buildings here were all moved from their previous sites to save them from the path of the St Lawrence Seaway and include a tavern, mill, church, store, etc., all of which are fully operational. Vehicles are not allowed. Daily 9.30am-5pm mid-May to mid-Oct; $12.75.

KINGSTON A small, pleasant city situated at the meeting place of the St Lawrence and Lake Ontario. Early Kingston was built around the site of Fort Frontenac, then a French outpost, later to be replaced by the British Fort Henry, the principal British stronghold west of Québec. This was, ever so briefly, the capital of Canada (1841-44) and many of the distinctive limestone 19th century houses still survive.

The town is the home of Queens University, situated on the banks of the St Lawrence. The Kingston Fall Fair, which in fact happens in late summer, is considered 'worth a stop'. Kingston is also a good centre for visiting the picturesque **Thousand Islands** in the St Lawrence.

ACCOMMODATION
Hilltop Motel, 2287 Princess St, 542-3846. S-$65 D-$85.

Louise House Summer Hostel (Hi-C), 329 Johnson St, 531-8237. $18 dorm, open May-Aug only. Check-in 4pm-8.30pm, bfast incl.

Queen's University Victoria Hall, 533-2529, has rooms May-Aug. Rsvs pref. $18 w/student ID, Non-student rates S-$48.50, D-$58. Bfast available.

Camping: Lake Ontario Park Campground, 542-6574, 2 miles W on King St. May-Sep. Sites for two $16 w/hook-up, XP-$2. Also, **Rideau Acres**, 546-2711 on Hwy 15 (north of exit 104/exit 623 on Hwy 401). Sites $20.

FOOD
Chez Piggy, 68 Rear Princess St (walk thru Courtyard), 549-7673. Brunch dishes all under $8, are interesting and different—lamb kidneys with scrambled eggs and home fries, Thai beef salad, along with the more typical brunch fare. Sun brunch served 11 am-2.30pm. Rsvs recommended at wknds. Mon-Sat 11.30am-midnight, Sun from 11 am.

Kingston Brewing Company, 34 Clarence St, 542-4978. The oldest brewing pub in Ontario, with true British ale served from a hand-pump. Produces own lager and Dragon's Breath Ale. Burgers, sandwiches and main courses under $8. Locals come here for the charbroiled ghetto chicken wings served with spicy BBQ sauce and the smoked beef and ribs plus typical bar fare. Back courtyard garden and sidewalk patio. Tours of brewery available. Mon-Sat 11am-1am, Sun from 11.30am.

Farmer's Market, Market Sq, is open Tue, Thu & Sat.

Morrison's, 318 King St E, 542-9483. 'Best value set meals at $4-$7.' Daily 11am till 7.30pm.

Pilot House, 265 King St E, 542-0222. Beautifully fresh fish and chips and expensive English beer (12 kinds of draft). Daily 11.30am-2am.

OF INTEREST

Fort Frederick, Royal Military College Museum, 541-6000, ext. 6652. On RMC grounds ($^1/_2$ mile E of Hwy 2). Canada's West Point, founded in 1876. The museum, in a Martello tower, features pictures and exhibits of Old Kingston and Military College history, and the Douglas collection of historic weapons. June through Labour Day. $2.50.

Murney Tower Museum. 18 Barrie St, 544-9925. Martello tower, used to serve as military housing. Now run by the Kingston Historical Society. Daily 10am-5pm May-Sep. $2.

Old Fort Henry, E on Hwy 2 at junction Hwy 15. The fort has been restored and during the summer college students dressed in Victorian army uniforms give displays of drilling. Daily 10am-5pm, $9.50. The fort is also a military museum. For info call 542-7388. John A MacDonald, Canada's first Prime Minister, lived in **Bellevue House**, 545-8666, 35 Centre St. The century-old house has been restored and furnished in the style of the 1840s. Known locally as the 'Pekoe Pagoda' or 'Tea Caddy Castle' because of its comparatively frivolous appearance in contrast to the more solid limestone buildings of the city. The house is open daily, 9am-6pm summer, 10am-5pm winter. $2.75.

Marine and Pump House Steam Museum, on Ontario St, 542-2261. A restored 1848 pump house now housing a vintage collection of working engines. Also marine museum and coastguard ship. $3.95, $3.45 w/student ID for each attraction, or combined rates avail. Mid-June-Sep, 10am-5pm Tue-Sun for Marine Museum, coastguard ship, 4pm for the Pump House.

North of the city the **Rideau Lakes** extend for miles and miles. The Rideau Hiking Trail winds its way gently among the lakes. You can take a free ferry to **Wolfe Island** in the St Lawrence. Ferries leave from City Hall. Once on the island it is possible to catch another boat (not free) to the US.

Thousand Islands Boat Tours, 549-5544. Departing from Crawford Dock at the foot of Brock St in downtown Kingston, there are additional tours of the harbour and Thousand Islands. $12-$17, or lunch cruise, 3 1/2 hours, $31.

Gananoque Boat Tours. From Gananoque Quay, 20 miles from Kingston, on Hwy 2, 382-2144. Trip lasts 3 hrs, $16, one hour for $11. Tours 9am-3pm, mid May-mid October.

ENTERTAINMENT/SPORT

Stages Nightclub, 390 Princess St, 547-3657. Bands and disco.

Canadian Olympic-training Regatta Kingston (CORK). Annual event, held during the last week in Aug; one of the largest regattas in North America. Call 545-1322 for exact dates, or check *www.cork.org*

INFORMATION

John Deutsch University Centre Union, University Sts. Ride board, shops, post office, laundry, etc.

Visitor & Convention Centre, 209 Ontario St, 548-4415. Summer daily 8.30am-8.30pm; otherwise 9am-5pm, Sun 10am-4pm.

INTERNET ACCESS
Kingston Frontenac Public Library 130 Johnson St, 549-8888. Open Mon-Thu 9am-9pm, Fri/Sat 9am-5pm, and in winter only Sun 1pm-5pm.

TRAVEL
VIA Rail Station, Princess & Counter St, 544-5600. Take #1 bus downtown.
Bus Terminal, 175 Counter St, 547-4916. Daily 6.30am-9pm. Take #2 bus downtown.

ST LAWRENCE ISLANDS NATIONAL PARK The park is made up of 17 small islands in the Thousand Islands area of the St Lawrence between Kingston and Brockville, and Mallorytown Landing on the mainland. The islands can be reached only by water-taxi from Gananoque, Mallorytown Landing and Rockport, Ontario, or from Alexandria Bay and Clayton in New York State. Park is open daily, mid-May to mid-Oct. Free.

It's a peaceful, green-forested area noted chiefly for its good fishing grounds. Camping facilities are available on the islands, $10. Visitors Centre is located at **Mallorytown**, (613) 923-5261.

TORONTO 'Trunno,' or 'Metro' as the natives call their city, is the most American of the Canadian cities, having many of the characteristics of metropolitan America but without all of the usual problems. It's a brash, cosmopolitan city with some 100 different languages on tap around town, sprawling over 270 square miles, with many fine examples of skyscraper architecture, good shopping areas, excellent theatre, music and arts facilities, a vibrant night life and fast highways. Yet it's a clean city, with markedly few poor areas, and the streets are safe at night.

Perhaps out of envy, Toronto is also nicknamed 'Toronto The Good'; 'more like Switzerland than North America', remarked one reader. 'Good' in that the city has yearned to be as stylish as New York without the poverty and dirt, and may have succeeded. You can get a great haircut, great clothes, great movies, great drinks, great music and a great job here. They also have a great polar bear section at the zoo where you experience a polar bear diving into the water two inches from your face.

Then take a look at the windows of the Royal Bank building. The golden glow emanating from them is real gold dust, mixed with the glass. That also is proof of how rich Canada is, and most of the wealth and power, the envy of the other provinces, is situated right here on Bay Street.

This is also a good centre from which to see other places in Ontario. Niagara Falls and New York State are an hour and a half away down the Queen Elizabeth Way (QEW), to the north there is Georgian Bay and the vast Algonquin Provincial Park, while to the west there are London and Stratford.

Toronto Life, www.tor-Lifeline.com/ includes restaurant guide, events calendar and the best of the city. *The telephone area code is 416.* Good links can be found at *From Toronto with love* at *www.angelfire.com/on/fokes/*

ACCOMMODATION
For assistance on finding accommodation in Toronto, contact **B&B Homes of Toronto**, 363-6362; **B&B Registry**, 964-2566; **Downtown Toronto Association of B&B Guesthouses**, PO Box 190, Station B, Toronto M5T 2W1, 368-1420; and **Econo-**

Lodging Services, 101 Nymark Ave, 494-0541.

Canadiana Guest House and Backpackers, 42 Widmer St, (877) 215-1225 or 598-9090. $21 up. A.C., bfast, TV lounge 'Good value.'

Chisholm Hospitality Home, 120 Leslie St, 469-2967. Dorm $19, $35 private room; ask for backpackers' rates. 'Very friendly.'

Global Village Backpackers Hostel, 460 King St, 703-8540. $23.50 dorm. Bar, laundry, kitchen. 'Bright and cheerful.'

Karabanow Tourist Home, 9 Spadina Rd, at Bloor St W, 923-4004. Rooms with shared bath and free parking: from S/D-$52-62. Discounted weekly rates Oct-May. TV, next to subway. 'Clean and very helpful.' email: 7.1663.3131.@compuserve.com

Leslieville Home Hostel, 185 Leslie St, 461-7258. 'Run by British couple. Great atmosphere but a 15 min streetcar ride from centre.' Rsvs essential in summer. Heavily discounted rates Nov-April. $16 dorm, S-$37, D-$47. Bfast $2.50.

Marigold International Travellers Hostel, 2011 Dundas St W, 536-8824. Closest hostel to the Canadian National Exhibition. TV room, free morning coffee and donut buffet. Dundas and Carlton street cars pass in front of door; close to Roncesvalles eateries. $20. Mixed reports. Check in after 2pm.

Neill-Wycik College Hotel, 96 Gerrard St E, (800) 268-4358. Try here first. Good facilities, baggage storage, central, 5 mins from subway. No AC in rooms but AC lounges and TV. Dorm $19; S-$34; D-$44 (10% weekly discount; also w/student ID, ask for backpackers' rates). Bfast $4. 'Recommended.' May-Aug only. Airport shuttle. 'High rise hospitality.'

HI Toronto Hostel, 76 Church St W, 971-4440 En-suite bathrooms, private rooms avail. Centrally located, a few minutes from the Eaton Centre. Rsvs advisable in summer. Dorms $17.95.

University Residences: University College, 85 St George St, 978-8735. Summers only. Also suggested are **Trinity** and **Wycliffe Colleges** on Hoskin Ave, and **St Hildas** on Devonshire Place. About $80 weekly. 'Pleasant and clean.' Renovated in '99, check for new rates.

University of Toronto: Scarborough campus, Sir Dans, 73 St George St, 287-7367. 'Fantastic student residence.' Under $100 weekly (min 2 week stay). 17 May-25 Aug. 'Parties, sports facilities.' 'Basic Uni accommodation, have to clean own rooms.' 'Excellent setting/location, full of other travellers/BUNACers in summer.' 90 mins from downtown; for shorter stays, the Uni **Conference Services** 287-7309, can arrange group housing; townhouse to sleep four, $84 per night.

University of Toronto Housing Service, 214 College St, 978-8045. Has list of accommodations available in student residences, summer only. $30-50 range.

YWCA, 80 Woodlawn Ave E, 923-8454. Yonge-University subway to Summerhill, walk two blocks north. For women only. Dorm $20. From S-$47, D-$52.

Camping: Indian Line Tourist Campground, 7625 Finch Ave W, (905) 678-1233/off-season 661-6600 ext. 203. This is the closest area to metropolitan Toronto. Sites $19, $24 w/full hook-up. Showers, laundry. May-early Oct. Rsvs recommended July-Aug. Also, try **Glen Rouge Park**, 7450 Kingston Rd (Hwy 2), 392-2541. Near hiking, pool, tennis courts and beach. Showers/toilets. $17, $24 w/hook-up.

FOOD

Over 5,000 restaurants squeezed into this city! Fave dining areas to eat out in include **Bloor St W, Chinatown** and **Village by the Grange**, the latter being home of super-cheap restaurants and vendors.

Druxy's Famous Deli Sandwiches, 385-9500, a cafeteria-style eating place with locations all over Toronto, is a good spot for salads and sandwiches.

Fran's Restaurants, 21 St Clair Ave W, 2275 Yonge, 20 College. Spaghetti, fish and chips, burgers. 24 hrs. Under $12.

Java Joe's, Yonge & Shephard (in the Nestle Bldg), 221-9032 and Gerrard St W (corner of Bay). Serves up bfast of bagel and coffee/tea for $1. Lunch specials for $4-5. 'Good value, pleasant surroundings.' Yonge St open Mon-Fri only.

Lick's Homeburgers and Ice Cream, 362-5425, call for various locations; on Yonge south of Eglinton and on Queen St E in the Beaches. For the messiest, yummiest burgers around in a fun atmosphere, from $4.

Loon Fong Yuen, 393 Spadina. Unpretentious Chinese eatery, meals from $7. Lots of places in Chinatown (around Dundas & Spadina) offer meals at reasonable prices.

The Midtown Café, 552 College St W, 920-4533. Play pool or relax and eat whilst listening to music. Large *tapas* menu at wknds. Eats for $3-$5. Daily 10am-2am.

Old Spaghetti Factory, 54 Esplanade, east of Yonge, 864-9761. Huge old ware-house. From $7. 'Very delicious. Excellent value and service.' Daily 11.30am-11pm / midnight Fri-Sat.

Sneaky Dees, 431 College St, 603-3090. Serves a bargain bfast for $3.85 from 3am-11am. Doubles as a night-time hot spot. Closes 4am / 5am Fri/Sat.

Swiss Chalet, a chain with numerous outlets, has 'great' barbecued chicken and ribs at very reasonable prices.

Toby's Goodeats, Locations across the city (including Yonge & Bloor, Bloor & Bay, the Eaton Centre, Yonge & St Clair). Toby's serves up some of the best-value meals in the city. Meals for under $10.

Markets: Westclair Italian Village (little Italy) along St Clair Ave W btwn Dufferin and Lansdown. Sidewalk cafes and restaurants. Don't miss 2 good markets, for fresh produce and a wide variety of food:

Kensington Market, Dundas St West to College St, Spadina Ave to Augusta St.

St Lawrence Market, 95 Front St East. Over 40 foodstalls in this historic 1844 build-ing, Toronto's first city hall.

OF INTEREST

Art Gallery of Ontario, 317 Dundas St at McCaul, 977-0414. Rembrandt, Picasso, Impressionists, large collection of Henry Moore sculptures, plus Oldenburg's 'Hamburger,' and collections by Canadian artists. 'Don't miss the Art Gallery shop!' Tue-Fri noon-9pm, Sat/Sun 10am-5.30pm. Summer; (mid May-mid October) closed Mon. Winter; closed Mon/Tue. 'Pay what you can' for permanent collection (suggested $6), around $10, $7 w/student ID for temporary exhibits.

Bata Shoe Museum, 327 Bloor St, 979-7799 ext. 225. The only shoe museum in North America, displaying over 9000 pairs from Elton's platforms to ancient Egyptian sandals. Tue-Sat 10am-5pm, Thu till 8pm. Sun noon-5pm. $6, $4 w/student ID. Free 1st Tue of the month.

Black Creek Pioneer Village, 1000 Murray Ross Parkway, 736-1733, on the north-ern edge of Toronto at Jane St and Steeles Ave. A reconstructed pioneer village circa 1860. Costumed workers perform daily tasks in the restored buildings. Daily 10am-5pm; closed Jan-Apr. Open daily 10am-5pm, longer in summer months; check for details; $9 or $7 w/student ID. If travelling there by subway and streetcar, allow about 1 hr each way from the city centre.

Canada's Wonderland, 30 kms north, Rutherford Rd, off Hwy 400, for info (905) 832-7000. Ontario's answer to Disney? Includes 5 theme areas, a 150-ft man-made mountain complete with waterfalls, 'splashworld' and all the usual rides and entertainments. $43.27 for a day pass, $25.73 if don't want to use the rides. May-Sep 10am-10pm.

Casa Loma, 1 Austin Terrace (Davenport at Spadina), 923-1171. An eccentric chateau-style mansion built by the late Sir Henry Pellatt between 1911 and 1914 at a reported cost of $3m. It was restored in 1967 and the proceeds from the daily tours go to charity. 'Fantastic.' Daily 9.30am-4pm, year round. $9. *www.casaloma.org*

Spadina Historic House, 285 Spadina Road, 392-6910, next-door, is also open to the public, daily noon-5pm except Mon. Must take a guided tour, which leave every

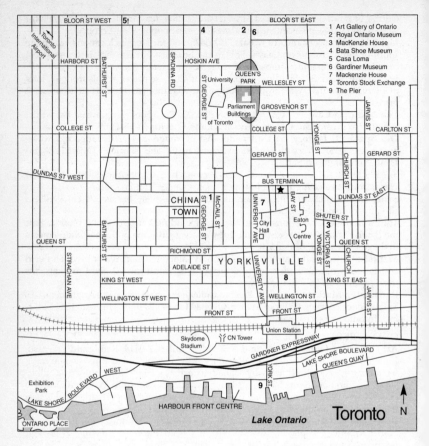

1	Art Gallery of Ontario
2	Royal Ontario Museum
3	MacKenzie House
4	Bata Shoe Museum
5	Casa Loma
6	Gardiner Museum
7	Mackenzie House
8	Toronto Stock Exchange
9	The Pier

hour until 4pm, $5. Gardens are open same hours, no admission charge. 'Play croquet in the gardens'. 'Take subway to Dupont'.

Chinatown, along Dundas West and China Court, Spadina, south of Dundas. Usual mixture of tourist and 'real' Chinese. Good place to eat.

City Hall, 100 Queen St at Bay St, 392-7341. $30m creation of Finnish architect Viljo Revell, perhaps most impressive when lit at night. Brochure available for self-guided tour, Mon-Fri 8.30am-4pm. The reflecting pool in **Nathan Phillips Sq** becomes a skating rink in winter, and is also home to various special events. Call the **Events Hotline**, 392-0458.

CN Tower, 301 Front St, 360-8500. At 1815 ft the tallest free-standing structure in the world, and one section has a glass floor you can walk across. The observation deck is open in summer 9am-midnight. Elevator to observation deck $16; $20 inclusive to go to the Space Deck. Classy 360 Restaurant and plenty of other eateries, tourist shops and simulator rides, as you would expect for one Canada's premier tourist attractions. 'Can get in at a discount $6.50 if YHA member—came across discount by accident!' 'The CN Tower has a great view, but don't eat there unless the Air Show is on, when you can have a front row seat and the planes are so close that the pilots wave to you.' 'Expect queues!' *www.cntower.ca*

Gardiner Museum of Ceramic Art, 111 Queen's Park, 586-8080. The only museum of its kind in North America, with a vast collection of pottery and porcelain. Mon-Fri 10am-7pm, Sat 10am-5pm, Sun 11am-5pm. $5, $2 after 5pm. Free 1st Tue of the month.

Harbourfront, 410 Queen's Quay West, 973-3000 Infoline. 92 acres of restaurants, antique markets, art shows, films, theatre, etc., on Lake Ontario. Free Sun concerts. Great place to spend a sunny summer afternoon, or free ice skating in the winter (charge for skate rental). *www.harbourfront.on.ca*

Mackenzie House, 82 Bond St, 392-6915. Georgian home and print shop of William Lyon Mackenzie, first mayor of Toronto and leader of the Upper Canada rebellion in 1837. Now restored to mid-1800s condition. Tue-Sun noon-5pm, closed Mon; $3.50. Take a guided or self-guided tour.

Metro Toronto Zoo, off junction Hwy 401 and Meadowvale Rd, 392-5901. Year round daily from 9am; closing time varies with season. $12. Take bus #86A from Kennedy Subway station.

Old Fort York, 392-6907. On Garrison Rd, the Fort was built in 1793 and was the site of the 1812 battle of York when American forces beat British/Canadian and Native defenders. In retaliation British forces later burnt down the White House in Washington DC. The fort now houses restored army quarters and a collection of antique weapons, tools, etc. Guided tours and 'historical activities,' open daily 10am-5pm, or 4pm in winter; $5.

Ontario Place 995 Lakeshore Blvd (on the lakefront), 314-9900. A complex of manmade islands and lagoons, with marina and attractive parkland. Films at Cinesphere on what was once the 'largest screen in the world'; multimedia presentations of Ontario are shown in several unusual pavilions; get lost in the mega-maze, and lots of water-based activities. There's an amazing children's fun village and fairly cheap food available in several different eating places. Well recommended by previous visitors. Open daily, grounds till midnight in the summer, 5pm in winter. All day pass $22; includes rides, films etc., or grounds only $10—pay for activities as you go. Less in the off-season. Take #511 Bathurst streetcar or #121 Front Esplanade bus from Union Station. Also served by Go Transit rail. *www.ontarioplace.com* Opposite is the **Canadian National Exhibition**, 393-6000 *www.theex.com*. Otherwise known as CNE or 'The Ex', held annually next to Ontario Place during the 18 days before Labour Day. Admission around $30. Free admission to Ontario Place from the CNE during this time. A sort of glorified state fair, Canadian style, and the largest annual exhibition in the world. Cheap food in the Food Hall, and site of the Hockey Hall of Fame. 'Fabulous.'

Ontario Science Centre, 770 Don Mills Rd and Eglinton Ave E, 696-1000. A do-it-yourself-place which is 'part-museum, part fun fair.' Includes 'Mindworks' exhibition on the science of human nature. 'Breathtaking.' 'An absolute must.' 'Definitely worth going to.' Daily 10am-5pm, 6pm July/Aug. Closed Mon in winter. $10, $15 w/OMNIMAX film. *www.osc.on.ca*. Take Yonge Subway to Eglinton, then Eglinton East bus to Don Mills Rd.

Provincial Parliament Buildings, Queen's Park ($^1/_2$ block N of College St, University Ave), 325-7500. Completed in 1892, the Legislative Buildings once provided living accommodation for its elected members. Building open daily 8.30am-5.30pm in summer, Mon-Fri in winter; chambers close 4.30pm. Free guided tours, including a $^1/_2$ hr visit to the Public Gallery. Free gallery passes available at main lobby info desk 1.30pm.

Royal Ontario Museum, 100 Queen's Park, 586-8000. Has the largest Chinese art collection outside China and fine natural history section. Mon-Sat 10am-6pm, Tue till 8pm, Sun 11am-6pm. July/Aug $14, $7 w/student ID, rest of year $12, $7 w/student ID. Free for last hour or after 4.30pm on Tue. *www.rom.on.ca*

Sky Dome, 1 Blue Jays Way, 341-2770. Located at the foot of Peter St, this impressive structure boasts the largest retractable roof in the world and numerous bars and restaurants. Catch a football or baseball game here starring Toronto's Argonauts or the much-loved Blue Jays. Tours available, $9.50. If the roof is open, get a great view from the top of the CN Tower.

The Pier, 245 Queens Quay West, 338-7437. Toronto's Waterfront Museum, plus lots of stuff for kids. Maritime history incl. 1930's restored shipping warehouse. Open May-Oct, daily 10am-6pm, $5. Take streetcar #510 (Harbourfront LRT) from Union Station or Spadina St.

Toronto Stock Exchange, The Exchange Tower, 130 King Street West, 947-4670. Stock Market Place Visitors Centre has interactive exhibits, be a broker for day! $5, $3 w/student ID. Mon-Fri 10am-5pm, Sat May-Oct. *www.tse.com*

University of Toronto, west of Queens Park, 978-5000. The largest educational institution in the British Commonwealth. Free 1 hr historical walking tours of the campus available June-Aug, starting from Nora McDonald Visitors Centre, 25 Kings Cross Circle; Mon-Fri 10.30am, 1pm & 2.30pm.

Parks: The best of the city's parks and open spaces are **High Park** (free swimming), **Edwards Gardens, Don Mills, Forest Hill** and **Rosedale**. The ferry ride to **Centre Island** in the harbour costs $4 rtn. Or take a stroll along the boardwalk in the Beaches, south of Queen St E, east from Woodbine. The car-free islands can be explored on foot or bike via the bridges.

ENTERTAINMENT

Check the *Globe and Mail*, *Toronto Star* and *Toronto Sun* for daily entertainment guide, as well as the free weekly guides, *NOW* and *EYE*. Also look for *Key to Toronto*, monthly. There are many bars situated along Queen St W, some of which feature nightly live entertainment: check out especially the **Bamboo**, 312 Queen St, 595-5771; closed Sun, and the **Rivoli**, 332 Queen St, 596-1908. Also, **Lee's Palace** on Bloor St W, just east of Bathurst for bands, 532-1598, and the **El Mocambo** at 464 Spadina (cnr with College), 968-2001.

The Big Bop, 651 Queen St W, 504-6699. A multi-storey dance club with bands and different styles of music on each floor and a sofa-lounge upstairs, air-hockey tables/pool tables. Popular with students. Wed-Sat 8pm-3am. $8, on Wed $2.50 and all drinks $3. Must be 19 or over.

For free tkts to **CBC TV shows** and info on tours, call 205-3311, Mon-Fri 9am-5pm.

Cineplex Odeon, 1303 Yonge St, 964-3625 the largest cineplexes in the world; cheap tickets all day Tue. Tkts go fast for the evening performances of new movies so buy early.

The Docks, 11 Polson St, 461-3625, restaurants, bars, club and golf! Spookily enough, all down by the waterfront. *www.harbourfront.on.ca* On the #510 streetcar route.

Harbourfront, 235 Queen's Quay West 973-3000. Concerts plus movie theatre showing oldies, horror movies, and other classics.

Molson Indy, at the Canadian National Exhibition, 872-4639 for tkts. $75-$110 for 3 days. It varies every year, but usually during the second half of July. 'This race has been on the Indy car circuit since 1986 and has grown more popular each year.'

Hummingbird Centre, 1 Front St E (cnr w/ Yonge), 393-7469. Opera, ballet, concerts, jazz, drama. Student rush seats available on night of performance.

St Lawrence Centre for the Arts, 27 Front St E (cnr w/Scott), 366-8243. Drama, dance and opera. Season usually ends in May; have some performances during the summer.

Yuk Yuk's, 2335 Yonge (cnr w/ Eglinton), 867-6425, offers a night of amateur stand-up comedians. Dinner available. Features excellent nightly shows. 'Canadian humour at its best.' $5-15 cover.

Festivals: Toronto International Film Festival, first Thu after Labour Day, tkts available at box office, College Park, 444 Yonge St, call 968-3456. *www.bell.ca/filmfest*.
Toronto International Dragon Boat Race Festival held over 2 days in mid-June. Celebration includes traditional performances, foods and free outdoor lunchtime concerts.

SHOPPING
Queen St, west of University Ave, is renowned as the **alternative student shopping area**. 'Vibrant.' Also, check out:
Bee Bee's Flea Market Inc., St Lawrence Market, 92 Front St at Jarvis. Most Sundays all year, 10am-5pm. Antiques, crafts. Free coffee or tea.
Eaton Centre Shopping Mall, Yonge and Dundas, 598-8762. An impressive multi-levelled, glass-domed complex of stores, eating places and entertainment. 'Definitely worth a visit.'
Honest Ed, Bloor & Bathurst, 537-1574. 'Just about everything at 40% reduction.'
Sam the Record Man, Yonge and Dundas, 977-4650. 'Huge selection of cheap records.'
Beneath the **Toronto Dominion Bank** complex, Bay and King Sts, there is a wealth of shops and restaurants, bustling during the day but closed at night. Interconnects into the subway system, the Royal York Hotel and Union Station.
World's Biggest Bookstore, 20 Edward St at Yonge (1 block from Eaton Centre), 977-7009. 17 miles of shelves with over 1 million books. Open daily.
Yorkville, north of Queens Park east of Avenue Rd. 'Lively, open till about 1am on Sat night—street theatre, music, etc.'

INFORMATION
Access Toronto, Government Info only, 392-7341.
Post Office at Front and Bay Sts.
Tourism Toronto, 207 Queen's Quay W, Harbourfront Centre, (800) 363-1990 / 203-2600. More convenient office in the Eaton Centre on the lower floor. Watch out for the roving visitor information van as well. Mon-Fri 8.30am-6pm, Sun from 9.30am.

INTERNET ACCESS
The Electric Bean Cybercafe, 10 Eglinton Ave (at Yonge St), 481-2100, can't miss it—it's the bright yellow building. Summer hours; Mon-Thu 8am-midnight, Fri 8am-1am, Sat 10am-1am, Sun noon-10pm. $15/hr.
There are a **public libraries** at City Hall, Nathan Phillips Square, 100 Queen St W, 393-7650, 11am-4pm Mon-Fri only, or at 2161 Queen St E, 393-7703 (book time up to 24 hrs in advance) Mon-Fri 10am-8.30pm, Sat 9am-5pm. Closed Sun.

TRAVEL
Travel CUTS student travel office, 187 College St, 979-2406. Smaller office at 74 Gerrard St E, 977-0441. Both open Mon-Fri 9am-6pm.
Airport Express / Pacific Western (905) 564-6333, buses between airport and downtown every 20 mins, $12.50 o/w. Also service from Islington, Yorkdale and York Mills subways to the airport every $1/2$ hr, $7-12.
Allo Stop, 975-9305 ride share service. $20 to Ottawa; $26 to Montreal. $6 membership. *www.allostop.ca*
Bike rentals: **Brown's Sport and Cycle Shop**, 2447 Bloor St W, 763-4176. $18, $35 w/end, $49 weekly, $200 deposit! Mon-Sat 9.30am-6pm, Thu-Fri to 8pm.
GO Trains, 869-3200, commuter trains to Oshawa, Hamilton etc.
Greyhound Bus Terminal, 610 Bay St at Dundas, call 367-8747 for info.
CanaBus Tours, 74 Gerrard St E, (877) CANABUS / 226-2287. Fun Ontario tours, 7 days, $277. Tue and Sat departures. *www.canabus.com/*
The Last Minute Club, 1300 Don Mills Road, 441-2582. 'Best place to get really cheap flights.' Mon-Fri 9am-8pm; Sat/Sun 10am-4pm. $40 membership.

Toronto Driveaway Service, 5803 Yonge St, Suite #101, 225-7754. Open 9am-5pm.
Toronto Transit Commission (TTC) bus and subway, 393-4636. Standard fares operate on this integrated transport system and it is cheaper to buy tokens. Current fare is $2, 10 tokens $17, monthly pass $88.50. Free transfers, valid btwn subway and bus lines. Exact fare required for buses and streetcars. Day pass $7. Bus drivers do not give change. Some routes have night buses / streetcars which run from 1am-5.30am. Route maps available from ticket booths. City buses run to airport (Terminal 2 only) every hr from Lawrence West subway. $2. *www.city.toronto.on.ca/ttc/*
VIA Rail Canada, 366-8411. Trains from Union Station to Niagara Falls; same day return $32 if booked 5 days in advance, $49 on the spot.

HAMILTON   Situated on the shores of Lake Ontario roughly midway between Toronto and Niagara Falls, Hamilton is Canada's King of Steel. The city is home to the two principal steel companies in the nation, Stelco and Dofasco, and like its US counterpart, Pittsburgh, is in the throes of an urban cleanup and renewal in the wake of the steel giants. The air and the water are cleaner here these days and many new and interesting buildings have gone up around town. Hamilton is working hard to improve its image.

The city is also blessed with one of the largest landlocked harbours on the Great Lakes, as a result handling the third largest water tonnage in the country. Although primarily a shipping and industrial centre, Hamilton does offer a variety of non-steel related activities to the visitor. It is also within easy reach of Niagara, Brantford, Stratford and London. *www.city.hamilton.on.ca/.*
The area code is 905.

ACCOMMODATION
McMaster University, 1280 Main St West, 525-9140, ext. 24781. Shared bath, kitchen facilities, indoor pool. From S/D-$32, S-$189 weekly, approx. $390 monthly (call to check prices). Discounts for longer stays. May-Aug.
Pines Motel, 395 Centennial Pkwy, 561-5652. Close to Confederation Park, water-slide and wave pool. From S/D-$68, TV.
YMCA, 79 James St S, 529-7102. S-$29 + $12 key deposit. Men only.
YWCA 75 MacNab St S, 522-9922. S-$29 + $5 deposit. 'Rsvs a good idea.'

FOOD
Barangas, 380 Van Wagner's Beach Rd, 544-7122. Food with an international flavour, dishes $7-18. Daily 11am-2am.
Black Forest Inn, 255 King St E, 528-3538. A festive atmosphere for good budget dining. Sample all kinds of schnitzels and sausages, all served with home fries and sauerkraut. Try the Black Forest cake for dessert. Main courses $6-12. Tue-Thu 11.30am-10.30pm, Fri-Sat till 11pm, Sun noon-9.30pm. Closed Mon.
Farmers Market, central Hamilton. The largest such market in Canada.
McMaster University Common Building Refectory. Open during the summer, June through Aug. 'Meals from $4.'
The Winking Judge, 25 Augusta St, 524-5626. Convivial crowd esp. at lunchtime and wknds when the piano player is about. Sample the veal piccata, prime rib and barbecue ribs. Most pub fare items $4-10. Mon-Thu 11.30am-midnight, Fri-Sat till 2am, Sun noon-11pm.

OF INTEREST
African Lion Safari and Game Farm, W off Hwy 8, S of Cambridge, (800) 461-9453 / (519) 623-2620. 1,500 exotic animals roam this drive-through wild-life park, incl. the white tiger. 'Look deep into the icy blue eyes of these rare large cats!'

www.lionsafari.com. $17.95 plus $4.95 if you don't have your own vehicle. 10am-7.30pm, daily May-Oct.

The Bruce Trail extends more than 700 km along the Niagara escarpment. Good for hiking, pleasant walks. 'Gorgeous.'

Canadian Football Hall of Fame, 58 Jackson St W, within City Hall Plaza area, 528-7566. Push button exhibits. Tue-Sat 9.30am-4.30pm, Sun from noon. $3, $1.50 w/student ID.

Canadian Warplane Heritage Museum, 9820 Airport Rd, Hamilton Airport, Mt Hope, (800) 386-5888 / 679-4183. Museum houses the world's largest collection of planes remaining from WWII-Jet Age which are kept in flying condition. Watch the 'Flight of the Day', browse the archive exhibit gallery and memorabilia and experiment with video/audio interactives. Daily year-round 9am-5pm, Thu till 8pm. $7, $6 w/student ID. *www.warplane.com.*

Dundurn Castle, 610 York Blvd, 546-2872. Restored Victorian mansion of Sir Allen Napier MacNab, Prime Minister of United Canada, 1854-1856. In August, be sure to hang around for the annual Aug event *An Evening in Scotland—A Celebration of Scottish Heritage* which features music and dance. Mansion open daily 10am-4pm June-Sep, winter Tue-Sun noon-4pm. $6, $5 w/student ID. Includes tour and admission to the Military Museum also in Dundurn Park.

Hamilton Art Gallery, 123 King St West, 527-6610. Canadian and American art. Tue-Sun 11am-5pm. Free.

Hamilton Museum of Steam and Technology, 900 Woodward Ave, 546-4797. May-Sep daily 11am-4pm, otherwise noon-4pm. Closed Mon; $3.75.

Hamilton Place, 50 Main St W. An impressive $11m showcase for the performing arts and part of the downtown renewal project. Home of Hamilton Philharmonic, one of Canada's finest. Call 546-3100 for schedules.

Hess Village, 4 blocks btwn King & Main Sts. Restored Victorian mansions in a 19th century village. Stroll alongside the trendy shops, antiques, restaurants, etc.

MacMaster University. Has one of Canada's first nuclear reactors and a planetarium. There is also an art gallery on campus in Togo Salmon Hall.

Royal Botanical Gardens, 680 Plains Rd W, 527-1158. Both natural and cultivated landscapes. Wildlife sanctuary called 'Cootes Paradise' where trails wind through some 1,200 acres of marsh and wooded ravines. Open from dawn to dusk daily. $7, $6 w/ student ID. A maple syrup festival is held here in March. *www.rbg.ca*

INFORMATION/TRAVEL

Hamilton Street Railway (local transit), 527-4441. Basic fare $2. Ticket office at Hamilton GO Centre, 36 Hunter St E.

Tourist Information Centre, 127 King St E, 546-2666. Mon-Sat 9am-5.30pm, Sun noon-5pm. 'Very helpful.'

Greater Hamilton Tourism and Convention Services, 1 James St South, 3rd Floor, (800) 263-8590 / 546-4222.

BRANTFORD Chief Joseph Brant brought the Mohawk Indians to settle here at the end of the American Revolution, the tribe having fought with the defeated Loyalist and British North American armies. Her Majesty's Chapel of the Mohawks was built in 1785 and ranks as the oldest church in Ontario and the only royal chapel outside the United Kingdom. King George III himself was pleased to donate money for the cause. Chief Brant's tomb adjoins the chapel.

The town's other claim to fame is **Tutela Heights**, the house overlooking the Grand River Valley where Alexander Graham Bell lived and to which he made the first long distance telephone call, all the way from Paris, Ontario, some eight miles away. The call was made in August 1876, following Bell's first call in Boston.

The annual **Six Nation Indian Pageant**, depicting early Indian history and culture, takes place at the beginning of August. Visit the Six Nations Reserve to see how Native Indians really live. Go online at *www.city.brantford.on.ca*

The telephone area code here and the area west of Toronto between the lakes is 519.

OF INTEREST

Bell Homestead National Historic Site, 94 Tutela Heights Rd, (800) 265-6299 / 756-6220. Bell's birthplace and museum, furnished in style of the 1870s. Daily 9.30am-4.30pm, $3, $2.50 w/student ID.

Brant County Museum and Archives, 57 Charlotte St, 752-2483. Indian and pioneer displays. Wed-Fri 10am-4pm, Sat/Sun 1pm-4pm. $2, $1.50 w/student ID. Also, **Museum in the Square**, is another part of the County Museum, Market Square Mall, 752-8578. Changing exhibitions, Mon-Fri 10am-6pm, Sat till 5.30pm. Donations only.

Brantford Highland Games, held early July. Pipe bands, dancing, caber tossing.

Chiefswood, 8 miles E by Hwy 54, near Middleport, on Indian reservation, 752-5005. 1853 home of 'Mohawk Princess,' well-known poetess Pauline Johnson, daughter of Indian Chief Johnson. Her works include *Flint and Feather* and *Legends of Vancouver*. Tue-Sun 10am-3pm until Canadian Thanksgiving, closed in winter. $3, $2 w/student ID, includes guided tour.

Woodland Cultural Centre and Museum, 184 Mohawk St, 759-2650. Collection of artefacts of Eastern Woodland Indians. Mon-Fri 9am-4pm, Sat/Sun 10am-5pm. $4.

INFORMATION

Visitor Information Centre, 1 Sherwood Drive, (800) 265-6299 / 751-9900. Daily 9am-4.30pm. Organises daily tours of town. Also info centre in the **Wayne Gretzgy Sports Centre** just off hwy.

NIAGARA FALLS   The Rainbow Bridge (25c) which spans the Niagara River connects the cities of Niagara Falls, NY, with Niagara Falls, Ontario. Whichever side of the river you stay on, the better view of the Horseshoe Falls is definitely from the Canadian vantage point. It's an awe-inspiring sight which somehow manages to remain so despite all the commercial junk and the jostling crowds you have to fight your way past to get there. Try going at dusk or dawn for a less impeded look, and then again later in the evening when everything is floodlit. Snow and ice add a further grandeur to the scene in winter. Hydroelectric schemes, however, have reduced the flow, and consequently slowed the erosion that moved the falls 11km in 12,000 years. Since 1950, it has been possible to effectively 'turn down' the Falls at night with the water flow reduced to just 50 per cent. The environmental impact is still unknown. In the nineteenth century the Falls once stopped altogether, due to a build-up of ice up-river. The next-door town of **Niagara-on-the-Lake** is also worth a visit. This was the first capital of Ontario and home of the first library, newspaper and law society in Upper Canada, and it has a certain 19th century charm. The drive along the Niagara Pkwy from Niagara-on-the-Lake to the Falls is recommended. (*See Niagara Falls, NY, for further details.*) The official website for the Niagara Region of Ontario is *www.community.niagara.com/.* and lots of information can also be found at niagaraparks.com

The area code is 905.

ACCOMMODATION

Tourist homes are the best bet here. Suggest you call first, many tourist homes offer a free pick-up service from the bus depot. Beware of taxi drivers who try and take you to motels or the more expensive tourist homes. 'If arriving on the US side be aware that it's a 45 mins walk with bags and there are no buses.' For accommodation assistance, phone the visitors centre on 356-6061. NB: Rates increase at weekends and during the summer.

Edgecliffe Motel, 4181 Queen St (at River Rd), 354-1688. From D-$30 (Sep onwards)—$70. Up to 4 people. Pool, free breakfast coffee.

Henri's Motel, 4671 River Rd, 358-6573. Will try to put people who arrive on their own into a dbl. room to bring down cost. D/T/Q-$45-65. 'Very friendly.' 'Decent rooms.'

Maple Leaf Motel, 6163 Buchanan Ave, 354-0841. 'Near Falls and very comfortable.' S/D-$50.

Olympia Motel, 5099 Centre St, 356-2614. 'They gave us a student discount.' From S-$59, D-$69, less for longer stays. 'Very friendly.'

HI-Niagara Falls Hostel, 4549 Cataract Ave, (888) 749-0058 / 357-0770. 2 blocks E of bus and train stations; 30 min walk to Falls. Amenities include 2 kitchens, common area, bike rentals, laundry facilities and lockers. Discounts available at the Maid of the Mist, the Whirlpool Jetboat and other locations. Diners, grocery stores and post offices in the vicinity. 'Very cosy and friendly.' $16.

Niagara Falls Backpackers International Inn, 4219 Huron St at Zimmerman, 357-4266. $18. Nr bus sta. 20 mins to Falls. 'Friendly welcome.'

Camping: King Waldorf Tent & Trailer Park, 9015 Stanley Ave near Marineland, 295-8191. 4 miles from Falls. 'Very friendly, Scottish owner, 2 pools, laundry, free showers.' $24 for two, XP-$3. May-Oct.

Riverside Park, 9 miles S on Niagara River Pkwy (on Niagara River banks), 382-2204. Laundry, pool, showers. Sites $20 for four w/hook-up. May-Oct.

OF INTEREST

The **Explorers Passport Plus**, $18.65 allows a combined entrance for three of the Niagara attractions (although not the most famous—the *Maid of the Mist*) and unlimited travel on the **People Mover** buses that travel Apr-Oct on a 19 mile loop between the Falls and Quesston Heights Park. The attractions are the Great Gorge Adventures, Journey Behind the Falls and the Niagara Spanish Aero car. Information on (877) 642-7275 / 371-0254, or *www.niagaraparks.com*

Casino Niagara, 5705 Falls Ave, (888) 946-3255. If you have travelled all the way to one of the seven natural wonders of the world and want to stay inside and lose all your money—this is the place for you! Newly opened and a big draw for many American visitors. Open 24 hrs, must be over 19. *www.casinoniagara.com*

Great Gorge Adventures, 4330 River Road, 374-1221, scenic boardwalk alongside the whitewater rapids, $5. Apr-Oct only, 3km from Horseshoe Falls.

Journey Behind the Falls, 356-8448. Elevator and walk through tunnels from Table Rock House, $6. Daily 9am-10.30pm, shorter hours during winter. 'Very amusing.' 'Worth it to hear and feel the force of the Falls.' 'Amazing.'

Maid of the Mist boat trip, 358-5781. The boats pass directly underneath the Falls. Waterproofs provided. 'Make sure yours is dry or you'll be miserable.' $10.65. Definitely recommended. 'Most memorable thing I did in North America.' Boats run every 15 mins. Daily 9am-7pm Apr-Oct.

Marineland, 8375 Stanley Ave, 356-8250. Dolphin and sealion shows, killer whales and rides. 'Rollercoaster, Dragon's Mouth, incredible.' $26.95. Daily 9am-6pm.

Minolta Tower, 356-1501. 665 ft tall with a restaurant at the top. $6.95. Open till 11.30pm.

Niagara Helicopters, 3137 Victoria Ave, 357-5672. $80 for a 9 min tour. 'Expensive, but an amazing experience and impressive views.' *www.niagara-helicopters.com* has a $10 discount voucher.

Niagara Spanish Aero Car, (877) 642-7275 / 356-2241. Cable car crossing the Niagara river 3 miles from the Falls, views of the whirlpools below. $5.25, open daily Apr-Dec.

Skylon Tower, 5200 Robinson St, 356-2651. One of the tallest concrete structures in the world. See-through elevator; revolving restaurant at 500 ft. 'Arrive first around sunset and see the Falls floodlit by night and then by day.' 'Excellent view.' $7.95. Daily 10am-10pm winter, 8am-1am summer.

Nearby Niagara-by-the-Lake; Fort George, 468-4257. Reconstructed 18th century military post. Daily 10am-5pm, May-Oct only, $6. The **Shaw Festival**, Apr-Nov annually is the season of George Bernard Shaw productions. Tkts from $35, $15 for lunchtime theatre. Call box office on (800) 511-7429 / 468-2172. *www.shawfest.sympatico.com*

INFORMATION

Visitors and Convention Centre, 5515 Stanley Ave, (800) 563-2557 / 356-6061. 'We phoned here as suggested and the helpful staff provided us with various names and numbers of places to enquire regarding cheap accommodation. Very successful!' Daily 9am-5pm, Wknds till 6pm.

TRAVEL

VIA Rail Canada, 366-8411, 2 hr journey from Toronto to the Falls. $49 day rtn ($32 if bought 5 days in advance). 'A great day trip.' 'Don't catch shuttle bus from station to the Falls. It costs $3.75 and it's only a 10 min walk.'

KITCHENER-WATERLOO   A little bit of Germany lives exiled in Kitchener-Waterloo, a community delighting in beer halls and beer fests. The highlight of the year is the Oktoberfest, a week-long festival of German bands, beer, parades, dancing, sporting events and more beer.

Waterloo is often referred to as the 'Hartford of Canada' since the town is headquarters of a number of national insurance companies. The best days to visit K-W (a fairly easy 69-mile excursion from Toronto) are Wednesday and Saturday in time for the farmers' market where black-bonneted and gowned Amish and Mennonite farming ladies and their menfolk sell their crafts and fresh-picked produce. Sixteen miles north at **Elmira**, there's the annual Maple Syrup Festival, held in the spring.*www.kw-visitor.on.ca* *The area code is 519.*

ACCOMMODATION

There are plenty of reasonable motels on Victoria Street in Kitchener. Res rec during the Oktoberfest.

Kitchener Motel 1485 Victoria St N, 745-1177. From D-$50.

Wilfrid Laurier University, 75 University Ave. W, **Waterloo**, 884-1970. May-Aug 20th (approx.), $30.

Camping: See **Bingemans,** below. $24-26 without hook-up—3 day packages avail. incl. waterpark entrance, from $90.

OF INTEREST

Kitchener is the site of **Woodside National Historic Park**, 528 Wellington St, 571-5684, boyhood home of **William Lyon Mackenzie King**, Prime Minister from 1921-1930 and 1935-1948. His former home and grounds are open to the public during the summer, 10am-5pm daily, May-Dec. $2.50, $1.50 w/student ID.

Bingemans, 1380 Victoria St North, **Kitchener**, (800) 565-4631 / 744-1555. Water park featuring wave pool, water slides, bumper boats etc. $18.95, $12.95 after 5pm, or pay as you go for individual attractions. Open daily 10am-8pm. *www.bingemans.com*

Doon Heritage Crossroads, RR2, **Kitchener**, 748-1914. Re-creation of rural Waterloo County village of 1914. Daily May-Dec 10am-4.30pm, after Labour Day only Mon-Fri. $6, $3.50 w/student ID.

Oktoberfest, K-W Oktoberfest Inc., PO Box 1053, **Kitchener**, 570-4267. Now attracts more than 700,000 people annually for 9 days of celebration, early Oct. Festival halls and tents serving frothy steins of beer and sauerkraut, oompah music, Miss Oktoberfest Pageant, archery tournament, ethnic dance performances, beer barrel races! $5 or up to $30 for an all-you-can-eat-all-night Bavarian smorgasbord.

INFORMATION
Kitchener Chamber Tourism, 80 Queen St N, Kitchener, (800) 265-6959 / 745-3536.

GEORGIAN BAY ISLANDS NATIONAL PARK
A good way north of Toronto on the way to Sudbury, this is one of Canada's smallest national parks. It consists of 59 islands or parts of islands in Georgian Bay. The largest of the islands, **Beausoleil**, is just five miles square, while all the rest combined add only two-fifths of a mile. Hiking (trails on Beausoleil Island), swimming, fishing and boating are the name of the game in the park.

The special feature of the park is the remarkable geological formations. The mainly Precambrian rock is more than 600 million years old and there are a few patches of sedimentary rock carved in strange shapes by glaciers.

Midland is the biggest nearby town for services and accommodation but boats to Beausoleil Island go from **Honey Harbour**, a popular summer resort off Rte 103. On Beausoleil, once the home of the Chippewa Indians, there are several campsites. /.$3 Park Entrance fee from May-Sep. *www.huronet.com*

The telephone area code is 705.

ACCOMMODATION
Chalet Motel, on Little Lake, 748 Yonge St W, **Midland**, 526-6571. From S-$65, D-$72.

Park Villa Motel, 751 Yonge St W, adjoining Little Lake Pk, **Midland**, (800) 257-0428 / 526-2219. From S-$48, D-$52. Heated pool.

Camping: Many campgrounds within the Park, one of the most popular is **Cedar Spring Campground**, nr the Visitors Centre, on **Beausoleil**, $15, most other campgrounds $11. Need to take a water taxi onto the island, a number of companies will do this, try **Honey Harbour Boat Club**, 756-2411, $32 each way, res rec.

OF INTEREST
30,000 Island Cruise, at Midland Dock. 2$^1/_2$ hr trip among the islands of Georgian Bay at 10.45am, 1.45pm, 4.30pm (from June-Sep) and 7.15pm (mid July-Sep). $15. Call for rsvs and info on 526-0161 ext. 310.

Huronia Museum and Indian Village, 549 Little Lake Park Rd, **Midland**, 526-2844. Daily summer 9am-6pm, till 5pm winter. Last admission leaves an hour before close. $6. Human history of the area.

Sainte-Marie Among the Hurons, 3 miles E of **Midland** on Hwy 12, 526-7838. Re-creation of Jesuit mission which stood here 1639-1649 plus Huron longhouses, cookhouse, blacksmith, etc. Orientation centre offers a film about the mission and the excavation work involved in the project. Daily Apr-Oct 10am-5pm (last admission 4.45pm). $9.75, $6.25 w/student ID.

Wye Marsh Wildlife Centre, Hwy 12, 3 miles E of **Midland**, 526-7809. Guided tours, animals, exhibits, floating boardwalk. Daily 10am-6pm, 4pm in winter. $5.

INFORMATION
Georgian Bay Islands National Park, Box 28, Honey Harbour, ON, P0E 1E0, 756-2415.
Midland Chamber of Commerce, 208 King St, (800) 263-7745 / 526-7884. Mon-Fri 9am-6pm, Sat/Sun 9am-6pm.

LONDON   Not to be outdone by the other London back in Mother Britain, this one also has a River Thames flowing through the middle of the city. London, Ontario, also has its own Covent Garden Market. It's a town of comfortable size, and a commercial and industrial centre. Labatt's Brewery is perhaps the town's most famous industry.

London also offers the visitor a thriving cultural life. It is physically a pleasant spot, known as 'Forest City,' and is situated midway between Toronto and Detroit. The University of Western Ontario is here and is said to have the most beautiful campus of any Canadian university. You will find it on the banks of the Thames, in the northern part of the city.

London Pageone is the definitive guide to the city of London; *www.london.page1.org/. The area code for London is 519.*

ACCOMMODATION
For B&B accommodations priced from $45-$75 a night, contact the **London Area B&B Association**, own B&B is about 5 miles out of town, they also make res for others; 851-9988.
Uni of Western Ontario, Alumni House, University Drive, Housing Services, 661-3547. Features include laundry, pool, continental bfast. Rsvs required. From S-$28 student, $35 non-student. May-Aug.

FOOD
Fatty Patty's, 207 King St, 438-7281. Burgers, fries and salads in huge portions. Mon 11am-7pm, Tue-Sat till 9pm, closed Sun.
Joe Kool's, 595 Richmond St, 663-5665 'right in centre—ask a local.' Tortillas, burgers, etc.; 'good music.' Open till 1am Sun-Thu, 2am Fri/Sat.
Prince Albert's Diner, Richmond St at Prince Albert, 432-2835. 50s-style diner with great cheap meals.
Spageddy Eddy, 428 Richmond St, 645-3002. Copious canneloni, seas of spaghetti with lashings of lasagne. Tue-Sun 11am-9pm.

OF INTEREST
Children's Museum, 21 Wharncliffe Road South, 434-5726. World cultures, communications, music and crafts. Children and adults alike can explore, experiment and engage their imaginations. More up-to-the-minute experiences can be enjoyed in the computer hall, at the photosensitive wall or the zoetrope. 'Excellent.' Mon-Sat 10am-5pm, Sun from noon; winter closed Mon; $4.
Double Decker Bus Tour of London, (800) 265-2602 / 661-5000. 2 hr city tours during the summer months.
Eldon House, 481 Ridout St, 672-4580. London's oldest house and now a historical museum, and close by **London Regional Art Gallery**, 421 Ridout St N. Both Tue-Sun noon-5pm, donation only.
Fanshawe Pioneer Village, 2609 Fanshawe Pk Rd E, off Clarke Rd, 457-1296. Recreation of 19th century pre-railroad village. Log cabins, etc. Daily 10am-4.30pm; $5, $4 w/student ID.
Museum of Indian Archaeology and Lawson Prehistoric Indian Village, 1600 Attawandaron Rd, 473-1360. Museum contains artefacts from various periods of Native Canadian history—projectiles, pottery shards, effigies, turtle rattles etc. On-site reconstructed Attawandaron village. Daily 10am-4.30pm. $3.50, $2.75 w/student ID.

Royal Canadian Regiment Museum, Wolseley, on Canadian Forces Base, London, 660-5102. History of Canadian forces from 1883. Tue-Fri 10am-4pm, Sat, Sun from noon. Free.

ENTERTAINMENT
Barney's, 671 Richmond St, 432-1232. The local hangout which attracts the young professional crowd. Cheap draught beer in the Ceeps. Arrive early to get a spot on the patio in the summer.
Call the Office, 216 York St, 432-4433, east of Richmond. Live bands.
Grand Theatre, 471 Richmond St, 672-9030. Features drama, comedy and musicals from mid-Oct-May. The theatre itself, built in 1901, is worth viewing.
The Spoke Tavern, Somerville House, University of Western Ontario, 661-3590. A popular campus pub.
Western Fairgrounds, Home of the **Western Fair**, an agricultural show with rides and games. Held annually in mid-September. **Harness racing** takes place from Oct-June Wed, Fri and Sat. Call 438-7203 for more info.

INFORMATION
Tourism London, 696 Wellington Rd S, 681-4047. Daily 8am-8pm, Sep-May Fir-Sun only, 10am-1pm & 2pm-6pm.
Visitors and Convention Services, 300 Dufferin Ave, City Hall, 661-5000. Daily 8.30am-4.30pm.

TRAVEL
Greyhound, 101 York at Talbot, (800) 661-8747.
U-Need-A-Cab, 438-2121.
VIA Rail, on York east of Richmond, 672-5722.

STRATFORD
In 1953 this average-sized manufacturing town, on the banks of the River Avon some 50 kilometres north of London, held its first Shakespearean festival. The now world-renowned season has become an annual highlight on the Ontario calendar. The festival lasts for six months of the year, from May-Nov, attracting some of the best Shakespearean actors and actresses, as well as full houses every night.

Based in the Festival Theatre, but encompassing several other theatres too, the festival includes opera, original contemporary drama and music, as well as the best of the Bard. In September the town also hosts an international film festival.

There's not much else of interest in Stratford except a walk along the riverside gardens and a look at the swans. Heading west there is **Point Pelee National Park** before going to Windsor and crossing to the US. For online info to 'The Shakespearean Festival City,' hook-up to *www.sentex.net/~lwr/strat.html. The telephone code is 519.*

ACCOMMODATION
The Festival Theatre provides an accommodation service during the summer. You are advised to contact them first, call 271-4040. Also, the **Festival Accommodations Bureau**, 273-1600, can tell you where to go.
Burnside Guest Home, 139 William St, 271-7076. Turn of the century home, this is the budget traveller's best bet and offers a great view of Lake Victoria. B&B rooms $50-70; student rooms $35; call ahead.
Camping: Wildwood Conservation Area, 7 miles W on Hwy 7, 284-2292. Access to beach, pool and marina. Tent sites $19, open May-Oct.

ENTERTAINMENT

Art in the Park, Lakeside & Front Sts, June-Sep outdoor exhibitions of art and crafts for sale.

Festival Theatre, (800) 567-1600 / 273-1600. Tkts from $21-69, Festival Theatre, Third Stage and Avon Theatre. The Festival Theatre is at 55 Queen St, Avon Theatre on Downie St, Third Stage on Lakeshore. Order from: Festival Box Office, PO Box 520, Stratford, ON, N5A 6V2. Special student matinees ($11-13) in Sep and Oct often swamped by high school parties. 'Get there early on the day of the performance for returns.'

Jazz on the River, Mon & Fri eves from 6.30-8pm, mid-June to early Sep.

Lake Victoria, (Avon River) at the middle of town, offers tranquillity to take in the outstanding views and have a leisurely stroll.

Stratford Farmers' Market, Coliseum Fairground, Sat mornings.

INFORMATION

Tourism Stratford, 1 York St, (800) 561-7926, open Tue-Sat 9am-8pm, Sun/Mon 9am till 5pm, during the festival season. At other times, there is another office at 88 Wellington St, top floor, 271-5140. Mon-Fri 8.30am-4pm. Will send free a visitors guide if you call ahead; willing to help walk-ins. *www.city.stratford.on.ca*

POINT PELEE NATIONAL PARK About 35 miles from Windsor, Point Pelee is a V-shaped sandspit which juts out into Lake Erie. On the same latitude as California, the park is the southernmost area of the Canadian mainland.

Only six square miles in area, Point Pelee is a unique remnant of the original deciduous forests of North America. Two thousand acres of the park are a freshwater swamp and the wildlife found here is unlike anything else to be seen in Canada. On the spring and fall bird migration routes, the park is a paradise for ornithologists. There are also several strange fish to be seen and lots of turtles and small water animals ambling around.

Point Pelee is quite developed as a tourist attraction and there are numerous nature trails, including a one-mile boardwalk trail. Canoes and bicycles can be rented during the summer months and the Visitor Centre has maps, exhibits, slide shows and other displays about the park. Entrance to the park is $3.25. There is no camping in Point Pelee, although there are two sites in the nearby town of Leamington. Park info: 322-2365.

SUDBURY Sudbury is some 247 miles northwest of Toronto and the centre of one of the richest mining areas in the world. The city is often referred to as the 'nickel capital of the world' due to the proliferation of the mineral to be found close to the surface. The local Chamber of Commerce will tell you that Sudbury enjoys more hours of sunshine per year than any other city in Ontario (and we have no reason to doubt them), but this is not a pretty area. Part of the empty landscape looks so like a moonscape that American astronauts came here to rehearse lunar rock collection techniques before embarking on the real thing. Be sure to see the lunar landscape of Sudbury basin, a geological mystery that may have been caused by a gigantic meteor or volcanic eruption.

Away from the immediate vicinity of the town there are scores of lakes, rivers and untracked forests to refresh the soul after witnessing the ravages of civilisation.

The telephone area code is 705.

ACCOMMODATION

Cheapest in the Ukrainian District, around Kathleen St. Your other best bets for lodgings are the chains—**Comfort Inn**, **Ramada Inn**, **Venture Inn** and **Sheraton Caswell Inn.**

Laurentian University, Ramsey Lake Rd, 673-6597. They are helpful and provide accommodation in summer till the beginning of Aug, $28.

Plaza Hotel, 1436 Bellevue St, 566-8080. For the very budget conscious only—rents by the week only, mainly for transient workers, approx. $65 per week. Not recommended.

OF INTEREST

There is really only one attraction; **Science North,** 100 Ramsey Lake Rd, 1 mile from Hwy 69 S, (800) 461-4898 / 522-3701. Has a number of exhibits, mainly located at this site. The **Science Centre,** inside you can conduct experiments, such as simulating a hurricane, monitoring earthquakes on a seismograph, or observing the sun through a solar telescope. Also, a water playground, space exploration and weather command centres, and a fossil identification workshop. There is an **IMAX Theatre**, **Virtual Voyages** simulator ride, a cruise on **Lake Ramsey**, and a 10 min drive away, **Big Nickel Mine,** at Hwy 17 West & Big Nickel Mine Dr. Tour of the mine and surface exhibits. Summer hours are 9am-6pm, winter 10am-4pm, daily. May change for individual exhibits and holidays. Single 'attractions' range from $6.50-$9.95 each or an all day passport is $24.95. There is a website at; *sciencenorth.on.ca*

INFORMATION/TRAVEL

Convention and Visitors Service, 200 Brady St, Tom Davies Sq, (800) 708-2505 / 673-4161.

SAULT STE MARIE First established in 1669 as a French Jesuit mission, Sault Ste Marie later became an important trading post in the heyday of the fur trade. Today 'The Soo,' as locals call the town, oversees the great locks and canals that bypass St Mary's Rapids. The **Soo Locks**, connecting Lake Superior with St Mary's River and Lake Huron, allow enormous Atlantic ocean freighters to make the journey 1748 miles inland. From special observation towers visitors can watch the ships rising and falling up to 40 ft.

The town is connected to its US namesake across the river in Michigan by an auto toll bridge. If you're going north from here, 'think twice about hitching.' Lifts are hard to come by, the road is long and empty. It's probably best to get as far beyond **Wawa** as possible. Thunder Bay is 438 miles away to the northwest. Two of the most popular local events are the **Bon Soo Winter Carnival**, which runs from January to February, and the **Northern Triathlon** in August. From late September to mid-October, the foliage colours are spectacular and the weather is perfect for hiking. Ideally, see it all from the **Algoma Central Railway.** *www.sault-canada.com/. Telephone area code is 705.*

ACCOMMODATION / FOOD

Whatever you do, make your lodging reservations in advance.

Algoma Cabins & Motel, 1713 Queen St E, 256-8681. From D-$47, cabins $63, weekly rates available.

Algonquin Hotel (HI-C), 864 Queen St E, 253-2311. A youth hostel, but all private rooms. Cooking facilities, linen included, on-site parking, bar / restaurant. From S-$21 (AYH members)—D-$35.

Ambassador Motel, 1275 Great Northern Road (Hwy 17), 759-6199. From D-$69. Heated indoor pool

Camping: KOA Sault Ste Marie, W on 5th line off Hwy 17, (5m north of town), 759-2344. $21.50 without hook-up.

For food, try **Ernie's Coffee Shop**, 13 Queen St. 'Big, cheap meals, excellent value.'

OF INTEREST

Agawa Canyon Train, (800) 242-9287 / 946-7300. Runs on the Algoma Central Railway. Central Railway Station, Bay St, next to Station Mall on the waterfront. Day trip north through spectacular scenery, or the entire line takes about 2 days, to the town of **Hearst**. Around $50 for the day trip, res rec, esp. in the autumn.

Ermantinger Old Stone House, 831 Queen St E, 759-5443. Completed 1814 and a rare example of early Canadian architecture, costumed guides will tell you all about Ermantinger, a fur trader, who married an Indian Princess and lived in the house with their 13 children. Daily 10am-5pm. $2.

Lake Superior Provincial Park. A fair ride north of here up Hwy 17—some 130 kms—but nonetheless worth the trip to this rugged wilderness park. Includes nature trails, moose hunting in season, Indian rock paintings, beaches, dozens of small lakes, canoeing and hiking. Three main campsites. Park can be accessed from Agawa Canyon Train. Call park info on 856-2284.

Lock Tours Canada Boat Cruises, 253-9850. 2 hr cruises through the American (one of the world's busiest) and the Canadian locks. Departs from the Roberta Bondar Pavilion on the waterfront. Also takes in St Mary's River. Runs daily in summer, $17.

Waterfront Boardwalk 759-5311, from the glamorous sounding Great Lakes Power Plant to the **Roberta Bondar Park.** The latter is the site of a huge tent-like pavilion. Farmers Market held here on Wed & Sat during the summer.

INFORMATION

Sault Ste Marie Chamber of Commerce, 334 Bay St, 949-7152.

THUNDER BAY On the northern shore of Lake Superior and an amalgam of the towns of Port Arthur and Fort William, Thunder Bay is the western Canadian terminus of the Great Lakes/St Lawrence Seaway system and Canada's third largest port. Port Arthur is known as Thunder Bay North and Fort William is Thunder Bay South. The towns are the main outlet for Prairies grain and have a reputation for attracting swarms of huge, and hungry, black flies during the summer.

The city's new name was selected by plebiscite and is derived from the name of the bay and Thunder Cape, 'The Sleeping Giant,' a shoreline landmark. Lake Superior is renowned for its frequent thunderstorms and since in Indian legend the thunderbird was responsible for thunder, lightning and rain, that was how the bay got its name. The city is 450 miles from Winnipeg to the west, and about the same distance from Sault Ste Marie to the southeast.

For those essential listings and information on special events and recreational activities, go to *www.tourism.thunder-bay.on.ca/*.

The telephone area code is 807.

ACCOMMODATION

Circle Inn Motel, 686 Memorial Ave, 344-5744. 'Reasonably close to the bus terminal.' From S-$71, D-$73.

Confederation College (Hi-C), Sibley Hall Residence, 960 William St, 475-6381. Mid May-mid Aug only. From $10. res req.

Pinebrook B&B, Mitchell Rd (Hwy 527 left on Mitchell Rd on Pine Dr), 683-6114. D-$55-75.

Thunder Bay Backpackers Hostel, 1594 Lakeshore Dr & McKenzie Stn Rd, 983-

2042. Hostel is a central point in the **Backpackers Hostels Canada** network. Run by world travellers and teachers, full of artefacts from around the world. 'World class skiing.' The owner is more than happy to provide information on places to stay all over the country. 'Friendly, warm hostel, baths, TV.' 'The best in Canada.' Close to Sleeping Giant. $17, all private rooms. Tent sites $12, for two $16. email: *candu@microage-tb.com*; website: *www.backpackers.ca*. If coming from the east ask bus driver to let you off at the hostel.

Camping: Chippewa Park, south off Hwy 61, 623-3912. A wooded park on Lake Superior with a sandy beach, picnic grounds, a fun fair and wildlife exhibit. Daily, late June-Sep. $14 without hook-up.

OF INTEREST

Amethyst Mine. 35 miles on Trans-Canada Hwy, then north on E Loon Lake Rd, 622-6908. Self-guided or guided tour, gift shop. Daily May-Oct 10am-7pm; $3.

Centennial Park, Centennial Park Rd, east of Arundel St, 683-5762. Animal farm, a museum and a reproduction of a typical northern Ontario logging camp of the early 1900s. Daily 10am-7pm summer, till 5pm winter. Free.

Hillcrest Park, High St. A lookout point with a panoramic view of Thunder Bay Harbour and the famous **Sleeping Giant,** he of the Indian folk legends from whom the town derives its name. Impressively visible across the bay in Lake Superior.

Old Fort William. On the banks of the Kaministiquia River, 577-8461. Once a major outpost of the North West Trading Company, now a 'living' reconstruction. Craft shops, farm, dairy, naval yard, Indian encampment, breadmaking, musket firing, etc. Daily 9am-5pm. $10, $8 w/student ID. *www.oldfortwilliam.com*

Thunder Bay Museum, 425 E Donald St, 623-0801. Indian artefacts and general pioneering exhibits. Tue-Sat 1pm-5pm (winter), daily June-Aug 11am-5pm. $2, pay-what-you-can on Sat.

INFORMATION

Tourism Thunder Bay, 500 E Donald St, (800) 667-8386.

Pagoda Info Centre, Water St, 345-6812. 8.30am-8.30pm daily in summer, otherwise 9am-5pm.

TRAVEL

Greyhound, 815 Fort William Rd, by SKAFF, 345-2194. Open daily, $117 to Toronto o/w (book 7 days in advance).

Harbour cruises from Port Arthur Marina, Arthur St, 344-2512. Several cruises, daily, mid-May to Oct, from $14. Call for exact times.

ONTARIO'S NORTHLANDS
Going north out of Toronto on the Trans-Canada Hwy, you can carry on round the lakes westwards to Sudbury, Sault Ste Marie and Thunder Bay, or else, at Orillia, you can get on to Rte 11 which will take you due north up to North Bay, and from there to Ontario's little-explored north country. **North Bay** is 207 miles from Toronto and is a popular vacation spot as well as the accepted jumping off point for the polar regions.

There's not much in North Bay itself, but there is ready access to the **Algonquin Provincial Park,** a vast area of woods and lakes good for hiking, canoeing and camping, and also to **Lake Nipissing.** Pressing north, however, there is **Temagami,** a hunting, fishing, lumbering, mining and out-fitting centre. The Temagami Provincial Forest was the province's pioneer forest, established in 1901 and providing mile upon mile of sparkling lakes and rugged forests. It's quiet country up here; even with modern communication systems, people are few. It's also mining country.

Cobalt is the centre of a silver mining area and **Timmins** is the largest silver and zinc producing district in the world. You can visit mines and mining museums in both towns.

At **Cochrane**, 207 miles north of North Bay, the northbound hwy runs out, and the rest of the way is by rail. The **Polar Bear Express** runs daily during July & Aug except Fri, up to Moosonee on James Bay, covering the 186 miles in $4^{1}/_{2}$ hrs (approx. $48 rtn). After September, the **Little Bear** does the same route (approx. $79 rtn). It's a flag stop train so will stop anywhere; hail a train the way you would a taxi! Except it only runs three times a week; Mon, Wed & Fri northwards, southbound a day later. Rsvs required, call (800) 268-9281 / (416) 314-3750. It's a marvellous ride, the train packed with an odd assortment of people, everyone from tourists to miners, missionaries, geologists and adventurers. **Moosonee** counts as one of the last of the genuine frontier towns and is accessible only by rail or air. Since 1673 when the Hudson Bay Company established a post on nearby Moose Factory Island, this has been an important rendezvous for fur traders and Indians. It's also a good place to see the full beauty of the Aurora Borealis.

This is as far north as most people get, but there's still a lot of Ontario lapped by Arctic seas. Over 250 miles north of Moosonee, accessible only by air, is **Polar Bear Provincial Park**. This is a vast area of tundra and sub-arctic wilderness. The summer is short and the climate severe. The rewards of a visit here can be great however. There are polar bears, black bears, arctic foxes, wolves, otters, seals, moose and many other varieties of wildlife.

ACCOMMODATION

All the towns mentioned above have small hotels or motels, none of them especially cheap however. If planning to come this far off the beaten track, it is advisable to give yourself plenty of time to find places to stay. Remember that if everything is full in one town your next options may be several hours' driving further down the road. There are many campgrounds in this part of Ontario, but again the distances between them are often considerable.

Orillia; Orillia Home Hostel (HI-C), 198 Borland St E, (705) 325-0970, $13. Close to bus and train station, kitchen, laundry etc.

Algonquin area: Portage Hostel, 1352 Barren Canyon Rd, **Pembroke**, (613) 735-1795. $25, open year round.

The Portage Store, Box 10009, Algonquin Park, **Huntsville**, (705) 765-5784. Not a traditional hostel, but an outfitting company. Tents are provided, canoeing, trekking and mosquitoes! Best park scenery in Ontario, moose and other wildlife.

Temagami area: Temagami Hostel, Smoothwater Outfitters, Box 40, Temagami, (705) 569-3539. Located 14km N of the town, on Hwy 11. Canoe rentals, cross-country skiing. $25.

QUÉBEC

Québec is the largest province in Canada—its area is seven times that of the United Kingdom—and it really has a character all its own. The vast majority of French Canadians live here in La Belle Province, and the French culture is apparent in all walks of life—from the French-only street signs in Montréal and Québec City to the smaller, rural towns where the only language you'll hear is French interspersed with expressions in 'joual'—a dialect used mostly in Northern Québec. Some Québeçois may seem reluctant to speak English to the visitor; in the bigger cities, however, the shopkeepers will understand enough to serve you, and you may find the younger Québeçois eager to practice their English.

The name of the province is derived from the Algonquin Indian word 'Kebec,' meaning 'where the river narrows'. This reference to the St Lawrence River indicates both the important role the river played in the development of the province in the 18th and 19th centuries and its continued importance for Québec's economy today. Four-fifths of the province lies within the area of the barren Canadian Shield to the north. The atmosphere in the smaller, unassuming rural towns contrasts sharply with the cosmopolitan sophistication of Montréal and the Old World charm of Québec City. *www.yahoo.com/Regional/Countries/Canada/Provinces_and_Territories/Quebec.* **National Parks**: Forillon, La Mauricie, Minguan Archipelago, Saguenay-St Lawrence Marine Park.

MONTRÉAL Canada's largest city is built around the mountain, Mount Royal, from which it derives its name. Located on the archipelago at the junction of the Outaouais and Saint-Laurent Rivers, Montréal is a natural meeting point for overland and water passages.

Jacques Cartier arrived here in 1535 to find a large Indian settlement, Hochelaga, believed to have been where McGill University now stands. When Champlain arrived, nearly 100 years later, the Indians had gone, and the French subsequently settled there. Their city is now one of the world's greatest inland ports, boasting some 14 miles of berthing space. Since the opening of the St Lawrence Seaway in 1959, the city's port-based industries have greatly expanded and increased, making Montréal one of North America's most important commercial, industrial and economic centres.

More than two-fifths of the total population of Québec live in the Montréal metropolitan area. Two-thirds of Montréalers speak French, and as a result their city is second only to Paris in terms of French-speaking population.

Host city for Expo '67 and the 1976 Summer Olympics, Montréal is forever improving, expanding, renovating. Theatre and the arts flourish. There is always something to do here, and Montréalers consider their city to provide the best of everything in Canada—the best restaurants, shopping, nightclubs, the best bagels, and the best smoked-meat sandwiches (the last of which may in fact be true). This is a cosmopolitan vibrant city whose liveliness is epitomised in Vieux Montréal, on Crescent Street, or on Rue St Denis where you can mingle with the French Canadians and discover a part of the culture and joie de vivre that is neither North American, nor European, but unique unto itself. Walking tours, restaurants and other insights can be found at *Montreal—A Celebration*; the website is at *www.cam.org/~vpress/montreal.html*
The telephone area code is 514.

ACCOMMODATION

For info regarding hostels, hotel and *chambres touristiques* (rooms in private homes or small guest houses), your best resources are the **Québec Tourist Office**, the **B&B Breakfast à Montréal** network, PO Box 575, Snowdon Station, H3X 3T8, 738-9410;

and the **Downtown B&B Network**, 3458 Rue Laval, H2X 3C8, (800) 267-5180, which lists homes available downtown. Wander down **Rue St-Denis** for least expensive options. *Tourisme Quebec* will send an excellent list of accommodation for the whole province; (800) 363-7777 if calling within Canada / USA, 864-3838 from elsewhere. On the web, see *www.bbcanada* for a list of many B&Bs.

Alternative Backpackers of Old Montréal, 358 Rue St Pièrre, 282-8069. 'The best hostel I've stayed in, right in the old town. Decor inside very arty. Spacious, clean, very friendly owners. 24 hr access. Definitely recommended.' Dorms $17.

Auberge de Montréal (HI-C), 1030 Rue Mackay, 843-3317. Convenient location, great service and upbeat staff who will gladly assist with nightlife ideas and outings. Dorms each have private shower/toilet. Kitchen, A/C ride board and twice weekly pub crawl. 'Clean, safe, friendly.' $18. MUST be a HI member. Private rooms from around D-$50.

Hotel de Paris, 901 Rue Sherbrooke Est (hotel), and hostel across the street at 874 Rue Sherbourne, 522-6861. Renovated Victorian house, dorms $16, kitchen facilities, linen $2. 'Very cramped and no privacy.' S-$48-58, D-$68-80 for non-hostel private rooms. Nr Old Montréal.

Hotel Amèricain, 1042 Rue St-Denis, 849-0616. Highly recommended. 'Friendly people, large rooms, and close to Old Montréal.' From S-$42, D-$45.

Hotel la Residence du Voyageur, 847 Rue Sherbourne Est, 527-9515. S/D-$50-85, all rms have private bath, incl. bfast; free pkg. *wworks.com/~resvoyager/*

Hotel Le Breton, 1609 Rue St Hubert, 524-7273. 'A gem in the city's budget accommodation crown.' Clean, comfortable but rooms fill up quickly. S/D-$45-80, TV and A/C, shared or private bath. *www.contact.net/publix/breton/*

Hotel St-Denis, 1254 Rue St-Denis, (800) 363-3364 / 849-4526, in the heart of the latin quarter, prices include bfast, from S- $59, D-$65. *www.hotel-st-denis.com*

Hotel Travelodge Montreal Centre, 50 Blvd Rene Levesque Ouest, (800) 578-7878 / 874-9090. Next to Underground Montreal, rooms fit up to 4 people, S/D $60-100.

Maison André Tourist Rooms, 3511 Rue Université, 849-4092. 'Clean and comfortable.' Non-smokers pref. Satisfied guests have been returning every year. S-$26-35, D-$38-45, XP-$10. Rsvs recommended.

YMCA Downtown, 1450 Rue Stanley, 849-8393. Co-ed. Small rooms with TV and phone. Cafeteria open daily 7am-8pm. From S-$35, $2 discount w/student ID. Busy June-Aug. No rsvs June-Sep. From $28.

YWCA Hotel, 1355 Rue René Lévesque Blvd Ouest, 866-9941. Clean and safe, located downtown. Kitchen/TV on each floor, gym, laundry, lounge and computer room. From S-$22. Rsvs accepted. Women only. *www.ywca-mtl.qc.ca*

University Residences: NB: Both Concordia and McGill are English-speaking universities.

Collège Français (Vacances Canada 4 Saisons), 5155 Rue de Gaspé, 270-4459. 'Clean and simple.' Take Metro to Laurier. No laundry or kitchen. $12-13 dorm. Weekly rates available, open all year round.

Concordia University, 7141 Sherbrooke Ouest, 848-4755. S-$36, D-$48, w/student ID $27.

McGill University, Bishop Mountain Hall, 3935 Rue de l'Université, 398-6367. Shared washroom, laundry, kitchenettes, common room with TV and laundry. Garner bldg has best views. Full bfast $5 daily. $39, $32 w/student ID. Weekly rates available. Mid May-mid Aug only.

Université de Montréal, 2350 Rue Edouard-Montpetit, 343-6531. Easy access by bus. Located on the edge of a beautiful campus; East Tower has best views. 'Highly recommended for value, location, ambience and comfort.' Inexpensive cafeteria on campus. Laundry. Phone/sink in each room. Mid-May-August. $23-$38, discount w/student ID. Weekly rates available.

Camping: KOA Montréal-South, 130 Monette Blvd, St. Phillipe de Laprairie, 659-

8626. 15 miles from city, take Autoroute 15 S over Pont Champlain. Sites for two $19, XP-$4. Pool laundry, store, showers and daily shuttle available.

FOOD

For cheap eats, best to look within the **Rue St-Denis** area. St-Denis, the centre of numerous clubs, bars, cafes, and restaurants, reflects Montréal's French culture and is frequented by a heterogeneous group, including many students from neighbouring universities. A preppier crowd tends to gravitate towards Crescent St. There are many **Greek** restaurants on Prince Arthur Est between St Laurent and Carré St Louis. Definitely worth a try. Also, try perusing the free *Restaurant Guide*, published by the Greater Montréal Convention and Tourism Bureau, 844-5400, which gives ideas of where to go depending on what type of cuisine you fancy. Note: Rues Prince Arthur and Duluth both have 'bring your own wine' restaurants (Fr. *apportez vin*) who will cool and serve any bottle you bring. Great meals for $10.

Amelio's, 3565 Ave Lorne, 845-8396. Italian-style pizza and pasta, average meal $6-9. McGill 'ghetto,' 'intimate atmosphere.'

Ben's, 990 Maisonneuve Ouest, 844-1000. Cheap deli, open 24 hrs. Famous for its Montréal smoked meat. 'Cheerfully tacky deli which is packed at all hours.'

Carlos & Pepe's, 1420 Peel, 288-3090. Spicy assortment of Mexican delicacies—burritos, salsas, sangria plus a live band. Average meal $10-$15. Daily till 1am, except Thu-Sat till 3am.

L'Anecdote, 801 Rachel Est, 526-7967. Great burgers and vegetarian tofu hot dogs. Daily 9am-9.45pm.

La Cabanne, St Laurent, 843-7283. Cheapish shish-kabab-type food in good atmosphere. Upstairs is the Bar St Laurent where you can play pool and drink beer.

La Paryse, 302 Ontario E, 842-2040. 'Best hamburgers in Montréal.'

Le Faubourg Foodhall, 1616 Ste Catherine Ouest, 939-3603, filled with various cafes and shops selling fresh produce and serving Montréal Bagel Bakery.

Mazurka, 64 Prince Arthur Est, 844-3539. 'Good, cheap Polish and continental style food.' $5 specials.

Peel Pub, 1107 Ste Catherine Ouest, 844-7296. Old-fashioned tavern, serves fish and chips, beer by the pitcher. Big student hangout. Strongly recommended by past readers. 'The place to go if on a budget.' Bfast only a meagre $1.69. Daily specials, e.g. pizza, for 99¢.

Markets: Atwater Market, Marché Maisonneuve, Marché St Jacques and **Marché Jean-Talon** all sell everything from soup to boutiques, handmade articles, fast food and produce for your own preparation. Open daily. Go and haggle. For info on the markets, call the Admin offices for times; 937-7754.

OF INTEREST

NB: **Montreal Museum Pass** gives entry to 19 city museums. A one-day pass (if you could stand it) is $15, or a 3-day pass (valid over 21 days) is $28. Available from the **InfoTouriste Centre**, 1001 Dorchester Sq, at the museums themselves, or by calling 873-2015 / (800) 363-7777.

Vieux Montréal. Situated on the Lower Terrace, this area includes business and local government sectors. In recent times the buildings lining the old narrow streets have received facelifts, funds being provided from the public, as well as private, purse. The squares and streets are best explored on foot. **Notre-Dame De Bonsecours,** and **St Paul** make for pleasant strolls. Not to be missed, particularly if you don't plan to visit Québec City. During the summer months Montréalers are avid walkers and there is street activity until all hours of the night. Pick up excellent walking tour leaflets from the city's information bureaus. To get there: metro to Champ-de-Mars, Place d'Armes or Victoria.

The Upper Terrace. Flanking the southern edge of the mountain, the area includes a considerable part of the city stretching east and west for several miles. At its heart was the Indian town of Hochelaga, discovered by Cartier in 1535, standing not far

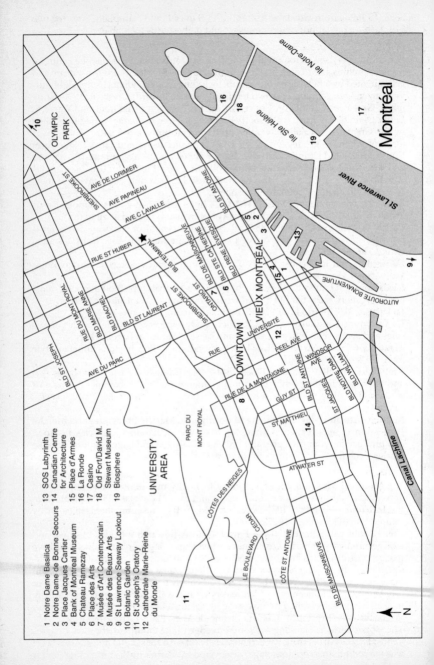

Montréal

1 Notre Dame Basilica
2 Notre Dame de Bonne Secours
3 Place Jacques Cartier
4 Bank of Montreal Museum
5 Chateau Ramezay
6 Place des Arts
7 Musée d'Art Contemporain
8 Musée des Beaux Arts
9 St Lawrence Seaway Lookout
10 Botanic Garden
11 St Joseph's Oratory
12 Cathedrale Marie-Reine
   du Monde
13 SOS Labyrinth
14 Canadian Centre
   for Architecture
15 Place d'Armes
16 La Ronde
17 Casino
18 Old Fort/David M.
   Stewart Museum
19 Biosphere

from the present site of **McGill University**. The high-rise area through which run **Rues Sherbrooke**, **Maisonneuve**, and **Ste Catherine**, and **Dorchester Blvd** is the urban centre where metro, bus and rail lines converge. It is also where the major hotels and shops are situated. Beyond Blvd St Laurent, Montréal is entirely French. On the western half of the Upper Terrace is the City of **Westmount**, famous for its stately mansions, fine churches and public buildings.

AML Cruises, 842-3871, 2 hour cruises on the St Laurent river, May-Oct daily, call for timings and res, $19.95.

Bank of Montréal Museum, 119 Rue St-Jacques Ouest, 877-6892. Coins, documents and general banking memorabilia tracing Montréal history as the country's financial centre. Mon-Fri 10am-4pm, closed noon-1pm. Free.

Botanical Garden and Insectarium, 4851 Rue Cherbourg Est, 872-1400. One of the most significant (2nd largest) in the world: 30 specialised gardens spread out over 65 acres, a vast complex of greenhouses, the largest collection of Bonsai and Penjing trees in the western world, a 1700 species orchid collection, a Japanese Garden and a Chinese Garden. **Insectarium** is unique in North America, it combines science and entertainment and is home to 350,000 insect specimens from 88 countries. Daily 9am-7pm, shorter in winter. $9.50 summer, $6.75 winter, $15 combined with Biodome.

Canadian Centre for Architecture, 1920 Rue Baile, 939-7000. This museum and architecture centre dedicated to the art of architecture is considered to be a world-class institution. Its collection includes 42,000 drawings and master prints, a library with 180,000 books, 50,000 photos as well as important archival finds. Tue-Sun 11am-6pm, Thu till 9pm; $6, w/student ID $3.50. Free for students on Thu. Closed Mon in summer, Mon/Tue in winter.

Canadian Railway Museum, 122A St-Pière (alias Rte 209) in **St Constant**, (450) 632-2410. 28 km from Montréal. Largest railway museum in Canada. 120 vehicles dating from 1863. Streetcar demonstrations daily. Bilingual tours geared to non-specialist. Note: public transport to St Constant is a disaster. Call museum to arrange group transportation. Daily 9am-5pm May-Labour Day, then wknds only till mid-Sep; $6.

Cathedrale Marie-Reine-Due-Monde, (Mary, Queen of the World), Rue de la Cathedrale on Dominion Sq. Small-scale version of St Peter's in Rome. Built 1878. Daily 7am-7pm.

Chapelle de Notre Dame de Bonsecours, 400 Rue St-Paul Est, 282-8670. Overlooking the harbour and known as the 'sailors' church.' Built in 1771 and the oldest church still standing in the city, it was once an important landmark for helmsmen navigating the river. There is a fine view from the top of the tower. It has been dedicated to sailors since the original chapel was erected in 1657.

Château Ramezay, 280 Rue Notre-Dame Est, 861-3708. Built in 1705 by Claude de Ramezay, a governor of Montréal, the building is a prime example of the architecture of the time and contains a wealth of furniture, engravings, oil paintings, costumes and other items relating to 18th century life. Open daily 10am-6pm, in winter till 4.30pm. Closed Mon Sep-May. $6, $3.50 w/student ID.

Lachine Rapid Jetboat Tours, 284-9607. From Clock Tower, 2 hr trips daily May-Oct, 10am-6pm; $49. 'Excellent fun.'

Museé d'Art Contemporain, 185 Rue Ste Catherine Ouest, 847-6226. The only institution of its type in Canada dedicated exclusively to all forms of contemporary art including paintings, sculpture, multimedia and performance art. Lots of temporary exhibits. Tue-Sun 11am-6pm, Wed till 9pm (free after 6pm), closed Mon. $8, $5 w/student ID.

Museé des Beaux-Arts, 1379 Rue Sherbrooke Ouest, 285-1600. The oldest established museum in Canada—founded in 1860—housed in a magnificent neo-classical edifice built in 1912. An extensive permanent collection, including many treasures and decorative arts which date from 3,000 BC. Sculpture Garden and terrace. Tue-Sun 11am-6pm, Wed till 9pm, half price admission form 5.30pm on Wed, closed Mon. $12, $6 w/student ID.

Notre Dame Basilica, Rue Notre Dame Ouest, 849-1070. Built in 1829, the wonderful vaulted starry ceiling, extraordinary wood work and beautiful stained-glass windows never fail to impress. Also houses one of the largest Casavant organs ever made. The gilded interior threatens to 'out-Pugin Pugin.' 'Interior decor is breathtaking.' June-Sep 7am-8pm; otherwise till 6pm. Tours available. Also houses a small museum, 842-2925, $2 entry fee.

Place Jacques Cartier. Once Montréal farmers' market, the restored **Bonsecours Market** building is on the south side of the square. This square also features the first monument to Nelson erected anywhere in the world. You can buy food at the stalls or sit at a street cafe and listen to a jazz band. 'Touristy.'

SOS Labyrinth, Old Port of Montreal, King Edward Pier, Hangar 109, 859-9030. A labyrinth—they change around the passageways weekly—to explore either by day or at night. 'Great fun; a really good way to spend an afternoon.' $8, or free if it's your birthday.

St Joseph's Oratory, 733-8211. On the north slope of Westmount Mountain which is separated by a narrow cleft from Mount Royal. The Oratory dome is a marked feature of the Montréal skyline. The world's largest pilgrimage centre, includes a remarkable 'way of the cross,' the original chapel and two museums containing memorabilia of founder Brother Andre and religious art. Also famous for its cures said to have been effected through the prayers of the 'Miracle Man of Montréal.' Daily 6am-10pm; free. Museum is open 10am-5pm. Donations appreciated. St. Joseph is the patron saint of Canada.

Underground City, entrance at Place Ville-Marie and various subway stations, 31 km of shops, transport and hotels.

Parks: Olympic Park, 4141 Pierre-de-Coubertin Ave., 252-4737. Site of the 1976 Olympic Games, the **Olympic Stadium** is now home to Montréal's baseball (the Expos) and soccer teams. Daily tours at 12.40pm & 3.40pm in English; $5.25, $4.25 w/student ID. 'Better value: savour a sporting event.' 'Very disappointing—certainly not worth the bother.' 'For lovers of modern architecture only.' 'Go and see a baseball game—much better than the tour.' Next door is the **Montreal Tower**, offering spectacular views and a cable car ride to the top of the world's tallest inclined tower. Open daily 10am-6pm winter, till 9pm Sun-Thu during the summer, and 11pm Fri/Sat; $9. Still within the Park is the **Biodôme**, 4777 Pierre-De-Coubertin Ave, 868-3000. Offers the chance to explore the 1001 wonders of Naturalia from all remote corners of the planet. Tropical Rainforest, Desert, Polar and Sea Worlds all under one dome. Daily 9am-5pm, till 8pm in summer. $9.50, w/student ID $7.

Parc des Iles is the name for the two smaller islands in the St Laurent river, connect to each other and the main island by bridges and the metro Ile Ste Helen. The park stretches over both islands; 'Take picnic for a quiet day away from the city.' Also houses many of the buildings for the 1967 Expo, and hiking / biking trails.

The larger island, **Ile Ste Helen** itself, is home to a number of attractions:-
Biosphere (not to be confused with the Biodome, above), 283-5000. Housed in part of the '67 Expo, the dome is concerned with the ecosystems of the St-Laurent river and great lakes, and all things watery. Open daily, May-Labour day, 10am-6pm, check timings for winter; $6.50, $5 w/student ID. The **Old Fort** and **David M Stewart Museum**, military and colonial history, open daily 10am-6pm (summer), till 5pm winter. $3. **La Ronde**, 872-872-4537, an amusement park at the eastern end of the island—'sensational waterskiing shows.' Rollercoaster, Le Monstre—'very scary.' Open wknds only in May, daily June-Sep 10.30am-11pm, $24. The second island, the **Ile Notre Dame** was man-made for the '67 Expo, and is home to the **Casino**, 392-2746.

Maisonneuve Park: 4601 Rue Sherbrooke Est, 525-acre park with a botanical garden, golf course, picnic areas and skating rink.

Mount Royal Park: Remembrance Rd or Camillien-Houde Way. On a fine day the views from the 763 foot slope are spectacular. The view encompasses St Lawrence and Ottawa Rivers, the Adirondacks (New York State), and the Green Mountains (Vermont). It is also an excellent place to admire the nightscape of Montréal. Locally called 'La Montagne'. During the summer: open-air concerts, winter: skiing and skating.

Tour of Montréal Harbour: Miss Olympia Tours, 842-3871. Summers, starting May through mid-Oct, lasts 2 hrs. $19-40. 'Outstanding.'

Festivals: Montréal is a vibrant theatrical centre with enough performances and styles to suit most tastes.

Montréal International Jazz Festival. Held at the beginning of July annually, this is a festival of music and fun throughout the city. Around 200 live shows, many free, with many top-name performers.' An ecstatic jazz party that transforms the city into something so beautiful and bizarre that even the locals sometimes feel like tourists.' *www.montrealjazzfest.com*

At the end of Aug / beginning of Sep, try to catch the **World Film Festival,** *www.ffm-montreal.org*. The largest celebration of film in North America, ranked with that of Cannes, Berlin and Venice. Lots of freebies as well, 848-3883.

ENTERTAINMENT

Read the free *Montréal Mirror* or *Voir* for what's going on. For some real night-time fun, hang out on St-Paul to see street performers, artists and the like. Theatre is big here, so naturally there is a wide variety of theatrical groups, including the **Theatre du Nouveau Monde**, 866-8667 (French) or **Centaur Theatre**, 288-3161 (English) for tkt info.

Café Campus, 57 Rue Price Arthur Est, 844-1010. Drinking, dancing, French students. Cheap. Free on Wed nights.

Studio Lezards, 4177 Rue St-Denis, 271-7670. Eclectic, arty, lively disco situated in the heart of the city. 'Wall and body painting!' From $5 cover. Open nightly 10pm-3am.

DJ's Pub, 1443 Crescent St, 287-9354. On Thu nights here you can get 6 mixed drinks for under $15. Open till 3am daily, happy hour noon-8pm.

Jello Bar, 151 Rue Ontario Est, 285-2621. Martinis and lounge, maybe a spot of jazz. Very cool.

Le Bifteck, 3702 Rue St-Laurent, 844-6211, studenty bar / venue, all types of music. St Laurent metro then #55 bus north.

Les Foufounes Electriques, 87 Rue Ste-Catherine Est, 844-6211, means 'the electric buttocks!' Alternative bands, young clientele, terrace garden in summer.

Le Pub de Londres a Berlin, 4557 Rue St-Denis. Very boho atmosphere, draught beers, pool tables, free popcorn.

Le St-Sulpice, 1680 Rue St-Denis, 844-9458, good bar, with terraces for people-watching.

Place des Arts, 175 Rue Ste Catherine Ouest (main entrance), box office at 150 de Maisonneuve Blvd, 790-ARTS. Montréal's cultural complex. Features concert, dance and theatrical performances in five theatres and studios.

INFORMATION

InfoTouriste, 1001 Dorchester Square, 873-2015 / outside Montréal (800) 363-7777. Free city guides and maps, and extensive food and housing listings. Summer; daily 9am-7pm, winter till 5pm. *www.tourism-montreal.org*. In Old Montreal at 174 Rue Notre Dame Est.

Tourisme Jeunesse, 4008 Rue St Denis, 844-5246. Youth hostel membership, free maps, hostel info and advice.

INTERNET ACCESS
There is an internet cafe at **Cybermac Cafe**, 1425 Mackay, 287-9100.
The **Bibliotheque Centrale** (Main library) is at 1210 Rue Sherbrooke Est, 872-5923.
Open Mon/Thu 10am-6pm, Tue/Wed 10am-10pm, Fri noon-6pm, Sat 10am-5pm,
Sun (summer only) 1pm-5pm.

TRAVEL
Airports: Mirabel Airport, 55 km from city centre, international flights, and
Dorval Airport, 21 km from city centre, domestic and US flights. Info for both at
394-7377. Shuttle bus from downtown, call **Gray Line / Autocar Connaisseur,** 934-
1222; $9.75 to Dorval, $18 to Mirabel from downtown.
Allo Stop, 4317 Rue St Denis, 985-3032. Connects travellers with rides. Female
drivers may be requested. Membership $6, drivers $7. 'More reliable than hitchhik-
ing, cheaper than bus or train.' Average fares $15 to Québec City, $26 to Toronto,
$10 to Ottawa. *www.allostop.com*
Bike Rental; Velo Aventure Montreal, Conveyor Pier at the Old Port of Montreal,
847-0666; or **Bicycletterie JR**, 151 Rue Rachel Est, 843-6968, $14 per day, $12.60 for a
second day. Lots of good cycle paths especially down by the river.
Central Voyageur bus terminal, 505 Blvd de Maisonneuve and Berri, 842-2281. For
Greyhound call 287-1580. Metro; Berri-UQAM.
Central Station (Gare Centrale), 895 Rue de la Gauchetière Ouest, under Queen
Elizabeth Hotel. Served by **VIA Rail**, (800) 561-9181, and **Amtrak**, (800) 872-7245.
Metro: Bonaventure.
Gray Line City Tours / Autocar Connaisseur, depart from 1001 Metcalfe, 934-1222.
From $23.50 to $60 depending on tour. Call for info on various tour permutations.
Metro: Peel.
Royal Tours, 871-4733, $22 for 3hr tour of the city, $29 to get on and off where you like.
STCUM Metro and Bus public transport, (built for Expo '67). The metro is fully
integrated with the bus system, it whispers along on rubber tyres. Public transit
with flair. 'A joy after New York.' Current fare: $1.90, $8.25 for 6 tkts. Tourist passes
give unlimited travel, $5 day, $12 for 3 days. Ask for transfers (honoured on both
buses and metro). Daily 5.30am-12.30am. For info call 288-6287. Free maps available at certain stations. *www.stcum.qc.ca*
Taxi Pontiac, 761-5522.

LES LAURENTIDES (THE LAURENTIAN MOUNTAINS)   This region
of mountains, lakes and forests is located just north and west of Montréal
via Autoroute 15 and Rte 117. Proximity to Montréal and Québec City
ensures that amenities are well developed. A resort area in both winter and
summer, it is known for camping, hiking, and skiing.

Ste Agathe, built on the shore of Lac des Sables, is the major town of the
Laurentians. Water sports and cruises are major pastimes here. Other towns
of interest include: **St Donat,** the highest point in the area (which consequently attracts both climbers and skiers); **St Sauveur des Monts,** an arts
and crafts centre; **Mont Laurier,** a farming area; and **Mont Tremblant,** a
year-round sports centre which caters to those interested in fishing, water-
sports and hiking in the summer. In winter, it's probably the most popular
ski resort in the area.

In the hills to the northeast of Montréal, north of **Trois Rivières**, and
accessible off Hwy 55, is the unspoiled **La Mauricie National Park**, (819)
538-3232, $3.50 entrance. The park's rolling hills and narrow valleys are
dotted with lakes. Canoeing and cross-country skiing are extremely popular
here. Moose, black bear, coyote and a great variety of birds are indigenous to

the area. The park is open year-round. Camping is available May-Oct, $22, res on (819) 533-7272.

Accommodation is plentiful, although somewhat costly. The area is very busy in the summer and from December to March, so it is wise to book ahead. There are a lot of B&B places, inns and lodges to choose from. It is also possible to make day trips out to the Laurentians from Montréal which is a little over an hour away. Information and reservation service at the **Tourist Association**, 14142 Rue de la Chapelle, RR1, Mirabel, Quebec J7Z 5T4, (800) 561-6673 / (450) 436-8532, *www.laurentides.com*

QUÉBEC CITY The focal point of French Canada is in fact two cities. Below Diamond Rock, Lower Town (*Basse Ville*) spreads over the coastal region of Cape Diamond and up the valley of St Charles. Atop rugged Diamond Rock, 333 ft above the St Lawrence River, is Upper or Old Québec. Originally a fortification located in the heart of New France, it remains the only walled city in North America. It's joined to the charming Quartier Petit Champlain by a 200ft funicular railway.

In 1759, General Wolfe and his British troops scaled the cliffs in pre-dawn darkness and took Montcalm and his French troops by surprise, thereby securing Canada for the British. The site of this attack, the Plains of Abraham, is now a peaceful public park.

Despite the outcome of that battle, Québec remains quintessentially French; only five percent of its inhabitants speak English as a first language. Walking around narrow, winding streets past the grey-stone walls, sidewalk cafes, and artists on the Rue du Trésor, it's easy to believe you have been transported across the Atlantic to the alleyways of Montmartre. The town is best explored on foot and details of a walking tour are available from the Tourist Bureaux. Montréal is situated 150 miles due west.
The telephone area code is 418.

ACCOMMODATION
Auberge De La Paix, 31 Rue Couillard, 694-0735. Friendly staff, co-ed rooms with big clean mattresses. Kitchen facilities. Close by great bars/restaurants on Rue St Jean. Free bfast 8-10am, all you can eat. Curfew 2am. $19. 'Central location, clean.'
Auberge St Louis, 48 Rue St Louis, 692-2424. From S/D-$55, bfast included.
B&B Chez Marie-Claire, 62 Rue Ste Ursule, 692-1556. From D-$83 bfast included. 'Central location, bright, clean rooms, friendly hostess.'
Bonjour Québec, 3765 Blvd Monaco, 527-1465. A B&B agency that will set you up with a place to stay, from S-$46, D-$52.
Centre International de Séjour de Québec (HI-C), 19 Rue Ste Ursule, 694-0755. Laundry, microwave, TV, pool, ping-pong tables, living room, kitchen, cafeteria, limited street parking, linen provided. 'Very nice and well situated.' From $16.
Hôtel Manoir Charest, 448 Rue Dorchester Sud, 647-9320. S/D-$55. 'Clean and friendly.'
Le Manoir Lasalle, 18 Rue Ste Ursule, 692-9953. From S/D$30-$70, bfast included.
Hotel la Maison Acadiènne, 43 Rue Ste Ursule, 694-0280. From S-$47, D-$51, bfast included. *www.maison-acadienne.com*
Maison du Général, 72 Rue St Louis, 694-1905. 'Very well situated.' No rsvs taken; call or show up after noon (check out time). S/D-$33. May-Oct only.
Maison Ste Ursule, 40 Rue Ste Ursule, 694-9794. 3 rooms with kitchen facilities. From S-$38, D-$47.

YWCA, 855 Ave Holland, 683-2155. For women and couples only. From S-$27, D-$40.

Camping: Aéroport Camping, 2050 Rue de l'Aéroport (off Rte 138), **Saint-Foy**, 871-1574. $14-$23 camping with pool. May-Oct.

Camping Piscine Turmel, 7000 Blvd Ste Anne (off Rte 138), **Chateau-Richer**, 824-4311. May -Sep. $18 a night. Showers, laundry, pool, auto mechanics and ice cream parlour. 'Clean and well kept.'

Municipal de Beauport, 95 Rue Serenite, **Beauport** (off Rte 40 E), B, 666-2228. Campground on hill, overlooking Montgomery River. Pool, canoes, showers and laundry. $16 w/hook-up, $85-$120 weekly, May-Sep.

FOOD

Stroll alongside the cafés around **Rue St Jean** and **Rue Buade**. Complete 3-course meals (répas complêt), are recommended as being quite economical. Try the traditional *Québeçois* food and the inexpensive *croque-monsieurs*.

Café Buade, 31 Rue Buade, 692-3909. All day bfast, entrees $5-$12. Open 7.30am-11pm.

Café Ste-Julie, 865 Rue des Zouaves—off St Jean, 647-9368. Big filling bfast $4, burger lunch $4.75. Daily 6am-8pm.

Casse Croute Bréton, 1136 Rue St Jean. Many choices of fillings for your 'make-your-own-crêpe.' Bfast special $3, lunch specials (11am-2pm). Sun-Thu 8am-1am, Fri-Sat 9.30am-2am. 'Excellent crêpes.'

J A Moisan, 699 Rue St Jean, 522-0685. A cheaper alternative to eating out, buy groceries here for your own food concoctions. Daily 8.30am-10pm.

La Fleur de Lotus, 38 Cte de la Fabrique, across from the Hôtel de Ville, 692-4286. 'A local favourite.' Thai dishes $3.50-$10. Mon-Fri 11.30am-10.30pm, Sat & Sun from 5pm.

Le Commensal , 860 Rue St Jean, 647-1236. One of Canada's largest chain of vegetarian restaurants. Self-service hot and cold buffet, pay by weight.

Marché de Vieux Port open-air market, 160 Rue St André. Daily Mar-Nov.

OF INTEREST

La Citadelle, on Cap-Diamant promontory, 694-2815. Constructed by the British in the 1820s on the site of the 17th century French defences, the Citadel is the official residence of the Governor General and the largest fortification in North America still garrisoned by regular troops. Changing of the Guard ceremony by the 'Van Doos' at 10am daily May-Sep, and 'Beating the Retreat' at 6pm in July/Aug. Includes the **Royal 22nd Regiment Museum**, 648-3563; exhibits of military objects such as firearms, decorations, and uniforms. Museum and Citadelle are open daily April to Oct; 9am-6pm high summer, shorter hours toward season beginning and end – call for times. Tours last 1 hr, $5.50.

The **Fortifications de Québec** are also worth a visit. This is the stone wall that encircles Vieux Québec. Frontenac erected this wall in the late 17th century in order to fortify the city and guard against British invasion. Tours available. May-Oct daily 10am-5pm, with restricted hours the rest of the year, $2.75, $2.25 w/student ID. There are great views of the city from the walkways along the wall. Information (800) 463-6769 / 648-7016.

The Plains of Abraham. Battlefields Park was the scene of the bloody clash between the French and British armies. A Martello Tower, part of the historic defence system of walled Québec, still stands. Interpretative Centre, National Battlefields Commission, 390 Ave de Bernieres, 648-4071. There are a number of other historic sites in this 250 acre park including the Wolfe Monument and the Jardin Jeanne d'Arc. Also here is the **Museé du Québec,** Parc des Champs-de-Battaile, 643-2150, which houses the original hand copy of the surrender by Montcalm and displays Québec art and the old city jail. Daily 10am-5.45pm, Wed till 9.45pm; $7, $2.75 w/student ID.

Outside the Walls; **Basilique-Cathedrale Notre Dame de Québec**, 16 Rue Buade, 692-2533/4. Restored many times, the basilica was first constructed in 1650 when it served a diocese stretching from Canada to Mexico. All the bishops of Québec are buried in the crypt. Daily 9am-6pm. Get there early. Tours of the basilica and crypt are available 10.30am-5pm, from May to Nov. Free. Sound and light show, 3 times daily. $7, $4 w/student ID. 'An atmospheric introduction to the history of the city.'

Château Frontenac, Rue St Pierre. Named for the 'illustrious governor of New France', this hotel is one of Québec City's most prominent landmarks; looks more like a castle than a hotel. There is a spectacular view of the St Lawrence from the Promenade des Gouverneurs.

Ile d'Orléans. This island in the St Lawrence is a slice of 17th century France. Wander around the old houses, mills, churches. Also known for its handicrafts, strawberries and home-made treats. Reached by the bridge from the mainland, with a 67 km round-island drive; various picturesque towns along the way.

Museé du Fort, 10 Rue Ste Anne, 692-1759. Diorama sound and light show. Re-live the six sieges of Québec. In summer daily 10am-6pm. $6.25, $4 w/student ID.

Notre Dame Des Victoires, Place Royale, Basse Ville, 692-1650. Built in 1688. Eighty years before its construction, this is where Champlain established the first permanent white settlement in North America north of Florida. The church itself gets its name in honour of two French military victories. Its main altar resembles the city in that it is shaped like a fortress complete with turrets and battlements. Guided tours mid-May to mid-Oct. Free. Mon-Sat 9am-4.30pm.

Parliament Buildings, on Grande Allée at Honore Mercier, 643-7239. The main building built in 1884, is in Second Empire style. The bronze statues in front represent the historical figures of Québec. June-Sep, daily 10am-4.30pm, winter Mon-Fri only. Free. Includes **L'Assemblée Nationale**, completed in 1886. From the visitors gallery you can view debates in French. While in the area, check out the architecture of the buildings on Grand Allée and stop for a café au lait at one of the sidewalk cafes lining the street.

Place Royale has undergone considerable restoration under its current owner, the Government of Québec. In the summer, the roads are blocked off and restricted to pedestrians only, and many plays and variety shows are put on in the parks of the area. This is one of the oldest districts in North America.

The Ramparts, Rue des Ramparts. Studded with old iron cannons, probably the last vestiges of the Siege of Québec in 1759. Good views of the port.

Winter Carnival, 626-3716, first two weeks in February, is the best-known of Quebec's festivals; features ice-sculptures, dog-sled races, parades and a snow-bath! *www.carnaval.qc.ca/*

INFORMATION

Centre d'information, 835 Rue Wildfred-Laurier, 651-2882, Bilingual advice, accommodation, tourist attractions, etc. Daily 8.30am-5pm.

Office du Tourisme, 399 Rue Saint-Joseph Est, 2e etage, 522-3511, *www.quebecregion.com*

Tourisme Jeunesse, Place Laurier, (800) 461-8585 / 651-5323. Maps, travel guides, hostel membership and insurance sold. Make rsvs here too for hostels. *www.tourismej.qc.ca*

TRAVEL

Allo Stop, 467 Rue St Jean, Québec, 522-0056. Ride share. *www.allostop.com*

Central bus terminal (Gare Centrale d'Autobus), 320 Rue Abraham-Martin. Daily 5am-1am. Also, **Ste Foy bus terminal**, 925 Ave de Rochebelle. Both 525-3000. Operating from here are **Greyhound Canada** (800) 661-8747, and **Orleans Express** (to Montreal) 395-4200.

Coop Taxis Québec, 525-5191. Around $25 to airport.
Ferry across the St Lawrence, 644-3704. Daily departures from the wharf 6.30am-3am. Fare: $1.50. Nice views of Québec, especially at sunset.
Jean-Lesage National Airport, Ste Foy, Blvd Hamel to Blvd de l'Aéroport, 640-2600. 14 miles (23 km) from city centre. Mainly domestic flights.
Pelletier Car Rental, 900 Pièrre Bertrand, 681-0678. Mon-Fri 7.30am-8pm, Sat/Sun 8am-4pm.
VIA Rail, Gare du Palais, 450 Rue de la Gare du Palais, 692-3940 (in Quebec), or (888) 842-7733. Also **Gare de St Foy**, 3255 Chemin de la Gare, 658-87982.

LA GASPÉSIE (THE GASPÉ PENINSULA) This is the bit of Québec Province jutting out above New Brunswick into the Gulf of St Lawrence. The word Gaspé is derived from the Micmac Indian word meaning Lands End. You'll appreciate this when standing on the shore at Gaspé for there's nothing but sea between you and Europe. Picturesque fishing villages line the Peninsula; slow, pleasant places in summer, rugged in winter. Inland it's farming country although a large area is taken up by the Gaspésian Provincial Park.

The route from Québec City to Gaspé runs along the mighty St Lawrence where the scenery closely resembles that of the Maritime Provinces. The North Shore is a more interesting drive, but at some point, you have to take a ferry to get to the South Shore. (The narrower the river at the point of crossing, the cheaper the ferry ride.) You can, for instance, take Rte 138 out of Québec City and pass by the **Chute de Montmorency,** the impressive 250ft waterfall—higher than Niagara. Then through **Ste Anne de Beaupré,** destination of millions of pilgrimages yearly since 18th century ship-wrecked sailors believed Ste Anne was their saviour. Next, continue through to picture-postcard **Baie St Paul** where there is an interesting collection of old-time French Canadiana. **The Centre d'Art de Baie St Paul** is at 4 Fafard, and opposite is the Centre d'Exposition; well-known for showing local arts and crafts and contemporary art. Further on at **St Simeon** there is a ferry crossing **to Riviére du Loup**.

Take Rte 132 as far as **Trois Pistoles.** Long before Canada was officially 'discovered', Basque whale hunters built ovens here to reduce whale blubber to oil. The remains of the ovens can still be seen at the **Parc de l'Adventure Basque en Amerique**, at the ferry wharf. Open daily in summer, 10am-5pm; $5. Along the south shore of the St Lawrence through the fishing villages; the ever changing seascapesprovide an attractive drive. Inland, the **Gaspésian Provincial Park** is called the 'sea of mountains' and includes the highest point in the province, 4160 ft **Mount Jacques Cartier.** A great view of the scenery is almost guaranteed from the hike to the top, and perhaps even a sight of the caribou who make this area their natural habitat. Mornings are the time you are most likely to see them. The park is open year round—for info, call 763-7811 (summer) or 763-3301 (year-round), *www.sepaq.com/En/Park/gaspesie/gaspesie.html*. Round the top of the Peninsula is **Gaspé** itself where Jacques Cartier came ashore in 1533 and set up a cross to stake France's claim to Canada.

Nearby is **Forillon National Park,** 368-5505, $3.75 entry. Forillon scenery is typified by jagged cliffs and fir-covered highlands. The park is criss-crossed by many hiking trails and on the way you may see deer, fox, bear or moose. Large colonies of seabirds such as cormorants, gannets, and gulls nest on the cliff headlands and it is possible to see whales and seals basking offshore. Naturalists offer talks and slide presentations at the Interpretative Centre on Hwy 132 near **Cap des Rosiers.** There are also reception centres at Penouille and L'Anse-au-Griffon. Camping at the park is available in the summer at Cap Bon Ami, Des Rosiers, and Petit Gaspé. All three have good recreational facilities. Call 368-6050 for res, needed 48hrs in advance in July/Aug; $16.50.

The views all around the coast are fantastic but none better than a few km south at **Percé.** The village takes its name from **Rocher Percé**, the Pierced Rock, which is just offshore. You can walk there on a sandbar at low tide, and also a good point for whale-spotting Apr-Dec.

From Percé boat trips go to nearby **Ile Bonaventure,** where there is a bird sanctuary. Information in the area from the **Tourism Association**, 357 Route de la Mer, Sainte-Flavie, (800) 463-0323 / 775-2223, *www.tourisme-gaspesie.qc.ca* For a directory of outdoor pursuits in the area, check out *www.ojori.com/outdoor/er02.htm* The telephone code is 418.

ACCOMMODATION
Auberge Le Balcon Vert Backpackers Hostel, 22 Cote du Balcon Vert, **Baie St-Paul**, (408) 435-5587. Open June-Sep, $16, $14 w/ student ID, $40 for private cabin, $16 campsites. High up in the hills, has nice views. *www.balconvert.charlevoix.net*
Auberge de Cap aux Os Hostel (HI-C), 2095 Blvd Grande-Grève, **Cap-aux-Os** (actually within the Forillon National Park), 892-5153. $18. Laundry, linen & bike rental;$15. 'Very friendly, bilingual but mostly French'. Take coach or train from Québec City to Gaspé, 25 kms from hostel.
Auberge du Château Hostel (HI-C), 152 Blvd Perron, **Pointe à la Garde**, 788-2048. Castle with a hostel built by the owner, Jean. Laundry, linen rental, free bfast. Dinner served in castle, $8, or afternoon tea on the terraces. 'Excellent atmosphere, excellent food, excellent host.' 'Phone before going to get exact location.' Dorms $17.
Auberge Internationale l'Echouerie, 295 1e Ave Est, **Ste-Anne-de-Monts**, 763-1555, shuttle runs into Gaspesie Parc during the summer. Kitchen, baggage stoore, parking; $15.
Motel Fort Ramsay et Pavillions Anna Mabel, 254 Blvd Gaspé, **Gaspé**, 368-5094. May-Sep. S/D-$45. Kitchen facilities.

THE PRAIRIE PROVINCES

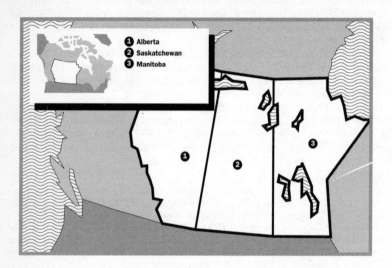

1 Alberta
2 Saskatchewan
3 Manitoba

The terrain in Alberta, Manitoba and Saskatchewan is primarily prairie, with countless sunflowers and endless acres of wheat. Even as western Alberta rises up to meet the glorious Canadian Rockies, you might hear locals sigh, 'the Rockies are nice, but they get in the way of the view'. Grain was once the foundation of the economy of these provinces, but today mineral wealth and tourism are the leading industries.

Although the major cities of the prairie are fast-growing centres of commerce and culture, a rough frontier edge remains. Vast areas of virgin wilderness are still there for the intrepid to explore and conquer; it's even possible to travel for days in some places without ever seeing another human being.

ALBERTA

Once an agricultural backwater region with an economy dependent solely on wheat, Alberta is still reeling in the proceeds the multi-billion dollar oil and gas boom of the '70s and '80s. The former small-town farming centres of Calgary and Edmonton are now thriving metropolitan areas, their skylines dotted with looming corporate high rises. With 85 percent of Canada's oil and gas on tap, Albertans enjoy the lowest taxes and unemployment rate and the highest per capita income in the country.

Alberta's prosperity is not without political backlash. Only 30 percent of the seats in the federal Parliament are meted out to Alberta, the three western provinces and the two territories. As a result, many westerners feel deprived of power by the more populous East. It is not only in Québec that the idea of separation arises.

Cattle and grain ranching complement the corporate side of the Albertan landscape and character. The Albertan ranches produce some of the finest beef in the world. As the saying goes here: 'If it ain't Alberta, it ain't beef.'

Of all the Canadian provinces, Alberta has the greatest variety of geographical features, from the towering Rockies in the southwest to the rolling agricultural land north of the US border to the northern wilderness lands of lakes, rivers and forests. Although it gets hot in summer, cold, snowy weather can linger into May before returning again as early as September.
National Parks: Waterton Lakes, Banff, Jasper, Elk Island, Wood Buffalo (not developed, no access by road, no accommodation). *www.yahoo.com/ Regional/Countries/Canada/Provinces_and_Territories/Alberta.*
The telephone area code is 780 for Edmonton and Jasper, 403 for Banff and Calgary.

EDMONTON   Edmonton's close proximity to the highly productive Leduc, Redwater and Pembiano oil fields made it one of the fastest growing cities in Canada during the oil boom. Coal mining, natural gas, and—a couple of throwbacks to Edmonton's origins—fur-trading and wheat, also played a part in the rapid expansion. With the downturn in world oil prices, those heady days are now over. Edmonton is in the process of re-assessment.

During the Klondike Gold Rush, Edmonton was a stopping place for prospectors hoping to strike it rich. The provincial capital joyfully celebrates its gilded age every July with **Klondike Days** when the place explodes with pioneer spirit. The other 51 weeks of the year, it's a sober, hard-working spot, the most northerly major city on the continent with a wealth of attractions. It's home to a progressive university, the only subway system in western Canada, the world' s largest indoor shopping mall and some of the finest sporting facilities anywhere.

Edmonton is nestled in the heart of Alberta. It's a good place to launch a trip up north or a westward journey into the Rockies. Jasper is 228 miles away, but you can stop first at Elk Island National Park, just 30 miles east.
The area code is 780.

ACCOMMODATION
Cecil Hotel, 10406 Jasper Ave, 428-7001, downtown. S-$29, D-$40. TV, phone, private bath.
Commercial Hotel, 10329 82nd Ave, 439-3981. S-$28, S-$35 w/ bath, D-$31, D-$39 w/bath, key deposit $5. South, in trendy Strathcona.
Edmonton HI Hostel, 10647 81st Ave, 988-6836. Common room, snack bar, showers, kitchen/laundry. $15 AYH, $20 non-member. Cycling in river valley, summer festivals. 'Easy walk from downtown. Comfortable.' Bike hire, $12 day.
Grand Hotel, 10266 103 St, 422-6365. S-$42, D-$51, $5 key deposit. Handy location-across from Greyhound bus station. Breakfast included.
St Joseph's College, 89 Ave at 114 St near University of Alberta, 492-7681. A better alternative to the more institutionalised and expensive uni accom nearby. S-$29, weekly $179. Full board S-$40, weekly $246. Meals available. Rsvs in summer.
Klondiker Hotel, 153 St and Stony Plain Rd, 489-1906. West End location. From S-$44, D-$49.

North American Baptist College Residence, 11525-23rd Ave, 437-1960; S-$20. Winter rooms also available.

University of Alberta Residence, Lister Hall, 87th Ave & 116th St, 492-4281. Open to non-students May-Aug, call for rates.

YMCA, 10030 102A Ave, 421-9622. Dorm rooms $17, S-$34, $10 key deposit.

YWCA, 10305 100 Ave, 423-9922. Dorm rooms $14.50, S-$32-$37, D-$45.

Camping: Bondiss Skeleton Lake Scout Camp, 14205-109 Ave, 454-8561. 500 acres, 3 km of shoreline, swimming, hiking.

FOOD

Downtown along 104 St is **"Restaurant Row"** with over fifty places within walking distance of each other and an abundance of coffee shops.

Whyte Ave, from 99 St to 109 St, there are lots of eateries along this stretch—close to Uni of Alberta campus. **Strathcona Square,** located at 8150 105 St, is a restored Victorian building containing several restaurants worth looking at.

Bones, 10220 103rd St, 421-4747. Specialises in ribs, $8. Sun-Thur 11:30am-10pm, Fri 'til 11pm, Sat 4pm-11pm.

Chianti's, 10501 Whyte 82 Ave, 439-9829. Italian dishes, ranging from pasta to seafood, and daily speciality wines. Sun-Thur 11am-10pm, Fri/Sat 'til 11pm.

David's, 8407 Argyll Rd, 468-1167. Come dine here for the true taste of Alberta beef. Mon-Sat 7am-11pm, Sun 9am-9pm.

Earl's, various locations. Generous servings—one on Uni of Alberta campus.

OF INTEREST

Alberta Government House, 128 St & 102 Ave, 427-2281. Originally built in 1913 as a residence of the Lt. Governors, the building has also seen service as a WWII Veterans hospital. It's open to the public on Sun only, 1pm-5pm.

Chinatown & Avenue of Nations, 102 Ave & 97 St. See the impressive gate that opens into the heart of the Edmonton Chinese community. Be sure to roll a ball in the lion's mouth for good luck.

Edmonton Art Gallery, 2 Sir Winston Churchill Sq, 422-6223. More than 30 exhibitions each year include contemporary and historical art from Canada and around the world. Mon-Wed 10.30am-5pm, Thur & Fri 'til 8pm. Sat/Sun & hols 10am-5pm. Thur 4pm-8pm, free. $3, w/student ID $1.50.

Edmonton Space Sciences Centre, 11211 142nd St, 452-9100 (info)/451-7722 (recording). Over $2 million worth of exhibits, IMAX film theatre, exhibit gallery and science shop; $7.50 day pass, combo tkt w/ IMAX admission, $13. Open daily 10am-9pm.

The John Walter Museum, 10627 93rd Ave, 496-4852, was built of hand-hewn logs in 1874. The house was the district's first telegraph office. Four historic buildings on original site. Sun 1pm-5pm, free. Different activities each Sun, sometimes with free food.

Legislature Bldg, 97th Ave & 108th St, 427-7362. On the site of the original Fort Edmonton. Built at the beginning of this century. Free tours every $1/2$ hr. Open daily, 9am-4pm.

Old Strathcona Historic Area, 10324 Whyte Ave, 433-5866. Buildings in this historic district date back to 1891. They've since been converted into antique stores and restaurants. The visitors centre has maps available for walking tours; open Mon-Fri 8:30am-4:30pm.

Provincial Museum, 12845 102nd Ave, 453-9100. Features displays of Alberta's natural and human history, including native people, pioneers, wildlife, and geology. Open daily 9am-5pm, $6.50 (half-price on Tue).

Muttart Conservatory, 9626 96A St, 496-8755. Four glass pyramids nestled in the city centre feature more than 700 species of plants from arid to temperate climates. Mon-Fri 9am-6pm, Sat-Sun 11am-6pm. $4.50, $3.50 w/student ID.

Ukrainian Canadian Archives and Museum of Alberta, 10611 110 Ave, 424-7580. Traces history of Ukranian pioneers in Alberta. Includes costumes, paintings, folk art. Tues-Fri 10am-5pm, Sat from noon. Hours subject to change, phone prior to visit.

Shopping: West Edmonton Mall, 170th St & 87th Ave. World's largest indoor shopping mall with over 800 stores. Employs 15,000people, and features water-slides, dolphin tank, full size replica of Santa Maria, skating rink, a petting zoo, 10aviaries and the world's largest indoor mini golf course—you name it! 'Mind boggling.' 'A must see.'

Parks: Fort Edmonton Historical Park, corner of White Mud and Fox Dr, 496-8787. Reconstruction of the original and a replica of a Hudson's Bay Co Trading Post. 'Worth a visit.' Mon-Fri 10am-6pm, shorter hours in winter. $7; discounts for HI members.

Polar Park, 22 kms SE on Hwy 14, 922-3401. Preserve for cold-climate and hardy African animals. Cross country trails and sleigh rides in winter. Daily 8am-dusk, $5.

Nearby: St Albert, N of Edmonton on the St Albert Trail, is the oldest non-fortified community in Alberta. You can tour the **Arden Theatre, City Hall** and **Musee Heritage Museum** daily; free. Also in St Albert is the **Father Lacombe Chapel**, St Anne St, 427-3995. Built in 1861 by the missionary for which it's named, the chapel is the oldest building in Alberta. Open 10am-6pm daily; $2. Next door to the Chapel is the **Vital Gradin Centre**, a museum dedicated to the early missionaries. For information on St Albert, call 459-1724.

ENTERTAINMENT

Edmonton presents a very talented opera and symphony. For performance infor-mation, call the **Edmonton Opera** at 424-4040 or the **Edmonton Symphony** at 428-1414.

Festivals: Jazz City International Festival, late June. Canadian and overseas jazz musicians. Running simultaneously is **The Works**, a celebration of the visual arts.

Edmonton Folk Music Festival, mid-Aug, Gallagher Park. Features traditional and bluegrass music, country, blues and Celtic music—all under the bright Alberta sun.

Edmonton Queen Riverboat, 424-2628, offers a variety of cruises on the North Saskatchewan River. Call ahead for schedule and prices; rsvs required.

Edmonton Street Performers Festival, mid-July. Downtown streets come alive with magicians, jugglers, clowns, mime artists, musicians and comics.

Fringe Theatre Event, 448-9000. For 10 days in mid-Aug, Old Strathcona is trans-formed into a series of stages for alternative theatre, a rival to Edinburgh's festival. More than 65 troupes attend from around the globe.

Klondike Days. Edmonton returns to the 1890s for Klondike Days, 10 days in mid-July. It's a whirlwind of street festivities, capped off with the great Klondike Days Exposition at Northlands Park. 'Excellent entertainment.' The show at MacDonald Hotel, Jasper & 98th St, during this time, is 'not to be missed'. Free entrance to the Golden Slipper Saloon. Immense 'Klondike breakfasts' are served in the open air, massed marching bands compete in the streets, and down the North Saskatchewan River float more than 100 of the weirdest-looking home-built rafts ever seen. 'Where most students drink; good entertainment.'

INFORMATION

Chamber of Commerce, 832 Connaught Dr, 852-3858.

Edmonton Tourism, 9797 Jasper Ave, (800) 463-4667. *www.tourism.ede.org*.

Visitors Information Centre, 9797 Jasper Ave (lobby level), 426-4715. Mon-Fri 8am-5pm; winter: Mon-Fri from 8.30am. Another **info centre** at 2404 Calgary Trail Northbound SW, 496-8400. Mon-Fri 8am-9pm, Sat-Sun 9am-5pm, 8.30am-4.30pm after Labour Day.

INTERNET ACCESS
Bistro.web, 8711 82 Whyte Ave, 468-6983; $5/hr.
Bytes, in the West Edmonton Mall, 444-SURF, Mon-Sat 10:30am-11pm, Sun noon-6pm; $6/hr.
The Node Room, 118 Ave & St Albert Trail, 432-9982, Open daily noon-midnight; $6/hr.
Planet Cybercafe, 10442 82 Ave, 433-9730, Open 24 hrs; $6/hr.

TRAVEL
Edmonton International Airport, 890-8382, 18 miles S of the city on Hwy 2, about a 45 minute drive.
Sky Shuttle runs Mon-Fri 5.40am-10.45pm, Sat & Sun 6am-10.15pm and departs every 20-30 mins from MacDonald Place, various downtown hotels and the Arrivals Terminal. $11 o/w, call 890-7234 for more info.
Greyhound, 10324 103 St, 420-2440/(800) 661-8747.
Edmonton Transit System Info, 496-1611 for info. Operates the city buses as well as the new, silent, streamlined and comfortable LRT (Light Rail Transit). Basic fare: $1.60.
Red Arrow Express, 425-0820. Coach service btwn Edmonton and Calgary 6 times daily (6:30am, 8:30am, 12pm, 2pm, 4pm, 6pm), also 8pm on Fri & Sun, o/w $42.
CN/VIA Rail Station, 12360-121st St, (800) 561-8630 in Canada, (888)842-7733 elsewhere.
Co-op Taxi 425-8310 or 425-2525.

ELK ISLAND NATIONAL PARK This 75 sq mile park is the largest fenced wild animal preserve in Canada. Apart from the elk, moose, mule deer and the countless tiny critters that live here, there is a herd of some 600 buffalo. Though impressive to behold, it's a trifling number compared to the millions that once roamed the North American continent; the buffalo were hunted almost to extinction by the end of the 19th century. The herd here at Elk Island has been built up from about 40animals since 1907.

It is possible to observe the buffalo at close range, but only on the other side of a strong fence. Walking on the buffalo range itself is discouraged! North America's largest buffalo herd, 12,000 strong, is contained in **Wood Buffalo National Park** in the far north of Alberta. This area, however, remains relatively undeveloped.

Elk Island is open throughout the year. The Visitor Centre, just north of Hwy 16, 922-5790, features exhibits and displays. Walks, hikes, campfire talks and theatre programmes are offered by the park rangers. Recreation facilities, including swimming, golf and hiking trails, are available on the east shore of Astotin Lake. There are camping facilities in the park. Admission $8 per vehicle.
www.parkscanada.pch.gc.ca/parks/alberta/elk_island/elk_islande.htm.

OF INTEREST
Ukrainian Cultural Heritage Village, on Hwy 16, 662-3640. Russian immigrants played an important role in taming western Canada and this open-air museum portrays pre-1930s life of the Ukrainian settlers. The authentic buildings have been moved here and then restored. Daily 10am-6pm. $6.50, Tues free. After Labour Day 10am-4pm, $3.25.
Vegreville, 25 miles E of the Ukrainian Village, is where to find the world's largest Ukrainian Easter Egg, towering over 30 ft tall! Constructed in 1974 to commemo-

rate the 100th anniversary of the arrival of the Royal Canadian Mounted Police in Alberta, it is possible to camp around the egg. Arrive early July and watch the annual **Ukrainian Festival** with singing, music and leg-throwing folk dances.

JASPER NATIONAL PARK   Jasper National Park takes its name from Jasper Hawes, the clerk in the first trading post at Brul Lake in 1813. It's 4200 square miles of lofty, green-forested, snow-capped mountains, canyons, dazzling lakes, glaciers and hot mineral springs. Within the park are the Miette Hot Springs, one of which gushes forth at a temperature of 129°F and, in contrast, the huge Columbia Icefields whose melting waters empty into the Atlantic, Pacific and Arctic Oceans.

Accessible from Edmonton by Rte 16 (The Yellowhead Hwy), Jasper lies along the eastern slopes of the Canadian Rockies and bumps against Banff, a neighbouring national park. This vast mountainous complex of national parkland is an extremely popular resort area throughout the year.

One of the park's biggest attractions is the 17-mile-long **Maligne Lake,** the largest of several beautiful glacial lakes in the area. The tour to the lake from the township of Jasper comes highly recommended by previous visitors.

Within the park it is possible to drive through some of the West's most spectacular mountain scenery. **Mt Edith Cavell** (11,033 ft) and **Whistler's Peak** (7350 ft) are two of the more accessible points from Jasper township. The aerial tramway has put Whistler's Peak within reach of even the most nervous would-be mountaineers. The cable car hoists you up to the top of the towering Peak, but the distance between the tramway and the ground below never exceeds 450 ft. Once at the top, the view is tremendous. In winter, this is a favourite skiing spot.

Sixty-five miles from Jasper on the Icefield Hwy between Jasper and Banff (Rte 93) is the **Columbia Icefield**, 130 impressive square miles of glacial ice. You can walk across parts of the glacier, but it's better seen by snowmobile. Bring a sweater, even if it's warm outside. Several glaciers flank the beautiful highway as they creep down from the icefields. Snowmobile trips are available on **Athabasca Glacier**, just a mile from the road.

In addition to being the Jasper National Park Headquarters, the resort village of **Jasper** is also an important CN railroad junction. Should you arrive by train, take note of the 70-ft Raven Totem Pole at the railway depot. The totem was carved by Simeon Stiltae, a master carver of the Haida Indians of the Queen Charlotte Islands.

www.worldweb.com/parkscanada-jasper/index.html.

ACCOMMODATION

Past visitors have recommended contacting the tourist homes/B&Bs for very reasonable rates. The **Chamber of Commerce**, 632 Connaught Dr, 852-3858, has a list of hotels in the area; and **Parks Canada Information Office**, Town Info Centre, 852-6176, provides a list of approved tourist homes.

Youth Hostels general info: contact 10926 88th Ave, Edmonton, T6G 0Z1. To make reservations at any of the Alberta hostels, call 852-3215. Check out website: *www.HostellingIntl.ca/Alberta*. The Pika Shuttle Company runs a shuttle service btwn hostels in Alberta; call (800) 363-0096 for info. Fares vary according to distance. Also check out **Hikers Wheels** and **The Rocky Express** under Banff *Travel* section.

Athabasca Falls HI Hostel, 852-3215, 32 km S from Jasper on Hwy 93; E side of Hwy 93. Propane heating and lighting. Volleyball, basketball, horseshoes, and Athabasca Falls nearby. $10 members, $15 non-members.

Beauty Creek HI Hostel, 87 km S of Jasper; W side of Hwy 93, 439-3089. Cycling destination, and close by Stanley Falls, Columbia Icefield. Partial closure Oct-Apr; in winter pick up key. $9-$14.

Jasper HI Hostel, PO Box 387, Jasper, AB T0E 1E0, 852-5560. 7 km SW of Jasper on Whistler's Mountain Rd, off Hwy 93. Hiking, biking, skiing, barbecue. $15 members, $20 non-members.

Maligne Canyon HI Hostel, 11 km E of Jasper on Maligne Lake Road, 852-3215. Propane heating/lighting. Across the road to Maligne Canyon, access to Skyline Trail. $9-$15.

Mt Edith Cavell HI Hostel, 26 km S of Jasper; 13 km off Hwy 93A (10¹/₂ km straight uphill, not accessible by car in winter or spring). Near Angel Glacier, Tonquin Valley & Verdant Pass. 'Superb area for hiking/skiing.' Partial closure Oct-June. $9-$15.

Camping: Several campgrounds in the area, the nearest ones to Jasper being at **Whistler's** on Icefield Pkwy S (852-3963), and **Wapiti**, also on Icefield Pkwy (852-3992). Approx $17-$24. Firewood available for $4. Gets very cold at night. May-Oct.

OF INTEREST

Columbia Icefield, 762-6700. Snowmobile trips available daily, mid-Apr-mid-Nov, weather permitting, $23.50. Open 9am-5pm daily (shorter hrs in winter). Ice walks are also available for those who'd rather journey by foot. Tours last 3-5 hours, $31-$37. Call 852-5595.

Jasper Heritage Folk Festival, held annually in early Aug. This folk festival, set amid the unparalleled grandeur of the Canadian Rockies, includes blues, jazz, bluegrass and country.

Jasper Raft Tours, 852-3332. 3 hr trips on Athabasca River running through May-Sept at 9am and 12.30pm; $41. Tkts available at the Brewster Bus Depot and Jasper Park Lodge. Also, **Rocky Mountain River Guides**, 852-3777, offer a 1-day trip white-water rafting trip, approx $60. 'Excellent! The trips are very well organised and the professional raft guides make you feel safe and at ease. Very safety conscious.' Shop around for the best deal. Don't forget to buy a photo as a souvenir.

Jasper Tramway, 852-3093. 2 miles S via Hwy 93 and Whistler Mountain Rd. Canada's longest aerial tram. Daily mid-May-Oct, 8am-10pm July through Aug; $16. Bus connections from RR station, or just walk there.

Maligne Lake Boat Tours. 1¹/₂ hr tour ($32), 852-3370. Views of Maligne Narrows. May-Oct, hourly 10am-5pm.

FOOD

Buckles Restaurant and Saloon, 925 Connaught Dr, 852-7074. Open daily 7am-midnight.

The Jasper Pizza Place, 402 Connaught Dr, 852-3225. Popular with locals, licensed and very reasonable. Under $10 for pizza, burgers, salads and tacos. Open 11am-midnight.

Mountain Foods and Café, 606 Connaught Dr, 852-4050. Extensive selection of sandwiches that are perfect for bfast or lunch. Sun-Thur 8am-9pm, Fri-Sat 'til 10pm.

Scoops and Loops, 504 Patricia St, 852-4333. Sandwiches, pastries, sushi, udon noodles and ice cream all available here to be eaten up! Mon-Sat 10:30am-10:30pm, Sun 10am-10pm.

INFORMATION/TRAVEL

Brewster Transportation and Tours, 852-3332. Provides local transportation and

sightseeing. June-Sept, two tours daily. 'Quite pricey.' 'Predictable.' 'A last resort.'
Jasper National Park Interpretive Centre, 500 Connaught Dr, 852-6176. Guided walks, trail maps and information. Daily 8.30am-7pm in summer; winter 9am-5pm. Or find them on the Internet: *www.worldweb.com/parkscanada-jasper.*
Jasper Chamber of Commerce, 632 Connaught Dr, 852-3858. Mon-Fri 9am-5pm. Courtesy phone available for accommodation; very helpful and friendly staff.
Travel Alberta is in the same office. Daily 8am-7pm.
Heritage Taxi, 611 Patricia, 852-5558.

BANFF NATIONAL PARK   Banff, Canada's oldest national park and the third oldest in the world, was established in 1883, when 3 Canadian Pacific Railway workers stumbled upon a cave on the side of Sulphur Mountain. The cave wasn't just your run of the mill cave; it was dispatching a steady stream of piping hot mineral water. Taking in 2546 sq miles of the Rockies, the park radiates a sense of alpine-style grandeur, but it's the dry, equable climate and hot mineral springs that have brought Banff fame and fortune. **Banff** and **Lake Louise** are the main resort towns. The park gets its name from Banffshire in Scotland, the birthplace of Lord Strathcona, a past president of the Canadian Pacific Railroad.

Cable cars that take visitors high into the mountains operate year round. Both the **Sulphur Mountain Gondola** and the **Mt Norquay Chair Lift** offer fantastic views, but to ride the Mt Norquay lift in winter you have to plan on skiing down. During the summer months, hiking is popular on the many trails that encircle the mountains. It can be tough going, though, and the inexperienced shouldn't tackle the trails without a guide.

It is possible to walk up **Mt Rundle** or **Cascade Mountain** during the summer, but you must first register with a park ranger. If you're on Mt Rundle, make sure that you're on the Sulphur Mountain Trail. It's easy to mistakenly take the less scenic one, which runs along the river valley. It takes 1hr, 30 min to walk up the **Sulphur Mountain Trail** from the **Upper Hot Springs**. The gondola takes around 8 mins and costs $14. If you walk up, the ride down is free! Call 762-2523.

At the Upper Hot Springs there is a pool fed by sulphur springs at 40 degrees centigrade. Great for relaxing, although it will cost you $7. You can also hire towels for around $1.

If you don't have much time in Banff, there is a beautiful trail walk along the glacial green Bow River to **Bow Falls** near the Banff Springs Hotel. The hotel, the pride of the Canadian Pacific railway, is built in the style of a Scottish baronial mansion. The scenery really is spectacular and the area is not overrun by tourists, especially in winter. Although the cold temperatures cause the Bow Falls to freeze, they are still breathtaking. You may also see herds of elk tiptoeing on the ice further down the valley. An alternative short walk is the trail up Tunnel Mountain, which takes about 1¹/₄ hrs from bus station to the summit.

Glacial lakes are one of the most compelling features of the park. **Peyto Lake** (named after Bill Peyto, famous explorer and guide of the 1890s) changes from being a deep blue colour in the early summer to an 'unbelievably beautiful turquoise' later in the year as the glacier melts into it. Tourists have been known to ask the locals whether the lake is drained each year to paint the bottom blue! The glacier which feeds the lake is receding at 70 ft a year.

'The jewel of the Rockies,' **Lake Louise** lies in a hanging valley formed during the Ice Age. Don't let the invitingly placid waters fool you; the water is a chilly 10 degrees centigrade. The town of Lake Louise is 36 miles from Banff on the Jasper highroad. From town, journey 9 miles to **Moraine Lake** (once pictured on the back of the Canadian $20 bill), the **Valley of the Ten Peaks** and back through **Larth Valley** over **Sentinel Peak**, or walk out to the **Plain of the Six Glaciers** via **Lake Agnes**. You will need lots of time and a pair of sturdy shoes (or snow shoes in the winter—several feet of snow is the norm). Also worth a mention is the **Great Divide,** located near the picnic area at the park. From this geographic point, all waters flow either west to the Pacific or East to the Atlantic. You can actually see where the split occurs.

Be careful of the black and grizzly bears who live in the park. They are out and about in full force in summer, but are occasionally seen in winter as well. You may also see moose, cougars, coyotes and Rocky Mountain goats and lots of elk—beware the mean-spirited elk! The park is also home of the southernmost herd of the endangered woodland caribou. The lakes and rivers of the park are excellent for trout and Rocky Mountain Whitefish fishing, although you may need a permit to fish in some areas.
www.worldweb.com/parkscanada-banff/index.html

BANFF   Situated 81 miles W of Calgary and 179 miles S of Jasper, the village of Banff is always buzzing with activity. With excellent downhill skiing in the winter—a choice of three ski areas within easy reach—and hiking, cycling, golfing, and mountain climbing in the summer, visitors to this little town are rarely at a loss for something to do. Banff is also a lively arts centre— home of the Banff School of Fine Arts and host of a variety of arts festivals in summer and at Christmas time.

Over recent years Banff has become the favourite playground of Japanese tourists; many of the town's signs are printed in both Japanese and English. This sudden interest in Banff partly stems from a Japanese soap opera that uses the famous Banff Springs Hotel as its backdrop. As a result, the hotel is constantly full of honeymooners from the Pacific Rim. 'Really touristy but a very attractive town with spectacular surroundings.' For live webcam views from the top of Sulphur Mountain, go to *www.banffgondola.com/.*

ACCOMMODATION
Accommodation options in and around Banff are generally expensive. However, there are many hostels in the area and for the budget traveller they are undoubtedly the best bet. **Central Reservations**, (800) 661-1676. Will find accommodation for a $10 fee. **NB:** Not advisable to arrive in Banff on Sun eve without rsvs.

Banff HI Hostel, Tunnel Mountain Rd, 762-4122. 3 km from downtown, 45 min walk from train or bus station. 'Excellent hostel. Comfortable, friendly and near some great hikes.' Close to Whyte Museum and Banff Hot Springs, plenty of outdoor sports. Pika Shuttle btwn Alberta hostels can be reserved from here. $20 member, $24 non-member.

Castle Mountain HI Hostel, Hwy 1A and 93 S, 762-4122. 1.5 km E of junction of Trans-Canada and 93S. 25 km E of Lake Louise. Access to Norquay, Sunshine, Lake Louise, trails, springs and falls. $13 member, $17 non-member.

Hilda Creek HI Hostel, 762-4122. 8.5km S of Columbia Icefields Visitors Centre, 120 km N of Lake Louise on Hwy 93. Close by Mt Athabasca, Saskatchewan Glacier, skiing, telemarking. Hostel has wood burning sauna. 'Basic, but great hiking.' Partial closure Oct-Apr. $12 member, $16 non-member.

Lake Louise HI Hostel (Canadian Alpine Centre), Village Rd, 522-2200. Kitchen/laundry, cafe, mountaineering resource library, guided hikes, fireplace, sauna. Book early in high season. 'A palace!' $21 member, $25 non-member, private rooms available $27 member, $31 non-member.

Mosquito Creek HI Hostel, on Hwy 93, 26 km N of Lake Louise next to Mosquito Campground, 762-4122. Hiking, mountaineering, cross-country skiing. $13 member, $17 non-member.

Rampart Creek HI Hostel, 12 km N of Saskatchewan River crossing on the Icefields Pkwy, 762-4122. 'Loads of atmosphere but no common area. Handy for ice climbing and saunas followed by a dip in the creek!!' Hiking, volleyball, mountaineering, ice climbing, wood burning sauna. Partial closure Oct-Apr. $12 member, $16 non-member.

Ribbon Creek HI Hostel, 762-4122, 70 km W of Calgary on Hwy 1 (Trans Canada Hwy), then 25 km S on Hwy 40, turn right at Nakiska Skill Hill access, cross the Kananaskis River and left 1.5 km to the hostel. Hiking, biking, skiing, golfing, rafting, near Kananaskis Village. $13 member, $17 non-member.

Tan-Y-Bryn, Mrs Cowan, 118 Otter St, 762-3696. Continental bfast included. 'Super guest house.' S-$45, D-$50-$67.

Whiskey Jack HI Hostel, 27 km W of Lake Louise in Yoho National Park. Hiking to Emerald Lake and President Range. Closed mid-Sept-mid-June. $15 member, $19 non-member.

Y Mountain Lodge, 102 Spray Ave, (800) 813-4138. Laundry, cafeteria, meeting space. Operated by YWCA team. Dorms, $20. Private rooms available for budget rates (although higher in summer), call to enquire.

FOOD

For unbeatable value, try **Safeway** (on corner of Banff Ave & Elk St). For more upmarket possibilities, there's **Keller's** on Bear St, where they offer free coffee while you select your purchases. Pick up a copy of *Dining in Banff* for more options. On **Caribou**, check out **Aardvark Pizza**, 762-5500. 'Cheap, tasty and handy for post pub munchies!' Open daily, 11am-4am; **The Fine Grind**, (403) 762-2353, great coffee, hot chocolate and snacks served daily 7am-11pm, 'til midnight on w/ end; and the **Magpie and Stump**, 762-4067, authentic local cuisine and decor. Reasonable prices; noon-2am daily.

Athena Pizza, Banff Ave, (403) 762-4022. 'Large deep pan, $22.50 feeds 4pp.' Open daily, noon-1am.

Cascade Plaza Food Court, 317 Banff Ave (lower level). 'Great Chinese/Japanese food. $3.50 for a big plateful.'

Guido's, Banff Ave, 762-4002. 'Generous 3-course meal $8.50-$15. One of the best eating places in Canada.' Daily 5pm-11pm.

Joe's Diner, 221 Banff Ave, 762-5529. 50's style decor & music. 'Good and cheap.' Open daily, 8am-9pm.

Melissa's Misteak, 218 Lynx St, 762-5511. Varied menu, large portions, nice atmosphere. Open daily 7am-10pm.

Tommy's Neighbourhood Pub, 762-8888. Good food, friendly staff and 2-for-1 specials on five nights a week! Open daily 11am-2am.

OF INTEREST

Buffalo Paddock. On the Trans-Canada Hwy $1/2$ mile W of eastern traffic circle. A 300-acre buffalo range. You have to stay in your car. Free.

Icefields Snowmobile trips. See under Jasper.

The Indian Trading Post, 762-2456. A museum-like store which sells everything on display. Indian crafts and furs. Daily 9am-9pm, summer.

Lake Louise Gondola, 522-3555, off Trans-Canada Hwy. Daily 7.30am-6pm June-Labour Day. $10 r/t. Bfast, lunch also available. Skiing Nov-May.

Luxton Museum, 1 Birch Ave, 762-2388. Chronicles the history of the region's original inhabitants. Daily 9am-7pm, $6, $3.75 w/ student ID.

Natural History Museum, 108 Banff Ave, 762-4652. Geology, archaeology and plant life of the Rockies plus films. Sept 10am-8pm May, 10am-6pm rest of year; free.

The Park Museum, 92 Banff Ave, 762-1558. Details flora, fauna and geography of the park. Daily 9am-6pm, (winter 'til 5pm); $2.50, $1.50 w/ student ID.

Sulphur Mountain Gondola Lift, Banff, 762-2523. You can see 90 miles around on a good day. Daily May-Oct. $16.

Upper Hot Springs, Banff, 762-1515. Pool temperature is usually around 39 degrees centigrade. Daily 9am-11pm in summer, 10am-10pm in winter. $7, towel hire $1.25.

Whyte Museum of the Canadian Rockies, 111 Bear St, 762-2291. Library, art gallery, history of Rockies. Daily 10am-6pm in summer. $4, w /student ID $2.

ENTERTAINMENT
Banff Ave is the centre of the local universe, and the shops are consequently over-priced and tacky. Try **Canmore** for a more relaxed shopping experience. (22km towards Calgary on the Trans-Canada Hwy). The local rag, *The Crag & Canyon*, has info on local events.' Locals nights' and happy hours should keep you going from Sun-Thur! On Tues it's only $4 for the **Lux Cinema** on Bear St, 762-8595. Some of the more popular bars and clubs include:

Eddy's Back Alley, off Caribou, 762-8434. Chart and rock music, dead cheap on local nights. Open daily 8pm-2am.

Melissa's Bar, 218 Lynx St (upstairs), 762-5511. Stuff yourself with free popcorn while drinks get cheaper by the hour. Daily 7am-10pm.

Rose and Crown Pub, 202 Banff Ave, 762-2121. Live music nightly, darts, pool and great food. Home away from home! Open 11am-2am.

Wild Bill's, 201 Banff Ave, 762-0333, 'Best value in town and live music nightly.' Try your hand at line dancing! Open 11am-2am.

INFORMATION
Banff-Lake Louise Chamber of Commerce, 762-0270.

Banff National Park Interpretive Centre, Banff Ave, 762-1550. *www.worldweb.com/parkscanada-banff*.

Lake Louise Info Centre, 522-3833.

TRAVEL
The Banff Explorer, 762-8421, is a transit service within Banff. Leaves Banff Springs on the half hour and runs the length of Banff Ave. Every 15 mins a bus leaves for **Tunnel Mountain**, $1.25, summer only.

Big Foot, (888)244-6673, offers overnight adventures from Vancouver to Banff. Stay overnight in hostels; they provide the transportation. $106 for 2 days.

Brewster Transportation, 762-6700. Banff to Jasper, scenic route $85 o/w, $118 r/t; to Yoho Valley and Emerald Lake (recommended, fantastic scenery) from Lake Louise, or from Banff. 'Unless you have a car, forget trying to see both parks.'

National Car Rental has an office in town at Lynx and Caribou Sts, 762-2688.

Canoes/Rowing Boats are on hire at Banff and Lake Louise; and at Lake Minnewanka and Bow River motor boats are available. Motor boats are not allowed on Lake Louise. Hostel and the Y run rafting trips, approx $50. During winter, hiring skis/snowboards is easy and good deals can be found almost any-where. The buses to the ski areas can prove to be expensive, so if you're staying for the winter season, a pass is the best option.

Bactrax:, 225 Bear St, 762-8177. Mountain bikes available from $5p/hr, $19p/day 8am-8pm.

Rocky Express, (888) 464-4842, ' A wilderness adventure you' ll never forget' —and it lives up to its promise. Departs Weds, Fri, Sun from Calgary & Banff hostels; fun, flexible tours for small groups covering Banff and Jasper National Parks. Stay in hostels en route; price includes transport only but, at approx $185, is a good value way of seeing the maximum in short amount of time. (Total around $330 for six days).

Saddle horses from **Martins Stables, Banff, Banff Springs Hotel** and **Chateau Lake Louise**. Hired horses cannot be ridden in the park without a guide escort.

Hitching between Banff and Lake Louise could not be easier and it' s very popular. More difficult getting to Jasper, drivers like to view the many wonders of the **Icefield Pkwy** on their own. Not impossible, but be patient.

KANANASKIS COUNTRY

Tucked away between Banff and Calgary, Kananaskis Country is a recreation area that contains sections of three provincial parks (Bow Valley, Peter Lougheed and Bragg Creek). This 4,000 sq km back country area offers skiing, snowmobiling and windsurfing. There are excellent hiking trails and plenty of unpaved roads and trails for mountain biking.

Canmore, an old pioneer town, is situated at the north-western tip of Kananaskis Country. While retaining the haunting presence of the early settlers, Canmore displays a more modern side with the Nordic Centre, built for the XVth Olympic Winter Games. The centre is open year-round, drawing flocks of mountain bikers, roller bladers and hikers in the summer. The **Canmore Heritage Day Folk Festival** is held the first weekend in August. This cosmopolitan event is an annual tradition where each year families, locals and Calgary music lovers venture forth to enjoy the sights and sounds.

www.calexplorer.com/bckana01.html is a fun online article that lists many of the local activities.

ACCOMMODATION
Ribbon Creek HI Hostel, (403)762-4122, 70km W of Calgary on Hwy 1 (Trans Canada Hwy), then 25 km S on Hwy 40, turn right at Nakiska Skill Hill access, cross the Kananaskis River and left 1.5 km to the Hostel. Hiking, biking, skiing, golfing, rafting, near Kananaskis Village. $13 member, $17 non-member.

CALGARY

This fast growing city of 714,000 enjoys a friendly rivalry with Edmonton, 186 miles to the north. Known as the oil capital of Canada, Calgary, like Edmonton, went through a massive urban growth explosion during the late seventies. Calgary's growth has since stabilised, and the gleaming office towers that went up during the boom years are now the Canadian headquarters of the world's largest oil and gas exploration companies.

At one time Calgary's only claim to fame was the internationally-known Stampede, ten days of annual revelry devoted to the city's homesteading, steer wrestling, and bull riding heritage. But in 1988 Calgary busted out of its cowboy breeches and became a city of international standing by hosting the Winter Olympic Games. The legacy of the games lives on at various winter sports facilities, including 70and 90 metre ski jumps, bobsleigh and luge tracks, and an impressive indoor speedskating oval. If you are adventurous, you can rent a pair of speedskates and try your luck.

Geographically, the city is huge. Once annexation plans are complete, Calgary will be the largest city in Canada. In addition to excellent roads, there are over 100 km of bicycle paths that span the length and width of the city. Navigation is made even easier by Calgary's fast light-rail transit (train) system.

Despite its northerly location, Calgary seldom sees a rain cloud and gets less snow than New York City. Local weather is determined by the Chinook, a mass of warm air rushing in from the Pacific that can instantly send the temperature from minus 10°C to plus 15°C.

www.lexicom.ab.ca/calgary/index1.html is a useful source of attractions and events listings.

The area code is 403.

ACCOMMODATION

Contact the **B&B Association of Calgary**, on 531-0065 for info; it is never too early to make rsvs, especially for stays in July.

Calgary HI Hostel, 520 7th Ave SE, 269-8239. $15-20. Located downtown, this modern, pleasant hostel resembles a ski lodge. 'Excellent facilities.'

Travelodge, 9206 Macleod Trail S, 253-7070. From S/D-$69.

St Louis Hotel, 430 8th Ave, 262-6341. From S/D-$28.

YWCA, 320 5th Ave SE, 263-1550. S-$35, D-$45; both $5 extra w/bath. $5 key deposit. Includes use of gym and pool.

University of Calgary, **Kananaskis Hall** and **Rundle Hall**, 220-5100. From S/D-$24. Students only, no rsvs. Monthly rates available. 'Good facilities, gym, cheap meals.'

Camping: KOA Calgary W, 288-0411, 1.6 km W on Hwy 1; and **Langdon Park**, about 20 miles E. Sites $24, $26 w/hook-up, XP-$2.

FOOD

Downtown's food offerings are concentrated in the **Stephen Avenue Mall**, 8th Ave S btwn 1st St SE and 3rd St SW.

17th Ave SW, btwn 1st and 14th Sts. Lots of places 'sandwiched' among interesting shops.

Earl's, various locations. 'Great burgers, great prices.'

Electric Avenue, 11 Ave SW btwn 4th & 6th Sts—trendy night-club area with lots of eateries.

Joey's Only, fish & chips and seafood. All-U-can-eat chips. Inexpensive, good food. For locations call 243-4584.

Kensington's Delicafe, 1414 Kensington Rd NW, 283-0771. Earthy atmosphere, live entertainment, Wed-Sat. Open Tues-Sun 11:30am-2pm and 5pm-10pm.

Kensington—Louise Crossing area—Memorial Dr. and 10th Ave NW. Several restaurants to choose from, all reasonably priced.

Nick's Steak House and Pizza, 2430 Crowchild Trail NW, 282-9278. Close to Uni of Calgary, across from McMahon Stadium. Open daily 11:30am-11:30pm.

North Hill Diner, 80216 Ave NW, 282-5848. Open daily 7am-midnight.

Smitty's Pancake House, for locations call 229-3838—big bfasts.

Terra Bakery, 1600 90 Ave SW, 259-5864. Open 8am-6pm daily.

OF INTEREST

Calgary Tower, 101 9th Ave at Centre St South, 266-7171. Offers fantastic views of the city and the Rockies. Daily 7.30am-midnight, $6.15, $2.50 w/student ID.

Calgary Zoo and Dinosaur Park, Memorial Dr & 12th St E on George's Island, 232-

9372. Has a fine aviary and a large display of cement reptiles and prehistoric monsters including one 120-ton dinosaur. Daily 9am-6pm, w/ends and rest of year 'til 8.30pm, $10.

Centennial Planetarium and Alberta Science Centre, Mewata Park, 11th St & 7th Ave SW, 221-3700. Phone for show times in planetarium. Museum has vintage aircraft, model rockets and a weather station. $9 for any two shows. Daily 9:30am-5:30pm, Fri & Sat 'til 10.30pm.

Energeum, 640 5th Ave, 297-4293. Hands-on science centre about energy resources, oil and gas, coal, and hydro-electricity. Free. Mon-Fri 10.30am-4.30pm.

Fort Calgary Interpretive Centre, 750 9th Ave SE, 290-1875. Calgary's birthplace. Traces early Northwest Mounted Police life and prairie natural history. Daily May-Oct 9am-5pm. $5.

Glenbow Museum, 130 9th Ave SE, 264-8300. Art and artefacts of the west with a large collection of Canadian art and native artefacts. Daily 9am-5pm. $8, w/student ID $6.

Parks: Canada Olympic Park, Hwy 1 W, 247-5404. Bus tour of bobsleigh, luge runs, and Olympic ski jumps. In the winter the public can try bobsleigh and luge. Also the **Olympic Hall of Fame** with a heart-stopping audio-visual ski-jump simulator that allows visitors to experience the sensations felt by the athletes. Daily 9am-9pm., $7, bus tour $10.

Heritage Park, 1900 Heritage Dr, 259-1900. Calgary was once the Northwest Mountie outpost; this and other aspects of the city's past are dealt with in the park. The reconstructed frontier village includes a Hudson's Bay Co. trading post, an Indian village, trapper's cabin, ranch, school, and a blacksmiths, $11, $18 w/ rides included. Daily 9am-5pm.

Prince's Island Park, on the northern edge of downtown has special events and is just nice for sunbathing, etc.

Nearby: Bar U Ranch, 395-2212, located near the Rockies. A National Historic Site, the Bar U features displays and demonstrations about the history of ranching in Canada. Guided tours and authentic cowboy grub available. Open daily, 10am-6pm.

ENTERTAINMENT

Electric Ave, 11th Ave SW (see under *Food*) is an action packed strip of real estate that comes alive at night, guaranteeing you rockin' times! 'Try **The Warehouse, The King Edward Hotel**, and the **Tasmanian Ballroom**.'

Calgary Centre for Performing Arts, 205 8th Ave. Calgary Symphony Orchestra and live theatre. Call the 24 hr show info line, 294-7444.

Ranchman's, 9615 Macleod Tr S, 253-1100. A Honky-tonk, saloon, restaurant, nightclub and rodeo cowboy museum. Boot stompin' country music and dance hall. Open Mon-Sat 11:30am-2am.

Festivals: Afrikadey, held annually every Aug. Featuring the music of the entire African Diaspora: Africa, the Caribbean, and the North and South Americas, this festival of African arts and culture is a banquet of sights and sounds.

Calgary Folk Music Festival, held annually, last w/ end of July. This 3-day festival, set on the river in a beautiful inner-city park, balances traditional Canadian folk music with the sounds of acoustic and electric folk to Celtic, world beat and country.

Calgary International Jazz Festival, last week of June annually. The 10 days of the Calgary International Jazz Festival fit the city like an old glove.

Calgary Stampede. Second week in July. Calgary returns to its wild cowboy past. Rodeo events, chuckwagon races, free pancake breakfasts, bands, parties and tons of Texas two-steppin'. A tradition since 1912. For info & tkts, call 261-0101; for tkts only call (800) 661-1260. '10 days of fun and enjoyment.'

INFORMATION
Calgary Tourist and Convention Bureau, 237 8th Ave SE, 2nd floor, 262-2766/263-8510. Daily 8am-8pm.
Calgary International Airport, 735-1372, at the 'Chuckwagon' on Arrivals level. Daily 7am-10pm.
Talking Yellow Pages, 521-5222, provides a wide range of info for only the cost of a local call.
Travel information/accommodation rsvs: (800) 661-1678. *www.visitor.calgary.ab.ca.*

INTERNET ACCESS
Cinescape, Eau Claire Mkt, 200 Barclay Parade, 265-4511. $5/half-hour, $8/hr. Open 11:30am-midnight Mon-Thur, Fri-Sat 'til 1am, Sun 'til 10am.
Cyber Choice for the Virtual Reality Cafe, 26 Crowfoot Terr, 208-8787. Open Mon-Thur 9am-10pm, Fri 'til 11pm, Sat 10am-11pm, Sun 11am-9pm. $3/ 15min.
Screen Play Cafe, 3919 Richmond Rd, Glamorgan Shopping Centre, 246-8750. Open daily 7:30am-10pm. $5/ half-hr, $7.50/hr.
Wired-The Cyber Cafe, 1032 17th Ave, SW, 244-7070. Open Mon-Thur 9am-10pm, Fri 'til midnight. Sat 10am-12am, Sun noon-8pm.

TRAVEL/TOURS
Calgary International Airport, 735-1372, is located 12 miles N of the city. The **Airport Direct**, 291-1991, bus leaves every 30 mins from major downtown hotels, $10, 9am-midnight. A taxi will cost about $20-$25: **Checker Cab**, 299-9999and **Yellow Cab**, 974-1111.
Greyhound Bus Station, 850 16th St SW, (800) 661-8747. Leave terminal by 9th Ave exit and take #79, 103, 10, 102 bus to town, $1.50. 'The only bus south out of Calgary to the USA leaves at 7am, arriving Butte, Montana, at 7pm.' $87.
Hitchhiking is illegal within city limits.
Rocky Express, 6-day adventure tours through the Rockies; 912-0407. $199, plus extra for food and lodging.

DRUMHELLER In the Drumheller Badlands, north-west of Calgary, the 30-mile **Dinosaur Trail** leads an excavation site where more than 30 skeletons of prehistoric beasts have been found. Everything from yard-long bipeds to the 40-ft-long Tyrannosaurus Rex has been found in this mile-wide valley.

The valley has more to offer than just dinosaur fossils— there are also petrified forests and weird geological formations such as hoodoos, dolomites and buttes. The yucca plant, another survivor of prehistory, is found here, also in fossil form. The **Tyrell Museum**, 823-7707 in Midland Provincial Park on Hwy 838 is one of the largest palaeontology museums in the world. Daily 9am-9pm, $7.50. For more information, contact the visitors centre at 823-8100.

ACCOMMODATION
Alexandra HI Hostel, 30 Railway Ave N Drumheller, 823-6337. Located inside a refurbished hotel built in the 30's. Close by Royal Tyrell Museum. Games and meeting rooms inside hostel. $17.50 member, $20 non-member.

WATERTON LAKES NATIONAL PARK The other bit of the Waterton/Glacier International Peace Park (see also under Montana). Mountains rise abruptly from the prairie in the south-western corner of the province, giving way to magnificent jagged alpine scenery, several rock-basin lakes, beautiful

U-shaped valleys, hanging valleys and countless waterfalls.

There are more than 100 miles of trails within the park for walking and riding. It's also a good spot for fishing and canoeing. The park also features four campsites, along with several cabins and hotels for a not-quite-so-rustic experience. The high elevation and frigid glacial water conspire to make Waterton's lakes too cold for swimming but a heated outdoor pool is open during the summer in Waterton township.

A drive north on Rte 6 will take you close to a herd of plains buffalo. Go south on the same road and you cross the border on the way to Browning, Montana. You can also reach the US by boat. The *International* sails daily between Waterton Park townsite and Goathaunt Landing in Glacier National Park. Park admission $4per person or $8per carload. The park headquarters is located in **Waterton Park** townsite on the west shore of Upper Waterton Lake. The park information office is open daily during the summer. Park rangers arrange guided walks and tours and give talks and campfire programmes, etc, about the flora and fauna of the area. **Visitors Centre**, 859-2224, daily 8am-8pm.
www.worldweb.com/parkscanada-waterton/.

MEDICINE HAT   A town whose best claim to fame is its unusual name. Legend has it that this was the site of a great battle between Cree and Blackfeet Indians. The Cree fought bravely until their medicine man deserted them, losing his head-dress in the middle of the nearby river. The Cree warriors believed this to be a bad omen, laid down their weapons and were immediately annihilated by the Blackfeet. The spot became known as 'Saamis,' meaning 'medicine man's hat'. Discover the *Pure Energy* of Medicine Hat, *www.city.medicine-hat.ab.ca/.*

ACCOMMODATION
Assiniboia Inn, 680 3rd St SE, 526-2801. S-$30, D-$36.
El Bronco Motel, 1177 1 St SW, 526-5800. S-$45, $125/ wk, D-$50.
Trans-Canada Motel, 780 8th St, 526-5981. S/D-$30-$34, all rooms have kitchens and two beds.

OF INTEREST
Medicine Hat Museum and Art Gallery, 1302 Bomford Cr, 527-6266. Indian arte-facts, pioneer items and national and local art exhibits. Daily in summer Mon-Fri 9am-5pm, Wed 7pm-9pm, w/ends 1pm-5pm, $3 suggested donations.

INFORMATION
Chamber of Commerce, 513 6th Ave SE, 527-5214; Mon-Fri 8.30am-4.30pm.
Information Centre, 8 Gehing Rd SE, 527-6422. Daily 8am-9pm in summer, 9am-5pm after Labour Day.

WRITING-ON-STONE PROVINCIAL PARK   In the south of the province, 40 km from the small town of Milk River on Hwy 501, is this park of great biological, geological and cultural interest. The site, overlooking the Milk River, contains one of North America's largest concentrations of pic-tographs and petroglyphs. Inscribed on massive sandstone outcrops, these examples of plains rock art were carved by nomadic Shoshone and Blackfoot tribes.

This site is open year round but access is only on the one and a half hour guided tours, daily from May through beginning of Sept. Call for info on special events, 647-2364. Camping $11.

HEAD-SMASHED-IN BUFFALO JUMP   If the name isn't enough to pique your curiosity, then the fact that this historical interpretative centre is a UNESCO World Heritage site may. The Plains Indians who once inhabited this area hunted buffalo by driving herds of the massive beasts over the huge sandstone cliffs to certain death below. According to legend, a young Indian brave tried to watch one of the hunts from a sheltered ledge below (somewhat like standing underneath a water-fall). So many animals were driven over the cliff that, after the hunt, his people found him with his skull crushed by the weight of the buffalo. The startlingly illogical name makes perfect sense.

The centre is located 18 km NW of Fort Macleod on secondary Hwy 875, 175 km S of Calgary, 553-2731. Daily 9am-7pm, 'til 5pm in winter. $6.50. The home page, *www.head-smashed-in.com/* documents the buffalo hunting culture of aboriginal peoples of the plains.

MANITOBA

Situated in the heart of the North American continent, Manitoba extends 760 miles from the 49th to the 60th parallel, from the Canada-United States border to the Northwest Territories. In spite of its seemingly central location, the province has a 400-mile-long coastline on Hudson Bay, where the port of Churchill can be found.

Although Hudson's Bay Company, Canada's oldest business enterprise, was not formed until 1670, the first European settlers reached Hudson Bay as early as 1612. You cannot travel far in Canada without becoming aware of the power of the Hudson's Bay Company and its influence in the settlement of the country. At one time its territory included almost half of Canada, its regime only ending in 1869 when its lands were annexed as part of the country. These days the company is relegated back to its origins—you will see the name on a chain of department stores across Canada.

By 1812 both French and British traders were well established along the Red and Assiniboine Rivers. In that same year, a group of Scottish crofters settled in what is now Winnipeg. The present population of Manitoba includes a large percentage of German and Ukrainian immigrants, although the English, Scots and French still predominate. Manitoba became a province in 1870 after the unsuccessful uprising of the Metis (half Indian/half trapper stock) had been quashed. After the rail link to the east reached Manitoba in 1881, settlers flocked to the new province to clear the land and grow wheat. Winnipeg became the metropolis of the Canadian west.

Though classified as a Prairie Province, three-fifths of Manitoba is rocky forest land. Even this area, however, is rather flat. If you're travelling across the province, the landscape can get pretty tedious. Infinite prairies stretch out to the west and endless forests and lakes abound in the east. There are an astonishing 100,000 lakes in all, the largest of which is Lake Winnipeg at 9320 square miles.

National Park: Riding Mountain. *www.yahoo.com/Regional/Countries/Canada/ Province_and_Territories/Manitoba/.*
The telephone area code is 204.

WINNIPEG A stop here is almost a necessity if you're travelling across Canada. Canada's sixth largest city, this provincial capital has plenty to offer, especially if you can time a visit to coincide with one of the festivals happening in and around Winnipeg in the summer months. Among these are the Winnipeg Folk Festival, held annually at Birds Hill Park in July and Folklorama, Winnipeg's cultural celebration, held every year in early August. Sports fans' eyes were glued to Winnipeg in 1999, as the city played host to one of the world's premiere athletic festivals, the Pan-American Games.

Winnipeg (from the Cree word 'Winnipee' meaning 'muddy waters') is very 'culture-conscious', with good theatre, a symphony orchestra, the world-renowned Royal Winnipeg Ballet, plus an ample supply of museums and art galleries. It's also a major financial and distribution centre for western Canada, hence the vast grain elevators, railway yards, stockyards, flour mills and meat packaging plants.

The Red River divides the city roughly north to south. Across the river from downtown Winnipeg is the French-Canadian suburb, St Boniface. This community retains its own culture while mixing well with the Anglophones in Winnipeg. Many services are, therefore, offered in both languages. Winnipeg is known for its long and brutally cold winters, but summer daytime temperatures are comfortably in the high 70s and 80s before cooling off in the evenings.

ACCOMMODATION
Backpackers Guest House Int'l, 168 Maryland St, 772-1272, (800) 743-4423. $14-$16 dorm, private rooms, S/D-$35. Bike rentals $5 per day. 'Highly recommended.' 'Lovely, friendly guest house.'
Ivey House Int'l Hostel, 210 Maryland St (Broadway & Sherbrooke), 772-3022. $16-HI, $20 non-HI. Bike rentals. Check-in 8am-10am and after 4pm. Rsvs recommended. 'Very friendly.' Central.
McLaren Hotel, 514 Main St (across from the Centennial Centre), 943-8518. S-$35, Room for two, w/wash basin $40. En suite, $45. Very central.
University of Manitoba Residence, 26 MacLean Cr, 474-9942. May-Aug, co-ed, $18-$20pp. Small fee gives access to pool and sports facilities on campus. There are many **B & B** places in Winnipeg. The tourist office has a complete listing, or call 783-9797 for rsvs. Daily 8am-8pm.

FOOD
The multicultural background of Winnipeg's 650,000 citizens is manifested in its diverse culinary offerings. Choose from over 1000 restaurants serving everything from Ukrainian and Japanese to regional cuisine.
Alycia's, 559 Cathedral Ave, 582-8789. Ukrainian cuisine, 'try the pirogies, pan fried pasta stuffed with potato and cheese, delicious'. Dishes come separately or in combinations, $4.50-$8.50. Mon-Fri 8am-8pm, Sat 'til 9pm.
Blue Boy Cafe, 911 Main St, 943-1308. Cheap bfast and lunch, $3 up. Mon-Fri 6:30am-8pm, Sat 8am-4pm, Sun 8am-8pm.
Fat Angel, 220 Main St, 944-0396. 'Funky, colourful dining spot'. Entrees, light meals, vegetarian food and pizza, $3-$15. Lunch Mon-Fri 11.30am-2.30pm, dinner Mon-Thu 5pm-midnight, Fri 'til 1am, Sat 6pm-1am.

Grand Garden, 268 King St, 943-2029. Authentic Chinese food including regional specialities, sizzling plates and hot pot selections. Entrees $3-$17. Lunch Mon-Fri 10am-3pm, w/end 10am.

Kelekis, 1100 Main St N, 582-1786. Renowned deli. Good and cheap. Open Sun-Thur 8am-7:45pm, Fri-Sat 'til 9:45pm.

Montana's Cook-house Saloon, 665 Empress St, 789-9939. Open Mon-Fri 11am-1am, Sat-Sun from 10am.

Nikos Restaurant, 740 Corydon Ave, 478-1144. Bistro style setting for home-style Greek and Canadian fare. Everything from moussaka to subs. Entrees $6-$9. Daily 10am-10pm, Thur-Sat 'til 11pm.

Old Market Cafe, Old Market Square. Numerous speciality kiosks feature a variety of foods. Good in summer. Outdoor patio. Next door is **King's Head**, a British style pub.

Sweet Palace, 1425 Pembina Hwy, S of downtown, 475-7867. Indian specialities including over 35 desserts. Lunch buffet $7, dinner buffet $10. Tue-Thur 11am-9pm, Fri-Sat 'til 10pm.

OF INTEREST

Walking tours of historic Winnipeg begin in the renewal zone of the 1960s and wind through the streets and around the buildings of the Exchange District, where the city's commercial and wholesale history began. Tours depart on the hour, 10am-3pm, Tue-Sun, from Old Market Square, and last approx $1^1/_2$ hrs, $5. Call 942-6716 for more information.

Winnipeg's most popular walking tour is **Art Walk**, which begins at the Winnipeg Art Gallery and includes stops at 10 museums and galleries. Tours run Wed-Sat, 10am-3pm; $5. Call 786-6641 to reserve a place.

Assiniboine Park, Corydon Ave W at Shaftsbury, 986-3130. On the Assiniboine River with miniature railway and an English garden. The lush foliage makes this park very popular in the summer. There is always some sort of production here, be it Shakespeare, the symphony, or the ballet. In winter activities shift to skating, sleigh rides and tobogganing. Also located within the park is a sculpture garden dedicated to the works of local artist Leo Mol, 986-6531. Open Tue-Sun, 10am-8pm; free.

Assiniboine Park Conservatory, 986-5537, houses the tropical 'Palm House' and a gallery featuring works by local artists. Daily 9am-8pm, free. **Assiniboine Park Zoo**, 986-6921, one of the world's most northerly zoos housing native wildlife. There's also a statue in honour of Winnie the Pooh, who was named after Winnipeg. 9am-8pm daily, $3

Centre Culturel Franco-Manitobian, 340 Blvd Provencher, 233-8972, and its resident cultural groups, promote French culture through live musical entertainment, art exhibitions, theatre, art courses and a unique gift shop. Taste French-Canadian cuisine in **Le Café Jardin** or on the garden terrace, Mon-Fri 11.30am-2pm. The centre is open Mon-Fri 9am-8pm, Sat-Sun 1pm-5pm, free.

The Forks, 983-6757. This development at the confluence of the Red and Assiniboine Rivers celebrates the transformation of the Canadian west. Attractions include **Johnston Terminal**, formerly a 4-storey warehouse, now home to a variety of shops and restaurants.

Forks Market, a vast array of ethnic cuisine, local and national arts and crafts.

The Forks National Historic Site, 9 landscaped acres on the west bank of the Red River offers festivals and heritage entertainment from May 'til Labour Day. Also features an open-air amphitheatre, picnic area and dock. For event schedules call 957-7618.

Legislative Building, Broadway and Osborne, 945-5813. Completed in 1919and built from native Tyndal stone, this neo-classical style building houses, as well as the legislative chambers, an art gallery, a museum and a tourist office. It is set in a

30-acre landscaped park and the grounds contain statues of Queen Victoria, statesmen and poets. The Golden Boy perched atop the dome of the building, sheathed in 23.5 karat gold, symbolises 'Equality for All and Freedom Forever'. Created in a Paris foundry that was bombed during WWI, the Golden Boy spent 2¹/₂ yrs in the hold of a troop ship before making his way to Winnipeg. 8am-8pm daily, guided tours 9am-6pm on the hr, grounds tours 11am-4pm on the hour, free.

Living Prairie Museum and Nature Preservation Park, 2795 Ness Ave, 832-0167. See what the prairie looked like before the settlers came. Daily July-Aug, 10am-5pm. Free. Tours available. The prairie is open daylight hours. 'Take insect repellent!'

Lower Fort Garry, on the banks of the Red River 19 mi N of Winnipeg on Hwy 9, 785-6050. This National Historic Park is the only stone fort of the fur-trading days in North America still intact. It has been used at different times for various purposes. Originally the fortified headquarters of the ubiquitous Hudson's Bay Company, it has also been used as a garrison for troops, a Governor's Residence, a meeting place for traders and Indians, and the first treaty with the Indians was signed here. The park is open daily from May-Sept, 10am-6pm, tours available, $5.50. There is also a museum with nice displays of pioneer and Indian goods, maps and clothes. To reach the fort take the Selkirk bus from downtown Winnipeg, $4.25 o/w, Beaver Bus Lines, 989-7007.

The Museum of Man and Nature, 190 Rupert Ave, 956-2830, next to the **Centennial Centre** concert hall, 956-1360. Features provincial history and natural history of the Manitoba grasslands. Includes dioramas depicting Indian and urban Manitoban history and a replica of the 17th century sailing ship *Nonsuch*, that sailed into Hudson Bay in 1668and returned to England with a cargo of furs, resulting in the founding of the Hudson's Bay Company. Daily in summer, 10am-6pm, Thur 'til 9pm. Tues-Sun 10am-4pm in winter, $5.

Oseredok— Ukrainian Cultural and Education Centre, 184 Alexander Ave E, 942-0218. Folk art, documents, costumes, and history. Mon-Fri 9:30am-5:30pm, Sun 2pm-5pm, donation appreciated.

Riel House National Historic Park, 330 River Rd, 257-1783. Built in 1880-81, the Riel home has been restored to reflect its appearance in the spring of 1886. Louis Riel is noted as the founder of the province of Manitoba and lead the Metis revolt of 1870. Although he never actually lived in the house it was here his body was laid in state following his execution in 1885. Daily 10am-6pm, May-Aug only; Suggested donation $2.

River Interpretive Tours, 986-4928, boat tours exploring the city's waterways. The cruise follows the beginnings of the fur trade, the early forts and shows the importance water transportation played in developing Winnipeg. Tours depart from Forks Historic Docks Site Mon-Fri 9am, 10am, 1pm and 3.30pm, w/end 10.30am and 12.30pm. 1¹/₂ hrs, $5.

Royal Winnipeg Ballet, 380 Graham Ave, 956-2792. Canada's oldest ballet company. Founded in 1939, the RWB has grown to take its place among the world's great companies. Tkts $8.25-$48.

Royal Canadian Mint, 520 Lagimodiere Blvd, 257-3359. One of the largest and most modern mints in the world, strikes all Canadian coins as well as coins for several other countries. Tours every ¹/₂ hr. May-Aug Mon-Fri 9am-5pm, last tour 4pm. Sat 10am-noon, Jun-Aug only for self guided tours, $2.

St Boniface. Across the Red River, the city's French Quarter is the largest French-Canadian community in Canada and is the site of the largest stockyards in the British Commonwealth. A historic and cultural cornerstone of the city, it is the birthplace and final resting place of Louis Riel and original site of the Red River Colony.

St Boniface Museum, 494 Ave Taché, 237-4500. Built in 1846, it was originally a convent for the Gray Nuns who arrived in the area in 1844 and founded the **St Boniface General Hospital**. One of the oldest buildings in Winnipeg and the largest oak construction in N America, it houses displays centred around French-Canadian heritage, the Metis and missionaries who served them, recalling the early days of the Red River Colony. Guided tours by appointment. Mon-Fri 9am-5pm, Sat 10am-4pm, Sun 'til 8pm; $2 adult, $1.50 w/ student ID.

St Boniface Cathedral 190 Ave de la Cathedrale, 233-7304. The oldest basilica in western Canada, originally built in 1818 has been destroyed several times by fire. The latest structure was built in 1972 and still has the facade of the 1908 basilica that survived the fire. Open Mon-Fri 8:15am-5pm, Sat 10:45am-6:45pm.

Steinbach Mennonite Heritage Village Museum, 40 mi outside Winnipeg, 326-9661. E on Hwy 1, S on Hwy 12. This re-creation of a turn-of-the-century Mennonite village comes complete with mill, store, school, and costumes of the day. Also a good restaurant. May 1-Sept 30, Mon-Sat 10am-7pm, Sun noon-7pm. $3.25. Accessible by Greyhound or Grey Goose Bus Lines.

Upper Fort Garry Gate, the only bit remaining of the original Fort stands in a small park S of Broadway off Fort St. This stone structure was Manitoba's own 'Gateway to the Golden West'. A plaque outlines the history of several forts which stood in the vicinity. Free.

Winnipeg Art Gallery, 300 Memorial Blvd, 786-6641. One of the world's largest Inuit art collections. Traditional, contemporary and decorative Canadian, American, and European works. Rooftop jazz concerts on Thur eves throughout summer, $17, $16 w/ student ID. Call for schedule. Daily 10am-5pm, Wed 'til 9pm. $4, $3 w/student ID, free on Wed.

SHOPPING/EVENTS

Osborne Village, between River and Corydon Junction. Boutiques, craft and speciality shops and eating places. Look for the Medea, a co-op art gallery found in the Village. The **Exchange District** and **Old Market Square** are also interesting places to shop. Portage Ave is the main downtown shopping area. Portage Place has shops, restaurants, and IMAX theatre, 956-4629, with a gigantic 55ft x 70ft screen. S-feature tkts $7, D-feature $10.50

The **Winnipeg Folk Festival** takes place annually at the beginning of July in Birds Hill Provincial Park. This internationally renowned festival features the best in bluegrass, jazz, and gospel music. The park is accessible from Hwy 59 N of Winnipeg or through Winnipeg Transit.

Folklorama, (800) 665-0234, is Winnipeg's multi-cultural celebration held in early August. This two week-long festival highlights the ethnic diversity of Winnipeg with over 40pavilions featuring the food, dance, and culture of different nations. Day passes available.

Jazz Winnipeg Festival, 989-4656. Features the best in international, national and local jazz performers on free outdoor stages at locations throughout downtown and the Exchange District. Takes place mid-June.

The Fringe Festival, 956-1340, presented by the Manitoba Theatre Centre and held in the Exchange District in mid-Jul. 10 days of theatre performances including, mimes, jugglers, comedy and drama. All shows less than $8.

INFORMATION

Manitoba Visitors Reception Centre, Room 101, Legislative Building, 450 Broadway at Osborne, 945-3777. Maps and literature. Open in summer Sun-Thur 10am-6pm, Fri-Sat 10am-8pm, 8:30am-4.30pm rest of year. Pick up a copy of *Passport to Winnipeg* for up-to-date information.

INTERNET ACCESS

Networkx, 510 Portage Ave, 779-9000. Open Mon-Sat 10am-midnight, Sun 2pm-10pm. $7/hr, discounts for longer blocks of time.

TRAVEL
Bike hire: several locations in Assiniboine Park: ask at Visitors Centre.
Greyhound 487 Portage Ave, 783-8840, (800) 661-8747, 301 Burnell St, for **Grey Goose Bus Lines**, 784-4500.
Splash Dash Water Bus, 783-6633. 30 min water taxi tours along the Red and Assiniboine Rivers depart from the Forks Historical Harbour every 15 mins from May-Oct, 11.30am-midnight; $7.
VIA Rail, Broadway and Main St, 949-7400, (800) 561-3949. The train to Churchill takes a day and a half and must be booked 7 or more days in advance. R/t $211.
Winnipeg International Airport, 20 mins W of downtown, is served by the local transit buses, 986-5700. Take 15 (Sargent Airport) from Vaughn and Portage, $1.55. A taxi will cost around $13 o/w, call 925-3131.

RIDING MOUNTAIN NATIONAL PARK   The park occupies the vast plateau of western Manitoba's Riding Mountain. As it rises to 2200 ft, breathtaking views of the distant prairie lands unfold.

The total area of Riding Mountain Park is about 1200 square miles. Although parts of it are flagrantly commercialised, there are still large tracts of untamed wilderness to be explored by boat or by taking one of the hiking and horse trails. You'll see a fair amount of wildlife here; deer, elk, moose and bears abound, and at **Lake Audy** there's also a herd of bison. It's also a good spot for fishing.

Clear Lake is the part most exploited for and by tourists. The township of **Wasagaming** (an Indian term meaning 'clear water'), on the south shore of the lake has campsites, lodges, motels and cabins as well as many other resort-type facilities, right down to a movie theatre built like a rustic log cabin.

The park is reached from Winnipeg via Rte 4 to Minnedosa, and then on Rte 10. Daily admission $6.50, $15 (4 day pass). 848-7275.
http://parkscanada.pch.gc.ca/parks/manitoba/riding_mountain/riding_moun-taine.htm

CHURCHILL   Known as the 'Polar Bear Capital of the World', Churchill is the only human settlement where polar bears can be observed in the wild. It's known for more than just its great white inhabitants, though. Churchill has been a trading port since 1689 and served as the launching point for the first settlers to Manitoba. Today it's still the easiest part of the 'frozen north' to see. During the short July-October shipping season, this sub-arctic seaport handles vast amounts of grain and other goods for export.

The partially-restored **Prince of Wales Fort**, the northernmost fort in North America, was built by the British in 1732. It took 11 years to build and has 42-ft-thick walls. Despite this insurance against all-comers, the garrison surrendered to the French without firing a single shot in 1782.

Churchill is a great place to view some of the wonders of nature. From September to April, the beautiful **Aurora Borealis** (northern lights) are visible and good for picture-taking. Churchill has made it even easier for you to watch its sky explode with colour; the **Tundra Domes** offer clear, comfortable viewing from plexi-glass seating areas. Perhaps it isn't as authentic, but it beats sitting out in the cold. The summer daylight ruins the viewing conditions. To make up for it, whale watching is best in the summer months, from July-early September. The beluga whales come in and out with the tides. Polar bears are most frequently seen roaming around the city in September and October and are periodically air-lifted to other regions. The large numbers of polar bears sparked the decision to grant National Park status to Wapusk National Park, one of the world's largest polar bear maternity denning sites. On the tundra, lichens and miniature shrubs and flowers bloom each spring and autumn and a short distance inland there are patches of *Taiga*, sub-Arctic forest.

Note that Churchill is only accessible by plane or train (no automobiles). Look into the package deals put together by VIA Rail (see Winnipeg).

ACCOMMODATION
Northern Lights Lodge, 101 Kelsey Blvd, 675-2403, S-$68, D-$78, $10 more in Nov for bear season. TV, bar.
Polar Inn, 15 Franklin St, 675-8878, D-$90, more during bear season.

OF INTEREST
The **Eskimo Museum**, next to the Catholic Church on LaVerendrye St, 675-2030. Fur trade memorabilia, kayaks and Canadian Inuit art and carvings dating from 1700 BC, that are among the oldest in the world. Tues-Sat 9am-noon, 1pm-5pm, Mon 1pm-5pm. Free. 'Worth visiting.'
Fort Prince of Wales National Historic Park, 675-8863, at W bank of mouth of Churchill River, built by the Hudson's Bay Company in the 1700's to protect their interests in the fur trade. After its partial destruction by the French in 1782, it was never again occupied. Now partially restored. Open daily. The fort is only accessible by boat and the Sea North Tour is your only choice. The package includes harbour tour and whale watching and lasts 2 1/2 hrs, $45. Boat departs at a different time each day, tides and weather permitting, Jun-Sep. Call 675-2195 for schedule.
Wapusk National Park, 675-8863, is one of the newest addition to the Parks Canada family, established in 1996. Located south and east of Churchill, the park is a haven for polar bears. Tourists flock to see the bears' arrival from their summer ranges before moving onto the ice for winter. To see the bears, it's best to climb aboard one of the specially-designed tundra vehicles. Call the park office for more information.

INFORMATION/TRAVEL
Parks Canada, Manitoba North Historic Sites, Bayport Plaza, 675-8863. Daily 1pm-9pm.
North Star Bus Station, 203 La Verendrye, 675-2629. Local bus company offering 4-hr tours of the town, $45.
Tundra Buggy Tours, (800) 544-5049, offers tours into the tundra. The most safe and efficient way to bear-watch. Full day tours, $130.

SASKATCHEWAN

It's no wonder Saskatchewan is known as the 'Wheat Province.' It's responsible for over half of the wheat grown in Canada. Wedged between Alberta and Manitoba, Saskatchewan is the keystone of the Canadian prairie. Although the Trans Canada Hwy winds through seemingly endless, flat expanses of wheat fields in southern Saskatchewan, the province does have a more diverse geography. From the scenic hills of the Qu'Appelle Valley to the Cypress Hills in the Southwest and the badlands in the Southeast, Saskatchewan is anything but wholly flat.

Given the flatness of the terrain and the purity of the atmosphere, visibility in the south can be up to 20 miles. Watch the sky—sunrises and sunsets are beautiful, and cloud formations during wild prairie storms can be spectacular. As you travel north of the prairies past Hwy 16, the yellow landscape gives way to green rolling hills, and, still further north, to rugged parkland—lakes, rivers and evergreen forests.

Saskatchewan derives its name from 'Kisiskatchewan', a Cree word meaning 'the river that flows swiftly.' The river in question was, no doubt, the South Saskatchewan, where generations of Northern Plains Indians gathered to hunt and fish. The earliest written records of what is now Saskatchewan date to 1690, when Henry Kelsey of the Hudson's Bay Company became the first European to explore the region. Other explorers soon followed, opening the area to fur trade. More recently, oil exploration in the south has led to the discovery of helium and potash, as well as large quantities of 'bubbling crude.' In the summer, the weather is hot and dry while the winters are long, cold and snowy
*www.yahoo.com/Regional/Countries/Canada/Provinces _and_Territories/
Saskatchewan/.*
National Parks: Prince Albert, Grasslands.
The telephone area code is 306.

REGINA Nestled in the heart of the wheatlands, Regina is the universally-accepted stopping place between Winnipeg and Calgary. The present-day capital of Saskatchewan, Regina served a brief stint as capital of the entire Northwest Territories in 1883, just one year after it was established. Situated along the railroad, the town was a government outpost and headquarters for the Northwest Territories Mounted Police until the province of Saskatchewan was created in 1905.

The town was christened Regina after Queen Victoria in 1882 when the Canadian Pacific Railway completed its track across the Pacific. Prior to Regina, the town had a more poetic moniker, Pile O'Bones (a reference to the Indian buffalo killing mound at the site), a name considered inappropriate for a capital city. Thanks to the addition of a manmade lake and 350,000 hand-planted trees, the Regina landscape is more picturesque than one might expect.

ACCOMMODATION
B & J's B & B , 2066 Ottawa St, 522-4575. S-$30, D-$40. Weekly rates available. Free coffee and pastries in the morning.
Empire Hotel, 1718 McIntyre St, 522-2544. S-$25, D-$31. Shared bathrooms.
Turgeon Hostel (HI-C), 2310 McIntyre (at College), 791-8165. $14-HI, $19 non-HI. Near downtown, 1¹/₂ blks from Wascana Park. Cooking facilities, laundry, common room, library. 'Great place—clean, convenient.' Closed Jan.
University of Regina—College West Residence, Wascana Pkwy & Kramer Blvd, 585-4777. S-$30, D-$38, bath, TV. May-Aug only. Rsvs essential.
YMCA, 2400 13th Ave, 757-9622. $18p/night, $5 key deposit. Men only.
YWCA, 1940 McIntyre St, 525-2141. $35p/night, $2 key deposit. $168 wk, $285 mth plus $125 damage deposit. Rooms have basin, fridge; shared kitchen facs, showers, laundry.

Camping: Fifty Plus Campground, 12 km E on Hwy 1, 781-2810. 'Clean, quiet and quaint', 1 km off the hwy. Recreation hall, heated pool, laundry, showers, store. Sites, $13-$19, XP $1. May-Oct.

Kings' Acres Campground, 1km E of Regina on Hwy 1, N service road behind Tourism Regina, 522-1619. Sites $12, $16 w/hook up, XP-$1. Indoor recreation facility, large heated pool, showers, store. March-Nov.

FOOD

City Hall Cafeteria, 359-3989, on main floor, McIntyre and Victoria. 'Best lunch bargains in town,' $3-$5. Mon-Fri 7am-4pm.

Geno's Pizza and Pasta, Albert St N at Ring Rd and Gordon Rd at Rae St, 949-5455. Inexpensive Italian. Open Sun-Thur 11am-2am, Fri-Sat 'til 3am.

The Novia Cafe, 2158 12th Ave, 522-6465. A trendy Regina tradition. 'Don't miss the cream pie.' Open 7am-5pm Mon-Fri, Sat 9am-3pm.

Regina Farmer's Market, 1900 block of Scarth St, 949-8353. A great place to buy fresh produce and local bakery favourites. Wed & Sat only.

OF INTEREST

Government House, corner of Dewdney Ave and Pasque St, 787-5773, official residence of the Lieutenant Governors from 1891-1945. Explore rooms that have been restored to Victorian elegance. Tue-Sun 10am-4pm, free.

RCMP Centennial Museum, Dewdney Ave W, 780-5838. The official museum of the RCMP portrays the history of the force in relation to the development of Canada through equipment, weapons, uniforms, archives and memorabilia. Daily Jun-Sep 8am-6.45pm, Sep-May 10am-4.45pm. Tours in summer only, Mon-Fri 9am-11pm and 1.30-3.30pm. Donations appreciated. The **Sergeant Major's Parade,** is held on the Parade Sq at the Training Academy, 780-5900, Mon-Fri at 1pm. The **Sunset Retreat Ceremony,** also at the Academy. Colourful ceremony centred around the lowering of the flag and drill display by troops. Every Tue at 6.45pm Jul-Aug.

St Paul's Cathedral, 12th Ave and McIntyre St, 352-8931. The oldest house of worship in Regina, dating back to 1894. Open daily 10am-4pm, call ahead for tours. The area around the cathedral swells with quaint shops, restaurants and coffee houses— a lovely place to pass the afternoon.

Wascana Centre, in the heart of the city, this 2300 acre park built around Wascana Lake, is home to many of the province's top attractions. A place of government, recreation, education and culture. Home to the provincial **Legislative Building,** 787-5357, built in 1908 and designed to reflect the architecture of English Renaissance. Daily May 19th-Sep 2nd, 8am-9pm, tours every 30 mins, free. The **MacKenzie Art Gallery,** 3475 Albert St, in the SW corner of Wascana Centre, 522-4242. Historical and contemporary works by Canadian and American and international artists. Daily 10am-6pm, Wed and Thu 'til 10pm, free. The **Royal Saskatchewan Museum:** 787-2815. First Nations Gallery traces 10,000 yrs of Aboriginal culture, the Earth sciences Gallery depicts over 2 billion yrs of geological evolution. Features traditional and contemporary Aboriginal art, books and crafts. Daily May-Sep 9am-5.30pm, daily Sep-Apr 'til 4.30pm. $2 suggested donation. The **Saskatchewan Science Centre,** 791-7900, in the park features over 80 hands-on exhibits, live demonstrations and visiting exhibits. Next door is the **Kramer IMAX Theatre,** 522-4629, watch breathtaking films and special effects on the huge 5 storey screen, 7 shows daily. Mon-Fri 9am-6pm, w/end 10am-6pm. Museum $6.50, IMAX $7, combo tkt $12. Finally, the **Diefenbaker Homestead,** 522-3661, the boyhood home of the former Prime Minister of Canada, is also in the Park. Daily 9am-6pm. Free.

Willow Island, at the N end of Wascana Lake, is accessible only by ferry which departs from the dock off Wascana Dr, 522-3661, $2 r/t. The island is a popular picnic and BBQ site, and home to a **Waterfowl Sanctuary**. May-Sep, Mon-Fri noon-4pm. Part of the **University of Regina** campus is also located in the park. **Guided tours** of Wascana Centre can be arranged through the guide office, 522-3661, wk/days 9am-4pm, summer only. Bike rentals are available at park Marina.

Buffalo Days are held in Regina Exhibition Park, Dewdney Ave W, 781-9200, late Jul-early Aug. A celebration of Saskatchewan traditions such as chuckwagon races, logging contest, agricultural fair and exhibition. Also midway rides, grandstand shows, free entertainment stages and casino. The **Buffalo Days Parade** displays over 40 floats in carnival atmosphere. Entrance $7. There is also a three day **Folk Festival** held at the University of Regina in Jun. One of Saskatchewan's biggest attractions is the **Big Valley Jamboree**, 352-2300, in **Craven**, 26 mi N of Regina. In mid-July, the population of this small town swells nearly one hundred-fold as thousands congregate for North America's largest country and western festival. Following the festival is Saskatchewan's largest rodeo, the last weekend in July, 565-0565.

INFORMATION/TRAVEL
Regina Convention and Visitors Bureau, Hwy 1E, 789-5099. Mon-Fri 8am-7pm, Sat & Sun 10am-6pm. After Labour Day Mon-Fri 8.30am-4.30pm.
Saskatchewan Transportation Company, 2041 Hamilton St, 787-3340, (800) 661-8747. Bus to Saskatoon, 3 daily, $26.
Regina Airport is reachable by cab only. Call 586-6555, $8-$10.

INTERNET ACCESS
Cafe Ultimate, 1852 Scarth St, 584-2112. Open Mon-Thur 8am-midnight, Sat from 9am, Sun 1pm-11pm; $6.50/hr.

SASKATOON   Saskatoon started in 1883 as the proposed capital of a temperance colony. An Ontario organisation acquired 100,000 acres of land and settlement began at nearby Moose Jaw. Something about the prospects of living on the Canadian prairie without alcohol didn't quite catch on. The population of Saskatoon failed to increase, and plans for the temperance colony were essentially scrapped. Nevertheless, the city continued to develop as a trading centre. There are still a few dry establishments today, however.

The scenic South Saskatchewan River cuts right through the middle of the town; the parklands along its bank make Saskatoon a really pretty place, especially in the summer. It's an easy-going town with friendly residents. Saskatoon is 145 mi N of Regina, in the heart of the parklands.

ACCOMMODATION
Patricia Hotel, 345 2nd Ave N, 242-8861. S-$34, D-$38, w/bath, Q-$46. Rsvs recommended. The hotel also runs a year-round **hostel**: $13-HI, $19 non-HI.
The Senator, 3rd Ave S at 21 St E, 244-6141. S-$56, D-$71. TV, bath. Rsvs recommended. Very central.
YWCA, 510 25th St E, 244-0944. $38, $120 weekly, $285 monthly. $10 key deposit. Includes use of pool. Women only. Call to reserve.

FOOD
David's Lounge and Restaurant, 294 Venture Cr off Circle Drive North, 664-1133. Good for big hearty breakfasts. Open Mon-Sat 7am-10pm.
Louis' Campus Pub, on the University of Saskatchewan campus, 966-7000. Named

CANADIAN WILDLIFE

With so much remote and relatively uninhabited land, Canada is rich in wildlife. Due to increasing urbanisation, however, many of Canada's native species are known to be extinct or endangered, with most of their decline attributable to habitat destruction. When camping or travelling in wilderness areas, keep a clean and tidy camp, do not intentionally feed wild animals and stick to designated trails. These are some of the more common and/or interesting types the visitor to the backwoods or mountains may come across.

Bears—the dangerous **grizzly**, found in BC, Alberta and the Yukon, is very fast but doesn't see well, can't climb trees and runs slowest downhill. Bears are one of the few big game animals in BC for which a spring hunt is still allowed. As a result, the grizzly population is fast declining. Smaller **black and brown bears** are found all over and often visit campgrounds and dumps—keep your food locked away and never in the tent! Largest of all is the **polar bear**—that's the white one found only in the far north, where it's common to see them strolling around town! The **beaver** is one of Canada's symbols and is found all across the country. They are most likely to be seen chewing through logs or washing in the very early morning or early evening.

The massive, mean-looking **buffalo** still exists; Wood Buffalo National Park in the Northwest Territories is home to the world's largest free roaming herd. Buffalo are huge, powerful and, above all, not to be tampered with.

When out in the prairie at night you may hear the howl of a **wolf** or **coyote**. The coyote is a small, timid animal, more of a scavanger than a hunter. The larger, silver grey wolf native to BC and Yukon has been getting better press of late. One of the ecosystem's most important predators, wolves are seldom a threat to humans. Sadly, their numbers are dwindling due to government control programs, wolf bounties and the elimination of wolf habitats.

Found all over the country, the **lynx** is a large grey cat with mainly nocturnal habits that hunts small animals. **Deer** of many kinds can likewise be found everywhere. Canada's **cougar** population once mirrored that of the deer, its chief food supply. This large predator with its distinctive long tail is common only now in the west. Moose, too, are found throughout Canada but are most common in the northern woods and around swamps. A large brown, shy animal, the moose is a popular target for hunters. Their distant cousins, **caribou** (or reindeer) live in herds only in the far north. Overhunting and radioactive fallout severely reduced the caribou herds, but now they are more carefully monitored. Some Inuit still use caribou for food and for their hides. Smaller animals such as the **squirrel**, **chipmunk**, **raccoon** and **skunk** are found almost everywhere in Canada and may well be seen around campsites. Although marmots are common all over the country, the **Vancouver Island Marmot** is found only in the mountainous areas of the Island. One of the world's rarest mammals, their population is now less than 200. The marmots can be recognised by their unusual features: chocolate-brown fur with contrasting white faces, buck teeth and their high pitched whistle (for which they've earned the local nickname, 'whistle pig').

If on either the Pacific, Atlantic or Hudson's Bay coastline, **whale-watching** may appeal. Canada is a fisherman's paradise; northern **pike**, **bass** and **trout** are the most common **freshwater fish. The** highly prized **salmon** can be found on the east and west coasts, with that of British Columbia being the best.

One of the most mournful and memorable bird calls heard in Canada is that of the **loon**. Hear one over a northern Ontario lake in the late evening, and you'll never forget it. More info on Canadian wildlife/wilderness areas via the following sites: *www.cwf-fcf.org*, and *parkscanada.pch.gc.ca/parks/ main_e.htm*.

after the rebellious Louis Riel. A favourite summertime haunt. Lunch on the patio. Open Mon-Thur 11an-7pm, Fri 'til midnight.

Saint Tropez Bistro, 238 2nd Ave S, 652-1250. 'Nice light meals downtown.' Open Mon-Sat 5pm-11pm.

OF INTEREST

Stretching 19 km along both sides of the South Saskatchewan River, near Spadina Cres, the **Meewasin Valley Trail**, cuts right through the heart of Saskatoon. Picnic areas, BBQ sites, lookouts and interpretative signs along the way. The trail head is at **Meewasin Valley Centre and Gift Shop**, 402 3rd Ave, 665-6888. Learn about Saskatoon's history and the river through interactive displays and exhibits. Gift shop sells local arts, crafts and souvenirs. Mon-Fri 9am-5pm, 10:30am-5:30pm w/end and hols. Also in and around the park is the **Mendel Art Gallery**, 950 Spadina Cres, 975-7610. Mendel's permanent art collection and changing exhibitions of international, national and regional artwork. Daily mid-May-mid-Oct, 9am-9pm, rest of year noon-4pm. Free. For a change from the ordinary, try Shakespeare prairie-style at the **Shakespeare on the Saskatchewan Festival**, 653-2300, early Jul-mid-Aug, in the park. Buy tkts in advance. The **University of Saskatchewan**, 996-6607, is home to many attractions including the **Biology Museum**, 996-4399, the **Gordon Snelgrove Art Gallery**, 996-4208, **Museum of Antiquities**, 996-7818, and the **Museum of Natural Sciences and Geology**, 996-4399, to name but a few. Call for individual opening times, all attractions are free, donations appreciated.

Musée Ukrainia, 202 Ave M South, 244-4212. Ethnographic collections representing the spiritual, material and folkloric cultural heritage of the Ukraine. Daily June-Aug, Mon-Sat 10am-5pm, Sun from 1pm, $2.

Ukrainian Museum of Canada, 910 Spadina Cres E, 244-3800. Folk art, photographs and exhibits depicting the history of Ukrainian immigrants in Saskatchewan. Summer, Mon-Sat 10am-5pm, Sun 1pm-5pm, closed Mon rest of year. $2.

The Western Development Museum, 2610 Lorne Ave, 931-1910. Turn of the century 'Pioneer Street'—family life, transportation, industry, agriculture, etc. The museum's collection is 'said to be the best of its kind in North America'. 'Good.' Daily 9am-5pm; $5, $4 w/student ID.

SaskTel Saskatchewan Jazz Festival, 652-1421, held in downtown Saskatoon. Emphasis on mainstream jazz and a wide variety of other styles from Dixieland and blues to contemporary fusion and gospel. Over 500 musicians and 200performers, plus workshops and seminars. Dates change annually, call for details.

Harvest Fest, 931-7149, held in conjunction with the **Saskatchewan Exhibition**, early July. Midway, casino, grandstand, tractor pulls and other contests. The town's biggest event of the year. At Exhibition Grounds south of Lorne Ave.

INFORMATION/TRAVEL

Visitors and Convention Bureau, 6305 Idylwyld Dr N, 242-1206. Open Mon-Fri, 8:30am-7pm, Sat-Sun 10am-7pm.

The *Saskatoon Lady*, 934-7642, sails from behind the Delta Bessborough Hotel daily. Cruise along the river and take in the local attractions. Boat departs, 10.30am, 1.30pm, 4.40pm and 7.30pm, $10.

Saskatchewan Transportation, 50 23rd St E, 933-8000, (800) 661-8747. Bus to Regina, 3 daily, $26.

Saskatoon airport is reachable by taxi only. Call 653-3333, $12-$14.

INTERNET ACCESS

Coffee Dot Com, 269B 3rd St S, 651-2923, Open Mon-Sat 6.30am-10.30pm, $7/hr.

PRINCE ALBERT NATIONAL PARK This 1496-square mile park typifies the lake and woodland wilderness country lying to the north of the prairies. It's an excellent area for canoeing with many connecting rivers between the lakes. From 1931-8 it was home to Grey Owl, one of the world's most famous park naturalists and impostors. Born Archibald Belaney, old Grey was an Englishman who came to Canada to fulfil a boyhood dream of living in the wilderness. Donning traditional clothing, he presented himself as the son of an Apache woman and carried out valuable research work for the park. Visit the cabin he lived in for 7 yrs. Accessible by boat or canoe across the lake or on foot in summer. Entrance to the park is $4, $8 per car load.

Accommodation in the park includes campsites, hotels and cabins. **Waskesiu** is the main service centre where most hotels and motels can be found at some expense. Saskatoon is 140 mi S. For **Park info: Prince Albert National Park**, 663-4500; or **Prince Albert Convention and Visitors Bureau**, 953-4386. In the park **camping: Beaver Glen**, $13, $16 w/hook-up. You can also brave it and camp in the back country for $3. **Sandy Lake** and **Namekus**, $10. Campers must register, 663-4522.

parkscanada.pch.gc.ca/parks/saskatchewan/prince_albert/prince_alberte.htm.

THE PACIFIC

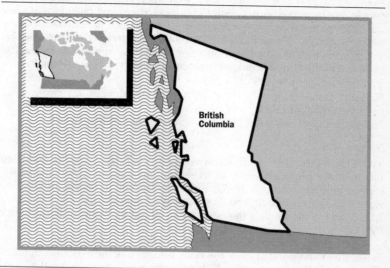

British Columbia

BRITISH COLUMBIA

Arguably Canada's most scenic province, British Columbia lies sandwiched between the Pacific Ocean and the Rocky Mountains and is bordered to the south by Idaho and Washington State, and to the north by the Yukon and Northwest Territories. This is an almost storybook land of towering snow-topped mountains, timbered foothills, fertile valleys, great lakes and mightier rivers. The spectacular coastline has long deep fjords dotted with islands and ranges of craggy mountain peaks that in some cases exceed 13,000 ft.

Inland there is a large plateau that provides British Columbia's ranching country. This is bounded on the east by a series of mountain ranges extending to the Rocky Mountain Trench. From this valley flow the Fraser, Columbia and Peace Rivers. The south-western corner of British Columbia is considered one of the world's best climatic regions with mild winters and sunny, temperate summers, and is consequently popular with Canadian immigrants.

This vast and beautiful province, which is about four times the size of the United Kingdom, was, however, a late developer. As recently as the 1880s there was no real communication and no railroad link with the east. The Rockies formed a natural barrier between British Columbia and the rest of the Confederation. Although both Sir Francis Drake, searching for the mythical Northwest Passage, and Captain James Cook came this way, there was no real development and exploration on the Pacific coast until the mid-1800s. Vancouver Island was not designated a colony until 1849 and the mainland not until 1866. British Columbia became a province in 1871.

The whole province still only has a population of three and a half million people, but in recent years British Columbia has enjoyed one of the highest standards of living in Canada thanks to its abundance of natural resources. About 50 percent of provincial moneys comes from timber-related products and industries but BC also has an amazing diversity of minerals on tap as well as oil and natural gas. Fishing and tourism are other major money-makers.

www.vacationsbc.com

National Parks: Yoho, Glacier, Kootenay, Mount Revelstoke, Pacific Rim.

parkscanada.pch.gc.ca/parks/main_e.htm

The telephone area code is 604 in the Vancouver area. Elsewhere it's 250.

VANCOUVER   This rapidly-growing West Coast city rivals San Francisco for the sheer physical beauty of its setting. Behind the city sit the snow-capped Blue Mountains of the Coast Range; lapping its shores are the blue waters of Georgia Strait and English Bay; across the bay is Vancouver Island; and to the south is the estuary carved out by its magnificent Fraser River.

Metropolitan Vancouver now covers most of the peninsula between the Fraser River and Burrard Inlet. Towering bridges link the various suburbs to the city and downtown area which occupies a tiny peninsula jutting into Burrard Inlet with the harbour to the east and English Bay to the west. Once downtown you are within easy reach of fine sandy beaches (or ski slopes in winter) and within the city limits there are several attractive parks. Most notable of these are the Queen Elizabeth Park, from which there is a terrific view of the whole area, and the thickly wooded 1000-acre Stanley Park.

Again like San Francisco, Vancouver is a melting-pot, with English, Slavs, mid-Europeans, Italians, Americans, and the second largest Chinatown in North America. The politics are very west coast: some people are rabidly right wing, and some are rabidly left wing.

Canada's 'Gateway to the Pacific' has a harbour frontage of 98 miles but the railroads too have an important part to play in Vancouver's communications system; one of the most spectacular rides is that into Fraser Canyon, once the final heartbreak of the men pushing their way north to the gold fields with only mules and camels to help them. If you're heading back east from here, this is the route to take.

Vancouver's climate is mild, but it does rain a fair amount. January is the coldest month although temperatures then are only about 11° Centigrade cooler than in July. Snow is rare and roses frequently bloom at Christmas. Altogether a great place to visit.

Vancouver hosted Expo '86 with the theme of transportation and related communications and technology. You can visit the site and the buildings down at the harbour. The city has become the location of choice for many American film-makers. This 'Hollywood to the north' provides a diverse backdrop for all types of movie sets and at lower costs than US locations.

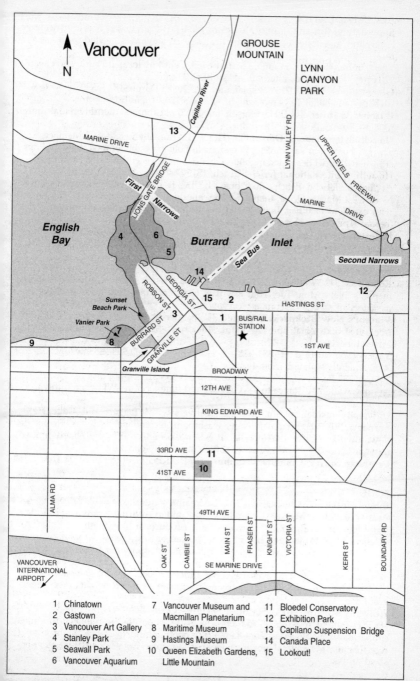

Vancouver

N

GROUSE MOUNTAIN

LYNN CANYON PARK

Capilano River

MARINE DRIVE

LYNN VALLEY RD

UPPER LEVELS FREEWAY

13

First Narrows

LIONS GATE BRIDGE

MARINE DRIVE

English Bay

4

6

5

Burrard

Inlet

Sea Bus

Second Narrows

12

ROBSON ST

GEORGIA ST

14

15

2

HASTINGS ST

Sunset Beach Park

3

1

BUS/RAIL STATION

Vanier Park

7

8

BURRARD ST

GRANVILLE ST

1ST AVE

9

Granville Island

BROADWAY

12TH AVE

KING EDWARD AVE

33RD AVE

11

41ST AVE

10

49TH AVE

ALMA RD

OAK ST

CAMBIE ST

MAIN ST

FRASER ST

KNIGHT ST

VICTORIA ST

KERR ST

BOUNDARY RD

VANCOUVER INTERNATIONAL AIRPORT

SE MARINE DRIVE

1 Chinatown
2 Gastown
3 Vancouver Art Gallery
4 Stanley Park
5 Seawall Park
6 Vancouver Aquarium

7 Vancouver Museum and Macmillan Planetarium
8 Maritime Museum
9 Hastings Museum
10 Queen Elizabeth Gardens, Little Mountain

11 Bloedel Conservatory
12 Exhibition Park
13 Capilano Suspension Bridge
14 Canada Place
15 Lookout!

ACCOMMODATION

Supernatural British Columbia Tourism, (800) 663-6000, makes rsvs in Vancouver hotels and sometimes has discounted rates. A credit card is needed to secure the reservation.

The Cambie Hotel, 300 Cambie St, 684-6466. Centrally located, 'basic and cheap'. $20 pp w/hostelling or international student ID card.

Globetrotters Inn, 107 W Esplanade, 988-2082. Dorm-$18, S-$30, D-$40, $45 w/bath (twin beds). Rsvs recommended. 'Small and friendly.'

Hazelwood Hotel, 344 E Hastings St, 688-7467, in Chinatown. Mthly rentals only, $375, $425 w/bath.

Hostelling International Downtown (HI-C), 1114 Burnaby St, 684-4565. Members $20, $24 non. Located in Vancouver's W end, metropolitan neighbourhood, close to shops, attractions, Sunset Beach and nightlife. Open 24 hrs, 'excellent'. Rsvs recommended.

Hostelling International Jericho Beach, 1515 Discovery St, 224-3208. $17.50 CYH. At foot of Jericho Beach. Take bus #4 UBC from Granville Station to 4th & Northwest Marine Drive, then a 5-min walk downhill to Discovery St. Big hostel with excellent facilities. Book ahead in summer. 'A great place but arrive early' (before 11pm). Bike rental $20 per day. 'Beautiful area.'

Kingston Hotel, 757 Richards St, 684-9024. S-$45-$75, D-$55-$85. Bfast incl. Very European. Swedish sauna. Cafe outside, TV lounge, laundry. 'Nice place.' 'Good people.'

Patricia Hotel, 403 E Hastings, 255-4301. D-$70 incl tax. 'Close to downtown.'

Roomies, 1542 W 8th Ave, 732-4350. Roommate referral service, furnished apartments, sublets. Mon, Tue, Thu, Fri 10am-6pm, Sat 11am-3pm. Closed Weds. $50 basic fee. info@roomies.com, *www.roomies.com*

Vincent's New Backpackers Hostel, 347 Pender St, 688-0112. Centrally located, free coffee, bike rental, 2pm check out. $10 dorm. S-$25, D-$35. Discounts available. Mixed reports.

YMCA, 955 Burrard St, 681-0221. S-$43, $45 w/TV, D-$53, $55 w/TV. Co-ed. 'Conveniently situated, friendly staff.'

YWCA, 733 Beatty St, 895-5830, downtown. D-$53-$106, T-$94 and up. Co-ed, TV, laundry, walking distance to YWCA pool and fitness centre. Wkly and mthly rates available.

University residence: Simon Fraser University, McTaggart and Gage Halls, Burnaby, 291-4503. Shared kitchen, washroom, recreational facilities, 15 min to downtown and close to Wreck Beach. $20 pp, no linen. $33 pp w/linen, limited number of double rooms available, $50 w/linen. May-end Aug.

Camping: Surrey Timberland Campsite, 3418 King George Hwy, 531-1033. $16 incl tax.

FOOD

Burger Heaven, 77 10th St, 522-8339. 'Good atmosphere, reasonable prices.'

Granville Public Market, Granville Island underneath the Granville St Bridge. Daily 9am-6pm. Exceptional quality fresh produce, fish and other edibles. An excellent place to stop and have lunch. You can browse the market and be entertained, and then enjoy your meal of Fukomaki (sushi, under $3), Indian Candy (smoked salmon, about $2), fresh fruit, or any of a rainbow of other varied and exotic choices while your eyes feast on a difficult to beat view of sailboats, the city of Vancouver and the mountains rising up to snow-capped heights in the background.

Heavenly Muffins, 601 W Hastings, 681-9104. Open Mon-Fri 6am-7pm.

JJ's, 644 Bute St, 682-2068. 'Products of cooking school sold to public. Good main course about $6.' Breakfast 7am-8am, lunch noon-3pm.

Keg Restaurants, several locations. Inexpensive; salad bar, seafood, burgers. 'Keg-sized drinks.'

Milestones All Star Cafe, 2966 W 4th Ave, 734-8616. Pizza, burgers, salad, subs. Dinner $11-$15.

Old Spaghetti Factory, 53 Water St, 684-1288, in Gastown. Large portions and reasonable prices.

Sophies Cosmic Café, 2095 W 4th St, 732-6810. 50s and 60s style café serving burgers, pastas and Mexican dishes. Sophies has also become an institution for old fashioned bfasts, and serves the 'best chocolate shake in town'.

Subway, Univ of BC, Students' Union Bldg, 822-3461. Cafeteria style, $4 up for subs.

Taf's Cafe, 829 Granville St, 684-8900. 'Arty atmosphere cafe. Reasonably priced. You can leave messages and luggage here.'

The Only Cafe, 681-6546, 20 E Hastings. 'Basic but tasty meal. A Gastown institution.' Complete meal $8-$12. 'Queues, popular with locals.'

The Tea House, Stanley Park, west side, 669-3281. Only when you want to splurge. Very expensive, but really lovely.

UBC Campus Pizza, 2136 Western Pkwy, 224-4218. Close to university.

White Spot Restaurants, several locations, 731-2434. Good and cheap.

OF INTEREST
The Downtown area
Canada Place, at foot of Burrard St. Unusual building resembling a cruise ship; the Canadian Pavilion during Expo '86, it's now Vancouver's Trade and Convention Centre. A 5-storey IMAX theatre is also housed here, 682-4629. For the domed OMNIMAX experience, go to **Science World**, 268-6363, 1455 Quebec St, a short SkyTrain ride away. Science world $11.75, OMNIMAX $10, both $14.75. Open daily 10am-6pm, shows Sun-Fri 10am-5pm, Sat 10am-9pm.

Chinatown, on Pender St, between Gore and Abbott Sts. Gift and curio shops, oriental imports, night clubs and many Chinese restaurants.

Gastown, in the area of Water, Alexander, Columbia and Cordova Sts. The original heart of Vancouver. In 1867 'Gassy Jack' Deighton set up a hotel in the shanty town on the banks of the Burrard Inlet. His establishment became so popular that the whole town was dubbed 'Gastown'. Now an area of trendy boutiques, good restaurants, antique shops, and pubs.

Lookout!, 555 Hastings St, 689-0421. Ride the glass elevator 167m up to the observation deck of this tower for a superb view of the city and surroundings. All day tkt $8, $5 w/student ID. Free if you dine at the revolving restaurant!

Robson St, between Howe St and Broughton St. European import stores and continental restaurants. 'Vibrant. Great at weekends.'

Stanley Park. The largest of Vancouver's parks occupies the peninsula at the harbour mouth and has swimming pools, golf courses, a cricket pitch, tennis courts, several beaches, an aquarium, an English rose garden, and many forest trails and walks. A nice way to see the park is by bicycle. You can hire a bike just outside the park entrance, around $5 p/h. Rollerblading around the park is another option—'the best thing I did in North America!' If you're walking, a recommended route is the **Sea Wall Walk** past Nine O'clock Gun, Brockton Point, Lumberman's Arch and Prospect Point. Near the eastern rim of the park is a large and very fine collection of totem poles. Free.

Vancouver Aquarium, 659-3474, located within the park. Features Ocra and blue whales, several performances p/day, daily 9.30am-7pm, $13. 'Brilliant. Could have watched the whales for hours.'

Vancouver Art Gallery, 750 Hornby St, 662-4719. Small but innovative collection of classic and contemporary art and photography and lunch time poetry readings. Daily 10am-5.30pm, Thu 'til 9.30pm. $10, $6 w/student ID.

Vancouver West. Reach Vanier Park by ferry, ($2, $3.50 r/t, every 15 mins, 10am-8pm), or take bus #22 or #2 and visit:

Hastings Mill Museum, 1575 Alma Rd, 734-1212. One of the few buildings remaining after the Great Fire of Jun 13th 1886, this is now a museum with Indian artefacts, mementoes of pioneer days and pictures of the city's development. Open daily 11am-4pm. Sep 16-May 31, Sat and Sun only, 1pm-4pm. Donations.

Macmillan Planetarium, 1100 Chestnut St, 738-7827. Runs numerous star shows throughout the day and laser shows set to music. Show times vary, call ahead. Rsvs recommended, $12.50.

Maritime Museum, ft of Cypress St, 257-8309. Exhibits include the RCMP ship *St Roch*, the first ship to navigate the Northwest Passage in both directions and to circumnavigate the continent of North America. Open daily, 10am-5pm, $6.

Queen Elizabeth Gardens, Little Mountain. When you enter the park keep left for the side with the views overlooking the North Shore mountains and harbour. There is a good view from the Lookout above the sunken gardens. Also, **Bloedel Conservatory**, 257-8570, on top of the mountain has a fine collection of tropical plants and birds. Entrance $3.50. To get to and from Little Mountain, take a #15 Cambie bus from Granville and Pender Sts and get off at 33rd and Cambie. Open Mon-Fri 9am-8pm, Sat-Sun 10am-9pm.

University of British Columbia, at Point Grey, has a population of some 23,000 students. There is a good swimming pool, cafeteria and bookshop. Also an **Anthropological Museum**, 822-3825, $6, the **Nitobe Japanese Garden** and **Totem Park** which has carvings and buildings representing a small segment of a Haida Indian village. To get to the campus take bus #4 or #10 from Granville and Georgia. No charge for museum on Tue after 5pm.

Van Dusen Botanical Garden, 37th and Oak Sts, 878-9274. 55 acres of gardens and lakes, hedge maze and nice view of the city. Open daily in summer 10am-9pm, $5.50.

Vancouver Museum, 1100 Chestnut St, 736-4431. Large circular building fronted by an amazing abstract fountain. Traces the development of the Northwest Coast from the Ice Age through pioneer days to the present. Displays artefacts from native cultures in the Pacific NW. Sat-Wed 9am-5pm, Thu-Fri 9am-9pm. $8, $5.50 student.

Vancouver East, Burnaby

Exhibition Park, bounded by Renfrew, Hastings and Cassiar Sts, is the home of the **Colliseum** and the site of the annual **Pacific National Exhibition**, 253-2311. The PNE takes place mid Aug-early Sep. $6 p/day. 'Fantastic. Includes lumberjack competition, rodeo, Demolition Derby, exhibitions, fair, etc.'

Simon Fraser University, atop Burnaby Mountain. Constructed in only 18 mths, the giant module design of this ultra-modern seat of learning makes it possible to move around the university totally under cover. The views from up here are superb. To reach the campus catch a #10 bus on Hastings east, change at Kooteney Loop to the #135-SFU.

Vancouver North

Beaches: Near UBC is Wreck Beach, free and nude; other recommended spots are English Bay, Tower Beach (also naturist), Spanish Banks (watch the tides), Locarno, Jericho and Kitsilano.

Capilano Suspension Bridge, 985-7474. Going north, the bridge is on the left hand side of Capilano Rd. The swinging 137-metre long bridge spans a spectacular 70-m-deep gorge. Entrance to the rather commercialised park costs $10, $6.35 w/ student ID. 8.30am-8.30pm. 'Not worth it unless you have time to walk the trails.'

Grouse Mountain, 984-0661. The skyride is located at the top of Capilano Rd and you can ride it to the top of the mountain for incredible views, a cup of coffee or a quick hike. Make sure the weather is clear before you go. 'Take food with you and make a day of it'. 'Spectacular. Not to be missed. Best thing I did in North America.' 'We went on a cloudy day and had an amazing time walking in the clouds.' The gondola costs $17, operates daily 9am-10pm.

Lynn Canyon Park, 981-3103. Less exploited than Capilano and free. The bridge swings high above Lynn Canyon Creek. Swimming in the creek is nice too and there is an 'excellent' ecology centre by the park entrance. To get there: catch the Seabus at bottom of Granville. At Grouse Mountain take a 228 bus to Peters St and then walk. By car, take the Upper Levels Hwy to Lynn Valley Rd and follow the signs. 'Peaceful and uncrowded.' Open daily 10am-5pm summer; weekdays winter.

Whistler Mountain, lies just north of Vancouver and is easily accessible from the city by bus or train. This area of incredible natural beauty is ideal for hiking, biking, rafting or horse-riding and boasts skiing conditions ranking among the best in the world. Even in summer it is possible to ski on the glacier. Trains leave from North Vancouver Rail Station daily at 7am, take $2^{1}/_{2}$ hours and cost $31 o/w, incl breakfast. Greyhound, 482-8747, runs a $2^{1}/_{2}$ hr bus service 6 times a day from Vancouver depot next to VIA rail station $18 o/w.

Whistler Hostel (HI-C), 932-5492, is a timber cabin on picturesque Alta Lake and a good base from which to explore the area. Members $18.50, $22.50 non. Great facilities and just 10 mins from the main resort.

ENTERTAINMENT

Jolly Taxpayer Pub, 828 W Hastings St, 681-3574.

Luv-A-Fair, 1275 Seymour St, 685-3288. Downtown Vancouver. Vancouver's hottest club. Hip-hop and alternative music, 'favourite haunt of visiting celebrities in the past.' '80s night on Tue really draws the crowds.' Cover charge $2-$6. Open 9pm-2am. Sun 'til midnight.

Purple Onion, 15 Water St, 602-9442, Gastown. 'A little bit of everything to please everyone.' 2 rms of live music and DJs. Open daily from 9pm, cover charge $5-$9.

The Roxy, 932 Granville St, 684-7699. Downtown Vancouver. 'Good atmosphere, extremely popular with locals'. 'Great in-house band.' Cover $4-$7. Open 7pm-2am.

Sea Festival, second wk in July. A week long celebration on the shores of English Bay featuring bathtub races, sand castle competition, parades, parties, and the city's biggest fireworks display, 'spectacular'.

Vancouver Folk Music Festival. Held in mid-July at Jericho Beach Park, 602-9798, features over 45 acts from across Canada and around the world. Tkts $35 Fri, $50 Sat, $100 w/end. *www.thefestival.bc.ca*

Vancouver International Comedy Festival. From street theatre to cabaret to stand-up, it's all there late Jul-early Aug at Granville Island, 683-0883. Some performances are free, otherwise tkts $7-$25.

Yuk Yuk's Comedy Club, 750 Pacific Blvd S, 687-5233.

INFORMATION

Chamber of Commerce, World Trade Centre, Suite 400, 999 Canada Place, 681-2111.

Supernatural British Columbia Tourism, (800) 663-6000. Info kiosks at airport, Gastown and Eaton's department store. Read *Georgia Straight* and the *Westender*, free from the Tourist Info Centres, for what goes on generally.

Vancouver Travel Information Centre, 683-2000. Waterfront Centre, 200 Burrard St. Open daily 8am-6pm.

INTERNET ACCESS

Central Branch Public Library, 350 W Georgia St, 331-3600. There are only 2 free computers available for those w/o library cards, but you can use the 5th floor computer centre, $5/55 mins.

Digital U, 101 - 1595 West Broadway, 731-1011. $9.50/hr.

Kitsilano Cyber Cafe, 3514 W 4th Ave, 737-0595. $6/hr

TRAVEL

Hitching is legal and common in Vancouver but no safer than anywhere else in North America. Exact-fare buses (currently $1.50-$3) operate in the city. The **Skytrain**, a light rapid transit system runs between downtown and New Westminster and connects to the bus system. The ultra-modern **Seabus** also connects to the bus system. A Daypass costs $6, available at 7-11, Safeway, Syktrain stops. You can ride anywhere, all day, after 9.30am. Take a ride from the bottom of Granville St to N Van, for stunning views en route. Catch bus #236 to Grouse Mountain.

BC Ferries, (250) 386-3431/(888) 223-3779 in BC. Regular boat service from mainland to surrounding islands. Schedules and prices vary depending on destination, call for details. Victoria $9 o/w.

BC Rail, 1311 W Pemberton St, 984-5246/(800) 663-8238, just over Lion's Gate Bridge, in N Vancouver Serving surrounding area and points North, Whistler, $31.

BC Transit Info, 521-0400. Schedules change every 3 months so call first. There is a free, direct line to BC Transit in the Skytrain stations.

Greyhound Bus Terminal, 1150 Station St, 683-8133/(800) 661-8747. Calgary $106, Seattle $34.

Gray Line Tours, 879-3363, leave at 9.15am and 2pm daily for 3 1/2 hour city tours in a double-decker red London bus. They will pick you up from any downtown hotel as long as you call the day before to rsv, $43.

Vancouver International Airport is reached via Hwy 99, Grant McConachie Way. Take city bus #20 from Granville St to 70th Ave. Change to the Airport #100 bus which takes about 45 mins. Charter Bus Lines Airporter Service, 270-4442, runs 25 min services every 1/2 hr from the Sandman Inn, Skytrain and Seabus stations, Canada Place and other downtown locations. $10 o/w.

VIA Rail located at 1150 Station St, at 200 Granville St, and 1311 West 1st in N Vancouver, (800) 561-8630, in US (800) 561-3949.

'Downtown to Downtown' **Vancouver to Victoria** bus service (via ferry) on Pacific Coach Lines, 662-8074, $51 r/t. However, it is much cheaper to go by public transport all the way using the ferry services. Take #601 bus, change at Ladner Exchange to #640 or #404 bus to Tsawassen ferry terminal. Ferry costs $9. From Swartz Bay take #70 PAT bus to Victoria.

VANCOUVER ISLAND   The island, and the Gulf Islands which shelter it on its leeward side, are invaded annually by thousands of tourists attracted by the temperate climate and the seaside and mountain resorts. Vancouver Island is a fisherman's paradise, with mining, fishing, logging and manufacturing the chief breadwinners. There are good ferry and air connections with the mainland. (See Vancouver and Victoria sections.)

Victoria, the provincial capital, is situated on the southern tip of the Island. **Nootka**, on the Pacific Coast, was the spot where Captain Cook landed in 1778, claiming the area for Britain. In the ensuing years, despite strong Spanish pressure, Nootka became a base for numerous exploratory voyages into the Pacific. The Spaniards were finally dispersed as a result of the Nootka Convention of 1790 but a strong sprinkling of Spanish names on the lower coast bear witness to the past.

Long Beach, 12 mi of white sand west of **Port Alberni** on the Pacific Coast, is recommended for a bit of peace. To get there take Rte 4 from Port Alberni across the mountains towards **Tofino**, the western terminus of the Trans Canada Highway. The beach is part of the now fully developed **Pacific Rim National Park**. Also in the park is the Broken Island Group in

Barkley Sound and the 45-mi-long Lifesaving Trail between Bamfield and Port Renfrew. There are campsites in the Long Beach area and on the Ucluelet access road, as well as at Tofino.

The Pacific Ocean is too cold for swimming here, though it's great for surfing or beachcombing. **Hot Springs Cove** reputedly has the best hot springs in Canada. The least known too, for you can only reach the springs by boat from Tofino and then walk a one-mile trail. The springs bubble up at more than 85° C and flow down a gully into the ocean. The highest pool is so hot that you can only bathe in winter when cooler run-off waters mix with the springs. Sneakers (as protection against possible jagged rocks underfoot) are the only dress worn while bathing.

Back over on the south-eastern side of the island there is a superb drive from Victoria north to **Duncan**, where the Forest Museum offers a long steam train ride and a large open forestry museum. Going further north you come to **Nanaimo**, the fastest growing town on the island. (By ferry to Vancouver $9.) Lumbering and fish-canning are the main occupations in town and it's worth taking a look at Petroglyph Park with its preserved Indian sandstone carvings thousands of years old. Nanaimo is also a bungee jumping centre (the only real place to do it in North America) and the starting point for the annual Vancouver Bathtub race across the Georgia Strait in mid-Jul. There are 'mini hostels' in Duncan and Nanaimo.
The area code for this region is 250.

ACCOMMODATION
Port Hardy: Betty Hamilton's B&B, 9415 Mayors Way, 949-6638. S-$45, D-$55-60.'Really nice after all my hostels and Betty certainly looked after you.'
Nanaimo: Nichol St Mini Hostel, 65 Nichol St, 753-1188. On bus route, communal kitchen, laundry facilities, showers. Registration 4pm-11pm. Open May 1st-Sept 1st only. S/D-$15, cottage-$38. Camping $8. Great downtown location, offers discounts to area, BBQ.

VICTORIA   Former fort and trading post of the Hudson's Bay Company and now provincial capital, Victoria is noted for its mild climate and beautiful gardens. This small, unassuming little town is located at the southern tip of Vancouver Island on the Juan de Fuca Strait. As a result of its attractive climate, it's a popular retirement spot and popular with British immigrants. Victoria has the largest number of British-born residents anywhere in Canada, and likes to preserve its touch of Olde Englande for the benefit of the year-round tourist industry.

Afternoon tea, fish n' chips, British souvenir shops, tweed and china and double-decker buses all have their place, but if you can get beyond all that, you will find Victoria a pleasant place to be for a time with plenty to explore around the town and out on the rest of the island. There are ferry connections from here to Vancouver and Prince Rupert as well as to Anacortes and Port Angeles, Washington.

ACCOMMODATION
Difficult to find in summer. Book ahead if possible.
Cherry Bank Hotel, 825 Burdett Ave, 385-5380. S-$54, $70 w/bath, D-$63, $78 w/bath. Bfast incl. 'Comfortable, central, recommended by locals.'
Craigmyle Guest Home, 1037 Craigdarrock Rd, 1 km east of Inner Harbour, 595-

5411. S-$65, D-$80-$95, T-$140. All rms have private bath/shower, full English bfast inc.

Hotel Douglas, 1450 Douglas St, 383-4157. S-$50-$80, D-$60-$95, XP-$10. City centre, close to City Hall.

Ocean Island Backpackers Hostel, 791 Pandora Ave, (888) 888-4180/385-1788. New hostel; $16 dorm, $40 double. No curfew, open 24 hrs, kitchen facs.

Selkirk Guest House, 934 Selkirk Ave, 389-1213. Dorm $18, linen included. Private rms available. S-$40. XP-$10. D-$60 (w/kitchen and bath). Kitchen/laundry, rowboat and canoe available for use.

Univ of Victoria Residence, 721-8395. May-Aug, students and non-students. S-$38, D-$60 incl full bfast. Stays over 14 days, $26.80 pp.

Victoria Backpackers International Hostel, 1608 Quadra St, 386-4471. Shared rooms $12 p/night, $10 key deposit. Private rm w/bath-$35-$40. 'Very spacious rooms'. 'A great place to stay. Really friendly and run by a complete lunatic!' Open 7.30am-1am.

Victoria International Hostel, 516 Yates St, 385-4511. $20, $16 CYH. Kitchen, laundry, linen rental, lockers, hostel-based programmes. Rsvs essential. Close to bus station and the train station. 'Priority given to members; if you are not one, you'll have to wait until 8pm to see if there is a bed.'

Victoria Visitors Bureau, 812 Wharf St, 953-2033 or 387-1642, can help find accommodation for you.

YWCA, 880 Courtney St, 386-7511. Dorm- $20 incl tax, S-$38.50 incl tax, D-$55 incl tax. 'New building with coffee shop.'

FOOD

Chinatown. Fishgard St and Government. Inexpensive Chinese eateries.

Fisherman's Wharf, St Lawrence and Erie Sts. Great place to buy seafood.

James Bay Coffee Co and Laundromat, Menzies St, 386-4700. 'Instead of watching clothes go round in the laundromat, hang out in the cafe next door—fabulous idea!'

London Fish & Chips, 5142 Cordova Bay Rd, 658-1921. Has the great British 'chippy' successfully crossed the Atlantic? Decide for yourself—but you'll still have to order 'french fries'. $10 for 2 fish and fries.

Scotts, 650 Yates St, 382-1289. Open 24 hr. Meals from $4.50.

Tomoe Japanese Restaurant, 726 Johnson St, 381-0223. 'Delicious, cheap food.'

OF INTEREST

Anne Hathaway's Thatched Cottage, 429 Lampson St, 388-4353. 'Authentic' replicas of things English, plus 16th and 17th century armour and furniture. Tours daily 9am-7pm in summer, 10am-3.30pm rest of year, $7.50.

Art Gallery of Greater Victoria, 1040 Moss St, 384-4101. Includes contemporary and oriental sections. Mon-Sat 10am-5pm, Thu 'til 9pm, Sun 1pm- 5pm. $5, $3 students w/ID. Thu 5pm-9pm free, Mon by donation.

Bastion Square overlooks the harbour. There is a **Maritime Museum** in the square, 385-4222, (open daily 9.30am-4.30pm, $5, $3 w/student ID) also a number of other renovated 19th-century buildings housing curio shops and boutiques. 'Nice place for just sitting, sometimes there is free entertainment around noon.'

Beacon Hill Park, 'Nice for walking and having a peaceful time by the lake.'

Butchart Gardens, 14 mi north of the city off Hwy 17, 652-4422. An English Rose garden, a Japanese garden and a formal Italian garden are the chief features of Victoria's most spectacular park. Floodlit in the evening in summer. Also houses a number of restaurants. Summer hrs, 9am-11.30pm, last admission 10.30pm, otherwise 9am-4pm or dusk. $15.75. 'Definitely worthwhile.' 'Don't take the special tour bus.'

Christ Church Cathedral, Quadra and Rockland Sts, 383-2714. One of Canada's largest cathedrals, built in Gothic style. Started in the 1920s and completed in 1991. The bells are replicas of those at Westminster Abbey in London, England. Stewards are on hand inside the cathedral to show you to places of interest. Open 8.15am-5.15pm daily. Donation appreciated.

Craigdarroch Castle, 1050 Joan Crescent St, 592-5323. Sandstone castle built in late 1880s by Scottish immigrant Robert Dunsmuir as a gift for his wife, Joan. Now a museum with stained glass windows, Gothic furnishings, original mosaics and paintings. 9am-7pm. $7.50, $5 w/student ID.

Market Square, off Douglas St. Attractive pedestrian mall with shops, fine restaurants and bars.

Parliament Buildings, Government and Belleville Sts. The seat of British Columbia's government is a palatial, turreted Victorian building topped by a gilded seven-foot figure of Captain George Vancouver, the first British navigator to circle Vancouver Island. Guided tours available daily throughout summer months.

Royal BC Musuem, 675 Belleville St, 387-3014. British Columbia flora and fauna, Indian arts and crafts and a reconstructed 1920s BC town. In summer daily 9am-5pm. $9.65, $4 w/student ID. 'Great museum.'

Thunderbird Park, Douglas and Belleville Sts. The park contains the world's largest collection of totem poles, a Kwakiutl Tribal Long House, its entrance shaped like a mask, and a flotilla of canoes fashioned from single logs of red cedar.

The Undersea Gardens, Inner Harbour, 382-5717. You can look through glass at a large collection of sea plants, octopus, crabs, and other sea life. Also scuba diving shows with Armstrong the giant octopus. Daily 10am-7pm May-Sept; rest of year 10am-5pm. $7.

INFORMATION
Tourism Victoria Info Centre, 812 Wharf St on the Inner Harbour, 953-2033 Open daily in summer 8.30am-7.30pm. 9am-5pm rest of year.

INTERNET ACCESS
Central Library, 735 Broughton, 382-7241. $3 fee (pay $5, get $2 back when done) for non-Victoria residents, up to 2 half-hour sessions per day.
Cyber Station, 1113 Blanshard St, 386-4687. $10/hr.
Victoria Cyber Cafe, 1414B Douglas St, 995-0175. $.14/min.

TRAVEL
Victoria Clipper, 382-8100, catamaran service to Seattle. $58-$66 o/w, $79-$109 r/t. Takes 2$^{1}/_{2}$ hrs.
BC Ferries, 386-3431/1-888-223-3779 in BC only. Serving Victoria, surrounding islands and the mainland. Vancouver $9 o/w.
BC Transit, (604) 521-0400. New schedule every 3 months so call first. (There is a free, direct line phone to BC Transit in the Skytrain station.)
Gray Line Tours, 388-5248, Double-decker bus tours of Victoria (1$^{1}/_{2}$ hr, $17) and Butchart Gardens (3 hrs, $36.75) depart the Empress Hotel; city tour buses depart every 30 mins.
Pacific Coach Lines, 700 Douglas St, 385-4411/ (800) 661-1725. Buses and connections to and from Victoria and other cities. Vancouver $26.50 o/w, $51 r/t.
Victoria Regional Transit, local bus, 382-6161 $1.75 one zone, $2.50 two zones.
VIA Rail, (800) 835-3037/(800) 561-3949 in the US, information and rsvs. From Victoria to Courtenay: the train journey is beautiful—in a small-one car including engine train—spectacular scenery, high bridges. The train stops over Nanaimo's bridge so you can watch the bungee-jumpers, $30 incl tax.
From Courtenay to Port Hardy, you can only go by bus. Ladlaw Coach Lines, on 27th St, 334-2475, $49. Ferry goes from here to Prince Rupert, 15 hrs, $104, call BC Ferries, 386-3431.

KELOWNA   Back on the mainland and going east out of Vancouver, Rte 3 takes you over the Cascade Mountains and down into the Okanagan Valley. One-third of the apples harvested in Canada come from this area. Good therefore for summer jobs, or if you're taking it slow, for a nice holiday just lying by the lake in the sun. The **Kelowna Regatta** is held during the second weekend in August, with accompanying traditional festivities.

Beware of the local lake monster. It goes by the name of Ogopogo, and is like the Loch Ness Monster but with a head like a sheep, goat or horse.

Not to be missed are the local wineries. **Mission Hill Winery**, 768-7611, is one of the best, free tours and sampling 10am-5pm daily. The **Kelowna Centennial Museum**, 763-2417, on Queensway Avenue has nice displays of Indian arts and crafts. Tue-Sat 10am-5pm. Donation appreciated.

ACCOMMODATION
CYA Hostel, Gospel Mission, 251 Leon Ave, 763-3737. $12 p/night, includes meals. Men only.

Kelowna International Hostel, 2343 Pandosy St, 763-6024. $15 dorms, private rms D-$35. Kitchen/laundry, bike rental available.

Same Sun Hostel, 730 Bernard Ave, 868-8844. Rms-$35 member, $39 non-member, Dorm (up to 6 people) $15 member, $17 non-member. Showers, downtown location, beach views. Another location on Harvey Ave, 763-9814, same dorm rates, private room $39 first person, $10 each extra person.

Willow Inn, 235 Queensway, 762-2122. $75 for 2, $99 for 4. Downtown, close to lake and park.

Hiawatha Park Campground, 3787 Lakeshore Rd, 861-4837. Sites $28 for 2, $30 w/hook up. XP-$8. Laundry, store, pool, hot dogs.

INFORMATION/TRAVEL
Kelowna Chamber of Commerce and Tourist Info, 544 Harvey Ave, 861-1515. Mon-Fri 8am-7pm, Sat-Sun 9am-7pm in summer; 9am-5pm winter. *www.kelownachamber.org*

Greyhound, 2366 Leckie Rd, 860-3835/(800) 661-8747. To Vancouver 6 runs p/day, 5¹/₂ hrs, $51.47.

Kelowna City Bus Transit, 860-8121. $1.25 one zone, $1.50 two zones, $1.75 three zones.

KAMLOOPS   The Trans Canada Highway takes the Fraser Canyon/ Kamloops/Revelstoke route through the province. The highway, at 5000 miles long, the longest paved highway in the world, crosses Rte 5 here, making Kamloops an important communications centre. Two rail lines also connect in Kamloops.

Kamloops is useful as a halfway stopover point between Vancouver and Banff or else a possible jumping-off point for visits to the Revelstoke, Yoho, Glacier, and Kootenay National Parks. The **Kamloops Museum,** 828-3576, on Seymour Street deals with the region's agricultural and Indian history. Kamloops is a popular place for skiers and trout fishermen.

ACCOMMODATION/FOOD
Bambi Motel, 1084 Battle St, 3 blks west of Yellowhead Bridge, 372-7626. $50 for 2, $70 for 4; kitchen available.

Kamloops Old Courthouse Hostel, 7 W Seymour St, 828-7991. Dorm $15 members, $19.50 non, private rooms $35-$50. Downtown location. Kitchen, laundry, TV.

Thrift Inn, 2459 E Trans Canada Hwy, 374-2488. $49 for 2, $53 for 4, pool, AC, TV.
Mr Mike's Broiler Restaurant, 2121 E Trans Canada Hwy, 828-0151 and 23-750 Fortune Dr, 376-6843. 'A place for a pig-out. Don't be put off by the exterior.'

INFORMATION/TRAVEL
Greyhound, 725 Notre Dame, 374-1212/(800) 661-8747. Open 7.30am-9pm. Vancouver $47.
Kamloops Visitor Centre, 1290 W Trans Canada Hwy, 374-3377. Mon-Fri 8am-6pm, Sat-Sun 9am-6pm.
Kamloops City Bus Transit, 376-1216. $1.25.
VIA Rail, (800) 561-8630/(800) 561-3949 in the US, information and rsvs.

MOUNT REVELSTOKE NATIONAL PARK   The park, midway between Kamloops and Banff, Alberta, is situated in the Selkirk Range. The Selkirks are more jagged and spiky than the Rockies and are especially famous for their excellent skiing facilities. The summit drive to the top of **Mount Revelstoke** is a 26 km parkway with scenic views. At the summit there is a 9 km trail winding through forests and meadows with fantastic views of distant peaks, glaciers and mountain lakes.

The Trans Canada runs along the southern edge of the park following the scenic **Illecillewaet River**. There are 2 self-guided tours available. One is a tour of the rain forest, with its huge cedar trees, and the other of the rare skunk cabbage plants. You can see it all without ever getting out of the car. Park services are provided in the town of **Revelstoke**, a quiet, pretty place set amidst the mountains. Entrance to the park is $4, and includes same-day entrance to Glacier National Park.

ACCOMMODATION
In **Revelstoke**:
Frontier Motel, at jct of Hwys 1 & 23 N, 837-5119. $58 for 2, $75 for 4. Price includes 4-course bfast.
Mountain View Motel, 1017 First St W, 837-4900. S-$40 up, D-$45 up, XP-$5; kitchens available in some rooms. AC, cable TV. Central location.
R Motel, 1500 1st St W, 837-2164. S-$49, D-$54.
Camping: Canada West Campground, 2¹/₂ mi west of Revelstoke, 837-4420. $16 for 2, $20 w/hook up, XP-$2; laundry, showers, outdoor heated pool, cappuccino bar. Free firewood.
Canyon Hot Springs Campground, about 15 mi east of town, 837-2420. $19 for 2, $25 w/hook up, XP-$2.

OF INTEREST
Canyon Hot Springs, 837-2420, 15 mi east of town on Hwy 1. 39°C mineral waters, or a swim in a pool of 26°C. $5, daypass $7.50.
Revelstoke Dam, Hwy 23 N, 837-6515. Self-guided tours, Mar 18th-Jun 16th, 9am-5pm; Jun 17th-Sep 10th, 8am-8pm; Sep 11th-Oct 29th, 9am-5pm. Free.
Revelstoke Museum and Art Gallery, Boyle Ave and 1st St, 837-3067. Mon-Sat 10am-5pm, $2 suggested donation.
Three Valley Gap Ghost Town, 837-2109, about 10 mi west on Trans Canada Hwy 1. Near site of original mining town of Three Valley with historical buildings moved here from various places in BC. Open daily 8am-4pm in summer. $6.50. Also has accommodation, $90 for 2.

INFORMATION
Tourist Info, Hwy 1 and 23 N, 837-3522. Open daily 9am-7pm.
Chamber of Commerce, 24 Campbell Ave, 837-5345. Mon-Fri 8.30am-5pm, Sat 10am-5pm.
Mount Revelstoke National Park, 837-7500. Open 7am-10pm.

GLACIER NATIONAL PARK From Revelstoke continue eastwards along the Trans Canada and you quickly come to this park. As its name tells you, Glacier is an area of ice fields and glaciers with deep, awesome canyons and caverns, alpine meadows and silent forests. There are many trails within the park and, like Revelstoke, this too is a skier's paradise. The Alpine Club of Canada holds summer and winter camps here.

The annual total snowfall in the park averages 350 inches and sometimes exceeds 600 inches. With the deep snow and the steep terrain, special protection is necessary for the railway and highway running through Glacier. Concrete snow sheds and manmade hillocks at the bottom of avalanche chutes slow the cascading snow, while artillery fire is used to bring down the snow before it accumulates to critical depths. Travellers through Rogers Pass in winter may feel more secure in the knowledge that they are passing through one of the longest controlled avalanche areas in the world.

Eight popular hiking trails begin at Illecillewaet campground, 3 km west of Rogers Pass. The **Meeting of the Waters** trail is short and easy and leads to the dramatic confluence of the Illecillewaet and Asulkan Rivers. The longer **Avalanche Crest** trail offers magnificent views of Rogers Pass, the Hermit Range the Illecillewaet River Valley.

Admission to the park is $4 pp daily and climbers and overnight walkers must register with the wardens at **Rogers Pass Info Centre**, 837-7500. Park services and accommodation are available at Rogers Pass. The Info Centre also has displays and exhibits on the history and national resources of Glacier National Park.

ACCOMMODATION
See also under Revelstoke.
Golden Municipal Park, in Golden on Kicking Horse River, 344-5412. $13, $15 w/hook up. Hot showers, outdoor pool. There are **National Park sites** at **Illecillewaet River**, 3 km W of Rogers pass summit, $13; **Loop Brook**, 5 km W of Rogers Pass summit, $13. Both campgrounds have firewood, toilets and shelters. Open Jun-Sep. Back country camping at **Mountain Creek** and **Rogers Pass** is available with a permit, $6. Campers must register at Rogers Pass Info Centre.

INFORMATION
Golden Chamber of Commerce, Caboose, 500 10th Ave N, 344-7125. Open 9am-8pm.
Glacier National Park/Rogers Pass Info Centre, 837-7500. Open 7am-9pm, winter hrs vary.
Tourist Info, Hwy 1 and 23 N, 837-3522. Open daily in summer 9am-7pm, 9am-5pm in winter.

YOHO NATIONAL PARK Still going east, Yoho National Park is on the British Columbia side of the Rockies adjoining Banff National Park on the Alberta side. It gets its name from the Cree word meaning 'how wonderful'.

Yoho is a mountaineer's park with some 250 miles of trails leading the walker across the roof of the Rockies. Worth looking at are the beautiful alpine **Emerald** and **O'Hara Lakes**, the curtain of mist at **Laughing Falls**, the strangely shaped pillars of **Hoodoo Valley**, and **Takakkaw Falls**, at 800m one of the highest in North America. The spectacular **Kicking Horse River** flows across the park from east to west. Entrance to the park is $5 pp.

ACCOMMODATION

There are 5 **campgrounds** and various cabins within the park. The campgrounds are at **Chancellor Peak**, open May-Sep, $13; **Hoodoo Creek**, open Jul-Sep, $14; **Kicking Horse**, open May-Oct, $18; **Takakkaw Falls** (walk-in), open June-Sep, $13; and **Monarch**, open Jul-Sep, $13. Each campground charges an extra $4 if you want to build a fire. Yoho operates 6 backcountry campgrounds, 4 in the Yoho Valley and 2 in the Ottertail Valley, $6 pp. Call the **Field Visitor Centre**, 343-6783. Alternatively, Yoho is easily visited from either Lake Louise or Banff. Tours of the park are available from both places.

Whiskey Jack Hostel, 13 km W along the Yoho Valley road (which begins at the Kicking Horse Campground) and 22 km W of Lake Louise on Hwy 1 (Trans-Canada Hwy). $15, $19 non-members. No phone - call the Banff International Hostel, (403) 762-4122, to make rsvs.

INFORMATION

Yoho National Park, 343-6324. Visitor Centre open 8.30am-4.30pm. *www.world-web.com/parkscanada-yoho*
Yoho Field Visitor Centre, 343-6783. Open 8.30am-7pm.

KOOTENAY NATIONAL PARK   Lying along the Vermilion-Sinclair section of the Banff-Windermere Parkway (Hwy 93), south of Castle Junction, Kootenay is rich in canyons, glaciers and ice fields as well as wildlife. Bears, moose, elk, deer and Rocky Mountain goats all live here. The striking **Marble Canyon**, one of several canyons in Kootenay, is formed of grey limestone and quartzite laced with white and grey dolomite and lies just off the highway. Park Info: 347-9615.

The western entrance to the park is near the famous **Radium Hot Springs**. There are two pools with water temperatures at almost 60°C. Springs are open daily in summer and entrance is $4. Admission to the park is $5 pp; visitors must obtain a park motor vehicle license at the entrance before driving through. There are campgrounds and motels within the park (beside the Springs and other locations) and accommodation is available in the town of Radium Hot Springs. Camping at **Redstreak Campground**, 2.5 km from Radium Hot Springs, $17, $22 w/hook-up. Open May-Sep; **McLeod Meadows**, 27 km N from W Gate entrance, $13. Open May-Sep: and **Marble Canyon**, 86 km N of W Gate entrance, $13. Open Jun-Sep.

PRINCE GEORGE   This fairly uninteresting town has become the takeoff point for development schemes in the wilderness Northwest. Travellers en route to Alaska from Jasper use the Yellowhead Hwy (Rte 16). At Prince George change to Rte 97 to Dawson Creek and the Alaska Hwy or Hwy 37 for Alaska or continue on Hwy 16 winding over the Hazelton Mountains to Prince Rupert on the coast. If you are travelling north from Kamloops, Rte 5 picks up the 16 at Tete Jaune Cache.

ACCOMMODATION
Prince George Hotel, 487 George St, 564-7211. S-$46, D-$61. English pub, TV.
Blue Spruce Campground, 4433 Kimball Rd, 964-7272. $15.50 two people, XP-$2.

BARKERVILLE   The settlement of British Columbia started here on 21 August 1862 when Billy Barker, a broke, bearded Cornishman and a naval deserter, struck the pay dirt that, within a short time, earned him $800,000, and all from a strip of land only 600 ft long. As a result of his find Barkerville became a boom town.

The shaft that started it all is now a part of the restored gold rush town at **Barkerville Historic Park** located 55 mi east of Quesnel and 130 mi south of Prince George. You will need a car to get there.

In Barkerville you can do some panning, call in at the Gold Commissioner's office, visit Trapper Dan's cabin in Chinatown, have your photograph taken in period clothes and visit the same type of shows the miners once enjoyed at the Theater Royal. A fine museum in the park tells the whole saga of Barkerville with photos, exhibits and artefacts. For info call 994-3332. Open daily 8am-8pm.

There is a campground near the park and fairly inexpensive motel accommodation in nearby **Wells**. Park admission is $5.50. The park is open year-round with reduced opening hrs and no guided tours after Labour Day.

DAWSON CREEK   A small, but rapidly growing town north-east of Prince George on Hwy 97 which marks the start of the Alaska Highway (see also Alaska). The Zero Milepost for the Highway is the centre of town.

Dawson Creek was settled in 1912 when the railroad was built to ship wheat from the area. A much older settlement, **Fort St John**, about 50 miles north, was established in 1793 as a fur trading outpost and mission. Today the town thrives on the expanding gas and oil industries in the area.

ACCOMMODATION
Cedar Lodge Motel, 801 110th Ave, 782-8531. S-$41, D-$49.
Camping: Mile 0 Campsite, 1 mi west of jnct Alaska Hwy next to golf course, 782-2590. $10, $15 w/hook up. Hot showers, laundry.

OF INTEREST
South Peace Pioneer Village, 1 mi south-east on Hwy 2, 782-7144. Turn of the century village incl log schoolhouse, trapper's cabin, blacksmith's shop, etc. Daily 9am-6pm, Jun-Sep. Donations.
Historical Society Museum, 900 Alaska Ave, 782-9595. In renovated 1931 railway station; local wildlife and history exhibits. Open in summer, daily 8am-7pm; Tue-Sat 9am-5pm in winter. $1 suggested donation.

INFORMATION
Tourist Info, 900 Alaska Ave, 782-9595. Open in summer, daily 8am-7pm.

FORT ST JAMES NATIONAL HISTORICAL PARK   Back on Hwy 16 (the Yellowhead Hwy) and heading from Prince George to Prince Rupert, it is perhaps worth a small detour at **Vanderhoof** to the shores of **Stuart Lake** to visit this former Hudson's Bay Company trading post. The 19th century post features restored and reconstructed homes, warehouses and stores. The park is open daily, 9am-5pm, May-Oct, and entrance is $4. Info: 996-7191.

PRINCE RUPERT   Known as the 'Halibut Capital of the World', Prince Rupert is the fishing centre of the Pacific Northwest. The season's peak is reached in early Aug and this is the time to visit the canneries.

This area was a stronghold of the Haida and Tsimpsian Indians and the **Museum of Northern British Columbia,** 624-3207, on First Avenue contains a rare collection of Indian treasures. In front of the building stands a superb totem pole. Inside, there are more totems, masks, carvings and beadwork.

Prince Rupert is marvelously situated among the fjords of Hecate Strait and at the mouth of the beautiful Skeena River. There is also a reversing tidal stream fit to rival the falls at Saint John, New Brunswick. You get a good view of the Butz Rapids from Hwy 16, en route from Prince George. The town is also a major communications centre being the southernmost port of the Alaska Ferry System, the northern terminus of the British Columbia Ferry Authority and the western terminus of VIA Rail.

ACCOMMODATION
Accommodation tends to be expensive. The **Visitors Information Bureau** may be able to help.

Aleeda Motel, 900 3rd Ave, 627-1367. S-$53 up, D-$70 up, XP-$6.

Pioneer Rooms, 167 E 3rd Ave, 624-2334. S-$27, D-$43. 'Small, clean and cosy.'

Raffles Inn, 1080 3rd Ave W, 624-9161. S-$50, D-$56, Q-$72. 'Comfortable and clean.' Near ferries & bus station.

Park Ave Campground, 1750 Park Ave, 624-5861, $10.50. 1km from ferry terminal. Covered areas for cooking and eating.

OF INTEREST
Museum of Northern British Columbia, 1st Ave and McBride St, 624-3207. Mon-Fri 9am-8pm, Sun 9am-5pm, winter hrs vary, $5.

North Pacific Cannery Village Museum, Port Edward, 628-3538. Old, original cannery buildings, wooden fishing boats, fishing exhibits, $6.

Queen Charlotte Islands, west of Prince George. Miles of sandy beaches. A place for taking it easy. Accessible from Prince Rupert by plane or boat.

Hazelton. A village north-west of Prince Rupert off Hwy 16, Hazelton is worth a stop for the interesting **Ksan Indian Village and Museum**, 842-5544. This is an authentic village and consists of a carving house and four communal houses. The houses are decorated with carvings and painted scenes in classic West Coast Indian style, $2. Tours daily May-Sept, $8.

Prince Rupert Grain Elevator, tours of the most modern grain elevators in the world. Rsv through Visitors Info Bureau.

INFORMATION/TRAVEL
Visitors Information Bureau, 100 1st Ave W (at McBride), 624-5637.

Ferry: The nicest way to approach Prince Rupert is undoubtedly by sea. A ferry, 386-3431, calls here from Port Hardy on Vancouver Island, making the trip on odd days of the month, $104, about 15 hrs. Leaves 7.30am-arrives 10.30pm. The scenery is magnificent and if you can afford it, it's a great trip. **Alaska Marine Highway Ferries**, (800) 642-0066, leave here for Haines, Alaska, 1 1/2 days, US$103. If you want a shorter trip, take the one to Ketchikan, passing through glaciers and fjords en route, 5 hours, US$38. 'Very beautiful.'

THE TERRITORIES

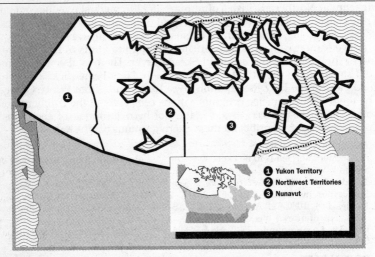

1. Yukon Territory
2. Northwest Territories
3. Nunavut

The Northwest Territories, Nunavut and the Yukon were originally fur-trading areas of the Hudson's Bay Company, only becoming part of Canada in 1870. These are territories, not provinces; the distinction is largely political. The lands are sparsely populated, and they don't have full status in parliament. The land masses that approach the Arctic Circle may not have a unified voice in parliament, but they do have a rich linguistic heritage, boasting more than eight official languages. If planning a trip to the Northwest Territories, Nunavut or the Yukon, be sure to contact the tourist office in advance. They can send you more detailed information so that you can take advantage of the many package tours available. Call Northwest Territories Arctic Tourism: (867) 873-7200/(800) 661-0788, Tourism Industry Association of the Yukon, (867) 668-3331, or Nunavut Tourism at (867) 979-6551/ (800)491-7910.

National Parks: Auyuittuq, Nahanni, Wood Buffalo and Kulane in Yukon. *www.yahoo.com/Regional/Countries/Canada/Provinces_and_Territories/Northwest Territories (or Yukon)/, www.nunatour.nt.ca*
The telephone area code for this section is 867.

NORTHWEST TERRITORIES

The Northwest Territories is on the verge of a name change. In 1999, the land mass formerly known as the Northwest Territories was split into two. The resulting eastern territory has taken the name Nunavut ('our land'), a tribute to the natives who fought for over twenty years for the right of self-government. Now that the territories have been halved, we can expect the remaining western 'Northwest Territories' to pick a new name.

The western territory takes in an area of 550,000 square miles, larger than France, Spain, and Germany combined. Despite the magnitude of its size, it's a vast, mostly unexplored, lonesome wilderness. The sparse population of 40,000 is scattered in 32 communities located on historic trade routes, the Mackenzie, Liard and Peel Rivers, and along the Arctic coast. Almost half of the population—18,000 people— make their home in **Yellowknife**, the territorial capital.

The territories are not, however, entirely perpetual ice and snow. Although half the mainland and all the islands lie within the Arctic zone, the land varies from flat, forested valleys to never-melting ice peaks; from blossom-packed meadows to steep, bleak cliffs and from warm, sandy shores to frigid, glacial banks. Both the region's highest and lowest temperatures were recorded at **Ft Smith**, where it bottomed out at -71 degrees F and soared to 103 degrees F!

European explorers looking for a water route to the Orient came here as early as the 16th century. Sir Martin Frobisher founded the first settlement on what is now called **Iqaluit**, previously **Frobisher Bay**, in 1578. Henry Hudson and Alexander Mackenzie both explored the area in search of greater trading outlets and profits. After a lapse of several years, settlement of the area picked up in 1934 when gold was discovered in **Yellowknife**.

With the more recent discoveries of rich mineral deposits and the promised exploitation of the oil and gas fields, life in the Territories is beginning to change. Many believe it's changing for the worse. Fur trapping is still the principal economic activity of the Inuit and other native people, but continued development and exploitation of natural resources could threaten their traditional ways of survival.

It's a long, long way north (a mere 3,655 miles from New York City to Yellowknife), but if you've decided to go, there are a variety of ways to get there. Flights depart regularly from Edmonton, Winnipeg and Montreal into the Territories. Once within the Territories, flights are available from Yellowknife to the remoter parts of the Arctic. By road, the Mackenzie Highway starts 250 miles inside the Alberta boundary, then saunters up to **Hay River** on the Great Slave Lake before striking west to **Fort Simpson**. From Hay River it's another 600 miles to Yellowknife. Buses from Edmonton, Alberta leave daily for Hay River and three times a week for Yellowknife. When travelling in the Territories, always carry ample supplies of food and fuel since it can be hundreds of miles between towns with few, if any, services enroute.

The Northwest Territories are rich in history and culture. Traditional and modern arts thrive among indigenous communities. Along the Arctic coastline Dene elders are recognised for their skills in producing traditional clothing, snowshoes, baskets and drums. The works of Dene and Metis painters and carvers are collected across North America. Communities along the Mackenzie River produce everything from moccasins and jewelry to canoes and moosehair tuftings. Old time fiddle musicians and young local bands can be found 'shaking their thang' at the dances and festivals held throughout the year. **Raven Mad Daze**, (867) 873-8389, in Yellowknife and **Midnight Madness**, (867) 777-2607, in Inuvik celebrate the summer solstice with entertainment in the streets, late night sidewalk sales, traditional drum dances and native cuisine. The **Midway Lake Festival**, (867) 952-2330, takes place in McPherson in late July.

The Territories are a place of vast natural beauty, with half a million square miles of unspoilt wilderness, wild rivers, mountain forests and sweeping tundra. **The Canoe Heritage Trail** offers some of the most challenging hiking in North America. A route bushwhacked through the mountains to Yukon during WWII, it's famed for its wildlife and for the spectacular natural formations in its valleys. The skies fill with the sinuous dance of **Aurora Borealis**, the northern lights. A giant electrical storm in the upper atmosphere radiates sheets of coloured light, typically ranging from greens, through yellows and pinks to subtle purples, across the night sky. Visitors come from around the world to witness one of nature's most marvelous spectacles, as familiar here as the summer sun or winter snow. Inuits thought the lights were a gift from their ancestors to light up long winter nights. Light-starved travellers may very well agree. The lights are best seen on clear nights from September to January.

The **Mackenzie,** Canada's longest river, is one of the world's greatest rivers. It twists and turns for 1200 miles from the **Great Slave Lake**, one of the largest and deepest lakes in the world, to the Arctic Ocean. As it winds across the Territories, it offers access to hundreds of navigable miles on the Slave River, the Nahanni, Liard, the Peel and Arctic Red Rivers, and on Great Bear Lake. During the ice-free months (end of May to October), tugs and barges ply up and down the river. The hardiest canoeists and trailer-boaters can join them for one of the loneliest, loveliest trips in the world.

The **Great Slave Lake** is the jumping-off point for the vast developments underway to the north. **Hay River** is a vital freight transportation centre being the transshipment point between rail and river barges.

Yellowknife, the territorial capital, is less than 300 miles from the Arctic Circle on Great Slave Lake. The city takes its name from the copper-bladed knives used by its original inhabitants. As the site of Canada's largest gold mine, Yellowknife keeps up its precious metal heritage. Other mineral treasures have been discovered nearby; in 1991, diamonds were discovered in **Lac de Gras** (150 mi NE). Tonalite gneiss, the oldest rocks in the world, at 3.98 billion years old, can also be seen near Yellowknife. Although you won't find any kryptonite here, Yellowknife is the hometown of Margot Kidder, famous for playing the role of Lois Lane in the *Superman* movies. You can even take a stroll down 'Lois Lane', named in honor of Kidder.

Despite its 'wild frontier atmosphere,' Yellowknife has been the seat of territorial government since 1967. The legislative building, built in 1993, features Canada's only round assembly chamber— a symbol of the consensus style of government. Since this is the most highly developed region in the Territory and the hub for travel to remoter areas, it is also quite expensive. Yellowknife is the second-fastest growing community in Canada, so lower prices for visitors are likely on the horizon. B&Bs seem to be the best bet for a cheap room, S/D-$50-$75. In June, it's possible to take part in a 24 hour golfing marathon, since the sun doesn't set here for the whole of the summer. It is also possible to visit the underground gold mines. Tourist information is available from the **Chamber of Commerce**, 4807 49th St, (867) 920-4944, and from **Northwest Arctic Tourism** 52nd St and 49th Ave, (867) 873-7200. One other place to visit is the **Prince of Wales Northern Heritage Centre**, 48th St, (867) 873-7551, which has exhibits and crafts on the history and cultural developments in the Northwest Territories. Open daily 10.30am-5.30pm. Free.

Fort Smith, just across from the Albertan frontier and once the territorial capital, is a sprawling mixture of shacks, log cabins and modern, government-built establishments. The Hudson's Bay Company established a trading post here in 1874, and the town later became a stopping place for gold-seekers on their way to the Yukon. The **Northern Life Museum**, 110 King St, 872-2859, relates the human history of the area and boasts an impressive collection of dinosaur bones and mammoth tusks. Open Tue-Fri, 1pm-5pm. Fort Smith is also the headquarters of **Wood Buffalo**, Canada's largest National Park and the second-largest national park in the world. Straddling the Alberta/Northwest Territories line, Wood Buffalo was established to protect the only remaining herd of wood bison. The end result is an excellent example of boreal forest with streams, lakes and towering cliffs, perfect for cross-country skiing or snow-shoeing. The park's unusual geography also yields one of North America's most extensive landscapes of sinkholes, underground rivers, caves and sunken valleys. There are several trails within the park and rangers sponsor guided nature hikes in summer. Camping is permitted: try **Pine Lake**, open May-Sept, $10p/site. Camping is available elsewhere in the park but a back country pass is required, call (867) 872-2349, for details.

Nahanni National Park, (867) 695-2310, is north-west of Fort Simpson. This wilderness area of hot springs, waterfalls, canyons and river rapids is shrouded in an enduring Yukon Gold Rush mystery. In the early 1900s the three McLeod brothers reputedly discovered gold nuggets the size of grapes near the present day park. Three years later, their beheaded bodies were found in a valley. The vein of gold which the McLeods tapped has never been found again, and their mysterious deaths remain unsolved. Here you will find **Virginia Falls**. At 312 ft, it's more than twice the height of Niagara Falls. This park is also inaccessible by road; die-hards have been known to hike into the park then canoe down the watershed of the S Nahanni river. Unless you have a death wish, take the plane. Jet connections are available from various points, including Fort Simpson. The **Visitor Centre** in **Fort Simpson** features extensive displays on the history, culture and geography of the area, free. Park entrance $10.

The third largest city in the Northwest Territories is **Inuvik**. Tucked away in the northernmost corner, it's the town furthest north on the continent that can be reached by public highway. A boom town, Inuvik is ever alert for news of oil strikes. The city is an interesting mixture of old timers, traders, delta Eskimos, Indians, oilmen and entrepreneurs. True to its heritage, gold and diamond mining continues to be the economic mainstay of the community. Look out for the cold temperatures, even in summertime. Church-going residents have poked fun at the cruel temperatures by constructing **Our Lady of Victory Church**, shaped like an igloo. There are three hotels, all expensive, but camping is possible if you can stand the cold.

NUNAVUT

A separate Canadian territory since only 1 April 1999, and situated in the far north-east of the country, Nunavut is much closer geographically and culturally to the arctic environment of Greenland than to anywhere else in North America. Even the far reaches of Alaska seem tame in comparison to the northern isles of Nunavut. Formed from the eastern portion of the Northwest Territories, Nunavut has achieved self-rule for the Inuit, the native people who make up 85% of the population. It was a struggle that lasted a quarter of a century, and that finally became a reality in 1993 when the Nunavut Act was passed. Nunavut means 'Our Land' in the Inuit language.

The landscape is typically arctic, and most of the province lies above the tree-line. It can be both stark and beautiful at the same time, and varies from dramatic mountains and fjords on the shores of **Baffin** and **Ellesmere Islands**, to lakes and tundra further west. The climate ranges from -40c in the far north during winter, to between the much more bearable temperatures of 2-10c (and almost 24 hrs of sunshine) during the summer. Snow flurries are a possibility year round; in summer, so are bugs, and some form of insect repellent is advisable.

The new territory covers one fifth the land mass of Canada, spans four times zones geographically (but only uses three - from 5-7 hours behind GMT) and has a population of under 25,000 for its 1.9 million square miles. It has three official languages, English, French and Inuktitut.

Sadly, in common with other North American counterparts, the sudden dominance of western culture has not blended happily with traditional life. The region has a 60% unemployment rate, where previously the population was employed full-time in sheer survival. In the 1950s there was forced relocation of the Inuit to permanent settlements instead of their previous nomadic existence. Local arts and crafts are highly regarded and have so far provided some income, but even this has recently fallen into decline. The creation of the Inuit peoples' own government is, however, seen as a positive step, and expectations are high for the future.

For the territory's official website, see *www.nunatour.nt.ca* They can also be contacted at Nunavut Tourism, PO Box 1450, Iqaluit, NT, X0A 0H0. There is also an excellent site written mainly by the Inuit about their history and culture and landscape, appropriately called 'Changing the Map of Canada' at *www.nunavut.com/nunavut99/english/ index.html. The area code for Nunavut is 867.*

Iqaluit the new capital is by far the largest community with a grand total of around 4000 residents. Previously known as **Frobisher Bay**, it is located amid majestic tundra landscapes on the southern coast of Baffin Island. Since 1954 and the establishment of the Early Warning Line, this has also been an important defence and strategic site and a refuelling stop for military and commercial aircraft. There is an **Unikkaarvik Visitors Centre** which gives information on day hikes and on arctic wildflowers, which are especially prevalent in July. Also a **Visitors Centre** and **Museum**, next to each other on the beachfront. The museum houses many artefacts relating to south Baffin Island.

Previously Eskimo Point, **Arviat** is situated on the western side of Hudson Bay, and one of the closest communities to 'the South' (Manitoba).

South of the community lies **Wolf Esker**, which is a good introduction to tundra flora and fauna, and there are several archaeological sites in and around the town. An old coastal supply boat, the *Qulsittuq*, dating from the 1920's is beached here.

For the more adventurous, **Auyuittuq National Park**, 473-8828, is nearest the Inuit settlement of **Pangnirtung** on Baffin Island, and is renowned for its spectacular fjords, active glaciers, mountains and archaeological sites. Inaccessible by road, it is an adventure in itself reaching the park. It is possible to arrive either by boat or snowmobile from **Broughton Island** and Pangnirtung, after flights from Iqaluit (First Air, Air Nunavut, $75-$200 p/p). You must register your entry at one of these places, and park entry costs $15 p/day or $40 for 3 nights. Even more inaccessible is the remote northern park of **Ellesmere Island National Park**, 473-8828. This is the site of deep glacial valleys and mountains and remnants of the last continental glaciation that covered most of North America ten thousand years ago. Several nunataks (peaks protruding through the icecap) are over 2,500 m (8,250 ft.) above sea level. To get here, you will need to be determined and rich. You can take a scheduled flight to Qausuittuq (Resolute Bay) with First Air / Canadian, but will have to charter your own flight to the park from here (cost around $18,000 for 10 passengers!).

ACCOMMODATION

Inns North is a chain run by the native people, and has 19 locations throughout Nunavut and the Northwest territories. (204) 697-1265.

TRAVEL

As expected of an arctic area, the climate can be unforgiving, and transport around the territory is limited to air travel. Nunavut boasts only 21 lonely km of roads. This would seem to render pointless the great local argument as to whether Nunavut or Northwest Territories should keep the distinctive polar bear licence plate (the only non-rectangular licence plate on the continent). A compromise was eventually reached, and both retain it, with separate wording.

Flights are available from Ottawa, Winnipeg and Edmonton (via Yellowknife). Carriers include:- **NWT**, 920-2500, (800) 661-0789 *www.nwtair.nt.ca*, **Calmair**, (204) 778-6471 *www.calmair.com*, **Canadian North**, (416) 798-2211 / (800) 665-1177 *www.cdnair.ca*, and **First Air**, (613) 839-3340 *www.firstair.ca*

Likewise, travel between communities in Nunavut necessitates further air travel. Try **First Air** or **Air Nunavut**, 979-2400. This is another area where a specialised tour company might be a good idea. Companies include **Wilderness Adventure Co**, RR#3 Parry Sound, Ontario, P2A 2W6, (888) 849-7668, offering 7/14 nt treks to Ellesmere Island. **Northwinds Arctic Adventures** offer dogsledding tours amongst other things, PO Box 820, Iqaluit, Nunavut, X0A 0H0, (800)549-0551, *www.northwinds-arctic.com*

THE YUKON TERRITORY

Fur-trading brought Hudson's Bay Company into the Yukon in the mid-1800s but it was the Klondike Gold Rush of 1898 that really put the area on the map. Thousands of gold-seekers climbed the forbidding Chilkoot and White Passes and pressed on down the Yukon River to Dawson City. In two years **Dawson City**, at the junction of the Klondike and Yukon Rivers, grew from a tiny hamlet to a settlement of nearly 30,000. Dawson City became known as the Paris of the North.

There's not much gold around anymore, however. Instead there's silver, copper, zinc, open-pit mining and a big hunt for oil. Following the Gold Rush, the Yukon practically settled back into its pre-gold hunting and trapping days, once again a remote spot on a map in northwestern Canada. When the Japanese occupied the Aleutian Islands in WWII, another rush to the Yukon was on. Army engineers constructed the **Alaska Highway** as a troop route in 1942, passing right through the Yukon and up to Alaska.

The 1523 mile Highway begins at Dawson Creek, British Columbia, and winds its way, via the territorial capital of **Whitehorse** to **Fairbanks**, **Alaska**. Services are provided at regular intervals along the route.

Above Whitehorse, many prospectors lost their lives in the dangerous Whitehorse Rapids. Later, the White Pass and Yukon narrow gauge railway, now in restored operation, took the prospectors as far as **Skagway**. For info call: (800) 343-7373 or (907) 983-2217. Round trip excursions from Skagway, $95, and through connections to Whitehorse.

You can also fly into Dawson City or Whitehorse, or else travel by cruise ship as far as Skagway, Alaska, and from there drive on a year-round highway to Whitehorse. Hitching is said to be reasonable.

Sixty percent of the Yukon's population lives in **Whitehorse**—also the leading shipping and transportation centre and the headquarters of the Territory Mounties. A visit here should include a stop at the **WD McBride Museum** on 1st Ave and Wood St, (867) 667-2709, to look at Gold Rush and Indian mementoes including a steam locomotive, a sleigh wagon, guns. shovels, etc. Audio-visual presentations on Yukon history are offered, $4. Open daily, 10am-6pm May 15-Sept 30 (summer); Sunday, 1pm-4pm (winter). You can also ride the Yukon River through turbulent **Miles Canyon** on the *MV Schwatka*, named after the explorer, 668-4716. 2 hrs, $18. Be sure to visit the **Whitehorse Power Dam** to see the salmon leap in August. The restored *S. S. Klondike* , 667-4511, on S Access Rd, is a dry-docked 1929 sternwheeler that recalls the days when the Yukon River was the city's sole means of survival. Tkts from the info booth at the parking lot for video and guided tour, $3.50. Open daily June-Sep, 9am-7pm (last tour at 6pm). The **Whitehorse Airport** is home of the world's largest weather-vane— a DC3 aircraft that rotates on a pedestal. The famous plane belonged to the Yukon Airlines fleet from 1946 to 1970.

ACCOMMODATION
High Country Inn, 4051 4th Ave, 667-4471. D-$89, up to 4 people. Cooking and laundry facilities, shared room.
98 Hotel, 110 Wood St, 667-2641. S-$30, D-$45 (+$10 key deposit). 16 units (w/out private bath). Open 24 hours, year round.
Robert Service Campground:, 1km from town on S Access Rd, 668-3721. Beside the Yukon River, a convenient stop for campers, sites $12.

In **Dawson City,** some of the buildings hurriedly thrown up in 1898 still stand. At the height of the Gold Rush more than 30,000 people lived in Dawson, at the meeting point of the Yukon and Klondike Rivers. Gold dredging concluded in the 1960s, and the population plummeted to a mere

350 full-time residents. The population has climbed up a bit since then, capitalising on the tourist trade with things like an old time music hall and gold panning for $5 a pan. Picks, pans, and even bags of unrefined gold are all on view. Food and accommodation prices are high.

ACCOMMODATION
The Bunkhouse, Front and Princess St, 993-6164. Recently built, downtown location. From D-$50.

Gold Rush Campground, 5th Ave and York St, 993-5247. Showers, laundromat, TV, store. Convenient downtown location. Sites $15, $19-$26 w/ hook-up. Open 7am-10pm, Jun-Aug; 9am-9pm, May & Sept.

OF INTEREST
The Dawson City Museum, 5th Ave, 993-5007. The Yukon's first museum, was established in Dawson City in 1901 in conjunction with the local library. The museum has the largest single collection of recovered artifacts in the Yukon. Its collection of early narrow-gauge locomotives includes a 'Vauclain-type' Baldwin engine, the last one in existence. Historic films and slides are shown nightly during the peak season. Open daily, 10am-6pm, June 1 to Sept 3; by appointment only in the winter. $4, $3 w/student ID.

In the southwestern corner of the Yukon is the mountainous **Kluane National Park**, 634-2345. The park has extensive icefields and Canada's highest peak, **Mt Logan** (19,850 ft), as well as a great variety of wildlife. The rugged, snowy mountains of Kluane typify the storybook picture one has of the Yukon. But the territory is not a perpetual winter wonderland. Summers here are warm with almost total daylight during June and although winters are cold, they are generally no more so than in many Canadian provinces. The 'Green Belt', along the eastern boundary of the park supports the greatest diversity of plant and animal life in northern Canada. The Alaska Hwy, near the park's NE boundary, provides an easy way to view the eastern edge of the park and glimpse the spectacular peaks beyond. 'This is Big Country to beat Montana.' **Camping** is available at **Kathleen Lake**, 27 km S of Haines Junction off Haines Rd, 634-2251. Good hiking and fishing area, free firewood. Open Jun-Oct, sites $10. If foraging for provisions doesn't appeal to you, you're in bread nirvana. Located next to the visitor centre is **Village Bakery**, 634-2867, home of the original sourdough bread.

Watson Lake, 536-7469, is the commercial and transportation center for the southern part of the Yukon Territories. Here the **Alaska Highway Interpretation Centre** chronicles the building of the great highway in 1942. During the war period, homesick service men and displaced construction workers erected sign posts pointing in the direction of their hometowns. The tradition stuck, perpetuated by today's visitors, so that now a veritable forest of road signs grows behind the Centre.

The Yukon government provides and maintains more than 50 **campgrounds** throughout the territory, mostly in scenic places along the major highways. Hotel/motel accommodation is available in all the towns mentioned above but it's on the expensive side.

3. MEXICO

BACKGROUND

This guide is intended primarily for 'on the road' travel in North America and so this chapter concentrates on selected areas of Mexico deemed likely to be of greatest interest for visitors primarily spending time in the USA and Canada. For longer stays, further reading is recommended and necessary, but for a brief visit this chapter gives you valuable general background information and highlights selected areas to visit from the USA.

BEFORE YOU GO

Mexico is anxious to keep formalities to a minimum for the border hopper with dollars to spend. Anyone content with a visit of three days or less to a border town (by land) or seaport (by sea) need only present a passport and pay a new tax of $15.00 at the crossing point.

For trips further afield, a **tourist card** is needed. If you try to leave the border area without one, you may be stopped and sent back at customs posts 20 miles inland. Cards are issued by Mexican embassies, consulates and tourist offices, by certain travel agencies and at the border itself: if you are flying in, the airline will handle the formalities. All you need is a valid passport, or for US and Canadian nationals, other proof of citizenship. Travelers under 18 also require an authorization signed by both parents and witnessed by a Commissioner for Oaths or Notary Public. The tourist card suffices for citizens of the UK, most other European countries, the US and Canada, but nationals of Australia and New Zealand are required to obtain full visas. Those in doubt should refer to their nearest consulate. At the port of entry, both card and passport must be shown, together with a cholera certificate if you have been in an infected area during the preceding five days. No other vaccinations are required, but we recommend the vaccination for hepatitis B and tetanus.

European visitors receive a card valid for 90 days from the date of entry. US citizens are given 180 days, but in both cases *Migración* officials can vary the duration at whim, often stamping the card with a 30 day limit, as well as charging for the privilege on occasion. The card must be used to enter Mexico within 90 days of the issuing date. So if planning to spend several months in the US first you should obtain the card there at the end of your stay, rather than from the home country. There are Mexican Consulates in most US cities and border towns.

If you are likely to need an extension, request a longer validation when first applying; doing it within Mexico is time-consuming and may involve a trip back to the border to get a new card. In Mexico City you can try your luck at the Visa Renewal office, located at Ave. Chapultepec # 284, Col. Roma , México D.F. Ph. (5) 626-7200. Be prepared for a long wait. The card is issued in duplicate: one part is taken from you on entry, the other as you leave. Once in Mexico you are obliged by law to carry it with you at all times, and you can be fined quite heavily for overstaying the expire date, particularly if you have a car.

If you are on an Exchange Program Visa, do not let US officials take your IAP-66, or any other visa documentation, when you cross into Mexico. You need it to get back into the US! In London, the Mexican Consulate is at: Ground Floor, Wakefield House, 41 Trinity Square, London EC3N 4DJ. (020) 7488 9392. In the US the Mexican Embassy is at 1911 Pennsylvania Ave NW, Washington DC 20006, (202) 728-1600.

GETTING THERE

Most travellers (and certainly the overwhelming majority using this guide) will be visiting Mexico via the US. Major American, Mexican or international carriers fly from Los Angeles, Chicago, New York, Miami, San Antonio and other US and Canadian cities to Mexico City and elsewhere in Mexico. It is usually cheaper to fly to the US and shop around there for a flight to Mexico, rather than fly direct from Europe. But because of the continuing devaluation of Mexican currency, the cheapest way to travel is generally to cross into Mexico by land and then travel on domestic flights purchased in pesos.

The most popular (and often fully booked) flight, at present costing about $229 one-way, $400 round trip, is Mexicana's flight from Los Angeles to Mexico City. Mexicana has offices in most US cities: for up to date information in the UK contact Mexicana Tour, 215 Chalk Farm Rd., Camden Town, London, NW18AF, (171) 284-2550. Fax (171) 267-2004.

Tijuana to Mexico City costs about $340 round-trip although it may be possible to find a cheaper fare by shopping around closer to the time of departure. For info, call Mexicana: 1 (800) 531-7921 or Aeromexico: 1 (800) 237-6639. For brief round-trips from the US, it is worth checking with the various airlines as they all offer competitive (and, at press time, largely unpredictable) fares. Major US carriers flying to Mexico include American, Delta and Continental.

Special deals offering discounts on internal flights within Mexico for those with international return tickets are of limited interest, since they typically apply only to trips originating in Europe, not the US, and carry time and other restrictions. Airlines impose a US$17.50 departure tax on passengers leaving Mexico.

There are 12 major and a number of minor crossing points along the US-Mexico border. The most important are Tijuana (12 miles south of San Diego), Calexico-Mexicali, Nogales (south of Tucson), Douglas/Agua Prieta, El Paso/Ciudad Juárez, Eagle Pass/Piedras Negras, Laredo/Nuevo

Laredo, Hidalgo/Reynosa and Brownsville/Matamoros. If you have a car, the smaller border crossings (such as Tecate, 40 miles east of San Diego) are often less bureaucratic. Car travellers should avoid Tijuana, especially on weekends. There are generally long delays caused by extensive searches for drugs and aliens. El Paso/Ciudad Juárez border is often mentioned by readers as the easiest crossing: Less traffic. Matamoros is the crossing point closest to Mexico City (622 miles/996 kms); after you pass the border you will encounter checkpoints.

Amtrak goes to the border at El Paso and Laredo from where you make your own arrangements by bus or plane.

CAR RENTALS

Reservations for car rentals in Mexico can be made in the US with the major companies (Hertz, Avis, Budget, Dollar, Thrifty and National, etc.). The major international car hire companies, plus of course many Mexican companies, have offices throughout the country. In theory all the companies in Mexico charge the same rates for any given car type, as rates are set by the Government, but shopping around, especially among smaller local companies, can often get you significant savings. The official rates are based on time plus kilometres at inland towns and daily rates including 200 km/day on the coast. Be sure to check on extra costs for insurance, and to determine whether you are dealing in miles or kilometres. Car hire is not especially inexpensive in Mexico. Expect to pay at least around US$35 or $45 per day.

When you drive in Mexico you need to carry a proof of Mexican auto liability insurance which is usually provided by the car rental company. An international driver's license should be used, available from AAA in the US and Canada or in the United Kingdom from RAC or AA.

AAA members can get free road maps and guides. The AAA in Mexico can assist you, call (5) 588-7055.

GEOGRAPHY AND CLIMATE

Running from north to south, the two chains of the Sierra Madre dominate and dictate the country's geography and climate. The vast central plateau lies between the mountain ranges and drops to the Rió Grande valley in the north. Around the area of the capital, just south of the Tropic of Cancer, there is a further jumble of mountains, finally petering out in the narrow and comparatively flat Isthmus of Tehuantepec. From Tijuana in the northwest to Mérida in the Yucatán, Mexico stretches for 2750 miles.

Between the altitudes of 5000 and 8000 feet the climate is mild. The descent to sea level corresponds to an increase in temperature, so that the lowlands are very hot in summer as well as being very warm in winter. The Central Plateau, where Mexico City is located (altitude 7350 feet), enjoys a pleasant, spring like climate. It is warm and sunny throughout the year, although regular afternoon showers or storms can be expected from June to October, the Rainy Season.

In the deserts of northern Mexico and throughout Baja California, temperatures of over 100°F are to be expected during the summer months. It is similarly hot on the coast, although the sea breezes are cooling. But in the lush tropical jungle lands to the south of the Tropic of Cancer, humidity is

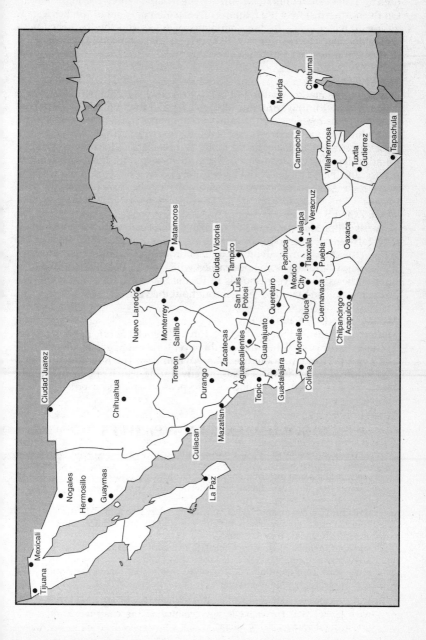

high and the annual rainfall is nearly as great as anywhere else in the world. On the northern side of the Isthmus of Tehuantepec, rainfall reaches a staggering 10 feet a year. The large numbers of rivers and the frequency with which they become rushing, swollen torrents make the land impassable by permanent rail or road systems.

WHAT TO WEAR
Light clothing made of natural fibers (cotton, etc.) is recommended. Bring a jacket or something warmer for Mexico City and the Central Plateau's cool evenings, plus raingear for the rainy season. Shoes, rather than sandals, are a necessity for uneven streets and climbing up pyramids.

Lavenderías automáticas (laundromats) and *tintorerías* (dry cleaners) can be found in larger towns and cities. Many hotels also offer their own laundry service. In smaller places you'll have to rely on two stones and the washing powder you have remembered to pack along with the spare plug for the sink.

TIME ZONES
Virtually all of Mexico, from the Yucatán to the Pacific due west of Mexico City, falls within the zone corresponding to Central Standard Time in the US. The west coast from Tepic up to the border, and including the southern half of Baja California, is an hour earlier, while the northern half of Baja is an hour earlier still and corresponds to Pacific Standard Time in the US. The Mexicans stay on Standard Time throughout the year.

MEXICO AND ITS PEOPLE
Modern Mexico is the product of three distinct historical phases: pre-Columbian (or pre-Cortés) Indian, three centuries of Spanish colonial rule, and since 1821 independent Mexican government. The Revolution of 1910 was followed by ten years of near-anarchy during which one in every eight Mexicans was killed, and although the peasants played a crucial role in

---

SOME MEXICAN WEBSITES

www.diegorivera.com: Information about Diego Rivera, his wife Frieda Kahlo, and their works.

www.indians.org: Information on ancient Mexican cultures.

www.metro.jussieu.fr: 100001/bin/select/english/mexico/mexico: Information on the Mexico City subway system.

www.mexico-travel.com: Maintained by the Mexican Ministry of Tourism, this site purports to contain over 40,000 pages of information on all topics related to travel to Mexico.

www.mexnet.com: Extensive information about Copper Canyon.

www.travlang.com: Foreign language information for travelers.

www.wotw.com/mundomaya: Extensive information about the Mayan region, including photos and maps.

You can also obtain information about any Mexican state by visiting www.[State].com. For example www.chihuahua.com contains information about the state of Chihuahua.

overthrowing the corrupt aristocracy, in the end it was (and is) the middle classes who have benefited from the uninterrupted tenure of the Institutional Revolutionary Party (PRI) since 1929. There is at present a higher percentage of landless peasants than when the Revolution began, and the poor live in overcrowded slums where illiteracy is common, malnutrition rampant and basic services often non-existent.

There are, however, some indications of slow improvement. The country is not as desperately poor as it was and the government appears to be making real efforts to root out some of the social ills. Until now the benefits of industrial and agricultural development have been defeated by the explosive population growth. Although the area of harvestable land has doubled since 1940, the population has risen from 20 million to over 86 million in the same period, and half of these are under fifteen years of age.

Despite relatively successful efforts made to increase earnings from tourism and manufacturing industries, Mexico's economy still relies heavily on oil exports. Mexico is the world's second largest debtor with its external debt at a level of over US$100 billion. It is, however, considered a model debtor by the International Monetary Fund and the international financial community in general, as it has not declared a moratorium on its debt and has implemented a series of economic austerity programs.

Despite gestures of independence, most notably the nationalization of the oil industry in 1938, Mexico seeks foreign investment and to a great extent is economically dependent on its neighbor to the north. Currently, hopes are pinned on NAFTA—the North American Free Trade Agreement—which will give Mexican business direct access to the US and Canada, and vice versa. The relationship, however, remains epitomized by the ceaseless flow of undocumented immigrants across the US border, and by the steady growth of *maquiladora* (in-bond manufacturing) industries on the Mexican side whereby US companies can take advantage of cheap Mexican labour to produce US products.

POLITICS

At first glance, Mexican politics appears to be an alphabet soup of letters with the parties known as PAN, PRD, PDM, PRT, PARM and of course, PRI. PRI is the Partido Revolucionario Institucional. The party is not very revolutionary but is certainly institutional since it is the most popular and largest party in Mexico, having ruled the country since 1929. The participation and activity of the opposition parties have increased considerably in recent years but as yet they have been unable to topple the PRI's domination. President Ernesto Zedillo Ponce de León won the 1994 election. Mexican presidents cannot be re-elected and hold office for six years. Zedillo got off to a difficult start, being snubbed by the opposition parties, the PRD and PAN, and having to deal with continued unrest in the province of Chiapas.

CULTURE

Mexico is a fascinating and colourful country, physically and culturally, bridging the gap between America North and South. It is a feast of art and history, with more than 11,000 archaeological sites, temples, pyramids and palaces of bygone civilizations, and many museums which are generally regarded as being among the best in the world. (See box) Although Mexico City and resort towns like Acapulco have their share of tall buildings, expensive hotels and general North American glitter, rural Mexico is something else again and the whole pace of life visibly alters the moment you cross the border from the United States.

Three centuries of Spanish rule have left their mark not only on the lifestyle of the country but also on its appearance. The fusion of Spanish baroque with the intricate decorative style of the Indians produced the distinctive and dramatic style called Mexican Colonial. A number of towns rich in Mexican Colonial buildings are preserved as national monuments and new building is forbidden. The most important colonial towns are: Guadalajara, León, Guanajuato, San Miguel de Allende, Morelia, Taxco, Cholula, Puebla and Mérida.

Despite its Spanish architectural and linguistic overtones, Mexico has a distinctly Indian soul: fatalistic, taciturn, reflective and strong on tradition and folklore. You will notice this most sharply in the villages, where it is easy to misinterpret the dignified shyness of the villagers as coldness. Various towns stand out as being Indian in character: Querétaro (where the Mexican constitution was drafted in 1917), Pátzcuaro, Oaxaca, Tehuantepec and San Cristóbal de las Casas. Not to be missed are Indian market days and festivals. Toluca, an hour's drive from Mexico City, has an outstanding Indian market.

MONEY

The exchange rate with the US dollar is (at press time) about N$9.50 Considering the continuous drop in the Mexican peso against the dollar since December 1994, this rate may easily vary in the coming months. The prices given in this section use the above exchange rate.

The Mexican peso is denoted by the symbol N$, meaning *peso nuevo* (new peso). This is to differentiate the new currency from the old peso (still in circulation, although in small amounts). Mexico introduced the new currency in 1993, to simplify calculations. One new peso equals 1000 old pesos. Banknotes in 10, 20, 50, 100, 200, and 500 N$ denominations and coins units of 1, 2, 5, and 10 new pesos are in circulation.

Mexico uses the $ sign for the peso, unfortunately the same as the US dollar sign; where necessary the two are distinguished by the addition of the suffixes MN (*Moneda Nacional*) for pesos and US or 'dls' for dollars. Important note: all peso prices in this section are written as—pesos. US dollar prices are given as US$.

Shop around for the best exchange rates, especially in the large cities and resort areas. Generally the best rates can be obtained at the *casas de cambio* (money exchanges). Try to avoid the hotels for changing money if possible. Many larger stores and some market vendors will accept dollars but check carefully on the rates they are using.

Banks: Banking hours are 9am-5pm Monday-Friday. (The *casas de cambio* are usually open till around 5pm.) The larger banks (Bánamex, Bancomer) are the best for changing money if there are no *casas de cambio* around in the provinces. Major credit cards are accepted in most places but the cheaper hotels and restaurants may not take them. Don't take it for granted—always ask first.

DISCOVERING MEXICO'S ANCIENT CIVILIZATIONS

Aztecs, Mayas, Mixtecs, Olmecs, Toltecs, Zapotecs—great civilizations have flourished in Mexico for at least 4000 years. To discover their fascinating remains and share their drama, you'll have to journey to the south of the country, where each state's tourism secretariat can provide you with maps, information on tours, brochures and other assistance about the main sites and how to get to them.

Highly recommended, before going to the field, is a first stop in Mexico City at the excellent Museo Nacional de Antropologia, located at Paseo de la Reforma en Chapultepec, Polanco. Tue-Sun 9am-7pm. Admission US$2.50. For information, call (5) 553-1902. Also look in at the Museo Nacional de Culturas Populares, located at Calle Hídalgo #289, Colonia Coyoacan, also in Mexico City. Tue-Sun, 10 am-8 pm. For information, call (5) 658-1265.

Mexico's pre-Columbian heritage is often divided into three distinct periods: pre-classic (2000 BC to 200 AD); classic (200 AD to 900 AD); and post-classic (900 AD to the Spanish conquest in 1521 AD).

PRE-CLASSIC—2000 BC to 200 AD

The Olmecs founded one of the earliest great civilizations of Mesoamerica, which is often considered the "mother culture" of the region. Early advances in agriculture led to the rise of Olmec towns and ceremonial centers in what are now the states of Veracruz and Tabasco. Staple crops of the Olmecs included beans, corn, and squash, though the Olmec diet may have at times included other humans. The Olmecs domesticated dogs and turkeys, had elaborate religious ceremonies and structures, and are famous for their stone carvings, including monumental stone heads between 1.5 and 3 meters tall weighing up to 20 tons.

The primary Olmec cities were Tres Zapotes and La Venta. La Venta, 84 miles west of Villahermosa in Tabasco, is still an interesting site to visit, even though the archaeological finds were transferred in toto to escape destruction from oil drilling in the 1950s. Many colossal Olmec heads of basalt can be seen at the archaeological museum in Mexico City, the Tabasco Museum in Villahermosa, and at Parque Museo La Venta, on Rte. 180 near the airport. Apart from three large stone heads, La Venta has stelae, altars, mosaics and a model of the original city. Self-guided tour map, US$1, daily 8:30am-3pm and 6pm-9pm. For tourist information in Villahermosa, call (93) 16-28-89, Avenida Los Rios #203, in front of the newspaper building Tabasco Hoy. Tourist information can also be found at tourist information booths in the bus stations, railway stations, airport, and around town.

The Zapotecs inhabited what is now Oaxaca in southern Mexico. Their primary city was Monte Albán (the 'White City'), the elaborate ruins of which can still be explored today. The region was later conquered by **the Mixtecs**, who were skilled craftsmen in precious metals, ceramics, and mosaics. For information and maps in Oaxaca, call (951) 6-07-17 or 6-01-23. Sectur: Ave. Independencia 607 Zona Centro, Open 9am-5pm. Mon-Fri.

CLASSIC —200 AD-900 AD

The dominant influence of the classic period is the **Mayan** civilization. The Maya were the largest homogenous group of Indians north of Perú, and their society stretched from present-day Honduras throughout the Yucatán peninsula. Approximately 6 million Maya inhabit the area today. The Maya built massive pyramids throughout Central America, including the impressive sites at Uxmal and Chichén Itzá at the tip of the Yucatán and at the ancient partially excavated city of Palenque. For maps and information on reaching these sites call (99) 24-8002 or (99) 24-8925 Secretaria de Desarrollo Industrial y Comercial. Located in 59

St. # 514 by 62 and 64 St. Central Zone, Open Mon-Fri. 8am-2pm and 5pm-7pm Mérida, Yucatan.

UXMAL and CHICHEN ITZA Along with Palenque, Uxmal was one of the chief Mayan cities and the showpiece of that civilization's finest architectural accomplishments. Chichén Itzá, on the other hand, was first a Mayan city and later occupied and built on by the belligerent Toltecs, becoming in the process the most stupendous city in the Yucatán.

Fifty miles of good road lead from Mérida to **Uxmal**, where the clean, open lines of the ancient city create an impression of serenity and brilliant organization on a par with the greatest cities of either Eastern or Western civilization at that time. As white as marble and gilded by the sunshine, the limestone complex of the Nunnery Quadrangle, the Palace of the Governor and the Pyramid of the Soothsayer has a fascinating and almost modern beauty. The friezes of the palaces are decorated with stone mosaics in intricate geometric designs. Daily 9 am-5 pm, US$7.50, with show included free on Sundays.

In the 10th century the peaceful Mayan world was disturbed by the war-like Toltecs, who came down from their northern plateau capital of Tula to conquer the Yucatán cities and make **Chichén Itzá** their southern capital. The monumental constructions you see there are both Mayan (eg. El Caracol, the circular observatory) and Toltec (eg. the Court of a Thousand Columns). The city is dominated by the Great Pyramid, the Temple of Kukulcán, with its stairways of 91 steps on each of four sides, making a total of 364. That figure plus one step round the top totals the days in the year. Other points of interest include the Ball Court and its inscriptions and the Sacred Well into which human sacrifices were hurled. Admission US$ 7.50.

PALENQUE About 130 Km inland from Villahermosa are the jungle ruins of the classic Mayan sacred city of Palenque, which flourished AD 300-700. Built on the first spurs of the Usumacinta Mountains, the gleaming white palaces, temples and pyramids rise from the high virgin jungle. Its visually compelling site, compact size (the excavated portion is about three-quarters of a mile by half a mile, out of the 20-square-mile extent of the city) and its dramatic burial chamber make Palenque, to many minds, more outstanding than Chichén Itzá. The 1950 discovery of an ornate crypt containing fantastically jade-bedecked remains of a Mayan priest-king revised archaeologists' theories about Mayan pyramids, which were earlier believed to be mere supports for the temples on top. Although it's a hot, steep and slippery journey, you should climb the Temple of the Inscriptions, descend the 80 feet into its crypt to view the bas-reliefs: chilling and wonderful. Maps and site information are available in Palenque or Chiapas, call (961) 2-45-35 or (961) 3-93-96/99.

The Maya developed advanced mathematics, astronomy, and writing systems. Religious ceremony was central to Maya culture, which at times included human sacrifice. Losers of sporting events might also expect to be beheaded, or tied into a ball and rolled down the steep steps of a pyramid. Although the ancient Maya shared a common culture, like the ancient Greeks they were politically divided into as many as 20 sovereign states, rather than ruled by a unified empire. Such division may ultimately have led to constant warfare and the eventual downfall of their civilization. In addition to the main Mayan sites mentioned here, there are many smaller ruins scattered throughout the Yucatán, such as those at Tulum on the Caribbean coast. Tour information call (967) 8-28-18

POST-CLASSIC—900 AD-1521 AD.
The Toltecs were mighty warriors who occupied the northern section of the Valley of Mexico. Their primary city was Tula, approximately 80 km north of Mexico City, where the Temple of Tlahuizcalpantecuhtli was built (yes,

Tlahuizcalpantecuhtli). Giant stone warriors, standing nearly 5 meters high, guard the temple.

The Toltecs conquered the city of Teotihuacán, near present-day Mexico City. Teotihuacán is one of the most important ceremonial centers in ancient Mesoamerica, and includes the massive Pyramid of the Sun, 63 meters high, and the Pyramid of the Moon, 42 meters high. The Toltecs spread the cultural influence of the Teotihuacanos, including the cult of Quetzálcoatl (the 'Sovereign Plumed Serpent'), throughout their empire. The rise of the Toltecs, however, transformed much of Mesoamerica from a theocracy to a warrior aristocracy.

The Aztecs, who sometimes referred to themselves as the Mexicas, created the most complex culture in all of Mesoamerica. Their primary city was Tenochtitlán, built in 1325 on small islands in Lake Texcoco where modern-day Mexico City is located. According to legend, the site was chosen when the wandering Aztecs came upon an eagle perched upon a cactus eating a snake, fulfilling a prophecy. Today, the Mexican flag incorporates this scene.

Influenced by the Toltecs, the focus of Aztec life was war and conquest. Only the Incas in Peru had a larger empire in the Americas. However, the Aztecs also built great cities, developed a sophisticated calendar, devised a system of imperial administration and tribute, and made great advances in agriculture. Among their many gods, the Aztecs continued to worship Quetzálcoatl. When the Spanish arrived in Mexico in 1519, with their light skin and hair, horses, muskets, armour, and great

Cortés, aided by Indian tribes who had been mistreated by the Aztecs, was able to conquer Tenochtitlán and overthrow the mighty Aztec empire.

Unfortunately, the Spanairds did a thorough job in eliminating much of the Aztec civilization. Virtually nothing remains of the giant pyramids dedicated to Tlaloc the rain god and Huitzilpochtli the sun god. Some minor remains of the ancient city of Tenochtitlán are located in the suburbs of Mexico City, and some smaller pyramids can be found at Santa Cecilia, Calixtlahuaca, and particularly Malinalco, some 48 km from Toluca, where there are temples dedicated to two Aztec military orders, the Knights of the Jaguar and the Knights of the Eagle. Other Aztec artifacts can be viewed in the Museo Nacional de Antropologia in Mexico City.

WHAT TO SEE NEAR MEXICO CITY

The **Pyramids of Teotihuacan** and **Temple of Quetzálcoatl**. Take Metro to Indios Verdes (last station on north end of line 3), then take bus US$5.50 marked 'Pyramids'. (NB: no backpacks on Metro.) Frequent buses from Terminal del Norte direct to site, called Teotihuacanos, every 15 Minutes US$ 2 each way takes 1hr to get there. The temples are part of the ruins of the once-great city built by the mysterious Teotihuacanos, about whom very little is known other than that they were a militaristic, highly regimented society. At its peak in about 300 A.D., Teotihuacan was the world's sixth largest city, bigger than Rome, and only 10% of the city has been excavated. For reasons yet to be uncovered, the Teotihuacan civilization disappeared between 600 and 700 A.D., and it was not until hundreds of years later that the Aztecs assumed control of the site, naming it Teotihuacan, "The Place of the Gods.". The Pyramid of the Sun is 216 ft high (248 steps to the top where the sacrifices were made) and the older Pyramid of the Moon, one half km away, although less vast, is just as impressive. The Temple of Quetzálcoatl is about 1km from the pyramids and has some superb Toltec carvings. Daily 8 am-5 pm, US$4 except holidays and Sundays. When climbing pyramids, take care—they're very steep. Traders everywhere—even at the top of the pyramids selling fake artifacts that 'they made at home'. *Son et lumière* six nights per week, in English at 7 pm (not June-Sept). For tour information call Viajes Orlyn (Mexico City) (5) 531-9497 also call (5) 956-0276 pyramids information.

Tipping and Tax: 10-15 percent is the standard tip. Service charges are very rarely added to the bill when you receive it so they must be determined by the total before tax. Almost everything you have to buy or pay for, including hotels and restaurant food, has IVA (*Impuesto al valor agregado*)—value added tax—on it which may be included or shown separately.

HEALTH

Medical services are good, and in Mexico City it's easy to find an English-speaking doctor. Fees are reasonable compared to the US, and some hospitals will examine you and give prescriptions free. Nevertheless, where a fee is likely you should ask for a quote beforehand, and insurance is advisable. 'If you travel in the US before Mexico, you'll hear many ghastly tales of internal infections and uncontrollable bacteria, even though the water is so chlorinated that you're more likely to kill off your own bacteria than find any new ones.'

For the long term traveller, acclimatization is the best policy, but it can take from three days to four weeks. If needed, you can stop *turista* spoiling a brief trip by using Lomotil (which delays the symptoms but will not remove the cause), or Pepto-Bismol, the antibiotic Bactrim, or Kaomycin. Entero-Vioform may still sometimes be on sale, despite being banned everywhere else. It makes you go blind.

If you have decided *not* to 'get used to it', then be cautious. Drink only bottled water. If you are not sure about the water, boil it for 30 minutes or use purification tablets. Be careful when buying food from street vendors: is the fat rancid? Beware of ice cream, salads, unpeeled fruit and vegetables washed in impure water. Eating plenty of garlic, onions and lime juice (which act as natural purifiers and preventatives) may help, but need to be taken in large quantities. *Té de Perro* (dog tea), fresh coconut juice and plain boiled white rice are the native Mexican recommendations.

Anti-malarial drugs are advisable in tropical and southern coastal areas—but as Mexico denies (perhaps rightly) that it has malaria, it's difficult to get any drugs for it there, so bring them with you. It wouldn't hurt to have inoculations against yellow fever, cholera, typhoid and polio, especially if you travel to coastal areas in the south.

'It helps to warn people but hopefully they won't be frightened off.' It is better to travel with health insurance.

LANGUAGE

The more alert among you will have guessed by now that it's Spanish, although in some areas Indian languages are still spoken—e.g. Mayan in the Yucatán. The point is, you should learn some Spanish, especially the words for numbers, food and directions. 'Well worth learning some Spanish if you can: don't expect too many Mexicans to know English.' Your efforts in Spanish will normally be encouraged and appreciated by the local people.

COMMUNICATIONS

Mail: Do not have mail sent *Lista de Correos* (Poste Restante) unless you are sure of being able to collect it within 10 days. After that time it is likely to be 'lost'. Letters or postcards to North America are US$0.45; to Europe, US$0.60; to Australia and New Zealand, US$0.70. Important mail should be sent registered mail from a post office, and never put in an ordinary letter box. 'Send mail only from post offices—letter boxes not reliable.'

Chances are that packages sent in or out of the country will not make it to their destination. There are telegraph offices (*Telegrafos Naçionales*) in all cities and towns and many villages too. Domestic cables are cheap and a good way to communicate with other travellers. International cable service is also good and the 'night letter' service, sent after 7pm, is a good value. Public telex and fax facilities can be found in the larger cities.

Telephones: Public phone booths are found in most cities and larger towns. Elsewhere make use of telephones in stores, tobacco stands, hotels, etc. Public phones with direct dial long distance service (national and international), identified as 'Ladatel' are now being installed in the larger cities. To make a call from one city to another in Mexico, dial 91 + the city code + and the number. Note that the number of digits in phone numbers is not standardized across Mexico. From other public phones dial 02 for the long distance operator for calls within Mexico or 09 for the international operator. In smaller towns look for the '*Larga distancia*' sign outside a store or cafe in the centre of town. Collect calls (reverse charges) are called *llamadas a cobrar*.

Some important phone numbers used throughout Mexico are: emergency assistance—(5) 250-0123 & (5) 250-0151; local information 04; countrywide information 01. For calls to the UK, Ireland or other European countries the code is: 98. For the US or Canada the code is: 95.

PUBLIC HOLIDAYS
Mexico's religious and political calendar supplies many excuses for public holidays. Expect everything to close down on the following dates:

January 1	New Year's Day	November 1**	All Saints' Day
February 5	Constitution Day	November 2	All Souls' Day
March 21	Juárez Birthday		(or Day of the Dead)
March-April*	Holy Thursday	November 20	Revolution Day
March-April*	Good Friday	December 12**	Our Lady of
May 1	Labor Day		Guadalupe Day
May 5	Battle of Puebla Day	December 24**	Christmas Eve
September 15**	Declaration of	December 25	Christmas Day
	Independence	December 31**	New Year's Eve
September 16	Independence Day	*Date varies with year.	
October 12	Día de la Raza	**Usually working half a day.	

On top of these, every town has its own festival and fiesta days, with processions, fireworks, and dancing in the streets. Local tourist authorities will fill you in on the details.

ELECTRICITY
All Mexico is on 110V, 60 cycles AC—in common with the rest of North America. It's a good idea to take a small torch as electricity can be uncertain, especially in small towns.

SHOPPING

The favorable rate of exchange and colorful markets will tempt even those who hate to shop. Mexico is famous for its arts and crafts and the markets guarantee some of the best entertainment anywhere. Look for woven goods, baskets, pottery, jewelry, leather goods, woodcarving, metalwork and lacquerware. A number of towns or states specialize in a particular craft or style. The government-run FONART shops feature some of the best local works and will give a general idea of price variations. FONART shops are generally a bit higher and will not bargain, but sometimes the quality is superior to what is available in the market. Prices and quality vary. Be sure to look over everything carefully. The vendor may guarantee that the sarape you're holding is '*pura lana*', pure wool, but you know acrylic when you see and touch it. Bargaining is a fine art and expected.

'The cheapest market by far for sarapes, ponchos and embroidery is Mitla, near Oaxaca. Knock them down to one-third the asking price, and make rapid decisions in order to keep the price down.'

THE METRIC SYSTEM

Mexico is metric. See appendix.

INFORMATION

There are Mexican Government tourist offices in most US cities and border towns. Here are the main addresses:

New York: 405 Park Ave. Suite 1401, New York, NY 10021, (212) 755-7261, FAX (212) 753-2874; *Houston:* 10440 W. Office Drive, Houston, TX 77042, (713) 780-3740, FAX (713) 780-8362; *Los Angeles:* 2401 W 6th St., 5th Floor, Los Angeles CA 90057, (213) 351-2069, FAX (213) 351-2074..

Washington, DC: 1911 Pennsylvania Ave NW, Washington, DC 20006, (202) 728-1600, FAX (202) 728-1758. *Toronto:* 2 Bloor St W, Suite 1801, Toronto, Ontario M4W 3E2, (416) 925-0704 or (416) 925-1876, FAX (416) 925-6061. *Florida*: 128 Aragon Ave., Coral Gables, FL 33134 (305) 443-9160, FAX (305) 443-1186. *Illinois:* 300 N Michigan Ave, 4th Fl, Chicago IL 60601, (312) 606-9252 , FAX (312) 606-9012.

For information 24 hrs a day, call 1-800-482-9832 .

In London, the Mexican Consulate is at 42 Hertford Street Mayfair, W1Y7TS, (0171) 499-8586 or 495-4024. Fax (0171) 495-4035 and the Mexican Ministry of Tourism is at Wakefield House, 41 Trinity Square, London EC3N 4DJ, (020) 7488-9392.

Once in Mexico itself, tourist information is provided at federal, state and local levels and most towns on the tourist track have at least one information office. Bear in mind that the level of service provided is extremely variable, and in particular do not presume that English will be spoken. You might also find maps, directories and brochures available for free at the border (look for the booth under the name of **Modulos Paisanos.**

NATIONAL PARKS

'Both Mexican and foreign visitors are admitted from 8am-5pm throughout the year', according to the official tourism handbook, but most National Parks are without visible regulation and either merge imperceptibly with the surrounding farmland or are undeveloped and inaccessible wilderness. Don't expect the services of Yosemite or Yellowstone. NB: all beaches in Mexico are federally owned and free.

ON THE ROAD

ACCOMMODATION

The range of **hotel accommodation** in Mexico is wide, from ultra-modern marble skyscrapers, and US-style motels along the major highways, to colonial inns and haciendas to modest guesthouses, called *pensiones o casas de huespedes*. There is also a marked difference between north and south Mexico. In the north of the country hotels tend to be older, often none too clean with bad plumbing, and large noisy ceiling fans to hum you to sleep. In southern Mexico hotels 'are a joy'. They are rarely full and often offer a high standard of comfort and cleanliness at low rates. It is fairly common to find hotels which are converted old aristocratic residences built around a central courtyard. Hoteliers will probably offer you their most expensive room first. A useful phrase in the circumstances is: *Quisiera algo más barato, por favor* (I'd like something cheaper, please). Ask to see the room first: *Quiero ver el cuarto, por favor.* Of course a double room always works out cheaper per person than two singles, but also one double bed—*cama matrimonial*—is cheaper than two beds in a room. On the other hand, cheaper hotels often don't mind how many people take a room. 'Travelling in a group of four, considerable savings are possible. Most hotel beds are big enough for two people; therefore a double-bedded room can accommodate four.'

Prices are fixed, and should be prominently displayed by law; though inflation is moving so fast you should not be surprised if your bill bears little relation to the posted rate. In general you should expect to pay about US$13-$20 per person per night in a basic but tolerable hotel a few blocks from the centre of town. An intermediate standard hotel should cost US$20-$35. It should rarely be *necessary* to pay more than this, though if you want to pay US$140 and up for a US-style resort hotel, that's possible too.

Hotel rates may vary between high and low season. High season extends from mid-December to Easter or the beginning of May, the remaining months being low season. Seasonal variations will be more marked at coastal resorts. *As most travellers using this Guide tour North America, including Mexico, in the summer months, low season rates have been quoted.*

'We notice that cockroaches are mentioned by people assessing places to stay. Even the best hotels are full of them—they are part of the scene and should not be regarded as unusual.'

'As it is rare indeed for Mexican wash basins to have plugs, I would recommend travelers to be equipped with this useful item.'

Hostels: There are two youth hostel organizations, the Mexican 'Villas Deportivas' chain and the International YHA-backed SETEJ establishments. The hostels offer cheap dormitory accommodation and we list them here only when a viable option for the tourist.

In general, however, hostels tend to cater more to a Mexican high school clientele, are some distance from town center's, and are rarely worth the small amount saved compared with a cheap hotel room in a better location. For details contact Turismo Juvenil o Causa Joven Cerapío Rendón #76 Col. San Rafael, México D.F., tel: 1-800-716-0092 or (5) 546-7805 ext. 167 & 199. Young travellers can also obtain a discount card for free, useful for saving on some hotels, museum and buses. You need to be 18 years old: call 1-800-482-9832.

Camping: Hotels are so cheap it is difficult to justify taking a tent. Where campsites exist, they tend to double as trailer parks and be some distance from areas of interest. Camping independently in the middle of nowhere is definitely pushing your luck, though in some of the beach resorts, nights under the stars are a feasible option. Those who insist on doing things the hard way should get *Traveler's Guide to Camping in Mexico*, by Mike & Terry Church, US$ 19.95. The Secretaría de Turísmo publishes a useful brochure: go to Ave. Presidente Mazarik # 172, Col. Polanco (5) 250-8555 ext. 111.

FOOD AND DRINK

Because high altitude slows digestion, it's customary to eat a large, late, lingering lunch and a light supper. (You may be wise to eat less than usual until your stomach adjusts.) Do not eat unpeeled fruit and avoid drinking tap water, unprocessed milk products and ice cubes.

Stick to bottled mineral water, bottled juices, soft drinks or the excellent Mexican beer. Mexican milkshakes or *licuados* are made with various fruits and are delicious; probably best to avoid *licuados con leche* (those made with milk). Go to a *jugos and licuados* shop for *Watershake*, and home-made fruit ice creams.' 'The most important thing is to eat plenty of limes, garlic and onions—all "natural disinfectants"—we didn't have any stomach troubles.'

Mexican cuisine is much more than tacos and beans but the basic menu revolves around ground maize (first discovered by the Mayans), cheese, tomatoes, beans, rice and a handful of flavourings: garlic, onion, cumin and chilies of varying temperatures. The ground maize flour is made into pancake-shaped *tortillas*, which appear in a variety of dishes and also on their own to be eaten like bread. *Tortillas* are also made with wheat flour: restaurants will customarily ask, '*De maíz o de harina?*' (Do you want corn or flour tortillas?) Enchiladas are tortillas rolled and filled with cheese, beef, etc., baked and lightly sauced. *Tacos, tostadas, flautas* and *chalupas* all use fried tortillas, which are either stacked or filled with cheese, beans, meat, chicken, sauce, etc. *Tamales* use softer corn dough, filled with spicy meat and sauce and wrapped in corn husks to steam through. Other dishes to sample: *pollo con mole* (chicken in a sauce containing chocolate, garlic and other spices), fresh shrimp and fish (often served Veracruz style with green peppers, tomatoes, etc). Beans and rice accompany every meal, even breakfast. A good breakfast dish is *huevos rancheros*, eggs in a spicy tomato-based sauce. Mexico is also noted for its pastries, honey and chocolate drinks.

There are over 80 types of chilies in Mexico ranging in taste from sweet to steamroller hot. The different sauces are served from little containers found on tabletops so the diner can determine how mild or hot the dish will be. Best bargain for lunch is *comida corrida* or *menu de hoy*. This can be a filling four-course meal and cost as little as US$4.50

breakfast: *desayuno*

coffee and a roll: *café con panes*

lunch: *almuerzo* (lighter) or *comida*

dinner/supper: *cena*

fixed-price meal: *menú corrida*

eggs: *huevos*

fish: *pescado*

meat: *carne*

salad: *ensalada*

fruit: *fruta*

beer: *cerveza*

soft drink: *refresco*

mineral water: *agua mineral*

bread: *pan*

potatoes: *papas*

vegetables (greens): *verduras*

bacon: *tocino*

ham: *jamón*

cheese: *queso*

I want something not too spicy, please: *Quiero algo no muy picante, por favor*. The best-known hard liquor is tequila, a potent clear drink made from the maguey plant tasting 'similar to kerosene'. The sharp-spiked maguey is also the source for other highly-intoxicating liquors such as aguamiel, pulque, and mezcal. Look for the fat worm at the bottom of mezcal. It guarantees that you have the real thing. If you don't drink it (and by the time you reach the bottom of the bottle you won't know or care), some people like to fry them for snacks. Margarita cocktails are made with tequila but are primarily popular with turistas. The Mexicans prefer to take their tequila neat with a little salt and lime on the back of the hand. Mexico produces some decent wines but is famous for its beer; don't pass up Dos Equis dark.

TRAVEL

Now for your basic Spanish travel vocabulary: please—*por favor*; thank you—*gracías*; bus—*autobús*; train—*tren* or *ferrocarril*; plane—*avión*; auto—*carro*; ticket—*boleto*; second class—*segunda clase*; first class—*primera clase*; first class reserved seat (on trains)—*primera especial*; sleeping car—*coche dormitorio*; which platform?—*cuál andén*? which departure door/gate?—*cuál puerta*? What time?—*A qué hora*? And inevitably: How many hours late are we?—*Cuántas horas de retraso tenemos*? Street—*calle*; arrival—*llegada*; departure—*salida*; detour—*desviación*; north—*norte*; south—*sur*; east—*este* or *oriente* (and abbreviated *Ote*); west—*oeste* or *poniente* (abbreviated *Pte*). Junction—*empalme*; indicates a route where one must change buses/trains; avoid *empalmes* at all costs. Also, these will be useful : I need your help—*Necesito que me ayude, por favor*; Where is the bathroom, please—*Dónde está el baño, por favor*?

Bus: Bus travel is the most popular means of transportation for Mexicans. Buses cost a bit more than trains, but will cut travelling times by anything from a quarter to a half and in any case are absurdly inexpensive by American or European standards: Tijuana to Mexico City (1871 miles/2995 kms) costs about US$235 r.t. All seats are reserved on first class (*primera*) buses, but 'beware of boarding a bus where there are no seats left—you may be standing for several hours for first class fare'. Sometimes it's advisable to book for second class also although in southern Mexico a reader advises: 'Normally there are no standby passengers on first class and you get a reserved seat; on second class buses this is rarely the case'. Standards of comfort, speed, newness of buses, etc., vary more between bus lines than between first and second class, although second class will invariably be slower (sometimes days slower with attendant expenses) and cheaper on longer runs. 'Mexico City to Mazatlán, on a second class bus, took 24 hours. Scenery superb, driving horrifying. Great journey.' Travelers generally recommend deluxe or first class buses: 'By far the best—quite exciting, cheap, fast'. Most towns have separate terminals for first and second class buses. Always take along food, a sweater (for over-air-conditioned vehicle) and toilet paper.

When making reservations you are always allotted a particular seat on a particular bus so if you want a front seat book a couple of days ahead. No refunds are made if you miss the bus; and be careful of buying a ticket for a bus which is just pulling out of the bus station! No single carrier covers the whole country and in some areas as many as 20 companies may be in competition, and while this doesn't mean much variation in fares, it can mean a big difference in service. Greyhound passes are not valid in Mexico, though by waving a student card you can sometimes get a substantial discount—though really this is only for Mexican students during vacations.

Though you shouldn't have too much faith in the precision of its contents, ask for *un horario*—a timetable—showing all bus lines and issued free. **Bus Information** from Mexico City.

Central del Norte: (5) 587-1552
Central del Sur: (5) 689-4987
Central del Oriente: (5) 133-2124
Central del Poniente: (5) 271-0038 or (5) 271-4519

Rail: The trains are operated by Mexican National Railways ('N de M' or simply 'Ferrocarriles'). They only provide services to Veracruz (US$ 9 one way, 11hrs.) and to Saltillo (US$ 18.50 one way, 15 hrs). For reservations, call in Mexico City (5) 547-1084 or (5) 547-6685.

Particularly recommended routes are: from Chihuahua through the spectacular Tarahumara (or Copper) Canyon (four times wider than the Grand Canyon) and down to the west coast at Los Mochis. Enroute the train passes through 87 tunnels, crosses over 36 bridges, crosses the Continental Divide three times, and climbs to 8071 feet at the track's highest point. The Canyon is the home of the semi-nomadic Tarahumara Indians. Stop off at Créel if you want to visit them. (See box.)

Air: If time is short you may well want to consider city hopping by air. Although obviously more expensive than bus or train, the plane wins hands down for comfort and will give you more time in the places you really want to visit. Mexicana operates the largest number of domestic services (see the 'Getting There' section). Other destinations are served by Aeromexico (which also flies to Paris and Madrid as well as several US cities), AeroCalifornia and Aerolitoral.

Car: Taking a car to Mexico offers the prospect of unlimited freedom of movement, but `also of unlimited hassles if you fall afoul of Mexican bureaucracy. First, you need a car permit, which is issued with your tourist card, and the card itself is specially stamped. (The permit is not strictly necessary for Baja-only trips.) You cannot then leave Mexico without your car; if called away in an emergency, you must pay Mexican customs to look after it until your return, and in theory if the vehicle is written off in an accident it must be hauled back to the border at your expense. Airlines are not allowed to sell international tickets to visitors with the special card, without proof that the vehicle has been lodged with the authorities.

At the border you must produce a valid license and registration certificate. A UK license is likely to produce incomprehension in the average Mexican traffic cop: an international one is recommended.

Only Mexican **insurance** is valid in Mexico. You can get it at the border where 24-hour insurance brokers exist for the purpose. It is advisable to increase public liability and property damage coverage beyond the minimum. If you are involved in an accident, the golden rule is to get out of the way as quickly as possible before the police arrive: they tend to keep all parties concerned—whether responsible or not—in jail until claims are settled. A convincing level of insurance may assist your quick release.

Some practical concerns: do not try to drive your Cadillac or BMW from Los Angeles to Oaxaca. Choose a rugged vehicle and take plenty of spares: basic VWs, Dodges and Fords are manufactured in Mexico and are most easily repairable. VW buses are the best for small groups. All main roads are patrolled by the Green Angels fleet, radio coordinated patrol cars with English speaking two man crews (*Angeles Verdes*) in Mexico City (5) 250-8555 ext. 297 and 130; Monterrey N.L, contact Direccion de Turismo (8) 344-4343 or 340-1080 and they will connect you. Chihuahua Chih: (14) 29-33-00 ask for ext.1815; Acapulco (74) 83-84-70. They are equipped to handle minor repairs, give first aid and supply information: a raised hood will convey your need of assistance.

Garage repairs are reported as 'often incredibly cheap, particularly if you avoid 'authorized dealers', where you should expect to pay through the nose. Get a quote first!' Although you are not permitted to sell your car in Mexico, in theory you can do so in Guatemala and Belize, though these days purchasers are hard to find.

Pemex, the nationalized gasoline supplier, produces two grades of petrol. 'Don't buy cheap gas. Pemex Nova caused our car to shudder and stall. A mixture of Nova and the (better quality) Extra was a vast improvement.' Extra is however hard to find outside the larger towns, and some travelers modify their vehicles to take low-grade fuel.

It's important to note that all US cars manufactured after 1975 require unleaded gasoline. Outside the big cities unleaded petrol is undependable or not to be found and the use of anything else may damage the catalytic converter and ruin the entire engine. Garage attendants are notorious for swindling tourists: watch the dial carefully. Fuel itself is very cheap, at about US$0.45 per litre. 'Never let the gas level go low, and fill up at every opportunity. Gas stations are few and far between in remoter areas.'

Mexico has good main highways. Petrol stations (Pemex) are infrequent on the road, but most villages will have a 'vendor de gasolina', who will sell you a can-full and syphon it into your tank. Ask: *Dónde se vende gasolina aquí, por favor?* Once off major highways, be on the alert. Branches or rocks strewn across the road are an indication of a hazard ahead. Watch for pot-holes, rocks and narrow bridges (*puente angosto*), and slow down in advance of the sometimes vicious 'speed bumps' (*topes*) near roadside communities. Unless absolutely necessary, *do not drive at night*: many Mexican drivers rarely use headlights, and wandering cattle, donkeys, hens and pedestrians never do.

Car theft is a frequent occurrence: it is worth paying extra for a hotel with a secure car park. And US plates tend to attract the meticulous attention of traffic police. 'You are considered fair game for police along the road, who will stop you and fine you for 'speeding'. Haggle with them—they always come down to five to ten dollars. One man was asleep in his car in Nuevo Laredo when he was arrested for speeding: the car was parked at the time.' 'Drivers should be warned that after entering the country there is a 'free zone' of about 100 miles, with three or four customs stations along the road. You will have to bribe at least one official in order not to have your car ripped apart. But once you leave the 'free zone' you will have no more problems with customs and hardly see any police.'

Mexico's principal highways lead from Nogales, Juárez, Piedras Negras, Nuevo Laredo, Reynosa and Matamoros, all on the border, to Mexico City. The most expensive road in the world is the new toll highway from Mexico City to the Pacific-coast resorts, including Acapulco. It costs US$100 to drive the full length.

The most scenic road in Mexico is the well-maintained 150D which sweeps through the Puebla Valley past the volcanic peaks of Popocatépetl and Orizaba, climbs into lush rain forests and down through foothills covered with flowers and coffee plantations, to end up in the flat sugarcane country around Veracruz. Note, however, that wherever a car is a definite advantage over the comprehensive bus network, a pretty sturdy vehicle is often needed: this is particularly true in Baja, where a four wheel drive is a major asset.

Some signs: *Alto*—Stop; *No se estacione*—no parking; *bajada frene con motor*—steep hill, use low gear; *vado a 70 metros*—ford 70 metres; *cruce de peatones*—pedestrian crossing; *peligro*—danger; *camino sinuoso*—winding road; (*tramo de*) *curvas peligrosas*—(series of) dangerous curves; *topes a 150 metros*—speed bumps 150 metres; *Ote* (abbr.)—east; *Pte* (abbr.)—west.

Urban Travel: Most cities of any size have a good public transport service on buses, minibuses or converted vans. The flat fare is usually about US$0.60. When choosing a destination note that *Centro* is the centre of town and *Central* is the bus station.

Hitching: Can be hazardous with long waits (not just for a lift but for a car to come along) in high temperatures. However . . . 'found hitching pretty easy in northern Mexico. If you don't speak Spanish at all (like me) show a sign saying *estudiante* and giving your destination. Plan your trip with a map and accept rides only to places you know, unless the driver can make it clear to you in any other language.' 'Water in the desert, I never realized how important it was. Anyone hitching should take a water canteen.' Hitching is *not* recommended for women.

For Women Alone: For better or worse, *machismo* is alive and well in Mexico. The causes and results of *machismo* are frequently discussed and written about but it still doesn't make things any easier for women. Males from 8 to 80 feel compelled to remark on a woman's (and especially a foreigner's) legs, arms, breasts, hair, eyes, etc. In a country of dark-haired people, light or blonde hair has come to symbolize sexiness or higher status. Bare arms and legs, no bra and a casual manner signify that a woman is free and easy. Use common sense—don't hitchhike or enter cantinas. The best way to deal with hassles is to say nothing and continue walking. If possible, travel with a male friend (although *machos* will still try to pick you up) or a couple of women friends.

'I travelled alone and despite many warnings (mostly from US citizens!) I felt very safe. Mexicans seem more curious and friendly than anything else. Not at all like southern Europe.'

FURTHER READING

For anyone planning more than a brief trip to Mexico the following are recommended for additional information.

Let's Go: Mexico is an annually updated, group-researched 617 page guide, full of detailed background and essential practical information. Price £11.20.

The Hungry Traveler's Menu Translator and Food Guide to Mexico, by Marita Adair, price £5.60.

Eat Smart in Mexico describes how to decipher the menu, know the market foods and embark on a tasting adventure, by Joan & David Peterson, £8.0.

Access Mexico by Harper Perennial, £11.80, contains 43 detailed maps to help you get around.

Traveler's Guide to Mexican Camping by Mike & Terry Church, £19.95.

Insight Guide to Mexico, is a well written and illustrated combination travel guide and historical/sociological portrait, by John Wilcock, £12.00.

Insider's Guide to Mexico by Peggy Bond, £11.80.

NORTHWEST MEXICO

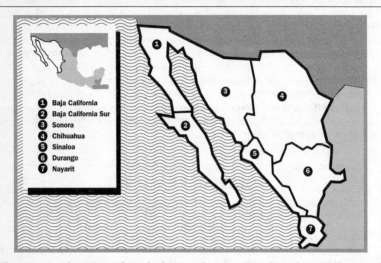

1 Baja California
2 Baja California Sur
3 Sonora
4 Chihuahua
5 Sinaloa
6 Durango
7 Nayarit

This vast arid region of stark desert, sharp mountains, deep valleys and canyons contains the states of Baja California, Sonora, Chihuahua, Durango, Nayarit and Sinaloa.

The nearness of Mexico to the US is deceptive once you learn that one way or another, you must cross many miles of thinly populated and largely dull terrain in this northern sector in order to get anywhere more interesting.

The coastline offers some relief, especially from Hermosillo southward as it gradually becomes greener, until you reach the lush and humid jungle around Tepic and San Blás.

Baja California has its own peninsula to the west; poorest of Mexican states, beautiful in a bare-bones sort of way, especially on its eastern coast on the warm Sea of Cortéz (also called the Gulf of California).

BAJA CALIFORNIA

TIJUANA   Previous editions of this guide have dismissed Tijuana and the other border towns; yet more of its readers visit 'TJ' than anywhere else in Mexico, numbering themselves among the millions of day trips passing through the city each year. You will do Mexico an injustice if you judge it by the border towns, but you will do yourself an injustice if you fail to take the opportunity provided by a free day in San Diego, El Paso or Laredo to experience an abrupt cultural discontinuity available in few other places on the planet. The most cursory trip across puts into sudden perspective everything the traveler has taken for granted in the course of a trip round the US.

Tourist trap, home of cheap assembly plants, staging post for illegal immigrants en route to El Norte, Tijuana's every aspect depends on its proximity to the border. Possessing few Mexican virtues but pandering to most American vices, the town has long functioned as a commercial and sexual bargain basement for southern California, and although a municipal clean-up campaign has edged the more blatant prostitution and sex shows to the outskirts, hustle is still the name of the game for the storekeepers, street traders and taxi drivers competing for your attention.

There are bargains to be had if you bargain ruthlessly: good deals likely for leather goods, blankets and non-Mexican items such as cameras and name brand clothing. 'You can knock all goods down to a third of the asking price. Take US dollars.' 'Some great buys if you enjoy haggling.' 'If you go in a spirit of sociological inquiry, remember to have fun. Well worth a day visit.' 'I enjoyed every minute of it.'

ACCOMMODATION
Tijuana has over a hundred hotels: those in the southeast section of the city are reputedly the quietest and most salubrious. Expect to pay US$24-$42, and be prepared to haggle. 'Lower prices possible if you don't mind sleaze.' There are several small, inexpensive hotels on Ave Madero, to the left as you leave the old Tres Estrellas de Oro bus station.

Hotel Cesar, Revolución & Calle 5, (66) 85-16-06, S-US$32, D-US$43.

Unidad Deportiva Crea, Cayon Aviacion y Via Rapida Oriente, (66) 82-90-67 or (66) 34-30-89, Zona del Río, near the bridge, about US$5 for dormitory bed, make reservation before going down and ask for Mr. Bonifacio Estrada Montes.

Hotel Nelson, Revolución 721, (66) 85-43-02 or (66) 85-43-04. 'Clean, decent bathrooms, relatively expensive. S/D-US$ 37. Also has a good restaurant.'

FOOD
Nelson (see Hotel Nelson). Reasonable prices for full-scale Mexican meals.

La Especial , Revolución in btwn 3 & 4 , (66) 85-66-54 open 9am-11pm.

La Placita, Revolución in btwn 3 & 4, (66) 88-27-04.

Carnitas Uruapan, Blvd. Aguascalientes #1650, (66) 81-61-81 or (66) 81-14-00. Deep-fried pork (carnitas) in various combinations. Popular with locals and tourists. One order US$7.50.

OF INTEREST
Centro Cultural FONART, Paseo de los Heroes & Calle Mina, Zona Río, (66) 84-11-11. New cultural museum of striking modern design with archeological, historical and handicrafts displays. Auditorium with multimedia show in English (afternoons) and Spanish (evenings), also theatre, art shops, and restaurant. Daily 10 am-9 pm. Show admission US$4.00—includes free pass to museum.

ENTERTAINMENT
Jai Alai. Fronton Palacio Revolución and Calle 7, (66) 85-36-87. Fast and furious version of squash using arm baskets to hurl hard rubber ball against court walls. Exhibitions only Fri. & Sat. 7pm-10pm, Free admission.

Bullfighting. Toreo de Tijuana en el centro de la ciudad. The season changes every year, but is from May-Oct. approximately. In one of two rings. Tkts US$8 to US$156 sold in advance at Mexicoach: Ave. Revolución #1025 central zone (66) 86-14-70. 'Amazing and disgusting.'

Racetrack (*Hipódromo*), Agua Caliente Blvd. in front of Calimax, (66) 33-73-06. Moorish-influenced building containing enclosed and open-air stands. Races on Tues, 1pm-5pm matinee, Sat & Sun 2 pm-5:30 pm. Free admission.

INFORMATION
State Tourism Office, Paseo de los Heroes # 1089, (66) 34-39-61 or (66) 34-65-74.

TRAVEL
To Tijuana: see section on San Diego, California. From SD Amtrak terminal, the San Diego Trolley will take you to US border suburb of San Ysidro (approx. US$6); then 20 minute walk to centre, or the local bus from the border to Avenue Revolución (Tijuana) costs no more than US$4. Some local buses are: Volante, Diamante & ABC. 'Taxi from border should cost no more than US$8.' If passing straight through, get either the shuttle bus from Amtrak or the Greyhound service from LA and San Diego: these both take you to the new so-called 'central' bus station on the eastern edge of town. The old Tres Estrellas terminal near the border has poor connecting service and a 3 new peso taxi ride is the only other option. Mexicoach offers an excessively expensive centre-to-centre service from San Diego.
Onward: frequent bus services to Ensenada (2 hrs), Mexicali (3 hrs), Santa Ana (11 hrs), Los Mochis (22 hrs), Mazatlán (28 hrs), Guadalajara (40 hrs), Mexico City and points between. Six buses daily to La Paz (22 hrs).

MEXICALI   Inland border town located 136 km east of Tijuana and departure point for bus and rail routes to West Coast destinations. One of the hottest places in Mexico, with few concessions to tourists or to anyone else: accommodation choice is between three hotels priced at US levels or Zona Rosa sleaze. However, for even the short stay border-hopper the trip from Tijuana (the new terminal) is recommended: the three hour ride gives an acceptably brief taste of the starkness of Northern Mexico, and the descent on the eastern side of the mountains towards Mexicali is both hair-raising and dramatic.

ACCOMMODATION
Hotel Plaza, Ave Madero 366, (65) 52-97-57 or (65) 52-97-59. S-US$32, D-US$39. Excellent 24 hr restaurant.
Hotel La Siesta Inn, Blvd Justo Sierra #899, (65) 68-20-01. S-US$61, D-US$71.
Hotel Del Norte, Ave Madero 205, (65) 52-81-01 or (65) 52-81-03. S-US$33-D-US$42.

FOOD
Cafe Samborns, Calz Independencia inside Plaza Fiesta, (65) 57-02-12.
Las Campanas Restaurant, Calz Justo Sierra & Calle Honduras, Col. Cuahutemoc, (65) 68-12-13.
El Chalet Restaurant, Calz Justo Sierra #899, (65) 68-20-01.

ENTERTAINMENT
Desert Biking. Behind Hotel Riviera, quarter-mile down road on right. US$15 p/hr, US$20 deposit. 'Three wheeler fat tyre motorcycles for desert tracks and sand dunes. Great fun for novices.'
Bodegas de Santo Tomás, Mexico's largest winery, tours and tastings offered Mon-Sat.
Mexicali Museum: Alvaro Obregon #1209, (65) 53-5044.
Museo Regioanal de Mexicali: Ave. Reforma y calle E, zona centro, (65) 54-19-77 or (65) 52-57-15. Gives a comprehensive introduction to Baja California history and culture. Admission US$0.73

INFORMATION
State Tourist Office : (65) 57-23-76.

TRAVEL
The bus station is near Mateos and Independencia, a mile south of the border: no need to enter the town itself. Buses every 30 mins to Tijuana takes 3 hrs and cost US$13 o/w, hourly to the south.
San Felipe: A 2 hr, 125 mile drive from Mexicali, through desert and beautifully harsh mountains. San Felipe is a likeable, ramshackle fishing village with miles of white sand beaches and superb fishing. After this an unpaved road continues south to join Route 1 from Ensenada.

ENSENADA   Slightly hipper version of Tijuana, 70 miles south via a new toll road. A thriving fishing industry fails to impart authenticity to anything but the cheap and tasty seafood. The town is full of Californians, especially at weekends, and is one of the few towns where you will get better value from US dollars than from pesos. But 'the drive to Ensenada along the coast is beautiful—well worth crossing the border just to experience the complete change of environment'.

ACCOMMODATION
'Reservations vital for Saturdays. We didn't have one and spent the night on the streets.' In general expect to pay S-US$16, D-US$32.
Hotel America, Ave López Mateos #1309 Esq. con Espinosa S-US$20, D-US$27, (61) 76-13-33.
Hotel Bungalows Playa, Ave López Mateos #1847, S-US$16, D-US$21, (61) 76-14-30.
Hotel Colón, Ave Guadalupe #174, (61) 76-19-10.
Hotel del Valle, Ave Riveroll #367, S-D US$32, (61) 78-22-24.

FOOD
El Charro, Ave López Marcos #475, (61) 78-38-81.
La Holandesa, Ave López Mateos #1797, (61) 77-19-65.
Mi Kasa, Ave Riveroll #872, (61) 78-82-11.
Victor's Restaurant, Blvd Lázaro Cárdenas #178, (61) 76-13-13.

OF INTEREST
Shopping: **FONART** store, next to tourist office, Mateos 885, (61) 78-24-11. Daily 9am-7pm. High quality textiles, silver, ceramics, etc. No bargaining. Most goods from southern Mexico: a good place to buy if not going further.
El Nuevo Nopal, on northern edge of Ensenada, offers similar range.
BS Beauty Supply (Calle 4 & Ruíz) and **La Joya** (Calle 5 & Ruíz) specialises in tax-free imported goods.
La Bufadora. Spectacular natural geyser, shooting water into the air from underground cavern. 20 miles south of town, and off the main road; own transport needed.
Agua Caliente Hot Springs. 22 miles E on Rte 3. Unpaved but navigable road.
The Tourist Zone. Is located at Ave López Mateos where you will find souvenirs, shops, restaurants and bars.

INFORMATION
Sectur, Blvd Costera y Teniente Azueta #540, frente a la gasolinera de Pemex (61) 72-30-22 or (61) 72-30-00. A good tourist guide for Ensenada is Mr. Roberto Gonzales (61) 78-41-07, Tour Bajarama (61) 78-35-12 or (61) 78-32-52., Tour Calibaja (61) 78-16-41.

BAJA BEYOND ENSENADA   After Ensenada the paved but narrow and variable quality Transpeninsular Highway (Mexico 1) leads the bus traveller to the tip of Baja at the resort center of Cabo San Lucas, 1,000 dusty miles and 20 hours further on. Known for its sport fishing and beautiful beaches, this is where the Gulf of California and the Pacific Ocean meet. To explore most areas of interest en route you need a car, and often a four-wheel drive vehicle: buses do not prolong their rest stops at the roadside towns, which in most cases is no great loss. Expect visions of desolate beauty and long passages of tedium, especially when the road loses sight of the coast.

OF INTEREST

The mountains, forest and trout streams of **San Pedro Mártir National Park** lie two hours away from **Colonet**, 74 miles from Ensenada. Superb hiking and climbing but check at the turn off that the dirt road is open all the way. Further down the highway, the agricultural town of **San Quintín** offers good markets and restaurants. **Bahia San Quintín**, five miles away by dirt road, has fine beaches, expensive motels and excellent seafood.

The next 250 miles or so consist of bleak inland desert. Those with an interest in salt evaporation plants will enjoy **Guerro Negro**, at the border of Baja California Sur: otherwise its only virtue lies in its proximity to **Scammon's Lagoon**, breeding ground for gray whales and an incredible spectacle during the breeding period of late December-February. Four wheel drive needed for the 20 mile trek.

San Ignacio, is a delightful oasis village with date palms imported by its Jesuit founders in the eighteenth century, a reconstructed mission, and its own wine. But more and cheaper accommodation will be found 50 miles further on at **Santa Rosalía**, a copper mining town of interest for its friendly inhabitants, ugly galvanised steel church, and thrice-weekly ferry to Guaymas on the mainland, the shortest and cheapest crossing. Boats depart (subject to change): Sun & Wed at 8 am, arrive 3 pm. Transboradores Terminal (115) 2-00-14 or (115) 2-00-13. The 7 hr trip costs US$15 salon class, US$29 tourist class, and US$166 for cars. See below for further details.

The desert oasis of **Mulegé** has hotels and restaurants and two hours away by four wheel drive Baja's best cave paintings. Between Mulegé and **Loreto** are a number of beaches accessible by car. Loreto itself was founded in 1697, but most in evidence now is work-in-progress on the Government-sponsored tourist resort.

La Paz follows after another 200 miles of boring inland desert. For years an isolated pearl-fishing centre, the ferry service and completion of Hwy 1 have turned La Paz into a major tourist town, but the centre at least preserves a relaxed charm. Not much to see except the famous sunsets, some good beaches and snorkelling, but many good restaurants and hotels, and the zócalo (main plaza) is spectacularly lit at night. Tourist Information Office, Obregón & 16 de Septiembre, (112) 40-100 or (112) 40-103. Daily 8 am-8 pm.

Ferries: Sematur is located at Guillermo Prieto & 5 de Mayo, (112) 5-88-99 ext. 109 operator, Travel Agency Viaxtur (112) 5-38-33 or 5-46-66. Thurs-Tues services at 3 pm to **Mazatlán**, arrive 9 am. US$22 salon class, US$31 tourist class. From La Paz to **Topolobampo (Los Mochis)**, US$15 salon class, US$20 tourist class. Wed & Thurs departs at 10am, arriving at 7 pm. For more information call 1-800-696-9600.

Cabo San Lucas lies 120 miles further south at the tip of the peninsula, and is a purpose-built tourist town with little time for the budget-conscious, who will have better luck at **San José del Cabo**. The whole southern tip has beautiful and—so far—unspoiled beaches, a couple of which, on Rte 9 out of San Lucas, are accessible to campers. **Sierra de la Laguna National Park**, reached by dirt road from Pescadero, offers pine forests and the occasional puma. The San Lucas-Puerto Vallarta ferry, a gruelling 20 hr trip, is currently suspended. In any case the La Paz-

Mazatlán route, followed by the bus, is the more tolerable alternative.

Ferries: The Baja-mainland routes make few concessions to tourist convenience or comfort. You must queue for tickets several hours before they go on sale, and be prepared for long waits and customs hassles. Salón class is incredibly cheap, but involves a long and rowdy voyage with two hundred or so others crowded together on bus seats. Tourist class cabins are still a bargain, but frequent air conditioning breakdowns often make them unendurable. Taking a car across demands a willingness to wait several *days* (commercial vehicles always get priority) and pay substantial bribes. As if all this wasn't enough, the food is awful too. The ferry service has recently been privatised and hopefully will improve. Remember that flights duplicate most ferry routes and are definitely a less exhausting, albeit more expensive, option.

OTHER BORDER TOWNS

CIUDAD JUAREZ Over the bridge from El Paso, and seemingly part of the same urban sprawl, this is the city about which Bob Dylan wrote his most depressing song ever (*Just Like Tom Thumb's Blues*). Souvenirs, gambling, racetracks and brothels, and it's easy to get lost in the rain. But still worth a quick visit (the market is recommended), rather than cowering on the other side of the border: 'it's easy to make the crossing for a much, much cheaper hotel room than you'll find in El Paso.'

ACCOMMODATION
Singles average US$25, doubles US$30.

Hotel Monaco, Paseo del Triunfo de la Republica # 335, (16) 16-16-77 or 16-31-54. S-US$25, D-US$33.

Hotel Continental, Ave Lerdo #112 Sur, (16) 15-00-84, or (16) 15-01-44, S-US$28, D-US$31.

Hotel Suite Jose Marti, Calle Jose Marti #2881, (16) 13-70-38 or (16) 11-49-02, S-D-US$29.

Hotel Plaza Consulado, Ave.Lopez Mateos #1020, (16) 11-48-84/85, US$ 33.

INFORMATION
State Tourist Office, Libertad #1300 primer piso Edificio Agustin Melgar Colonia Centro, (14) 29-33-00 Ext.5610.

Tourist Booth, Ave Juárez & Azucena. (16) 14-92-52.

Mexam Tour: (16) 13-00-30 or 13-00-20

Turimex de Chihuahua: (16) 13-56-57 or 13-28-58

TRAVEL
By bus to Chihuahua, Mexico City or most other destinations. Instead of direct route to Chihuahua it is possible to go via **Nuevo Casas Grandes**, impressive ruins (pyramids, ball courts) of 1000 AD agricultural community. 'Get up early to squeeze this trip into a day.' 'Beware of low flying taxi drivers.'

NB: Mexican buses to Chihuahua and Mexico City also depart from El Paso Greyhound terminal. By air, Gonzalez Airport to Mexico City, about US$363 r/t. Call Aeromexico, 1-800-237-6639.

CHIHUAHUA The first major town on the route down from El Paso, Chihuahua is a prosperous industrial and cattle-shipping center, once famous for breeding tiny, hairless and bad-tempered dogs of the same name. The city is of interest primarily as the inland terminus for the dramatic **Al Pacífico** train ride from Los Mochis on the coast through the Barranca del Cobre (Copper Canyon). This is one of the world's most spectacular train rides.

ACCOMMODATION
Singles average US$9, doubles US$20.
Hotel Del Carmen, Calle 10 #4 Col. Centro, (14) 15-70-96 S-US$9, D-US$12.
Hotel San Juan, Calle Victoria 823, (14) 10-00-35. Off the Plaza Principal. 'Clean and friendly.' 'Lovely patio.' S-US$10, D-US$15.
Hotel del Parque, Calle Ocampo #2400 Col Centro, (14) 15-15-58. S-US$12, D-US$13.
Hotel el Campanario, Blvd. Diaz Ordaz # 1405, (14) 15-45-45 or 15-49-79. S/D-US$20.

OF INTEREST
The Chihuahua Cathedral, one of the most beautiful churches in Northern Mexico, was built in 1727. Construction began in 1772, and was not completed until almost a 100 years later. Built in colonial style, the cathedral overlooks the Plaza Principal.
The Palacio de Gobierno, where Miguel Hidalgo, the 'Father of Mexico', was executed at 7 am July 30th 1811, is decorated with 'lovely lurid Murals'.
Quinta Luz, The Museum of Pancho Villa is a fortresslike 50 room mansion, Villa's home and hideout, at Calle 10, #3010 Col. Santa Rosa, (14) 16-29-58. Take bus from Plaza Principal to Parque Lerdo. Calle 10 (unmarked so ask for Calle Diez) is opposite the park, running SE of Paseo Bolívar. Tues-Sat 9 am-1 pm, 3 pm-7 pm, Sun 9 am-5 pm, US$1. Now state-run, after being in the hands of Villa's 'official' widow for many years: see Villa memorabilia including weapons and the bullet-scarred car in which he was assassinated in 1923.
Archeological Site Paquime: The most important prehispanic archeological site in northern Mexico is Paquime, located in the valley of Casas Grandes, Chihuahua, about 321 km from the city. For more information (169) 2-41-40.

INFORMATION
State Tourist Office, Calle Libertad #1300, Col. Centro, (14) 29-33-00 ext. 4511 or Fax (14) 29-34-21. General Information (14) 15-77-56.

TRAVEL
For information about travel to the Copper Canyon, see separate box.

LOS MOCHIS A dull agricultural city, of interest only as the southern terminus for the ferry connections with La Paz in nearby Topolobampo. Tourist office: (68) 15-10-90.

ACCOMMODATION
Hotel Posada Real, Gabriel Leiba y Rafael Buelna #38 sur zona centro, (68) 12-23-63 or 12-12-79. S-US$42, D-US$47.
Hotel Catalina, Ave Alvaro Obregón, #48 zona centro, (68) 12-11-37 or 12-12-40. S-US$16, D-US$19.
Hotel Beltran, Hidalgo # 281 Pte., (68) 12-07-10 or 12-06-88., S-US$20, D-US$23.

FOOD
Cafeteria Fenix: Calle Angel Flores #385 sur zona centro, (68) 12-26-25 or 12-26-23.
Restaurant Chic's: Blvd. Rosales y Alvaro Obregon zona centro, (68) 15-47-09.

THE COPPER CANYON

Copper Canyon (Mochis and Chihuahua) The spectacular Copper Canyon was formed some 20-30 million years ago, when intense volcanic activity raised the Sierra Madre mountain range. Copper Canyon is 300 feet deeper and four times wider than the Grand Canyon. In the high parts of the canyon there is an impressive variety of vegetation and wildlife. During the summer the climate is cool, and during the winter the temperature can drop below freezing. The temperature at the base of the canyon is hot, and the plant and animal life markedly different. The descent to the bottom of the canyon can take two days, and those who make the trek should be in good physical condition. It is recommended to make the descent in winter or spring, to avoid the summer heat of the canyon floor.

The canyon is populated by Tarahumara Indians. Despite the tourism, they live in largely traditional ways and are known for their basketry and long distance running abilities.

How To Get There: The best way to reach and experience the canyon is by train. There is an incredible trip from Chihuahua to Los Mochis, which takes 14 hrs one way. The train passes through 86 tunnels, over 37 bridges and covers more than 400 miles. The train stops at many different points along the way, allowing passengers to see and photograph the spectacular views. Train No. 74 from Chihuahua to Los Mochis costs US$90 and leaves at 7am daily, Train No. 73 leaves Los Mochis at 6 am daily. For more information, call Ferrocarriles Nacionales de Mexico at `(14) 15-77-56, 6 am-10 pm Monsun. Chihuahua to Los Mochis US$90 one way Chihuahua to Creel train runs every day at 6:30am and 3:15pm. Tours of the canyon and accommodations can be arranged in Chihuahua by (1) Turísmo al Mar (14) 16-92-32 or (14) 16-65-89, contact Mr Cobarrubias or Mr Colmenero; (2) Viajes Dorado de Chihuahua (14) 14-64-38 or (14) 14-64-90, contact Mr Juan Rodriguez; (3) Turísmo Gema (14) 15-65-07 or (14) 15-28-98, contact Mr Jesus Gonzalez or (4) Temsa (14) 16-16-46. Other tourist information can be obtained from the Mexican Secretary of Tourism at (14) 15-91-24 ext. 4512. For information about Los Mochis you can contact the Mexican Secretary of Tourism at (69) 16-51-60/65.

Where To Stop Off And Why: **Créel Station**: This is the doorway to the Sierra Tarahumara. From here you can get to the Tarahumaras Caves, Arareko Lake, rock formations in the Valley of the Mushrooms, the Elephant Stone, and the Valley of the Frogs. Four km from the nearby town of Cusarare are the Cusarare waterfalls. Local tours offer horseback rides and trips to the waterfalls. Tours run between US$12 and US$28. Camping is also possible but bring a tent (summer is rainy season).

Batopilas: One of the more beautiful parts of the Copper Canyon, Batopilas has a descent from 2,200 metres to 460 metres above sea level. From the vantage point of Bufa you can appreciate the splendor of this magnificent canyon.

Divisadero Station: An impressive view of the canyon is located at an altitude of 1300 meters, at the Urique River. There is a path to the bottom of the canyon, and an excellent opportunity to experience the variety of vegetation from pine forest to tropical.

Basaseachic National Park: This park has two of the highest waterfalls in Mexico. Basaseachic Falls is 254 metres high and Piedra Volada is 456 metres high. The **Candamena Canyon** is located here, and excursions to the bottom are offered.

TRAVEL
The Bus Station: " Los Mochis ", (68) 82-05-77, (68) 82-19-49, (68) 81-36-80.
Trains leave Los Mochis at 6 am. Tickets (see under Chihuahua for prices) on sale from 5:45 am: (Only for the Copper Canyon Tour). For information call Viajes Flamingos, (68) 12-16-13. Starting from Los Mochis end reportedly gives best views; sit on the right. Station is 3 miles out of town—allow plenty of time for local bus or taxi. Los Mochis station uses Chihuahua time, one hour earlier than local time.
Ferry for La Paz, if operating (see Baja section), leaves from **Topolobampo** for the 8 hour trip, Mon-Sat at 10 pm. Salón class US$15. Often sold out 24 hrs ahead. Nowhere to stay in Topolobampo, but 'a night out under the stars is fun. Fishermen cook freshly caught fish and shrimp over wood fires and invite you to partake. But buying even basics is difficult—don't count on it for food for the ferry.' Going straight from the ferry to the Al Pacifico, or vice versa, is logistically difficult and an exhausting trip: a stopover in Los Mochis is recommended.

MAZATLAN Big, boisterous and a major gringo tourist town, Mazatlán offers a ten mile strip of international hotels and some superb game fishing: to the south of this, the old section of the town has more affordable hotels, local colour and an element of risk. The El Cid Hotel rents out windsurfers, sailboats, catamarans and snorkel gear. A 10-12 minute parachute/sail along the beach averages US$20. **Piedra Isla**, a tiny island just offshore, has good beaches, diving and camping possibilities: very congenial after the last boat leaves at 4.30 pm.

ACCOMMODATION/INFORMATION
Best value around the bus station and in Old Mazatlán on Aves Juárez, Aquiles Serdán and Azueta.
Hotel Fiesta, Ferruquilla #306, tel. (69) 81-78-88, S-US$13, D-US$15.
Hotel Plaza Gaviotas, Calle Bugambilias #100 Zona Dorada, (69) 13-44-96, S-D-US$48.
Hotel las Arenas, Ave. del Mar #1910 Fracc. Telleria, (69) 82-00-00, S-US$38, D-US$43.

FOOD
Restaurant Canada, Zona Turistica, Ave. del Camaron Sabalo esq. con Ave. de las Garzas, Zona Dorada (69) 13-69-77 , international and regional.
Restaurant Panama, Calle Benito Juarez y Canisales, Col. Centro, (69) 85-18-53.
Restaurant Costas Marineras, Privada del Camaron y la Florida, Zona Dorada, (69) 14-19-28, o 16-15-99.
Tourism Office, Ave Camaron Sabado & Tiburon Fracc. Sabalo Contry, tel. (69) 16-51-60.

TRAVEL
Local bus, 'Zaragoza', 8 pesos from bus station into town. Ferry leaves 5 pm, daily to La Paz, a 16 hour trip. Be at terminal before 8am to get ticket. 'The route (Mexico 40) from Mazatlan to Durango is absolutely breath-taking. Although it's just over 300 miles, it took us a long time to cover as the road twists and turns up to 7000 ft where it crosses the Continental Divide. A part of Mexico that should not be missed.' Take Transportes Monterrey-Saltillo bus for the 6 hour trip.

SAN BLÁS An hour's drive off the highway just north of Tepic takes you through increasingly lush tropical country to San Blás, once a sleepy seaside village, but no longer. 'Signs advertising granola and yogurt, expensive hotels and food, dirty beaches and medium surfing.' 'Very hippified but nice with a good swimming beach.' 'Bring lots of insect repellent—famous for its gnats.' 'We really liked it here. The beach is lovely and the town is small but pretty with nice places to sit and eat.'

ACCOMMODATION

Hotel Bucanero, Juárez 75, near plaza, (328) 5-01-01. 'Clean, popular with young people.' S-US$16, D-US$21.

Hotel Garza-Canela, Paredes #106 sur. Zona Centro. (328) 5-04-80. S-US$48, D-US$60.

Motel Marino Inn, Ave. H.Batallon y Ave. Islitas, zona costera. (328) 5-03-03. S-US$25, D-US$37.

Hotel Posada del Rey, Campeche #10 camino rumbo a la playa, (328) 5-01-23, S-US$26, D-US$32.

FOOD

Try the little cafes along the beach for inexpensive fish, oyster meals. Also check to see if the pool in the bar of the Torino restaurant still has 4 crocodile residents. Restaurant-Bar **La Familia**, Ave H. Batallón 16, (328) 5-02-58. Open 8 pm-10 pm.

INFORMATION/TRAVEL

Tourist Info, opposite plaza, has useful booklet with maps, lodgings, etc. Buses from Tepic to San Blás run fairly regularly. 'Interesting jungle scenery enroute.' The bus station is on Calle Sinaloa, tel (328) 5-00-43. Take a small boat trip into the jungle lagoons and creeks behind the town. Dawn is the best time for you to catch the animals (or vice versa).

NORTHEAST MEXICO

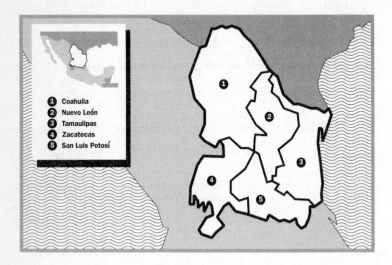

1 Coahuila
2 Nuevo León
3 Tamaulipas
4 Zacatecas
5 San Luis Potosí

The northeast states offer little worth tarrying for. The border towns east of Juárez- Nuevo Laredo, Reynosa and Matamoros- provide similar experiences to the others, and are worth a quick visit but no more. 'Nuevo Laredo is a corrupt dump and an insult to Mexico'; Matamoros has either exceptionally friendly people or unbelievably officious and venal immigration officers, depending on whom you listen to. All three cities offer flights to Mexico City (about US$144 one way), and bus route via Monterrey.

Another route south is the Pan American Highway, Mexico 85, taking you from Nuevo Laredo to Monterrey, Nuevo León.

MONTERREY

NUEVO LEÓN This state is an important economic centre of Mexico. In addition to its modern capital city of Monterrey, one of the three largest cities in Mexico, Nuevo León also has interesting deserts, vegetation, waterfalls, caverns, and museums.

In Monterrey you can find the famous **Macro Plaza** also known as the Gran Plaza, comprising 100 acres in the heart of the city. Completed in 1985, it is one of the world's largest squares. Nearby are shops, restaurants, important government buildings, museums, and downtown hotels. In the center of the Macro Plaza is the large Fountain of Life ('La fuente de la vida'), one of several fountains in the plaza.

OF INTEREST

Museum of Contemporary Art (Marcos Museum). This amazing museum is located in the heart of the Macro Plaza in the old town at Zuazua and Padre Raymundo Jordon, (8) 342-4820. The museum was designed in contemporary Mexican style by the famous Mexican architect Ricardo Legorreta. It has 11 galleries that display the art of Mexico, Latin America, and other parts of the world. Tue & Sun 9am-7pm. US$1-$2, free on Weds & Sat.

Obispado Museum, (8) 346-0404. The Obispado was built by the Catholic church in 1788. Sitting on a hilltop overlooking the city, it was used as a fort during the Mexican-American War in 1847, the French Intervention in 1862, and the Mexican Revolution in 1915. Today the building is used primarily as a museum. Tue-Sun 10am-5pm, US$2.

In **Monterrey** you can also find the **Planetarium Museum of Science, Art, and Technology**, complete with an Imax theatre, as well as Plaza Sesamo, an amusement park inspired by the children's TV programme, *Sesame Street*.

Also near Monterrey is the **Parque Nacional Cumbres**, where the famous 75 ft **Horsetail Falls** ('Cascada de Cola de Caballo') is located. The falls can be reached by foot, horseback, or carriage. From Monterrey, take hwy 85 NW for 145 km. Daily 8am-7pm, US$1.50.

South of the city of Monterrey you will find the interesting **Grutas de Garcia** caves that are some 500,000 years old. These caves were once submerged by an ancient sea, and marine fossils can be seen in the walls. To reach the caves, take Hwy 40 west from Monterrey for 40 km to Saltillo, then 9 km on marked road to the caves. Daily 9 am-5 pm, US$ 5.00.

INFORMATION

State Tourism Office, (8) 345-1500, ext.165 & 167 or (8) 345-6805, Zaragoza sur 1300 piso A-1 Building Kalos Suite #137, Monterrey NL.

Tour: Around the city contact Osetur (8) 347-1533 or 347-1599, Lomas Grandes St. #2700 San Fco. Building, 5th Floor Col. Lomas Largas.

Saltillo, 50 miles up in the hills to the west, is preferable if you need to break your journey. Further on towards Mexico City, **San Luis Potosí** is a gold and silver mining town of considerable historical interest and with a distinctive regional cuisine.

Zacatecas is the capital city of the state of the same name and is built on the side of a 7000 ft mountain. It's still a silvermining centre and is famous for its baroque cathedral and the Quemada ruins. Yes, those are rattlesnake skins for sale in the market. For 'marvellous views' of the area take a ride on the cablecar (*teleferíco*) north of the plaza. US$2 r/t.

Secretary of Tourism (Sectur): Prolongacion Gonzales Ortega y E. Castorena, Col. Centro (492) 4-05-52

OF INTEREST

Rafael Coronel Museum, also known as ex-canvento de Sn Fco open Mon-Tue & Thu-Sat. from 10am - 2pm & 4-7pm. Admission US$1.

Zacatecas Museum, Explanada del cerro de la bufadora next to the patrocinio Sanctuary. (492)2-80-62.

Francisco Goitia Museum, Enrique Estrada #102, Col. Sierra Alicia. (492)2-81-16.

Teliferico, Will take you from the old town to the **Bufa** (great view) (492)2-56-94.

Don't go without visiting **Hotel Quinta Real** built in the old colonial style, inside of what used to be a Plaza de Toro (beautiful) also go to the **Jerez de Zacatecas** where the high society of Zacatecas used to live.

CENTRAL MEXICO

❶ Aguascalientes	❻ Querétaro	⓫ Morelos
❷ Jalisco	❼ México	⓬ Tlaxcala
❸ Colima	❽ Guerrero	⓭ Puebla
❹ Guanajuato	❾ Hidalgo	⓮ Oaxaca
❺ Michoacán	❿ México DF	⓯ Veracruz

Mexico seems to save itself scenically, culturally and every other way, in order to burst upon you in central Mexico in a rich outpouring of volcanic mountains, pre-Columbian monuments, luxuriant flowers, exuberant people and picturesque architecture. This is the region where the Mexican love of colour manifests itself and the air is cool and fresh on the high Central Plateau. Be prepared for mugginess on either coast around Acapulco and Veracruz, however.

Mexico City lies in the centre of this region, surrounded by a dozen tiny states from Tlaxcala to Guanajuato. Northwest of Mexico City is the orbit of Guadalajara, second largest city and home to the largest colony of American expatriates. That fact makes its outlying satellite towns of Tlaquepaque, Chapala, Ajijic and so on, quite expensive.

MEXICO CITY The Aztec city of Tenochtitlán had a population of 300,000 by 1521, when stout Cortés demolished it to build Mexico City from the remains. Today that figure represents the number of new residents the city acquires *each year*, making it likely that total population will reach 20 million during the lifetime of this guide.

México DF (pronounced 'day effy', for Distrito Féderal) is the nation's cultural, economic and transportation hub, with most of the country's people living on the surrounding plateau. As well as being the largest city in the world, it is probably the most polluted, with a smog level to make LA seem positively bracing and a crime level to make New York City seem like the Garden of Eden on a Sunday afternoon: be alert, especially away from the centre. The altitude—7400 ft—together with the crowds, suicidal traffic and incessant din, can quickly exhaust the unacclimatised traveller.

For a time, the earthquake of September 1985 overshadowed these problems. In addition to the thousands of deaths, 250 major buildings were toppled and the whole country's communication network was seriously disrupted. The city has now fully recovered from the destruction caused by the earthquakes, except for a few damaged buildings still in the process of demolition and clearance.

Visit the city for its striking architecture from Aztec through Spanish Colonial to modern, from pyramids to enamelled skyscrapers, from modern subways to archeological finds preserved *in situ* at Metro stops. Great wealth and poverty exist side by side but residents at all economic levels tend to be the most hospitable of Mexicans. 'North America is incomplete without a visit to this vast and fascinating city.'

ACCOMMODATION

Singles average US$13, doubles US$15-35. Best area for low price accommodation is around Alameda Park, especially Revillagigedo Street, Plaza San Fernando, Zarazoga, and (further west just before Insurgentes) Bernal Díaz and Bernadino de Sahagun. Also try the area immediately surrounding the Zócalo. Be prepared to add 25% to these prices during summer: during this period pressure on a diminishing reserve of low cost hotels is intense, and a room in Cuernavaca, about an hour away by bus, may be the only viable option.

Hotel Bajío, Tonala # 357 Col Roma, (5) 564-0468 or (5) 264-1455.

Hotel Boston, Brazil #113 Centro, (5) 526-1408.

Hotel El Gran Cosmos, Lázaro Cárdemas 12, (5) 521-9889. Metro Bellas Artes. Central, D-Q room with or without bath. 'Ask for a room with a patio.' S-US$20, D-US$35.

Hotel Congreso, Allende # 18, (5) 510-4446/51. Small rm w/TV and private bathroom. S-US$16, D-US$22.

Hotel Guadalupe, Calzada Guadalupe #152, Col. Hipodromo de Peralvillo, AC, shower, TV, (5) 537-1779.

Hotel Montecarlo, Uruguay #69, (5) 521-9363. 'Clean and friendly.' Built in 1772 as an Augustine monastery. DH Lawrence briefly lived here. S-US$13, D-US$17. Nearby are two restaurants, Vips & Sanborns.

Villa Juveniles Conade: Glorieta Insurgentes local # G-11, Col Juárez, (5) 705-6072 or 533-1291 full almost all the time, call first. Charge US$3. Also recommended are **Hotel Paraiso**, Calle I. Mariscal #99 Col. Revolucion (5) 566-8077,(5) 566-8432, S-US$13.

Outside Mexico City: See Villa Juvenil Canade.

FOOD

Mexico City is a good place to taste frothy Mexican hot chocolate, a drink once so prized that only the Aztec and Mayan nobility drank it, to the tune of 50 tiny cups a day. A dish invented locally and now popular all over Mexico is *carne asada a la tampiquena* (grilled beef Tampico style). Due to reports of rude waiters and rapacious mariachis, Plaza Garibaldi is no longer recommended as 'best and cheapest'. 'Good cheap eating at small restaurants around Glorieta Insurgentes situated where Insurgentes crosses Avenida Chapultepec. Fewer mariachis than Garibaldi but you can sit in greater comfort to hear them.'

Cafeterias Sanborn's are all over Mexico City and they are excellent for breakfast, lunch or dinner. Some of the locations are: Insurgentes Nte. # 70 Col Sta Maria La

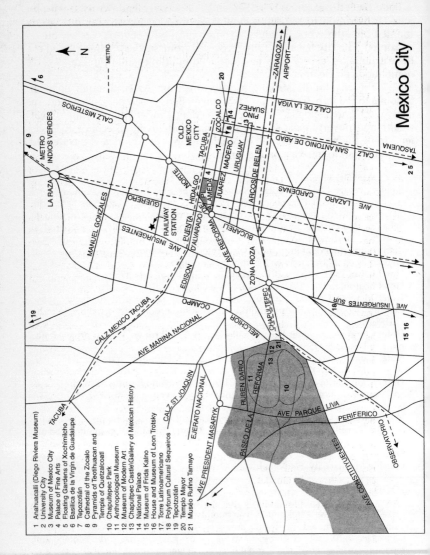

Mexico City

1 Anahuacalli (Diego Riviera Museum)
2 University City
3 Museum of Mexico City
4 Palace of Fine Arts
5 Floating Gardens of Xochimilcho
6 Basilica de la Virgin de Guadalupe
7 Tepoztlan
8 Cathedral of the Zocalo
9 Pyramids of Teotihuacan and
  Temple of Quetzalcoatl
10 Chapultepec Park
11 Anthropological Museum
12 Museum of Modern Art
13 Chapultepec Castle\Gallery of Mexican History
14 National Palace
15 Museum of Frida Kalho
16 House and Museum of Leon Trotsky
17 Torre Latinoamericano
18 Polyforum Cultural Sequeiros
19 Tepoztotlán
20 Templo Mayor
21 Muséo Rufino Tamayo

Riviera, (5) 591-0444. Ave Insurgentes # 1605 Col San José Insurgentes, (5) 662-5077. Insurgentes Sur : Quicuilco # 3500 Col. Pena pobre (5) 665-4982. Parroquia # 179 Col del Valle, (5) 534-7226. Ave Fco I Madero #4, (5) 512-9820. Salamanca # 74 Col Roma, (5) 533-3242.

Cafeterias Vips also all over Mexico City and also great for breakfast, lunch or dinner. Some locations are: Madero # 54, Col. Centro (5) 521-6448, Calle Uruguay # 53, Col. Centro, (5) 510-3765, Insurgentes Nte.# 131 (5) 535-2334,. Insurgentes Sur # 14, (5) 705-1673 and Insurgentes Sur # 496, Col. Roma. (5) 272-1732.

Taquería Beatriz, Londres 179, (5) 525-5857. 'All kinds of tacos. Try the tepache.'
'Zona Rosa' is a pleasant place to go strolling and there are some cheap restaurants among the plush sidewalk cafes.
For real Mexican tacos (not to be confused with the Tex-Mex variety found in most parts of the US), try **Beatriz** (several branches downtown and near the Zona Rosa) or **El Caminero**, Ignacio Ramirez #17 Col. Tabacalera near Revolution Monument (5) 566-3981.

OF INTEREST
Anahuacalli (Diego Rivera Museum), Ave. del Museo #150 Col. San Pablo de petlalpa, (5) 617-4310 or (5) 617-3797. Diego Rivera-designed black lava building housing his large collection of Aztec, pre-Columbian artefacts. Open Tue-Sun 10am-2pm, 3pm-6pm. US$1.27, closed Mon.
Polyforum Cultural Sequeiros, Ave Insurgentes Sur & Philadelphia, Col. Napoles, (5) 536-4220/24 in the Hotel de Mexico. A monument designed by and in honor of the artist. 'The March of Humanity mural is indescribably wonderful like being inside an opium dream.' Open 9am-7pm. Sound and light show in the evening.
University City, home of UNAM, the Universidad Nacional Autonoma de México. 11 miles south, Located at Insurgentes Sur # 3000 inside the cultural center of the city, reached by buses from downtown or trolley bus from Eje Central Lázaro Cárdenas. Famous for its modern design and colourful murals, mosaics and basreliefs by Rivera, Juan O'Gorman, Siqueiros and others. Mon-Sun, 9am-6pm.
Torre Latinoamericano, corner of Cárdenas and Madero #2 Col. Centro (5) 512-5315 or 510-4994. Miniature Empire State building that floats, with a magnificent view (smog and weather permitting) from its 44th floor. Open 10 am-midnight. Small admission charge.
Museum of Mexico City, Pino Suárez 30, three blocks south of Zócalo, (5) 522-3640 or 542-0083. Built and rebuilt on site of razed Aztec temple (only cornerstone remains), museum provides excellent introduction to city's history with models, murals, photographs. Good background at the start of your visit. Tues-Sat 10am-8pm, Sun. 10am-4pm. Closed Mon.
Palace of Fine Arts, Ave. Hidalgo 1, Col. Centro, (5) 512-2593 or (5) 521-9251 ext. 232 . This heavy white opera house contains Mexico's finest art collection. Upstairs are some of the best murals by Orozco, Sequeiros, Rivera and Tamayo. 'Worth every centavo.' Open Tues-Sun, 10am-7pm. Small admission fee.
Floating Gardens of Xochimilco (so-chee-meel-coh), 15 miles south. Cheapest to catch 31 or 59 bus from downtown. If you get on, you almost certainly won't get a seat. Very crowded weekends, boats take you around lake, other boats sell food, drink. 'A complete waste of time—muddy canals and gardens.' 'Smelly canals full of refuse.' Boat prices: 'Take one-third off first price quoted.'
Basílica de la Virgin de Guadalupe. Take bus to La Villa, on Reforma, or Metro to Basílica. The holiest of Mexican shrines, it honours the nation's patron saint, The Virgin of Guadalupe. Legend has it that she appeared to an Indian, Juan Diego, in 1531. Devout visitors show their faith by walking on their knees across the vast, cement courtyard. Indians, dressed in national costume, dance and parade by on her feast day, December 12. The old cathedral leans in all directions and is slowly sinking into the soft lakebed soil. The new basilica was designed by Pedro Ramírez Vásquez, architect of the National Museum of Anthropology.
Tepotzotlán, 25 miles north by *auto-pista* (expressway). Buses from Terminal del Norte, or Metro to Indios Verdes then local bus. Has a magnificent 18th century **church**, possibly Mexico's finest, with a monastery and an interesting collection of colonial religious art. Open Tue-Sun 10 am-6 pm.
Alameda. A park since 1592, it lies west of the Palace of Fine Arts between Avs. Juárez and Hidalgo. Originally the site of executions for those found guilty by the Spanish Inquisition, it is now the scene of popular Sunday concerts and family

outings. On June 13, Mexico's single women line up at the Church of San Juan de Dios and plead with St Anthony to find a husband for them.

Zócalo, or Plaza de la Constitución, has been the centre of the country from Aztec times. Second only in size to Red Square, vehicular traffic is restricted. The Cathedral, National Palace, Templo Mayor, and much more, are all within 5 minutes of each other.

The Cathedral at the Zócalo is the oldest church edifice on the North American continent and was built on the ruins of the Aztec temple. Has plumb-line showing how the cathedral has shifted. On the east side of the Zócalo is the **National Palace**, begun in 1692, interesting on its own and for its enormous and impressive murals by Diego Rivera. For more information: (5) 510-4737 ext. 1351.

Templo Mayor. Just off the corner of the Zócalo, between the Cathedral and the National Palace, is the excavated site of the Aztec Templo Mayor—really twin temples and several associated buildings. Although only the lower and internal parts remain, the ruins are extremely impressive. At the rear of the site is the recently inaugurated Muséo del Templo Mayor which houses many of the artifacts recovered during the excavations, (5)542-4784 or (5) 542-4786. Open Tues-Sun 9am-6pm. Admission US$2.00 except Sun. Guided tours available in English Mon-Fri 2 pm-6 pm. Not to be missed.

Pyramids of Teotihuacán and **Temple of Quetzólcoatl:** for details see 'Ancient Civilisations' box.

Chapultepec Park. Most of the city's important **museums** are in the park, but it is also an attraction in its own right, especially on Sundays when all the families in the city seem to parade there. 'Should be a compulsory visit—very colourful.' Free **zoo** contains the first captive pandas to be born outside China. Metroline 1 to Chapultepec or line 7 to Auditorium.

Anthropological Museum, (5) 656-4553/62/66. The claim that this is the finest museum in the world is well-founded; 'certainly one of the world's top ten'. Contains Mexico past and present. The Museum has recovered some of its most prized treasures which were stolen in December, 1985, but they are not displayed yet. 'Deserves every accolade thrown at it. Worth going here *before* you visit the pyramids at Teotihuacán.' Cameras but no tripods allowed, so bring fast film or flash. 'Worth taking your own photos, since postcards of exhibits are very poor and few (as in all Mexican museums I've visited).' Open Tue-Sat 9 am-7 pm, Sun 10 am-6 pm. Closed Mon. US$4, free Sun. Take Metro to Chapultepec or yellow and brown bus #76 on Reforma Paseo.

Gallery of Mexican History, a cleverly designed building within Chapultepec Castle, with a first-rate presentation of Mexican history since 1500. Open 9am-6pm daily.

Museum of Modern Art. Has Mexico's more recent masterpieces. 'Excellent collection, not only of Orozco, Rivera, etc, but some charming primitive paintings.' Be sure to see *La Revolución* by Lozano. Open 10 am-6 pm daily except Mon. Fee US$0.65, At the entrance of Chapultepec park, corner of Reforma and Ghandhi Street, (5) 211-8045 or (5) 211-8331. Metro Line 1: Chapultepec. US$2, Sun free. Open Tues-Sun 10am-6 pm, closed Mon.

Chapultepec Castle, old castle with original furnishings and objets d'art. Found fame in 1848 when young Mexican cadets fought off invading Americans here. Rather than surrender, the final 6 wrapped themselves in Mexican flags and jumped from the parapets to their death. Unless you want to copy them 'beware stone parapets and banisters, both very unsafe. Castle not impressive but worth visiting for the murals'.

Muséo Rufino Tamayo. Reforma y Calzada Ghandhi, Bosque de Chapultepec. Exhibitions of modern art and sculpture, including the personal collection of Mexico's best known living artist, Rufino Tamayo. The building itself is worth a visit. Located opposite the Museum of Modern Art. Open Tue-Sun 10 am to 5.30 pm, (5) 286-6519. US$2.

Two museums in the southern suburb of **Coyoacán**. Take 23A bus south on Burcareli marked Coyoacán or Col del Valle and the journey takes an hour.

House and Museum of León Trotsky, Rio Churubusco #410, Col. Del Carmen Coyoacan, (5) 658-8732. Ring door buzzer to be let in. This is where Trotsky was pickaxed to death in 1940; his tomb is in the garden. His house is preserved as he left it. Open Tue-Sun 10 am-5 pm, closed Mon. US$2. 'Really interesting museum.'

Muséo Frida Kahlo, 5 min from Trotsky house, corner of Allende and Londres #247, (5) 554-5999. Metro Coyoacán (or sometimes called Bancomer), line 3. Open Tues-Sun 10 am-5.30pm. Closed Mon. US$1.15, Guided tours at 11 am. Frida was Diego Rivera's wife and a prominent artist in her own right. Their colonial style house is filled with their effects and many of Frida's works. The **volcanoes of Popocatépetl and Iztaccihuatl** can be seen on a clear day in the east, although 'for good views take bus to Amecameca from ADO Terminal'. The peaks are some 3000ft higher than Mts Rainier or Whitney in the USA. 'Mind-blowing view when sitting on the right-hand side of bus from Mexico City to Puebla.'

Mexican Independence Day celebrations, 15 Sept at 11 am. President gives traditional cry of liberty to crowd in the Zócalo amid churchbells ringing, fireworks firing, confetti floating, much rejoicing.

Military parade, 16 Sept down Reforma.

ENTERTAINMENT

Jai Alai, the fastest game in the world, nightly at 6 pm except Mon and Fri at Fronton Mexico, on Plaza de la Republica. Fee. Jacket preferred. Complex betting system; stick to the pre-game parimutual.

Bullfight season runs Nov to March; other times of year, you can see *novilladas* (younger bullfighters, younger bulls) which are cheaper and may please you just as well if you know nothing of bullfighting. Fights Sun at 4 pm; booking in advance recommended. Take 17 bus down Insurgentes Sur to Plaza California, 1 block from the Plaza. Monumental (also known as Plaza México) is at 50,000 seats the biggest in the world; buy '*sol*' seats in *barrera* or *tendido* sections to see anything, (5) 563-3961. Tickets from US$8 to US$130.

Ballet Folklorico at the Palace of Fine Arts Ave. Juarez y Eje Central Lazaro Cardenas, Sun at 9.30 am and 8.30 pm; Wed at 8.30 pm. 'A real must—not classical ballet but a series of short dances representing Spanish, Indian and Mexican cultures.' Incredible costumes! Reserve in advance, (5) 512-2593. Tickets from US$28 to US$33.

Casa del Canto, Plaza Insurgentes. Music from all over Latin America, cover charge about US$2.00. 'Terrific.'

Plaza de Garibaldi. Nightly after 9 pm, mariachi music, sometimes free, sometimes not. Can be dangerous—be careful.

Candelero Dinner & Dance, Insurgentes Sur # 1333, (5) 598-0055. Has an eating place inside and plays lots of good music only from Thu-Sat.

SHOPPING

Many good markets including the Saturday market at **Plaza San Jacinto** in the suburb of San Angel; **San Juan market** on Ayuntamiento is a city-run market with many Mexican handicrafts and a good place to practice haggling; the **Handicrafts Museum** is on the Plaza de la Cuidadela at Avenida Balderas and has lots of trash and treasures; the **Thieves Market** (adjoining the Mercado La Lagunilla on Rayón between Allende and Commonfort) is open on Sundays. **La Lagunilla** is also especially interesting on Sundays when vendors come from all over the city to set up booths. Books, guidebooks, American mags: **American Bookstore**, Madero 25.

INFORMATION

Post Office on **Lázaro Cárdenas** and **Tacuba**, has a *poste-restante* section where letters are held up to 10 days for you. (5) 521-7394. Open weekdays 8 am-10 pm, Sat 8.30 am-8 pm, Sun 8 am-4 pm.

Mexico City News is an all-English newspaper with a good travel section.

Mexican Government Tourist Bureau, Presidente Masaryk 172, (5) 250-8555, north of Chapultepec Park—rather out of the way. Otherwise (5) 250-0123 for English-language tourist information. Open Mon-Fri, 8 am-6 pm. 'Go there in the morning.'

Tourist Police. Located at Florencia St. #20 Col. Juarez, Zona Rosa for more information (5) 625-8154 or (5) 242-6341 also available in Acapulco and Puerto Vallarta.

Radio VIP—CBS Affiliate Station, 88.1 FM.

MEDICAL SERVICES

American-British Cowdray Hospital, Observatorio and Calle Sur # 136. Call (5) 230-8000 or in emergencies, (5) 515-8359 or (5) 230-8136. Open 24 hours.

EMBASSIES

Britain: Calle Río Lerma #71 Col. Cuahutemoc. (5) 207-2149 or 207-2089. US: Paseo de la Reforma # 305 Col. Cuahutemoc. (5) 209-9100 ext. 3573, 3405 and 3404. Canada: Scheller # 529, Col. Polanco. (5) 724-7900.

TRAVEL

Taxis: 4 types, drivers described as '99.9% cheats—best to find out roughly how much the journey should cost before taking it. Wherever possible, fight to the death!' Regular taxis (yellow) have meters, and you pay 10% more at night. Jitney or 'pesero' taxis (green) cruise the main streets; the driver's finger held aloft indicates that he has space among the other passengers, who fill the taxi like a bus. Sitio taxis (red) operate from ranks on street corners; agree on fare beforehand if possible. Outside hotels, etc, you'll find unmetered taxis; always agree on fare beforehand. 'Taxi meter or not, arrange price beforehand. Hard to bargain, you get overcharged all the time.'

Buses: Municipal buses cost US$0.50, Peseros (white and green mini buses) US$.30. If time is short, take this incredible Tour by Gray Line Tours: (5) 208-1163 or 208-1415. **City tour** costs US$ 45p/p. If staying any length of time it is suggested that you get a street map and a Metro guide.

The Mexico City Metro, opened in September 1969, now carries some 4.6 million passengers daily at a ridiculously low price. 'The world's best transport bargain.' 'Use wherever possible, the streets are choked with traffic.' But avoid during rush hours (7-10am, 5-8pm) and be prepared to jostle with the rest of them at other times. Work out connections in advance—no overall plans inside stations. Backpacks, suitcases and large packages are *banned* during rush hours (7-10 am, 5-8 pm)—this can be strictly applied. Women and children should take advantage of separate queues and cars provided at worst times, and everyone should beware endemic bag-snatching and slashing. Some stops have artifacts uncovered during excavation: Aztec pyramid foundation at Pino Suarez, more artifacts at Bellas Artes and Zocalo. 'Clean, fast and incredibly simple to use.' When leaving the city, it is best to consult the Tourist Office for info.

Rail: Estacion Buenavista, Insurgentes and Mosqueta, 4 blocks from Guerro Metro. Bus on Insurgentes Norte to downtown. Train information (5) 547-1097 to some city 547-6593, English information call (5) 547-1084.

Air: Benito Juárez International Airport, (5) 571-3600 or 784-4811. Flights to all Mexican destinations. For international flights remember the US$17.50 departure tax (pesos only). From the airport take the official yellow taxis, buying a fixed price ticket to your destination from desks at the end of the arrivals building. You can also call this service for transport to the airport, but it costs the same or more than a regular taxi. Or, Metro to 'Terminal Area line 5'—but transfers involved and

OTHER SITES OF INTEREST IN MEXICO

Gray Whales at Baja California Baja California is the only place in the world where gray whales immigrate from Alaska to breed and give birth. These fascinating animals usually come down by the end of December and stay until March. When the water starts getting warm, they return north. The best spots to watch the whales are Ojo de Liebre and San Ignacio Lagoon, both near **Guerrero Negro**. Another good spot is La Paz, Baja California at **Magdalena's Bay**. Tours can be arranged by Eco-Tour Malerrino in Guerrero Negro (115) 7-01-00 with Mr. Luis Enrique Anchón or Turísmo Express in La Paz (112) 5-63-10 with Mrs. Alma or Lorena Barajas. The cost of the trip ranges from US$95pp.

Cliff-diving at La Quebrada in old Acapulco, Guerrero The famous **high-dive act** takes place off the rocks at the far end of La Quebrada located at 187 Costera Miguel Aleman. The floodlit drops are 25 and 40 metres into 2-metre-deep water, and the *clavadista* hits the water at about 60 mph, timing his dive to meet the incoming surf. Divers wear different types of costumes and often jump with the Mexican flag or torches. You can enjoy the show with dinner at the Mirador Restaurant. Admission is free, but there is a one (expensive) drink minimum. Or you can go down the steps to La Plazeta, located below the restaurant, where admission is US$1. Shows are Sat and Sun only, at noon, 7.30 pm, 8.30 pm, 9 pm, 9.30 pm,10 pm, 10.30 pm and 11 pm. For more information, call the Secretary of Tourism (SECTUR) at (74) 84-26-02 or (74) 84-24-23.

Los Voladores de Papantla in Veracruz The 'Flying Indian' religious ceremony of the Totonacs, dating back hundreds of years, is still performed in the traditional style. The dance can be seen every Sunday in the main square of Papantla. Four performers climb to the top of a very tall pole that has four extended arms at the top. One performer stands on the ground, dancing and playing traditional pipe music. The other four, dressed to represent the colourful plumage of the macaw, the symbol of the sun, secure themselves by the ankle with ropes and leap into the air. All four fly around the pole exactly 13 times, representing the 52 year cycle of ancient Mesoamerica. For more information, call the Secretary of Tourism (SECTUR) in Jalapa at (28) 12-73-45.

Paquime, a city founded around 1050 A.D., was an important pre-Hispanic religious and commercial center that dominated the northern regions of Mexico and extended its influence into parts of the United States including Texas, Arizona, Colorado, and New Mexico. The architecture of Paquime included multi-storied apartment-type buildings, complete with running water and a drainage system. The city suffered a terrible fire around 1340 and was later looted by the Spainards and abandoned. Extensive and fascinating ruins of Paquime were only recently excavated, and it is estimated that over 75% of the city remains unearthed. Paquime is located near **Casas Grandes, Chihuahua.** You can reach the archeological site by bus from Chihuahua City to Casas Grandes, which will take you to the main plaza from where you take a taxi to the ruins (taxis may be arranged by calling 4-08-13, 4-01-87, or 4-15-75). Museum and site open from 10 am to 5 pm. Admission US$1. For more information, contact Secretary of Tourism (SECTUR) at (14) 28-33-00 ext. 4511.

remember baggage limitations. For buses getting into or out of Mexico City: 4 terminals, each located near a Metro stop. *North* arrivals/departures at Terminal Central del Norte, (5) 587-1552, change at La Raza and go to Autobuses del Norte, line 5. (Also get there by bus, Insurgentes Norte then Cien Metros.) *South:* Terminal Sur, at the Taxquena Metro stop, southern end of line 2, (5) 689-4987. *West:* Terminal Poniente, (5) 271-4519 at Observatorio Metro station, west end of line 1. *East:* Terminal Central del Oriente (also known as ADO), (5) 133-2124, at the San Lázaro Metro station, to the east on line 1.

Mexico City travel and tourist info from DF tourist office, Amberes and Londres in the Zona Rosa, (5) 525-9380 or (5) 525-9380. Open only in the morning.

BEYOND MEXICO CITY   *All the places mentioned below can be easily reached from Mexico City by bus or car, or, in the case of those towns in the Yucatán Peninsula, also by air.* **Queretaro**, a lovely, lively town, loaded with history, lies about 140 miles to the northwest of the capital. It's a bit off the usual beaten tourist track and is recommended for its freshness, friendly townsfolk and the numerous hidden plazas and cobblestoned by-ways tucked away off the main streets. The Treaty of Guadalupe Hidalgo ending the US-Mexican War was signed here and the present Mexican Constitution was drafted here in 1916.

To the west of Mexico City is the university city of **Morelia** known for its colonial architecture and fine candies! **San Miguel de Allende**, a big draw for American students, writers and artists, is a treasurehouse of art, past and present, put together on the backs of the fortunes made from silver. The town's mountainside setting adds to the charm. To the west is **Guanajuato**, another Spanish colonial town whose silver mines once supplied one-third of all the world's silver. There's an international arts and music festival here in October and November.

About an hour's drive west of Mexico City, and with some magnificent scenery in between, is **Toluca**. Sitting at 8760 ft, Toluca is the highest city in Mexico and is famous for its main attraction, the **Friday market**. Local Indian stall-keepers come from miles around to sell you local specialties like straw goods, papier mache figures and sweaters. Bargain without mercy but first check out the prices at the government store next to the **Museum of Popular Arts and Crafts**, east of the bus station. You can often do better here than at the market.

The centre of modern Mexico's silver industry is **Taxco**, about 130 miles from Mexico City and sitting high up in the Sierra Madras. The views around here are marvellous and the city is preserved as a national monument thus preventing the construction of modern buildings.

To the east of the capital is **Puebla**. Situated amidst wild and mountainous scenery, Puebla is renowned for its ceramics as well as the snow-capped volcanoes of Popocatépetl (dormant) and Ixtacoihuatl (extinct) and nearby **Cholula**, a pre-Columbian religious centre. Puebla is also the home of *mole*, an unusual sauce made up of the odd combination of chocolate and chilli—usually served over turkey or chicken—and, apparently against all odds, quite delicious.

When the sea beckons, head east to Mexico's chief port since the days of the Spanish invasion, **Veracruz**. Cortes landed here in 1519 and with the advent of the gold and silver trade to Europe, Veracruz became a frequent point of attack by British and French forces. These days, it's a sometimes rough and raucous port city with influences split between old Spain and the Caribbean.

For a more typical resort-type experience, hop on a bus (or drive the very expensive toll road) and head west to **Acapulco** and the other gringo resort towns like **Manzanillo** or **Ixtapa**. Although hit hard by Hurricaine Pauline in October 1997, the beach area of Acapulco escaped any lasting damage.

Aiming south from Mexico City, there's **Oaxaca** and the nearby Zapotec centre of **Monte Albán** or the Mixtec site at **Mitla** to explore. (See *Ancient Civilisations Sites* box.) Moving further southeast into the most beautiful, lush and untouched territory in Mexico, you are in the land of the Maya. The astounding Mayan ruins at **Palenque**, **Chichén Itzá** and **Uxmal** (see Box in *Mexico/Background* chapter) contrast sharply with the modern Caribbean resort towns of **Cancun** and **Cozumel**.

Prices in Cancun are at New York levels, the hotel strip is as gaudy as anywhere in Florida, but the beaches are beautiful and free and the sea is deep blue, warm and inviting. A perfect end to a trip to Mexico? Perhaps, especially if you can combine soaking up the sun on the beach with an excursion to **Tulum** on the coast, or **Chichén Itzá** inland.

Appendix I   TABLE OF WEIGHTS AND MEASURES

Conversion to and from the metric system

Mexico employs the metric system. **Canada** has almost completed the changeover to metric, and the **United States** as yet uses it only sporadically and within its National Parks.

Temperature

50°C	120°F
45°C	110°F
40°C	100°F
35°C	
30°C	90°F
25°C	80°F
20°C	70°F
15°C	60°F
10°C	50°F
5°C	40°F
0°C	30°F
-5°C	20°F
-10°C	10°F
-15°C	0°F

Fahrenheit into Centigrade/Celsius: subtract 32 from Fahrenheit temperature, then multiply by 5, then divide by 9. *Centigrade/Celsius into Fahrenheit:* multiply Centigrade/Celsius by 9, then divide by 5 then add 32.

Linear Measure	0.3937 inches	1 centimetre
	1 inch	2.54 centimetres
	1 foot (12 in)	0.3048 metres
	1 yard (3 ft)	0.9144 metres
	39.37 inches	1 metre
	0.621 miles	1 kilometre
	1 mile (5280 ft)	1.6093 kilometres
	3 miles	4.8 kilometres
	10 miles	16 kilometres
	60 miles	98.6 kilometres
	100 miles	160.9 kilometres
Weight	0.0353 ounces	1 gram
	1 ounce	28.3495 grams
	1 pound (16 oz)	453.59 grams
	2.2046 pounds	1 kilogram
	1 ton (2000 lbs)	907.18 kilograms
Liquid Measure	1 US fluid ounce	0.0296 litres
	1 US pint (16 US fl oz)	0.4732 litres
	1 US quart (2 US pints)	0.9464 litres
	1.0567 US quarts	1 litre
	1 US gallon (4 US quarts)	3.7854 litres
	3 US gallons	11.3 litres
	4 US gallons	15.1 litres
	10 US gallons	37.8 litres
	15 US gallons	56.8 litres

The British imperial gallon (used in Canada) has 20 fluid ounces and 4 imperial quarts and is equal to 4.546 litres.

Speed	25 km/h	equals (approx.)	15 m.p.h.
	40 km/h	equals (approx.)	25 m.p.h.
	50 km/h	equals (approx.)	30 m.p.h.
	60 km/h	equals (approx.)	37 m.p.h.
	80 km/h	equals (approx.)	50 m.p.h.
	100 km/h	equals (approx.)	60 m.p.h.
	112 km/h	equals (approx.)	70 m.p.h.

Appendix II   SOME BUDGET MOTEL CHAINS IN THE US

Budget Host Inns, PO Box 14341, Arlington, Texas 76094, (800) 283-4678. *www.budgethost.com*

Chalet Susse International, Chalet Dr, Wilton, NH 03086. (800) 524-2538. *www.sussechalet.com.*

Days Inn, 339 Jefferson Rd, PO Box 278, Parsippany, NJ 07054-0278. (800) 325-2525. *www.daysinn.com.*

Econo-Lodges of America (Choice Hotels), 10750 Columbia Pike, Maryland 20901-4494. (800) 553-2666. *www.hotelchoice.com.*

Exel Inns, 4202 E. Town Blvd, Madison, WI 53704. (800) 356-8013.

First Interstate Inns, PO Box 760, Kimball, NE 69145. (800) 462-4667.

Friendship Inns/Choice Hotels, Address as Econo-Lodges (above). (800) 553-2666. *www.hotelchoice.com.*

Hampton Inn/Promise Hotels, 755 Crogsover Lane, Memphis, TN 38117. (800) 426- 7866. *www.hampton-inn.com.*

Hospitality International, 1726 Montreal Circle, Tucker, GA 30084. (800) 251-1962. *www.reservahost.com*

Knights Inn, HSS 339 Jefferson Road, PO Box 278, Parsippany, NJ. 07054-0278 (800) 722-7220. *www.knightsinn.com*

Motel 6, PO Box 809103, Dallas, TX 75380. (800) 466-8356. *www.motel6.com*

Quality Inns (Choice Hotels), 10750 Columbia Pike, Silver Spring, MD 20901. (800) 424-6423. *www.hotelchoice.com.*

Red Roof Inns, 4355 Davidson Road, Hilliard, OH 43026. (800) 843-7663. *www.redroof.com.*

Rodeway Inns, Address as Econo-Lodges (above). (800) 228-2000.

Super 8 Motels, PO Box 4090, Aberdeen, SD 57402-4090. (605) 225-2272, or (800) 800-8000. *super8motels.com*

Travelodge Forte Hotels, See Knights Inn above. (619) 448-1884, (800) 255-3050. *www.travelodge.com.*

Contact any of the above for their directories of motels, containing full information on rates, facilities, locations and often small maps pinpointing each motel.

INDEX

CORRECTIONS AND ADDITIONS

The detail, accuracy and usefulness of future editions of this Guide depend greatly on your help. Share the benefit of your experiences with other travellers by sending us as much information on accommodation, eating places, places of interest, entertainment, events, travel, etc., as you can.

These printed forms are supplied to get you started. Additional information can be sent on separate sheets of paper. *Please do not write on the back of these forms, nor on the back of your own sheets.* When making remarks, bear in mind that a comment on a hotel like 'Quite good' or 'OK' conveys little to anyone—be as descriptive and as quotable as you can, but please also be concise. If suggesting new hotels, eating places etc., please give **full** information: ie. **correct name, address, phone numbers, price** etc. **This is very important**. Without complete information your special 'hot' tip may not get published.

Please use these slips *only* for this guidebook information and not for any other BUNAC publications. Completed slips and other information should be sent to: General Editor, *The Moneywise Guide to North America*, BUNAC, 16 Bowling Green Lane, London EC1R 0QH, England.
In the USA: BUNAC, PO Box 430, Southbury, CT 06488.

The deadline for information to be included in the 2001 edition of the Guide is 10th October, 2000.

EXAMPLE

Place: LONE PINE, CALIFORNIA	Date: 20 August 2000
Subject: ACCOMMODATION	Page no: 351
Correction/Addition	Comments
Redwood Hotel, 123 Spruce Ave. [(209) 976-5432 $28 single, $32 with bath. $35 double, $40 with bath.	Clean, bright, though simply furnished. Vibrating water bed. Friendly and helpful. Turn left out of bus station and walk two blocks.

Place: _____ Date: _____

Subject: _____ Page no: _____

Correction/Addition
(Please give complete information)   Comments

Place: _____ Date: _____

Subject: _____ Page no: _____

Correction/Addition
(Please give complete information)   Comments

Place: _____ Date: _____

Subject: _____ Page no: _____

Correction/Addition
(Please give complete information)   Comments

Place:	Date:
Subject:	Page no:
Correction/Addition (*Please give complete information*)	Comments

Place:	Date:
Subject:	Page no:
Correction/Addition (*Please give complete information*)	Comments

Place:	Date:
Subject:	Page no:
Correction/Addition (*Please give complete information*)	Comments

Place: Date:
_____   _____

Subject: Page no:
_____   _____

Correction/Addition
(*Please give complete information*)   Comments
_____|_____

                                    |
                                    |
                                    |
                                    |
                                    |

Place: Date:
_____   _____

Subject: Page no:
_____   _____

Correction/Addition
(*Please give complete information*)   Comments
_____|_____

                                    |
                                    |
                                    |
                                    |
                                    |

Place: Date:
_____   _____

Subject: Page no:
_____   _____

Correction/Addition
(*Please give complete information*)   Comments
_____|_____

                                    |
                                    |
                                    |
                                    |
                                    |

Place: _____   Date: _____

Subject: _____   Page no: _____

Correction/Addition
(*Please give complete information*)   Comments

Place: _____   Date: _____

Subject: _____   Page no: _____

Correction/Addition
(*Please give complete information*)   Comments

Place: _____   Date: _____

Subject: _____   Page no: _____

Correction/Addition
(*Please give complete information*)   Comments